THE LODESTAR

Also by Pamela Belle

Wintercombe

The Lodestar

PAMELA BELLE

St. Martin's Press
New York

For my father, and for Steve

Library of Congress Cataloging-in-Publication Data

Belle, Pamela.
The lodestar / Pamela Belle.
p.   cm.
ISBN 0-312-02945-4
1. Richard III. King of England. 1452–1485—Fiction.   2. Great
Britain—History—Richard III, 1483–1485—Fiction.   I. Title.
PR6052.E4474L6 1989
823'.914—dc19
89-31066
CIP

First published in Great Britain by The Bodley Head Ltd.

First U.S. Edition

10 9 8 7 6 5 4 3 2 1

INTRODUCTION

The brief reign of Richard III is at once one of the most intensively researched, yet least documented periods of English history. There are, for instance, only two reliable contemporary accounts, one by an Italian, Mancini, who probably spoke no English and who recorded only the events of the few months between April and July, 1483, and the other by a cleric who had access to court information but who was biased against the King, largely because of his northern power-base. Reading these scanty descriptions, it becomes clear how much of most historians' accounts are in fact based very largely on opinion, conjecture, prejudice and the highly fanciful 'history' written by the man referred to by Josephine Tey as 'the sainted More'.

In writing my own fanciful history, I have tried to use the *known* facts as the bones of my tale—but, being a historical novelist and not a historian, I have had of necessity to flesh out the story with conjecture. There were Herons at Bokenfield, although their history for the fifty years either side of 1500 is, conveniently, obscure. My version of the fate of the Princes in the Tower was inspired by a tradition handed down in the Tyrell family to this day, and first printed in the book by the late Audrey Williamson, *The Mystery of the Princes*, published by Alan Sutton, a work which poses some splendidly awkward questions. The battle of Bosworth has no contemporary description whatsoever, and my version of events on that day is an amalgam of the theories of the most recent historians of the period.

As well as the work of Mrs Williamson, I would like to pay grateful tribute to the many members of the Richard III Society, who have contributed so much in the field of fifteenth-century research, and whose articles in the society's magazine, 'The Ricardian', have been of enormous help. I am also indebted to their sales officer, Miss A. Smith, who very kindly gave up a great deal of her spare time to check my typescript for errors—I am not a specialist in fifteenth-century history. As always, my mother struggled with my almost illegible handwriting to eliminate other, more basic mistakes: and so I take full responsibility for the accuracy, or otherwise, of what follows.

The quotations at the head of each chapter and section are taken from *Le Morte d'Arthur*, by Thomas Malory.

PAMELA BELLE

'Loyalty binds me'

(MOTTO OF KING RICHARD III)

THE DESCENDANTS OF EDWARD III

(very much simplified)

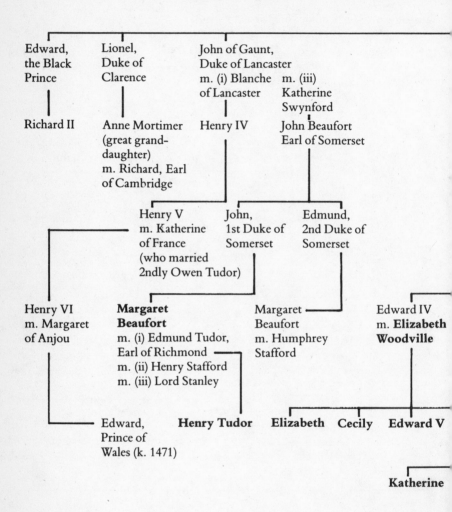

(Bold Names are of those featured in the story)

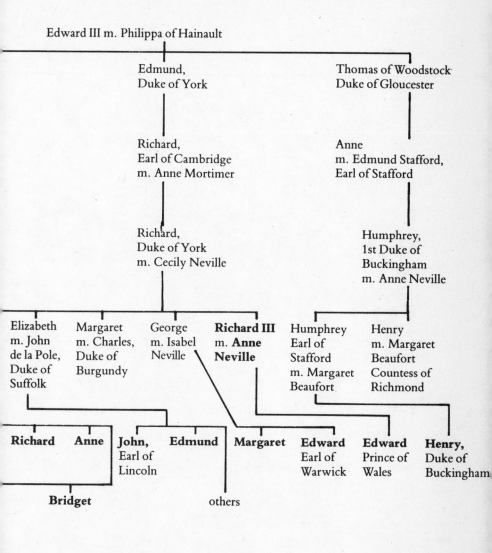

PART
I
1481–82

THE YOUNG SISTER

**'The most valiant and fairest lady
that I know living'**
(BOOK 3, CHAPTER 1)

**'Had he none other succour, but rode
so forth himself alone.'**
(BOOK 3 CHAPTER II)

'You *can't* marry him!'

The statement, thick with appalled disbelief, was perhaps louder
and more forceful than the speaker had intended, but had no more
effect on the girl at the window than it had on the threadbare, faded
arras hanging that disguised the rough stone walls of the room
where they stood. She looked down at the embroidery she was
holding, and then with an air of calm certainty sat in the window-
embrasure and took up her needle again. The man watched it slide
expertly in and out of the heavy velvet girdle perhaps three or four
times, holding hard to his patience and his temper: it had never been
of any use, ever, to threaten, cajole, bribe or blackmail his sister
Meg, and yet she was the only person who could disturb his own
habitual self-control.

She knew it too well: the calm smile on her face as she raised it
from her sewing to look at him had a touch of mischief about it.
'Why not? Why can't I marry him? And don't talk so loud—Father
will hear you.'

'You know as well as I do that our revered father is as deaf as a
rock to anything else when he's discussing money. All his attention
will be on your precious Sir Robert, and how big a jointure he can
grasp without paying over too much dower—even if the dower
isn't his.' He took the three steps necessary to carry him to the
window and stood over the girl, fighting the desire to shake her out
of her decision. 'Meg—you can *not* marry that man! He's as cold
and predatory as a pike. He's more than twice your age, he has
daughters near as old as you, and they say his first wife died of a
melancholy, if not worse.'

'There's small chance of me doing that,' said Meg, unintimidated, her needle glinting in a shaft of the pale November sun. 'I
might die of melancholy here, though, if I have to endure much
more of this.' Her wide blue eyes flashed up at him, and suddenly
real feeling, real anger, suffused her face. 'You of all people should
understand that! The boredom of it—sewing, cooking, having to

[3]

obey Elizabeth, listening to Father rambling on and on and on about the Scots and the harvest and his horses and the Prior of Brinkburn and all the other tedious people he thinks have done him an injustice—I can't bear it much more, Christie, I really can't. Sooner or later I shall say something to Elizabeth—oh, I've been very good up until now, "Yes, sister, no, sister, of course I will, sister," but if she reminds me just once more of how lucky I was to be placed at Alnwick and how little advantage she thinks I've taken of it, I swear I shall lose my temper.'

'I don't think I've ever seen you lose your temper before,' said her brother, diverted, an unholy gleam appearing suddenly in his eyes. 'Do me the service of warning me in advance, will you? I'd like to be there when you do.'

He had always been able to make her laugh. Meg's perfect, pale-skinned face crinkled suddenly with amusement, and she gave the delighted, delightful gurgle that had enchanted any man who heard it, all her life long. It had led to her eventual departure from the Percy stronghold at Alnwick, where she had been in service to the Dowager Countess of Northumberland since her childhood: for although both Meg and Christie Heron had Percy blood through their mother Alianor, their father's second wife, it was not legitimate. Alianor Percy had been a bastard daughter of the third Earl, sired in his youth before his marriage, but always a favourite both of himself and his wife, now Dowager. It was for her sake, after her early death, that her son Christie and daughter Meg had been brought to Alnwick and reared in the luxury of the most powerful household in the North, an opportunity far beyond the reach of the children of most small landowners. Enormous possibilities of advancement had thereby been opened to them, and Christie, sharp-witted and as urgent as Meg to escape from the coarse, petty, uncultured world that his father and half-brothers and sister inhabited, had grasped every crumb thrown his way. He had impressed the Master of the Henchmen with his prowess at swordsmanship, riding and the arts of war, of hunting and jousting and all the other martial skills at which a prospective knight should excel. Nor had he neglected his books, and the elderly cleric who struggled to instil into a half-dozen rough and ready, uncouth sprigs of Northern nobility and gentry the rudiments of reading, writing and other essentials found that the quiet, reserved boy, the poor relation who would have been despised by the others had he not had the firm approval of the Master of Henchmen, was a notably brilliant pupil

[4]

who far outstripped his companions and bid fair to overtake his teacher. So Christie Heron, who had long ago determined that he would never return to the narrow confines of his father's rule, came to the notice of his uncle, Henry Percy, the fourth Earl, who had decided that such a mind could be usefully harnessed in the cause of Percy aggrandisement. He had been despatched to the Temple in London, and now had a lawyer's training, and a glorious future beckoning him: service with the Percies, riches, an heiress perhaps, all had seemed possible at the age of twenty-one.

But his father had beckoned instead. The eldest son, John, now in his thirties, had not had the benefit of a Percy education and would always be a limited, surly Border ruffian like so many around their pele-tower, Bokenfield, suspicious of words and wit and music, ever ready with sword or dagger, barely able to write his name. Gerard, his next brother, was cast in the same mould. Elizabeth, lacking the beauty and the handsome Percy dowry that would advance Meg, kept the house, bitter and envious of her half-sister's good fortune. William, Sir Lyell Heron's youngest surviving son by his first wife, was a simpleton who mouthed and dribbled in a corner, and whose survival to the age of twenty-four was both a marvel and a burden.

Then, tragedy had struck. Gerard, newly wed, had been killed by marauding Scots in one of their incessant raids across the Border. Sir Lyell had looked at his remaining family, and at John's three pale cowed daughters and ailing, now-barren wife who refused inconveniently to die so that her husband could marry a younger and more fertile woman to breed Heron heirs for Bokenfield, and was forced to the unwelcome realisation that the future of his line might well depend upon the brilliant, arrogant, accomplished stranger who was also, astonishingly, his youngest son.

And so Christie Heron, poised on the brink of his future—tantalising possibilities of travel to Burgundy or Italy, service at Alnwick, even, dazzlingly, the remote chance of a post at Court—had been summoned home by his bereaved sire. Left to himself, he would undoubtedly have ignored that peremptory, ill-written order: but Sir Lyell, with the devious cunning that was his greatest similarity to his youngest son, had taken care that the Percies knew of his plight, and would add their weight to his request. Without Percy favour, Christie Heron was nothing: and so he left glittering, enticing London, and travelled the long miles north to Bokenfield, the gloomy primitive tower that had been Heron property for a century, and to the family that he had seen perhaps three or four times in a dozen years.

Meg, though, he knew far better, for she had been at Alnwick too, in the Dowager Countess's bower, until she had quite innocently attracted the notice of a married Percy cousin, a situation which pleased nobody, least of all Meg. She had agreed with the Dowager, a kindly but implacable woman, that a return to Bokenfield might be best for all concerned, and had the promise of a rich dowry to sweeten her departure. That promise had not sweetened her jealous sister Elizabeth, but it had brought Sir Robert Drakelon to Bokenfield, Sir Robert, friend and retainer to the Earl of Northumberland, friend to the Duke of Gloucester, friend to the King, friendly to all and in particular to those who might act to his advantage. Christie had known him at Alnwick, and disliked and distrusted him instantly: recognising, perhaps, just such another as himself.

And recognising also, as he had beheld Sir Robert's cold blue eyes dwelling on the flushed, laughing face of Meg Heron, dancing at Alnwick, that it would not only be a Percy dower that would attract the attentions of a prospective bridegroom, even one so cold and unemotional as Sir Robert Drakelon.

'But you haven't answered me—*why* don't you want me to marry him?' Meg's quiet, reasonable voice broke in on his thoughts. 'You know as well as I do that I have no other way of escape from here.'

'I'm not arguing against your marriage,' said Christie, trying, successfully, to match her imperturbable air of calm. 'But there are other fish in the pond besides your precious Sir Robert. Mother of God, there must be dozens of men in Northumberland, Herons, Lisles, Lumleys, even a Percy or two, who'd be glad to take you, someone young, to make you laugh—if you marry him, you'll be exchanging one prison for another.'

'I doubt it,' said Meg, unshaken. 'He has talked of taking me to Westminster, to Middleham, to York—Christie, I have only ever been to Alnwick and the other Percy castles, the Dowager does not travel elsewhere, and I want to *see* something of life, not be mewed up in another tower like Bokenfield, wife to some young cut-throat like poor Gerard was, supplementing his farming by doing a little quiet cattle-reiving over the Border on moonlit nights. That isn't what I want, just as you don't want to spend all your days here at Father's beck and call, just to have Bokenfield at the end of it. I want

[6]

to see London, and perhaps dance at Court, I want to be merry and laugh and have conversations with intelligent, cultured people —just as I did at Alnwick. And who else can give me that, save Sir Robert?' A smile of pure, delightful mischief appeared suddenly on her face. 'And besides, I don't think it is only my dower that interests him.'

He wanted to hit her, to shake her as he had done when they were children, before Alnwick and the sophistication of London had glossed over such immature impulses with a sheen of civilisation. Instead he looked at her, the annoying, infuriating, loving, amusing, exasperating little sister who had always been his closest friend, the only one who could see beneath that gloss to the real Christie, now so deeply buried by ambition and education that no-one else knew of his continued existence, and saw her with the eyes of a stranger. She was beautiful, and knew it, had always known it and revelled in it, using those huge blue eyes and tumbled riotous mass of yellow-gold hair to charm anyone into granting her childhood desires, using them now to snare the husband who would bring her the life she wanted. They were not much alike, physically, save in their height, both being tall and long-boned, Christie lean and Meg slender: her gold curls were subdued in him to a light brown, his eyes a paler colour, almost silver grey, and her fine, delicate features translated very inaccurately to his thin, clever face with its strong bones and long narrow mouth and eyes. He had none of her good looks, yet the kinship between them was obvious: and the likeness in their minds was far more strongly marked. They were two of a kind, both charming, both ruthless, knowing quite well what they wanted from life and prepared to use every means at their disposal to obtain their desires. Even if it meant marriage to Sir Robert Drakelon, whose middle-aged lechery she had actively encouraged.

'Oh, Meg,' he said softly, knowing that there was no hope of dissuading her, but unable to conceal his unhappiness. 'Is there *really* no other way? Are you honestly set upon this? You're only seventeen, you have a fine dower, there'll be plenty of others if you refuse him, you don't *have* to accept him—Father will shout and swear and bluster and lock you in your chamber for a week and have a score of eligible young men lined up outside your door at the end of it—you know he will accept it eventually, he favours you because you've always reminded him of Mother. You have only to be stubborn for just a little while, Meg—Sir Robert isn't your only escape.'

[7]

'But I know that,' said Meg, calmly certain. 'I am telling you, Christie, I *want* to marry Sir Robert. I am sure I shall be perfectly happy with him, and if you don't give over trying to persuade me otherwise—and you of all people must know I can't be persuaded *at all*—then I shall think seriously about sticking this needle into the first part of you I can reach. And I am only partly joking.'

He was silent then, recognising defeat. It had been a lost cause from the start, he knew, but at least he had tried. And he could be generous, for Meg was the only true friend he had, and he would not lose her out of petty spite. He smiled at her, a genuine smile of a kind that few people apart from Meg had ever seen. 'Well, I shall retire in disarray, mauled by your superior tactics and weaponry, and concede you the field. I hope your choice turns out to be the right one—and I hope very much that you are happy.'

'Of course I shall be,' said his sister positively, as he gave her a kiss on the pale, flawless curve of her cheek. 'I want to be happy, and when have you ever known me fail to have what I want?' She smiled brilliantly. 'I wanted you to wish me well, and so you have—and will you do one more thing for me? Before Father comes in—they must surely have come close to completing all their business by now. Will you play for me?' And her eyes were hungry, knowing that although Sir Robert Drakelon could command good musicians, although King Edward's singing boys and choirs were famed not only in England but throughout Europe, her brother Christie had a gift that few could match.

It was a gift that was appreciated more in Alnwick than in Bokenfield, however, as Sir Lyell Heron had early made abundantly clear. It was bad enough that his youngest son had emerged from the Percy nest an elegant, accomplished, arrogant popinjay with scarcely a garment able to withstand the daily rigours of Border life, and no knowledge whatsoever of essentials such as cattle-rearing, barley-growing and raiding the Scots (and in this, as in much else, Sir Lyell had grossly underestimated Christie), but that he should play his lute with a skill only a lowly professional minstrel should properly command, and sing effeminate French and Italian love-songs into the bargain—that was a disgrace to the proud, tough name of Heron, and Sir Lyell had curbed his disgust only because he needed his son's services far more, alas, than his son needed him.

But although Christie's father was realist enough to pretend to ignore his ignoble accomplishment, Sir Lyell's terrifying sudden rages were legendary, and Meg saw a wary, considering look appear on her brother's face. She said quickly, 'I don't think Father will hear you, the walls are so thick. Please, Christie, please—I haven't heard you play for so long.'

And because she could always, in the end, persuade him to do what she wanted, he slipped up the spiral stairs to the chamber he shared with poor, slobbering William, and brought down the only thing he loved, apart from her.

His lute was Italian, no English maker having the skill to produce something so fragile and so lovely, and it was immensely valuable: needless to say, Percy money had paid for it, and in fact it had been a gift of the Dowager Countess, who loved fine music and had been the first to recognise the great talent for it in her young protegé. For six years Christie Heron had guarded it and treasured it as others, more sentimental, might cherish a woman, and for him it sang. He drew it carefully from the soft doeskin bag and set about tuning it, a process so prolonged that, the popular joke went, a minstrel might spend fifty years of his allotted span of seventy, purely in adjusting the strings of his lute. It required great skill to know the limits of the slender top course, and to stretch it to just within those limits, and a fine ear to tune the other four courses in keeping with its pitch. Meg, whose musical ability was well within conventional bounds, watched her brother's face as he tested each pair of strings, adjusted, and tried again, seeing him laid defenceless before her, utterly absorbed. He had a depth to him, a capacity for passion and feeling that she, considering herself a realist, thought that she lacked, but recognised reluctantly in him. He had tried to suppress it, to channel all his energies into his own advancement: but what would happen, she wondered, if he ever met a woman who could arouse his emotions to the levels that his music reached?

And then he began to play, without a plectrum in the new, soft Italian manner, slowly and quietly at first because he lacked practice, and then with increasing assurance as his fingers regained their suppleness. There were tunes from France and Burgundy and Italy that she had heard before, at Alnwick, although she knew no words to match them, and then, suddenly, something that she did know, their own special song.

> I have a young sister,
> Far beyond the sea,
> And many be the dowries
> That she sent unto me.

[9]

She sent to me a cherry
Without any stone,
And so she sent a dove,
Without any bone.

She sent to me a briar
Without any leaf:
She bade me love my leman
Without any grief.

How should any cherry
Be without a stone?
And how should any dove
Be without a bone?

How should any briar
Be without a leaf?
How should I love my leman
Without any grief?

Meg's voice, high and loud and deceptively pure, soared above his own as the last two verses made the riddle plain.

When the cherry was a flower,
Then had it no stone,
When the dove was in the egg,
Then had it no bone.

When the briar's in the seed,
Then hath it no leaf:
When a maiden hath her love,
Then she is without grief.

'You see?' said his young sister, smiling, as the last fragile notes shivered and died on the strings of his lute. 'I will have what I want, and I will be happy.'

She could not see Christie's face: it was bent over the tuning-pegs, adjusting the thin top course. For a while there was silence: then he said, still tuning, 'If—if it should not be so—if you should ever need me, Meg, or my help, you have only to ask, wherever you might be, wherever I might be—send me word and I will come to you, I swear it.'

'I won't need it, of course,' said his sister, with the unshakeable confidence of her seventeen years. 'But thank you, all the same.'

Aware that her answer might not seem properly appreciative, she added hastily, 'Don't stop playing, please. Sing something happy, something I know well.'

For a while still, Christie was silent, apparently absorbed in his tuning, and Meg was visited by a pang of guilt. What was he thinking? Had he really forgiven her for her determination to marry Sir Robert? She realised, belatedly, that his offer of help, should she ever need it, had come uncharacteristically from the heart. And she had lightly turned it aside.

A door slammed below them, signal that Sir Lyell had ended his discussion with his future son-in-law. Christie's head came up, and his pale eyes met hers, wild with sudden mischief. 'Something happy, little sister? How does this sound, then?'

And 'this' was the tune, though fortunately not the words, of a song she did know, and had heard sung at Alnwick when the winter evenings grew riotous and uninhibited at Christmas time: it was ostensibly about a cockerel, but actually concerned something else entirely. Meg, her feet tapping in time with the swift infectious rhythm of the tune, felt her spirits lift in unison, and began first to hum and then, more confidently, to sing the words.

> I have a handsome cock
> Who comes of noble kind:
> His comb is of red coral,
> His tail is of Ind.
>
> His legs are made of azure,
> So graceful, and so small.
> His spurs they are of silver while,
> Down to the root withal.
>
> His eyes are made of crystal
> Bedded all in amber,
> And every night he percheth him
> Within my lady's chamber.

And the door opened abruptly as the song ended, to reveal both Meg's father, Sir Lyell Heron, and her intended husband, Sir Robert Drakelon.

It was evident from Sir Lyell's mottled, indignant face that his negotiations with his daughter's future husband had not gone particularly well. True, most of the girl's handsome dowry, some four hundred marks, had been provided by the Percies, but he did not see why he must pay all of it over to this chilly, correct, unemotional man who, unaccountably, appeared to lust after his pretty youngest child to the extent of offering her marriage. Mind you, he himself had lusted after the girl's mother, long ago, and Meg greatly resembled her: he could understand that any man, even one so impersonal as Sir Robert, would look on her with favour. Moreover, in marrying her, he would be allying himself still more firmly with the centre of Northern power at Alnwick: the girl was half a Percy, after all, even if on the wrong side of the blanket, and niece to the present Earl. He had deviously drawn Sir Robert's attention to Meg's various advantages, but the man's knowledge was frighteningly complete. He was well aware of those advantages already, or, he made it clear, he would not have deigned to enter this barren, draughty little tower: and he proceeded instead to interrogate Sir Lyell as to the exact proportions of her dowry while making it plain that he was well aware of the size of the Percy contribution. Sir Lyell had hoped to keep back just a little, some forty or fifty marks perhaps, to endow his other daughter, whose bitter tongue had long ago overcome the usefulness of her housekeeping abilities, but Sir Robert had implacably demanded it all, and Sir Lyell, thinking of the Percy wrath hanging over his head like a baleful thundercloud, ready to strike him should he attempt any deceit, had acknowledged defeat. He was a realist to his bones, but it did not make the pill any sweeter to swallow—outgunned and outmanoeuvred by a man young enough to be his own son!

The sounds of merry music filtering through the thick oaken door had done nothing to ease his temper, and his fury rose as he recognised the bawdy tune and, worse, his supposedly innocent, pure and virginal daughter singing the words. Praying that she did not understand their import, he flung open the door, and the music died.

Meg, flushed, mischievous and happy, bobbed a curtsey, and her eyes went at once to Sir Robert: like a bitch on heat, the hussy, thought her father sourly. He swallowed his bile and said with an attempt at bluff cheerfulness, 'All is concluded, daughter. The contract has been drawn up, and Sir Robert and I are agreed. He has signed it, and you are free to become his wife.'

'So I hope I may kiss my dear bride?' said that gentleman. Without waiting for an answer, he slid with practised ease past Sir Lyell's bulk and took Meg in his arms, with rather more enthusiasm than might properly have been expected from him.

Christie watched the slippery-looking black head bent towards his sister's, and knew that he could not bear to stay longer in this stifling little place, narrow, repressive, brutal and limiting of ambition. Without Meg, his life here would descend to the level of an unpaid lackey, expected to do his father's bidding in unsavoury lawsuits, and in breeding heirs, in return for his scanty bed and scantier board. Meg would break free, even if she had sold herself to do it, and he knew, as the happy pair plighted their troth, that he would not delay long in following her example.

*

The marriage date was set, the ink dry on the wedding contract, and Sir Robert, after a rather less resplendent dinner than those he was usually offered, had ridden back to Alnwick, where he was the Earl of Northumberland's guest. And after his departure, Sir Lyell was free to give full rein to the spleen that had been festering all day within his ample chest. He found fault first with Elizabeth's housekeeping: the meat she had served had been tough, old, the sauces not spicy enough, or too spicy, the sweetmeats coarse and mean, the table poorly dressed. Sir Robert would think they were pauper peasants, instead of an old proud knightly family. Meg was the next to face the increasing severity of his wrath. What in the name of the Devil did she think she was doing, singing a bawdy song? A good thing it was that Sir Robert had heard it after, and not before, the contract had been signed: he must think her nothing but a light loose woman, given over to lechery and idle thoughts. Meg sat calm and still as he berated her, saying nothing: it was obvious that she feared him no longer.

'I don't think Sir Robert minded much,' said Christie, quietly and caustically into the spluttering pause as his father ran for once out of words. 'I doubt he wants Meg for her holy purity.'

Sir Lyell thumped the table so that the pewter dishes, the finest they had, jumped and rattled: a winecup overturned, and Elizabeth, her thin lips tightening, watched the red stain disfigure the only unpatched tablecloth in the family's ownership. 'Who asked you to speak, puppy? You did enough harm, playing that obscene song.'

'Any obscenity is in your mind, Father—it's about a cockerel, no more, no less.'

'Don't try to bandy words with me, my boy—you know very well what it's about! Encouraging your sister in bawdry, yes, I heard you! Don't you want her to marry Sir Robert? Finer match

[13]

than you'll ever make, you insolent idle good-for-nothing! Why weren't you at Brinkburn? I told you to go there this morning!'

'Because it's a fool's errand.'

The room was suddenly very quiet. Meg and Elizabeth, united for once in their apprehension, exchanged glances. Their brother lounged on his stool, one leg crossed over the other, the dark blue hose immaculate, not a stain nor a crease on the quiet good taste of his blue velvet doublet, assured and at ease, playing with his father's choleric nature, Meg realised, as a cat with a mouse, arousing to fury as much by his manner as by his words. And Sir Lyell, not naturally a subtle man, rose unerringly to the bait. 'A fool's errand? A fool, am I? A fool, eh? We'll see who's the fool, boy, when the Earl hears of this. Why won't you go to Brinkburn, then? Is your dainty arse too soft to sit a horse?'

The Priory was perhaps four miles away, easy riding along the River Coquet. Christie paid no heed to the insult: he brushed a speck of dust from his sleeve and said, his eyes not flinching from his sire's suffused, angry face, 'The Prior has the right of it. The land is his, lawfully. It was given to him by your father, and he had every right to do it. The fact that you want it back makes no odds. It belongs to the Priory, their title to it is plain, and they need it more than you do. They're one of the poorest hereabouts, and that's saying a good deal. You have quite enough to support you and your family in all this splendour.'

Meg drew in her breath, at once appalled and admiring. She had never been one for confrontation, preferring to get her way by more devious methods—but then so had Christie. What his purpose in this deliberate baiting was, she could only guess: and if she was right, she hoped very much that he had some plan for his future, for the Percies would hardly tolerate him now, useful to them though he might be.

Their father seemed incapable of speech as Christie's ironic hand encompassed the mouldering tapestry and dented pewter, his sisters' threadbare gowns and Sir Lyell's own patched sweatstained leather jack. The older man's mouth worked convulsively, spittle frothing at the corners, and his colour changed alarmingly to a still deeper shade of red. At last, his voice forced its way past the rage lodged across his throat. 'How dare you—you parasite, look at you, prinked up like a woman, singing filthy effeminate songs, corrupt, immoral, I know what goes on in London—you're nothing more than an arse-licking blood-sucking whore-loving leech.

Where would you be without the Percys, eh? At least all this was gained with honest toil.'

'It's the first time I've heard raiding the Scots called that,' said Christie. He pulled his dagger from its sheath and with studied care cleaned the nails of his left hand while his father stared at him, impotent and helpless in his rage, and spluttered. Meg, though aware that it was a vain task, decided to intervene. 'Don't quarrel, please, Christie—it's my betrothal we've been celebrating, it should be a happy day.'

'Happy? To see you shackled to that hypocritical pike of a man? There's more feeling in a block of ice.'

He does not mean it, thought Meg, staring into her brother's inimical grey eyes. He's just provoking Father through me—and I will not be used in that way. Aloud, she retorted, 'More feeling than in you, perhaps—the only time you ever come to life is when you strum that wretched lute.'

'Margaret!' Sir Lyell's voice was shatteringly loud in the cramped stone-walled room. 'Shut your mouth, girl, this is no concern of yours. And as for your precious lute, my boy, I've a good mind to break it over your thick pate—and then perhaps you'd have more leisure to do my bidding.'

'If you lay one finger on it,' said Christie, his voice suddenly deadly quiet, deadly furious, 'I swear I'll break your fat neck, you uncouth ignorant stinking old peasant. And you needn't think I'm bluffing, either—I can, and I will.'

The silence was appalling. Sir Lyell, his breath coming in noisy gasps, saw the intent in his son's pale eyes—like a snake's, thought Meg in fear—and, visibly, shrank before it. His mouth gobbled futilely for a moment, and then he said, his words thick with rage and humiliation, 'Get out. Go on, get out. You're no son of mine, d'you hear? You're not wanted here, never were—don't know who spawned you, some devil's get you are, you're none of mine—so go on, get out, I never want to see you again!'

Christie rose, and stretched, with the insolent grace of an alley-cat. 'The prospect doesn't grieve me very much,' he said. 'I hadn't intended to stay here to be your lackey, doing your dirty work for you and using the law to frighten innocents and feather your own nest, so don't worry—I don't think you will ever find me darkening your door from now on.'

Sir Lyell rose also, his fists planted huge on the stained tablecloth, his chin thrust forward. 'And I'll make sure the Earl hears of

[15]

this—you'll not find yourself welcome at Alnwick either—they won't want an insolent puppy who dares threaten his own father, and insult him at his table—I'll see the gate's barred against you there, and then where will you go, eh? There'll be no place for you anywhere in the North, I'll see to that—you'll rue this day, boy, if it's the last thing I do, I'll see you'll rue it!'

'I hadn't thought of returning to Alnwick,' said Christie, casually, his eyebrows raised. 'So I shouldn't waste your time going there, Father. The true power in the North is Richard of Gloucester, and he'll be in need of men for the Scottish invasion next summer. I'll take service with him at Middleham, and I doubt your influence will stretch so far. Really, Father, you have no need to concern yourself with my welfare any longer.' And with a last, deeply ironic bow, he was gone.

*

Meg found him in the stable, perhaps fifteen minutes later, saddling his horse. She saw with a pang how few his possessions were: just a bundle of clothing, and another containing the precious lute. He had covered the fine blue doublet with a worn leather jack, and pulled on a pair of old but still serviceable riding-boots. Bareheaded, and unarmed save for his dagger, he looked uncharacteristically vulnerable in the gloom of the stable, and Meg felt a stab of grief. She understood, none better, his need to go—but why do it in this manner, and leave Bokenfield an outcast, never to return?

He glanced at her as she stood in the doorway, and she caught the glimmer of his smile as he answered her unspoken question. 'You look very wan, and there's no need. I had to quarrel with him, little sister—I had to, or I would never be free of him. If I hadn't turned him against me, he would have tried to hold me here by any means he could—blackmail, bribery, threats, Northumberland, any weapon he could find to hand. He needs me for my lawyer's mind and he also needs me to breed his heirs, now Gerard's dead—can you see poor Agnes giving him a grandson after those three feeble daughters? No—but I could, and he'd already started to cast around for a wife for me. And when I want to wed, I'll do my own choosing.'

She could see the logic of it, the reasoning behind his actions, she would probably even have done it herself in his position, but still she was disturbed by his cold-blooded manipulation of their father's failings. Not so great the difference between Christie and

Sir Robert, she thought wryly, despite their evidently mutual dislike: her future husband and her brother had treated each other all through dinner with an elaborate, chilly courtesy that barely hid their malice. To conceal her disquiet, she said lightly, 'Which wife had he found for you?'

Christie finished tying the bags to the back of the saddle. His horse sidestepped, snaking its head wickedly, and Meg stayed well out of its reach. She was competent with horses, but she had never liked or trusted this brute. It was a rich, bright bay, a handsome colour around a great raking gaunt frame that looked only fit for the shambles, and with a certain irony her brother had christened it Bayard. The noble name sat ill on the ugly, bad-tempered animal, but it had the reputation of being the fastest horse ever foaled at Alnwick.

'One of the Manners girls was mentioned,' said Christie, slapping Bayard's bony rump: the horse, Meg noticed, moved out of the way instantly. 'They're co-heiresses since their brother died. I didn't relish the thought of exchanging one draughty heap of stones for another, still less doing it at my father's bidding. You take a piece out of me, you evil old villain, and I'll have your hide on my feet before the week's out.'

'I can't think why you keep that brute,' said Meg, as a brisk cuff on the drooping red nose deflected it from her brother's arm. 'He must surely be dangerous.'

'Oh, he and I deal well enough together—we understand each other, we're two of a kind, and better the devil you know—and he's trained for war, which could be useful. No self-respecting knight would look twice at him, but he's better than most war-horses supposedly worth twice the money. And he has no equal anywhere for speed and strength, and that could be useful too. Move over, you ugly old devil.'

'Then you really are going to fight for Gloucester in Scotland?' said Meg. Somehow, she had not quite believed it: she could picture Christie as a lawyer, as an efficient if ruthless steward or administrator, even, should disaster strike, earning his bread as a minstrel, but not as a soldier. He had excelled at the arts of war, as a child at Alnwick, because he had found it an easy way to win the acceptance, if no more, of the other boys: but she knew that he preferred more peaceful and devious pursuits. He was not knighted, he had no sword: how would he survive?

But Christie, of course, would always survive: it was one of his many talents. She watched him check Bayard's girth and then, ready at last, turn to give her his farewell. He said, his voice unusually gentle, 'Do me the service of not fearing for me, will you? You know full well that I can always manage to fight clear of trouble.'

'Except when you deliberately make it,' said Meg, thinking of the impotent, raging, defeated old man she had left up in the bleak loneliness of his tower. 'But take care, Christie—please take care.'

Her brother laughed. 'When have you ever known me not have any care for myself? But you look to yourself, little sister,' he added, more seriously. 'When I told you a few hours ago, that if you ever needed me, I would come to you—I was not joking. It was a solemn and serious vow that I made to you, and though there was no sacred relic to swear it on, I hold myself as bound to it as if there was. So please, take care of yourself as well—and let me know if you should ever want my help. You will, won't you?'

This time, she accepted his concern with a nod of her head. 'Oh, yes, Christie, of course I will—you know I will.' And as the thought struck her only now, that this could be the last time that they would ever meet, she added hesitantly, 'I shall write to you, at Middleham, if I should ever have news for you. And you—you will write to me, Christie? If you send a letter to Denby, it's in Yorkshire, that's where his chief manor is—it should reach me in the end.' She discovered to her shame that tears were stinging her eyes, that her nose was running, and that she had nothing to wipe her face save her sleeve. 'Goodbye,' she said, her voice wobbling, and obeyed a sudden, childish impulse to hug him, ignoring the malevolent presence of the horse. Then she stepped back, ashamed of her sentimental weakness, and gave her brother, and only friend, her bravest smile. It drew one from him in return, and Meg knew that, though he did not show his feelings so readily, he was as moved as she. 'Goodbye,' he said, and kissed her gently on both cheeks. 'I must be gone before Father changes his mind and tries to chain me here. Take care of yourself—remember my vow—and be happy.'

She stood in the mud and ordure of the barmkin, within the circle of tower and stable and barn and byre, and watched him mount the great ugly bay horse and ride away from her out of the gate, with just one backward glance and a wave of his hand: and although he was soon out of sight amongst the trees, she stood there for a long,

long time before turning, a sad, forlorn figure robbed of all her vaunted self-reliance, and trudged back inside the tower.

*

Christie also felt some sadness, but it was soon gone as he gave Bayard his head along the rutted mired track that led westwards from Bokenfield. In a few moments, they came to a much wider road that crossed their path. He reined the horse in with some difficulty, for the animal had not had an extended gallop for some days, and looked to right and to left along the river of mud and ridges, puddles and ruts, that was dignified by the name of Great North Road. To the right lay the Scots, Berwick, and the Percies at Alnwick, his old life, an old road he had travelled so often before. And to the left, the south, London, the soft green of a more kindly country than his native Northumberland. And, not so far, Middleham in Yorkshire, where Richard Plantagenet, Duke of Gloucester, kept his court and his council and ruled the North for his brother King Edward.

His future beckoned. With confidence, and certainty, and an overwhelming sense of freedom at last attained after a lifetime spent under others' rules and restrictions, Christie Heron turned his horse's head and rode south, towards Middleham.

CHAPTER TWO

**'A mighty Duke, and many
goodly men about him.'**
(BOOK 4, CHAPTER 24)

It had been raining all day, a heavy miserable downpour accentuated by gusts of bitter November wind. The road was a quagmire, pitted with ruts melting into puddles, streams flowing into miniature lakes. Dark was approaching, and the bleak landscape was deserted: not a sound anywhere save for the raindrops beating on the few remaining leaves and branches of a skeletal oak tree, and the harsh desolate cawing of a rook.

Perkin Hobbes sat under the oak, sheltered to a small degree by its bulk, by a stand of brown wet bracken, and by a thick woollen hood covering his lank dark hair. He was cold, he was so hungry that food occupied his thoughts almost to the exclusion of all else, he had forgotten when he had last tasted meat or had a hot meal, but despite these deprivations he was not uncheerful. If Perkin had been of sufficiently exalted birth to merit a motto, the most appropriate one would have been, 'Something will always turn up'—and up until now, something always had. He had begged, borrowed and thieved his way from his native London to these barren and inhospitable parts, although without any clear sense of direction or purpose: and now, destitute, soaked, starving, he sat under the oak tree and debated the relative merits of returning to Durham, where he might be recognised to his cost, or continuing to move north. There was always Newcastle—he still had his pipe, he could juggle with any item of rubbish that came to hand, he had a good voice and a vast repertoire of bawdy songs. Failing that, he could always steal his bread. Something would be bound to turn up.

His ears, always acute, picked up a new sound amidst the heavy plop of raindrops. A horse, a slow tired horse, squelching through the mire of the road. Very carefully, Perkin turned his head towards the sound, parting the bracken fronds with grimy cautious fingers. In the rainy gloom, the bright bay of the animal's hide was almost extinguished by rain and mud, and even Perkin, no horseman, could see that this beast was not of knightly quality. Its rider slouched in the saddle, either very weary or half asleep, muffled within a large grey riding-gown, unfashionably plain but practical, and with a broad-brimmed hat pulled well over his eyes against the rain. Neither horse nor rider were in any way alert, and Perkin, sorely tempted, fingered the dagger at his belt. No-one else was about: surprise would be on his side, and desperation too. A lone traveller would probably not be wealthy, but a horse, serviceable clothes, perhaps a chinking purse, all represented staggering riches to a boy with nothing at all save what he wore or could carry.

The horse was almost up with him. The rider gave no sign of movement: Perkin could not see his face, could not tell if he were old or young, though his hunched posture rather suggested an elderly man. No sign, either, of any weapon. It was too good a chance to miss: Perkin, young, agile and desperate, would surely be more than a match for some tired old fool without the sense to ride abroad in company and good daylight.

He waited until the horse had passed him, going south, and then stealthily, using the skills developed by years of picking pockets and robbing houses, market stalls, passers-by, travellers, he slid from his hiding place. The damp rustle of the bracken was drowned by the rain: light-footed, he leapt from rut to rut across the puddles and without a sound hurled himself at the horse's sagging rump and the drenched gown swaying above it.

He never did discover exactly what happened next: he knew only that the supposedly exhausted elderly man erupted into a most un-aged life, that his intended victim employed a series of brisk, ruthless moves that he had not expected in anyone not bred in the gutter, and that he was abruptly divested alike of his dagger, his advantage and his dignity and propelled from the horse, to land with a soggy splash on his stomach in one of the larger puddles. Gasping, winded, Perkin choked on muddy iced water and struggled desperately to regain his feet and run.

The neck of his ragged doublet was grasped and twisted, nearly throttling him, and he was wrenched up out of the mud, crowing for air. 'Here's a nice fish,' said a voice unpleasantly. 'Wriggle, and I'll spit you.'

Perkin, never one to put his life in unnecessary danger, obediently hung still in his captor's grip. Cautiously, he opened his eyes, still blurred with thick slimy mud, and took stock of the traveller he had thought to rob. Too late, he realised the extent of his error: the somnolent old man was in fact young, tall and possessed of considerable strength, judging by the ease with which he had hold

[21]

of Perkin's clothing. In the gloom he could see little of the man's face, but the eyes were noticeable even in this light, being a chilling cold pale grey. Most telling of all, however, was the long, plain, extremely sharp dagger resting against his scrawny belly. Perkin, aware of the point rubbing gently just below his navel, put some effort into controlling his breath. At least he was not dead yet: although, to judge by the implacable look on the tall man's face, it would not be long before he was. He essayed a cheerful grin, and said, in the ineradicable accents of London, 'Sorry, sir—I mistook you for someone else.'

'For someone worth robbing,' said his captor coldly. Perkin rattled on, his voice bright and cocky. 'Didn't mean no 'arm, sir, 'ope I didn't frighten your 'orse, like, I was only practising my tumbling, sir.'

'You *what?*' Disbelief was plain in the other man's voice: and something else. Perkin, suddenly aware of an unlikely sliver of a reason for hope, said cheerfully, 'My tumbling, sir. 'S what I do, like. For a living. I was practising, sir, and it went wrong—didn't mean no 'arm, sir, honest.'

For a long, long moment, those strange, compelling eyes stared at him. Perkin, emboldened, wiped his streaming face with his sleeve. The dagger did not move. Then the other said, in a conversational tone, 'A little dangerous, don't you think?'

'Eh? Dangerous?'

'Yes, I'd have thought it most unwise, not to say risky, to practise your tumbling with a dagger in your hand. Wouldn't you say the same?' And he indicated with a jerk of his head the spot where Perkin's own notched and humble weapon lay half-submerged in the mud.

'That, sir?' Perkin, now committed, saw no option but to brazen it out. 'Oh, that! Yes, it's mine, sir, but I don't rightly know what it's doing down there. Must've fallen from my belt when I was leaping, sir.'

The silence was punctuated by the rain. A large drop fell from the end of Perkin's insignificant nose. Astonishingly, the other man gave a sudden shout of genuine, delighted laughter. 'Mother of God, you've the Devil's own insolence! Are you or are you not going to admit you were doing your best to rob me?'

Perkin stared at him, for a moment lost for words. Then he said, 'What if I was? You're going to rip me up anyway.'

'Wouldn't risk blunting the blade—your hide must be tougher

[22]

than my horse's. Let's have one thing understood—I am not going to kill you. I generally need a better reason than failed robbery. But if you run—well, have you ever seen a thrown knife?'

Perkin shook his head, mute. In one swift, accomplished movement, the other man turned the dagger so that the blade was in his fingers and flung it. Perkin's eyes followed it to its target, a split in the oak tree's bark some thirty feet away, where it rested quivering gently. The hair prickled on the back of his neck, and his stiff fingers sketched the sign of the cross.

'I'm no sorcerer—I merely take the trouble to practise my skills,' said the tall man. He let go of the boy's doublet and picked up Perkin's own weapon, fingering its edge with resignation. 'Not so dangerous, this—I doubt it'd cut through cloth, never mind skin and bone.'

'I know,' said Perkin, more cheerfully. 'How could I juggle with it if it was sharp, eh?'

His captor let out a curious sound that sounded suspiciously like a snort. 'No wonder it's notched. How old are you, boy?'

'I was born the year after King Edward married the Woodville woman,' said Perkin. 'That's what my mother said, anyway. She reckoned she was married the same month as him, and I was born the next year. June, it was, St Peter's day,' he added. 'Though everyone calls me Perkin. Perkin Hobbes, sir, of the Red Lion in Aldgate, in the fair City of London, at your service.' And he bowed, with a flourish.

'At my service? I doubt it. So you're sixteen, perhaps, and you juggle and thieve—what else do you do?'

'I pipe, sir, and I sing. Not badly, people say, sir,' Perkin added, with a certain pride.

'Well, I won't ask you for a demonstration of your talents—not here, anyway. Why did you leave London?'

A certain shiftiness passed over Perkin's face. 'I had a—a disagreement with my mother, sir. She turned me out.'

'What did you do? Thieve her gold?'

'No, nothing like that, sir—it wasn't hers, I wouldn't steal from my own mother, sir. It was the foreign gentleman from Lombardy —he had so many florins, beautiful they were, I didn't think he'd miss one or two,' said Perkin, with a wistful sigh at the thought of all that glittering, perfect gold. 'He did, though, mean old bastard, and my mam found one on me. I'd spent the rest,' he added. 'Bought meself a nice new velvet doublet, but I had to sell that when

I got to York. Nice city, York, though not so fair as London—are you going to York, sir?'

'No—to Middleham. I have business with the Duke of Glouces-ter.' In the gathering dark, those pale eyes looked Perkin's slight, mudsoaked, disreputable figure up and down. 'And what shall I do with you? Turn you loose to raid the next unsuspecting passer-by? Hand you over to the Durham Justices? A spell in the pillory would be the least punishment you could expect, I'd reckon. Or are you known in Durham already?'

'They might know me again, I suppose,' said Perkin, carelessly. Even the advancing gloom was no protection against the expression on the other man's face, and he decided on what passed in him for honesty. 'It wasn't nothing serious, sir—truly, I didn't try to steal nothing—it was the rain did for me in Durham, all set nice I was and then it bleeding *pissed* down and washed 'em all off.'

The silence was deafening. Perkin hurried to fill it. 'Me sores, sir. I was begging, thought I'd get more money if I looked a bit, well, shabby, pathetic, like. So I painted sores on me face. A whore gave me a smear or two, nice little girl, though I couldn't understand hardly a word of what she said, they talk foreign up here. And I was sitting there doing quite nicely thank you, penny or two in me hood, and then it started raining and before I knows where I am, it's in the pillory with a dead cat's guts round me neck and then kicked out and told to try me tricks elsewhere. That was the day before yesterday,' he added. 'And I ain't had nothing to eat since.'

'And not a lot in the last few weeks either, by the look of you,' said the other man. 'Well, Perkin Hobbes of the fair city of London, failed thief, failed beggar, failed tumbler—I think I may be able to help you. How would you like to be my servant?'

'Eh?' Perkin's scanty jaw dropped in total disbelief. Of all the possible outcomes of this unfortunate—or perhaps not so unfor-tunate—encounter, this was the least likely, the most improbable, the most outrageous. What had he done to deserve it? As the man—the gentleman—had said, he was a failure, half-starved, desperate, hundreds of miles from the home he had left in disgrace years ago, a creeping maggot of humanity on the wild desolate face of Northern England, without any future and only a store of unreasonable, foolish optimism to sustain him. And to have that hope justified almost destroyed all his cheery, shallow, hard-won confidence, and turned his world upside-down. Suddenly tears stood in his eyes, shamefully, and his nose began to run: with an effort, he closed his mouth, and said in a hoarse gasp, 'Why? Why, sir? In God's name, *why?* You're joking, sir, you must be. *Me? Me a servant? Why?*'

'Because I like you. Because I need a servant. Because, in a life full of nice calculations, it is pleasant to give way to an impulse now and again,' said his benefactor, walking forward to retrieve the knife from the oak-tree. Perkin, slipping and squelching in the mire up to his ankles, followed without understanding. 'But me—I'm a thief, a vagabond, you said it yourself—what's to stop me robbing you and making off?'

'*I* will,' said the other man, turning, dagger in hand, so abruptly that Perkin almost ran onto its point. 'And besides, I do intend to pay you, and clothe you, and feed you. As you're an inn-keeper's brat, I presume you have some knowledge of the duties I might want you to perform?'

Mendaciously, Perkin nodded. He had taken as little part as possible in the running of the Red Lion, preferring to roam the streets with a gang of similar urchins, and not even his healthy respect for the strength of his mother's arm had had much effect on his lack of conscientiousness. Something in the other man's ironic gaze made him realise that the stranger was well aware of this possibility, and he added with reluctant honesty, 'But I don't know that much of servanting, sir. I learn quick, though.'

'Good—or you'll be back on the streets, or in the stocks. Do you think we can reach Durham before the curfew?'

Perkin stared. 'It's two–three mile at least, and it must be close on sunset. You'll never reach it—the gates'll be shut.'

'We'll see,' was the laconic response. 'Have you ever sat a horse?'

'A little, sir—I've ridden me mam's mule a few times.'

'In that case, I doubt you'd have got very far on Bayard. Come on, Perkin Hobbes—if you want a nice cosy inn and not a cold bed in a ditch, there's no time to lose!'

*

Perkin thought, afterwards, that it was a two-fold miracle that they had ever managed to reach the warm comfortable Durham inn where, astonishingly, he was to sleep that night, instead of on the cold ground with the rain and sky for a roof. Yet here he was, in an upstairs room with painted plaster walls—the Mermaid Chamber, it was called—and a feather bed for his master, a truckle bed for himself, and above all, a sight from which he could scarcely tear his

[25]

eyes, a glowing, crackling, lusty, even uncomfortably *hot* fire. He had not been so close to such a one for weeks: his hands crept out towards it of their own accord, while he pondered the astonishing events of the afternoon, and still more the nature of the man he must now call master. Christopher Heron, he had said his name was, and easy enough to see how that name had been come by, if all his family were as long and lean as he. But of any family Master Heron did not speak, and Perkin, not given to whimsical flights of fancy, could not imagine this unfathomable, enigmatic, self-possessed and somehow menacing stranger in some cheerful manor house, surrounded by parents, brothers, sisters, even a wife and children. He had shown no emotion but amusement, and Perkin had sensed, chillingly, that he was well-nigh impossible to outwit.

But Christopher Heron could have killed him so easily, and none would have blamed him for the slaying of a common thief in self-defence: indeed, he would have been commended for it, or for turning the robber over to justice, and a probable hanging. Instead, he had made him his servant.

There was a price to be paid for such benevolence, though, and it was being set out at this moment by an astonished and mystified chamberlain: a tub, soap, and several large pails of hot water from the kitchen. Perkin, hardly able to credit his ears, heard his master order him to strip, step into the tub and wash himself.

'Wash? Me? Oh, no, sir, please, sir, it lets in cold and sickness, don't—' His voice tailed away as he saw the look on the other man's face. 'In. Or you'll be turned out on the streets as you are.'

The dreadful rent, stinking, mud-soaked doublet and disgraceful footless hose were carried away at arm's length by the unfortunate chamberlain. Reluctantly, Perkin hunched his scrawny, undersized body into the tub. He had not seen his belly for days, and noted with weary interest the fresh crop of flea bites scattered brightly across his chest, glowing through the sticky smears of mud. Perhaps it would be better washed after all, and he might be rid of the passengers for a while.

Christie Heron sat on the bed, his back propped against the carved headboard, watched his servant gingerly soaping his arms with unthorough fingers, and marvelled at himself. Why in God's name had he attached this unsavoury fugitive from justice to his person? What was there in that pinched face and unlovely London voice that had prevented him from handing over the boy to his richly-deserved fate? A pick-pocket, thief, descended to the gutter even if he had not been bred there—there had never been less promising material for a faithful servant. And yet, he had liked the boy—liked the spirit, the cheerfulness in the face of all odds, the inventive mind, the bright spark of desperate courage he had sensed beneath the filth and rags.

And it had been true—he had enjoyed his capitulation to a whim. He had played God, and snatched a brat from the gutter. After a lifetime at the beck and call of others, Percies and Herons, he was striking out on his own. A servant was symbol of the status he hoped to attain, in the service of Richard of Gloucester, and Perkin Hobbes, cleaned up and put into decent livery, might be a passable example of the breed.

He stared absently at the boy, who was attempting unsuccessfully to dowse his undeniably lousy head, and met narrow, bright blue eyes staring dubiously back between streams of dirty, soapy water. 'You ain't one of *those*, are you?' said Perkin, suddenly wary. 'You ain't one of those unnatural buggers what like young boys? Is that why you got me here? He stood up, scattering water everywhere, and looked round wildly for a means of covering himself. Something in the set of Christie's face calmed him: he sat down again slowly and muttered, 'Sorry, sir.'

'I shouldn't worry, Perkin,' Christie said: he was having some trouble concealing his amusement. 'I'd feel more lust for a plucked chicken.'

'I bin called many things,' said Perkin, after a startled silence, 'but not that.' He wiped the water from his face, leaving a dirty smear with his fingers, and went on with uncharacteristic earnestness. 'All right, sir, I believe you.'

'For which benison, many thanks,' said Christie. The irony was not lost on his servant, who shot him a suspicious glance before continuing. 'But you see, sir, I don't know nothing about you, do I? All I know is your name, and where you're going. I don't know where you come from, or whether you have a nice wife waiting for you in some nice snug little manor somewhere, and a quiverful of sons—I don't know *nothing* about you! You could be the Devil himself for all I know.' He crossed himself as an afterthought: it made a grimy mark on his chest.

'And you feel you ought to know something of me before entering my employ?' said Christie, the beginnings of a smile on his long mouth. 'I'd always been under the impression that the situation is usually the other way around. I don't know very much about you—but enough, I think, to trust my judgement. I don't think you will rob me, or murder me in my bed.'

'I dunno how you can say that so certain,' Perkin pointed out. 'I can't even say it for sure meself—when I see gold, or silver, something comes over me, I can't stop meself. I will *try*, though,' he added. 'And you still haven't told me anything of yourself, sir.'

'Only after you've washed your hands, you revolting brat—you're just spreading the dirt around yourself.' And as Perkin, with a shamefaced grin, obeyed, Christie went on, with a brevity that concealed a wealth of discordant, unwelcome emotions. 'I quarrelled with my father and my sister is soon to be wed and I have decided to offer my services to the Duke of Gloucester at Middleham. I have no wife, no manor, no children that I know of, no land—nothing save what I wear and carry and ride. I may not be the best master for you, Perkin Hobbes—my past is no use to me, and my future is uncertain.'

'You could say the same of me—we're in the same boat,' Perkin muttered. He had not missed the change in tone and expression as Christie spoke: he added unwisely, 'What of your sister?'

The look that Christie turned on him would have withered a basilisk. 'Meg? I told you. She married.' And said no more: Perkin, suddenly afraid, devoted himself with unwonted energy to his ablutions, while his master lay silent on the bed and thought of the beautiful, calm, calculating girl who held such a dear place in his heart, and who had somehow betrayed him. In a few days she would be wed, if she was not already: there was nothing he could do now to alter it. But he had vowed to give her his help, should she ever need it. Please God, she would not, but he did not trust Sir Robert, with his black slippery hair and blue sliding eyes, and the honeyed soothing voice. He himself was no angel, he knew that and none better, but he had his own code, and would live by it to the best of his ability. Sir Robert served none but himself: his greed and lechery had brought about the marriage, and Christie feared that it would also bring Meg to grief.

But he could do nothing, nothing at all, save to turn his back on her, and pray that she would never, ever have need of him.

*

Three days later, Meg Heron put on her best velvet gown, the blue one with no holes in it, and went with her golden hair flowing loose for the last time to her wedding in the chapel at Alnwick, a

[28]

celebration paid for with Percy money and attended by a veritable army of Percys and their retainers. She made her vows and became Dame Margaret Drakelon, Lady of Denby in Yorkshire: and on the same day, in the teeth of a rainstorm that blurred the heather-covered hills of Uredale, Christopher Heron and Perkin Hobbes came to Middleham, castle of the Nevilles and now the home of Richard, Duke of Gloucester, the King's youngest brother and Lord of the North.

They had spent the night at Ripon, at an inn whose comfort and price concealed from both Perkin and the innkeeper the fact that Christie's small store of coin was all but exhausted. It had already provided his servant with livery, a handsome doublet and hose, slightly too big, in the white and azure blue that richer Herons than those at Bokenfield affected, and a horse, small, spavined and inadequate, but seeming as a giant to poor Perkin. But he had only once taken a tumble, fortunately into a grass tussock with no gawping stranger ready to point a mocking finger, and now, on this the third day of his purgatory, and despite his aching stiff joints and the saddle sores in embarrassing places, he was beginning to enjoy this rich man's way of travelling, to look about him and mark the changing scenery and places and weather without having to grip his horse's sides and reins convulsively at the first signs of loss of balance. As for the horse, it was an old, tired, witless beast, grateful for the lightness of its burden and content to plod on all day in Bayard's lively, frothing, ill-tempered wake.

They had ridden up the River Ure from Ripon amidst unseasonable November sunshine: the earlier rain and wind had stripped the remaining leaves from the trees, and the bare branches glowed a warm brown in the morning light. They followed the track that wound alongside the river, sometimes crossing it, sometimes deviating some distance from it to avoid flooded water meadows. Often the road itself was flooded, and the horses were mired hock deep. And gradually, the woods and meadows, fields and stonebuilt villages gave way to a steeper, wilder landscape, and dark clouds came down to obscure the huddled shapes of the moors crowding the west, and hide the sun.

There was no guide, but the innkeeper had told them that it was a day's journey, no more, with God's help. The Deity had on the whole been kind until now, when the moors that concealed Middleham had themselves been hidden by cloud and rain, and the wind freshened and turned cold. Just ahead, the Abbey of Jervaulx, serene

[29]

and beautiful down by the twisting rushing river, promised lodgings in somewhat spartan comfort, but Perkin knew his master well enough by now to be resigned to the fact that they would not be receiving the good brothers' hospitality that night, but pressing on to reach Middleham. Weary, saddle-sore and aching with discomfort, Perkin glared at Christie's wide, impervious back and wondered why he had had the misfortune to be taken up by such an arrogant, pig-headed, unpleasant son of a whore.

But if he had not, his conscience reminded him promptly, he might very well be dead by now.

It would not have made him feel much more pleasantly disposed had he known of the thoughts inside his master's head. Christie had always, since early childhood, been adept at hiding his feelings: they were frequently of a depth and strength that accorded ill indeed with the facade of smooth, civilised courtesy and obedience which it was so necessary to wear in order to rise in the world. And rise he must, Bokenfield could not hold his ability or his ambition. He had abandoned his family, and his kin and benefactors the Percies with them, and was now about to cast himself on the mercy of Richard of Gloucester. It would not look or sound like that, of course, but if Gloucester would not take his service and his allegiance, he knew of nowhere else he could go. To return to Bokenfield was unthinkable, to the Percies, who had engineered that marriage for Meg, even more so. Without money he was nothing, and even the scanty coins sewn into his belt were of Percy origin. And the thought came to him, as he strained for his first sight of Middleham amid the approaching rain clouds, that he had never really liked the Percies. Great they were, and generous, but their generosity had not lacked a price, and that price had been unquestioning obedience to their will. He thought of his uncle, the fourth Earl, cold and hawkfaced and unbelievably proud, who held without question to the right of his family to rule the North as if they were the Kings of it. Only the Dowager, the woman his Percy grandfather had married after siring his mother, had shown him any warmth, any affection for him that expected no benefit for herself. She had marked his voice first, untrained and strongly true, and at the age of twelve as high and pure as Border air, and all else had followed. To the Countess Eleanor he owed the lute that jiggled softly against his thigh to the time of Bayard's hoofbeats, and all the music that was his passion and his only link left, now Meg had gone, between the Christie he was within, and the cold face he turned to the world.

He had heard that Richard of Gloucester appreciated music. Perhaps that was a good omen: he hoped so, for he knew no future save one at Middleham.

They came to the castle as darkness and rain alike were beginning to fall. Middleham was a substantial village that boasted stone-built houses, a broad square and a market cross: evidently the place had prospered greatly with the presence of the castle, tall and brooding and set with banners, glowering above it, dominating all around. At this hour, few were abroad, and no-one gave Christie and Perkin more than a cursory glance as they urged their tired horses up to the gatehouse that all but opened off the market square.

Perkin looked about him with interest and a well-disguised feeling of apprehension. He had never been within a castle's walls before, never dared to come so close to the strongholds of the greatest in the land—and Gloucester was the King's right arm in the North, as was well-known. He supposed, however, that his master was more familiar with the ways of the aristocracy and their minions, and certainly the manner in which Christie was now speaking with the gate-ward gave that impression. Authoritative and assured, he had already confirmed that the Duke was in residence, although this fact had been implied by the White Boar banner flying arrogantly from the keep, and had managed to give the impression, entirely erroneous, that His Grace of Gloucester would be expecting his arrival. Perkin, sharp-eared in the background, felt the first stirrings of pride. Christie Heron might have odd, not to say menacing, ways, but he certainly knew how to command, and how to handle the kind of petty-minded, obstreperous official usually to be found in gatehouses, whether in palace, city, castle or manor house.

Proof of that had arrived in the form of grooms, come to take their horses, and on their heels an elegantly-clad boy, a page or a squire, summoned by a servant to conduct this latest visitor to the keep, where even now supper was being made ready.

'I wish to speak with the Duke,' Christie said, an imperious note in his voice as if, thought Perkin admiringly, he had been born to command instead of spending a life at the beck and call of his father and the Percies: so much had Perkin deduced from the four days of their acquaintance. The page, a child of about eleven or twelve but already near his own height, was a round rosy well-fed boy who looked as if he had never known a day of hunger or thirst, rain or cold in his life. His gaze flicked shrewdly and contemptuously over

Perkin's insignificance: then, their horses left in the care of the grooms, to be housed in the stables in the outer ward to their left, the boy escorted them across the cramped bailey to the keep.

After the gracious, lordly space of Alnwick, Middleham seemed a crowded castle, packed with towers and buildings ranged against its walls, and Christie guessed that even in good daylight it would seem dark within these ramparts of deep grey stone: now, at dusk, the gloom was stygian save for the torches and cressets burning in their holders to light the bailey, and hissing as the rain struck them. The page led them perhaps thirty paces beyond the gate to a flight of steps which rose up to the first floor of the keep, and whose worn and irregular surfaces were half-hidden by the uneven torchlight. A porter's lodge in the thickness of the walls, half way up, sheltered a hunched chilly-looking man-at-arms, also with the white boar badge on his jerkin, who grunted in response to the page's cheerful greeting. Then they were ushered through a great doorway at the top of the steps, and into the Hall of Middleham Castle.

It was a scene of some confusion. The tables were being set up for supper, and servants, all with that ubiquitous white boar badge, scurried to and fro amongst knots of gentlemen and household officers, casually chatting beside the roaring smoky fire in the centre of the huge, shadowy room. A boy ran from cresset to cresset, lighting the torches and banishing the dark into the dim spaces of the beamed and gabled roof. Perkin, mindful of earlier instruction, resisted the temptation to spit or pick his nose: however, he could not help but stare like any bumpkin at the bustle and hubbub around him, in the largest chamber, outside a church, that he had ever seen. Fervently, he hoped that he would not disgrace himself or his master at the approaching meal: he had had several brisk lessons in the polite management of food and utensils in the days since he had entered Christie's service, but in such exalted company—even the servants seemed to be gentlemen born, and certainly better fed and educated than his humble self—he had no great hopes of success. He would just have to watch everyone else and copy them without making it apparent that he did.

The page left them to warm themselves by the fire, and soon an officer of the household approached, bade them welcome on his master's behalf and asked Christie his name and business. The Duke, it appeared, would be willing to speak with him after supper, and meanwhile there was a place for Master Heron at one of the higher tables, and another for Perkin amongst the other personal servants and menials, at the lower and draughtier end of the Hall, by the screens. The same page showed him his seat on the bench: under his breath, with some urgency, Perkin muttered the litany of good manners. Don't wipe your hands or nose or knife on the tablecloth, don't spit in the food, don't drink or talk with your mouth full, don't tell bawdy stories or get drunk, don't blow on your food, eat quietly and take small bites, don't put your elbows on the table—the list seemed endless, and he was almost relieved when the Duke, his lady and son entered, the trumpets sounded and they could eat. And once faced with food, Perkin forgot his worries and found that the polite consumption of pork and veal, venison and pigeon and sweetmeats, came somewhat easier to him than he had feared.

Only one thing spoilt his master's enjoyment of the kind of luxurious meal that he had not eaten since leaving Alnwick. This was the thready music of the minstrels, playing somewhat scratchily from the gallery above Perkin's table: Richard of Gloucester might be reckoned a great lover of music, but the standard of this particular ensemble left something to be desired. One of the lutes had half its strings out of tune, while the rebec player was hardly in time with the rest. Christie, well aware that he could perform far better himself, listened with interest to the comments of the men around him, all very similar to his own thoughts. He was informed by his neighbour that these were Lord Scrope's, and considered distinctly inferior to His Grace of Gloucester's own musicians, but out of courtesy and friendship to Lord Scrope, who lived at Bolton a few miles up the Dale, they must be given a hearing. 'Pity,' said the man on his right, thoughtfully dismembering his pigeon. 'For my money, a blinded cat would sound better.' He glanced shrewdly at Christie, who was removing some of the bones from his portion of pike, a fish that was an unwelcome reminder of his brother-in-law Sir Robert Drakelon. 'Come to take service with His Grace, have you?'

'Perhaps,' said Christie, his voice as unemotional as ever: impossible to guess at the feelings behind the flat tones and non-committal face, or the importance to him of the next two hours or so. The other nodded. 'Thought as much. Half of the North has been to kiss his hand and take his fees and favours, since the chance of glory in the Scots wars came along. If you have knowledge of arms, or of command, he'll not turn you away.' He cast his pigeon bones to one side of the plate and snapped his fingers: a servant came instantly to offer him another dish, and he chose the boiled beef. Cutting it with his knife, he added, 'I do not believe I have had the benefit of your name, sir?'

'Christopher Heron, of Bokenfield in Northumberland,' said Christie. He discovered in the course of ten minutes' conversation that his neighbour was one Ralph Bigod, of Settrington in the East Riding, related to Lord Scrope, and a gentleman of some substance who had been in the Duke's service for less than two years. He was two years older than Christie, a short thickset young man with a broad brown freckled face, his eyes and unruly hair of a very similar colour. It was not in Christie's nature to convey the expectations boiling within his impassive face after such a brief acquaintance, however open and friendly the other man appeared: so he was polite, non-committal, and gave nothing whatsoever away. Only his pale eyes flickered occasionally to the High Table where the man who, unknowing, held the key to his future was sharing a plate and cup with his Duchess, their son, a pale brown-haired child of perhaps six years old, acting as their page. What could be seen of His Grace of Gloucester amongst the shifting crowds of servants and diners was not discouraging: Christie caught a quiet smile for the little boy, and an affectionate handclasp with his delicate-looking wife. He had heard many reports of the Duke of Gloucester, some hostile—these mostly emanating from Alnwick, where his burgeoning power was resented and feared by some Percies—and the greater number favourable. Whatever else he could expect, it seemed at least that he would be granted a fair hearing.

Supper ended at last, with the withdrawal of the Duke and Duchess and the rest of their table. Amid the bustle as the servants set about clearing the remains of the meal, those who had no immediate duties remained to exchange tall tales of the Scots wars and to discuss Gloucester's plans, now far advanced, for the sieging of Berwick despite the coming winter. It was fast becoming apparent to Christie that, whatever his knowledge of the laws of the land, and his skills as a musician, his immediate value to Gloucester would be as a soldier.

A gentleman, obviously of some importance, approached to tell him that the Duke would now receive him. Christie was conscious of a certain surprise when Ralph Bigod, with obviously genuine friendliness, clapped him on the shoulder and wished him good luck. Then, with a quick glance around the Hall to locate Perkin, standing talking with some animation to another young servant by the screens, he followed the gentleman down to the door at the northern end of the Great Hall, which led to the chamber where the Duke conducted much of his less private business. Highly aware both of his own tension and of the need to hide it completely, Christie Heron was ushered into the presence of Richard Plantagenet, Duke of Gloucester.

The chamber was very large and high, and boasted a huge glazed window on its western side, that in daylight must command a fine view of the dale. In a heavy carved oak chair, his elbows on a table liberally spread with papers, the Duke sat, a man who must be a clerk or secretary on his left talking softly of some urgent-sounding business. The gentleman cleared his throat quietly, and announced, 'Master Christopher Heron, Your Grace.'

'Master Heron.' The Duke rose and came round from behind the table, his hand extended. Christie knelt to kiss it, in the act of humble courtesy that he had performed a thousand times to his haughty Percy uncle, and was raised to his feet, glad of the opportunity to study more closely the man who would, God willing, be his lord. The most immediately obvious thing of note was his comparatively small stature: he was shorter than Christie by half a head, and than his brother King Edward, whom Christie had often seen in London, by fully twice that amount. He was slender, and neatly made, and his face, with its broad brow and prominent nose and thin, rather stiff-looking mouth, was not displeasing. But he had none of the overflowing magnificence of his golden elder brother, nor any of the signs of dissipation and self-indulgence visible already in the King, though not yet forty. This dark young man contained within his slight frame an impression of controlled, powerful and yet nervous energy that was in its own way as imposing as the King's, though far less flamboyant. The narrow grey eyes studied the tall, self-contained man standing deferentially before him, cap in hand, plainly dressed and still bearing the marks of his travelling on hose and boots. Then he said, in a voice unexpectedly quiet, 'I understand you have business to discuss with me, Master Heron.'

Christie knew that he was being assessed by a man who had the reputation for being a shrewd judge of those who would serve him best. A great deal would depend on his answers to the Duke's questions: he said simply, 'I wish to enter your service and your household, Your Grace—and I believe I may be of some use to you, in Scotland.'

There was a brief silence in which he again faced the scrutiny of those perceptive eyes. 'You do?' said the Duke, without irony. 'Well, you may probably be right. Of what county are you, Master Heron? Your age? Have you training in arms? What learning have you? At the Temple, eh? You have some knowledge of the law, then?'

Christie, aware of sharpening interest, said that he did indeed.

'And was this training at your father's expense and behest?'

'No, Your Grace. The Earl of Northumberland paid for my place there. He is my uncle,' Christie added, knowing that here, if anywhere, would come the sticking-point: and saw Gloucester's eyes narrow. 'Your uncle? I have a fair knowledge of the Percy pedigree, and I know of no Herons amongst it—explain, if you will.'

'My mother was his bastard sister, born before his father married, and the Earl was so good as to take my young sister and myself into his household as children.'

'And had sufficiently good opinion of you to give you a lawyer's training? Why are you not now in his service, then?'

The simple truth, without evasion or embellishment, was best here, and Christie had long ago prepared his answer. 'My eldest brother has not yet produced an heir, and my second brother was recently slain by the Scots. My father looked to me to breed his heirs at Bokenfield, and had my lord of Northumberland's approval. So he ordered me home from London.'

Again, the shrewd, penetrating glance flickered over him. 'And I take it that you did not wish to be thus untimely wrenched from your studies?'

'That is true,' Christie told him, with some understatement. 'They were unfinished, and I felt that it would have been of greater profit to all concerned to let me remain at the Temple rather than hale me unwillingly home. And I felt also that life at Bokenfield with my father did not offer me sufficient scope for my abilities. Nor did I desire to return to Alnwick and enter the Earl's service. I knew of your need for men to invade Scotland, and I trusted that Your Grace could make use of me.'

'And you have of course your father's permission to come to Middleham?'

Christie's pale eyes met Gloucester's. 'I fear not, Your Grace.'

'And what of the Earl?'

'He does not know that I am here. I have signed no indenture

[36]

with him, Your Grace, and am neither his retainer nor his servant. I am free to give my service to you.'

There was silence in the chamber. The arras covering the walls flickered in the draughty candlelight, and the figures on them, knights and horses, paynims and infidels, seemed for a moment to be more alive than the two men standing facing each other in the centre of the rush-strewn floor. The Duke of Gloucester smiled suddenly. 'Some care may be required here—I fear the Earl your uncle is already something jealous of my influence in these parts, and the men I am able to attract. To have one of those his own nephew will not please him greatly, but if you have signed no indenture nor been retained by him, then you are indeed, as you said, free to enter my service, even if he has invested some money in your education and training. Do you have lands or tenants?'

'I fear not, Your Grace—I have but the one servant to call me master. I bring you nothing but myself and my skills and my brain,' said Christie, with a lack of humility that surprised the secretary, if it did not startle Gloucester. 'And I would not be speaking truthfully if I did not say that you may find them of some use to you, Your Grace.'

The darker grey eyes stared steadily into his, a crease between the straight, slightly winged dark brows. 'You may well be right,' said Richard of Gloucester, with a small, tight smile as if his mouth was not used to stretching thus. 'Master Heron, I welcome you to Middleham, and into my service. Master Kendall!' The secretary, a stout man in middle age with a balding pate and a furred gown, came forward. 'Your Grace?'

'I wish to take Master Heron into my household for the space of one year—in which time,' said the Duke, with a glance at Christie, 'I shall be well able to judge the truth of what you have said. He is to be a gentleman of the household, and to receive five marks a year, in addition to his livery and his meat and drink, and that of his servant and his horse. In return for this, he is to be at my service, and to ride and go and serve as I or my officers shall direct, and at my expense.' His gaze met Christie's again, and there was some warmth in his expression. 'And so I trust that our association will be a long and happy one, Master Heron. Are you agreeable to this arrangement?'

And Christie, calmly, said that indeed he was. As he stepped back from the table, there was no hint in his eyes or expression or bearing of the blazing triumph within. He had achieved his first ambition, he was in Gloucester's service: and now, if he were allowed to give

[37]

his gifts full rein without hindrance, who knew where his rise
would end?

❧ CHAPTER THREE ❧

'Such sorrow, that she
was nigh out of her mind.'
(BOOK 9, CHAPTER 19)

Dame Margaret Drakelon stood at the window of her solar, staring out at the rain which had interrupted her afternoon stroll in her garden—if such a word could so grace the straggly patch of overgrown herbs and leggy rosebushes that huddled against the rough stone of Denby Hall. In her hand, a bunch of sweet-smelling gillyflowers drooped sadly, clenched too tight, and her other fingers gripped the smooth worn ashlar of the window embrasure. The rain, uncaring, pattered in sharp gusts against the thick green-tinted glass, and obscured the distant trees and the tangled valley below the house. Slowly, the misery and dread almost suffocating her, she turned and made her way slowly across the rush and herb-strewn floor to the tall carved chair by the fire. Even in June, the house was cold, and the damp and draughts were barely kept at bay by the arras hung around the walls. Meg no longer noticed their splendid quality, the glowing colours and beautifully detailed stitchery. They had been bought from Flanders at huge expense for her wedding, and depicted the Marriage at Cana. There, water had been turned into wine: at her own marriage, gold had been transmuted into brass.

Such hopes she had had, in the chapel at Alnwick, when she had promised to take her husband for fairer and fouler, for better or worse—for what could possibly have been worse than her life at Bokenfield, an existence of lonely drudgery enlivened by her father's rages, her sister's spite, and the mindless mouthing and slobbering of her witless brother William?

This was worse. This bleak, isolated house in an unfrequented backwater many miles even from the nearest sizeable town, where it always seemed to be cold or raining or both (and only a month previously, it had snowed). A house where there were at least some creature comforts—glass, arras, chairs, fireplaces, garderobes, chimneys—but whose basic fabric had suffered long neglect and hasty repair. Sir Robert was not lacking in wealth, for there was iron to be found on his land, and the furnaces smoked by day and glowed by night like the images of Hell in her Book of Hours. The most immediately obvious reason for the poor condition of his ancestral home became clear when he brought his bride to Denby, a week after the marriage, and left her the next day, vowing to return by Christmas. That promise he kept, but in the five months since January Meg had seen her husband only four times, for a total of seventeen nights: he had been to London, to Windsor and Fotheringay and Pontefract and Nottingham, Alnwick and York and Berwick, while she had stayed here for the sake of the heir growing in her belly, and tried so urgently to keep herself from falling into the abyss of sickness and misery, lethargy and despair that yawned before her.

It had begun on the wedding night. Although of course still virgin, Meg knew fairly accurately what she must expect, and had looked forward with a degree of anticipation to the experience. It had left her bruised, bleeding, shocked and convinced that despite her husband's assurances, such demands and behaviour were not, could not be normal. She knew that it was supposed to hurt the first time—but not *every* time. And she could not rid herself of the suspicion that Sir Robert knew, and enjoyed, her pain.

She had tried to hide her surprise and dismay at the state of Denby Hall, the crumbling stonework and the smoky fires, the dirt and the general state of dilapidation: after all, Sir Robert's previous wife had been dead for some five or six years, his daughters were being reared in other households, and he had very frequently been at Alnwick and with the King in London. Smiling in the way that Christie so much distrusted, he had apologised for the short-comings of their home, invited her to admire the new arras that hid some of its defects, and admitted that he looked to his new, young, energetic wife to restore it to its former splendour—and to fill it with children.

And she had done her best, hampered by the bitter winter weather and by the household servants, who had done very little for too long and resented her instructions: bit by bit, chamber by chamber, Denby had begun to show a little of the fine estate that should be kept by a knight, and a King's knight at that. Meg had directed the cleaning and repair, supervised the steward's expenditure, restocked the kitchen and the still-room, employed more servants to assist in the running of the household, brewing and baking, in the stables and the fields. She had had a thorough grounding in the management of a large household at Alnwick, and

[40]

here there was the heady novelty of being in charge, at no-one's beck and call, of being able to direct others to do her bidding without fear of the kind of recrimination or petty fault-finding in which her half-sister Elizabeth had indulged so freely. And even her husband's absences were a relief, to her guilt, for her nights were free of pain and humiliation.

And then, late in March, she had realised that she was with child: and almost overnight, everything had changed.

Sir Robert, delighted, had insisted that she take especial care, both for the well-being of the baby and herself. She must eat only of the best, spend much time resting, refrain from riding or hawking: this last went hard with Meg, who enjoyed the wild afternoons with her little merlin on the commons around Denby, or on the fringes of the woods along the valley. But she had little choice in the matter, Sir Robert gave the stable grooms their orders, and she could go no further than the garden. But that she could have borne with equanimity: she knew the value of the child she carried, and that its presence ensured that her husband would not again force his attentions upon her until after its birth. It was the arrival of Mistress Slingsby that proved to be the fatal blow.

Mistress Slingsby was Sir Robert's sister, the widow of an impoverished York merchant, and the mother of several hopeful sons: it was presumably because of her experience of the birthing and rearing of children that Sir Robert had decided to ask her to foresake the household of her eldest son in York for a while, and to keep his young wife company until the child should be safely born. And in her brother's presence, Eleanor Slingsby was all affable smiles and kindly talk: it was when he left that his sister's manner changed. She was a long, lean woman, rather older than Sir Robert, with black hair dragged into a high-crowned headdress with an immaculate veil around her sharp, smooth face, signs of its true age kept at bay by, Meg suspected, the skilful use of cosmetics. It became swiftly apparent that Mistress Eleanor was a disappointed woman: disappointed in her husband, who had died untimely and left her such a pittance that she must depend on her eldest son for her bed and board, disappointed in her younger children, who were by her own account as ungrateful and graceless a brood as ever lived, and most of all, disappointed in Sir Robert. Mistress Eleanor had evidently assumed that her brother would make her eldest and favourite son Henry his heir, in the absence of a son of his own, and entirely disregarding the claims of his three daughters. She had lived for many years in this happy expectation, and to find him now married to a pretty seventeen-year-old who was already pregnant and could be confidently expected to produce a flock of heirs, was a grievous blow to Eleanor's hopes. She lost no time in taking her disappointment out on Meg: and to compound the girl's unhappiness, a few days after Sir Robert's departure, she fell ill. Every morning she was violently, uncouthly sick, and quite frequently during the day as well. Nothing she ate, not even the most tempting delicacies, seemed to quiet her rebelling stomach. Mistress Eleanor alternated between solicitous care, even going to the lengths of entering the kitchen to prepare a posset or a mess of eggs with her own hands, and brisk tirades to the effect that all women suffered such spasms, it was quite usual in the early months of pregnancy, and Meg should stop moping and apply herself to her household duties.

This, Meg would willingly have done had she still been in good health: for although the child within her seemed well enough, and was moving strongly, she herself had never in all her life felt worse. All her former energy and joy of living seemed to have leaked out of her, and the old calm confidence—in herself, in her future, in the choice she had made—had gone with the well-being that she had taken so much for granted. All her life, she had possessed unthinking good health and spirits, while so many around her suffered from a variety of greater or lesser ailments, and earned her disparagement thereby. Now she was laid low, and could not bear it, the nausea, the indignity, and worst of all, the unpleasant fact that stared back at her daily from her little silver mirror: her looks had gone. Her face and figure, save for the growing mound of pregnancy, were gaunt and strained, the golden hair hung as slack and dry and lifeless as straw, the rosy colour had vanished from her cheeks. And as well as fear for the baby, she knew fear for herself. Her husband had married her for her fresh beauty, her sweet young body and her youthful gaiety. How much more neglectful, how unpleasant would he become, when he saw her ugliness?

Mistress Eleanor played on that fear, urging her to tend herself, to use cosmetics, to wash her hair in chamomile water, for what would Sir Robert say when he saw her? But the heart and spirit had gone from Meg: without the energy to do more than walk a few steps in the garden—and even to rise from her bed took a supreme effort of will—she could spare nothing for arts that would only put garish paint on a withering flower. When not sewing, she read over and over again the few romances and histories she had brought with her from Alnwick, and gradually, strangely, began to feel that she, Meg, Dame Margaret Drakelon, was not real any more, but some figure in a story, a lady whose distress had once seemed so immediate and bitter, and who now had the shadowy remoteness of a Nicolette or a Guinevere or an Elaine. She had ceased to exist.

And then Mistress Slingsby was called away to York, late in May, to tend her son Henry, who had been taken ill. She was gone for ten days, and during that time, freed of her carping tongue and her undisguised hostility, Meg felt the first stirrings of energy and emotion for two months. The nausea and sickness swiftly diminished and disappeared after a few days, and she realised, with a thrill of delight, that outside, in the world she had ignored in her illness, it was almost summer—warm sunshine, growing grass, flowers and blossom and young animals. A scrawny yard cat, all sharp grey tabby bones, had a litter of five kittens in the stables, and Meg, aware of a strong feeling of kinship with this new mother, had them all, flea-ridden as they were, brought into her solar and installed in a basket by the fire. This delighted her maid, Joan, a sentimental girl of good but poor family, who had been chosen by Sir Robert for her plain face, her skill with a needle and with hair, and for the fact that she could read and write. And it was Joan, her head filled with the romances that she had read to Meg during the days of her illness, who first put into words the frightening truth that her mistress had ignored in the days since Mistress Eleanor's departure. 'You look so much better now, lady, just like you used to be when you first came here.' She took another strand of pale, glittering hair and stroked the brush down its length, again and again: when Meg had been married in her hair, as the saying went, the flowing, glowing golden locks had reached nearly to her knees. 'Your hair's shining again—that wash did it good.'

'It did me good,' said Meg, smiling into the mirror. She was still too thin, her face in repose was still gaunt and strained, but that smile had something of the old vitality about it, and if Sir Robert were to return from the Scottish Borders soon—and his last letter had seemed to suggest it—he would not be too dismayed at his wife's looks. No need now to pinch her thin cheeks to colour them: they had regained a little of their former glow, and every day that passed would improve them.

'I'll tell you who doesn't do you any good,' Joan continued, brushing the mass of hair back ready to be contained within the

[43]

hood that she wore in the privacy of her home. 'That Mistress Eleanor. Strange how you started getting better just after she left, wasn't it? Why, you could almost think she was poisoning you.'

There was a horrified silence. Meg's blue eyes, wide with shock, stared at Joan's hazel ones in the mirror. Then, she jerked round on the stool to face her maid. 'You—you can't be serious. *Poisoned?* In the name of all the saints, why?'

'Oh, that's plain to see,' said Joan, who was naïve enough to feel a certain amount of gratification at Meg's reaction: she had never been taken so seriously before. 'You're doing her precious Master Henry out of his inheritance, aren't you? That baby inside you, if it's a boy, will be Sir Robert's heir, and Master Henry won't get a penny. My guess,' Joan added, warming to her theme with a relish that took no account of Meg's horrified ashen face, 'is that she's trying to get rid of the baby. If you die as well, that's a bonus. It all fits, lady, don't you see, it all fits! All goes well until *she* comes along—then you fall ill. You get worse and worse, but you're strong, lady, thanks be to the Blessed Virgin, so the baby isn't harmed. Then her precious Henry falls sick, and she has to hurry back to York to tend him—he's more important to her than you are, after all. And as soon as she goes, you start to get better. Why, she's only been gone six days, and already you're a new woman, lady—or the old one, rather. Yes, she *must* be poisoning you— or bewitching you, perhaps. I could believe that one was a witch.'

As Joan spoke, Meg clung to the table on which the mirror was propped, her mind lurching into turmoil. Poison, witchcraft, bitter hatred, these belonged properly to the world of story and fable, not to her own prosaic reality. And yet—and yet, as Joan had artlessly pointed out, it all fitted. With a feeling that her world was closing in upon her, threatening not only her fragile happiness but her sanity and her life, she covered her face with her hands. 'I must be going mad—it can't be true, Joan, it can't! That sort of thing, it happens in stories, yes, but not here, not now—I can't believe it!'

'They say the Duchess of Clarence was poisoned,' Joan told her, eyes wide. 'By her own maid, too, and her baby son killed by witchcraft. If that can happen in the household of the King's own brother, why not here in Denby?' She leaned forward urgently, so far forgetting herself as to grasp Meg's thin shoulders. 'Oh, my lady, think on it! If you don't believe it, you'll play into her hands—she'll poison you, bewitch you, the baby will die, *you* might die! But you *must* believe it, you must—and then we can guard against her, that evil old woman.'

'How?' Meg, despite her doubts, was beginning to be carried along by Joan's desperate anxiety and her obvious belief in her theories. No use to point out that the Duchess of Clarence's unfortunate servant had been arrested and executed without trial by the Duke on what was almost certainly an imaginary charge of sorcery and poisoning—a scandal still quite fresh in everyone's memory. No use, either, to remind herself that this was Yorkshire, in England, and not one of those fabled Italian cities of sin and decadence where the administration of poison was a daily hazard for great and small alike. Even if she could not quite believe Mistress Slingsby, however strong her motive and hatred, to be capable of deliberately poisoning her or her unborn child, she knew too well her capacity for malice, and could easily imagine herself the subject of ill-wishing, if not worse. Suddenly the return of her tormentor, likely within the next few days, grew menacingly in her mind to become a threat of huge proportions. Even if she were innocent of all deliberate acts of malice, Mistress Slingsby's mere presence would be enough to make Meg ill again. For how could she possibly trust her, after this?

'I'll protect you, my lady, don't you fear,' said Joan, passionate in her sincerity. 'I'll eat everything you eat, I'll make sure she doesn't have the chance to do her evil work again, I'll guard you and the child, never fear! And when Sir Robert comes home again he'll send her packing, you'll see, lady, everything will be all right!'

But it was not. Sir Robert wrote that urgent business precluded his early return to his dear wife: he hoped she was well, and in good health and heart, and humbly begged her pardon for his unavoidable absence. He longed to be by her side, and was always her devoted husband. Meg, in an entirely uncharacteristic spasm of anger, disappointment and fear, threw the letter on the fire. Then Mistress Slingsby returned from York, jubilant at her restoration of her son's health: she expressed concern at Meg's wan looks, and spent an afternoon in the stillroom, brewing a cordial which, she confidently predicted, would hasten her sister-in-law's recovery. Meg, aware of Joan's meaningful looks, was careful only to pretend to drink it: but she could hardly give up eating. For a few days after Mistress Eleanor's return, she continued well, though in a sorry state of apprehension and confusion, for the older woman's malice and hostility were even plainer than before. Then, one morning, she awoke with a dreadful feeling of nausea. It had begun again: and this time her decline, because of her weakened body and anguished mind, was much more rapid. She could hardly walk, the flesh fell rapidly from her bones, and the sickness drained her energy and left her apathetic and spiritless. Joan did her best, but she was neither intelligent nor careful: Meg was told one afternoon, by a self-satisfied Mistress Eleanor, that she had sent the girl packing back to her family in disgrace. 'I always knew that girl was a baggage, and I had proof of it this morning—I found her in my chamber rifling my belongings, the insolent thieving jade!'

The last vestiges of hope left Meg: she stared despairingly at the sharp-faced woman standing by her chair, and tried to cope with the knowledge that now she was utterly alone. She could not denounce her sister-in-law, for it would only be dismissed as the hysterical ravings of a sick woman beset by the notorious fancies of pregnancy. She was alone, friendless, ill and in the depths of despair. But all that emerged from her terror-constricted throat was, 'But what am I to do for a servant?'

'You may share my Jennet,' was the magnanimous reply. 'She is not as skilled as that wretched girl at dressing the hair, of course, but she has other qualities—discretion, seemly modesty, mature wisdom. *She* will not fill your head with empty chatter, madam.'

And Jennet, who was approximately the same age as her mistress, sour-faced and tight-lipped, proved true to Eleanor's word. There was not one soul at Denby who could help Meg, who could befriend her, who could stop her slide into that miserable slough of illness and despair: no-one in the world, thought Meg now, the tears on her face a bleak echo of the rain on the window, who could save her.

Except one. She held a sudden picture in her mind of her brother Christie, tall and smiling in the gloom of the chamber at Bokenfield, saying, 'If you should ever need me, Meg, or my help, you have only to ask, wherever you might be, wherever I might be—send me word and I will come to you, I swear it.'

She had taken that promise far more lightly than had he, secure in the glorious self-confidence of her youth, her looks, her chosen future. Now, with all those things, perhaps even her life, in mortal danger, it came to her with renewed force. Christie would keep his vow: Christie would save her. She had only to write.

Only. It was a big word: in her condition of sick fear and misery, even the act of writing to her brother seemed fraught with danger.

She wondered if any of her previous letters to him or to Sir Robert had reached their destination: certainly she had had no reply at all from Christie, not even to her announcement of her pregnancy. She had sent it to Middleham, hoping that he had indeed taken service with Gloucester, but she had no certain knowledge at all.

She must word it so carefully, to avoid arousing suspicion: sweat broke out on her palms at the thought of it. Again the small voice whispered in her mind: what if all this is purely in your imagination? What if Mistress Eleanor is innocent of all but a certain malice?

But if that were true, she herself must surely be on the verge of madness. For a moment, terror rising in her throat, Meg covered her face with her hands, blocking out the world which had become such a dreadful threat. Then, with an air of calm resolution which utterly belied the turmoil within her, she turned and sent a servant for paper and quill and ink, to send her plea for help out of her private nightmare and into the daylight of ordinary reality.

*

The stone-built house in the centre of Berwick, not far from the silver-smooth waters of the River Tweed, had not welcomed such exalted guests for twenty years: not, in fact, since King Henry, of late lamented memory, his formidable Queen Margaret and their young son had sheltered in the castle after their defeat at the battle of Towton, and their entourage had been scattered through the better houses in the town. The great Earl of Warwick, maker and un-maker of kings, had occupied the house briefly during his short-lived tenure of the town a year or so later: now, his younger daughter's husband sat on the grass enjoying the evening sunshine, with a wide group of friends and retainers around him, replete after a splendid supper of Tweed salmon and Scottish mutton. There was an air of muted excitement and pleased anticipation about the group: they were to invade Scotland on the morrow. News had just arrived to the effect that the unhappy and incompetent King of Scots, on his way to relieve Berwick Castle and recapture the town, had been seized by his own nobles, who had hanged his low-born favourites from Lauder Bridge, and hurried him back to imprisonment in Edinburgh Castle. Now was the time for a show of English strength, and the great army which had been mustered outside the Castle for some days, drawn from all over the North and led by the Duke of Gloucester and the Earl of Northumberland, was to march to Edinburgh. At last, a chance of real battle, not the brief unsatisfying Border raids and harryings and skirmishes that had been all they had seen of action so far that summer.

Christie Heron, seated at the edge of the group, would welcome the chance of real battle more than most. He had as little stomach as any of them for the burning of poor peasants' hovels and the wasting of the sparse fields of oats and barley and rye that were their bulwark against starvation: after the abysmal harvest of the previous year, there would be a more bitter one yet for many farmers on the Borders. Chasing screaming women, slaughtering cattle and sheep and facing desperate men armed only with pitchfork or scythe left an unpleasant taste in his mouth: he understood very well the military necessity for such devastation, but that did not make the execution of the Duke's orders any more palatable.

He reckoned also that Gloucester himself had small liking for the raids. In the seven months since he had entered the Duke's service, Christie had grown to like, admire and respect the King's brother. His reputation for fair dealing and good lordship were widespread in the North, and Christie had discovered that reputation to be well-earned. To justify it, His Grace of Gloucester worked extremely hard, and expected a similar level of effort and commitment from those in his service. Christie in consequence had been exceedingly busy during those months, helping to raise the army, riding all over Yorkshire and beyond in his lord's wake or in his service, and by his own labour, diligence and reliability carving out a place for himself in the Duke's retinue. If there was a delay in supplying armour, difficulty in obtaining horses, even an urgent and confidential message to be delivered, it became common knowledge at Middleham that Christopher Heron was one of the best for the job. His reputation for impartiality, coupled with his lawyer's training, made him a frequent choice for the often difficult task of smoothing ruffled feathers, persuading local gentry to part with money, arms, men and horses, or arbitrating in disputes between other members of the household. It was all very different from the diminished glories of Alnwick, where no real power resided now, and Christie, secure in the knowledge of the merits of his past service—for which the Duke had several times commended him—and hopeful that the invasion of Scotland would bring him military glory, felt the satisfying stirrings of contentment. He had made some friends amongst the household at Middleham, none of course to share his heart and soul as Meg had done, but good companions nevertheless: he was respected, accepted and liked for his own sake as well as for his talents, and the achievement of his ultimate ambition, the acquisition of land to call his own so that he could be free of service, did not seem so impossible.

The Scots singer, hired for the evening on the recommendation of the house's owner, finished his interminable warbling of some old ballad of Border skirmishes: Christie had heard it sung better at Alnwick. Silence fell, save for muted laughter in a further corner of the garden, where some of the younger squires and pages were playing dice. The Duke dismissed the singer with a groat for his services, and his narrow eyes turned to Christie. 'Master Heron? Will you play for us now? I think your lute would follow well upon the ballad singer.'

He was being tactful, for the fat Berwick merchant by his side had obviously thought the singer's efforts to be the height of musical taste, but a half-smile twitched at the long tight mouth. Christie, an answering smile on his face, drew his lute from the doeskin bag at his side, tuned it with quick deft fingers, and turned back to his lord. 'What would you have me play, Your Grace?'

Over the months since it had become known at Middleham that Christopher Heron had a rare touch on the lute, he had often been asked to play both at supper in the Hall, and more privately for the Duke, his family and intimates. Gloucester was a great lover of music, kept singing boys in his chapel and troupes of minstrels, trumpeters and shawms: perhaps of all his household, Christie was the only one with whom he could converse knowledgeably about their mutual passion, and over the last few months the formal relationship between lord and retainer had become more and more diluted by friendship. It would be a long time before Christie achieved, if ever, the intimate status accorded to Gloucester's boyhood companions, Lord Lovell and Sir Robert Percy, but he had earned the Duke's trust, friendship and favour: it was far more than he had ever received from his aloof and haughty uncle, the Earl of Northumberland.

It had undeniably been awkward, not to say embarrassing, to meet his uncle again: the Earl was one of Gloucester's chief lieutenants in the army, and evidently not best pleased to see his nephew and erstwhile protege in Gloucester's retinue, wearing the silver boar badge instead of the blue Percy lion. He could do little, however, since Christie had never formally been bound to him by any tie save that of bastard kinship. A cool nod was the only acknowledgment of the years at Alnwick, although Sir Robert Drakelon, ever at the Earl's elbow with the slippery smile that Christie had always loathed and distrusted, was more forthcoming. From Sir Robert, he learned that his father was well, and that his brother John's wife Anges had at last died, leaving him free to marry again and breed Heron heirs for Bokenfield: this had gone some way towards assuaging Sir Lyell's fury at his youngest son's departure.

'And Meg?' Christie had asked, conscious that he had not yet answered her last letter: he had in truth had very little leisure to do so. Sir Robert, beaming, had assured him that Meg was well, the child was due in November, that he regretted bitterly that he was not able to be with her as much as he would like, but that his own dear sister was keeping her company until the baby's arrival. 'She could not be in better hands,' Sir Robert had declared, and in the face of his evident joy at the prospective birth of an heir, Christie's hostility had retreated somewhat. He still could not bear the man, but at least he seemed genuinely concerned for his beloved sister.

Thinking of Meg now brought a smile to his face, and in response to Gloucester's request for something loved and familiar, he struck the opening notes of the song they had called their own. 'I have a young sister, Far beyond the sea . . .'

The music dropped, crystalline, into the soft evening quiet of the garden: even the bees, patrolling the flowers in the last of the sunshine, seemed to lessen their busy humming in homage. He finished the song, in which several voices had joined, and at Gloucester's suggestion played a new Italian piece, complicated, beautiful and requiring him to stretch his skills to the limit. The reverent silence at its conclusion was more triumphant than any applause: Christie, filled with the exultation that always attended him when his playing went well, tuned an erring top course and turned again to his lord. There was an interruption, however: a man in the livery of the King's courier had come into the garden, dusty and tired from his journey, and bearing a bag full of letters and despatches, from the King in London and elsewhere. Since, unofficially, his bag would almost certainly also hold a number of private messages, there was a good deal of interest: and when Gloucester had received the bulk of the mail, the rest was distributed. Among those honoured was Christie: he felt at once a lift of the heart, and a pang of guilt, as he beheld his sister's familiar hand. He broke the seal, strolling away from the rest of the chattering crowd to gain some peace while he read: and at first he thought that it was another ordinary letter, full of Meg's crisp neat comment on her domestic struggles. Then, he realised that the tone of it, and the blotched urgent hand, were quite, quite different.

Dearest Brother, I write to ask you if you have received my earlier letters, for I have not yet had any reply from you, and I know not where you may be, nor even if you are with His Grace of Gloucester or no. I have sent this to Middleham in the hope that with God's help it will reach you, wherever you have journeyed, for I fear my earlier letters have gone somehow astray, and I long with all my heart to have word from you. You will know if you have read my last letter that I am with child, which I pray to the Blessed Virgin daily will be born safe in November, though I do fear for its life, and mine, for my health has not been of the best and I have suffered much from sickness. Mistress Slingsby, my dear husband's sister, tends me most solicitously, yet am I no better. I long to hear from you, to know how you are faring, and above all, my dearest brother, I beg you most urgently to remember and act upon that vow you did make to me, before you left Bokenfield, for it has become most important to me that you keep your promise and perform it now, as soon as ever may be—you know well which vow I mean, and beg you to remember your young sister,

Dame Margaret Drakelon.

'Bad news, young Kit?' a sympathetic voice said at his elbow. The use of the southern diminutive of his name was one which he was still unused to hearing: he turned to see, as he had suspected, the strong, steady figure of Sir James Tyrell, one of Gloucester's most able captains. He had known Tyrell for only two or three months, but already much liking and respect existed between the two men, though there was some fifteen years' difference in their ages. Tyrell was an essentially practical man, hardworking and conscientious, fond of presaging his comments with the remark, 'Of course, I'm nothing but a plain old soldier—' As all his friends knew, he was very much more than that, or he would not have earned Gloucester's trust and esteem.

'No, no bad news,' said Christie, staring at the strange letter, so hastily written and, to someone who knew Meg as well as he, scarcely hiding the hysterical note beneath it. His sister wrote as if she were afraid, but of what, in God's name? Meg was not given to womanish fancies.

[51]

'It's from my sister,' he added. 'She married Sir Robert Drakelon.'

'I know him—cold fish, that one,' said Sir James, frowning. 'Your sister not happy, eh? Wouldn't surprise me, it'd take a hot fire indeed to warm up Sir Robert's bed.'

'She certainly doesn't sound very content,' Christie said. 'And she seems to want me to go see her. Though she doesn't say so in as many words, the meaning's quite plain.'

'Well, you obviously can't,' Tyrell pointed out. 'We march into Scotland tomorrow—what would Gloucester do if half his army went gallivanting off to see their sisters? Is she breeding, perchance?'

'There's a baby coming, yes—Sir Robert was so pleased, I could almost have liked the man,' said Christie, with a wry smile. 'I urged her not to marry him, but she was set on it, and so was my father and all of Alnwick—it was like casting straws against a gale. She's made her own bed, and must lie there.' His voice sounded callous even to his own ears: he glanced at Sir James, but that bluff soldier was accustomed to plain speaking. 'Aye, you've the right of it. Breeding women often have strange fads and fancies—my own wife was four months gone with our first child, and would not let me rest until I could get oranges for her—I ask you, oranges! And they're not cheap, fetched from London all the way up to Gipping with the carrier—I told her those oranges would be the ruin of us,' said Sir James, grinning affectionately. For such a direct, earthy man, he was surprisingly uxorious, and wrote regularly to his wife in Suffolk, for which he was as regularly chaffed by his comrades. 'And when she was breeding James, that's our second, proper little lad he is, she'd got it into her head that if she didn't drink malmsey three times a day, he'd not grow inside her, and die. Nothing would do but malmsey; seven marks I had to pay for a butt of it, and it's not even as if I like the stuff—sickly sweet like sugared rosewater, fit only for drowning in—ugh!' Sir James's brown weathered face, all chopped lines and angles, creased with mock disgust. 'Don't you worry about your sister, for all she's wed to that oily mackerel of a man—why do you laugh, eh?'

'You call him a mackerel—I'd always thought of him as a pike,' Christie explained. 'No, you are probably right—though Meg was ever a calm, sensible girl, not given to such things, and I never did like the idea of that marriage.'

'And since Sir Robert has been so much in evidence with North-

umberland, these last few months,' Tyrell pointed out thoughtfully, 'it follows that your sister may feel herself neglected—and
certainly more by her husband than by yourself. Well, with a little
luck all this will be over by harvest time, and you'll be able to go see
her. Poor girl's probably lonely in that rotting old house in the
wilds—ever been there? No? It's a bleak spot, and when I saw it the
house obviously hadn't been touched for years. Let's hope Sir
Robert has provided her with some companionship.'

'Oh, yes, his own sister is with Meg. She says herself that this
woman is most kind. I'll go there when Berwick is taken,' said
Christie, ignoring the worm of doubt and guilt at the back of his
mind, and letting Tyrell's robust and cheerful good sense carry him
along. Of course there was no need to go to Denby now—Meg was
lonely and fanciful, that was all, and however solicitous, he could
not imagine any sister of Sir Robert's being much of a companion to
a young and lively girl.

And besides, there was the real, the overwhelming reason why he
could not leave the army. They were poised on the brink of real
achievement, victory over the Scots seemed likely, there were
battles and glory in the offing. To scurry away now on some private
errand would be to throw away all that he had worked for over the
last few months, and to discard his future, to forfeit the good will
and favour that he had won from the Duke for his past efforts and
present skills. It was madness even to think of it. He would write to
Meg, explain why he could not come now, but promising to be
with her as soon as he could. Meg would understand—she was after
all closer to him than to anyone else. She knew the ambition that
fired his soul. Surely she could wait a few weeks longer.

*

So the English army marched away from Berwick, at dawn the next
morning, leaving a thousand or more men under Lord Stanley to
continue the siege of the castle outside the town's walls, and swept
unopposed into Scotland, burning and harrying as they went, but
meeting very little resistance. There was an unfortunate incident at
a small settlement not far from Edinburgh, where a party of
belligerent Scots had barricaded themselves in a pele tower and
resisted all efforts to dislodge them. In the end, fire was used: it was
Christie's suggestion, knowing that vulnerability to be the chief
defect of tower houses such as this one, and Bokenfield. However,
four or five English soldiers were killed during the attack, and

[53]

several more wounded. Christie himself had a fortunate escape from that time-honoured defensive weapon, a cauldron of boiling water poured from the ramparts: another captain had not been so lucky, and was badly scalded. When the tower had been reduced to a blazing spear of flame, disfiguring the evening sky, Christie went to see him in answer to disquieting pangs of conscience.

Sir Thomas Bray had been carried to a house of some comfort nearby, deserted by its owners at the English approach. One of the nine surgeons sent north at the King's express desire had tended him, but he was still in great pain: much of his face was raw and red with weeping blisters, and his hands were bound and leaking ointments and unguents. The little bedchamber reeked of noxious remedies, and Christie advanced carefully to the bed, breathing through his mouth, to comfort his comrade.

Sir Thomas was a much older man than most of the army's captains: he must have been in his early fifties, and his already sparse hair was peppered with gray. Christie knew him by virtue of the fact that Bray, a staunch supporter of the House of Lancaster in his youth, had been a friend of Sir James Tyrell's father, also a Lancastrian, and had indeed stood godfather to Tyrell's older brother Thomas. He had been persuaded to join the Scots invasion because of his knowledge of siege cannon: given the short life of most men skilled in such a risky art, his knowledge must be great indeed. He was a big man, heavily built and broad in the shoulder, with a very old-fashioned and bristling moustache and beard: they were rumoured to hide a fearsome scar earned at the battle of Towton, where Lancaster had been routed some twenty years before. Old Lancastrian or not, Sir Thomas had served the House of York loyally for several years and was generally acknowledged to be an upright, honourable knight of the old school, who had transferred his allegiance at the death of Henry VI and his son, to the Yorkist King Edward, and was now a trusted servant of the crown. Christie had always felt some impatience at his slow, thorough methods, his emphasis on the importance of knightly behaviour and his inevitable nostalgia for the glorious days of Agincourt, and many of the less reverent young captains referred to him as a prosy old bore, or worse: but Sir Thomas had suffered in Christie's enterprise, and must be comforted.

He did not appear in much need of it: he was sitting up in the bed, clumsily and painfully spooning pottage into his mouth, with a page to wipe away the drips and a servant hovering anxiously in the

background. 'Ah, young Heron. Come to pay your respects, eh Well, I'm not dead yet, you know.' He slurped the last of the pottage noisily into his mouth and gave the bowl and spoon to the page. The child trotted away, and Christie said, repressing a smile, 'I came to see how you did, sir. I am very sorry for what happened —I should have warned you in time.'

'That doesn't matter—I should have kept a sharper lookout,' said Sir Thomas. 'My eyes aren't as young as they were, and after this they'll be worse—I can hardly see you, lad, come closer. What do you think? Surgeon says I'll live to frighten my wife—not that she's easily frightened, mind you. Think I'll keep my beauty, eh?'

Christie stared at the crusted, swollen eyelids and the weeping blisters, smeared with an evil-looking greenish ointment. 'You may, sir. I am no surgeon.'

'Doesn't matter anyway—my wenching days are done,' Sir Thomas said, and belched comfortably. 'I had far worse than this at Towton—remember Towton, lad? No, of course not, you're too young. Not born then, I suppose.'

'I was just walking, so I believe.'

'Ah, yes, I forget how many years it was—cold, so cold, a snowstorm blowing all day, and more froze to death than died an honest death in the battle.'

'I know—my grandfather died there.'

'Your grandfather? Oh yes, you're a Percy byblow, aren't you —you can always tell a Percy by the way they look down their noses,' said Sir Thomas, whose own nose under the blisters was a blunt and unaristocratic shape. He peered upwards through slitted, bloodshot eyes. 'Have I offended you? No, I thought not—you're not so much a Percy as all that, Hotspur's line or no, and you've broken free of that nest of vipers—not even Hotspur could be trusted, you know. They speak well of you, young Heron, in certain quarters—a coming man, they say.'

'Perhaps,' said Christie, his smile as controlled as almost every deed and word had been, for many months and years. 'I must leave you, alas, Sir Thomas, and go on with the army. Is there any service I may perform for you, any request you desire to make of me?'

Sir Thomas Bray grunted, and brushed a bandaged hand across the wreck of his face. 'I don't know . . . surgeon says I can't be moved save in a litter, and I will *not* travel in a litter, fit only for women and milksops—I'll stay here until I can see to ride like a man.' He peered up at Christie's impassive face. 'Don't you ever

[55]

show your feelings? You should meet my daughter—she has no false calm, no dissembling, all her thoughts show in her face and her words—I've spoilt her, I suppose, but a truer maid never breathed —if the castle falls and you are free from Gloucester's bidding for a space, will you ride and tell my wife, explain why I cannot be with her? Yes,' said Sir Thomas, an oddly wicked smile on his raw swollen lips, 'you should meet my Julian.'

*

They had set out from Berwick late in July, and two weeks later the army returned, sadly lacking in any experience of major battles, but jaunty with the heady feeling of victory. They had taken Edinburgh without bloodshed, and Gloucester had held the city at his mercy like a fist around an eggshell: they had only awaited his orders to crush it. But Richard of Gloucester was a man humane and prudent, and rather than risk the wrath of the Scots within their own country, was content to have the various lords and bishops grovel to him and to his absent brother the King. Promises were exacted and agreements signed, and Gloucester withdrew his army to Berwick, dismissed most of them with honours to the harvest, and settled down to the closer siege of Berwick Castle. It took just twelve days until the beleaguered garrison, starved and despairing of any rescue by their fellow Scots, surrendered: the tattered, exhausted little band marched out, and that night, the twenty-fourth of August, Gloucester and the captains of his victorious army supped in the Great Hall of Berwick Castle, English again after a gap of twenty years.

As the remains of the meal were being cleared away, Sir Robert Drakelon approached the window-embrasure where Christie was discussing the significance of the day's events with Sir James Tyrell, who had been made a Knight Banneret by a grateful Gloucester, along with several other new knights, including Ralph Bigod, who had distinguished themselves in the recent campaign. Christie had received nothing, and had not expected it: the Duke was not usually liberal with such honours, he had after all been in his service for less than a year, and while his birth was not humble, his present circumstances most emphatically were. He was still only twenty-two, and his time would surely come soon.

'Master Heron?' Sir Robert's honey voice, intruding on their conversation, came as a most unwelcome surprise to Christie, who had not seen his approach. The man seemed made of

shadows, he thought, and turned to face his brother-in-law. 'Yes, Sir Robert?'

'I wonder if I might beg a word with you—a private, family matter,' said Sir Robert, with a meaningful glance at Tyrell, who immediately excused himself and went to talk to Lord Lovell. Something in the expression on his brother-in-law's face, normally so smooth and bland, warned Christie to be on his guard. 'I trust that all is well with my sister?' he said politely, and saw the mask of Sir Robert's courtesy and unctuous flattery crack open with appalling abruptness to reveal what he had always known to lie beneath. 'Well? Your dear sister?' said that deceptively pleasant voice. 'I have one question to ask of you, Heron. Why was I not told of her madness?'

The word fell like a hammer on Christie's mind. He stared unbelieving at Sir Robert's bitter, distorted face. 'Madness? What are you talking about? Meg's no more mad than I am.'

'Then you are plainly lunatic,' the other man said, his voice hissing just above a whisper: already one or two in the Hall were glancing curiously in their direction. 'As lunatic as she—she has killed my son in her madness, and I have had her confined now —she is a danger to herself and to others, she has killed my son, I tell you, she killed my heir!'

To see the normally cold, unemotional Sir Robert reduced to this trembling figure of hatred was almost as appalling as the words he spoke. Christie's face seemed to have become like one of the stiff masks that disguisers wore at Christmas, Robin Hood or Saint George or the Angels at the Nativity: a wall behind which his thoughts boiled in rage and disbelief. Remotely surprised at the calm normality of his voice, he said quietly, 'I think you had better explain, Sir Robert.'

'Explain—' The older man's rather full, reddish mouth moved convulsively. 'You and your cursed family had best explain—oh, you hid it well, did you not? A sweet young maid, open and innocent and merry—and all the time her lunacy hidden! I tell you, you have saddled me with a madwoman—her wits are turned, she is as crazed as a pack of Gadarene Swine—and she has killed our son.'

None but the stoniest of hearts could have been impervious to the grief suddenly, nakedly displayed in those last few words: but Christie, knowing only that some appalling tragedy must have occurred, that Meg's letter had been a genuine appeal for help, and

[57]

that he had betrayed his own vow in ignoring it, was oblivious to all but his sister's plight, and the guilt that suddenly threatened to overwhelm him. He said, his voice hoarse, 'Tell me—tell me what has happened.'

Sir Robert stared at him. Something of his habitual calm had asserted itself: he pushed a hand across a brow beady with sweat, and repeated, as if to a very young child, 'I have told you—she killed our son.'

'So you have said—but how? How has all this happened?'

'She was with child,' said Sir Robert, his voice abruptly weary and despairing. 'I know that I left her too much alone, perhaps —breeding women are subject to fancies—but my own sister had the care of her! She was ill, yes, but breeding women often fall sick, it was nothing more than that. But when I went to see her—only last week—I found her raving—she accused my dear sister Eleanor of trying to poison her—and she had left the house and wandered off, against my orders, she was not found for half a day, and my son was born dead, three months too early—she killed him,' said Sir Robert, and the sorrow had hardened into bitterness and anger. 'She killed him in her mad wanderings, that was plain—she railed against me, she tried to strangle Eleanor with her bare hands—I tell you, Heron, your sister is mad in truth.'

The rigid mask still guarded Christie's horror. His own hands longed to rise to Sir Robert's throat, and his heart to run south to Denby, to make some amends for his callous and selfish betrayal: but his training did not desert him, as it had deserted Sir Robert, whom he had loathed for his lack of feeling. 'If you say she is mad, you are lying. Meg is no more crazed than you or I—perhaps you should look to your own neglect of her for your answer, or study your own sister more closely. Or maybe you do not wish to do that?' He took a step forward, his pale eyes staring bleakly into Sir Robert's own. 'Or perhaps you are casting round for an excuse to put Meg aside, and take another wife?'

'I would not put her aside,' the older man said. 'She is mad, I assure you—and if you do not believe me, then go see her for yourself—but my physician says that it may not last, or at least not until she breeds again.'

'Then I may go to Denby to see her?' Christie said softly, the menace in his tone quite plain still. 'You will not lock her away for ever, then?' And at last the grief and guilt and fury filling his soul spilled over into his face and voice. 'Dear God, man, she looked to you to give her the sort of life she had at Alnwick—she loved dancing and music and laughter—and you put her in a mouldering old manor no better than a nunnery—worse, in fact, for what companionship did she have? Do you wonder that she has turned to madness—if she is indeed mad, and I for one doubt it very much. She need not have chosen you, but she did, of her own free will, and you surely owe her more than slander and neglect!'

And he turned to push his way to the fresh air outside, knowing that if he stared into Sir Robert's untrustworthy face for one second longer, he would smash it to a pulp with his fists.

᪰ CHAPTER FOUR ᪰

**'He that hath a privy hurt is loth to
have a shame outward.'**
(BOOK 8, CHAPTER 14)

'By all the saints, what a Godforsaken place!' Perkin Hobbes sat his
brisk brown nag with considerably more ease than he had first
ridden a horse, and stared around at the bleak wind-ravaged
common that stretched about them. Ahead was an iron-working
furnace, a huddle of huts about a noxious pillar of smoke, and the
track on which they rode led past this evidence of the land's riches.
Their guide shouted something, and beckoned: Christie Heron dug
spurs into Bayard's sides and rode up with him, holding in his
wayward courser's head by dint of considerable strength and long
experience. 'Denby Hall, sir, over there, see?'

Christie stared past the intermittent raindrops, over the scrubland and scattered trees to a fold in the hillside where a grey
smoke-leaking chimney surmounted a confusion of grey gables and
roofs that merged into the trees. 'That is the home of Sir Robert
Drakelon?'

'Aye, though he bain't there now—folks reckon he be wi' the
Duke of Gloucester fighting the Scots.'

'He is. I wish only to speak with his wife—she is my sister.'

A knowing expression crossed the guide's face. 'Your sister, sir? I
hope you find her well,' he said, and with a bow and a smile for the
penny Christie tossed him, turned his ancient fat pony and set off
back to the village. Perkin, who knew a great deal more about this
affair than even Christie suspected, by virtue of his long hours
gossiping with other servants, looked at his master's bleak face with
some misgivings. They had taken only two-and-a-half days to ride
here from Berwick, he ached in every joint, and Christie, whose
moods during the months of Perkin's service had been on the whole
fairly affable, had retreated behind an icy laconic mask and become
again the dangerous, unnerving stranger of their first meeting. And
there was not even any laughter within him: none at all, however
bitter. Perkin had early abandoned his usual travelling monologue
of jokes, comments and amusing anecdotes, and had followed in his
master's miry wake in a dismal and apprehensive silence. It was

obvious that the man had a deep attachment to his sister, obvious that she was ill or unhappy or both, and not surprisingly given the nature and reputation of the man she had married: but Perkin, who could be perceptive, had realised that there was more to the tale than a miscarrying, and wedded misery. Some inner demon, of guilt or dread or rage, drove Christie onward: he had not slackened his pace since riding out of Berwick the morning after its surrender, and Perkin wondered that the horse Bayard, remarkable for speed and stamina though it was, could keep up such a rate. His own old horse had early foundered, and this was a hired nag, fresh from that morning's inn: even so, it had been hard-pressed to keep up. Perkin stretched his back and massaged an ache with his fingers. At least this Denby Hall seemed large enough to afford a comfortable lodging for the night, and he had come far enough from the ragged waif of ten months previously, to expect a decent pallet in a dry, rat-free, even flea-free chamber.

The rain stopped as they rode up to the gatehouse of Denby Hall. Christie stated briefly that he had come to speak with Sir Robert Drakelon: the steward who had come out to greet them was apologetic. Sir Robert was away, at Berwick, though he had been here only last week. Perhaps Mistress Slingsby, his sister, could help?

'Perhaps—if I may see her,' said Christie, realising that this must be the woman whom Meg had accused of trying to poison her. He gave his horse and Perkin's to a groom, and followed the steward within the ancient stones and timbers of the house that Meg now called her home.

Mistress Eleanor Slingsby received him in a small sunny solar, lit by watery rays from the west, and boasting a roaring fire as well as arras that glowed with life and colour. Christie, appreciative, glanced at the vivid scenes around the walls, noting that Middleham could show nothing finer, and then turned his concentrated judgement on the middle-aged woman who stood before him, her hands crossed at her waist and an expression of polite curiosity on her bland smooth face. It was easy to see that she was Sir Robert's sister, the likeness was marked in colouring and feature, and was strengthened in the even, pleasant, somehow cloying sound of her voice. 'I regret that my brother is from home, sir. How may I help you?'

Christie allowed his face to show some puzzlement. 'I dare say you may, Mistress, but does not Sir Robert have a wife? I know her, and would speak with her—this matter touches her closely.'

'I regret, sir, that Dame Margaret is at present—indisposed,' said the woman, with just a flicker of some emotion in her eyes and voice. 'She is not allowed visitors at present. My brother has entrusted all his more private business to me—you may speak quite freely, sir—I do not know your name?'

He ignored that question. 'But I must speak with Dame Margaret —it is most important that I do so.'

'Then I fear you will be disappointed,' said his adversary, a snap of malice entering her tone for the first time. 'I regret that my brother's wife is grievously sick in mind and body, and must for her own sake be restrained. He was adamant on that subject, and I must refuse you.'

'He has told me that I may see her,' said Christie sharply. 'She is after all my sister.'

For a moment, he saw an expression of alarm in the woman's face: then she was shaking her head. 'The poor girl is your sister? Then you knew of the sad condition of her mind, yet you still persuaded Sir Robert to marry her—a sin, sir, a wicked sin, as God is my witness!'

'I did no persuading, and she has ever been as sane as you or I,' said Christie grimly. 'Some dire event has overturned her mind, perhaps? She was never one for idle fancies—could her ravings be true, I wonder?' And as Mistress Slingsby, well aware of the covert threat, shook her head in alarmed denial, he added, 'I will see her now, or I shall know for certain that you wish her harm. By God's bones, Mistress Slingsby, I am her brother—and Sir Robert himself suggested that I come here to see her! Now show me where she is, or I'll search the house myself.'

*

Meg Drakelon had been two months confined to the little chamber above the garden. The room itself was comfortable, with a feather bed, fireplace, stools and table and the materials for her sewing and spinning. No books nor writing paper had been allowed her, and Mistress Slingsby's maid Jennet tended to her needs. For two months she had been a prisoner both in reality and within her thoughts, and the initial anguish and terror that had threatened her sanity, the fear for her child and herself that had driven her, ill and weak as she was, into her despairing flight from Denby and the

[62]

malevolent presence of her sister-in-law, had long ago quietened to a calmer acceptance of her circumstances. Raving and railing against Sir Robert and his sister would do her no good—in fact, had been the reason to keep her confined. She had lost the baby, and after the dreadful pain and illness that had attended her miscarriage, the peace of the little room was almost a haven. She was left alone, and there was no madness in her now. She had made the mistake, last week, of begging her husband, with tears and pleadings, to restore her to her true place as his wife, to send Mistress Slingsby back to York, and to begin again: but her obvious desperation had only convinced him that she was still crazed, and Mistress Eleanor had been well satisfied. While Meg was assumed by her husband to be still mad, no further children would be born, and Eleanor had also planted in her brother's mind the idea that Meg's supposed madness might be linked to pregnancy. The prospect of a wife who was turned in her wits every time she was breeding, was no incitement to lust, and Meg, well aware of this, could wonder with despair whether she would ever leave her prison.

She did not blame Sir Robert, save for his neglect of her, and that had been caused by his duties in Scotland—many wives received even less attention. She grew hot, now, to think of how she had hated him in his absence, how she had dreaded their nights together. She felt she could bear any pain now, if it would give her the child that would restore her to her rightful place at Denby. No, she knew where the blame for her present misery lay: she placed it firmly with Mistress Slingsby, the begetter of her misfortunes even if she had administered no poison—and Meg herself, looking back with a mixture of disbelief and anger, could not decide whether she had been guilty of that or not. And also she blamed, with the especial bitterness of the betrayed, her brother Christie, who had not answered her plea for help, who, if he had acted at once, would undoubtedly have prevented the death of her child and her present plight. She knew, from what her husband had said, that Christie was with Gloucester: he must have received her letter, he must!

And yet, if he had, then he had refused to answer it, and come to her, and had thereby broken the vow that he himself had made. And the thought that she could no longer rely on the love and support and help of her brother, her dearest friend all her life, was the most painful of all.

So when the key to her chamber door turned, one day of sun and showers late in August, and instead of Jennet or Mistress Eleanor,

[63]

her brother, beloved and hated both, stood there alone, her first words were of bitter anger. 'You're too late,' she said, schooling her face over the sudden grief and joy and rage that erupted within her. 'My need of you is gone.'

Christie stood still by the door, his face as impassive as hers: she would not have guessed at his thoughts, had she not known them so well, and they always so akin to her own. He was taller than she remembered, and the months of riding and action had laid more muscle and strength on his lean frame, bleached his hair almost to her own gold and darkened his pale skin. From this new colouring, his bleak eyes stared at her, silvery and unchanging: and she thought, for the first time in her life, that he would make an uncomfortable enemy. He said nothing, and Meg went on, her voice sharpened and bitter with the memory of betrayal. 'I wrote to you. I wrote you a letter. Did you receive it, at Middleham?'

'I had several letters. The last one arrived when I was in Berwick.' His voice was as flat and unemotional as she had heard it at Alnwick and Bokenfield, conversing with Northumberland or some other whom he disliked or mistrusted or did not know: it gave nothing away at all. And Meg remembered the laughter they had shared, and could for a moment have wept. She turned her eyes to her embroidery frame, the tiny intricate stitches on the border of what might become a seat or cushion cover, and her hand brushed across her forehead. Christie saw that it was trembling: he had been appalled beyond measure by the gaunt pale shadow of his lovely lively sister, and the loathing she had put into her voice. He took a step towards her, the burden of guilt and remorse threatening to crack his reserve: then she whipped round, her voice rising with her fury. 'You had that letter! You admit it! You know what I asked you to do—I was desperate, ill, that woman downstairs, if she wasn't poisoning me in fact then she surely was in thought—I *knew* you would come, I *knew* you would save me—and you did not,' said Meg, her voice suddenly dropping with the weight of her anguish. 'You broke your vow, and my baby is dead, and I am mewed up here until my husband decides that I am no longer mad. Oh, yes, I know that I was mad—mad with grief when I miscarried, and I was ill for weeks—and mad too when I realised that you would not come, and I was alone.'

'I could not come,' said Christie, and the unaccustomed hesitation in his voice revealed the extent of his own hurt. 'Meg, I could not have come to you then—my duties could not just be laid down

[64]

at a moment's notice—if I had left Gloucester then, I would never have won back his favour.'

The sun, stronger and redder now as it sank, touched Meg's hair around her face like a gilded halo, and put spurious colour on her thin cheeks and compressed lips. She laughed bitterly. 'Well, at least now I know that I am worth less than your towering ambition, my dear brother. It's not a year since you vowed to come to my call wherever you might be, whatever you might be doing. If you did not mean to keep your vow, why did you make it?'

'I did mean to keep it.' Christie had his voice under control now, but his eyes told her another story. She hardened her heart and gave full rein to her anger, all the rage and frustration and torment of the past few months spilling over into her words. 'You told me Sir Robert was not to be trusted—how much more rotten and false are you? Nothing is worth anything to you unless it's a means to rise higher. All you want from life is a knighthood and the lands Father couldn't give you and the money you've never been able to lay your hands on. I should have known, I should have known what you were really like when you sat at the table at Bokenfield and manipulated, yes, manipulated Father into rejecting you—and all for your own selfish ends—I didn't like it then but I never dreamed I'd be your next victim—and my child paid the price and lingers in limbo, unbaptised, unshriven—I was trying to reach you, I was trying to escape *her*—I thought *she* was poisoning me, all the signs were there—she even drowned my cat and her kittens.' Meg took a deep quivering breath, and drove the knife in up to the hilt. 'Yes, I was mad, for a little while, because I knew you'd betrayed me and I thought I needed your help to survive. Now I have had time, plenty of time to think, and I know that I do not need you, Christie Heron! I will win in the end by being sweet, and reasonable, gentle and moderate in all things, I will not give way any more to grief or hatred or even love, and Sir Robert will take me back to his bed and board and I will breed more children and *next* time I shall be stronger. I have survived poison and malice and torture and betrayal enough for a lifetime, in the past few months—I am strong now, I need nobody at all, and I most certainly don't need *you*. You obviously don't need me—you have your wonderful Duke of Gloucester, and your splendid ambition to nourish and sustain your greed and selfishness!' She saw with satisfaction that her words had gone home, and got to her feet with a surge of energy such as she had not felt for many months. 'Goodbye, Christie. I have no need

either of your apologies or of your justifications or your excuses
—they would only make me sick again, and I need to conserve what
is left of my health and my looks.' She pushed past him to pull upon
the door. Somewhat to her surprise, it opened: there was no-one in
the larger bedchamber outside, and she turned, her blue eyes
blazing, to hold it open for him. 'You have outstayed any welcome
I might have given you. I have proof you care nothing for me, so I
have ceased to care for you. Now go, before I call the steward and
the grooms and have you thrown out.'

It was not Meg, said a voice in his mind: it was not his calm
certain delightful young sister, standing there afire with vicious
fury, rejecting him, spurning all the years of their childhood and
since, denying the love and companionship that had brought them
so close. But it was not his nature to plead with her not to do this, to
urge her to listen to the excuses she had just derided. Every fibre in
his heart screamed at him to humble himself, to go down on his
knees to beg her forgiveness: but his pride was too great. He had not
shown such humility to Gloucester or Northumberland, he could
not show it even to his beloved sister, however great his love and
remorse, his deep knowledge of the truth of her words. When she
had had time to order her thoughts better, perhaps after another
child—

'Go!' said Meg again, and flourished the door with a vicious jerk
of her arm. But in the end he would not just leave so tamely: he had
to try to make amends, somehow. 'Meg—listen!'

'I have listened enough. Get out.'

'Meg—' He stared at her implacable face, blazing with life and
colour in her anger. 'Meg, will you not listen, not talk? Meg—'

'Go!' Her voice rose almost to a scream: there were distant sounds
from the rest of the house. He made one last desperate attempt to
reach her. 'Meg, please—if you should think again, change your
mind—'

'To summon you and have it ignored? Don't be a fool,' said his
sister with utter contempt: and he knew then that he had finally,
irrevocably lost her.

*

There was no comfortable bed for Perkin that night, only a straw
heap in the stable of a mean little inn in the village of Barnsley, the
only one they found which would offer accommodation so late: nor
did he sleep much. Over the months in Christopher Heron's

service, his early suspicion and mistrust of the man who had so casually hauled him from a ditch and given him a role in life, however humble, had changed to respect, and even liking. Christie would undoubtedly go far, and Perkin knew from the gossip and talk amongst the other servants and their masters at Middleham that Gloucester thought very highly of him. If his master's future seemed to shine brightly, Perkin was more than happy to be pulled upwards in his wake: and besides, he knew something of the complex, powerful nature that lay behind that notoriously uncommunicative face, and liked it. So it was with a mixture of disbelief and anxiety, hastily restrained, that he saw Christie settle down in the tiny but private chamber that was all that had been available, and proceed to drink himself into oblivion on the inn's raw, pungent wine. Perkin swallowed his protests: he had argued against leaving Denby in such haste, and had had the impression that his master was ripe for murder and that he, Perkin Hobbes, would suffice for a ready victim if he did not hold his tongue. He had duly held it at breakneck speed all the way to Barnsley, some five or six miles, and held it further as the jugs of wine were brought, and the fire made up: then Christie dismissed him for the night.

'To the stables?' Perkin enquired, feigning stupidity. He had seen his master the worse for drink before, but that was different: virtually every man in Middleham, with the notable exception of the Duke himself, had on occasion drunk too much at supper or dinner. This cold-blooded, purposeful quest for oblivion was something quite different: it chilled Perkin to the bone, and brought to mind a neighbour of his mother's, who had drunk himself to death one night, quite deliberately, swallowing bottle after bottle of wine and Dutch spirits. He had been found the next morning, dead in squalor, and the street had been convinced ever since that his lurching, incoherent ghost haunted that house. Perkin had no wish to find his master in similar circumstances, and glanced hopefully around for a truckle bed.

'Yes, to the stables,' Christie said. The uncertain candle-light shadowed his face, deepening the eye-sockets and accentuating the sharp bones of his face, so that the structure of the skull beneath was eerily apparent. He poured the wine into the pewter cup, and sent his servant a look that admitted neither argument nor protest. 'Or are you afraid of the rats?'

'No, sir,' said Perkin indignantly. 'But—ain't there a truckle under the bed?'

'If there is, you're not grovelling for it. Now get out and go to your hay before I kick you out.'

And Perkin, recognising defeat, left his master to the privacy of his thoughts and marched off to the stables, where he spent a restless and uncomfortable night dreaming of rats, and ghosts, and butts of malmsey. Christie was no Clarence, a well-known drunkard who had, it was rumoured, asked for and received a drunkard's end: but Perkin was surprised by the force of his anxiety.

He rose heavy-eyed at dawn, and threaded his way through the bustle of a rising inn, eager travellers breaking their fast early, smells of baking and scurrying servants, to Christie's chamber. To his relief, his knock received a reply, and he entered hesitantly.

'Come in, witless one,' said Christie. He was up, and dressed, and devouring bread and salt herring. 'You look as though you were expecting a ghost.'

'No, sir,' Perkin muttered, glancing covertly about the chamber. The bed had been made and the little group of wine-jugs, all apparently empty, were lined up neatly on the table with the cup and the expired candle. He looked closer at his employer and saw no signs of debauch, and none at all even of headache: indeed, Christie from his appearance had spent a much more comfortable night than had Perkin. He gave his servant the benefit of a cold smile. 'What were you expecting? A shambling grey-faced red-eyed wreck, clutching his head? I can hold my wine better than that. Eat your bread and herring and then go pack the gear—we've a long way to ride.'

'Back to Middleham?' enquired Perkin hopefully. He had a very high opinion of Gloucester's castle, and in particular the excellent food offered, and the cosy accommodation ranged around its walls. He was doomed to disappointment. 'No. We ride south, to Oxfordshire.'

'Oxfordshire?' Perkin stared at his master dubiously. 'Where's that, sir?'

'I would have thought that after your misspent youth begging around the country, you should have more knowledge of it than that. Oxfordshire, child,' said Christie with heavily ironic patience, 'is the name given to the country around Oxford.'

'Where's Oxford, then?' Perkin demanded brightly. This was more like the Christie he knew and liked the best, treating him with amused tolerance, almost affection: it was as if the unpleasantness at

Denby, and the harsh-strung tension of the ride from Berwick, had never been.

'Oxford? You don't know where Oxford is? Though as they chiefly breed scholars at Oxford, I'd be surprised if you did know. Follow the Thames upstream from London for many miles, and you'll come eventually to Oxford—two or three days' journey, perhaps. Now eat your breakfast.'

'Why are we going to Oxfordshire?' Perkin next asked, through a mouthful of coarse brown bread and bony salt herring. Christie finished the thick sweet ale and put the tankard down on the table. 'To visit the household of Sir Thomas Bray. I should keep at least one of my promises, after all. And has the ten months in my service taught you nothing of manners?'

'We ain't in company now,' was Perkin's prompt response, but he made sure his food was swallowed before he next spoke. 'How far is this Oxfordshire, sir?'

'A hundred and fifty, two hundred miles—I'm not certain. A week's riding, with good luck and good weather—and that's leisurely riding, so don't look so downcast. There's no need for haste now: His Grace of Gloucester has given me leave to be absent for a month, and to deliver certain messages on our route, but nothing too arduous. You'll have the chance to grow saddle-hard gradually.'

*

It took ten days in fact to reach their destination. They were ten pleasant days for Perkin: the novelty of travelling on horseback and spending comfortable—or not so comfortable—nights in hostelries along the way was still fresh enough for him to enjoy it, and the weather, as they journeyed south, turned warm and sunny, though they were passing into September. But for Christie, despite the apparently affable spirit in which he chaffed his servant or arranged the night's bed or conversed with fellow travellers, the memory of that journey would be ever afterwards inextricably tangled with the black thoughts that circled around and around his mind, and all concerning his sister.

It was many miles before he could even come to terms with her words, and acknowledge the truth of her accusations. He was selfish, utterly so: all his life had been the means to one end, his own advancement. The love and friendship he had shared with Meg had been delightful but unnecessary, and when his feelings and his vow had stood in the path of his ambition, he had ruthlessly sacrificed them. Now, he was paying the price, he had forfeited Meg's love, and he recognised now that it was deserved. Perhaps one day she would mellow, would realise that the bond between them was too strong to sever with angry words and broken promises: but he knew Meg, knew that she could be as implacable as himself, knew how little she could be persuaded. He must leave her alone, to change her mind if she would, and keep his bitterness and hurt, his grief and guilt to himself, behind that disguiser's mask.

He knew now, with remorse, that if by some miracle he could turn time back and receive that letter again, he would make some excuse to Gloucester and go to her. He had learned that his ambition and success were worth little beside his love for his sister, and hers for him. He had a bright future, but now it seemed as dust and ashes without Meg's friendship. He had thrown it away, and the loss of her, however deserved, was as bitter as any gall.

She had ceased to care for him, she had said: but he still cared very much for her, and would always wish her happiness, and joy, even if her chance of achieving it immured in that desolate house seemed bleak indeed. It hurt most grievously to know that she had rejected any support, help, companionship that he might have offered her in poor compensation for her loss: he could not blame her, his own sense of guilt would not allow him to do so, but he blamed himself, and the dark unhappiness within him was well-hidden by the cold face he turned upon the world. Only Perkin, who did not know the whole story, could guess: and he had early been warned against overmuch prying into Christie's private affairs.

*

The miles passed, over the bleak moors to Derby and then down into a kinder, greener country, Nuneaton and Coventry and to-wards Oxford. Christie had received precise directions from Sir Thomas Bray, who had returned to Berwick still in great pain, and whose injuries were proving reluctant to heal. Christie had only offered to go to his family as a pretext for visiting Meg: now, in the wreckage of that visit, this journey was a welcome distraction.

At last, on a sunny September evening, they came to a village called Adderbury, and asked where Sir Thomas Bray's house at Ashcott might be found: then it was but a mile's ride down into a green valley, all luxuriant grass and water-meadows and fat sheep and cattle, over a little stone bridge, and a turn to the right, towards the river's flow.

Three people on horseback, a man and two women, were in sight as Christie and Perkin walked their weary horses out of the trees that lined the track down the hill. Ahead of them lay Ashcott, a substantial stone manor house with a tower at either end and a high-roofed hall in the centre: it was walled round, but had none of the look of a fortress. Perkin stared at it approvingly, oblivious to the beauty of the golden stone, the mossy tiles and tall chimneys amid all that lush grass. It represented to him no more than the promise of a comfortable bed for the night, after a hearty supper —always supposing, of course, that his master did not ride away within the hour as if all the demons of Hell were jabbing at Bayard's heels with their pitchforks.

But Christie, comparing this lovely, peaceful, wealthy place with the crumbling grim grey stones and isolated situation of Denby, was conscious of a different feeling. He envied Sir Thomas Bray his house: and one day, if he rose as far as he desired, he meant to become the lord of a manor like this, so much more lush and rich than the poor starveling acres of Bokenfield. And because when he had the leisure for it, he loved beauty, whether in music or in a horse or hawk or in the marvellous pictures on a Burgundy arras, he found himself slowing Bayard to stare longer at the scene below him, the house in the wide steep-sided valley amidst rushes and willows and water. From the river, the gaunt long-shanked grey shape of a heron rose, its neck tucked in and its legs trailing, and he watched its flight with a smile unawares on his face, softening his features and making him seem, to Perkin's wary gaze, quite a different person entirely from his normal impassive self.

Then a voice, a child's voice, high and imperious, broke in: master and servant turned to see the three on horseback now only twenty yards or so away. The man, evidently a groom, had a hooded hawk on his gauntleted wrist, and one of the women, sidesaddle on a hackney, had the appearance of a waiting-maid: it was the third who had hailed them, and rode ahead of her servants on a handsome and very expensive-looking palfrey, dapple-grey with red harness. She was no more than a child, though big and well-grown, and many might have called her plump, not to say fat: the sky-blue cloth of her riding-gown was strained across an ample chest that showed no signs of womanly roundness. Most startling,

[71]

however, was her hair, which was bound in two plaits for convenience while hawking: in the red light of approaching sunset, it looked as crimson as blood, and it was only as she rode closer that Christie realised that its true colour was a subtle reddish brown.

There was nothing subtle, however, about her high voice: it demanded, 'What business do you have at Ashcott, sir?' The courtesy had evidently been added as an afterthought, and her tone was sharp. Beside her palfrey stood a dog, not the usual soft little lady's spaniel but a great fawn-coloured hound with a rough coat and a threatening appearance. It bared its teeth, and a hoarse rasping sound issued from somewhere within the fearsome-looking studded collar. 'Be quiet, Cavall,' the girl told it, and her eyes roamed disdainfully up and down Christie's shabby, travel-stained figure and ugly horse. He knew well enough who this must be: the likeness to Sir Thomas Bray, though not strong, was plain in the child's wide forehead and oddly peaked brows, and she had, unfortunately, inherited his broad build. Her father's description had misled, however: true, there was no hint of dissembling or deceit in the pale, hostile face, but her opinion of him was quite evident, and would have been more courteously hidden.

'I come for speech with Dame Alice Bray,' he said, deciding that Sir Thomas had at least been accurate in speaking of his only daughter as spoilt. 'I bring news and letters from her husband.'

Spoilt brat or no, there was no mistaking the genuine delight that suddenly infused her face. 'News? Of Father? Oh, is he coming home? I'll go tell Mother.' She dragged her palfrey's mouth around in a way that was sure to set any horseman's anger rising, and with a loud, piercing and unmaidenly hunting cry set it off at a gallop down the hill, the dog following with an easy lope. Over her shoulder, amidst flying chestnut plaits, came the cry, 'Show him the way, Robin!'

The groom, with a weary patience which revealed how often his master's daughter behaved thus unmannerly, bid Christie follow him, and in an uneasy and rather embarrassed silence the four remaining rode the rest of the way down the hill, under the ivy-clad stone of a gatehouse which, despite its narrow squint windows and well-oiled hinges and stout oaken door, did not look capable of withholding any determined force of attackers, and into a wide courtyard lined with barn, stables and kitchen. Here the groom took their horses and Christie and Perkin were led by the waiting-woman through the porch and into a high dim hall of a pattern, screens and dais and dusty rafters, to be found in almost every house or castle of any size in the land. And here, they were greeted by Sir Thomas Bray's wife.

The woman who confronted Christie bore a much stronger resemblance to her daughter than did her husband. With the girl standing beside her, the likeness was most marked: they shared the reddish hair, the dark eyes, rather heavy face, and above all their size. Dame Alice was a tall woman, much taller than Perkin (although ten months of good food had added a couple of inches to his height and several more to his girth), and strongly built with large hands and, probably, feet. She wore an ample dark red gown and a plain linen hood that emphasised her solid, formidable face. She looked like a woman who brooked no nonsense, and ruled with a rod of iron: whoever had spoilt the daughter, it was evidently not Dame Alice.

Courtesies were exchanged, and then Perkin was led to the kitchen quarters while Christie was ushered into a small pleasant parlour with painted and plastered walls, and there offered a generous tankard of ale, with bread and cheese. Throughout all this Dame Alice, whose voice was loud and booming, treated him with brisk politeness, enquiring as to his journey, the progress of the war in Berwick and finally, when his thirst was slaked and his hunger at least partly satisfied, asking in a matter-of-fact way about Sir Thomas, and the letters he carried. During the conversation, the child Julian had sat hunched in the window-embrasure, surrounded by cushions, fondling her dog's rough ears and munching her way through a pasty of a size unlikely to diminish her own. When Christie brought the letters from his pouch, she swallowed the last, much too large mouthful and sprang up with pleased eagerness to accept the small narrow rectangle of folded paper that was addressed to her.

Christie, with some amusement, watched her rip open the seal, unfold it and begin reading avidly. He had written both letters to Sir Thomas's dictation, for the older man's hands were still too sore and swollen to hold a pen without much pain and difficulty, and he had been struck by the difference in tone between them. His words to Dame Alice had been matter-of-fact, and devoid of any emotion bar the accustomed husbandly greetings: he had described his injuries, intimated that they were not serious, had given a concise account of the progress and success of the war, and had finished with a long series of instructions about the harvest, provisioning the house for the winter, selling off the season's lambs and calves, and the care of a favourite mare who was in foal. Julian's letter, by contrast, had opened with great affection and continued in the same vein, retailing humorous little incidents and stories, asking about the training of Cavall, the yellow dog. Christie glanced with interest at the girl, who did not look the sort to call a hound by the name that King Arthur had given his, in the romances. It was plain, though, that her father doted on her, and she on him: she was reading the letter with a fond smile on her face, transforming it into something approaching handsome. Mere beauty or prettiness would never be the outcome of those marked features, the straight jutting nose and firm chin, that would perhaps have been better on a boy, but without that imperious disdain her face was at least quite pleasant to look at. And since she appeared to be the only child, and therefore an heiress, there would be no shortage of offers for her, despite her nature.

At that moment she looked up, and the wide brown eyes stared curiously at Christie. 'Father says you play the lute. He says you play it surpassing well.'

Sir Thomas had painfully added a more private postscript to each letter, and his comments were therefore a surprise to Christie. He saw Dame Alice's mouth open to reprove her daughter, and said with a courteous smile, 'He does me too much honour, Mistress Julian. I play for my own amusement, no more.'

'He says you might play for us, if we ask you,' said Julian, in a manner which indicated that she thought of Christie on the same level as a common minstrel. With a mixture of amusement and exasperation, he wondered if she expected to toss him a couple of groats for his pains.

'Will you? Will you play for us after supper?' She had come closer: for a child of, he guessed, twelve or thirteen years she was very tall, her head passing his shoulder. Dropping her voice confidentially, she added, 'I play the lute too—did Father tell you? Perhaps you could give me lessons, while you're here. I'm sure we could reward you well.'

'Julian!' Her mother's voice roared its anger at this effrontery. 'Do not importune poor Master Heron any longer, you graceless girl—make your apologies and go to your chamber. You will need to change your gown for supper. If Master Heron does condescend to play for us, it will be entirely due to his own good will and not at all to your insolence—and as for asking for lessons—words fail

[74]

me!' As Julian, mutinous, opened her mouth to protest, Dame Alice added sharply, 'And don't you dare answer me back, you insolent hussy, or you'll know my reply. Now go.'

Scarlet with fury, Julian sent her mother a look that would have turned Medusa to stone, and ran from the room, leaving the door open. Dame Alice shut it with an indignant swish of skirts and turned to Christie. 'I must apologise for that girl's disgraceful behaviour. It was shameful to speak to you in that manner, and I'll punish her later.'

'I thought little enough of it,' Christie said, with some truth. 'She is but a child, and has not yet learned to school her tongue.'

'Not such a child—she was fifteen years old at Corpus Christi,' said Dame Alice, her full lips compressed. 'She is our only child to survive, and I fear my dear husband has sadly spoilt her. She was always the apple of his eye, she could do no wrong in his sight, and she has grown up disgracefully wilful and outspoken. I have many times resorted to the switch in my attempts to curb her, but she grows daily worse, and my husband when he is here indulges her every whim. Reading romances, hawking, that infernal dog, her lute, all fill her mind so there's no room for anything useful—how she'll run her husband's household I know not. If she had only been sent away to my cousin's house at a young age, all that nonsense would have been thrashed out of her early, but no, Sir Thomas must keep her by him, and you see the result.' Dame Alice glowered at the painted scenes of hunting on the walls as if they were personally responsible for the defects in Julian's character. 'Oh, we'll find her a husband, for she'll inherit all—but he'll have a sad time of it, I fear.' She sat down in the big settle by the empty fireplace, and indicated a stool. 'But I have run on enough with my own concerns, Master Heron. Pray be seated, and tell me something of yourself. How did you come to meet my husband?'

He had not particularly liked Julian, but it had been uncomfortable, to say the least, to have her mother discuss her so freely and detrimentally in her absence, and with a complete stranger. Christie began to understand the girl's wilful and undisciplined behaviour, and to take Dame Alice in some dislike. As their conversation progressed, this feeling was intensified: his hostess with every word and opinion she uttered revealed herself to be just as domineering as the girl, and she was as free with her views on life and politics as she had been with adverse comments on her daughter. It transpired from her talk that she was by birth a Clifford, cousin to that Lord

Clifford who had reputedly slain King Edward's younger brother, Edmund of Rutland, at the battle of Wakefield twenty years ago, and who had been slain in his turn by the men of York at the battle of Towton. It was evident that Dame Alice was very conscious of her proud lineage and references to her high-born cousins, now alas mostly dead or attainted, liberally peppered her talk. Discovering that Christie was a Northumbrian and had Percy blood, she grew somewhat warmer: his grandfather had died at Towton with her cousin, both fighting for King Henry, and she waxed warm on the hope that one day there would be a change of monarch, and those who had fought for poor witless Harry VI, his formidable wife and young son, would come into their own again. Since King Edward was in the prime of life with a brace of sons and a more than capable brother, and the only remaining Lancastrian pretender that Christie knew of was a penniless adventurer at the mercy of the whims of the Duke of Brittany, he thought this hope far-fetched to say the least, and the voicing of it to one in the service of the King's brother more than a little foolish. Indeed, Dame Alice herself seemed to realise that she had not been wise, and abruptly steered her talk into less dangerous waters, asking Christie many rather prying questions about his family connections. Having satisfied herself that he was of no wealth and little birth, despite being part a Percy, she lost interest: Christie reflected wryly that he evidently did not qualify for a position as prospective husband to Julian, and was not sorry.

Despite this disadvantage, he was shown every courtesy: Dame Alice with her noble forbears would not neglect her duty of hospitality. He was given a pleasant bed-chamber in the western tower, overlooking the deep moat and gardens to the rear of the house, and two perspiring servants brought up the tub and water for a hot bath before supper. There was a truckle bed for his own servant, and Perkin, whose attitude to cleanliness had undergone some alteration, was grateful for a wash in the tub after his master was done. Then Christie took a little time to tune his lute: it would need further adjustment before he played, but this would at least leave it nearly right. It had survived the journey remarkably well, but was after all much less delicate than it looked, having suffered years of similar treatment. He picked out a few notes almost at random, his fingers caressing the gut strings with love and pleasure, and only then realised that they were the first lines of 'I have a young sister'. He had not thought of Meg for hours: savagely, exorcising her hostile accusing phantom, he played the tune over and over again, six verses without words, and from that turned to a French piece he had learned long ago in London.

Perkin, brushing the travel-dust off his master's clothes before hanging them on the peg, heard the passion in the music and sighed apprehensively. It was all very fine being a personal servant, but with Christie Heron there was the grave risk of being the butt of whatever mood afflicted him: and Perkin knew that he saw much more of his master's private thoughts and feelings than did anyone else. Christie's friends at Middleham bore him some liking and more respect, he made himself pleasant without ever giving away very much of his real nature, and as a result Perkin bore the brunt of his angers and griefs, as well as his good humour. Hoping he would not be berated too much this evening, he deferentially suggested that his master's presence would be required soon at supper.

He had to repeat the question before his words penetrated the wall of music: then Christie played a wrong note, swore softly, and laid the lute aside, the strings shivering discordantly as he set it on the floor. 'So, Dame Alice and Mistress Julian await our presence below? I daresay St George went more eagerly to face the dragon, but we must do our duty. You may bring my lute, young Perkin, but if you drop it or knock it, or put your foot through it, I shall be playing my next tune on your guts.'

'Yes, sir,' said Perkin, deceptively meek, and, cradling the precious lute, followed his master down to the dragon's den.

The company was small—Dame Alice, her daughter, the steward, the priest, a couple of waiting women and Christie above the salt, and a motley collection of household servants, very subdued in blue and yellow livery, below it. The food was plentiful, but so highly spiced that it made Christie's nose run and a sweat break out on his forehead. In accordance with old custom, he must share a trencher with Julian, and to prove that, humble circumstances or no, he was nevertheless fully conversant with polite etiquette, he went through all the elaborate rituals of supplying the lady with meat and drink, wiping the pewter goblet and making courteous conversation. The irony of it was that the girl seemed totally unappreciative and wore, for the most part, a truly fearsome scowl. She answered him in surly monosyllables, and he was torn between amusement, irritation and the hope that Dame Alice, engaged in a discussion of her husband's agricultural instructions with the steward, would not overhear her daughter's rudeness. After his interested enquiry as to the provenance of her lovely little palfrey had met with a particularly graceless reply, Christie came to an abrupt and conscious decision that surprised him. If she behaved like a child, and a peculiarly ill-mannered child at that, he would treat her like one. With the charming smile that usually disguised his most hostile intentions, he met her inimical dark eyes and enquired innocently about her lessons. Doubtless she was now proficient in reading and writing?

Julian stared at him as if she could hardly believe her ears, a spoonful of spiced meat poised halfway to her open mouth. She put it down again and said, with shrivelling scorn, 'I can read very well in Latin now, and write it too. Can you say as much, Master Heron?'

He did, in that language, and had the satisfaction of seeing her scowl deepening. It lowered further as he added, 'Do you possess a lute of your own, Mistress Julian? Doubtless you have not been playing for long.'

'I've had a lute since I was ten years old,' said his adversary, rising unerringly to the bait. 'Father had a small one once made for me. I have a rebec as well, *and* a harp. I can play them all, and sing too.'

'What a very accomplished child you are,' said Christie, with a false and effusive sincerity quite alien to him. 'Such a prodigy, so young.'

Julian was evidently not entirely the self-obsessed fool she appeared. The round brown eyes narrowed: then she said with conviction, 'You're laughing at me!'

Christie, returned to his normal self, raised an eyebrow. 'I did not think you cared one jot for my feelings or thoughts. I admit, I was indeed making game of you—but then you are easy to mock, Mistress Julian.'

A hot humiliating wave of colour swept over the girl's face, leaving two bright spots of crimson on each plump cheek. She said, so low he could hardly catch the words, 'How—how dare you! How dare you laugh at me! You're—you're nothing but an upstart minstrel—you should be on the lowest table, not the highest!'

It was perhaps as well that Dame Alice chose this moment to call down the table to Christie, her loud voice stilling all the chatter. 'I see your servant has your lute, Master Heron. Will you not do us the great honour of playing for us, when supper is done?' And in a deliberately audible aside, she informed the steward that their guest played for none other than the Duke of Gloucester, whose standards were well-known to be high indeed. Christie, amused by this manifest desire to impress the steward and at the same time diminish himself, kept his counsel and engaged the priest on his left in a pleasant conversation about chapel music. Julian, her face still flushed with rage, sat stirring her spoon in a desultory fashion amidst the remains of her meal, while the great dog Cavall, obviously sensitive to his lady's moods, sat with his head on her lap, offering comfort. Christie hardened his heart: the girl was disgracefully spoilt, and must learn her lesson soon, or face much worse at the hands of parent or husband. He hoped that the suggestion that he give her lessons had been forgotten: he did not in the least relish the prospect of any time spent with this moody, wilful child and her exaggerated ideas of her own talent and importance.

But in that, he was proved wrong. With the meal at last ended, and the servants clearing the hall, the more exalted members of the household retired to the parlour and prepared to be entertained by their guest. Christie had often played for the King's brother, and for his uncle the Earl of Northumberland, and his accustomed repertoire for these occasions was small, varied and perfect. He played some simple ballad and carol tunes, both to loosen his fingers and to reaccustom them to their intricate task, and to give his audience something to hear with which they would undoubtedly be familiar. Then there would be a selection of more difficult pieces from Italy and Burgundy, courtly music, elaborate and stately, chosen to show off his mastery of technique, before a final flourish of dance music, fast and furious and likely to set feet and fingers tapping. Within that framework, he could vary the individual tunes or accede to requests for songs popular with his audience, and thus ensure that no two times did he play the same. Here, however, there were different considerations: he doubted if this humbler household would appreciate the intricacies favoured by the Duke of Gloucester's acute and practised musical ear, and he had no wish to appear too professional. He was a gentleman born who happened to play the lute quite well, in common with many others, men and women, of gentle birth, and he was no common minstrel, whatever Mistress Julian might think.

So he kept to the dance tunes and the carols and songs and ballads, and was rewarded with smiles, spontaneous singing of the more familiar words, and genuine appreciation as he finished. 'His Grace of Gloucester is indeed fortunate,' said the priest, a vigorous-looking old man with silvery hair and a ruddy face which testified either to his outdoor life or to his free consumption of ale, or both. 'But you showed a knowledge of the music of Burgundy when we spoke at supper, Master Heron—will you not give us just a taste of it now?'

So he had to take up his instrument again: he adjusted the top course, which had as ever gone a semi-tone flat, flexed his fingers, and perversely began on the most difficult piece in his entire repertoire, which he had learned when in London. It was short and exceedingly complicated, reputedly a favourite of the King's sister, the Dowager Duchess of Burgundy, and although he had not played it since before the expedition to Berwick, his fingers flew as if born to it, and his own desire for perfection was fully satisfied. And when he had finished, and the last notes had drifted away into the soft evening light, there was a faint collective sigh from the people in the room, as though they had heard something of rare beauty, and then a brief, rapt silence.

Julian, characteristically, was the one to break it. She scrambled up from her accustomed seat in the window and planted her solid bulk in front of Christie. Her eyes glowed, whether in appreciation or in challenge he could not guess. She said breathlessly, 'Master Heron—can I borrow your lute? I would like to play too.'

He glanced at the large, clumsy-looking hands, the nails all too obviously gnawed rather than cut, and his look of irony did not go unmarked. He did not mind in the least if she chose to make a fool of herself: just as her mother began a voluble protest, he handed his beloved instrument over to this graceless, unendowed child, with the mild injunction to be careful of it, and a soothing glance for Dame Alice: then, he leaned back on his stool, folded his arms and prepared to be bored.

But in that, he had done Julian an injustice. She might be lumpen and lacking in the civilized airs and graces, but for music she had a gift, and moreover, a singing voice that was strong and clear, and yet astonishingly sweet. She sang two or three French rondeaux, that properly demanded more voices than one, and a couple of English songs in fashionably woeful mood: then, with a triumphant glare at Christie, she embarked on a virtuoso performance of the Italian song, 'O Rosa Bella', with English words that showed signs of being self-crafted:

> Oh, lovely rose, oh, my sweet heart,
> For courtesy you must not let me die.

Alas, my woe brings death to be my part,
For having served and loved most loyally.
The god of love has pierced me with his dart,
My mistress has betrayed me and I cry—
Oh, love, come succour me with all your art,
My deepest soul, you cannot let me die.

The last plaintive notes of the song died away: her fingers sketched a quick light arpeggio across the strings, a very delicate movement for such clumsy-looking hands, and then she bent the chestnut head over the instrument as if acknowledging their due homage. Perhaps only Christie, the closest to her, could see how the music had affected her: those large bitten hands were very slightly trembling. Despite himself, he felt not a little admiration for her ability. To reach that standard of play needed long hours of dedicated practice and effort, not qualities normally possessed by spoilt fifteen-year-old girls. He still cared very little for Julian Bray, but he realised now that she was not so unpleasant and uncomplicated as he had supposed.

She lifted her head, threw him a supercilious, triumphant glance, and then with exaggerated courtesy returned him the lute. 'Did you like my playing, Master Heron?'

'I did indeed—and I feel you have very little to learn from me, Mistress Bray. I doubt the King's finest minstrel could play and sing so well.'

The glare which he received indicated that his double-edged compliment had gone home. Julian retreated to her windowseat, her chin defiantly raised, and her brown eyes snapping a warning. Her mother sent her a cold glance and a curt acknowledgment of her performance, echoed with rather more warmth by the priest. Dame Alice, ensconced in the only chair, a huge carved box affair that scarcely contained her bulk, then turned her beady gaze on her guest. It became plain that her seeming indifference to her daughter's accomplishment was but a pose, for she smiled graciously at him. 'You do play most beautifully, Master Heron. I hardly dare ask such a favour of you, especially on behalf of my graceless daughter, but her own playing could undoubtedly do with some improvement. Perhaps tomorrow morning, before you return to Yorkshire?'

He glanced at Julian. Her expression was masked by the shroud of her hair and the turn of her head as she gazed out of the window at the green valley, but he could see the tension in her hands as she gripped them together. He had no idea whether she wanted his tuition or not, and in any case his opportunity for correcting her play would be so brief as to be useless, unless to bring to her notice some glaring defect in technique. Everyone else was looking at him expectantly, Dame Alice in particular. He had a sudden and very vivid image of her boastful gossip to neighbours and acquaintances: my gifted daughter, tutored by the Duke of Gloucester's own minstrel! It was so ludicrous and unexpected that he almost burst out laughing: but only a twitch of a smile showed on his mouth as he gravely assured Dame Alice that he would be willing to do his poor best.

*

'Thought you said we was going at first light,' Perkin complained, shaking and folding Christie's better, red velvet doublet with an indignant snap that took no account of vulnerability to creases. 'What did you have to say you'd teach her for? She'll smash it over your head, most like.'

'You're paid to do my bidding,' said Christie. He stood at the window in shirt and hose, his light brown hair ruffled, paler at the ends where the summer sun had bleached it. Outside was the soft Oxfordshire dark, and an owl's call came faintly through the panes. He looked relaxed and at ease with the world, and Perkin, despite his grumbles, was highly relieved at this lightening of the black mood that had shadowed his master since leaving Denby Hall. He laid the doublet on the chest that stood at the foot of the simple wooden bed (though the mattress was feather, and luxurious), and said cheerfully, 'I knows that. That's why I don't want your head broke—and from what I've heard, she's likely to break it, that Mistress Julian.'

Christie stretched and turned, his lean bony face alight with sudden mischief. 'Well, Perkin my faithful servant, forewarned is forearmed, as they say—what have you heard? Or are you squeam-ish about passing on kitchen gossip? I thought not. Tell me about Mistress Julian.'

'Well—' Perkin's small face with its long lipless mouth and squashed-looking nose took on an unaccustomed thoughtfulness that was quite spurious. 'She's a right little madam by all accounts —well, not so much of the "little", she must be taller than me by three or four fingers. Her father spoilt her, let her do what she liked, couldn't say no to her, and her poor mother has to try and whip her in when the old man's away. You know that gentlewoman that attends her? She's the fifth our dear Mistress Julian's had in the last two years. No matter how desperate they are for a place, they always goes, sooner or later. She boxed the last one's ears, and pushed the one before that into the river. This one's lasted six months, and that's the longest so far. When she was only ten, she ran off to Banbury and was gone two days and all because her mother had given her the thrashing she deserved. Oh, her mother does her best, but it's not a lot of use when her father comes back in a few weeks and gives her sweetmeats and calls her his honey-pie, is it?'

'Do you know,' said Christie, when it was apparent that his servant's monologue had finished and that no answer to his final rhetorical question would be forthcoming, 'I find myself feeling rather sorry for the child. Oh, I don't like her, but does anyone ever treat her as an ordinary child? Her father dotes on her, and her mother alternately belittles her and tries to whip her into obedience. And no,' he added, glancing at Perkin's suddenly shrewd gaze, 'I have no knowledge of training children, but rearing horses or dogs can't be so different. And if you had a dog whom you petted one day and thrashed the next, neither of them for any particular reason, would you expect it to be obedient, trustworthy and loyal?'

'No,' said Perkin, grinning. 'I'd expect it to bite anyone it saw. Was *that* how you trained your horse?'

'Don't cast red herrings before me, or you'll rue it. But this Mistress Julian is like our imaginary dog—she bites everyone she meets. I've already been well nipped, and I don't doubt I shall depart from Ashcott tomorrow seriously mauled. As long as she leaves my lute intact, I don't care—I doubt our paths will ever cross again, and I'll probably take good care to see that they don't. Now pull out the truckle, and go to sleep like the good well-behaved gentleman's servant I'm trying so hard to change you into.'

*

Julian Bray stood at the window in the parlour, looking out at the bright sunrise, and absently chewing a large piece of bread. A bit fell to the floor, and Cavall, her faithful shadow, the only friend she had who was always loyal, always loving, always with her, walked forward unhurriedly and scooped it up off the rushy floor with tongue and teeth. She fondled his ears as he turned and leaned

[83]

against her in his characteristic gesture of affection, his long thin tail drifting to and fro with pleasure as she scratched beneath his chin. Her father had given him to her, at her earnest request, nearly two years ago, despite her mother's disapproval: a spaniel or a little lap-dog was suitable for a lady, not this great rough-coated fawn hound with, obviously, too much of the fierce alaunt in its makeup. But Julian, with her father's support, had insisted and the dog was now an accepted member of the household. With most people his behaviour was disdainfully indifferent, content to be stroked or petted by anyone, even the village children and babies who would pull themselves up on unsteady feet with handfuls of his coat and skin while their mothers watched in apprehension: but he had never so much as growled at them. It was to Julian that his whole fierce heart was given, and only in her protection that he showed aggression. Once he had badly bitten a head groom who had remonstrated with her for disobeying her mother's orders not to take her palfrey out: and Dame Alice always took care to lock the dog away when she had occasion to chastise her daughter. There was little doubt that Cavall was quite capable of tearing out the throat of anyone whom he saw as a threat to his beloved owner.

Julian finished the bread and turned back to the table to cut another hunk: she spread it liberally with butter and cheese, topped it with a slab of mutton and bit savagely into it. Her mother had often remonstrated with her about the amount she ate, predicting that she would grow fat and citing the awful example of a neighbour's daughter, so large she could find no husband, who had eventually retreated into a nunnery. Julian knew that, as her father's heiress, there was no chance of her taking the veil even if she had wanted it: she was required to marry well, and breed grandchildren to inherit Ashcott. There were several likely young men in the vicinity, but not all of them were as enthusiastic as her wealth and acres might warrant, for her reputation as a juvenile termagant was well spread abroad. Her father, moreover, was notably reluctant to let his only daughter escape early into the bonds of matrimony, and could be relied upon to pick his prospective son-in-law with uncommon care. Julian was quite happy with this situation: she loved Ashcott, its lush green meadows and the honey-coloured stones against which Cavall was almost invisible, the lovely rich valley and the familiar faces amongst which she had grown up, and marriage would almost undoubtedly mean leaving it all for another house, to return infrequently and as a stranger. The only reason she could possibly have to forsake her father and her home was to escape her mother: and that lady's harsh words, though not her beatings, meant very little to Julian now, after fifteen years of endurance. She had her own methods of escape, and she could usually ignore Dame Alice.

As if summoned, the door opened and her formidable mother swept in, accompanied by her gentlewoman and escorted by the steward, the priest, and Christie Heron. Too late, Julian realised the extent of her sin: eating before her mother, the household and her guest had entered, standing while she did it, her hair tangled and unbrushed—and she had not got up in time for Mass. She swept the crumbs from her blue gown and stood, head high and her mouth and hands clenched, while Dame Alice's strictures washed around her like the tide and receded, and the chief thought in Julian's head was, to wonder savagely how long she could keep herself from striking her mother.

'You were not at Mass,' the voice boomed, and Julian's wide brown eyes swivelled from contemplation of the arras to encounter Dame Alice's ferocious glare. 'Explain yourself.'

'Frideswide is ill, madam, and I forgot to ask Mary to wake me. So I overslept. And that,' Julian added, feeling that she might as well be hanged for a bullock as for a calf, 'is why my hair is not brushed. I was in too much of a hurry.'

'You're not in too much of a hurry to eat,' her mother observed, indicating the crumb-strewn floor and the remains of Julian's illicit breakfast. 'You can go to your chamber, girl—I'll see you later. And have that dog chained outside, if you please.'

It seemed that she had forgotten the arrangement of the previous night. Glad of it, Julian made her courtesy with less obvious resentment than might have been expected, and turned to go. Master Heron's voice stopped her. 'Am I not then to instruct Mistress Julian, Dame Alice? As I am to leave after dinner, I shall have no other chance.'

Curse him, thought Julian. Imprecations learned from the grandmother of one of her childhood playmates, reputedly a dabbler in witchcraft, spat in her mind, and she stared with unconcealed dislike at her tormentor. He sent her the kind of insincere smile commonly given to young children, and she realised that he was well aware of her feelings: in fact, they were most probably returned. Glowering, she listened as Dame Alice, trapped by her own greed for superiority, acceded to Master Heron's gentle persuasion with a speed that, despite herself, impressed her daughter. And then she was despatched to her room, after being told to summon Frideswide from her bed, ill or not.

Frideswide had the headache, and was reluctantly haled from her bed by her mistress. She was a placid girl of a good but impoverished family with five other daughters to place in the world, and she had long ago accepted that her lot in life would be one of struggle, service and poverty, without even the certain benefit of marriage at the end of it. She was twenty-four, no beauty with her low stature, sandy hair and poor skin, but she had kindness in abundance and, with her experience of looking after younger sisters, an astonishing tolerance of Julian's explosive and difficult moods. She had begun by feeling sorry for the girl, and had recently found herself actually liking her, somewhat to her astonishment, for Julian treated her for the most part with a mixture of contempt and indifference, and clearly thought nothing of heaping her with tasks. Frideswide bore it all with equanimity, and sewed and brushed and dressed and washed and escorted to the best of her ability, which was not inconsiderable. This morning, however, she looked decidedly unwell, the freckles standing out on her blotchy skin and her eyes sunken with fatigue. Even Julian felt a twinge of pity, but hardened her heart. 'Mother wants you to sit in the little parlour while Master Heron hears me play. Don't look like that, Friday, all you have to do is sit there—you can go to sleep if you like.'

'I think I will,' said Frideswide, crawling out of the truckle bed. 'Give me just five minutes, Mistress, and I'll be there.'

But it was twice that before she appeared, heavy-eyed and coughing, evidently about to succumb to a severe cold in the head: and by that time Julian had ordered one of the grooms to take Cavall to the kitchen, where he would undoubtedly be fed titbits and made much of, fetched her lute from her chamber and esconced herself in the little parlour. There was no fire and the room, facing west, was cold at this time of day: her fingers were stiff and she flexed them angrily, furious with herself, with her mother, with Frideswide and above all with Christopher Heron. How dare he presume to teach her? (She had completely forgotten that she herself had originally suggested it.) She had nothing left to learn—her technique was perfect, all she wanted was the time to practise and the music to play from, for her repertoire was pitifully small. For a wild moment, she contemplated asking Master Heron to write down for her some of the songs he had played the previous evening, and then dismissed it scornfully. He was doubtless self-taught like most minstrels, and had no knowledge of musical notation.

Frideswide Gower arrived behind a large square of linen into which she was blowing her nose. Behind her, his lute in his hand, an expression of amusement on his face, came Christie. Julian's mother was not with him, and she was profoundly grateful. She rose from her stool and made her courtesy, Frideswide sneezed copiously and huddled in the windowseat, surrounded by cushions: she sighed, and closed her eyes. Julian glanced at her irritably and turned her attention to Master Heron. He was pulling up a stool, having laid the lute carefully on the floor, and he smiled charmingly at her. 'I know exactly what you are thinking, Mistress Julian. You think I can teach you nothing, and that you know everything already.'

Julian's mouth had already been open to deliver a stinging comment: it dropped comically further, and she stared in surprise, the wind completely gone from her sails. Abruptly, she snapped her jaw shut and sat down on her own stool. 'No, of course I don't. But I don't think there's much point in trying to teach me anything in an hour or so.'

'My feelings exactly, but your lady mother is nothing if not insistent. Now, if you would take up your lute, Mistress Julian?'

Resentful of his exaggerated politeness, she did so, wishing she had the self-confidence not to be so careful of the way she held it. Despite her contempt for this upstart musician and messenger, she had no wish to allow him to point out any errors with, doubtless, much relish.

He did not. He gave the lute itself a keen glance: it was English made and very plain, but sweet of tone and light of touch, and Julian loved it almost as passionately as she loved Cavall. 'Now play me everything in your repertory, if you will. Start with those you know best, and go on to those you find harder.'

Julian stared at him, a hostile frown marring her high pale forehead: she would have liked very much to have told him where he could put himself and his lute, and it showed on her face. But it was an opportunity to show off her skill to a stranger which rarely came her way, and in the end her vanity won. With a final glowering look, she tossed the uncombed tangle of chestnut brown hair behind her shoulders and hunched over her instrument. 'I can't play so well if I don't sing.'

'Then sing,' said Christie: and she sang.

That voice was heartbreakingly pure, delightful, like a highly-trained chapel boy's: its soaring effortless treble contrasted very strangely with the mannerless brat that produced it, and the difference intrigued him. There was very much more to this child than appeared so readily on the surface, but where would she learn the grace, forbearance, tolerance, compassion that would mark true maturity? Assuredly not in Ashcott, from that domineering mother, and yet the sensitivity and imagination that showed so strongly in her music would surely wither here. He felt pity for her: it was an emotion very new to him, and, he realised with a wry, bitter inward smile, he had Meg to thank for it.

And strangely, at that moment, chiming with his thought, her fingers played the opening notes of a song both loved and hated, and she sang the familiar words:

> I have a young sister,
> Far beyond the sea . . .

He wanted to join her, to express his sorrow and regret in harmony with that glorious voice: he could only sit and watch this very different girl, not blessed with sweetness of face or lightness of heart, as she sang the song that meant so much to him. At its end she stopped playing to flex her fingers: the silence was filled by a heartfelt series of sneezes from the gentlewoman. 'Oh, do try and keep quiet, Friday,' said Julian unfairly, and then glanced back at the tall quiet young man sitting so impassively on his stool. 'I've played ten songs for you, and my fingers are tired and the lute's gone out of tune again. Have you heard enough? Aren't you going to say anything, or are you just going to sit there like a stuffed pudding?'

Something had happened inside Christie's head: as she spoke, he came to a decision which both surprised and amused him. He left her words hanging in the air as he got up, sparing a sympathetic glance for poor Friday snuffling in the window-seat, and went over to the mantel, which was ornately carved with, he supposed, the Bray arms, three fleur-de-lis on a bend, prominently featured. 'Well?' Julian demanded. 'Tell me what you think, I don't want to sit here all day.'

'What do I think?' Christie asked, a smile that Perkin would have recognised with alarm lighting his face with deceptive charm. 'What do I think of you, Mistress Julian? Well, you have the voice of an angel and your playing would not disgrace those Court minstrels you despise so heartily, though a little more practice would not come amiss. But as for you yourself, I have met many people in my life, and I can tell you that few of them have been as unpleasant, as impolite and as bad-natured as you. You're fifteen, you've been pampered all your life and your manners and your attitude to other people would disgrace a five-year-old street urchin. You've been taught music and reading and writing: has no-one ever taught you to be pleasant to people, to smile or laugh or behave gracefully to your servants or your parents, as a lady should? If it weren't for the fact that your mother has obviously already tried it and failed dismally, I'd be tempted to put you over my knee and thrash you myself. But think on it, Mistress Julian—just ask yourself why your mother has to resort to such methods, why your servants must loathe you, why you have no friends but that dog, and if you can do that then I've given you a much more important lesson than anything I could teach you on your precious lute.'

Throughout this, Julian's face had been growing more and more scarlet with rage and mortification: as he finished, she stared up at him, her mouth trembling, and then cried, 'How dare you! How *dare* you speak to me like that, you—you common jumped-up peasant! I'll have you whipped, I'll get Mother to throw you out, I'll—' Tears of rage spilled over onto her crimson cheeks, and she cast about wildly for something to throw. Fortunately, the nearest thing to hand was the cushion on which Friday had rested her aching head: she wrenched it away from her unfortunate waiting-woman, and hurled it at Christie. He dodged, surprised by her accuracy, and she threw another, and then another and then, her ammunition expired, stamped her foot in frustrated fury. Christie bent swiftly to pick up both lutes as her eye fell on them. 'Not a good idea, Mistress—you would regret it afterwards, they cost far too much to smash over my low-born head. Would you like me to leave?'

'Would I *like*—yes, you stinking bastard, go on, get out, out of here before I have you thrown out, I'll set my dog on you and you won't laugh then, I never want to see you again, get OUT!' She picked up her stool: as Christie bowed mockingly low she threw it, fortunately not quite so accurately as she had done the cushions, and it only chipped the painted plaster behind him. 'Mistress Julian, please!' came Friday's hoarse voice, and Christie, judging his moment, turned and walked from the parlour, still carrying his lute and hers. He shut the door not a moment too soon: a second later the other stool, by the sound of it, thudded against the wood and fell

[89]

with a crash. Smiling coldly, Christie went in search of Dame Alice.

He found her in the courtyard, talking with her steward. It was a perfect late summer morning, soft and golden: the sunshine fell kindly on her large-featured, heavy face as she turned to greet him. 'Yes, Master Heron? Is the lesson over?'

'It is,' said Christie. He had already decided to be circumspect: he went on, 'I regret that I left your daughter something overwrought. She asked me for my true opinion, and I gave it to her. She did not like what I said, and I am afraid that I was discourteous, madam.'

'I'll have her whipped,' was Dame Alice's predictable reaction. 'Wretched disgraceful girl, to treat a guest so—what did she do? Mother of God, did she throw anything?'

'Cushions only, madam. It was nothing.'

'She'll rue it,' said Dame Alice grimly, and looking at her savage face, Christie realised that Julian would. He regretted even mentioning the matter, as her mother continued. 'That girl has the devil in her—God help any man who takes her to wife . . . I regret this very much, Master Heron. Will you now be staying for dinner? You are very welcome, and I will make sure that shrewish daughter of mine does not set foot outside her chamber for a month.'

'Thank you, madam, but I think it would be best if I were to leave now,' Christie told her. 'And I beg you, please do not punish Mistress Julian on my account. Her offence was slight, for, as I said, I spoke to her with discourtesy, and deserved her reply.'

But Dame Alice was unlikely to mitigate her retribution. His first amusement had evaporated now, to leave an unpleasant taste behind, and he was conscious of an urgent desire to escape this unhappy place. With a show of reluctance and regret Dame Alice accepted his wish, Perkin, more resentful, was summoned, and in no more than ten minutes their baggage was packed, the horses saddled, and they were free to leave Ashcott.

It had been an encounter, like that earlier, darker one with Meg, that he would regret: and as Christie rode up the hill and away from that little golden manor that turned such a pleasant face to the world, and was so unhappy within, he hoped with some force that he would never have the misfortune to encounter Julian Bray again. Then, with success, he put it from his mind and turned Bayard to the North, and Middleham.

PART
II
1483

THE KING'S CHILDREN

'Then stood the realm in great jeopardy
long while, for every lord that was
mighty of men made him strong, and many
weened to have been King.'
(BOOK I, CHAPTER 5)

❧ CHAPTER FIVE ❧

**'So kind a king and knight . . . because of
his goodness and gentleness we bemoan him,
and ever shall.'**
(BOOK 10, CHAPTER 61)

The party from the castle had spent the afternoon hawking on the
moor and now, towards dusk, they were returning. In the west the
sun was hidden behind fluffy clouds, apricot and soft grey, and
there was a new springlike warmth in the air despite the chilly
breaths of wind that stirred their horses' tails and ruffled the feathers
of the birds. It had been a good day, with plenty of sport and one
superb contest between the Duchess of Gloucester's peregrine
and an agile curlew, which the falcon had eventually won. The
Duchess, her pale face flushed and happy, her fair hair falling down
from its confinement in her headdress, rode beside her husband,
talking in animated tones, while their young son, a delicate child in
good health for once, cavorted with some of his friends, pages and
children of local gentry, in a scuffle of ponies away to the left. Ahead
of them the grey grim bulk of Middleham fluttered its pennants in
the clear evening light, and behind them the hunched shape of
Penhill was still streaked with snow on its highest ridges.

Christie rode with the other less exalted members of the group,
Sir Ralph Bigod being one of them. A young man whose open,
friendly nature contrasted somewhat with the other's habitual
reserve, he was perhaps Christie's closest friend at Middleham.
They ate and worked and hunted and rode together, and talked of
war and hawking, horses and state affairs: but Ralph had never
heard of Christie's sister Meg, and no knowledge of the hurt and
sorrow that still lay deep in his friend's heart. It had made itself
know today, for she had loved April afternoons like this, and the
smiling Duchess with her falcon on her wrist had reminded Christie
inexorably, vividly of Meg, so different in her golden beauty from
the rather plain Anne Neville, and given the knife another twist.
What was Meg doing and feeling on this gusty bright day? Did she
ever think of him with less than hatred? He knew that it was quite
probable that they would meet again, for Sir Robert sometimes
visited Middleham, and one day he would probably bring his wife
with him. In cool, unelaborated tones he had had some news of her

from his brother-in-law, to the effect that she was now completely recovered, and they were living in accord as man and wife: but no more than that, and Christie knew that he had made an enemy both of his sister and her husband. In comparison with that loss, his friendship with Ralph seemed very shadowy, without real substance or heart.

They rode along the ridge that divided Coverdale, down on their right, from Uredale ahead and on their left, with Middleham on its slopes. The castle was quite close now, and as they rode down towards it an uncommon bustle about the bailey resolved itself into a man, most unusually, running towards them, with many others following. Even more remarkably, it became rapidly apparent that the figure was the solid clerkly shape of the Duke's secretary, John Kendall, his face red and perspiring from such unaccustomed exercise. Something was evidently very wrong: the Duke and Duchess urged their horses to meet with him, while the rest of the company fell in tightly behind them, closing ranks. And so they all heard the Duke's sharp question. 'What means this, John? What's amiss?' And louder, the astonished, unhappy, gasping voice of the secretary as he shouted his tidings. 'Your Grace, bad news— a messenger from London—Your Grace, your royal brother is dead—God rest his soul, King Edward is dead!'

*

The castle, after supper, was unusually subdued. Those who had black clothes were wearing them, and the order had already gone out to mercers in York for mourning cloth and garments. The Duke and Duchess, obviously much grieved, had retired to their private apartments, and their retainers and servants congregated about Middleham in small groups, buzzing with urgent talk as the full meaning of the King's death was discussed and the wide range of possible outcomes mulled over. It was not as though there had been no warning of this, for a false report of Edward's demise had reached York several days ago, only to be confidently denied by the next messenger, but those who had gone with Gloucester to Westminster at Christmas had commented on their return on the King's unhealthy looks, and now reminded their friends of this with gloomy satisfaction. Christie, Ralph Bigod and others, who had not been in London in the winter, had no patience with such prophets of doom: instead, they had retired to the castle garden, which occupied a small patch in the bailey, walled off from the bustle of stables and smithy, where they could not be overheard, for, as Christie had commented cynically, in times like these, who knew who was friend or foe? Ralph thought it unnecessary, and pointed out, with force, that all at Middleham were heart and soul for Gloucester. Christie, an eyebrow raised in dissent, asked how he could know. 'Unless, of course, you are in direct communication with the Deity.'

Ralph, noted for his devout attendance at Mass, grinned rather sheepishly. 'So—what will happen now? I still can't believe the King is dead, you know—it just doesn't seem possible. He was only forty—a man in the prime of life.'

'Too much eating, drinking and whoring will age any man,' said Richard Hoton, a rather strait-laced member of the household, whose elder brother, John, was in the Duke's service at Barnard Castle. 'Doubtless the likes of Mistress Shore burnt him out too early.'

'As they'll never do you,' said Christie affably. Dick Hoton was universally but gently ridiculed for his disapproval of dicing, drinking, gaming, riotous dancing and other less innocent pleasures. 'But there's little point in talking about how the King died. The question is, as Ralph said, what will happen now? The new King's a child of twelve. He's in his own household in Ludlow, surrounded by his Woodville relations, and his mother's in London. I can't imagine her so overcome with grief as to neglect taking full power as soon as possible, council or no council—and the word is that the King's wish was that the Duke be made Protector. For how long do you think the Woodvilles will sit back and allow him that office? They've all the meekness and forbearance of a pack of ravening wolves.'

There was silence. The Queen's numerous family, since their sister's scandalous elevation to the highest place in the land, had been eager to wind their tentacles into any conceivable office, marriage or title that might prove lucrative. Nearly every eligible heir or heiress of high estate had been married to a Woodville, thus antagonising large sections of the nobility, and at Court they were everywhere: the head of the family, the Queen's brother Lord Rivers, was the new boy King's governor at Ludlow, another brother commanded the fleet, sisters had been married respectively to the Duke of Buckingham, the Earl of Arundel, the Earl of Pembroke and sundry lesser lords. The standing joke in London asked why it was impossible to walk through Westminster without getting wet feet: the answer, that there were too many Rivers to wade through. The Queen's family had always disliked Richard of Gloucester, who had such power in the North, and his loathing of them had been increased by the death of his brother Clarence, which he had laid firmly at the door of the Queen and her kin. It was easy to see the appalling situation now looming: a child King in the hands and under the influence of his ruthless mother and her rapacious family, and the only threat to their supreme power the presence of the Duke of Gloucester, like a hovering falcon, in the North that was devoted to him.

'It's obvious,' said Ralph, his pleasant face suddenly very serious indeed. 'They can't let the Duke run free. They know he opposes them—mother of God, any sane man would, they're hardly fit to have charge of the King, let alone the country. They got rid of Clarence—why not murder Gloucester as well?'

'And the alternative to that is civil war,' Christie said bleakly. That spectre, laid to rest only by the last dozen tranquil years of Edward's rule, could all too readily be revived, to tear England's nobles apart again and claim the lives of so many great men. Nevilles, Percies, Cliffords, Beauforts, Plantagenets and many many others had died at St Albans and Towton, Tewkesbury and Barnet. Now was it all to begin again, because King Edward in the pursuance of his lust had taken for wife a beautiful, impoverished and rapacious young widow?

'So what do you think the Duke will do?' asked young Will Claxton, somewhat nervously, and glancing up and down the garden as if Woodvilles were to be found lurking behind the rose bushes or rearing their heads above the walls. Dick Hoton shrugged. 'I don't know, and I doubt he does. He was always so loyal to the King—it must be as if he has lost his lodestar. But whatever happens, he must act quickly, or there'll be a Woodville army at the gates of Middleham, or a Woodville summons to Westminster, and we can all guess what will happen then. Gloucester's not a lucky name for the uncles of young kings.'

They were silent, remembering stories of Humphrey, the Good Duke of Gloucester, most likely murdered by the young King Henry VI's fierce queen, Margaret of Anjou, nearly forty years ago, and the previous holder of the title, Thomas of Woodstock, similarly done to death more than eighty years before by his nephew, Richard II. After the years of complacent peace tended by King Edward, it was an abrupt and shocking prospect to contemplate a return to the uncertainties and dangers of a struggle for the throne, or at any rate for the power behind the throne. They had all been children at the time of the last battle, at Tewkesbury in 1471, and perhaps only Dick Hoton, at twenty-seven the oldest, had any memory at all of that confused, unsettling, lawless time before King Edward, a youth of eighteen, had first become King. Their loyalty was to Gloucester, they were in his pay and his service, and would go with him wherever he wished: but now that the King was dead, and the country's future suddenly clouded and uncertain, full of doubt and debate and strife, the course of their own lives seemed similarly unsure, and the dangers very plain. For if Gloucester fell, they would go down with him as surely as they had hoped to rise in his train.

'But if they try to exclude His Grace from government . . .' William Claxton said, too appalled even to voice the obvious corollary of his murder. 'If that happens, what will become of his followers?'

'Doubtless we'll survive,' said Christie, glancing at the timorous boy—he was only sixteen—with some contempt. 'Or most of us—the Woodvilles can hardly lay waste the whole of the North, they're not of the spirit of William the Conqueror. But I do know this: our own fate is small, compared to the fate of the realm. And for the sake of the peace and happiness and common good of all the people of England, the government must not fall into the hands of the Woodvilles—they're no better than the Duke of Suffolk and the rest of the leeches and vultures and kites who milked the country when Holy Harry was King. And the only man with the power and the ability to stop them plunging us all into war again is the Duke of Gloucester.'

*

It was something that the Duke himself had already, reluctantly, acknowledged, and his wife, who was after all the great King-maker's daughter, had pointed out the danger of his situation with some force. He could not expect to sit tight and unmolested in Middleham while the Woodvilles crowned their young King and then gathered their forces to attack him. He was too powerful, too well-known, too much respected to stand aloof from the changes in the country's rule. Even if he wanted to stay in the North, he would not be allowed to: at the first excuse he would be haled to London and judicially murdered, as had been his brother George before him. It was true that George, wild, irrational, inordinately ambitious and with the loyalty of a windblown weathercock, had to a large degree deserved his fate, but Gloucester could never forget the sordid prison death of the brother who had been closest to him in age, nor the identity of those he held to be responsible. He had had a terrible dream, soon after Clarence's death, in which Salome, with the silver-blonde hair and cold sweet smile of the Queen, had asked a Herod who closely resembled his eldest brother the King for the head of John the Baptist—and into the room had been borne a chased silver dish and cover which, removed with a flourish, had revealed instead the ghastly features of poor George, the blue eyes staring and the golden hair dabbled freely with blood . . .

It had been only a nightmare, unrooted in any literal reality, and yet the essential truth of it seemed plain to him. Clarence had been no friend to the Woodvilles, and in the end the Queen had persuaded Edward to have him executed on a trumped-up charge that glossed over his real offence: that he was an enemy of her, and her family.

As was the Duke of Gloucester.

He had no need of Anne's words to inform him of unpleasant political reality. Indeed, the change for the worse in his brother's health at Christmas had at least forced him to contemplate the terrible options that were open to him, should Edward die untimely. He had, basically, two choices: to stay in Middleham, to rule the North as his own kingdom, and hope, vain hope, that the Woodvilles would be too concerned in parcelling England's riches out amongst themselves to trouble with him. Or he could throw his own weight into the balance, and play for control of the child King, and the country.

There was no doubt where his duty, his loyalty, his heart lay. The country that his brother had brought to peace and prosperity could not in honour be left to the mercy of greedy, factious upstarts: nor could he allow the boy to come further under the thumb of his mother and her deeply unpopular relatives, to sully the child's own name and that of his father, who had been a king much beloved by his people. No, he must act, and act quickly, before the boy could be crowned and thus confirmed in his power, without the moderating weight of an appointed council to rule in his name and, hopefully, free of Woodville influence.

He could not, however, act on his own. He must have allies, both in Westminster and in the country at large. The obvious one was

Lord Hastings, Edward's Lord Chamberlain and his companion in vice: superficially a genial pleasure-seeker like his monarch and friend, he was also like Edward in that this affable exterior concealed a sharp intelligence and enormous political shrewdness. He was a powerful man, with many retainers at his command in the Midlands: and it was his servant who had brought the news of King Edward's death. He hated and feared the Woodvilles, and although loyal to the dead King's young son, would do his utmost to ensure that the government was kept out of the hands of the boy's relatives. Then there was Lord Howard, a wealthy East Anglian and a man with whom, despite a thirty years' difference in age, he had become friendly during the Scottish wars: Howard had much in common with himself, being a man of action who yet loved music and had a great respect for learning. And he had no love for the Woodvilles, who through Court intrigue had deprived him of the estates of the Duchy of Norfolk, to which he considered himself heir, and given them instead to the younger of Edward's sons, the nine-year-old Duke of York. The Earl of Northumberland could also probably be counted as an ally: he had several years before sworn to be Gloucester's good and faithful servant, and although by location and nature remote from the Court, was no lover of Woodvilles either. The men of the King's council, lords and prelates, and the officers of Edward's household would be loyal to his son, but not necessarily to his wife, and were men of shrewd judgement. He had good reason to know that they would not relish Woodville rule.

He knew what he must do, and yet the prospect appalled him, for he had no illusions about what would happen should his coup miscarry. He feared for his followers, for the North, and above all for his wife and his dear son, who would be the first after himself to suffer the Woodville vengeance. Nor did he have any illusions about the ruthlessness that he would undoubtedly have to employ in his bid to secure the young King, his nephew: a ruthlessness foreign to his nature, and yet utterly essential in the brutal, opportunist world of high statecraft. Whatever happened, the peace of Middleham was shattered. Never again could he ride as they had done that afternoon, free of care in the sunshine and wind, with happiness.

*

All over England the messengers scurried, from castle to castle and manor to manor and town to town, bearing the news: King Edward is dead, long live King Edward, his son, fifth of that name! And most people grieved sincerely, for the old King had been much loved, and had brought peace and strong government and prosperity, however dubious his initial assumption of the throne: and they hoped that this would continue under his son, though a boy of twelve, and known to be under the influence of his mother and her relatives. Many, however, were anxious, remembering that child kings often came to bad ends, amid strife and rebellion: did not the Bible say, 'Woe to the land whose King is a child'? But on the whole they were prepared to accept the boy with much joy and good will, for his father's sake.

Messengers left London in haste, bearing the warnings and advice of William, Lord Hastings. A succession of them rode for the North and Middleham, carrying the latest news, written with increasing urgency: it was obvious, Hastings informed Gloucester, that the Woodvilles were bent on obtaining supreme power, and that despite many doubters amongst the King's council, they seemed likely to succeed unless the Duke could halt their pretensions. One messenger also rode to Wales, to the Brecon lands of Henry Stafford, Duke of Buckingham, who had been forcibly married to a Woodville as a child, and reputedly loathed his wife and all her kin. The letter told Buckingham of his sovereign's death, and solicited his help against Woodvilles: so, a day or so later, another courier left Brecon and rode to Middleham, carrying a message which assured the Duke of Gloucester, his cousin, of his support in the struggle for power.

Like ripples from a stone cast suddenly into a still pond, the couriers crossed and recrossed from London to Middleham, Middleham to Wales, and from Gloucester to his nephew's governor, the Queen's brother Lord Rivers, suggesting courteously that he and the boy King meet the Duke on the road to London, so that they could all enter the capital together. Dick Hoton took that letter: Christie was one of those who, closer to Middleham, had the task of riding to the Duke's other castles, Sheriff Hutton, Richmond, Barnard Castle, Skipton, to gather men for the escort, or to the houses of his retainers up and down Yorkshire to enlist their services for the cavalcade south. It took the best part of a week to do this, and for the summoned men and their servants to gather at Middleham: for most of the inhabitants of the castle, it was a nerve-wracking time. No-one knew for certain what was happening in London, and in any case news reached

Middleham four or five days stale, even with the most furious riding: it seemed to take an inordinately long time to round up the men who were to escort Gloucester to London, to make them ready and supply their mourning livery, and yet it was obvious that speed was vital. If the Duke dallied too long, the boy King would slip through his hands, and the Woodvilles would win.

On Sunday 20 April, and ten days after the death of King Edward IV, his youngest brother set out from Middleham with an escort of some three hundred Yorkshire gentlemen, all clad in black and all, discreetly, armed: their purpose was not purely ceremonial. Such a large body of men could not move with any speed, especially on the muddy roads of spring: accommodation and food had to be arranged for them all each night, inns must be commandeered, landlords paid and the route cleared of obstructions such as slow-moving wagons, pot-holes or lakes. A great deal of the arrangements for the march fell on Christie's shoulders, and he took good care to do his job with seemingly effortless efficiency. It did not matter that he usually could snatch no more than four or five hours sleep each night, despite the increasing exhaustion both of himself and of Bayard, whose speed and endurance were rapidly becoming legendary. What did matter was the undeniable and gratifying fact that his work on the journey was marked and remembered by his lord, with whom he was coming into closer and closer contact. Christie had little leisure to contemplate what might lie at the end of their journey, when Gloucester would confront the Woodvilles: but in the Duke's preoccupied frown, the lines of strain already engraved around his eyes and mouth, the enormity of the gamble he was making showed plain. If this play for the Kingdom miscarried, the Duke was doomed: if it did not, he had won the King, and thus the realm. All or nothing, power or disgrace, death or exile: and Christie applied himself with diligence and energy to the task in hand, and grimly, deliberately, did not think of the possible outcome.

They were to meet Earl Rivers in Northampton, on the twenty-ninth of April: and a few miles outside that town, they were joined by the retinue of Henry Stafford, second Duke of Buckingham and, after Gloucester himself, the most important nobleman in the Kingdom.

The procession of retainers, bearing the badge of the Stafford knot, were something of a surprise to many of Gloucester's men: only those who, like Christie, were part of the Middleham household and had been closer to the comings and goings there since the King's death, knew that their lord had been in communication with Buckingham. They sat their horses and watched with lively interest as their leader, slight and unassuming on his favourite chestnut courser, rode forward to greet the man who was several times over his cousin, with a Beaufort mother, a Neville grandmother, and descent through the female line from the youngest son of King Edward III.

The Duke of Buckingham was a few years younger than Gloucester, and bore all the Plantagenet and Neville good looks that had distinguished Gloucester's brothers, in particular George, Duke of Clarence. Christie had seen Clarence, once, in London shortly before his execution, and to the undiscerning eye there was no resemblance between that unhappy Duke, his once-handsome face and figure bloated and fattened with drink and dissolute living, and this tall blond man with his wide easy smile and frank blue eyes. But Christie, watching Buckingham from his place amongst the foremost of Gloucester's men, was struck all at once by the similarity of height, colouring and above all of manner: the flamboyant sweep of an immaculate arm, the charm and friendliness, the cheerful laugh. Clarence, even in disgrace, had always had that easy eloquent way of talking, a knack of persuading each he spoke to that he was of great importance, a boon companion. And Christie remembered Clarence's true nature, and Clarence's fate, and watched this golden young man, so splendid in mourning, black velvet trimmed with sable, on a black horse richly caparisoned in purple, with a growing sense of mistrust. He had been in Gloucester's household long enough to know the essential qualities of his lord: a soldier first and foremost, a man honest and fair-minded in his dealings with the turbulent North, a man deeply loyal to his brother the King, who had never forgotten or forgiven the execution of his other brother, Clarence. He had, it was well-known, defended Clarence against his enemies, had been almost the only one to beg the King to show mercy towards him. Gloucester had always been susceptible to his brother George's spurious charm and vivid tongue: was he now to come under the influence of this man who would doubtless remind him poignantly of his executed brother?

Little of their conversation could be heard, but the tone was evidently most friendly. Beside Christie, Ralph Bigod's brown gelding shifted, chomping on the bit, and shook its head with a heavy slobbering sigh. Its rider, his eyes also on the two Dukes, said quietly to Christie, 'What do you know of Buckingham?'

'Very little. He has land in Wales, has a goodly portion of royal blood—his mother was a Beaufort and his grandfather and father were supporters of Lancaster. He's married to a Woodville and loathes her and all her tribe, he resents Earl Rivers' influence in Wales, and he's never been a haunter of Westminster. Like Gloucester, he's been content to stay on his estates.'

'Until now,' said Ralph, consideringly. 'Why do you suppose he's crawled out from under his Welsh stone now?'

'Simple. Our Duke moves against the Woodvilles. If Buckingham wants to have his inheritance restored and all the power he's bound to consider his by right of birth and position, he's more likely to get it by hitching himself to Gloucester than by joining the Woodvilles, even if he is married to one of them.'

'At least he's chosen the right moment to declare himself,' Ralph commented. 'There's small sign of anyone else deciding their actions till they've seen which way the wind blows. If His Grace is to succeed in this, he needs all the help he can muster.' His eyes lingered with approval on Buckingham's men, several hundred of them, and a most impressive and reassuring sight, and then moved round to contemplation of his friend's impassive face, sharply illuminated by the afternoon sun. 'You do not seem so sure?'

'I'll say nothing,' Christie told him, his eyes on the two Dukes, one plain and brown, the other gilded and brilliant, as they conversed animatedly. 'But think you on this. Our Duke is moved by self-preservation, and by loyalty to his brother and his family. His Grace of Buckingham, at the kindliest view, is moved by self-interest alone. If I were Richard of Gloucester, I would trust him no further than I could see him plain.'

*

The merry laughter of the Duke of Buckingham echoed through the door of the most sumptuous room in Northampton's most expensive and comfortable inn: after a few seconds, it was joined by the rather braying tones of Anthony Woodville, Lord Rivers, uncle and governor of the child King Edward the Fifth. There was no sound from Gloucester: Christie, entering the chamber at the head of a procession of chamberlains and servants bearing the most lavish supper the inn could provide, saw his lord at the head of the table, quiet and thoughtful, his smile reluctant, as if he considered that gravity were more appropriate to this occasion. Richard Grey, child of the Queen's first marriage and an unprepossessing young man, was already half-drunk, with a jug of wine in front of him and his brightly-flushed face at odds with his very fair hair, inherited from his mother. Lord Rivers, by contrast, was undeniably sober, and would doubtless remain so. He had none of the good looks of most of his family, being possessed of brown stiff hair and a long horse face with a naturally sombre expression, and coarse-grained skin that had the look of being always dirty, no matter how clean. His reputation was of a man pious to extremes—everyone knew of the hair shirt which he invariably wore under his splendid garments —rapacious in even the smallest property transactions, and exceptionally learned. He had translated religious books, wrote devotional poems, and excelled in the knightly arts of jousting and tournament. Christie, who had never encountered him before, gave him a considering glance as he supervised the serving of the food. Between the quiet solidity of Gloucester and the flamboyant grace of Buckingham, Earl Rivers seemed lost, out of place, and distinctly ill-at-ease despite his rather forced laughter. His learning and piety had made him an eminently suitable choice for the task of directing the young King's education, and his spiritual and moral welfare, but Christie was certain that in the brutal world of politics he would be more than a little out of his depth. It was not as if either of the two Dukes had much experience of affairs of state, but they would undoubtedly learn fast, from necessity. Rivers, like many learned and pious men, did not look as if he would even understand that necessity.

They were talking of the boy King, who was at Stony Stratford, some fourteen miles away, with the rest of his attendants. Gloucester had asked Rivers how the child had taken the news of his father's death and of his sudden elevation to the crown: the Earl, with a certain amount of proprietorial pride in his nephew, spoke of young Edward's natural grief, his precocious understanding of events, and his great resemblance both in looks and character to his lamented father. He went on at suspicious length, and Christie was interested to see that whereas the Duke of Gloucester listened with considerable attention, the Duke of Buckingham evidently had little patience with Rivers and his rather harsh voice rambling on, seemingly without end. He leant over to Grey, who was fumbling his way through the sauced capon on his plate, and said something *sotto voce* which made the Queen's second son roar with over-loud laughter: both Rivers and Gloucester glanced round, frowning, and the former said sharply, 'Richard, you forget yourself.'

'Wish I could,' said Richard Grey, belching cheerfully and taking another swig of wine. He held the cup out and Christie, waiting with the jug, glanced at his lord. Gloucester gave an almost imperceptible nod, and Christie stepped forward to fill it with the thick sweet wine that was the best the inn could offer, even to such exalted guests. Grey swallowed half the cupful in one draught, and returned to his food. A chunk of fowl impaled on his knife, he belched again. 'He's a good enough lad, my little brother, though too much of a prig and a milksop for my liking. Reckon Thomas and I will see to that, eh, uncle? Teach him everything his father knew.'

Lord Rivers looked at his nephew with some distaste. 'I hardly think that you and your brother are fit company for a twelve-year-old boy with pretensions to grace, gentleness and learning—even if you are all my dear sister's children. I begin to see the wisdom of our late monarch in placing his heir in Ludlow—it is certainly far enough distant from your debaucheries.'

'Well, he'll have to stay in Westminster now,' said Richard Grey, with the noisy laugh that was a drunken echo of Lord Rivers' bray. 'And when he's crowned and anointed, he'll have true power, full power—power to dismiss you, uncle dear, if he wants, and power to choose his own companions.' He drained the cup and held it out again in a hand that was less than steady. 'And the coronation's set for the fourth of May—next Sunday—and once crowned, the boy's king in fact as well as name.'

It was the evening of Tuesday 29 April. Five days until the coronation, five days in which Richard of Gloucester must act to save the Kingdom and himself from the Woodvilles. They had all known that the coronation had been planned in unseemly haste, despite the protests of Lord Hastings and the more prudent members of the council, and they had all been aware of the implications: but now, in the stuffy inn chamber, the shutters drawn against the dark fresh air and the myriad candles guttering gently in an occasional draught, the gravity of the situation struck home to Christie like a hammer blow.

The room was suddenly very quiet: Richard Grey, aware that perhaps he had said too much, belched and held out his cup again. Christie, wondering what other indiscretions might follow if Grey's tongue were loosened further, poured with a generous hand

and stepped back into the shadows, seemingly impassive, a man of stone who was in actual fact as alert and ready as an alaunt scenting the quarry. He watched as the conversation was steered by Lord Rivers, plainly embarrassed and angered by Grey's behaviour, into safer channels. A stilted discussion of Master Caxton's printing press ensued, in which Rivers led (he had had two or three works produced by this newfangled process), followed by Buckingham, whom Christie suspected of being largely ignorant of the subject, but spectacularly successful at giving the impression that he was not. Gloucester, whom he knew for certain to be interested in books, said little and seemed to have other matters on his mind, as well he might. Grey, swaying slightly in his chair, had reached the semi-comatose stage and let slip not a word, though several rather disgusting noises. On the surface, the mood of the gathering was convivial, even merry: the supper was cleared away, Grey retired, escorted by his servant, and Rivers lingered a little over his wine, his manner far more relaxed than had been the case earlier.

But Christie, glancing at Ralph Bigod, serving as carver that night, saw the wary, watchful look in his friend's face, so much less accustomed to dissembling than his own, and knew that his own sense of the tension beneath the talk and laughter around the table before them was not only in his imagination. What would Gloucester do now? The thought of Grey, and of his even more dissolute brother Thomas, Marquess of Dorset, becoming the intimates of the young King was certainly repugnant to him. Rivers, however disapproving of his sister's elder sons, would surely support them as he would the rest of his multitudinous family, against the Duke of Gloucester. And if the child was indeed to be crowned on Sunday, the old King's wish that his brother be Protector until the boy came of age would be set at naught. Crowned, young Edward would rule with full power under the control of a council probably comprised of Woodvilles and their supporters, with no place for the Duke of Gloucester and his friends. Doubtless this was why the boy had been taken on to Stony Stratford, fourteen miles closer to London and the coronation that would confirm his mother's family in their power, and fourteen miles away from the Duke of Gloucester, whom the Woodvilles had most reason to fear and mistrust: also why Rivers had returned to Northampton to welcome the Dukes and allay their suspicions. Grey's drunken indiscretions had not helped his uncle in the slightest, for both Dukes had been made aware now, even more than before, of the need to strike, and strike quickly.

At last Rivers, with a smile that sat oddly on his horse face, rose and tendered his thanks to the two Dukes for their hospitality: he would now retire to his own lodgings, in a hostelry just down the street, and bade them a very good night, adding that he would ride with them to Stony Stratford in the morning so that they could greet his royal nephew. The room seemed very quiet when he had gone: only Buckingham and Gloucester remained at the table, silent, while lesser servants removed the cheeses that had been set out, and mopped the spilt wine in front of Richard Grey's place. Ralph and Christie stayed at their posts, well aware that they had not yet been dismissed, knowing also that this night was not yet over. The last of the chamberlains withdrew, bowing, and it was not until the door had closed firmly behind them and the footsteps retreated towards the kitchens that Gloucester glanced up at his two attendants and snapped his fingers. 'Sir Ralph—Master Heron. We have much that we wish to discuss between ourselves. Be so good as to leave us—but do not go to your beds, we will summon you later.' He smiled, a rare smile that took up the lines of tiredness and stress in his face and made him seem youthful again. 'Do not fear: you'll get some sleep at least this night, for we have much to do to-morrow. My thanks for your service. You may wait outside, and ensure that no inquisitive stranger lingers too long near the chamber.'

It was a long wait in the outer room. There was at least a fire, and a bed and stools and cushions, and Christie went down to the inn kitchen and came back with a tray of leftovers from supper, cold but plentiful with huge hunks of bread. They ate in silence, both wondering what was being planned on the other side of the stout panelled door: but only the featureless murmur of voices could be heard, on and on into the night. The inn staff had long since gone to bed, and Ralph, who had made the mistake of lying down on the bed, had been sound asleep for an hour or more when the door opened and Gloucester stood in the gap, a flat black shape in front of the bright candles within. 'Master Heron! We would talk with you and Sir Ralph now.'

Christie rose from his stool. Ralph sat up, knuckling his eyes like a small boy, and leapt to his feet. Christie, a weary ache within all his muscles, wondered how long he could keep himself at this pitch of frenetic activity, days in the saddle and nights with little sleep, without faltering. But tonight, at least, the tension and uncertainty, the chance of taking a part in great events had ensured that, despite his exhaustion, he would not slacken now. He had found in the past that he had a well of hidden energy that he seemed to be able to call upon at times of great need, and he was tapping it now. Aware of the contrast between himself, relaxed yet alert, and the sleep-rumpled clothes and face and hair of Sir Ralph Bigod, he entered the chamber with his friend to await the orders of the Dukes of Buckingham and Gloucester.

The former lounged in his chair, one elbow on its arm, the other behind his head. In his splendid mourning garb, he looked every inch the prince—which he was not, nor had he one in his lineage for several generations back. Richard, Duke of Gloucester, brother and uncle of kings, by contrast seemed altogether slighter, smaller, less substantial in every way: and yet Christie was willing to lay long odds that it was Buckingham who was the lightweight. It was Buckingham who spoke now: his voice was as handsome as his person, pleasantly pitched, melodic and easy, and undoubtedly most persuasive. 'These men are to be trusted, Richard?'

'Implicitly,' said Gloucester, with another of those rare smiles for his two young attendants. 'I have men who have been with me longer, men who are older or of more experience. I can trust all of them, just as much as I trust yourself, Harry, and none more so than these. Gentlemen, you are to go quietly and rouse as privily as you can all of my men who are lodging here, without disturbing their servants if possible, and bring them to this chamber for their orders and yours. As quickly as may be—and remember, do it with all discretion.'

It did not take long: no more than fifteen minutes had elapsed before some twenty men, disguising their yawns and still straight-ening their clothing, were gathered in the chamber to hear the orders of Richard, Duke of Gloucester. As his lord's even, rather sharp voice issued his various commands, Christie felt the slow beginnings of excitement knot within his belly. This bold stroke was what had been essential—and, please God, the morning would see the end of the Woodvilles' pretensions to high estate, and the confirmation of the Duke of Gloucester's rightful place as protector and guardian of the young King.

*

Well before sunrise Christie Heron set out with the Dukes to Stony Stratford, and was glad of it. He wanted to take a full part in all that might follow, and not only because it would bring him hope of further advancement. Times were changing, great matters were stirring: the events of these days might well alter the course of England's history, and he would not sit on the edge and tamely watch. He felt sorry for Ralph, left at Northampton to guard Rivers who had been seized at first light that morning: for himself, he had so far forgotten his weariness—there had been perhaps three hours sleep that night—as to take his old delight in the fresh pink sky of the dawn, away to their left as they rode south to Stony Stratford, and to revel in the swift smooth contained gallop of Bayard, his black mane streaming and his great muscular body bunching and flexing under him. There were several hundred men around and behind him, but the Dukes led, their riding gowns whipped out behind them in the speed of their mounts: no ambling horses these, but fresh coursers chosen for their speed. And it took them no more than an hour to reach the little town where the twelve-year-old King of England was lodged.

They were in time. There was much bustle around the largest inn: the place teemed with soldiers, restless horses, pack animals, wagons, and in the middle of the crush a still centre in which sat a slender, fair-haired child on a richly-harnessed white palfrey. He looked round, startled, as the Dukes and their retinue clattered down the street and halted, their horses blowing and sweating, just outside the knot of retainers and officials. Gloucester's gaze, sharp and decisive, took in the situation in one long sweeping movement of his head: his arm stabbed briefly, to right and to left, and imperceptibly his men spread themselves more thinly, to make a circle around the boy and his attendants. It was neatly done, pre-empting any violent reaction by those of the King's retinue who were gathered there. Two thousand well-armed Welshmen had ridden from Ludlow with the boy: some were held in Northampton with Rivers, but those left in Stony Stratford still outnumbered the men commanded by the two Dukes. They had relied on surprise and speed to achieve their aim: and Christie, looking round from his position just behind Gloucester, could see no signs of aggression in the packed, curious faces. Gloucester, in accordance with the orders he had given earlier, gestured again, and his men dismounted, doffed their caps, and knelt on the cold dirty stone of the highway. From this position of obeisance and homage, Christie saw his lord and the Duke of Buckingham dismount and make similar reverence.

King Edward, the fifth of that name, stared at his uncle in transparent bewilderment, a frown between the pale, slightly arched brows. His voice was clear, high and unbroken, and carried some distance: all could hear it plainly. 'Greetings, uncle. We did not expect you so soon.' His eyes travelled restlessly along the ranks of bent heads, brown, grey, fair, in the early light, and returned to Gloucester. 'You do me—us—too much honour, uncle. Please —bid your men rise—and you likewise—and—' He peered at the deferential figure of Gloucester's companion, and an elderly man in a long furred gown, standing by the palfrey, whispered something. 'And Your Grace of Buckingham also,' the boy finished, his tone suddenly more confident. As the men rose to their feet, he studied their ranks again, and then, evidently at a loss, returned his attention to Gloucester. 'Please, I do not understand—where is my uncle Rivers?'

The silence amongst all that crowd of stalwart, well-armed men was broken only by the shuffling of horses' hooves and the chomping of bits. In the eaves of the inn behind the young King, an insolent bright sparrow set up a great chirping, and was joined by other birds, noisily attracting attention: and so it was that Gloucester and all his men saw the pale, horrified face of Richard Grey appear at the doorway of the inn, a mug of ale in his hand. It retreated in a flash, but none could mistake it, nor the look of grim satisfaction, of a Cassandra proved right, that illuminated the Duke's face. It was plain that Rivers had sent his nephew to Stony Stratford to urge the King to flee. He said to the boy, his voice eminently reasonable and gentle, 'I regret very much, Your Grace, that your uncle Lord Rivers has had to remain in Northampton. He sends his good will to you, however, and bids me do all I may for Your Grace's happiness and comfort. However, it is not now convenient nor politic for you to continue on to London today.'

'But Richard said—' the boy began, flushed, and glanced back into the inn before continuing, his face taut with rising alarm. 'My brother has told me—us—that my lady mother the Queen wishes me to travel in all haste. Our crowning is to take place on Sunday.' There was a wobble now in the high voice. 'Uncle, we must leave as soon as may be, and not delay any longer.'

Christie, glancing at the faces of the King's escort, saw the self-same feelings of surprise and fear in almost all of them. The situation hung on a knife-edge, for they far outnumbered the forces of the two Dukes, and one word from that handsome, suspicious child on the superb palfrey would set all those fierce Welsh retainers at their throats. But the boy was too young and inexperienced to take the initiative, and without Rivers the men were leaderless. They made no sound nor movement as Gloucester, with Buckingham at his shoulder and his most loyal retainers—Lord Lovell, Sir Robert Percy, Lord Scrope, Sir Richard Ratcliffe, Robert Brackenbury—immediately behind him, walked through their ranks to where young Edward still sat his horse, his bodyservants and attendant surrounding him. Christie, standing in the front rank of the Yorkshire men, could not hear their conversation clearly, though Gloucester was evidently stating his case with some conviction and urgency, and the boy, his face increasingly scarlet, was shaking his head. Then Buckingham intervened, the winning sweet tones of his voice plain enough even if the words were not, and the King suddenly capitulated. With an abrupt movement very eloquent of despairing anger and frustration, he kicked his feet clear of the stirrups, dismounted and stamped across to the inn, shoulders hunched and his whole posture so very reminiscent of Julian Bray in a tantrum that Christie almost smiled at the resemblance. Gloucester, with the ancient chamberlain and other retainers of both parties, followed him: but Buckingham turned to face the Welshmen, standing muttering and suspicious around the inn within the thin ring of Yorkshiremen. His beautiful persuasive voice rose into the morning air, silencing them. 'Gentlemen, now that the Duke of Gloucester has joined with the King's Grace his nephew, there is no further need for your loyal services. Lord Rivers has asked me, in the King's name and his own, to dismiss you all with his thanks for your service. You are free to return to your homes.'

Christie, listening, marvelled at the lying sincerity of the man, when Earl Rivers was at this moment under Ralph Bigod's guard at Northampton and had evidently placed much hope and faith in his Welsh escort. He marvelled also as Buckingham, seeing that these few words would not be enough, proceeded to elaborate on his story. It was beautifully done, and so persuasive that Christie himself almost succumbed to the urge to return in peace to his home: some of those on the fringes of the crowd began to turn away, calling to their fellows. But a stalwart core remained around Buckingham, while others, curious or aggressive, arrived from the further parts of the town. There was a discreet bustle around the inn doorway, a brief pause, and then an upstairs casement opened and the King, a quaver lost within his voice, and evidently close to tears, bade them go. Christie and the rest of Gloucester's men made way for them, and the two thousand Welshmen, whose presence had been intended to intimidate any foes and ensure the King's swift safe passage to London and his coronation, melted away like snow in June, leaving the Duke of Gloucester in sole charge of his brother's elder son.

*

'I don't understand,' said Edward, struggling to keep his composure. A second breakfast, the fine white bread still steaming from the oven, lay untouched before him and before his uncle, who in his haste had not eaten that morning. Buckingham, by contrast, had hungrily devoured all that was set in front of him and was dipping his fingers in the bowl held out to him by Christie, who had been summoned with a few others to serve them: it seemed the Dukes wanted only trusted men of discretion about them this morning, not inn servants of dubious loyalty. The Welshmen had departed, sullen and bewildered, and all Edward's close attendants, the men who had tended him throughout his childhood at Ludlow, had also been sent away: his chamberlain, Sir Thomas Vaughan, an old man with Woodville connections, had been so vehement in his protests that he had been placed under guard, along with Grey and one or two others. To all this, the boy had been a confused, angry witness, his frightened resentment increasing with each of his uncle's quiet, decisive orders until now, tears of rage standing in his wide blue eyes, he demanded again, 'I don't understand, uncle. *Why* have you dismissed them? Where is my uncle Rivers? Is he your prisoner too?'

His earlier formal dignity had utterly disappeared: next to his uncle and cousin, he was nothing but a fearful child in gorgeous clothes, and Christie, glancing at those unshed tears and the desperate remnants of pride in his trembling, taut body, felt a sudden and unaccustomed surge of pity. The boy must hardly know his uncle, and he had been reared by Woodvilles, who had doubtless taught him to fear Gloucester. God knew what terrible forebodings now tormented him, alone, bereft of all those familiar and dear to him, and compelled by pride to pretend to this pathetic royal dignity with men nearly three times his age and with many times his experience of the ways of the world and of state affairs.

'Earl Rivers is in Northampton, as I told Your Grace earlier,'

Gloucester said. He was plainly ill-at-ease with the boy, despite being quite accustomed to children. It would be a hard business indeed, to win the child over to him, and he obviously had little heart for this task. 'He spoke very well of your attainments, Edward—you are evidently studying very conscientiously.'

The boy ignored the compliment. He said, his voice quivering on the edge of panic, 'I don't understand. Tell me, uncle, for sweet Jesu's sake tell me—why have you sent them all away? Why? *Tell me!*' And he dragged a trembling hand across his eyes and then, mindful of etiquette, fumbled for a kerchief. Silently, his uncle proffered linen, and Edward, with a look of contempt, ignored it. Christie, taking pity on him, unobtrusively dropped a small square towel on the table by his side.

'Your Grace?' said Buckingham, his voice very gentle and deferential: the King, startled, turned his tear-stained face towards this other enemy, who presented himself in such a pleasant guise. 'Perhaps I may help your uncle to make the situation clear for you. We have done this with no thought in our heads but your own welfare and well-being, which is of the greatest concern to us both. And as to why we have dismissed your retinue, Your Grace—well, think you on this. Your late and much-lamented father is dead, a tragedy which has caused great grief to all the land, and in particular to your uncle here, who loved and served him with all his heart. And perhaps Your Grace could tell me, how old was your father at the time of his sad death?'

The boy stared at him, curiosity for the moment overcoming his other and more tangled emotions. 'He was forty years old.'

'And is that not a very early age for a man as vigorous and lusty as your father to die?'

Edward frowned his puzzlement. 'Yes, but—'

'He died untimely, Your Grace, and it is my unhappy duty to tell you that those same men we have just dismissed from your presence have contributed in no small manner to his death in the prime of life, when he should have had many more fruitful and happy years of rule before him. It is those men who were his companions in vices too unpleasant for me to speak of them in more detail to a child of Your Grace's tender years. Suffice it to say that by pandering to his lusty nature and fostering his natural inclinations to indulgence, they ruined his health, and led him to his early grave.'

Appalled and disbelieving, Edward stared at him. 'No! That isn't

[113]

true! My uncle Rivers isn't like that—he's well-known to be devout and high-minded, he would never—he didn't!'

'It is not your uncle Rivers of whom I speak,' Buckingham told him gravely. 'I know him to be blameless as far as debauchery and vice are concerned, though not in other matters—but your uncle Gloucester will tell you of that. No, I am thinking rather of your lady mother's two elder sons, the Marquis of Dorset and Richard Grey—amongst others.'

Edward swallowed convulsively. 'My brothers? You blame Tom and Richard for my father's death?'

'Amongst others, yes. And we are not the only ones who do not believe them to be fit companions and advisors to a king of your young years and necessarily limited experience of the world. I am sure, Your Grace, that if you are honest with yourself you will see the truth of what I say. It is not fitting that a child of your age should be forced to rely on such puny men to help govern this kingdom.'

The boy's face was of a sudden stricken with doubt: young as he was, he must have heard some talk of his father's activities, and known of the wildness and debauchery of his two half-brothers. He said slowly, 'If it is indeed as you say—but how can I trust what you say? And what of Sir Thomas Vaughan? He's my friend, he has grandchildren, *he's* not a man of vice. And my uncle Rivers, he isn't either!'

'I agree, he is not,' said Gloucester, speaking for the first time for some while. 'Edward, I am sorry to have to tell you this, but there has been a plot hatched in London, by certain of your mother's kin, against my life. Did you know that it was your father's wish that I be Protector of this realm until you are of an age to govern it yourself? No, I thought you did not. It has been kept from you, as has much else. And if you do not believe what I say, you may confirm this with members of your Council when we reach London, and discover the truth. And the truth is, that your half-brothers, amongst others, have plotted to ambush me, to have me killed, and to rule the country through you. You would have been their puppet, and danced to their bidding: they would have debauched you and led you into those same vices as they did your father. Do you really want such a sordid fate for yourself, Edward? Or will you follow your father's wish, and have me for your Protector until you come of age?'

There was silence, broken only by the crackle of the fire and the muted sounds of bustle elsewhere in the inn. Christie had heard nothing of any specific plots or ambushes: he could not be sure that such had existed, although he knew well that the Woodvilles wished Gloucester nothing but harm. His lord, though, was essentially honest—could he look his nephew in the face and tell him some fabricated tale of imaginary conspiracies? He doubted it, however pressing the need: Buckingham, on the other hand, could certainly convince a man that he had two heads, if necessary.

'My father chose my attendants,' said Edward, his voice showing a return of confidence. 'He chose them as he chose his own councillors, and I have faith in his judgement, uncle. I can't believe—I *can't* think they would plot against you, or me—they are *not* evil men, and I trust them, and I want them by me until you can *prove* that they're as wicked as you say. And you haven't shown any proof to me, yet, you've talked of it, but that's no proof, only words.' He looked from Gloucester's pale, still, careworn face to the gilded good looks of Buckingham, and added, 'And anyway, they have had no part in the governing of the kingdom, nor will they have, so you need not worry about that, uncle. I shall be too young to undertake that task myself for some years yet, but I have every faith and confidence in the powers of my lords and my council, and the Queen my mother—'

Buckingham's hand slapped down on the white napery covering the table. 'Your lady mother should not in no wise be concerned with the government of the kingdom, Your Grace. That's not a woman's business, and if she has any ideas on that score, she'd best abandon them with all speed—and so had you, Your Grace. It's for men to decide the fate of the country, not women, and they shouldn't meddle in what does not concern them. Look to your lords and your council for government, and let your mother restrict herself to domestic matters, where she belongs.'

Christie could not imagine that Elizabeth Woodville, whose urge to meddle was notorious, would be so easily discouraged as her son, who sat now at the table forlorn, desolate, all his impassioned pleas and arguments set at naught because he was a child, and had not the authority nor experience to deal with these powerful men who so abruptly had turned his sheltered, well-ordered little world upside down. Finally he said, the tears very close to the surface now, 'I see you are not to be persuaded, uncle, and there is nothing I can do—I am in your power, and must do your bidding. If—if my father did appoint you as my Protector, then of course I must submit to his wishes and yours.' He swallowed, holding on to his self-control with an all-too-visible effort, and added humbly, 'If it please you, uncle—since I have no attendants now, will you give me one or two of your own, until we reach London?'

'Of course,' said Gloucester, obviously relieved to be able to grant his nephew's request so easily. 'You may choose those you want, Edward, and as many as you feel you require.'

'I would like to have this gentleman to serve me,' Edward told him, and his hand indicated the tall impassive figure of Christie Heron, standing nearby with his basin and towel. 'He seems kind and pleasant—will you tell me your name and birth, sir?'

For once nonplussed, Christie stared at the child who was his sovereign, wondering why he should be thus singled out for attention, unless it were due to that kerchief: or perhaps his sympathy for the boy's plight had shown too clearly on his face. He said, 'My name is Christopher Heron, of Bokenfield in North-umberland, Your Grace, and I am the fourth son of Sir Lyell Heron of that place.' Some imp of mischief prompted him to add, 'You have just left the county of Shropshire, Your Grace. My great-great-grandsire was killed outside Shrewsbury, fighting with Welshmen.'

Edward's face took on animation and eagerness for the first time that day: with his fair hair and bright blue eyes, he was a handsome, if rather girlish-looking child, though his words had some spirit. 'At Shrewsbury? Did he fight for or against Glendower? What was his name?'

'His name was Harry Percy, and he was known as Hotspur,' said Christie, and had the satisfaction of seeing young Edward's eyes widen: Buckingham sent him a very sharp glance indeed, but said nothing. Gloucester smiled. 'You have chosen wisely, Edward: Master Heron, though young, has my wholehearted confidence and trust, and moreover plays the lute exceeding well. Do you like music, Edward?'

The boy's enthusiasm had quite vanished as his uncle began speaking. He glanced at Gloucester with suspicion, and lowered his eyes. 'Yes, uncle.'

'Then I do not doubt that you will enjoy his playing. But one attendant is not enough for your estate, Edward, and you must choose more before we return to Northampton.'

'We're going back to Northampton?' the boy demanded. 'Not to London? But you said we were going on to London!'

'And so we will, Your Grace,' said Buckingham soothingly. 'But there are still men at large in the countryside who mean to do you, and your uncle, harm. They may try to take your person by force, and kill your uncle. Northampton is a large town, stronger than Stony Stratford, with stout walls and a castle, well able to be defended. We will return there today, and await news from your council in London.'

'Then—then I am not to be crowned on Sunday?'

'I regret that it will not now be possible,' said the Duke of Gloucester, and his thin face was sad as he looked at the suspicion and dislike on his nephew's. 'Edward, it was your mother and her kin that were so eager to see you crowned, for then they could rule the kingdom through you, in defiance of your dear dead father's fondest wish. He left me as your Protector and guardian till you came of age: would you offend against his desires now he is dead?'

Mute, the boy shook his head. Buckingham took up the argument. 'Your Grace, you must trust our judgement. Did not your father trust your uncle's, and place every confidence in him, when he set out to win Berwick back from the Scots? Aye, and succeeded gloriously in his task. Your father leaned on your uncle Gloucester: he was his right-hand man. Will you not respect your father's judgement, and do the same?'

Like a trapped, frightened, bewildered young animal, Edward's haunted blue gaze swung from Buckingham to Gloucester and back again. It included Christie, somewhat to his surprise, for he did not consider himself to be in any wise the kind of man that children look to readily, as a friend or ally. He did not give the boy any further sign of sympathy, however: the child was obviously in the state of mind where, like Julian Bray, any overtures of friendship would be instantly treated with suspicion and hostility. Edward finally turned to study his uncle's face, although he must have known that there was no hope of Gloucester relenting: at last he bowed his head, and his assent came in a barely audible whisper. 'Yes, uncle, I will trust your judgement, and do your bidding.'

*

That night a messenger, riding hard, reached London with the news that Gloucester had snatched the King: and those who had most to lose by his swift and surprising action were thrown into an unedifying panic. The Queen and her eldest son, the Marquis of Dorset, made frantic and vain attempts to gather an army at Westminster. Such was the hostility they encountered, however, from the lords

[117]

and gentlemen they approached, that even the tenacious Elizabeth Woodville realised the weight of opinion lay firmly against her. She had made too many enemies during her years as Queen, too many had suffered from her greed and her meddling in political affairs, and now all her hens were come home to roost with a vengeance. Lord Howard had even gone so far as to tell her, with a soldier's bluntness, that he considered the Duke of Gloucester, a man well-known to live a quiet, sober, honest life, far more fit to have charge of the impressionable young King than the debauched and sinful Marquis of Dorset and Richard Grey.

Bereft of all those whom she had thought to win to her cause, save only her immediate family, the Queen recognised defeat. Gloucester had two of her sons, and she feared his intentions towards the rest of her children—in particular, the eldest, the Marquis of Dorset. The King's treasure, a very great quantity of gold, plate, jewels and coin amassed during the prosperous years of her husband's rule, was divided, the Queen's brother, Sir Edward Woodville, taking a large part of it with him to a pair of ships moored below the Tower, before escaping in them to join the rest of the fleet. Then the Queen, the Marquis, her brother the Bishop of Salisbury, her five daughters and her youngest son the Duke of York, fled in a panic from Westminster Palace to sanctuary next door at the Abbey, accompanied by servants, furniture, clothes, jewels, the rest of the royal treasure and everything to ensure a comfortable and secure, if restricted, existence.

And on the day once set for his coronation, her son the King entered London, royally clad in blue velvet, a figure of ethereal dignity and beauty on his delicate white palfrey, his fair hair shining in the May sunshine. Behind him rode his uncle of Gloucester and his cousin of Buckingham and their Welsh and Yorkshire retinue, all in deep black mourning garb. They made an impressive and sombre contrast to the red and murrey purple of the City mayor, his aldermen and some five hundred of the most important citizens of London. At the head of the procession were hauled four wagons piled high with Woodville arms seized at Stony Stratford and intended, so the criers shouted to the crowds packed into the narrow streets, to overthrow the rights of the Duke of Gloucester and the King's council. In the joyous tumult of the City's welcome, the tensions and fears of the past few days were forgotten: caps were flung in the air, the King's path was strewn with flowers, the sweet-smelling wallflowers that were also known as heart's ease, cowlips and violets, and the cheering seemed to rock the scattered clouds as men and women roared their relief at this peaceful accession, and their approval of the fair, nervous, shyly smiling boy who would be their King.

More than a mile away, in the cramped stone rooms of her apartments in the Abbey, the Queen heard the cheering, faintly, on the gentle warm breeze that brought also the odours of London and its unclean river. Savagely she ordered the windows shut and then wept, drawing her bewildered little children around her, for the death of her hopes and for fear of how the Duke of Gloucester, who would now surely be confirmed in the power she had craved for herself, would take his revenge on the family who had contrived his brother Clarence's death.

❧ CHAPTER SIX ❧

**'Though there was fair speech,
love was there none.'**
(BOOK 8, CHAPTER 14)

The Red Lion in Aldgate was a large and respectable inn of some repute, both for the comfort of its rooms and the excellence of its food, wine and beer. Some twenty or thirty guests, with their servants and horses, could be accommodated in degrees of comfort varying according to the lengths of their purses or their ambition, and at present, with a new King, the City packed with noblemen's retainers and their followers, and a Parliament session probable in the near future, it was full to its smart tarred eaves.

Perkin, and his master, were well aware of the story of the prodigal son, and the ironic parallels between that parable and his own case. Now that they had come safely to rest in London, with the boy King installed in the palace by St Paul's where the Bishop of London lived, there had seemed a sufficient halt to the headlong rush of recent events for both Christie and his servant to relax and recover from the stress and exhaustion of the journey from York-shire. There were many others now in attendance on the boy, and frequent visitors from Gloucester's household, amongst them the familiar sturdy figure of Sir James Tyrell, whose cousin Lady Darcy had been mistress of the old King's nursery. Her second husband, Richard Haute, a cousin of the Queen, had been a prominent member of young Edward's household at Ludlow, and dismissed with the rest of the boy's officials. Thinking that his nephew would like a familiar face amongst all the deferential, unemotional strangers who now accompanied Edward through his every hour, waking and sleeping, Gloucester had summoned her from her home in Kent whence she had retired some two years ago. She was a stern but kindly lady, well into middle age, and her appearance at the Bishop's palace had brought the boy perilously close to break-down. With hard-concealed pity, Christie had watched the reunion between the fair, delicate-looking child and the woman who had probably once been more of a mother to him than his own, and seen the desperate and almost successful attempts by the young King to keep his tears in check. He was twelve years old, and had been much sheltered, perhaps less loved. Christie, who had been kept at a distance by Edward during his days as his attendant, although he had played for him often, saw the true nature of the boy, his emotions and fears and desperate need for comfort, rawly displayed as, with a visible effort of will, he prevented himself from running into his former nurse's arms. And the thought was in his mind, despite his sympathy, as it must have been in Tyrell's, in Gloucester's, and in that of anyone who witnessed the touching, pathetic scene. What manner of king would this boy make, in the hands of his council?

But he was King by right of inheritance, and they would all have to guide and teach and mould this malleable, youthful material, as the Woodvilles had hoped to do themselves. The Queen had stayed in sanctuary with her daughters and her two remaining sons and her brother, and would not listen to entreaty: Gloucester was proclaimed Protector, as the dead King had wished, and various officers of high state, Chancellor, Keeper of the Privy Seal, Treasurer, were appointed. A Parliament was summoned, the coronation fixed for the fourth week in June, and it was decided, on the suggestion of the Duke of Buckingham, that the young King should be moved to much more appropriate and suitable lodgings, namely, the royal apartments in the Tower of London. By the middle of May, he was installed, and Perkin, who had taken two weeks to screw his courage thus far, asked for and received permission from his master to take an afternoon away from his duties to visit his mother.

Christie, as he had expected, was caustic. 'You'd best put your rags back on your back, or she'll be asking you for the coin you stole. Or she'll offer you her best bed. But you can put your best livery on, if you want to make an impression, and I'll wager it takes her ten minutes to recognise you.'

'I don't want to be robbed, thank you,' said Perkin, aware that the tempting sight of his azure velvet and silver lacing would possibly prove too much for just the sort of street urchin he had once been.

It was not far, along Woodroffe Lane and Hart Street, to the Red Lion in Aldgate. Perkin, wisely but wistfully, had rejected the azure velvet in favour of his plain black mourning doublet, matched somewhat unsuitably with hose in a startling shade of red. He was glad that Christie was not here to see him: he could well imagine the mocking comments about ladybirds that would undoubtedly have ensued, for his master's taste in clothes was somewhat quieter than his own. But today Perkin wanted to make a splash, create a good impression, and the red hose and black satin shoes would to his mind perform that task perfectly.

The Red Lion's principle rooms and entrance lay along the street, with an archway in the centre leading to a galleried courtyard with stables and further chambers: it was a big, rambling place, that had not altered at all in the two or three years since Perkin had seen it last. But he had changed greatly, as a glance in any mirror could tell him. He had left his mother's inn an irresponsible, unruly child, to live on his wits like a street urchin and survive starvation, abuse, disease, attack, robbery, and all the other multitudinous hazards of a wayfaring life. And through luck he had become a gentleman's servant and had rubbed shoulders with kings and nobles, the highest in the land, knew all the ways of the world great and small, and was well on the way to becoming a man of means and consequence. And he was not yet eighteen—what dizzying prospects might the world yet hold out for him?

He swaggered beneath the low entrance of the Red Lion, and was immediately accosted by a supercilious chamberlain, who did not recognise him. 'May I enquire the nature of your business, sir?'

Perkin, gratified to find that, far from being the scrawny runt, as of old, he overtopped the chamberlain by at least half a finger's breadth, looked the man in the eye and said in authoritative tones, 'I wish to speak with Mistress Hobbes.'

The chamberlain stared at him. 'She is very busy, sir. Upon what business?'

'Upon private and most urgent business,' said Perkin, suppressing an inconvenient desire to laugh. 'Be so good as to acquaint her of my arrival.'

The chamberlain was used to arrogant servants and their masters giving him orders, and the curt certainty in Perkin's voice convinced him: he bowed, and led him to a tiny parlour, where Perkin ordered a tankard of best beer, refused to give his name, and seated himself comfortably on a settle. He had barely half-drained his mug when the chamberlain returned. 'Mistress Hobbes will see you now, sir.'

Perkin was led through the familiar bustle in the courtyard to the little chamber by the kitchen, warm from the heat of the ovens, that his mother had always used as her business room. She had owned and run the Red Lion since the death of his father some ten years previously, and her strong and forceful personality had helped her to hold on to her possession despite the strenuous efforts of her husband's brother and nephews to wrest it from her. She had had her own children to look to as well: William, the eldest, was her rather stolid, unimaginative assistant, but the girls, Mary, Kate and Agnes, were much younger and in varying degrees unsatisfactory, while Perkin, who came last but one, had turned out worse than that: idleness, disobedience and finally, and unforgiveably, thieving from a guest had marked his progress, and she had only felt a few times any twinge of regret for the furious impulse with which she had turned him out of her house, and disowned him. But in these hectic, prosperous days she thought little of her disgraceful younger son: so little that when the immaculately-clad servant was ushered into her presence, she completely failed to recognise him, so much was he altered from the scapegrace undersized urchin she had ejected nearly three years before. She stared at him with mild curiosity, wondering why he was returning her gaze with such intensity, and said in the brisk sharp tones of an essentially practical woman, 'Well? And what may I do for you?'

A cheerful, insolent grin that was suddenly all too familiar spread across the stranger's face. 'Hello, Mam,' he said. 'Don't you recognise me, then?'

Very few people had ever seen Cis Hobbes totally at a loss for words: a small sparrow-like woman whose slight frame masked a keen tough brain and a right arm like whipcord, she had ruled her family, and the Red Lion, for ten years, and prided herself on her ability to deal with any situation that might arise, no matter how devastating the emergency. Now, faced with the elegant apparition that seemed to speak with the voice of her disreputable younger son, she sat at the paper-strewn table, mouth ajar, and an expression of lively dismay on her shrewd shrewish face. At last she said, hesitantly, 'Perkin?'

'The very same, as I live and breathe,' said her son cheerfully, to conceal the sudden awkwardness he felt: he had thought that nothing could disturb his mother's iron grasp of affairs, least of all himself: even her ejection of him had been for strictly practical reasons (she had had, after all, to consider the inn's reputation and consequently her own livelihood). And yet here she was, gaping at him like a country peasant faced with some freak at a fair.

'You've got the Devil's own insolence, coming back here,' said

Cis, recovering some of her command. 'And what are you doing all pricked and puffed up like that, eh? Up to your old thieving tricks again? And look at your doublet—so short it's indecent, boy, showing yourself off in the street like that—can't you dress modest?'

'It's my living,' said Perkin, with demure satisfaction. 'My master bought it for me.'

'Master? *Master?* You some lordling's fancy-boy, then?' Cis got to her feet and stalked round the table to glare at her son. 'Always said you'd come to the bad, didn't I? And you have and no mistake.' But the irascible tone of her voice carried no conviction, and her rather prominent blueish eyes were most uncharacteristically bright. 'Well, I can't say as I'm overjoyed to see you, young Perkin, but now you're back I'll just have to make the best of it.'

'This is just a visit, Mam,' said Perkin hastily, seeing the jaws of the Red Lion yawning suddenly. 'I'm a gentleman's servant, Mam, and he's a retainer of the Duke of Gloucester, attends the King—oh, you wouldn't believe the company I keep now. And I ain't stolen nothing for months,' he added, with honesty: his last attempt, to purloin a purse carelessly left in a York inn, had met with such a salutary tongue-lashing from Christie that he had vowed, so far successfully, to keep to the narrow, boring paths of virtue.

'That's a pity,' said Cis. 'Always said you was born to be hanged, and I don't like to be proved wrong.' She studied him critically, her head on one side: he had been her own height or less when she had last seen him, and now he overtopped her by some inches. 'Gentleman's servant, eh? Who's the well-born fool that's taken you in, or more likely have you taken *him* in?'

'He offered to have me as his servant,' said Perkin, aggrieved. 'It weren't none of my doing—I was starving in a ditch, Mam, and he said, "How would you like to be my servant?"—just like that. And of course I said yes.'

'And how long ago was that? Two weeks?'

'Nearly two years,' said Perkin, with a certain amount of satisfaction. 'Winter before last, it was.'

'And he's put up with you for nigh on two years? Mother of God, he must be a saint—or a simpleton. What's his name, then, this gentleman?'

'Master Christopher Heron, he comes from the North parts, he's in Gloucester's retinue and in the Tower with the King, and he's no saint—and for certain no simpleton either.'

[124]

'Heron? Never heard the name.' Cis stood, arms akimbo, surveying her son, her birdlike face all sharp angles and harsh lines until, suddenly, it was softened by a true and welcoming smile. 'Well, now you're back, you double-dyed-in-the-wool rascal, ain't you going to give your old Mam a welcoming kiss?'

And for once, Perkin swallowed his new dignity and did as he was told.

*

It was dusk before he returned to the Tower, having been regaled with his mother's best beer, a table spread and groaning with her choicest morsels, and the tale of all that had happened at the Red Lion since his departure. He had always known that he would be welcome, for his mother, despite her tough sinewy air of hard work and no nonsense, had a soft heart, even if it was never much in evidence, and she had always had a fondness for him despite his misdeeds. In return, he had told her something of his adventures before and after the eruption of Christie Heron into his life, and Cis had said, consideringly, into her foaming tankard, 'What's he like, then, this master of yours? Does he treat you right, like a good master? Or does he beat you as you undoubtedly deserve?'

'He hasn't beaten me at all, but I reckon he would readily enough if I'd done wrong,' said Perkin virtuously. 'There's no fooling him, Mam, he knows when I'm thinking of mischief afore I does myself, almost, but he's a good master—fair-handed, and he makes sure I'm looked after when we're journeying.' He did not mention the affable banter in which Christie habitually engaged his servant, for he doubted whether she would understand the peculiar and probably unique relationship between him and his master.

The nature of that relationship was amply displayed on Perkin's return to Christie's lodging within the bustling, spacious confines of the Tower. The young King had been practising with his bow, shooting at a couple of straw butts set up in a corner of the green, and now was discussing his performance with his attendants, while servants dismantled the targets and collected stray arrows. Christie was not amongst them, so Perkin turned towards his master's lodgings in the royal apartments south of the White Tower.

He found Christie sitting in the broad windowseat, his back propped up by a couple of ancient cushions, tuning his lute. Despite the open window and the warm evening, the chamber smelt musty and unused: it was a long while since a King had been lodged in the

[125]

Tower's royal apartments, and it had taken some time for the accommodation for Edward and his retinue to be made ready.

'And how was the prodigal welcomed? Fatted calf?' asked Christie, not looking up from the instrument: he twanged two strings experimentally, frowned and tried again. 'We're bid to Crosby Place for dinner tomorrow—or rather, *I'm* bid. You are to add to my consequence by attending me. I don't doubt that many of our Northern friends will be there—Lovell, Hoton, Brackenbury, Ralph Bigod—and don't you go getting into mischief with Bigod's servant, will you? I have a long memory.'

So had Perkin, and he squirmed uncomfortably. Ralph's man Jack was a well-known rascal and pursuer of women, wine and ill-gotten gains, and had several times previously led him into trouble. 'I'll avoid him,' he promised, with a quick glance at Christie to check the strength of his belief. It was not great: his master grinned, and put down his lute. 'If you can. Jack clings to his partners in crime like a leech. Well? Was she pleased to see you?'

Perkin opened his mouth to deny it, thought, and said with some surprise, 'Yes. Yes, I think she was. She gave me a right royal feast, anyway. And she'd like to see *you*, she said.'

'Oh?' One eyebrow flew up in a way Perkin recognised with an inward groan. 'Am I then to pass your mother's no doubt exacting standards before being permitted to continue as your master?'

'I dunno—I don't think so. But she reckons you're a saint or a simpleton, to put up with me for so long, and she never could resist seeing a marvel, she said.'

Christie snorted. 'A woman of taste and discernment, your lady mother! Well, perhaps after we dine at Crosby Place we can stroll round the corner into Aldgate and visit her. She sounds a redoubtable woman, my Perkin: she may want to meet me, but I must say I am somewhat curious about her. Does she brew good beer?'

'The best—and her wines are good too.'

'Then that settles it—we go to the Red Lion tomorrow.'

*

They must, however, dine at Crosby Place first. It was the house of a rich London draper who had died some years previously, and Gloucester had leased it for some years as his London house. The fact that a draper's mansion was large and opulent enough for a Royal Duke spoke something of the wealth and taste to which a humbly-born London citizen might aspire. Its gracious rooms of state, the Great Hall with its glorious carved and painted wooden roof, the council chamber, the beautiful intricate garden with its walks and hedges and carefully trained roses, were perfectly suited to entertaining ducal guests, receiving supplicants and suitors and courtiers, and for the lodging of his retinue. Christie, though comfortable enough at the Tower, had it in mind to ask his lord if he could rejoin his household: the young King had no personal need of him, and he had felt isolated from events, for Crosby Place was where most of the true business of government was carried out. True, Gloucester came most days to the Tower, always with the brilliant Buckingham at his side, to speak with his nephew, to go through various state papers and matters of government with him, to talk to his attendants and to watch him at play and to dine with him: but never once had the child, in Christie's presence at any rate, treated his uncle with any warmth. Edward, obviously, took his cue from his relatives in his suspicion and mistrust of his uncle. The Queen's refusal to emerge from sanctuary, or to allow her youngest son to join his brother in the Tower, had obviously had a great influence on the young King. He received visits daily from his mother's friends and supporters, though his half-brother the Marquis of Dorset was in hiding, having left the Abbey secretly, and his uncles Sir Edward Woodville and the Bishop of Salisbury respectively at sea and in sanctuary. It was plain that there was little that Gloucester could do in the few weeks leading up to the coronation to win his nephew's liking or trust, and Christie, who knew his lord well, saw that this disconcerted and saddened the Duke. It must also have been galling to find that Buckingham, with his ready wit and bright smile, could bring a cheerfulness to the child's pale unhappy face that his uncle could not.

But Christie mistrusted Buckingham still. He had been given almost royal power over Wales as a reward for his support of Gloucester against the Woodvilles, power rarely granted even to a Duke, and yet there was still something greedy about him, something slippery and deceptive in the frank blue gaze, the merry laugh and easy speech. There was nothing certain, nothing at which to point the finger, no word or deed that could be questioned, and yet deeply and instinctively Christie knew him to be false: a fair-weather friend, one who might well abandon his mentor and take himself, his retainers and his enormous power elsewhere, to someone who might pay better—although who could possibly improve on Gloucester's magnificent gifts?

Buckingham's golden head was almost the first that Christie saw as he rode Bayard through the narrow passage between lesser dwellings, through the gatehouse and into the great courtyard of Crosby Place. Duke Henry was conversing with a black-gowned cleric whom he recognised vaguely as the Bishop of Ely. The morning was sunny, and the big stone-paved quadrangle, with the Great Hall ahead, chapel on the right and further apartments on the left, was crowded with people, most of whom Christie knew. A groom took Bayard, who was restive from lack of exercise, with some misgivings, and Perkin melted into the background as Christie made his way through the throng of courtiers, attendants, retainers, servants and hangers-on to where Ralph Bigod was talking cheerfully to two well-remembered figures from the Scottish wars, Sir James Tyrell and Sir Thomas Bray.

Christie had seen Tyrell often in the last few weeks, for he had frequently visited the King, and his cousin Lady Darcy, in the Tower, but his last sight of Sir Thomas Bray had been nearly a year ago in Berwick, his face still hideously marred by the boiling water. The bristling moustache and beard, outlandish when all men of gentle birth went clean-shaven, must hide the worst of the scars: new pink skin gleamed like a baby's above it and around his eyes. He recognised Christie immediately, and his bellow of welcome sent heads turning all round the courtyard. 'Master Heron, as I live! Or have they knighted you yet? I hear young Bigod here was honoured.'

'Not yet,' said Christie, smiling. He was of insufficient estate for knighthood—£40.00 a year was deemed the minimum, and he could boast only the fees and rewards he got in Gloucester's service, amounting to barely a quarter of that sum: he would not grow rich on it. 'I am glad to see you look so well, Sir Thomas—have you quite recovered?'

'Oh, I'll never be young and handsome again,' said the older man, beaming cheerfully, 'and my hands are stiffer than an old washerwoman's, but at my time of life that doesn't matter. My thanks for your journey to Ashcott, Master Heron, it was kindly done, and I'm sorry that you were not as well received as you might have been.' He gave Christie a broad wink. 'Just what *did* you do to my daughter, eh?'

Christie's eyes opened very wide into an expression of innocence that his sister Meg would have recognised. 'Your daughter, Sir Thomas?'

'Yes, you rogue, my dear daughter Julian, comfort in her father's old age and scourge of her mother—I know I've spoilt her,' said Sir Thomas, his voice softening, 'but she's all I have, and she has great spirit.'

'Indeed she has,' Christie agreed, thinking that 'spirit' was not the word he would have used to describe the qualities of that rude, wayward, unhappy child. 'I upset her a little, I know—'

'Upset!' Sir Thomas laughed loudly and heartily. 'That's not how I'd have said it, young Heron, but, yes, she was a small trifle angry with you. I couldn't mention your name without her spitting at me like a cat. But whatever you said to her—and she'd die rather than tell me, though I've tried my best to persuade her—it's made a difference to her. She's grown up very much in the last year, she's not a child any more. I doubt you'd recognise her, quite the young lady she is.' He clapped Christie on the shoulder with a gnarled, scarred and furry hand, and added with a grin, 'She still detests you. Better not let her see you here.'

'She's here? At Crosby Place?' Christie felt suddenly and intensely curious—the thought of the graceless Julian transformed into a creature of refinement and elegance was impossible to imagine, and he was intrigued. Her father nodded. 'Aye—she and her mother came here from Ashcott about a week ago—couldn't resist the chance to spend my money, eh? We're lodging with John Harcourt and his wife, they've leased a house by Moorgate until after the coronation. Their boy Robert, he's a likely young lad, go far I reckon—about the right age for Julian.' He winked broadly, and Christie felt sympathy for the unknown Robert Harcourt, with the prospect of becoming the termagant's husband looking large in his future. Then Sir Thomas, still with that broad smile splitting his beard, asked him how he did since Berwick, and the conversation turned naturally to the events of the past few weeks. It became apparent that the older man very much disapproved of the Duke of Gloucester's actions in seizing the person of the young King, and still more his imprisonment of Earl Rivers, Richard Grey and the ancient Vaughan, now all confined in Northern castles. 'I know you two are close to Gloucester,' Sir Thomas said, glancing from Tyrell to Christie, 'but I'm an honest plain-speaking man and I don't believe in keeping quiet even if offence might be caused thereby—right is right and wrong is wrong, I've always said, and what your noble Duke did was wrong. Granted he don't care for the Woodville woman, who does? I certainly don't. But

Rivers is a good man, there's no call to fling him in some dank Northern dungeon simply because you don't like his sister.'

'There was rather more to it than that, Sir Thomas,' said Tyrell mildly. 'There was clear evidence of a plot to attack Gloucester —saw it with my own eyes.'

'Rivers? Plot against Gloucester? I don't believe it!' said Sir Thomas. 'And what's your Duke planning now, eh? He won't let go his grasp on power so easy now he's got it, you mark my words.' He looked at their carefully blank faces and coughed. 'Well, I suppose you both know that better than I do, being of his household, and I reckon I'd best keep my mouth closed in this company, who knows what offence it might cause?'

Tyrell, sounding rather indignant, assured him that what he said could be considered to be as between friends, and would go no further. An embarrassing pause ensued, during which Christie's eye was caught, then held, by a figure moving through the crowd towards them. He knew who it must be, and yet he could not quite believe the evidence of his eyes: this tall, self-assured young woman advancing so purposefully could not really be the same as that resentful undisciplined angry child he had left last summer at Ashcott. Yet the hair was the same, long and rippling chestnut over the gracefully flattering lines of her green gown with a wide collar baring her neck and part of her shoulders, and so was the brisk unwomanly stride, betraying her country upbringing. But she had grown, she had lost the childish layers of fat around her stomach and added generous curves to breast and hip, and the strong bones of her face stood revealed. She would never be beautiful, her personality was too marked and her height and sturdy build counted against her when the Queen's fair fragile loveliness was the conventional ideal, but she was a bold-looking girl, and eyes followed her from all around the courtyard, where there were few other women. Unfortunately, close behind her, the large features cast into an even more shrewish expression than Christie remembered, came the intimidating and unfortunately bulky shape of Dame Alice, a harbinger in all probability of what her daughter would be like in middle age—enough to discourage any prospective husband, Christie decided, and waited with interest to see what Julian's reaction to his presence would be.

It was obvious. The wide brown eyes swept across his face, paused, and returned narrowed with hostility. A hot flush washed over her pale skin: she halted, a familiar frown marring the high forehead, and said sharply, 'What are you doing here?'

'Master Heron is at present in the King's household, my dear, and is bidden to dine with the Duke of Gloucester, as are we,' said Sir Thomas. It was noticeable that his jovial masculine bonhomie had softened as his daughter approached: the expression 'apple of his eye' sprang to Christie's mind.

'Make your courtesy, child,' said Dame Alice in a fierce whisper, and evidently poked Julian from behind. With a pointed frown, the girl did as she was told, but ignored Christie. He could not really blame her: in her place he would also feel resentment towards a man who had humiliated and belittled her, and she with more pride than most. However, her undisguised loathing did make polite conversation rather difficult. He was relieved when another attendant arrived on the fringe of their group with the news that Gloucester wished to speak with him before dinner, and gladly took the opportunity to leave Julian's baleful glare in the courtyard and go to the Council Chamber, just off the Great Hall.

This was, if possible, even more crowded than the courtyard, and again Christie was able to acknowledge greetings from friends and fellow retainers as he made his way to the great stone-vaulted oriel window, where Gloucester stood with Lord Lovell and the ubiquitous Buckingham by his side.

'Master Heron!' His lord gave him the warm welcoming smile that was one of the reasons why he inspired such loyalty amongst his Northern followers, who knew him so well, even if the suspicious southerners were much more sparing of their trust and devotion. 'I'm glad to see you—your services have been missed.'

'Then I hope you will relieve me of my duties at the Tower, Your Grace,' said Christie, speaking formally in this public place, and feeling a pang of nostalgia for the breezy informalities of Middleham, where ceremony had not been the rule and the emphasis had been on plain practicality.

'Relieve you?' Gloucester favoured Christie with his dispassionate, assessing gaze. 'Is service in my nephew's household not then to your liking?'

'If I know Christie Heron,' Francis, Lord Lovell said, with a companionable grin in his direction, 'he's bored at the Tower and wants nothing better than an opportunity to exercise all that efficient energy on your behalf. Am I right, Christie?'

'You certainly approach the hub of the matter,' Christie said. He

[131]

met Gloucester's eye and added, 'It is chiefly, Your Grace, that I feel that you are at present better able to make use of me, and need me more, than does His Grace your nephew.'

'He's probably right, Dickon,' said Buckingham. The sun, streaming into the chamber through the oriel, lit his yellow hair with the colours of the stained glass that decorated it, red and amber, green and royal blue like a hugely-jewelled crown. It sparkled too on the stones decorating his doublet and made the rich blue satin gleam like a sapphire. Beside this richness, as ever, Richard of Gloucester, still in mourning for his brother, was a quiet slight figure seemingly of little account, his pale prematurely lined face colourless next to the flamboyant good looks of his cousin of Buckingham, lounging against the beautifully carved stone. 'The boy's unlively company for men such as Master Heron, and besides, there's plenty to keep him busy here, eh, Dickon?' He glanced significantly at the other Duke, but Gloucester was staring out of the window, abstractedly turning the signet ring on his finger round and round. It was an old habit which the Middleham fool had not been above mimicking, but Christie knew it for a sign of stress, and had noticed it much more frequently over the past weeks. Some men thrived on increased responsibilities and relished fresh and seemingly insuperable challenges, and Christie knew himself to be one of these, but Gloucester was too much of a perfectionist, too much of a worrier, to be truly happy under such a load. He would always do his duty to the utmost of his ability, but Christie knew that he hankered, with a longing too deep and impossible ever to be fully expressed, for that old life at Middleham, where matters had seemed simpler, and there were only three counties to tend instead of a large and quarrelsome kingdom beset by rival factions who must be soothed and juggled and rewarded in an endless courtier's dance.

'I would be happy to rejoin your household, Your Grace, if you, and of course the King, are agreeable.'

'I doubt Edward will notice,' said his uncle, and his voice was tinged with sadness. 'He has not yet forgiven me for dismissing his own household and arresting Rivers and Vaughan and Grey. I hope you won't take offence, Master Heron, but although he chose you as his attendant in Stony Stratford, you are just one more strange face amongst so many.'

'He is lonely,' said Christie, seeing in his mind's eye the small forlorn figure, surrounded by adults, bending his child's bow on the Tower green, or sitting solitary with his nose in a book, when a child his age ought more properly to be consorting with other children. 'It is a shame that his mother cannot be persuaded to allow his brother to join him—then at least he would have the company of another child.'

'That woman's more likely to give up her own life than young York,' said Buckingham, with a sudden flash of fury. 'God's blood, if I were you, Dickon, I'd break down the walls of sanctuary and get all the brats out, those girls as well. How in God's name does she think it will look if young Edward's crowned with all the rest of his family—saving yourself and your lady, of course—skulking in hiding as if you were some monster of depravity not fit to have them in your care? What does she think you'll do, have 'em all murdered?'

'Since she had my brother Clarence murdered, yes, she probably does,' said Gloucester. 'And I fear nothing will make her change her mind, unless we can wear her down with time—we have three weeks or more, remember. At present we are trying to persuade her at the least to accept my own right as Protector, and her place as Queen Dowager—but she's had a taste of government, and she's greedy for more, I fear.'

'The bitch would try and rule the whole world if the chance offered,' said Buckingham venomously. This was an aspect of his character that Christie had not seen before: he was usually so gracefully, elegantly persuasive, so much the pleasant conversationalist, that this malicious talk struck a jarring note. More than ever, Christie felt a deep and instinctive distrust of the Duke.

Gloucester, though, it was plain did not. He ignored that insulting reference to his brother's widow and turned to his retainer. 'Well, I have no objections to your return, Christie Heron, and if my nephew has none either, you may move your lodgings tomorrow. I'm sure the steward will find room for you, even if you have to share a chamber with young Ralph Bigod—do you think you can survive that? It won't be for long, his wife will join him shortly.'

'I've survived it before,' said Christie, remembering with a surprising affection Ralph's cheerful chatter, and even the somewhat strong savour of the feet of his unwashed hose. 'And I daresay I can screw my courage up to endure it again, Your Grace—and I thank you.'

'It is my pleasure,' said Gloucester, and smiled again: and even Christie's hard, pragmatic and essentially unsentimental soul was warmed by it. He had vowed to give his true loyalty to no man, save only himself and the burning ambition that was like a bright lodestar in his mind, but his respect and admiration for the Duke had grown so gradually, so imperceptibly that he had barely noticed the process of binding until now: when the realisation came to him quite suddenly that this man, diffident, quiet, thorough, essentially honest and fair-minded, was one he could and would follow loyally, always.

He was still analysing his feelings as he went into the Great Hall for dinner, with a sense of weary resignation. All his life, the mainspring of his actions had been himself, and all he had done had been with one end in view: to raise himself from his humble, impecunious origins to a position of power, wealth and property. To that end, he had employed his considerable gifts, with all the intelligence, charm and ruthlessness that he could command, and his rewards were growing: his future looked bright. He had switched his allegiance from Northumberland to Gloucester to suit himself, and alienated his uncle the Earl as well as his own family in the process: he had assumed that if he foresaw better fortune elsewhere, he would just as easily change his loyalty again. But that hard-headed shell had been first cracked last year, when he had seen what his ruthlessness had helped to do to his sister Meg: and since then he had become increasingly aware of the strength of his emotions. He had felt sympathy for Julian despite himself, and her, and he had felt much more for the little King. And now he found himself distrusting Buckingham because he sensed in him precisely those qualities he had once so nourished in himself: qualities entirely at odds with the impulse of loyalty and service which he now felt towards Gloucester.

I shall have to be careful, thought Christie wryly as the marshal approached to direct him to a table: for if I am not, all my ambition will vanish like snow in summer and I shall be left behind in the race for position and favour. There's small enough danger of that, though. He looked over to the occupants of the third table down from the top, where the Dukes and their most exalted guests and most intimate officers would sit, and saw with the mixture of amusement and annoyance which always seemed to be his reaction to this situation, that the only remaining place lay next to Julian Bray.

Julian, her awareness heightened by this, her first attendance at such a formal dinner in such high company, saw the hated, familiar figure, tall and long-legged and supple in the fashionably short skimpy doublet of mourning black, saw the marshall's hand pointing, and knew in her bones what was to come. She glanced at her left, seeing an elderly stranger, and beyond him and probably out of reach, her mother. Her father was on Dame Alice's further side, and thus even more distant from any appeal. She would have to cope with Christie Heron on her own, and she was not at all certain that she could. Away from the safe surroundings of Ashcott, as comfortable and familiar to her as her own skin, her customary sure arrogance seemed a hollow shell concealing, inadequately, the insecurities within, the fears and needs and terrible fervent emotions of a sixteen-year-old girl newly grown up, who knew only that something was missing from her life, and lacked the experience to know what it might be. She could foresee only too clearly the direction their talk might take, his barbed, humiliating comments, the cruel wit to which she had no response but anger and abuse, and if she had not been shored up with the pride he seemed to take delight in belittling, she would then and there have pleaded sickness and fled the Hall. But she sat, stubborn, her large freckled hands linked fiercely in her lap, so tightly that her nails drew blood, and her face set like pale stone between the loose flowing waves of her chestnut brown hair, from which the unfortunate Frideswide had spent all morning removing the tangles of neglect and three days' riding in May winds.

She thought of Friday, who had now outlasted all her other gentlewomen despite her neglect and mistreatment, with something like affection. During the past few months she had come to realise that her maid was a real person, with real thoughts, real feelings—even if they were not nearly so strong as the surges of emotion which afflicted Julian so devastatingly—and who could also, disconcertingly, hold opinions that were often at odds with her obedient, rather colourless presence. She had recently let slip, for instance, that at first she had disliked Julian intensely, and only the lack of any other option had dissuaded her from a precipitate flight from Ashcott in the first month. Julian, appalled—she had never considered at all what other people thought of her until Christie's tirade, which she had contrived eventually to push to the back of her mind—had somewhat hesitantly asked Friday if she liked her now. The older girl had deliberated in the rather slow way which had often maddened Julian, and then given her usual considered reply. 'Yes, yes, I suppose I do now. But you've changed, Julian. You're not so hasty as you used to be. It's as if you think about things more.' And she finished on a note of discovery. 'I think you must be growing up.'

And it was about time too, in all areas: Julian, looking at well-endowed neighbours' daughters two years younger than herself, had been uncomfortably aware of her child's flat chest, incongruously matched with her still increasing height. And then it had all seemed to happen quite suddenly: she had put on her last year's winter garments, had spectacularly burst out of them by Christmas, necessitating some expense, and found herself by April the proud possessor of a pair of most womanly breasts, generous hips and above all a long, comparatively narrow and deceptively graceful *waist*. Her mother, who could never be anything other than critical, still nagged her about her size, but the mirror told its own story, and Julian, adult at last, did not care, and because she did not care, ceased to eat at every available opportunity. She knew now, it was obvious at every gathering, that she was too tall, unforgiveably overtopping many men, that her hands and feet were too big and her features too large and her freckles too thickly sprinkled on her pale skin; that everything about her, the proportions of her body and her emotions and her intellect, her voice and even the impossible, luxurious tangle of her hair, had been dealt her by a much too generous hand. But she had seen men looking at her with interest, and after the long years of misery, of her mother's humiliating remarks, of knowing that she would never be the kind of beauty that turned heads or won hearts, she had relished that.

But Christie Heron, with one eyebrow slightly crooked in a way she remembered only too accurately, was about to sit by her, and her new-won confidence had shrivelled away to nothing. She braced herself in readiness for the first hurtful comment: but he smiled politely, expressed with doubtful sincerity his pleasure at the prospect of sitting next to her, and proceeded to attend to her needs with immaculate courtesy. He poured wine, heaped her plate —which most impressively was silver, not pewter—and offered to cut her meat with a solemnity that was, to Julian's biassed judgement, obviously spurious.

'No thank you, Master Heron, I can do that for myself,' she said, with similarly exaggerated politeness.

'I'm sure you can,' said Christie, neatly and efficiently dealing with his own gobbets of highly spiced and fragrant mutton. 'Tell me, how does your music progress?'

Julian, making rather less of a neat job of her capon, glanced at him suspiciously. 'It progresses very well, thank you, Master Heron.'

'And do you still find it difficult to practise sufficiently?'

'No,' said Julian, icily superior despite her quaking heart. 'I can set aside a great deal of time to play my lute, and my rebec. My father has just bought a dulcimer for me: it was made in Italy.'

'I have heard that a psaltery is better, more easy to play for one used to the lute.'

'Well, I manage perfectly well with a dulcimer,' said Julian scathingly, wishing that there was something she could say to disconcert him: but nothing seemed to alter that mockingly polite expression, or the cold amusement in his pale eyes, that in this light seemed almost silver, like a hawk's. She addressed herself to her food, but delicious though it was, it tasted like ashes in her mouth, and she had some difficulty in swallowing. She did not feel at all hungry, and when Christie, seeing her slowly emptying plate, enquired with that ironic politeness if she was feeling sickly, she looked him in the eye and said flatly, 'Naught ails me but the company.'

There was a little silence, as if both of them were contemplating that truth, suddenly raw amidst all the empty courtesy. Then Christie said quietly, 'It was last year, and both you and I have changed, I trust for the better. Will you not forgive, and forget?'

A great surge of anger overtook Julian, a physical feeling so strong that it almost suffocated her, and left her wishing, like the child she no longer was, that she could pummel out that rage with her fists and alter that insufferable infuriating impassive expression on his face. But she could not, of course, not with the Duke of Gloucester and the Duke of Buckingham and Lord Lovell and Lord Howard and all the other dignitaries and officers and nobles and knights and gentlemen looking on, not to mention her mother, and her father: so she hissed, cuttingly venomous, 'No, I can *not* forget—or forgive your insolence, you jumped-up northern barbarian. Who do you think you are, anyway? You're just hanging on to your precious Gloucester's heels as he rises—and he'll cling on to power like a leech and use you and your sort to do his dirty work for him, arresting people, murdering even, so who are you to judge me?'

At last, she saw with satisfaction, she had penetrated that amused, urbane manner, and her words had hit and hurt. His eyes narrowed, and his mouth tightened to a thin line: then he said softly, 'If you were a man, my dear Mistress Julian, you would pay for that insult to my lord and myself. As you very patently are not, and it seems have learned no discretion nor modesty, I shall restrict myself to avoiding your company and your conversation in the future.' And he pointedly turned his shoulder away from her and engaged the young lady on his right in talk, leaving Julian isolated, impotent, and scarlet with fury.

There was nothing she could do, nothing at all. At least, she had been given the sour pleasure of denting that overwhelming self-possession: and as eagerly and viciously as if it had been Christie Heron under her knife, she sawed at her cooling capon, and did not wonder, as an older and wiser person might have wondered, at the reasons for the extremes of feeling that each seemed to impel in the other.

CHAPTER SEVEN

'Elizabeth, that was called both good and fair.'
(BOOK 8, CHAPTER I)

Christie, who was both older and wiser than Julian Bray, and more given to bouts of introspection, walked with his servant at his side through the crowds in Bishopsgate, down to the end of the street, and left into Cornhill and thence to Aldgate. He felt raw with anger, and hurt, and astonishment that a rude, graceless and ill-mannered child could yet have the power to affect him so much. Why, if she meant nothing to him—and she undoubtedly did—were her words cutting him so deep? He was no barbarian, and his lord no murderer, unlike some people in high places. He should laugh, and think no more of Julian Bray, who had probably only been repeating like a brainless popinjay the words she had overheard from her mother. But try as he would, those words and the hot hatred in her large brown eyes still rankled bitterly. He wondered inconsequentially at the quality of those eyes: brown ones were supposed to melt, to languish and be gentle, but Julian's blazed and snapped like an undisciplined and savage alaunt. And he wondered at himself, for letting this stupid child affect his equilibrium as no other, save his lost and beloved Meg, had ever done.

He became aware that Perkin was speaking, and came back to reality in front of a substantial timber building with an archway and a sign with a red lion, decidedly rampant if not passant or guardant, somewhat inexpertly painted on it. 'I said, here we are,' Perkin repeated patiently but wearily, and with a tinge of pride woven in. Since it was evidently expected of him, Christie stared up at the prosperous timbers and shining glass and gleaming plaster, and remarked that it was a handsome building.

'It's the biggest in Aldgate—takes a lot of the east country travellers,' said Perkin, with a proud and proprietorial air that amused Christie, remembering his servant's avowed loathing of the place. 'If you will step this way, please, sir?' And Christie entered the warm dim interior, aromatic with beer and horse and spicy cooking, to meet the unknown and formidable person of Cicely Hobbes, Perkin's mother.

[139]

They had a private parlour this time, overlooking the courtyard where customers and their horses and baggage and servants constantly crossed and recrossed their vision through the thick greenish glass. London was packed these weeks before the coronation and the opening of Parliament, even gentlemen were having to sleep five or six to a room, and many of the horses had been taken out to fields on the edge of the city. A potboy brought tankards of frothing beer and a plate with slices of a cold meat pie, unnecessarily in view of the substantial meal which Christie and his servant had had at Crosby Place, and presented Mistress Hobbes' greetings and apologies—she was delayed, but would be joining them in a few minutes. Into the silence that followed the boy's withdrawal, Christie said, 'Does your mother manage this place on her own?'

'Oh, there's William, he's my brother—he helps, but he ain't much good,' said Perkin with some scorn. 'He's willing enough, much more than I ever was, but he's as thick-headed as an old mule—Will the ass, I used to call him when I was here. My father left the inn to me mam, until she dies, not to William—that's how much he thought of *him*! There's me sisters as well, but I think they're all married now, except for Agnes, she was the youngest of us. There's John Smyth, he's the chief chamberlain, he's a sour old bugger but he's good at his job,' Perkin finished, unaware that behind him the door had opened. 'And if he knows which side his bread's buttered he'll marry me mam and be set up for life.'

'Not if your mam has anything to do with it,' said Cis Hobbes, walking briskly into the parlour. She was in her customary black, and to Christie looked, with her beaky nose and pale blue eyes, very much like a shrewd sharp crow. Like Perkin, she was small, and had his wide lipless mouth and black hair, but there the resemblance ended. She stood in the middle of the floor, hands on her waist, eyeing Christie up and down, and then said, 'So you're the man fool enough to take my Perkin for a servant. Ain't he robbed you yet?'

'No—he knows full well what would happen to him if he did,' said Christie. Her lack of courtesy and her directness amused him: he made no attempt to bow, but indicated the only chair in the parlour, placed cosily next to the fireplace, which was empty on this sunny afternoon, the last but one in May. Cis, after a further shrewd glance at him, walked over and sat in it. 'Enjoyed your beer, then, Master Heron?'

'Yes, I thank you—most excellent, Mistress Hobbes.'

'You call me Cis,' said that lady immediately. 'I don't doubt you call Perkin Perkin—when you ain't calling him worse things, of course. And I'll continue to call you Master Heron, if you please, seeing as how you're of gentle birth, according to my Perkin, that is, and an easier liar never breathed—but that's by the way. From the North Parts, are you?'

'Yes—from Northumberland.'

'And close kin to the Percies!' said Perkin, who had not yet vanquished his desire to impress his mother—a lady alas impossible to overawe. Christie raised an eyebrow at him: Cis glanced from one to the other and grinned. 'How close? Closer than they'd like, I'll wager.'

'My mother was a bastard daughter of the third Earl on Northumberland,' said Christie imperturbably. 'I am thus nephew to the present Earl, who educated me at his castle at Alnwick.'

'And you're now with Gloucester?'

'No, mam, I told you, he's with the King in the Tower,' Perkin said with irritation. Cis sent him a look of such withering scorn that he quailed. 'I have more calls on my time than to remember every tit-bit of information you throw me, my lad. What's the boy like, Master Heron? I've heard he was much ruled by his mother's family, and it's also said he's a sad weakling, forever weeping or ailing.'

Christie took a heavy draught of the cool fresh beer, well aware that what he said could start tales travelling round half the city: Cis Hobbes looked like a woman who thrived on rumour and gossip, and he had no intention of being indiscreet, despite the fact that he already felt warm liking for her. He said slowly, 'He's no weakling, for certain. Oh, he's only twelve, and his world has been wrenched apart, but he has some spirit—he'll do well enough.' And again he saw in his mind's eye the lonely child at his pointless, forlorn exercise at the butts, or signing the government papers at his uncle's direction, King, yet at the beck and call of an adult he distrusted and disliked: saw also the increasingly frequent skin eruptions marring the boy's angelic beauty, and the night attacks that were not normal nightmares, for they left him struggling for breath. They were afflictions that a highly-strung, nervous child might well be prey to, and he remembered a boy his own age at Alnwick, one of the other pages, unmercifully teased because of his cracked raw hands and his wheezing breath at the slightest exertion: he had been sent home after a few weeks, and they later heard that he had died. They could not send young Edward home, and Christie knew that compared to the sufferings of that other boy, the King's trouble was but slight as yet: but he was under considerable stress, and it showed.

'I hope he does. Child kings are bad luck, and this one's got a feuding family to contend with, as well as a kingdom,' said Cis. 'D'you think he'll make a good King, then? Good as his poor father, God rest his soul?'

'I see no reason why not—he has intelligence, learning, good looks, all a young hopeful monarch could need,' said Christie. He noted the woman's sharp gaze, that could evidently see a great deal, and knew that she was aware that he had not told her the complete truth. She did not press the matter, however, but turned the conversation to other things: his opinion on the Scots wars, the Flanders trade and the chances of the unloved French King Louis XI soon expiring were all canvassed, while Perkin, oblivious to such matters, swigged his beer and tucked into the pie. In the time it took him to drain two tankards, his mother and his master had achieved a level of mutual understanding that was remarkable, given the disparity between them. To Perkin, realising it with a start of dismay, it was positively frightening that the two people who, between them, had had the most influence on his life, should be in such instant accord. But there they were, sitting either side of the cold fireplace, sipping beer and swapping jokes and anecdotes as if they had known each other for years instead of just half an hour. Perkin contemplated sneaking out under cover of their conversation, but decided that he would rather not risk that formidable pair of tongues both being turned in his direction. Fortunately, there was more beer in the jug, and he poured it out with a heavy, pointed sigh and consumed it in one long noisy gulp.

'Are you trying to get drunk quick, or telling us you're bored?' came his mother's acerbic voice. As Perkin, sheepish, put down his empty tankard, she went on. 'You'll be wanting to get back to your young King—soon be suppertime, I expect, and I'm a busy woman, can't sit here all day gossiping to your master. My congratulations, sir,' she added to Christie as he rose. 'You've turned my double-dyed-in-the-wool rascal of a son into something near human, and at great cost to yourself, I don't doubt.'

'It was nothing, Mistress Hobbes,' said Christie with spurious modesty: she caught his eye and winked. Perkin, uneasy, looked from one to the other and said bitterly, 'I'd like to know what chance I've got, set against you two. He's bad enough, but with you too, Mam, I'll never have a moment's peace.'

'Oh, I'm sure you will—well, one or two moments anyway,' said Christie. 'We must be going, Perkin my lad, supper at the Tower awaits us, and we can't be late for our King. Thank you for the excellent beer, Mistress Hobbes—your own brew?'

'Aye, and my own recipe too—handed down from my husband's father, and he had it from a Dutchman, what understood these newfangled hops. Now it's reckoned one of the best in London—if not *the* best,' said Cis, the same pride in her voice as had been in her son's when speaking of the Red Lion. 'So don't be afraid to come visiting, young Perkin, or you, sir, and remember, the beer's on the house!'

'It's an offer I cannot possibly refuse,' said Christie, and with a sudden warmth in his smile, he took Cis Hobbes's wrinkled workworn ink-stained paw, and raised it to his lips with great courtesy. 'Your servant, Mistress.'

'Ah, give over,' said Cis, contriving to look both pleased and embarrassed at the same time. 'Is he always like this, Perkin?'

Her son, quite at a loss, shook his head. 'No, Mam.'

'It's the effect of my beautiful eyes, must be,' said Cis, sighing. 'And at my age, too. Go on, off you go afore you're late, and my customers will be wanting me too, I don't doubt.' And as they were ushered from the inn to the street, she added in a hoarse audible whisper, ostensibly for Christie's benefit only, 'And don't you forget, sir, one show of trouble of insolence from young Perkin and you send him back to me—I'll soon thrash it out of him!' But as her son turned a face of dismay in her direction, she winked broadly, slapped the boy on his back, and bade them godspeed with warmth and kindness.

'I hope you didn't take no offence,' said Perkin anxiously as they walked down Hart Street towards the Tower. Christie had said nothing since leaving the Red Lion, and had walked so briskly that Perkin, with much shorter legs, had had to insert a hop and a skip into his stride to keep up. 'Me mam—should've warned you—she always talks to people like that. She'd talk to the *King* like that if she met him, I reckon. She don't mean no harm, sir, that's just her way. She don't stand on no ceremony, my mam.'

'I didn't take offence,' said Christie, sidestepping to avoid a group of noisy men-at-arms, wearing Lord Hastings' livery. 'On the contrary—I think your mother is a delightful woman. The only puzzle is, how in God's name did she come to produce such an unprincipled good-for-nothing rogue as you, my Perkin?'

[143]

'Sir!' His servant sounded indignant. 'I ain't stolen nothing for *weeks*.'

'Five weeks and three days, to be precise,' said Christie. 'I must congratulate you—it's the longest interval yet between your sins. Don't disgrace me before we leave the Tower, will you?'

'Leave the Tower? Where are we going to go, then?'

'Crosby Place—that's why I left Bayard there. The Duke requires my services again, I would like to return to his household, and the young King doesn't care who serves him if they are not his old friends from Ludlow. I shall have to ask his permission, of course, but I should think it'll be granted as a matter of course.'

But it was not so easy as that. After supper, during which he carved for his young monarch, Christie went to the boy's private apartments. The sunshine earlier in the day had vanished behind a pall of low cloud, and rain was threatening: certainly, there was insufficient light for shooting at the butts, his usual activity on these long summer evenings. There were only a few people in the chamber: young Edward sat on the deep windowseat, one knee propped up before him, the other swinging desultorily, kicking against the stone. He was eating from a basket of early strawberries with cracked, scaley fingers that were stained with their juice, and a bored, moody expression marred his pale, fine-featured face. 'Master Heron? You told me you wished to speak with me.'

'I have a favour to ask of Your Grace,' said Christie, thinking, treacherously, how absurd it was to bend the knee and stand on ceremony with a boy near half his age—and even more ridiculous when ancient grey-haired clerics like the Cardinal Archbishop of Canterbury must do it. He rose and said carefully, 'I crave Your Grace's indulgence in this. I have been of your household for a month now, and as there are no special duties for me to perform, I would humbly beg Your Grace's permission to return to the household of your uncle, the Duke of Gloucester.'

There was a silence, broken by Edward's foot kicking more viciously against the stone. A most unkingly petulance informed his voice when he spoke. 'I don't want you to go. I need you here.'

'Why, Your Grace?'

The boy's bright blue eyes flashed up at him: with surprise, Christie saw that he was close to tears. 'Because I want you to, that's why. Because I don't want you to go back to my uncle—everybody does that, half my household go to Crosby Place every day—I want you to stay here with me.' His eyes dropped, and he thrust the strawberry basket towards Christie. 'Have one. Go on, they're very good. The Bishop of Ely sent them, they're from his own garden.'

Deferentially, Christie took two of the tiny sweet red straw-berries, reflecting that his task would be made easier if Edward could behave more like a twelve-year-old boy and less like a bad imitation of a King. What threat did he feel, that he must retreat behind this wall of petulant dignity? It did not have to be like that: Edward's father had been famous for his common touch, for the ease with which he could converse with noble and commoner alike, for walking with only a few attendants about the streets of London and Westminster. It had not detracted from his royal authority —few men were as terrifying in anger as had been the Fourth Edward—but it had made him much beloved by his people. His son was young yet, and woefully inexperienced, but the omens were bad if he had inherited not his father's gracious bonhomie, but his mother's rigid, unperceptive and inflexible attitude to her inferiors.

'They're good, aren't they,' said Edward, popping a handful of the miniature fruits into his mouth: his eyes slid round to the other people in the chamber, all deferentially watching, and he added in a rush of confidence, 'Dr Argentine says they'll make my skin worse, but I haven't seen any difference myself.' He pushed the basket in Christie's direction again. 'Do you like them, Master Heron?'

'They're delicious,' said Christie, detecting a crack in the boy's brittle facade. 'I thank Your Grace—and I beg you, Sire, that you also have the kindness to release me from your service. I feel I am idling my days away here.'

'But everyone always seems so busy,' said his King, startled. 'They all rush to and fro—there's no time to stop and think and read and pray—there are always papers to sign and grants to approve and the coronation plans and the Council and everyone tells me different things—I am *always* busy,' the boy added, somewhat forlornly. 'It was quiet in Ludlow, I could study in peace, ride in the hills—I had friends and companions. Here there's no-one I know except for Dame Darcy—I mean Dame Haute, and a few men who used to be my father's, and Dr Argentine. I don't even know you.'

There was a small, sad silence. Christie said softly, 'Why, then, Your Grace, are you so eager to make me stay in your household?'

'I don't know!' Edward wailed. 'I don't *know*. I shouldn't even want you with me, you're one of my uncle's household, you're *his* man, not mine. And you're right, I don't need you at all. But you make music so well, and—and—I like you,' he said at last, with the simple directness of a much younger child. 'I think you understand—how—how—'

'How lonely you feel?' Christie prompted, very gently, and saw the tears grow and gather in the beautiful blue eyes. Edward Plantagenet, fifth of that name, by the grace of God, King of England and of France, and Lord of Ireland, surreptitiously smeared a hand across his face, drew a deep and rather ragged breath and nodded, evidently not trusting himself to speak. There was another pause, and then Christie said, watching the boy's silent struggle for control, 'If your lady mother would only release Your Grace's brother from sanctuary, you could have a companion near your own age.'

'She won't,' Edward muttered unhappily. 'She doesn't trust my uncle. She thinks—she thinks—' There was another quavering sob, barely muffled, and then he said in a desperate whisper, 'Her friends have told me that my uncle means us harm—that he wants to usurp the throne for himself!'

Involuntarily, Christie glanced around the tall arras-hung chamber, darkening swiftly now in the summer evening. Servants had brought candles: Dame Haute was sewing by their light, glancing up occasionally to keep watch on her charge's conversation, and the three male attendants, bored, were chatting and glancing out of the other window. They would have seen, if they had been looking, that their King was a trifle overwrought, but it would have taken exceedingly sharp ears to overhear Edward's last words. Dropping his voice to an even softer level, Christie said gently, 'You may rest assured on that score, Your Grace. I have served your uncle for some time now, and I know him for a man of honour. He loved your father, and his only wish is to ensure that you do not fall into the self-same trap that has ensnared other young kings, and place your trust in men who may take advantage of your youth and inexperience.'

'Like my uncle Rivers?' said Edward, with a sudden and alien bitterness. 'All men know him for a good and virtuous lord, Master Heron—and yet my uncle Gloucester keeps him mewed up in one of his castles. And my brother Grey is also in prison, and old Vaughan who never harmed a fly. What have they done?'

'They conspired against His Grace of Gloucester,' Christie said, patiently repeating the tale—and it was truth, though Lord Rivers had been only the reluctant and somewhat inept follower of the instructions relayed to him from his sister the Queen, via young Grey. 'Your uncle Sir Edward Woodville took a large part of the royal treasure, that your father had gathered for the governing of the realm, Your Grace, and your brother Dorset took most of the rest. It has not been recovered, and I doubt it will be. You have a natural affinity for your mother's kin, of course you have, but sooner or later you must realise that they may do you harm, and more damage to the realm.'

Edward was silent, his scarred hands plucking at a loose rush on the side of the basket. Finally he said, his voice haunted and taut with unshed tears, 'I wish my father had not died. He shouldn't have died so soon—why did he have to die and leave me alone? I don't really *want* to be King—not yet, not now, it's too difficult.' And then, so quietly and forlornly that Christie was not sure if he had heard it, 'Dickon would be a better King than me.'

He presumably meant his younger brother, the Duke of York. Christie had never met this child, but from comments dropped by other attendants had received the impression that the little boy in sanctuary at Westminster was made of altogether sterner stuff than his learned, sheltered, over-sensitive brother. What Edward said might well be true, but there was no altering the fact that he was the elder: Christie sought with urgency for words of comfort, and at last said softly, 'You are King because it is God's wish. You are the older brother, you were the first-born son, and so you must inherit your father's crown, just as your uncle of Gloucester's son Edward will one day be Duke of Gloucester, and the Earl of Northumberland's son have his title when he dies. It's the law of the land, and you can do nothing but accept, even if the burden seems heavy now—and of course it does, you're only a child, naturally you feel unhappy and confused, but you will soon be a man, older and wiser, and better able to cope with your duties as King. Old King Harry was much worse off than you, you know,' he added, with a smile intended to raise the boy's spirits. 'He never even knew his father, he was King while still a baby, and though he was a poor weak fish indeed and woefully unsuited to kingship, I don't think anyone ever heard him say that he wished to give up the crown.'

'His wife wouldn't have let him,' said Edward, a little more cheerfully: he had evidently been taught something of the recent tangled and unhappy history of the rival houses of York and Lancaster. 'She wouldn't have given up *her* crown for anyone, not even my grandfather York—and he was much better suited to kingship than poor old Harry the Sixth.'

'She knew that her husband was King, even though he was

mostly madder than a March hare, and she would not have him surrender his right so readily.' Christie saw the boy's frown and, aware that he was on dangerous ground, added, 'But all that is beside the point, Your Grace. I came here to ask a favour of you, and now that we seem to have come to a better understanding, I would ask you to reconsider your decision. You are lonely here, your attendants are mostly strangers—they are strangers also to me, all my friends are at Crosby Place. It's true perhaps that I know only too well how you feel, but I am sure there are others who understand as well as I do, if not better. Dame Haute, for instance.'

Edward's expression said that his old nurse, being a woman of advanced years, could not possibly have any insight into his feelings. Christie went on, pushing home ruthlessly any advantage he might have over the wavering boy. 'Perhaps, if I return to Crosby Place, I could go to Westminster with the men who are negotiating with your mother. If I could tell the Queen that you greatly desire the company of your brother, perhaps it might weigh a little in the argument.'

'You could do that if you were still in my household,' said Edward, mutinously: but it was obvious that he was tired, and heartsore, and wished the conversation at an end. He went on wearily, 'Oh, very well, since you're so set on it, Master Heron, you can go back to Crosby Place—there are plenty of my father's men who would be eager for your position, I can tell you. But will you promise to do what you said? To go to my mother? Please? I want it more than anything,' said Edward, King of England, sadly, 'to see my little brother Dickon again.'

*

'I said, do you want me to do your hair?' Cecily Plantagenet stood poised above her elder sister, brush in one hand and mirror in the other, and an irritated frown marring the ivory perfection of her flower-like face. When no reply came, she prodded her sister with a rather scuffed kid slipper, none too gently. 'Bess! Wake up!'

'I wasn't asleep,' Elizabeth told her mildly, turning her head away from contemplation of the unchanging monk-ridden court-yard outside the window. 'I was thinking.'

'Day-dreaming, you mean. Do you want me to brush your hair? It looks very tangled—and anyway, I want you to do mine.'

Elizabeth of York, eldest daughter of the late and much-lamented Edward IV, once betrothed to the Dauphin of France, seventeen years old and with now no affianced husband, sighed. She had indeed been day-dreaming, wondering wistfully what prince could be found for her now that her father was dead. It would largely depend on whether the little brother she hardly knew would concern himself at all with her affairs now that he was so abruptly thrust into kingship. She could not imagine that pale over-anxious child settling very well into the endless round of diplomacy, policy, the balancing of factions, the management of unruly subjects, and above all the sheer hard work entailed in the ruling of a kingdom. Young Dickon, now—that was another matter. She remembered her father once saying to her, in one of his paternal chats—she had always been the closest to him of any of his children—that it was a pity that Dickon had not been the elder boy, and Edward the younger, for Richard, Duke of York, was undeniably a chip off the father's old block. Dickon would have found her a prince to marry: she could swear by all the saintly relics she could find, that it would never enter Edward's head.

'You may brush my hair,' she said graciously. Cecily gave a snort and thrust the mirror into her hands. 'You sound just like Mother.'

Bess smiled sweetly into the mirror. A face more like her father's smiled in response: large hazel eyes, a rather small mouth, an oval face that could easily look heavy—thank the saints she had finally rid herself of that unflattering puppy-fat—and hair that was the true rich Plantagenet gold, rather than her mother's pale silver-gilt tresses. Cecily had all Elizabeth Woodville's beauty, the famous hair, the large long-lashed grey eyes, the perfect complexion, and had added to it a liveliness and sparkle that the Queen entirely lacked. She had been betrothed to the eldest son of the King of Scots, then very briefly to his wayward uncle the Duke of Albany, and now she had no husband in prospect either: but Cecily did not seem to be prey to the same nameless vague longings and yearning which so filled Elizabeth's head. She dropped the brush unceremoniously down on Bess's skull and dragged it through the thick waves of hair, humming under her breath. The older girl braced herself against the pull of the bristles, liking the familiar luxury of having her hair brushed for her, and yet apprehensive about Cecily's power to rip painfully through knots and snarls. That was her sister's major flaw, Bess decided with the maturity and wisdom of her three years' seniority: she had no sensitivity, no imagination, she lacked understanding of others' faults. Cecily would never yearn after possible husbands or handsome young courtiers, but neither would she weep for a dead puppy or give too generously to a starving beggar. Already, at fourteen, Cecily's view of the world echoed her mother's, and was entirely concerned with herself.

Two years ago, Bess would not have viewed her sister so critically, but then they had been three, divided in age by Mary, who was eighteen months younger than Bess and the same number older than Cecily. The three girls had been devoted, inseparable, their natures complementary to each other: sensitive, dreamy Bess, practical Cecily, wild Moll who loved to dance and sing and whose liveliness dragged them happily laughing in her wake. But just over a year ago—Bess had kept the anniversary silently, with pain and prayers and candles—Mary had died, of a sudden spring fever that had seemed no more than a head cold, until too late. At first the loss of their beloved sister had thrown Bess closer than ever to Cecily, but lately they had seemed to drift further and further apart into squabbles, boredom and indifference. It was a situation made worse by the family's flight from the commodious, comfortable Palace of Westminster with its good food and warmly-furnished chambers and troops of attendants, into the few bare rooms of sanctuary in the Abbey, where they all had to live cheek by jowl with each other and the Queen's brother, the Bishop of Salisbury, whom all his nieces detested. At first they had also had to share it with their half-brother Tom, but the Marquis of Dorset had early slipped away, taking with him quantities of the late King's treasure. Bess for one was secretly relieved: she had never liked Tom's overbearing manner, the drunkenness and lechery he did not bother to hide, and the lurking suspicion that, if he had not encouraged her father in so much late-night carousing, the King would still be alive today. The Bishop of Salisbury's sanctimonious pronouncements and his incessant concern with wealth and appearance were almost tolerable by comparison, but there were also the difficulties caused by living in unnaturally close proximity to the Queen.

As they grew up, tended by nurses and tutors in apartments of their own within the Palace, the children of Edward IV and Elizabeth Woodville had seen little of either parent save as a god-like figure who swept them on his knee, sang to them and gave them sweetmeats, or arrived pale and elegant at the nursery door to check on their progress in matters of learning, deportment and manners. The King, however, had been very fond of his children, and spent some time arranging their education: he had taken much more interest in the three elder girls as they grew up, and was in the habit of discussing political matters with Bess—the most thoughtful and intelligent—as if to a member of his Council, for might she not be Queen of France one day? But Bess, always uneasy in her mother's presence, had come to realise of late that the Queen's influence in matters of state was not entirely benign. This absurd flight into sanctuary, from a man whom Bess's father had always regarded as his most loyal and trustworthy servant, and his devoted brother, seemed to her to be ridiculous, even if her uncle Rivers and her brother Grey had been arrested and her little brother the King was now in the hands of Gloucester. There was no denying, however, that he had never been a friend to her mother and now, after failed conspiracy, vanished treasure and aborted attacks on his life, unlikely to revise his opinion. Cecily certainly shared her mother's fear, if not her guilt, and this was one of the chief bones of contention between the sisters: Bess yearning for freedom, unable to understand why they must stay cramped up in sanctuary with only a few servants and precious little comfort, and Cecily positive that their uncle Gloucester meant harm to all their family.

It was an old stale argument, and Bess did not raise it now. The initial longing for fresh air, for good music and hot food—their meals were sent in from the Abbot's kitchens, and were invariably unappetising and cold—had given way to a dull ache of boredom and lethargy that could not be dispelled even by looking after the younger children: Anne was seven, Katherine four, and little Bridget only two-and-a-half. The only person who remained cheerful, full of good fun and bright talk, was her brother Dickon, Duke of York: and as if on cue, the door of the chamber that Bess shared with Cecily, sleeping in the one bed, creaked open and he came in. 'Hullo. I thought I'd find you here.'

'There's nowhere else to find us,' Cecily pointed out, with a particularly vigorous pull of the brush. As her sister yelped with pain, she went on, oblivious. 'What do you want? And shut the door behind you.'

'There's another deputation from our uncle Gloucester, come to see Mother. She thinks it best if we're all there with her—*I* think she's thinking how appealing we'll all look together.'

Bess shot a startled glance at her brother. He was not yet ten, but his understanding of events and characters often astonished her with its maturity. He did not look like a precocious brat, though: his golden hair was unbrushed and curled wildly round his face, his nose was abundantly freckled and dirty, his doublet buttoned up wrongly and his hose wrinkled and torn. She said, smiling, 'I don't think *you* look very appealing—have you seen the hole in your knee? And your hands and face are filthy—what have you been doing?'

'You look like a beggar brat,' said Cecily more forthrightly. 'Go and put on clean hose, and at least wash those horrible hands—ugh! How you can get so dirty in just these few rooms is beyond me.'

'I was helping Jack clean the chimney in my chamber,' said Dickon, glancing down at his dishevelled garments. 'I suppose I had better change.' And with a rueful grin for Bess, and a rude face for Cecily, he went out again.

'Horrible little brat,' said Cecily briskly, though she did not really mean it. 'Nan and Kate and Biddy are much less trouble.'

This was patently untrue, as the three little girls, bored and filled with unexpended energy, screamed and squabbled and fought all day long, but Bess did not bother to contradict her. She said mildly, 'Are you done? If Mother wants us, we had better go.'

As her youngest son had so perceptively commented, Elizabeth Woodville, her six threatened children grouped around her, made a most pretty and affecting picture. Bess's sturdy golden leonine looks contrasted pleasingly with Cecily's demure pale loveliness, Anne with her shy gap-toothed smile and painstakingly straight back, the impudent Katherine, all tawny curls and dimples, and little Bridget, wide-eyed and sucking her thumb. The young Duke of York, the image of masculine protectiveness, was not a tall child, but stood squarely beside his mother, a bold and striking boy with his hair very neatly combed and his fresh hose undamaged and unwrinkled. In the middle of her brood, self-consciously maternal, Elizabeth Woodville sat, parading her touching anxieties about her children's future, so untimely deprived of a father in this threatening, uncertain and most wicked world. To Christie Heron, watching with other attendants, it was an excellent performance, but patently a performance none the less. He was fairly certain, both from her reputation and from the testimony of those who knew her personally, that this still-lovely, twice-widowed woman, now approaching fifty, and posing so touchingly with her children, had all the maternal feeling of a stone. The children, of course, were charming, as one might expect of the offspring of such handsome parents, and the two older girls were especially good-looking, but it was at the young Duke of York that his interest was particularly directed.

There was little resemblance between the brothers. Edward was tall for his age, pale, with a sensitive and rather girlish face: a glance at the Queen confirmed that it was his mother that he favoured,

[152]

rather than his dead father. But the child standing so solidly by Elizabeth Woodville's chair was stocky and quite small, with thick golden hair like the old King's. His face, however, was his own, an intriguing mixture of the urchin he still was and the man he would soon be, the firm bones and prominent nose and strong brows already taking shape beneath the freckles and childish roundness. Christie, mindful of the gossip, could see why people thought this boy more promising than his elder brother, and wondered what the situation between the two might be, when they were grown. Would the adult Edward trust his brother Richard as greatly and justifiably as their father had trusted Richard of Gloucester?

Lord Howard, grizzled soldier and sailor, loyal friend to the Duke of Gloucester and the leader of this morning's deputation, the latest in a very long line, was speaking to the Queen. In phrases obviously uttered many times before, he was reminding her of the unsuitability of her position in sanctuary, the slur—quite unjustifiable—that her refusal to emerge cast on the honour of the Duke of Gloucester, who had nothing but her own welfare and that of her children at heart, and was most concerned that the boy King's coronation should not take place while the rest of the royal family skulked in Westminster Abbey sanctuary. The line between the Queen's plucked brows deepened as the well-worn recital went on, reducing what was left of her famous beauty to a shrewish, irritated frown. Eventually she cut him short with a dismissive wave of the hand. 'All this has been discussed before, Lord Howard, and nothing you have said on your master's behalf has yet done anything to change my mind. Until I am assured of my own safety and dignity should I leave sanctuary, and above all until I know that my beloved children will be safe from harm and given all the benefits and privileges due their high rank—until I have those guarantees, neither I nor my children will emerge from here, though Gloucester himself go down on his knees to beg me, and you may tell him that. Have you anything new to offer?'

Howard glanced at the robed clerics, headed by the Bishop of Lincoln, the new Chancellor, who stood beside him, and turned back to the still, regal figure of the Queen. The younger children, despite their training and sense of duty and occasion, were becoming restless, and Anne was hopping from one leg to the other, but the two elder girls and the young Duke stood as still as rocks, used to years of rigid Court etiquette. As he looked at the pleasant face of Elizabeth of York, Christie wondered if perhaps she were a better person to receive the young King's message. Lord Howard, of course, would convey to the Queen the statement that the King wished to have the company of his brother, but Christie knew that Edward's message would have much more force if given informally by himself.

His opportunity came when the Queen, mindful of the fidgeting of the three little girls, rose to her feet and suggested that she and the senior members of the delegation retire to her privy chamber. A nurse was summoned and took the smaller children away, the three older remaining to make polite talk to the dozen or so attendants left. As the fretful wails of Bridget died away, diminished by the shutting of a stout oak door, he joined the little knot around Elizabeth of York.

She was evidently quite used to being the centre of attention, and was talking with animation to Sir Robert Percy, whom she must have met on similar occasions. Christie was presented, and waited for a suitable break in the conversation. It came quite soon, as the Princess Cecily, lively and lovely, joined them with some anecdote about little Anne's impudent chat, and Christie seized his chance. 'I would be grateful, my lady, if we may have a word more privily.'

Elizabeth's wide rather dreamy hazel eyes rested thoughtfully on him, and then she smiled. 'Yes, of course, Master Heron. The windowseat should suffice—shall we go stand there?'

She led the way, and he found himself, somewhat to his surprise, discovering in her a likeness to Julian Bray. It was not immediately obvious: their colouring was very different, of course, but they shared a certain generosity of feature, and still more their build, for Elizabeth was as tall as Julian, and as sturdy in her rich sombre mourning gown, the long waves of golden hair poured down her rather broad back. By the narrow window, looking out on to a shady courtyard, she turned and smiled again. 'What do you wish to tell me, Master Heron?'

'I have a message from your brother the King,' said Christie, and saw her eyes widen with surprise. 'From my brother? But you're wearing my uncle Gloucester's livery.'

'That is true, my lady—but for a while I was in your brother's household, from Stony Stratford until a few days ago, when he kindly granted my request to return to your uncle.'

'You were at Stony Stratford?' Elizabeth's rather low voice rose half an octave and then descended to a more seemly and private murmur. 'Were you? Please tell me—what *did* happen? We have heard so little, nothing but rumour, and my mother fears greatly for my uncle Rivers and my brother Grey.'

It was a diversion, but faced with those pleading hazel eyes and her evident concern and hunger for information, he gave her a brief account. She listened in silence, a frown between her arched brows that gave her a faint look of her mother, and when he had finished stood thoughtfully for a while, her eyes staring into space. He waited patiently, for it was evident that this girl, lacking the obvious sparkle and beauty of her younger sister, possessed a more mature and penetrating intelligence. At last she turned back to him, still with that earnest frown, and said, 'His Grace of Buckingham puzzles me. I hardly know him—he was seldom at Court, Father did not often mention him—the most clear memory of him that I can call to mind is when he and my uncle of Gloucester led poor little Anne Mowbray to marry my brother Dickon—I mean the Duke of York,' she amended, with a quick smile that revealed some girlish liveliness behind the dreamy, grave facade. 'And the chief thing I marked then was, how much he resembled my poor uncle of Clarence, who was even then in prison. It seemed so terrible to me, though I was only a child, that it should have been Buckingham who passed the sentence of death on him. I can remember it very well—it was four days before my twelfth birthday.'

There was a little pause, as her eyes strayed again to the window, though there was nothing of any interest there save a group of strolling, anonymously black-clad monks: then she said slowly, 'What do you think of His Grace of Buckingham, Master Heron?'

This required some thought: he trusted Elizabeth's good nature, but she was young, constantly in her mother's company, and he could not count on what he said going no further. He said carefully, 'You are right, my lady, he does remind me of your late uncle. He is a great lord, and has the Duke of Gloucester's trust and friendship, though they have worked together only for these last few weeks. He is obviously a man of wit and ability, or His Grace would not place so much confidence in him. But—I hope that his resemblance to the Duke of Clarence lies only in his face, and not behind it.'

Clarence, the plausible unstable brilliant rogue, whose life had been as the wild swinging of a loosed weathercock, spinning with the winds of fortune to whichever would reward him best—and his ultimate goal, to the bitter end of his brief, reckless and headlong career, the throne of England. Bess understood: her eyes studied him seriously, and then she favoured him with her slow smile. 'I pray for all our sakes that is not so, Master Heron. Now, I had almost forgot—what is this message you must give me from my dear brother? How is he? Is he well, and happy?'

'I regret to tell you, my lady, that he is neither,' Christie said to her gently, feeling that the truth was best here. 'He is lonely in the Tower, pining for the company of children his own age—oh, he has plenty of attendants, servants, even Dame Haute, who I understand was nurse to all your family. But he is not happy, and he asked me to tell you, or your lady mother the Queen, that he desires above anything the company of the Duke of York.'

'Oh, poor Edward,' said Elizabeth softly, and there was real distress in her eyes. 'He was happy at Ludlow with his books and plenty of other children: I doubt thoughts of kingship had ever entered his head. And now—you said he was not well. Have his night attacks returned?'

'They have, my lady,' said Christie, with a memory only a week old of that unhappy child, his face blue even in the candlelight, fighting for breath with the dreadful crowing gasps that were so frightening to everyone, though Dr Argentine had assured them all over and over again that there was no danger to the boy's life. Elizabeth nodded, biting her lip. 'He was always subject to them when he was little, especially if he was upset or ill. Then as he grew older, they stopped. He had bad skin then too, dry and flakey and sore—has that returned as well?'

'I fear it has,' said Christie. He had no wish to distress her, but knew he must paint as pathetic a picture as possible, the better to persuade the Queen to release her other son. 'His hands especially are painful, and I know that he finds it hard sometimes even to hold a pen.'

'Poor Edward,' she said again, and tears stood in the large greenish brown eyes. 'Oh, poor little Edward. Dame Haute will have an ointment for it that will do some good, but she could never cure it—the only thing that ever cured it was happiness.' She took a deep breath, and her wide eyes, suddenly wise and direct beyond her years, locked with Christie's and held. 'Master Heron, tell me the truth, if you will. Is he frightened?'

There was a chilly little pause, filled by the chatter and laughter of the younger attendants crowded around Cecily. Christie said at last, bleakly, 'Yes.'

Elizabeth drew another long quivering breath, like someone bracing themselves to face unpleasant realities. 'Is he afraid of my uncle of Gloucester?'

[156]

Christie would have liked to lie, to prevaricate, to tell her anything but the truth that he had seen in the little King's sidelong glances, the nightmares he had, the white strained face and staring eyes, like a nervy and terrified young colt, with which he always greeted the Duke. He wondered why he could not lie to the boy's so much steadier elder sister, even as he gave her the unpalatable truth. 'I regret it very much—but yes, he is. There's no reason for it, none at all, save that the King is young, and confused—all the certainties of his world have been ripped away, and he knows I think that he is King in name only—that your uncle holds the real power.' Carefully, he added, 'I think your uncle Rivers has been telling him tales. I know he is a sensitive boy, but his fear of his uncle Gloucester cannot be thus explained away.' And he added, on impulse, 'It is sad to see your uncle—he wants so much to have the King his friend, for your father's sake as much as his own, and all his advances are rebuffed or ignored. He is much hurt by it, I think.'

With a force that surprised and shocked him, the placid serious Princess turned and smacked her fist against the smooth stone around the window. As Christie exclaimed, she said something under her breath that sounded suspiciously like a curse, and then, her voice low but savage with grief and anger, 'Why, oh why did my father have to die? He was young, he should have waited, he should have lived until Edward grew up—Edward doesn't know what it's like to be King, he can read Latin and French and ride and hawk and converse elegantly, he's been beautifully educated in his little princedom at Ludlow,' said Bess bitterly, 'but he has no idea, no idea at *all*, of how to manage a kingdom, of reality, of what the world is *like*!'

'He's only twelve years old, my lady—he'll learn quickly.'

'Yes, but he's only a boy, he has no knowledge of the world, how can he tell wise advice from that given in malice or ignorance? A child king isn't bad in himself,' said Bess, with penetrating wisdom. 'The trouble begins when other people compete for his ear, and battle for power and the right to rule through him. Isn't that why my uncle Gloucester imprisoned my uncle Rivers? Isn't that why my mother is so opposed to Gloucester?'

'Are you opposed to Gloucester?' Christie asked her curiously. Elizabeth shook her head so vehemently that the yellow hair whipped against the wall. 'No, no—I know how much—how much my father loved and trusted him. I know he would not harm us—even though he doesn't care for my mother, he would never harm us—because of our father.'

It was good to hear this evidence of her trust and faith, even though, Christie thought, she was probably the only member of her family to harbour such feelings. But then a small robust figure arrived at their sides, with an engaging, friendly and rather lopsided grin. 'Master Heron, I understand,' said Richard Plantagenet, Duke of York. 'Sir Robert Percy has been telling me of your exploits against the Scots. Did you really save Sir Thomas Bray's life?'

It was impossible not to respond to the warmth and cheerfulness radiating from this very attractive child. Christie, without a trace of discomfort, found himself describing Sir Thomas's misfortune in some detail, and the boy listened with eager attention. He was evidently well acquainted with the worthy knight, who had often been at Court, and Sir Thomas had obviously taken an almost paternal interest in the little Duke, and had instructed him in the rudiments of gunnery. 'I like guns,' said Richard of York, with enthusiasm. 'They're so powerful—oh, I know there are all sorts of problems, barrels bursting, getting the range right, improving accuracy, all that sort of thing. But Father always said that they were the weapon of the future, and I think he was right. It'll change war completely—what use is a castle when a few cannon can batter its walls down inside a week? What good does wearing armour do you if a handgun can pierce it surer than any arrow? When Edward grows up,' said the boy fiercely, 'I hope he makes me commander of all his forces, just like Father made our uncle Gloucester commander in Scotland, and I'll win his battles for him—Edward isn't very good at fighting,' he went on, gazing earnestly from eyes that were surprisingly grey, like his mother's: it was the only Woodville thing about him at all. 'He fell off at the quintain three times in one day!'

'And you never fell off at all, I suppose,' said his sister, laughing. 'Dickon, you're as bloodthirsty as a Turk. Tell Master Heron what your ambition is.'

The Duke of York, who was two months and more short of his tenth birthday, drew himself up to his full, diminutive height and said proudly, 'When I grow up I'll win back France for Edward—all the lands that Harry the Fifth won, and Harry the Sixth lost. He is King of France, you know,' he added indignantly. 'He ought to rule more of France than Calais!'

And looking at him, small and bright and fierce as a flame, Christie thought that one day his boast might very well come true.

❦ CHAPTER EIGHT ❧

**'That is a great pity . . . that any man
or woman might find in their hearts to work any
treason against you.'**
(BOOK 4, CHAPTER 12)

'You are all here because you are men in whom we place implicit
and extraordinary trust.' The Duke of Gloucester stood by a broad
trestle table in the Great Chamber of Baynards Castle. On his right,
the heavy figure of Sir Thomas Howard, thumbs thrust into the belt
of his well-filled doublet, his narrow dark eyes scanning, in a
leisurely way, the score or so men standing in front of him. On the
left hand side, the side of the goats thought Christie irreverently,
the tall elegant Duke of Buckingham lounged against the table, his
blue gaze flicking from face to face, his golden hair lit by the bright
early morning sun. It was Friday, the thirteenth of June, and the
trusted men, summoned as they woke before sunrise, had arrayed
themselves in helmets and leather jacks, according to their instructions. The prevailing feeling amongst them, to judge from their
faces, was intense curiosity.

A mood of suspicion, of secret urgency, of events moving fast
behind the scenes, had for some days now infested Baynards Castle,
the London residence of Gloucester's mother, whence he had
removed his household for greater convenience, it being by the
river and thus handily placed for easy transport to Westminster and
the Tower. Christie, who made it his business to watch all the
comings and goings closely, could place exactly the beginning of
this darker period: it had started the day that the elderly Bishop of
Bath and Wells had had a most private audience with Gloucester,
and to which only the two Dukes had been privy. Since then,
Buckingham had seemed to gain vividness and stature: he
strode confidently about the Castle, and evidently commanded
Gloucester's absolute trust. The Protector, on the other hand, was
by contrast deeply worried and preoccupied, as if plagued by
doubts and uncertainties, or the promptings of an active conscience.
Then, a day or so later, messengers had set out in utmost haste to
various parts of the kingdom. Christie did not know the contents of
their summons for certain, but the general opinion amongst the
junior members of the household was that they ordered trusted

lords and cities such as York to send armed help. And such help could mean only one thing: the possibility of a Woodville conspiracy.

The Queen had proved so obdurate and inflexible that none of the Council had visited her for nearly a week now, but Christie was sure that the less official comings and goings at the Abbey sanctuary had not diminished. Failing to get her way by peaceful negotiation, it would be entirely in character for Elizabeth Woodville to conspire to dislodge her brother-in-law by more violent means. Christie, glancing round at the faces of those other trusted men, Robert Brackenbury, Ralph Bigod, Sir James Tyrell amongst all the familiar friends and colleagues, wondered who it was they were to arrest: for that was obviously the reason for their summons this morning. Rumour and speculation had been rife for some days, fuelled by the almost total secrecy surrounding the discussions of Gloucester, Buckingham, Lord Howard and one or two other intimates.

'It has come to my attention through the good offices of His Grace of Buckingham here, that certain persons have been conspiring against us and against His Grace the King, hoping to overturn the just and lawful goverment of this realm and seize the King's person for their own ends. It seems alas that the Queen has not been guiltless in this, and I understand that the harlot Shore is also concerned: but the chief mover in this plot is the Lord Chamberlain.'

There was total, appalled silence. The name of William, Lord Hastings, had been mentioned in the speculation and gossip, certainly, but not with any seriousness. It was well-known that he loathed the Woodvilles, and had had a long-running and bitter feud with the Queen's eldest son, the Marquis of Dorset, who shared Hastings' licentious nature without enjoying any of his affable and shrewd good sense. It had been Hastings, as was well-known, who had warned Gloucester, in his detailed and urgent letters from London when the old King died, of the Woodville plans to seize power in defiance of the dead King's wishes: and Hastings who had urged the Duke to take young Edward at Stony Stratford. His jubilation at the success of Gloucester's coup had been very public, and he had declared to all and sundry his satisfaction that it had been done without so much blood as would be shed from a cut finger. Christie had seen him almost daily at Baynards Castle, a short stout cheerful man in early middle age, with a ruddy complexion that owed more to consumption of strong French wines than to the soldiering he had done with the old King in their youth. He had been Edward's dear friend, his boon companion, a man of great power who had seen that power continued despite the change of King and Gloucester's position confirmed as the boy's Protector. Why, then, suddenly throw in his lot with the hated and despised Woodvilles?

A monstrous suspicion invaded Christie's mind, even as his lord continued speaking. 'To be betrayed by one so loved and trusted, both by myself and by my dear late brother the King—before God it is a most unnatural and dreadful crime.' His face was white and strained beneath the velvet cap, and his hand twisted his signet ring incessantly. 'And I thank the special efforts of the Duke of Buckingham and his associate, Catesby, who is also an agent of Hastings, and who brought his conspiracy to the notice of the Duke. I would never otherwise have suspected him.'

And Buckingham, glittering with sunlight and jewels, graciously inclined his head and smiled in sad agreement. Christie, watching him closely, thought he could detect just the faintest trace of smug, overweening satisfaction in that smile, and the monstrous suspicion grew in his mind, and would not be dislodged. But he had no time to ponder it, for more detailed instructions were now being given, and he must not miss anything. There was to be a Council meeting in the White Tower that morning, and another at Westminster comprised chiefly of prelates and church dignitaries who would discuss coronation matters. There was a room next to the Council Chamber: they would wait there in absolute silence, until they were needed. It was his intention to confront Lord Hastings with the evidence of his vile treachery, and if he was indeed guilty, they would be summoned to arrest him and the other parties to the plot.

It was a long wait in the bare room off the Council Chamber. Its windows faced north and east, and it was hot and stuffy, crowded with the twenty trusted men and the perspiring figure of Sir Thomas Howard, mopping his heavy face with an unsuitably small square of linen. Because of the need for secrecy, there would be several hours before they would be required: it was a measure both of their training and dedication, and their loyalty to the Duke of Gloucester, that they stayed still and quiet despite the heat and the boredom and the tension of waiting in silence. During those hours, Christie found his mind treading again and again, with dour and increasing familiarity, the paths of his suspicion. Either Hastings

[161]

had genuinely been plotting with the Woodvilles against the Protector, which seemed very unlikely given his past relations with them, or the Woodvilles had been plotting without his help, which seemed much more probable, indeed almost certain. But if Hastings was innocent, why should Gloucester accuse him, his beloved brother's dearest friend?

But Gloucester had not accused him. The Duke of Buckingham and his friend Catesby had accused him, had discovered the evidence against him, and convinced the Protector that Hastings must be seized. He must have had very strong proof, Christie thought, for his lord was too just a man to convict on flimsy evidence, no matter how convenient that conviction might be. And while there was no particular reason why Gloucester would want to be rid of Hastings, who with Lord Howard was his chief supporter on the Council, there was every reason for Buckingham to desire the removal of so powerful a rival for the Protector's ear, affection, and favour.

It fitted. Christie scratched his chin, unshaven in his haste that morning, and exchanged a wry grin with Sir Ralph Bigod, who like everyone else in the room was sweating profusely: he wiped a large drip off the end of his blunt freckled nose as Christie watched. He wondered if Ralph had reached the same conclusion, and doubted it: his friend, far less devious than himself, was much less inclined to seek ulterior motives in others.

And so was the Duke of Gloucester. Though an intelligent man, he was not versed in the serpentine coils of Court intrigue: after Clarence's death he had stayed in the North, coming to London only on essential business. It might not have occurred to him to doubt the likelihood of Hastings conspiring with his oldest and bitterest enemies. And, such was his reliance upon Buckingham, so great his confidence and trust, that he would never entertain the terrible suspicion that his chief supporter could seek to lay trumped-up charges against a loyal lord like Hastings, simply because he was a threat to Buckingham's pre-eminent position.

There was something else in this pot too, something to do with the ancient Bishop of Bath and Wells, Christie could feel it in his marrow—but there was no time left for contemplation, no purpose served by going to Gloucester and telling him of his suspicions: he would be disbelieved or worse, and he had no proof, no shred of evidence, only intuition. And then he heard, they all heard, the doors of the Council Chamber opening, loud and creaking through the thick wood of their own door, and the subdued murmur of the first councillors as they entered. They could not distinguish any words for certain, save when a voice came quite clearly through the oaken door, obviously from just the other side. 'I've had strawberries in my garden these last two weeks, my lord, and the little King said they were the best he had ever tasted.'

Ralph Bigod's mouth formed the words, 'The Bishop of Ely,' and Christie nodded. The Bishop, John Morton by name, was a wily old fox more statesman than churchman, with many years' service to Edward IV behind him, and more loyal service to Harry the Sixth before that. His reputation was of cunning, craft, and double-dealing, and he, along with the aged Thomas Rotherham, the Archbishop of York and known to be too good a friend to Woodvilles, and Lord Stanley, a jovial fat man whose eyes slipped away from every confrontation, was to be arrested with Hastings.

In the Council Chamber, an usher announced Their Graces, the Dukes of Gloucester and of Buckingham. There was a pause, filled doubtless with the bustle of greetings, of councillors finding their seats, while the listeners within the smaller chamber strained their ears to hear any signal.

Gloucester was speaking, his harsh abrupt voice instantly recognisable. Although no words could be distinguished, the serious tone was apparent. There was silence, then the sweeter, persuasive notes of Buckingham. A confused babble erupted on the other side of the door, topped by the Protector's voice, suddenly and drastically clear. 'Faced with that proof, do you dare deny it?'

Sir Thomas Howard was by the door, his sword at the ready, his fierce dark gaze, like a hawk's, holding them all still. Hastings' shouted angry protests soared above the noise from the councillors, and then came the cry of Gloucester for which Howard had been waiting. 'Treason! Treason, against the Protector and the King!'

The door was flung open by Howard, and the twenty trusted men, swords drawn, poured through into the Council Chamber. Almost first in the rush, Christie had a brief picture of the scene around the table, frozen as if in some Mystery Play tableau: Gloucester, his finger pointed unerringly at Lord Hastings, who had astonishingly and disgracefully drawn his dagger halfway from its sheath: and round the room, the appalled open-mouthed faces of the other councillors, aged clerics, barons, clerks. Then Howard had hold of Lord Hastings while Charles Pilkington, in one neat twisting movement, divested him of his weapon. In the silence,

[163]

Gloucester spoke, his voice abruptly quiet, and hoarse with strain. 'You are arrested on a charge of High Treason, my lord. Your attempt to use violence just now is sufficient proof of your evil conspiracy, even if I had not already had ample from other sources. Your harlot Shore will be arrested too, as will the other conspirators—the Archbishop here, the Bishop of Ely, and Lord Stanley.'

The two clerics were seized by the armed men, though in Archbishop Rotherham's case it was hardly necessary: he was quavering so much that his rich ecclesiastical robes rustled, and his lined face, framed in wispy white hair, was pale and slack with fright. Firmly, but not roughly, he was escorted from the chamber, followed by Morton, Bishop of Ely, whose strawberries were as famous as his cunning, which had availed him nothing. He was made of sterner stuff than the Archbishop, and his look of surprising satisfaction as he was taken away reminded Christie of the Duke of Buckingham, laying evidence of conspiracy before the Protector. It was a strange look for a man accused of High Treason. Stanley, blustering and protesting his innocence with suspicious fervour, was next, with Sir Ralph Bigod and half a dozen others hustling him away before his shouts could become embarrassing. And then there was only Hastings.

The ruddy complexion was but a shadow of his previous vigour: under it, the skin was a pale grey with shock and horror, and sweat trickled down his face in the hot airless room. He said to Gloucester, his normally cheery loud voice reduced almost to a whisper, 'What will you do with them?'

The treason, Christie noted, had not been denied by him: and amidst the agonising tension in the chamber, he had time to wonder at this. Then Gloucester said, his voice like a whip, 'That is not your concern, my lord. The more pressing question is, what is to be done with *you*?'

'He has committed treason,' said Buckingham, in a voice as soft and insinuating as a cat's. 'Treason proved beyond doubt, and moreover, he has drawn a weapon on you, in a Council meeting. He deserves to suffer the ultimate penalty, and quickly—*now*, before your resolve weakens.'

No-one else around that table said anything: the Chancellor, the Bishop of Lincoln, who might well have protested, was at Westminster discussing the coronation with other clergy. Lord Howard would not show mercy to anyone proved a traitor, however

[164]

previously favoured or honoured, and the others present were lesser men, more aged or of lower rank. A long dreadful pause swallowed all movement, all sound in the great Chamber, lined with arras, brave and beautiful, resplendent with armies under the leopards and lilies of England beating back the lilies of France. Christie was close enough to Hastings to see the sweat pouring down his heavy cheeks, the frantic pulse, urgent and greedy for life, beating wildly in his throat. He could also see the taut white face of Gloucester, the long mouth compressed, and all the muscles clenched in his jaw, the hard grey eyes almost hidden as he stared at Hastings: and the man who had been his brother's dearest friend, his nephew's most loyal subject and servant, stared back in mute, desperate appeal.

'He must die, Dickon,' said Buckingham, his voice gentle, plausible, persuasive. 'If he dies, and quickly, it will nip their rebellion in the bud. Waver, show weakness, and his friends will rise up and overthrow us all. Let this be their warning—let one death prevent the many.'

'I have committed no treason against the King,' Hastings cried, but Gloucester's arm chopped savagely in the air, waving him silent. 'I have heard enough, and have proof enough. Find him a priest, and then head him.'

*

All his life, Christie would remember that scene on the sunlit green outside the White Tower, as if burned on his eyes like a brand. The blue sky, slightly marred with high, wispy clouds, prophesying rain that Lord Hastings would never see or hear or feel. The bright fresh green of the trees and the grass, sprinkled with daisies and buttercups. The light blinding on the whitewashed walls of the great central keep, so that it hurt the eyes to look at it too long. The crowds of curious, jostling people: casual visitors, residents, servants, attendants, held back by a dozen men with halberds horizontal, peering past each other's shoulders to get a better view. Somewhere, too, though Christie did not dare look towards the royal windows, there might also be a white girlish face, framed in yellow hair, staring down, frightened and appalled, at the bright scene below, as unreal and unlikely as a Christmas disguising. His gaze, with that of all others, would be fixed on the makeshift block someone had made out of timber intended for the repair of a roof in one of the lesser towers—and on the heavy, richly-dressed, newly-shriven figure of Lord Hastings, blinking in the light and warmth, dazed with disbelief, hustled along between two brisk almost kindly soldiers, a young priest, evidently disapproving, following so close that his robes almost flapped against Hastings' dragging heels.

By the mercy of God, they had found, in a tavern, one of the official executioners: even drunk, he was likely to despatch his victim more cleanly with that huge hideous axe than one of the Protector's men. Christie was glad for Hastings' sake, and more relieved that he had not been called upon to do the task himself: it was just the sort of duty that his efficiency might earn him. And even now, he was unsure of Hastings' guilt, uncertain still of the part played in all this by the Duke of Buckingham.

The soldiers made Hastings kneel: he stared at the block, the headsman, the axe as if he did not believe in their reality. The priest prayed, monotonously, his brown hair drifting gently in the sweet summer breeze: it came from the south today, and brought the smell of fields and salty river mud, not the stink of London. Christie, with a moment of compassion for the man who was shortly to leave this life behind him, took a kerchief from his sleeve and said to the kneeling Chamberlain, 'Will you have a blindfold, my lord?'

Hastings squinted up at him: he was standing in front of the light, and the tall stooping figure, its hair turned unwontedly bright by the sun behind him, offering him a cloth to bind his eyes, was the last thing that Hastings saw clearly. Still bewildered, he nodded: the thick white linen shut off his sight: and someone else guided his head onto the rough splintery weathered baulk of oak. Then the axe rose, and fell unwavering with a dull chunk, and the headsman bent and grasped a handful of blood-dabbled, rather sparse brown hair, and waved it triumphantly aloft. 'The head of a traitor!'

But there was no sound from the people watching, only a few gasps and moans of horror or pity, here and there, for Hastings had been popular, and loved for his loyalty and generosity and comparative honesty: and all crossed themselves, and many prayed.

To Christie, unemotional and efficient, had fallen the task of overseeing the execution, and of afterwards gathering up the pathetic remains, paying off the executioner, dispersing the crowd and ensuring that none dabbled their kerchiefs in a martyr's blood by having sand sprinkled liberally over it and the myriad buzzing flies that had already congregated. He did it all with a curious sick feeling of detachment, as if the same sense of unreality which had protected Lord Hastings at the last had been transferred to himself. He had the sense of being adrift, uncertain, lost in a strange uncharted sea, a feeling he had never before experienced in a life he had always shaped to his own desires. He had been so certain that Hastings was innocent, until he had seen him accused, and the damning evidence of that drawn dagger. There were elements in this dark and sorcerous brew of which he was, and probably would remain, ignorant, but he would be willing to stake his next year's pay on the deep involvement of those wily foxes, the Bishop of Ely and Lord Stanley, and of His Grace the Duke of Buckingham. Whichever of them had been the instigator of this, whether Buckingham had, as he claimed, merely discovered the plot or played a darker role, he could not know and hardly guess: but he wondered that the Protector was not able to see what seemed to him so obvious.

And yet Buckingham was so plausible, utterly persuasive. Had he urged Hastings' instant death so that the conspirator would not reveal damning facts under interrogation? Or was it a genuine attempt to stifle rebellion before it had begun?

*

Unfortunately, the summary heading of Lord Hastings did not have that effect: it was more like throwing a stone into a hornets' nest instead of using it to block up the exit. The cry of treason had echoed up and down the city, and all that hot summer day people swarmed in the streets, frightened, alarmed, many carrying makeshift weapons. Such was the confusion and turmoil that the Protector sent his heralds out into the city, to proclaim everywhere streets met, at every conduit and cross and church door, that there had been a plot against the life of His Grace the Duke of Gloucester, Lord Protector: but that by God's help it had been discovered, and the chief mover, the Lord Hastings, executed for his crime. Out of respect for their cloth, the Archbishop of York and the Bishop of Ely had been merely imprisoned. There was no mention of Lord Stanley: he had, so it was rumoured in Baynards Castle, already persuaded the Protector and Buckingham that he had not been involved, and he was confined to his own comfortable lodgings while the other less-exalted conspirators—Oliver King and John Foster, both secretaries, and Mistress Elizabeth Shore, harlot, enjoyer of the successive favours of King Edward IV, the Marquis of Dorset, and Lord Hastings—were seized and imprisoned. The proclamation had the effect of calming the fears of some: but others, more suspicious of this fierce Protector and his Northern soldiers, many more of whom, it was rumoured, would swoop down on the city within a matter of days, were not convinced. The whispers spread abroad, and would not be stilled.

*

In the Abbey of Westminster, in her comfortless rooms, the Queen heard of Hastings' execution, and the imprisonment of the Archbishop and the Bishop, and her rage and lamentation filled the air and set her youngest children weeping too. Cecily and Bess had to comfort them, while their mother, in the privacy of her chamber, wept and stormed and threw cushions, so far had her cold assumption of royal dignity left her. Then she summoned all her children and told them, tearfully, that all hope was now gone and they were alone, their friends in captivity or dead, and only the lives of little Edward and Dickon standing between their wicked uncle and the throne of England. 'While you are here, you are safe!' she cried, clasping the Duke of York to her and stroking his rebellious hair. 'I shall never let you go, never!'

'I can't see what Uncle Richard would want to do to me,' said Dickon, and firmly, with his usual determination, disengaged his mother's arms and stepped back. 'Edward is lonely, Mother, and I hate being cooped up here. We've been here six weeks and I *want* to get out, Mother, I want to see grass and ride and breathe fresh air—please let me go!'

'You are safe here,' said Elizabeth Woodville fiercely: and her eldest daughter, looking at her frightened, greedy face, thought that she would not surrender him, for while she had him she had yet one more card to play.

She had no choice, though. The proof of Hastings' guilt and hers had been laid before the full Council, and they agreed with the Protector: the Duke of York must be released forthwith from his mother's custody and brought to join his brother. Everyone was aware, though none voiced it, of the young King's increasing ill-health. If the worst should happen, Elizabeth Woodville must not still be in possession of the presumed heir to the throne.

Accordingly, on Monday 16 June, three days after the execution of Lord Hastings, who now lay buried with dignity at Windsor alongside the monarch he had served so loyally, eight boats left the

Tower and rowed upstream to Westminster, bearing the Lord Protector, the Duke of Buckingham, Lord Howard and his son, the Cardinal of Canterbury and sundry other councillors, as well as a considerable body of armed men, amongst them Christie Heron.

His mind was still in a state of unfortunate turmoil and flux. He had told himself, over and over again, that the times were ruthless, and required desperate measures. But the Lord of Middleham would not have executed any man thus, without benefit of trial: nor would he have been so ready to listen to the persuasive words of a man so recently taken into his confidence, and so little tried. It was true that Buckingham had early demonstrated his loyalty to Gloucester, and been rewarded handsomely for it with a goodly portion of Wales: and also manifestly unfair that his physical resemblance to his cousin, the unfortunate Clarence, should lead Christie to mistrust him. But if he looked like a Barbary ape, Christie thought wryly, glancing over to those elegant satin-clad shoulders and flowing golden locks in the leading boat, I would still be wary of him: and by all the saints, I wish that Gloucester did not rely on him so much.

The boats arrived at Westminster, amid light drizzle that had come from a sky rapidly clouding over with afternoon: the sun emerged suddenly, and over the jumbled buildings of Abbey and Palace, a faint and hesitant rainbow appeared. Someone said something about fortune, a good omen, and there was muted laughter, sharp with tension. The Cardinal of Canterbury, a man very much venerated and respected, was to plead in person with the Queen to surrender the little Duke of York, even if she would not be persuaded to emerge herself, or to release her daughters. But the presence of the armed men was ominous, a threat that she would not be able to ignore, for after the death of Hastings no-one could doubt that Gloucester would not fail to make use of his soldiers if necessary, even to violate sanctuary. It had been violated before, after the battle of Tewkesbury, when the Duke of Somerset and other notorious supporters of the house of Lancaster had been dragged from their refuge in the Abbey and executed in the Market Square. Their judge had been the eighteen-year-old Richard, Duke of Gloucester: and Christie knew, as he looked at the grim serious faces around him, that he was not the only one thinking of the past.

Gloucester, his face still showing the extremes of tension and anxiety which had not lessened now for many weeks, went with an unusually quiet Buckingham and most of the Council to await the outcome in the famous and beautiful Star Chamber, where they usually met at Westminster. The Cardinal, an upright but frail-looking old man in his seventies, went with Lord Howard into the Abbey to see the Queen, while Christie and the men-at-arms under his command and Sir James Tyrell's, spread themselves around the Abbey gateway to await results.

It was never really in doubt. Faced with the implacable Lord Howard and his words of armed men, and the urgent pleas of Cardinal Bourchier, even Elizabeth Woodville must admit that she had no choice. Her plotting had failed her, and she must give up her son whether she liked it or not. The Cardinal, his voice trembling with emotion, begged her to surrender the boy peacefully, and not to tempt his uncle to violate sanctuary and take the child away by force, a terrible sin. Weeping for the ruin of all her hopes, Elizabeth stared defeat in the face and submitted at last.

So, surrounded by the tears and good wishes and prayers of his sisters and his mother, Richard, Duke of York, with a couple of attendants carrying his small baggage, emerged into the drizzle of the Abbey forecourt to a scattering of sardonic cheers from some of the less-disciplined men. Christie saw with a shock how small he seemed, surrounded by grown men: but, unintimidated, he acknowledged them with a generous wave of his hand and a wide lopsided grin. Then the Archbishop, not a tall man but seeming so beside the diminutive figure of the child, took him by the hand and guided him into Westminster Hall to greet his cousin of Buckingham and his uncle of Gloucester, before being escorted back to the boats and taken to join his brother in the Tower.

Behind him, his mother and sisters sat desolate in their cramped chamber, bereft of the boy whose brightness had lightened their gloomy days cooped up in sanctuary: and it was not only the Queen who wondered, in despair, if they would ever see him again.

*

'I don't care what you say, it's wicked.' Cis Hobbes punched the thick lump of cream-coloured dough as if it were the Lord Protector himself, pummelled it and twisted it and flung it down again with a thud that made the candlesticks rattle on the table. She always made at least one batch of the inn's bread each week, to keep her cooks up to the mark so she said: Christie, seeing her vigorous torture of it, suspected that her motives were more basic. With relish, she ripped the lump into four and set about those pieces in turn: still kneading, her angry accusing blue eyes on his, she went on. 'A wicked and evil thing to do, Christ and all his saints and his blessed mother bear me witness! To take the throne from that poor sickly child on an excuse as flimsy as a whore's honour—been planning it all along, I reckon. And you dare come here and ask me what I think—as if my opinion mattered a half-penny to the likes of you and him! Well, I've told you what I think and I don't suppose you like it—in fact, I can see you don't.'

'I don't mind,' said Christie wearily. It was morning, early, and he had had no sleep the previous night: over and over again his mind had wrestled in vain with the events of the last few days, and found no solution to the conflicts raging within him. And all the while his previous self, cool, hard, cynical, ruthless, had stood aside from this struggle, and commented in wonder on the unwelcome feelings surging inside his head, compassion, conscience, guilt, doubt. And there was no answer, would never be an answer: and so, in desperation, he had taken his thoughts and confusion to the one person in London with whom he felt he could speak freely, without fear or prejudice.

And he could not be surprised at her reaction: it must be the same across all the city. People had had suspicions of the Duke of Gloucester already: the malicious whispers had long suggested that, far from being the devoted uncle, he was in fact plotting to take the throne for himself, the brief office of Protector being too uncertain for full enjoyment of the power he supposedly craved. Now, those whispers had been justified, for the previous day, Sunday 22 June, less than a week after the Duke of York had been delivered from sanctuary, the Duke of Gloucester had ordered a sermon to be preached at Paul's Cross by Dr Ralph Shaw, a priest famous for the power and force of his eloquence. The text had been taken from the Book of Wisdom, to the effect that 'bastard slips shall not take root.' And to a stunned, suspicious, astonished crowd of Londoners, increasing by the minute as the word went round, he had said that King Edward IV, before his marriage to Elizabeth Woodville, had been betrothed to a daughter of the Earl of Shrewsbury. Trothplight being binding, the subsequent marriage was bigamous, the children of it bastards and not entitled to inherit. As the offspring of the Duke of Clarence were barred by the Attainder upon their executed father, it followed that the lawful king and the true heir of his father, the old Duke of York, was Richard of Gloucester.

The citizens, murmuring and uneasy, dispersed to their homes amid an atmosphere of extreme disquiet. The revelation, given Edward's well-known love of women, was all too plausible, though the lady concerned was now dead and had none to speak for her. There were many who had already thought, privately, that the Duke of Gloucester with his martial past and reputation for firmness and justice would make a better ruler for this troubled realm than an ailing twelve-year-old boy who would always be tainted and influenced by his mother's family. Those feelings, however, did not mean that they would give Gloucester their wholehearted support in his decision to usurp the throne: and there were many others who, like Cis, were aware of practical considerations, but could not stomach the disinheriting of Edward's sons, on the word of a bishop of mediocre repute: for it had been Stillington, the Bishop of Bath and Wells, who had laid the information at Richard's feet like a gift, two weeks before.

Christie had known of it since the day after the Duke of York joined his brother in the Tower, and had realised at once what it would mean: for a man would have to be a fool or a saint not to take advantage of the opportunity thus offered, and Richard of Gloucester was, emphatically, neither. At the best he could only hope for four òr five years as Protector before his nephew came into his own power: a power that would allow him to be rid of the uncle he feared on the slightest of pretexts. And so Gloucester, with reluctance but also with the relief of a man offered, at the last moment, a way out of an intolerable and insoluble dilemma, had heeded the urgings of Buckingham and Lord Howard and his friends and his wife, and made his claim known first to his attendants and his household, and then, through the medium of Dr Shaw and lesser preachers throughout the city, to the Londoners. Tomorrow, the Duke of Buckingham would address the Mayor, aldermen and chief citizens at the Guildhall, and his eloquence would doubtless prove even more effective than Dr Shaw's. Amid all the doubt, fear and confusion in the two months since Edward IV's death, the accession of Gloucester to the throne, on however thin a pretext, might be welcomed as a promise of some stability amid uncertainty and the threat of civil war. It was an argument likely to appeal to hard-headed merchants and traders and craftsmen.

It would not, however, appeal to Cis, who had her own ideas of right and wrong and was prepared to air them at length. She set the first of the lumps of dough aside to prove, and began on the next,

[172]

her mouth compressed. 'What do *you* think of your fine and overmighty master?' she enquired acidly. 'Still think the sun shines out of his ears?'

Despite himself, Christie smiled. 'Cis Hobbes, dear soul, I am not the one to think the sun shines out of anyone's ears. Gloucester is a man like all of us, and subject to normal faults and failings.'

'You said it yourself,' Cis muttered to the dough. Christie, patiently, went on. 'He'll make a good king without doubt. I know Yorkshire isn't England, but it's England writ small, and he ruled it well and fairly—you hardly know him here in the south, but in the north he is much respected, and loved. But as to the rights and wrongs of taking the throne—I don't know, Cis, I really don't know. You say this betrothal is an excuse, but I'm fairly sure that Stillington spoke the truth.'

Cis's only comment was a scornful grunt and the contemptuous tossing of the second lump of dough to join its fellow. Christie continued, wondering if it felt like this when beating your head against a stone wall. 'Think back to the year the Duke of Clarence was executed. Seventy-eight—more than five years ago. I was here, in London, at the Temple, and I remember it well. Clarence was killed in the Tower, drowned in a butt of malmsey wine, or so everyone said. Stillington was his friend and confidant. He was imprisoned too. No-one ever knew the real reason why Clarence was executed—oh, he'd been a nuisance for years, untrustworthy, a sot, an embarrassment, but every family has one. That's no reason for execution, and nor is wanting to marry the heiress of Burgundy. It's well-known that the Queen·desired his death, and that's one reason why Gloucester hates her—he suffered from Clarence's wild ways more than most, but he was too loyal to his family to have countenanced his execution.'

'And you reckon this bishop that was so friendly with Clarence told him that the King's marriage was bigamous?' said Cis sharply. 'Then why not kill the bishop too?'

He could feel her mind moving closer to his, seeking explanations and motives amongst the inextricable tangles of intrigue five years stale. 'Because he's a man of the cloth, and a nonentity, a silly old fool who's fathered several bastards and is easy to cow or buy off with a few fat sinecures. You couldn't buy off Clarence—he was totally unpredictable, unstable, and utterly selfish, and to cap it all he wanted to be King. And what better way to make himself King than to prove his brother a bigamist and his children all bastards?

[173]

That was why he was put to death so secretly, without a proper trial—in case he spoke out.'

Cis's breath exhaled in a long hiss. She had not touched the dough for some minutes, and her bright intelligent blue eyes stared thoughtfully into Christie's. 'It all fits, don't it, young sir. But how does Stillington know of this betrothal, then?'

'The word is, he witnessed it. It must have been all of twenty years ago, when King Edward had just come to the throne. He can't have been any older than twenty or twenty-one, and the talk at Baynards Castle is that she was a pretty young widow who asked him to restore to her some lands he'd taken—and he took her as well. And of course, being a high-born and virtuous lady, he could not have her without promise of marriage.'

'Which he conveniently forgot when he tired of her—and his eye fell on Elizabeth Woodville,' said Cis. 'His marriage to her wasn't exactly all shipshape and above board, was it? In secret in some tiny little country manor with a couple of servants to witness it—there's no doubt kings of all people shouldn't marry for love, it brings a mort of trouble in its train. Put the Kingmaker's nose properly out of joint, that did—he never forgave Edward for it.' She took up the third lump of dough, absently pulling at it with her small knobbly strong fingers. 'What has the Lady Eleanor to say to all of this, then?'

'Unless she can speak from the grave, nothing—she's been dead fifteen years.'

'Then why didn't our fine and handsome King Edward go through another marriage and make it all legal? Then the boys at any rate wouldn't be bastards—the young King's only twelve.'

'I don't know. Perhaps he did, but Elizabeth Woodville's unlikely to tell us.' Christie stared at Cis, his mind weary and heartsick. 'It *is* true, I'm sure of it. It's just the sort of thing Edward would have done to get the woman he wanted—God's bones, he's supposed to have put a dagger to her throat to persuade Elizabeth Woodville into his bed, and she refused unless he married her. Probably he went through much the same performance with Lady Eleanor. And it fits too well with what happened to Clarence and Stillington, five years ago. Probably the good Bishop was told never to mention it again on pain of death, but when Edward died he saw his chance to ingratiate himself with Gloucester. He knew what a revelation like that would mean. And he hates the Woodvilles.'

'Who doesn't? Well, it may all turn out for the best,' said Cis, in tones which indicated that she thought the reverse. 'For all he's a northerner, your Gloucester may be the best King for England —but that's not how we choose Kings here, is it? We take the eldest son, by the laws of inheritance, otherwise there'd be endless argument and worse—which is just what old Harry the Fourth started when he took the last King Richard's crown away from him, and ever since, off and on, there's been fighting over it when there's a king like Holy Harry, all God and no wits.'

'As there'd be fighting over it now, if the King were a child, and a sickly child at that,' said Christie. He knew the rightness of what she said, he knew that in the eyes of most men Richard of Gloucester would be nothing more than a usurper—but so had his brother Edward usurped the throne of Holy Harry twenty-two years ago, and nearly all now spoke of him with respect and affection, despite his multitudinous faults, and acknowledged that on the whole he had been a good king.

'Well, we'll let God be the judge,' said Cis. 'We'll know soon enough if He favours your Gloucester or not. If he prospers, then it's God's will he took the throne. But think on those children, Master Heron—those boys he's disinherited. Bastards or no, they've lived all their lives as King's sons, and the elder has seen the crown as his right. He can't do anything now, he's only a child, but what happens when he's grown, when his brother's grown? Will they stand tamely by while their uncle sits on the throne young Edward must think is his? Will they? If they're the true children of their parents, they won't. And what will your Gloucester do with them then? Or is he going to strike fast and soon, as he did with poor Lord Hastings, and justify two deaths—two small deaths, insignificant deaths, after all children die every day—because killing them now will save many deaths later?'

Christie stared at her. He found that his mouth had gone dry with anger. 'Is that what they're saying? Do they think he'll murder them? His own nephews? He'd be a monster if he did that—and he's no monster.'

'No, I'll grant you that. But he's tasted power, and the rewards of ruthlessness. He's already gone further than he ever intended, I'll warrant—and it's not such a big step, to keep hold of power and safeguard his own life and his son's. You thought you knew your lord,' said Cis. 'You now think otherwise. Can you swear to me

[175]

that it hasn't entered his head, how convenient it might be if they died?'

'I'll swear it hasn't,' said Christie. 'And before God, if you were a man I'd spit at you for what you've insinuated.'

Cis, looking at him, realised that she had thought him a self-possessed, even a cold young man. Now she knew better, and though she was an exceptionally level-headed, practical, sensible woman, for a moment she was frightened by the anger she saw glittering in his eyes. She said quietly, 'I'm sorry, lad. You know your lord, and you have your loyalty to think of—I'm well aware of that. I can see you don't think him capable of such a monstrous crime. But ponder this—how many folk here in London, in the south, know him as you do? He's just another great lord snatching ruthlessly at power, and they'll say what I've said—in fact, I've heard the whispers already. Let's pray that little Edward doesn't die of whatever he suffers from—for not one soul in London will believe it's a natural death.'

Christie stood staring at her still, but the tension and fury had ebbed from his face, leaving it pale and very tired, all the sharp bones standing out against the sunburned skin. He had not shaved, obviously, and the stubble gave him a disreputable, villainous look. Cis felt a twinge of sympathy, which she firmly suppressed. He was a young man of considerable maturity, and formidable gifts and energies: she had seen that from the first. He was quite capable of resolving this crisis, and reconciling the warring claims of his conscience and his common sense, without any assistance from anyone, least of all herself. He would not thank her for her pity, but all the same she wondered at his family, whoever and wherever they might be, and the pressures and influences that had produced someone so relentlessly self-sufficient—on the surface, at least. And she thought wryly of her own sons, both in their own way unsatisfactory—stolid William, delinquent Perkin—and found herself wishing that one of the three who had died as babies had turned out like this.

But of course Cis Hobbes and her husband Harry would never have produced the long, lean, arrogant and intelligent man standing in her kitchen looking at her as if she was some harbinger of doom. Some wild Border family, with a dash of illicit blue blood from the Percies—Perkin had told her all he knew about Christie's background, which was little enough—had engendered Christie Heron, and he and others like him, and his lord, had descended on fat, busy,

[176]

money-making, complacent London like starving falcons alighting on a pigeon house. It was a situation thick with menace, suspicion, misunderstanding and danger.

'I'm sorry,' he said, and he gave her a tired wry smile that would have sent her heart jumping, thirty years ago. 'I know you've been playing devil's advocate. I know you're right—that they'll always believe the worst of him here, many of them, because he's not one of them. And I think of the children too. I feel sorry for Edward, but he's a poor feeble thing, and he loathes his uncle—how much more will he hate him now? But the younger boy, he's worth two of his brother. When he's grown, Gloucester will find him a formidable enemy, if he has not won him over by then.' He added, reflectively, 'If he hadn't taken this chance—if he had been content to stay Protector and give way to Edward when he reached sixteen or so—the boy would have found some way to be rid of him. You don't need much of an excuse—remember what happened to Clarence. And even if he would risk it for himself, he has his wife and his son to think of, to save from Woodville vindictiveness.'

'It's all the old King's fault,' said Cis. 'If he'd married that lady of Savoy, like the Kingmaker wanted, none of this would have happened—*she* wouldn't have brought a pack of greedy debauched relations with her, snatching all the good marriages and grabbing land and gold so quick it'd shame a Lombardy merchant. But there's no going back, what's done is done as my old grandam used to say afore you was born, lad, and it looks as if your Gloucester will be King before the week's out. Are you glad?'

There was a long pause. Christie's eye fell on the dough: he said drily, 'It's not rising, Cis—it can't be warm enough in here.'

'Don't change the subject, lad. I said, are you glad or sorry?'

'I'd like to see you in the Council chamber—you'd even pin the Bishop of Ely to the wall, and he's the most slippery fish I ever saw. Glad? Yes, I'm glad for the kingdom, and for Gloucester—now he no longer has to decide, he's a different man. Glad for myself, if I'm honest, because he trusts and values me, and I mean to rise under him. But—' Christie paused, and then said quietly, 'I wish it had not been at the children's cost. I know that there was no other way but to disinherit them, and yet—I wish it had not been done. It's those boys in the Tower I am sorry for—what torment must they feel?'

*

[177]

Richard Plantagenet, Duke of York, known to his sisters as Dickon, had come to the Tower of London with a joyous heart. He had not been at all sorry to leave sanctuary—he was sick of quiet, of monks, of hushed voices and plainsong and his mother's overwhelming presence, her confusing mixture of distance and emotion. He would miss Bess, and Cecily, and even Anne: though not the little ones, who were an unholy nuisance, unsavoury, always cross or crying—how was a man supposed to live in comfort amongst all those bawling quarrelling girls? And now he was free, bobbing about in a boat on the windy Thames, seeing the river banks gliding stately past, Lambeth marshes on his right, the great houses of the Strand on his left, followed by the jostling wharves and spiky churches, towers and spires, of the City, and crowning it all, the magnificent bulk of St Paul's.

'Are you pleased to be out of sanctuary?' The voice of his uncle of Gloucester had broken in on his enjoyment of the open air, real life, sights, sounds, smells, the feel of the cold water bubbling against his hand as he trailed it over the side. Dickon turned, startled, and saw the pale face of his uncle, that had always been so severe and worried-looking, actually smiling at him. It was a rather hesitant smile, as if unsure of its reception. Perhaps he thinks Mother has turned me against him, he thought—but she hasn't, though she did her best. Filled with the same desire to hearten and reassure and cheer as he had felt with his sisters, he gave his uncle his happiest grin, unaware of the charm of his rain-drizzled hair, the crooked mouth and abundant freckles. 'Oh, yes, I haven't seen Edward for nearly a year—how is he? Bess said he wasn't very well, and that was one reason why he wanted me to join him. She says I'm very good at cheering up people who aren't happy.'

The truth of that artless statement could be seen on his uncle's face: the Cardinal, sitting opposite, thought benignly that he had not seen the Protector look so relaxed and happy for many weeks. But the child, it was plain, was one of those souls who, ablaze with light themselves, cannot help setting others afire with their own joy, their exuberance, their love of life.

'Will I be able to see the lions?' Dickon next asked. 'And I'd like to look at the guns—there *are* guns in the Tower, aren't there?'

'I shall ask Master De La Moyte, who is the master gunner, to show you all his pieces,' said Gloucester. This boy was such a marked contrast to his sullen sensitive sickly brother: he rather resembled his cousin, the Protector's own small Edward, but the flame that burned so fiercely in Dickon flickered with less certainty in his delicate only son. Something in the boy's glowing face made him add, very quietly, 'What has your mother said of me?'

'Oh, she's told us all sorts of things about you, how you're wicked and plotting to take the throne and all manner of nonsense like that,' said Dickon cheerfully. 'I don't take much notice of them, though. I remember what Father used to say about you, especially when you won Berwick back from the Scots. He said you were the truest, most loyal friend he'd ever had.' And he turned, smiling, to look at the Tower, its turrets pale and gleaming behind London Bridge, and so did not see the expression, at once desperate and haunted, on his uncle's face.

*

Edward was delighted to see him, but Dickon was appalled at his older brother's appearance, his pale face gaunt, unchildlike, with dark rings under his eyes and a curious, almost blueish tint to the lips. He was much taller than the last time Dickon had seen him, but his girth had not increased in proportion. With his pale hair he reminded Dickon, unfortunately, of a marigold Cecily had grown in a pot last year. She had left it in too little light, and it had shot up too tall, outgrowing its strength: eventually, the frail stem had snapped. Dickon, looking at his brother's thin frame, felt a sudden stab of fear.

With typical enthusiasm, he set about lightening Edward's life. The inhabitants of the Tower soon grew used to the sight of the King and his brother, shooting at the butts (there was much more point to this, Edward found, if he had a rival), getting under the feet of Master De La Moyte in the Armoury or, every day, peering fascinated from a safe distance into the cages on the wharf which held the dangerous animals of the King's menagerie. The official Keeper of the Lions was Ralph Hastings, brother to the late Lord: he, of course, did not sully his hands with meat, at a cost of sixpence a day for each lion, nor with cleaning out their malodorous cages. That task fell to one Bennett, with two or three to help him: a laconic middle-aged man suspicious of these beautifully-dressed children, always with a couple of anxious attendants in tow, he had so far relented by the third day as to allow Dickon to offer the smallest and youngest lion a large chunk of meat impaled upon a halberd, so that the royal child was out of reach of the animal's claws. Edward, hovering in the background, trying to hide his fear, could not be persuaded to emulate his brother's daring. They had already decided on their roles in life: Edward the King, just, wise, learned and devout, served most loyally by his brother, the soldier and knight-errant who would win back France, trounce the Scots and finally subdue Ireland.

It was a glorious dream: they talked about it, in the big bed they shared in the royal apartments, with attendants dozing on pallets outside the door, and the soft comforting dark all around. Dr Argentine confided to Dame Haute that the Duke of York had made the world of difference to his brother's health. There was colour back in the King's cheeks, he talked with animation, he even laughed: and for three nights now, there had been no attacks. Even his skin seemed to be improving.

And then the idyll was at an end.

So busy and happy had they been, that Edward had not noticed how the flow of visitors, great and small, had slowed to a trickle, and then almost ceased. Nor had he had any papers to sign, or discussions about state business. It was as if he had left off his kingship for a space, to become a child again: a much younger child, free to wonder and enjoy and participate in life, without undue formality or restriction or responsibilities. But when the Cardinal Archbishop and the Chancellor were announced, late on the Saturday afternoon, it had the effect of dragging both boys back to reality. Edward was King, after all, and had duties to perform: the coronation would take place in a few days, he now remembered, and the clerics were doubtless concerned with this.

Both men looked grave: the Cardinal, a kindly old man in his scarlet robes of state, appeared especially sad. Edward felt the old clutch of fear at his heart. Had someone died? What was the bad news they so evidently brought? He glanced nervously at Dickon, and saw his brother staring, serious for once, in puzzlement at the two churchmen.

'We have news for you, Your Grace,' said the Cardinal Archbishop Bourchier. 'News which may come as a grievous shock to you and your brother—I beg you, child, prepare yourself.'

'My mother?' Edward asked anxiously, thinking, please, God, don't take Mother too—and I haven't seen her for so long.

The Chancellor, a younger and altogether more severe man than the Cardinal, coughed. 'No, the Queen is as far as we know very well, and so are all your sisters. No, this news concerns yourselves, and your—situation.'

The boys, bewildered, exchanged glances, and it was Dickon, his voice suddenly too loud, who said sharply, 'Please sir—tell us and have done with it.'

There was a silence, and then the Chancellor said heavily, 'There has been a—discovery, concerning your late father—may God assoil him—and your mother the Queen. It has been revealed that their marriage was no marriage in the eyes of God and man, because your father was already espoused to another. It therefore follows that you, your brother and all your sisters are bastards, conceived and born within an adulterous union—and that you are therefore in law not your father's heirs. Accordingly, proclamation will be made tomorrow, asserting the right of your uncle the Duke of Gloucester, as the only true heir living of his father the Duke of York, to ascend the throne of England, France and Ireland—'

'No!' It was Edward's voice, high and strangled with disbelief. 'No—no, it's not true, it's not true! I'm King—*I* am, not my uncle! *I'm* the King!' He took a hoarse breath which turned into a paroxysm of coughing, and his brother, his face white and pinched under the freckles, smote him several times on the back until the spasm passed and he could regain control of his breathing. There were tears in his eyes, the Cardinal saw with compassion: he said gently, 'Believe me, Lord Edward, we would not bring this heavy news to you if it were not true. It grieves the Chancellor and myself most mightily that we must tell you this—I would not wish it, I would not wish it for the world.'

'But you're the Chancellor!' Edward's shaking, scabby finger pointed at Bishop Russell accusingly. 'Couldn't you have stopped him—Uncle Rivers was right—he *did* want the throne for himself, he wanted it all along, and now he's taken it and it's *mine*, *I'm* the King, *I* am, *I* am!' He burst into wild sobbing, and Bishop Russell stared at him, frowning. All very well for the child to protest his right, it was only natural, but it was not a kingly figure standing there in the rich black velvet, shaking and distraught. The younger boy was very white, but perfectly composed: he gave a quick glance at his brother, and then walked forward to face the two men, his hand resting on the little jewelled dagger he wore at his belt, and his freckled face tipped up to see them better. 'Is it true?' he demanded. 'Or are you telling us lies because you're afraid of my uncle?'

The Cardinal could only look at him helplessly: it was the Chancellor, Bishop Russell, who understood the question. 'That your father was betrothed to another when he married your mother, yes, I believe it to be true. Whether, of course, that gives your uncle the right to the throne must be confirmed by Parliament and Council. We, the Council, are already in agreement.'

'Why? Because you think he'll cut off your heads like he did to Lord Hastings, if you don't do as he says?'

'Your uncle is a just and merciful man, child,' the Cardinal protested. 'You must not say such things. I am so sorry for you and your brother—but I am afraid there is nothing you can do—nothing any of us can do. You are not the legitimate children of your father, and so cannot inherit.'

'Norman William was a bastard, and it didn't stop him,' said the boy fiercely. 'I wish my uncle Gloucester would come here and tell me himself, and then I'd tell him just what I think—that it's an excuse! He wants to be King, so he's made us all bastards—and because we're only children he thinks we can't do anything about it!'

'You must accept this terrible thing, child,' said the Cardinal. By the look of the boy, he would be quite capable of sticking his dagger into his uncle, should they meet: it was just as well that he himself and the Chancellor had volunteered to undertake this unhappy task. 'If it is God's will that your brother should not be King—'

'It's not God's will, it's my uncle Gloucester's!' Dickon's breath caught on a sob: he glanced round at his brother, who was crouched dazed, still weeping, on a stool. His shoulders came back, and his wide grey eyes stared commandingly up at the two venerable, priestly and very powerful men before him. 'Very well. I accept what you say. I don't like it, I don't even really believe it, but I haven't any choice—not now! But you tell my uncle Gloucester this—one day, one day, I'll win Edward's kingdom back for him, I swear it!'

At the sound of his name, his brother lifted his tear-streaked face from his hands, and stumbled to his feet to grasp Dickon's arm. 'Don't be such a fool, can't you see? Our dear uncle Gloucester hasn't any intention of letting us free, not now, not ever, if he thinks we'll take our revenge on him one day. He's going to kill us, murder us, it's obvious, Dickon, can't you see? He dare not let us live long enough to grow up!'

CHAPTER NINE

'For to be a true King, to stand with true
justice from thenceforth the days of his life.'
(BOOK I, CHAPTER 7)

On 22 June, Dr Ralph Shaw informed Londoners in his sermon that
the Queen was no Queen, King Edward IV having bigamously
married her, and that her children by him were bastards, and thus
unable to inherit the throne of England. On Tuesday 24, the Duke
of Buckingham spoke to the City dignitaries in the Guildhall with
his customary power, eloquence and charm. The content of his
speech, very similar in essence to Shaw's, met with silence, unease,
and very little open support. The next day, an assembly of Lords
and Commons, summoned to a coronation which would not now
take place, by a King declared by his uncle to be illegitimate, drew
up a petition asking the Duke of Gloucester to take the throne. And
on the day after, Thursday 26 June, this assembly, together with the
Mayor and his aldermen and other London dignitaries, went in
procession to Baynards Castle, the home of Richard of Gloucester's
mother, to deliver their petition and offer him the crown.

The result was never in doubt. Gloucester agreed courteously to
their request, and to signify his accession to the throne, rode to
Westminster Hall to take his seat upon the marble chair, the King's
Bench. And on Sunday 6 July, Richard Plantagenet, Duke of
Gloucester, was crowned King Richard the third of that name, in
Westminster Abbey.

'I mean to rise under him,' had said Christie Heron: and there
were many others who might echo that wish. One of the highest of
them received his due when, on 28 June, Lord Howard was given
the trappings of the Dukedom of Norfolk, to which he had long
made claim by right of his Mowbray mother, daughter of an earlier
Duke. It was an honour only a King could bestow, and a just reward
for the years of loyal service that Howard had given to both Edward
IV and his brother. No-one spoke of the young Duke of York, who
had been married at the age of four to the little daughter and heiress
of the last Mowbray Duke. He had become Duke of Norfolk in her
right, and continued so after her early death, against the natural
laws of inheritance and property. The two children in the Tower

were not spoken of at all, at least within the circle around Gloucester: the whispers, of course, would be hissing within the City like a
swarm of angry wasps that would not be stilled.

Lord Howard was made Duke, and his son Earl of Surrey, and
the latter celebrated the occasion by giving his monarch and benefactor a most splendid white destrier, named White Surrey after its
donor. Many loyal gentlemen received the dignity of knighthood,
and the King gave orders for his household. Amongst those dozen
or so appointed Esquires of the King's Body, was the name of
Christopher Heron.

He had known that favour would be shown to him for his
service, but had not expected such a great honour. An Esquire of the
Body was an intimate, privileged member of the Court, at his
monarch's side day and night. It was demanding work, dressing
and undressing the King at morning and evening, or on ceremonial
occasions: conveying his needs or wants to the chamberlain,
accompanying him wherever he might go. Of necessity, it was a
position only granted to those very high in the King's friendship
and trust, for they would be privy to many state affairs and royal
business that must be conducted with discretion: and for a diligent
servant, the rewards were high. Thomas Howard, now Earl of
Surrey, had been a Squire to Edward IV, and had done very much
better than the basic fee of seven pence for a day's service. Lands,
grants, lucrative positions as stewards of manors or constables of
castles were the usual rewards for a trusty and well-beloved squire:
Christie Heron, aware that fifty marks a year was a routine gift for
one in his position, knew that, at last he had his foot on the
lower-most rung of the ladder. Diligent husbanding of his resources would surely mean that he would be able to buy land, a
manor, somewhere to call home, a place where he could found a
new dynasty of Herons in a greener, kinder, less uncouth and more
civilized country than his native Northumberland.

The founding of a dynasty, however, normally required the
acquisition of a wife, and that was something he shied away from at
present. It was all very well sharing the intimacies of his life with
Perkin, who performed for him roughly the same offices as he
himself would for the King, but already Perkin knew too much
about him, was too sharp, saw more than Christie might wish him
to see. A wife, a young woman of intelligence—for he would not
marry a fool to breed up fools after him—would be in an unrivalled
position to slide subtly and insinuatingly beneath the hard armour

which he had constructed for so many painful painstaking years around his vulnerable, passionate soul. He had chinks enough in that carapace already—cracks made by Perkin, by Julian, by his King, by the children in the Tower, and above all by his dear, lost, beloved sister Meg. To admit this capacity for sympathy and compassion, and his deep unheeded sense of right and wrong and fair-dealing, would be to stifle his rise to fame and fortune almost before it had begun: and so, for the moment, he would not take a wife.

*

The Coronation of King Richard III took place on 6 July. On the Friday, two days before, he and his wife, now Queen of England, had moved from Baynards Castle on the waterfront, where they had been living for some time, to the Tower of London. They went by river, a short journey full of ceremony, the boats of the City of London, newly painted, gaily dancing on the sunlit bobbing water around the green and white royal barge. The brisk wind fluttered its ostrich feathers and set the ladies' headdresses whipping to such effect that many of them were forced to hold on to their flimsy veils and absurd caps in order to avoid losing them to the Thames. Up until the last minute, the King had been reluctant to move to the Tower: he was only too well aware, as were all his household and councillors and advisers, of the silent forlorn presence of his two small nephews, kept now under close watch in one of the lesser towers while their former chambers in the royal apartments were usurped by the man who had robbed them of their inheritance. There were fears that they might be the focus of rebellion, hence the changed attendants, the close guard, the smaller, more easily watched quarters in the Garden Tower by the Constable's lodgings and the water-gate. But the whispers in the City put another, more sinister interpretation on the fact that the old King's sons had been withdrawn into stricter confinement.

Not so strict, however, that they could not watch, with a mixture of fascination, anger and resentment, the grand procession being formed up in the inner wards of the Tower, on the Saturday afternoon. Their attendants, kindly but impersonal strangers, had done their best to persuade them back to their books—for the new King had been most emphatic that their education must not, even in these times, be neglected—but nothing short of main force would have dragged the two boys away from the window overlooking the inner ward, and the seething confused and glorious array of men and women forming up below them for the procession through the City to Westminster. The prevailing colours were scarlet and gold, a wonderful shifting bright tapestry of splendour and display and sparkle: beautiful horses, their true colours almost completely hidden under the richness of their trappings, urgent servants in livery giving last-minute adjustments to the robes of their lords and ladies. And everywhere, unavoidable, blatant, the hated white boar badge of their uncle of Gloucester, their father's most beloved brother, who had betrayed his trust and ousted his children.

There were tears of misery and rage in Edward's eyes as he stared at the scene, his scaley hands clutched convulsively on the stonework of the windowsill. Since his throne had been seized, he had suffered a drastic relapse: every night was shattered by his struggles for breath, and he wept a great deal for the most trivial of reasons. Much of his time, waking, was spent in prayer and he ate virtually nothing, even when not fasting. Dickon, glancing at his frail brother, felt irritation. It was certainly all very tragic, and wrong, and he hated Uncle Richard most bitterly himself, but tears would not win back the crown, and neither, thought Dickon with a practicality that would have brought a glint to his father's eye, was prayer likely to have much effect. To see justice done, they must survive, and at this rate of progress Edward would shortly decline into a premature grave. Well, even if he gives up, *I'm* certainly not going to, he decided fiercely, and stared intently down into the packed mass of humanity, looking for known faces. Lord Howard —the Duke of Norfolk now, and Earl Marshall of England—and the Duke of Buckingham were prominent. He recognised William Catesby, who had been his father's councillor, and John Sapcote, who had been one of his Esquires of the Body. And, of course, there was the loathed, glorious figure of his uncle, wonderful in blue cloth of gold and purple velvet furred with ermine: even on this hot day, and in those heavy robes, his face was pale and still. The horse, a lovely white destrier, was also arrayed in purple, red and gold. If ferocity of gaze and intensity of purpose could have worked as Dickon desired, his uncle would not have reached the outer walls of the Tower, never mind his coronation the next day: but with helpless, desperate deep-run fury, he must watch the procession ride out through the gate below them and into the City, unmolested by the hand of God, by retribution or by justice.

Edward, through his tears, saw a face amongst the mass of

knights and squires riding behind the King and in front of the Queen: in the ubiquitous livery, scarlet with the badge of the white boar upon his breast, there was something wrenchingly familiar about the thin, sharp-boned face and the light brown hair, sun-gilded, under the scarlet cap. Then he remembered the attendant who had shown such sudden, unexpected sympathy, whom he had asked to beg for the presence of Dickon, and who had assured him that his uncle meant him no harm. He put a name to the face—his father had had a genius for that. Christopher Heron, that was it: and as if his thought had summoned the man's attention, the thin face glanced up, briefly, and Edward knew that he and his brother had been seen. Suddenly sick at heart, he turned away and threw himself down on the bed.

*

All through that interminable day, on the long hot dusty procession through an unnaturally clean and sparkling city, bright with paint and gold and gorgeous with tapestry and painted clots hung out of all the windows, and the merchants and their wives in their best clothes, cheering the spectacle with a vigour that surprised and heartened him, Christie had those two small white faces, their hatred and unhappiness all too clear, hovering behind his eyes like unwelcome phantoms, the unpleasant reality beneath all this fabulous display that the worthy citizens were applauding with such enthusiasm. And he wondered, with bleak compassion, what was to happen to them, for they could not stay mewed up in that tower for ever. Perhaps the King would take them into his household, as he had done the other child claimants to the throne, the small son and daughter of the Duke of Clarence: perhaps they would be sent to Middleham, to be brought up with the King's own young son. But whatever he did, Richard must know that the children would have no love for him now: and Christie could see a most difficult situation developing.

That insinuation that Cis had made, about the convenience of their death, he resolutely ignored.

Whatever the rights and wrongs of Richard of Gloucester's assumption of the throne, the glory and symbolism and solemnity of the coronation service were intended to dispel all doubts and uncertainties: and this they emphatically did, even in the mind of Christie Heron, who witnessed the ceremony only from the body of the great Abbey church, along with hundreds of other members of the royal household. He had no more than brief and interrupted glimpses of the lengthy ritual, but the glorious singing of psalms and anthems by the choir of the Chapel Royal could be heard with wonderful clarity, and their voices quietened his inconvenient conscience, as he lost himself in the intricate variations of tone and pitch, point and counterpoint, the soaring purity of the boys' voices perfectly complementing the deeper tones of the men.

And the hand of God did not strike, as the King and Queen were anointed with the holy oil of St Thomas Beckett, and took on the sacred duties of monarchy. Nor did it strike afterwards, as Mass was sung, and Richard and Anne received the Sacrament, nor during the long interval as the great procession reformed for its return to Westminster Hall and the great banquet. Wryly, Christie decided that for the moment, at any rate, this monarch had divine approval. And he wondered, as he followed the King and Queen back to the Palace which would now be his home and theirs, what Elizabeth Woodville, declared an adultress and a mother of bastards, deprived of her honour and dignity as well as her sons, would think of this coronation of the man she hated most. He could imagine her, made of gilded stone, sitting with her five lovely daughters around her in the sanctuary only a few yards distant, and plotting vengeance. For Dame Elizabeth Grey, lately calling herself Queen, was most assuredly not the woman to stand idly by while all she had won over the years was snatched away from her. She might now be hidden, disregarded, in amongst the quiet and monks of the Abbey, but that cunning mind would not rest long. He knew that the last had not been heard of her: the only doubt was, when and where the result of her plotting might become apparent.

*

The festivities lasted for a week, with stately meals full of fanfares of trumpets and elaborate ceremonial, the King respendent in a fine doublet and gown of crimson, lined with green satin which matched exactly the colour of his Queen's new gown. Christie, remembering the old carefree days at Middleham where his lord's preferred riding dress had been a leather jack and boots of much age and greater comfort, and the Duchess Anne had cheerfully overseen the autumn salting in a gown whose true colour had long since faded to brown, splashed with anonymous stains, looked on this new, unwelcome but entirely necessary formality with resignation. It would not do for the King of England to dress like a plain

Yorkshire gentleman, even if more practical, and despite the iniquitous cost of crimson damask and purple velvet and cloth of gold. True, the King of France, now cheerfully reported to be on his deathbed at long last, was notoriously lax in matters of dress and, his plain old homespun covered in dog hairs, had, according to rumour, frequently been taken for a menial in his own palace. King Richard, however, was well aware of the values of display, pomp and ceremony, and had no desire to emulate the traditional enemy, much to the delight, and harrassment, of the Keeper of his Wardrobe.

And Christie, though realising that serving a Duke, albeit a royal Duke, was very different from the close personal service now demanded of him, found that first week of duty as a Squire of the Body most irksome. Anyone reared in a great household, as he had been, had the basic principles of etiquette and ceremony bred into their blood and bone, and he had compounded his training with those years at Middleham, which despite the times of informality had always been governed by the strict rules of a great lord's castle, without which only strife, disorder and lamentable waste and dishonesty could be expected. He was aware of the great honour done to him, a landless squire of dubious parentage, by the granting of such a favour, and could take a certain distant pride in the efficiency with which he discharged his duties. But the very nature of the tasks meant that he must present always this quiet, impassive, unemotional mask to the world at large. Since it was a mask he himself had cultivated over the years, he could not complain: and yet a restlessness stirred in him now, an urge to speak his thoughts, to show his emotions, even if unpleasing to those around him. It frightened him, this growing change and need in himself, as nothing had frightened him before: and the nature of that first busy week, full of jousting and feasting, accustoming himself both to the endless ingestion of over-rich food and too much wine, and the labyrinthine coils of a palace that seemed built for giant coneys rather than men and women, meant that he must resolve this increasing crisis alone. He could not leave his duties and take a boat down the Thames to speak with Cis Hobbes: neither did he feel able to discuss matters so nebulous and personal with the beady-eyed, inquisitive Perkin, who was revelling in the vastly increased status their residence at the Palace would bring him, and discovering a taste for back-stairs gossip that might at another time have amused Christie greatly. And there was no-one else he could talk to, at all.

It was at times like these that his grief for Meg arose and became almost a physical pain, gnawing deep within him. The old Meg would have loved the spectacle, the music, the wondrous clothes and the jousting and feasting and the glittering symbolic savagery of the tournament: he could almost picture her, dancing in the Hall on the night after the coronation with the other ladies, her golden hair hidden beneath a preposterous veiling headdress like the wings of a butterfly, and the silken folds of her gown gleaming blue in the candlelight. Almost, he saw her, save that the tall lady with the slender figure and the lively tread was not Meg, but the pretty wife of Lord Lovell. And such was his need, and so great the impossibility of revealing it to anyone at all, save her, that when his duties were ended for that day, and another man had taken his place, he spent long hours in the little chamber just off the Privy Garden, which had been allotted to him and his servant, writing to her in the same mood of despair and doubt with which she had once written to him. He knew as the badly-cut pen scratched across the thick paper, and his one waxen candle flickered sweetly towards its end, that he was a fool, that he had long ago forfeited any right he might have to a reply from her, even if she did him the favour of reading it. And when he had finished, and realised what he had written, how much he had revealed of things he had hardly known in himself, how he had laid his soul bare to her bitterness and hate, he screwed up the paper and thrust it with sudden self-disgust into the candle flame. The paper burned well: so did his finger. Singed, Christie swore quietly and dipped the burned digit into the half-full jug of wine that had formed part of his livery, the light refreshments served to everyone before they retired. A faint rattling snore from the pallet in the corner revealed Perkin to be safely lost in slumber. Christie crushed the smouldering twist of paper into anonymous ashes in his hand, and threw them into the hearth. Then, driven only by his envy of his servant's deep uninnocent slumber, he drained the wine to the lees, blew out the poor remnant of a candle and made his way to his own bed, to wait for a sleep that was too slow in coming.

*

Following the week of celebration at Westminster, the King and his Court removed to Greenwich. It was a palace smaller and quieter than the noisy bustle of Westminster, hard by the Abbey and its bells: in this spell of hot weather, it was also cooler and fresher, free of the noisome aroma of the common humanity that was packed round the walls of the King's chief residence. Here, he was able to discuss weighty matters in peace, to listen to the advice of his councillors, and to put matters in order before setting out on the planned progress through his kingdom. For as yet, most of the country would know only the vaguest details of the dramatic events of the last four months. They must be aware that they had a new King, and probably news had reached them by now that his name was Richard, and not Edward, but it was a matter of the gravest urgency that the new monarch should show himself to as many of his subjects as possible, in order to impress them with the splendour of his majesty and the wisdom and justice of his rule. Christie knew that the King set great store by the oath he had sworn at his coronation. Against tradition, it had been spoken in English, so that all who heard it might understand its solemnity: and he remembered, many times over the next weeks, his sovereign lord's harsh voice, echoing loudly in the lovely roof of the royal Abbey, swearing to grant and keep to the people of England the laws and the customs to them, as of old rightful and devout kings granted.

The royal procession left Greenwich on a sweltering hot, humid day, heavy with the promise of thunder. The over-dressed courtiers ran with sweat under their scarlet and crimson—for the need to make a great display was still paramount—and privately thanked their particular saints that the first part of the journey at least would take place on the cool waters of the river, where a flotilla of bright boats and barges waited to transport them. Into them were packed lords, justices, bishops, officials, their robes heavy and the collars of livery which all must wear in the service of the King, weighing uncomfortably around their necks: and then, accompanied by a bevy of less exalted and unofficial boats, and watched by crowds of citizens on the banks and wharves lining the river, King Richard III and his household left his capital for the unknown pastures of the provinces.

The cavalcade left the river at Kew, meeting its horses, baggage, servants and grooms, and made its stately way to Windsor: thence, leisurely, to Reading and on to Oxford. Here, there was a splendid reception given by the University, and, unfortunately, two very long and tedious disputations on moral philosophy and on theology. The princely sums and fine bucks which the King donated to the two disputants involved were a measure of his appreciation, not shared by all his household, who had some cause to regret their sovereign's serious cast of mind. Then the peaceful golden towers of Oxford were left behind, and King Richard moved on to the old royal palace at Woodstock: whence on the morning of Monday 28 July, many neighbouring gentry were invited to do homage to their new monarch.

Amongst them was Sir Thomas Bray. He had been absent from the coronation ceremonies, and Christie had discovered that his ostensible reason was ill-health. Yet here he was, large and jovial, his scarred face patched like a magpie's, the unburned skin tanned by the sun while the new flesh remained unhealthily pale. Beside him was his redoubtable wife, her sharp black gaze roving over the company. It came to rest with evident disapproval on the King, resplendent in his crimson gown lined with green—he had a fondness for that combination of colours, and it suited him well. Christie, going to greet them from courtesy—and he rather liked Sir Thomas—guessed instantly that his absence at the coronation was due more to disapproval of the King than to an illness he had obviously not suffered. Still, that was Sir Thomas's decision—or his wife's—and if he chose to incur Richard's displeasure, it was his affair. And Christie, uneasily, found that he could understand why a loyal servant of Edward IV should be unable to bring himself to attend the coronation of the man who had ousted his son and usurped the throne.

The good-natured Sir Thomas, looking at his livery collar, congratulated him on his new position and enquired after his rascally servant (Perkin's reputation during those early days at Berwick had been somewhat startling). Dame Alice, frowning, said not a word. Christie thanked Sir Thomas for his good wishes and asked, with some irony, about the progress of his recovery from his late illness. Sir Thomas, catching the gleam in the other's pale eyes, declared unblushingly that it had been a most painful attack of the gout, he had been sorry to miss the coronation and all that ceremony, but now, thanks to holy Saint Anthony, to whom he had prayed daily, he was as well as could be expected at his advanced age.

'And Mistress Julian?' Christie enquired demurely, with that gleam in his eyes that Perkin knew so thoroughly. 'I do not see her—is she also well?'

'She is well,' said Dame Alice, through shut teeth. 'I pray you excuse me, Master Heron—I must speak with Mistress Harcourt.' And she turned with an abruptness that verged on discourtesy, and

[192]

stalked over to another group of ladies and gentlemen, the stiff veils of her headdress jerking with her emphatic stride.

Sir Thomas, visibly embarrassed, coughed. 'You will forgive my dear wife, Master Heron. She is somewhat overwrought—we have had, er, a domestic upset.'

He would say no more, and diverted the conversation to less contentious matters. But Christie decided that the turbulent Mistress Julian had been the cause of some family dispute, and as a punishment had been left at home.

In this, he had not quite guessed correctly. There had indeed been an argument of cataclysmic proportions, but it had begun between Sir Thomas and his wife, and Julian had not then had any part in it. The decision to stay away from the coronation had been in essence that of Dame Alice, whose loud and constantly voiced suspicions about the motives of the Duke of Gloucester had at last, to her unbounded satisfaction, been proved correct. Sir Thomas, also unhappy about what he perceived to be the Duke's betrayal of his dead brother's trust, had taken little persuading during those last weeks of June, when confusion and rumour had been rife. But as the reports of a peaceful and glorious ceremony, with the apparently enthusiastic support of nobles and gentry alike, began to filter through to Oxfordshire, Sir Thomas began to regret his absence and consequent inevitable loss of royal favour. He was a Justice, the kind of man on whom the King must rely in order to govern the county according to his wishes, and the rewards for loyal service could be great: Ashcott had been extensively repaired and refurbished on the proceeds of the years under King Edward. If he were to further dower his daughter and provide for a comfortable old age for himself and his wife (although Sir Thomas sometimes found himself wondering whether any old age could be comfortable when shared with Dame Alice), he must continue to enjoy the benefits of royal patronage. Accordingly, when the summons to the gentlemen of Oxfordshire had gone out, Sir Thomas had announced to his family his intention of answering the call, well aware of the outcry it would provoke, but resigned to the fact that a little domestic discord was the price that must be paid for a return to profitable royal service, even if the man on the throne was not the one whom he might want.

Dame Alice, predictably, had been loud in her condemnation of his plan. He was being disloyal to the memory of King Edward, may God rest his soul, and more so to that poor little boy mewed up in the Tower. Julian, sitting in the parlour listening to her mother's tirade, had remembered similar outbursts against the lamented King Edward while he still lived, when Dame Alice's sympathies had belonged to the Lancastrian cause and her tears for the martyred saintly King Harry and his promising young son had flowed freely. Her mother's hypocrisy was breathtaking, she thought furiously: but at the same time, a little worm of doubt wriggled free in her mind. This reported earlier betrothal of the old King seemed nothing more than an excuse: in her heart she still acknowledged his bastardised son as the true King, and the man now on the throne as a usurper. And since one of his household was a man she unreservedly disliked, she could happily detest his lord and sovereign as well.

But, being Julian, she could not help but disagree with her mother: and unwisely did it aloud. 'I thought you didn't like King Edward. And you said when he died and we all had to pray for the Queen, that she was a haughty madam who had no more true royalty in her than Wat the hedger.'

There was a brief, appalled silence, and then, relentlessly, the stream of malice turned in her direction. Julian lowered her head in apparent but deceptive submission as the torrent raged around her, and she held fast to the knowledge that she had spoken, however rashly, nothing but the truth. Then, with her father's sad assent, she was despatched to her chamber and given a sound beating by her irate mother.

'You are your own worst enemy,' Sir Thomas had told her, much later, over a secret offering of wafers and sweetmeats. 'I know you spoke the truth, poppet, but you must have known how it would provoke your mother. It does not make my life any easier, you know.'

Julian bit into the crisp lightness of her wafer: she loved the way they seemed almost to melt on her tongue, and the floury taste mixed with the sharpness of the wine. She swallowed and said, looking directly at her father, 'I'm sorry. I didn't mean to make things difficult for you. I didn't think.'

Sir Thomas, who loved her more dearly than wife, house, lands, wealth, position, smiled at this apology (it was years since she had expressed sincere repentance to Dame Alice), and did not point out, as he might have done, that she never did think before she spoke. He went on, 'I am set upon going to Woodstock tomorrow. I must present my apologies to the King, though I must confess that it pains me to do it. But your dower might depend on it, my sweet, not to mention your chances of a good marriage, so I must bend the knee to the usurper and forget that he betrayed his brother's children. Your mother, my dear, doesn't always understand what is necessary as opposed to what is right. We all must live, after all—hankering after King Edward's poor little sons will do us no good at all. We must accept that what is done is done, and there's nothing we can do to change it.' He glanced sharply at his unusually silent daughter. 'You disagree?'

'Yes,' said Julian fervently, beginning on another wafer. Through the crumbs, she added passionately, 'I only said what I did because of mother—and it was the truth! But what the King did was wrong, you've as good as said it yourself, and nothing can alter that—wrong in the sight of God and man, to take the throne away from that poor little boy—who can't do anything about it at all! And on a feeble excuse, too—as if anyone really believes all that rubbish about the Lady Eleanor or whoever she was, anyway! And you just sit there and tell me you must accept it! Is everyone doing the same, all over England? You're following the usurper's sin with a bigger one, you're letting him take the crown away from that boy without even raising a voice against him! And then you're talking about going to Woodstock and *grovelling* to him like all the rest of the spineless gentry hereabouts. I think Mother was right,' she finished in a voice quivering with emotion. 'It's just because I don't like agreeing with her that I said what I did.' And then, seeing her father's face, suddenly old and slack with distress, she cried, 'Oh, I didn't mean it, I didn't mean to upset you!' And she flung herself into his arms, hugging him with the abandon of someone much younger, and sobbed against his broad chest, 'It's just that I wish you'd do what's *right*! I don't *care* about my dower, I don't *want* a good marriage, I want to be proud of you, and I can't be if you toady to that evil usurper.'

Many might have thought the same, in her position: only Julian could have said it so forthrightly, so hurtfully, in her own inimitable style. Sir Thomas, close to tears himself, stroked the thick chestnut brown hair, and murmured soothing words, and wondered bleakly about the future of his turbulent child, born late after a string of dead sons to a loveless marriage that was devoid even of the mildest affection, and adrift in a wild sea of confused emotions and loyalties. She would be much sought after, as the heiress of Ashcott, and indeed he had had many expressions of interest as it became apparent that there would be no more children, but he had never been able to bring himself to entertain any hopeful husband seriously, despite his wife's urgings. She was immature, she was too young, too childish: her body admittedly was now a woman's, but she had not yet learned to hide her thoughts and feelings in a properly adult manner. She was not ready yet for the responsibilities of directing a household, managing servants and children and a husband's affairs in his absence. Nor had any man yet presented himself who might give her the understanding and love she craved, though she might not know it. And in his heart of hearts, Sir Thomas had to admit that he could not bear to let her go, and face an existence at Ashcott alone, save for his shrewish intolerable wife.

And because he loved Julian so dearly, her words had pierced a small chink in his determined pragmatism. He wanted her to be proud of him, he wanted to be worthy of her love, and so, as he rode to Woodstock the next day, Dame Alice pouring a stream of discontented comment in his ear about the new King, his mind was unusually in turmoil. He made his obeisance to the King, spoke cheerfully to that pleasant young man who unaccountably seemed to have earned Julian's undying enmity, and successfully covered his doubts with a mask of jovial bonhomie: but to no avail.

And then he was taken aside by young John Harcourt, who lived not far away at Stanton Harcourt, and was a fellow Justice and official at the Court of the old King. Harcourt was in fact not so young, being in his thirties and the father of a son of seventeen: he had a long-standing grudge against the King, something to do with offices or revenues he thought the Duke of Gloucester had denied him, as well as an old family feud, and Sir Thomas had been somewhat surprised to see him at Woodstock. He listened to what Harcourt had to say, in his quiet sly voice, with growing interest. And on his ride home, Dame Alice this time ranting ceaselessly about some other Justice's wife who had supposedly snubbed her, a glow of enthusiasm woke within his shrewd, practical mind, still despite everything deeply emotional, and would not be stilled. At last, there was the chance to satisfy his honour, and Julian's, and avenge the betrayal of the old King's sons.

*

After Oxford, the weather broke, and turned thundery, with piled clouds grim and solid on every horizon, snowy white above and leaden lowering grey below. The Progress, alternately wet with perspiration and with rainwater, toiled along the roads of England, good, bad or indifferent according to the zeal, wealth and efficiency of each parish, moving steadily northwards. They stayed at Lord Lovell's beautiful house at Minster Lovell, its soft grey-gold stone set off perfectly by the green grass and willow trees along the River Windrush: it was a scene that reminded Christie forcefully of Ashcott, not so very far away. The brief sojourn—two nights only—began as an oasis of peace and coolness amid soft-falling rain, welcome on the parched fields and meadows, and ended in a sudden flurry of activity as word came of a failed plot, in London, to spirit away the young Princes from the Tower, raising fires in the City as a distraction. The plan had been discovered and its prime movers, including two minor officials of the royal household, arrested: they were to be tried by those members of the Council remaining in London, and executed if found guilty.

Then the Progress set off again on its ponderous way through a countryside rapidly becoming golden with harvest amid the lovely stones of the Cotswolds, their substantial villages solidly founded on the broad and woolly backs of their quantities of sheep. Gloucester, Tewkesbury, Worcester: each town filled with ringing bells, welcoming cheers, the evident delight of the people at this visible symbol of the monarchy, come amongst them in such brilliant splendour to brighten their humdrum lives. Christie rode a restive and fretful Bayard, who had not recently had the extended gallops necessary to rid him of fidgets, sidling, frothing around his bit and indulging in unlicensed but impressive cavortings half-remembered from his early training as a war-horse, that scattered squealing children and drew glances, some amused and others less so, from the rest of the cavalcade, who contrasted Master Heron's unfailing efficiency in other matters with his apparent inability to control his unruly mount. At every city and town, the King was greeted with joy and lavish gifts, which he usually refused, preferring instead to win the hearts of his people by granting them favours or requests. Thus, Gloucester received a charter of liberties, while Woodstock was given back some lands which King Edward had high-handedly added to his hunting forest at Wychwood. Everywhere there were pageants, feasting, the magnificent display not only of the royal entourage but of the various places on the route, freshly painted and gilded, hung with arras and cloth and tapestry and strewn with flowers and sweet herbs.

At Gloucester, the Duke of Buckingham left the Progress and

turned westward to his castle at Brecon: where lay, already conveyed there with comfort, but still captive, the Bishop of Ely, John Morton, the custody of whom the Duke had asked, and been given, at the time of Lord Hastings' execution. Christie watched the departure of the noble Duke, his entourage almost as splendid as the King's, with his badge, the Stafford Knot, as much in evidence as the White Boar, and felt some relief, and more misgiving. For some time now—in fact, ever since the execution of Lord Hastings—he had entertained suspicions about Buckingham's character and motives, and had felt deeply uncomfortable in his flamboyant presence. His duties had inevitably brought him into close contact with the King's intimates as well as with Richard himself, and at least he would not now have to listen to that mellifluous voice presuming on Richard's trust and friendship in a way that evidently irritated those like Lord Lovell or Sir Robert Percy, who had known him since childhood. Nor would he have his doubts fed by inconvenient memories of the beautiful Clarence. But the combination of Buckingham with that most devious man, the Bishop of Ely, a proven plotter, was one fraught with unpleasant and ever-widening possibilities, and Christie, remembering how Buckingham had asked for custody of the Bishop as a favour from the King, could not help but wonder anew at his motives for so doing.

But he could confide his doubts in no-one, least of all Richard, who had before he left London made Duke Harry Constable of England, Great Chamberlain, and restored to him his disputed half of the lands of his Bohun ancestors. It was evident that the King still placed the greatest reliance in the man who had done so much, by deed and word, to persuade him to the throne: and since Christie placed great trust in his sovereign's judgement, he must hope that his instinctive, nebulous suspicions about the Duke would prove to be unfounded.

At Warwick Castle, they stayed for a week: the Queen joined them from Windsor, bringing with her a Spanish envoy who had had time to conceal his surprise at being received by an adult King Richard instead of a child King Edward. It was noticeable how Queen Anne's arrival influenced her husband: in her presence his stern, serious mood lifted, he smiled and even joked a little, and the household at Warwick relaxed with him. The judges in the King's train heard local trials and disputes, as they had done all along their route, and the people of Warwickshire spread word of the fair justice and gracious generosity of the new King.

Then it was onwards towards York, which they reached by the end of August, still in a comparatively light-hearted mood: deceived by the evident and universal joy of the populace that all was well throughout the Kingdom.

*

In Brecon, amid the high blue hills of Wales, on the borders of the wild lands whence had sprung the rebellions of Owen Glendwyr, Llewellyn and other sons of Cymru, Bishop Morton and Duke Harry of Buckingham came early to an understanding. They were agreed on one thing, the necessity of unseating King Richard from his freshly-occupied throne as soon as might be. Their first attempt had failed, although it had admittedly got rid of Lord Hastings, one of their most important objectives. Buckingham then, knowing that the sons of Edward would be discredited, had bethought himself of his double line of descent from King Edward III, through his Beaufort mother and his great great grandfather, Thomas of Woodstock, whose arms he had acquired the right to bear, and had decided that he would make an admirable King. His claim was good, almost as good as the Yorkist brothers', and certainly better than that Welsh nonentity skulking at the Court of Duke Francis of Brittany in ignominious penury. And certainly he cut a much more impressive figure than the Duke of Gloucester, who was slight, dark-haired and rather pinched looking, with a conscientious face and premature lines of responsibility, anxiety and stress. Buckingham had always been vain of his tall, athletic body, his golden good looks and magnificent eloquence. He had won the trust and friendship of the most powerful man in England with astonishing ease: surely the hearts of the people would descend with equal felicity at his feet?

He had urged Richard on to take the throne at his nephews' expense, knowing of the resentment it would cause amongst the loyal members of the old King's household, not to mention the family of the Queen, amongst whom was his own wife. His marriage to her had been a stormy one, forced on him in adolescence, but it had strengthened and matured after the births of their children, and Katherine Woodville certainly shared the vaulting ambition of her sister the Queen. She would not throw away the chance of becoming Queen of England herself: and once Richard was on the throne, how easy to discredit him, to whip up discontent amongst the influential country gentry who had served his brother, how tempting to spread the rumour that the King meant harm to his nephews. One carefully-planned rebellion, even one act of assassination, and the way would be clear for the Duke of Buckingham to become King Harry the Seventh.

He had sailed through the coronation ceremony in his magnificent blue velvet with its design of gold-embroidered wheels: he had insisted on taking the chief part in its organisation, thereby displacing Lord Howard, now Duke of Norfolk, who as Earl Marshal of England would be expected to be in charge of the arrangements. The only unpleasant moment came when the crown was placed on Richard's straight dark hair, and he had been unable to look, so sick was he with envy: that heavy gold belonged on his own head, and none other, and he would not rest until his desire became reality.

The persuasive, practical tongue of the Bishop of Ely, over a cosy jug of hippocras in his privy chamber at Brecon, soon dashed all his hopes. If men were dissatisfied with the rule of King Richard, who at least had been able to style himself brother and uncle of Kings, how much less would they relish the rule of a Duke of Buckingham who could only claim distant kinship to royalty, however direct and legitimate his descent? The Bishop, looking at the handsome, vain, crestfallen face, smiled inwardly to himself and pressed home his advantage. The children did not matter. But if King Richard, and the Princes in the Tower, and Buckingham himself were discounted, there was another candidate for the throne of England: and moreover, one with an overwhelming advantage over the rest.

Buckingham, petulantly, demanded to know the name of this paragon, though he knew it already—there *was* only one other possible claimant, barring Yorkists. And Morton smiled a sweet, priestly smile that did not reach his narrow dark eyes. 'I am speaking, as you doubtless are aware, Your Grace, of Henry Tudor, Earl of Richmond.'

'Him!' said Duke Harry, with contempt. 'A penniless adventurer, shifted from pillar to post, his father a bastard—well, no-one ever proved that Queen Katherine married his grandfather—his mother a Beaufort, first cousin to my own mother, in fact. He only claims in his mother's right, whereas my claim comes not only from my mother but from Thomas of Woodstock in direct line of descent, without any taint of bastardy whatsoever. No-one in England, save the accursed line of the old Duke of York, has a better claim than I do!'

'I am not disputing your claim,' said Morton, with patient

[200]

reasonableness. The candles lit his shrewd face and gave it a quite spurious appearance of holy serenity. He sipped his hippocras and went on. 'There is no doubt that your claim to the throne is far in advance of the Earl of Richmond's—I am not disputing it. But, Your Grace, the Welshman has one overweening advantage over you, disagreeable though it may seem. He is not yet married.'

There was an explosive silence in the dim little room: the only other living creature in it a favourite hound of the Duke's, that lay always at his feet. Buckingham said, his voice carefully controlled, 'Why should that be such an advantage? My wife is the Queen's sister.'

'Pray consider the matter for a space,' said Morton, still so soft, so reasonable, so persuasive, trapping the unfortunate Duke in the coils of his eloquence. 'Henry Tudor is unwed, and a young man in his twenties will certainly require a wife—and if he aims for the throne of England, the matter becomes more urgent still, to breed an heir and a dynasty. And what better wife for him, to unite in one the houses of Lancaster and York and bring an end to all civil strife, than Elizabeth of York?'

With an inward cry of anguish and bitterness, the truth of what he said burst upon Buckingham like a thunderbolt. He sat staring at the comfortable, smiling Bishop, and felt much as the shepherd in the fable must have done, on finding a wolf under the sheep's skin. It was the perfect solution, and no doubt the perfection of it would strike others as it had struck him. He knew his own cause was doomed now: faced with that alternative, who would cry Harry of Buckingham for King?

'King Richard, of course, cannot marry his niece, and besides, he already has a wife. Nor can the sons of Edward marry their sister, nor can you put away your good Duchess after so many years of happy and fruitful wedlock.' As Buckingham squirmed involuntarily at the heavy irony, Morton continued. 'And so Henry Tudor must marry the Princess Elizabeth, as her father's heiress.'

'And the boys? You said they did not matter, but he cannot marry her and claim the throne while they are still alive,' Buckingham pointed out. He knew what the answer must be, had already contemplated it, awed and yet repelled by the boldness of such a stroke, but still the words when they came, so matter-of-factly spoken, put a chill on him.

'The Princes? Oh, they must be killed,' said Morton, the man of God, calmly. 'And if it can be done privily, no-one will believe that their uncle did not order it—rumour is rife already. And so he will be the more easily overthrown, and the way is clear for Richmond.'

There was a longer silence. Buckingham sighed, and quaffed his hippocras with a hand that was, he saw with surprise, trembling visibly. It was one thing to dream and plan in his own mind, quite another to have a fellow-conspirator who was so bold, so certain, so appallingly practical. For the first time, the Duke felt the faintest regret that he had not left well alone, and been content with the vast rewards he had received for his loyalty and assistance to the King. He said slowly, 'The children are closely watched, within the Tower. There has already been one failed attempt to free them, but they are too well guarded. How do you propose to—to do the deed?' He still could not bring himself to say the words 'kill', or 'murder'.

'I, Your Grace? A man of God, of peace, commit murder? For shame,' said the Bishop, with cold gentleness. 'You are after all the Constable of England. You have free access to the Tower. It is on your orders that they will be killed.' He saw the look on the Duke's face, and proceeded to draw in the line, his fish firmly hooked on the end of it. 'We have a man amongst their attendants. He knows what must be done, and waits only for the word. Your Grace, this is the price we must pay for victory. The children must not live to threaten us. If we can persuade the Queen that they are dead, she will gladly agree to our plan for her eldest daughter. Tudor's mother, the Countess of Richmond, has already been in contact with her.'

'The sanctuary has been well guarded since the plot to rescue the boys failed,' Buckingham pointed out. 'I myself gave the orders.' He knew he was being foolish, he knew that he was in too deep now to extract himself with safety, yet he could not help but struggle as the abyss opened beneath him. Though—what if they should succeed?

'My Lady of Richmond is a pious and charitable woman. She heard of the sickness of the little Princess Anne, and sent her own doctor to tend the child,' said Morton smoothly. 'Since the Queen reports her daughter still weak, though improving, the good Doctor Lewis has visited sanctuary many times. Doubtless he converses with the Queen as they watch over the child's sickbed: doubtless he relays her messages of thanks and good will to the Countess. More than that,' the Bishop finished slyly, 'cannot be proved. I have heard all this from the Countess's steward, Master Bray, who has corresponded with me.'

'You have indeed been very busy,' said Buckingham, staring with a mixture of alarm, admiration and hostility at this desperately devious old fox. 'You've also been very confident that I would agree to all this. As you well know, my original plans were quite different.'

The Bishop regarded him thoughtfully for a moment, and then smiled that peculiarly chilling smile. 'As I see it, Your Grace, you have little choice. Already there are some who might talk most revealingly—about your manipulation of poor Lord Hastings, for instance, may God assoil him.' He crossed himself piously. 'And the fact that I am more of a guest here than a prisoner, and that you have allowed me to correspond so freely with my friends in London and elsewhere. Not the close and careful watch that you promised the King, eh?' The smile became sharper, and the hard eyes, like chips of black flint, bored into Buckingham's recoiling blue ones. 'Make no mistake in this, Your Grace, you are deeply involved in conspiracy now. You are committed, utterly, to our cause. Oh, you may cherish your dreams of a Stafford dynasty to replace a Plantagenet one, but you know in your heart they are dreams only. We are together in this, Your Grace, *together*. Divided, each pursuing his own objective, the King must stand against us. But if we work together to place Henry Tudor on the throne, then and only then will the King fall. And Tudor, make no mistake, will confirm all that you have received from Richard, and add to it.'

Buckingham thought for an instant longer of his golden dream, the crown on his head, a figure truly regal in beauty and splendour, far more so than any Plantagenet or Tudor: then, reluctantly, he put it aside. But only for the moment, he told himself—he would see of what stuff this unknown Henry Tudor was made. With luck, he would be as easy to dupe as Richard of Gloucester. He smiled conspiratorially at the Bishop. 'Well, since your plans seem to be so far advanced, perhaps you will do me the service of enlightening me as to their extent.'

*

Utterly unaware of the clouds of betrayal brewing over Brecon, King Richard and his household entered York to the wild acclaim of the citizens, which he acknowledged with a series of uncharacteristically joyous smiles. These were his people, whom he had

[203]

governed fairly and wisely all his years in the North, the Lord of Middleham: and he had their love, as he knew in his heart he would never have the love of the rich green South. Reports had already reached him of unrest, from the Chancellor in London and other less exalted informants, but they were vague in the extreme, and he had expected something of the sort so early in a reign that had begun in less than auspicious circumstances. But Chancellor Russell was a capable man, the Duke of Norfolk was also in London, and he had full confidence in the abilities of both men to squash any rumblings of discontent. Besides, he had embarked on this Progress to show himself, his majesty and justice to precisely those of his subjects who might have doubts about them, and in this he had appeared to succeed beyond his wildest hopes. And now he was in York, where doubtless if he had appeared with ten wives (as long as they were all Nevilles), or a train of demons, they would still have cheered him to the echo, because he was one of their own. He was home, however briefly, his wife rode in state by his side, her long fair hair sparkling in the sun and her rather shy smile wider than he had seen it for months, and behind them, perched somewhat insecurely atop a dazzlingly white palfrey of impeccable manners, his eight-year-old son, a pale fragile boy with something of the spirit, though muted by ill-health, of his cousin Richard, once Duke of York. The reunion with his son had been the most moving, emotional moment of the Progress, and the King had decided, then and there, to create him Prince of Wales. The formal investiture would take place in ten days' time, on the Feast of the Blessed Virgin's Nativity, and frantic orders to the Royal Wardrobe, only now recovering from the strain of supplying the coronation robes, would shortly go south. Young Ned had been somewhat bemused by the news that he would shortly become Prince of Wales, a title he still associated with his cousin and namesake. Glancing back at the boy's thin face, smiling in surprise and delight at the cheering masses in the street as if he could not believe that they were applauding him, the King hoped that Ned's precarious health—he was much prone to infection and nosebleeds, and always seemed to be lacking in physical energy—would stand up to the exacting demands of the ceremony. Ned would do his best, he always did, but his parents could not help feeling anxious about him.

There was at least one member of his entourage who was also uneasy, though for an entirely different reason. Christie, riding a somewhat subdued Bayard, looked round at the familiar streets, all bedecked with arras and tapestries hung down from the windows, displays and pageants in glorious succession, and was aware that this was as much a homecoming for himself as for his King. He was back in the North, cool and wild, stubborn and dour, and he knew that his heart belonged here, however much his head might covet the lush rich pastures of the south. And he was also well aware that it was still home for Dame Margaret Drakelon, his beloved sister, and that one of those windows, crammed with the better sort who would not pack themselves in the streets with the common herd to watch the King and his train ride past, might well contain her. He knew there was a good chance he would see or even meet her during these days in York, and found that he was contemplating the prospect with a mixture of joy and dread. He knew Meg too well: she would have changed indeed if she did not ignore him completely or, perhaps worse, treat him with the coldness and indifference of a stranger. Meg's memory was long: there had been a girl at Alnwick, in their childhood, who had quarrelled with her over some minor juvenile matter, and Meg had never spoken to her again, in all the years afterwards. In such things she had shown a most unchildlike implacability, and he knew her too well to suppose that she had altered. Under that light-hearted, frivolous manner there was steel, his own steel, and she would not have forgiven him.

It hung on his mind to such an extent that at the first gathering of local dignitaries and their wives, in the noble surroundings of the great Guildhall by the edge of the River Ouse, he could have thought that every one of those ladies, in their trailing gowns of silk and velvet, might be Meg. More than once he almost approached a complete stranger: and so it was a greater shock when he turned in response to his name and saw Sir Robert Drakelon approaching, Meg on his arm.

She was pregnant, heavily so. It was the first thing he noticed about her, that grotesque disfiguring mound bulging out beneath her swollen breasts, and the shock was so great that something of his revulsion must have shown on his face, for the smile on Sir Robert's became rather fixed, and the open blue eyes narrowed. But they exchanged courtesies in civil enough fashion, and Christie, in perfect command of himself once more, congratulated his sister.

It was as he had most feared. The brilliant blue eyes turned coldly to his own. 'I thank you, sir,' said Meg distantly, as if he were unknown to her, instead of the brother who had been closer to her than anyone else alive. 'But I beg, if you will excuse me, husband, I must go sit down.'

Sir Robert escorted her to a chair, most solicitously. Christie stared at her misshapen body, knowing that a reconciliation between the couple must have been effected not long after he had, so disastrously, gone to see her. At least, he thought unhappily, she seemed now to be on good terms with her husband, and he could be sure that she would be tended as she deserved: certainly the cold Sir Robert was fussing over her like a mother hen with one chick. Doubtless he hoped that the child—due, obviously, within the month—would be the longed-for son and heir. Christie wondered, though, why he had brought her to York if she was so close to her time. He must know or guess that there was coolness between his wife and her brother: did he hope to mend matters?

But Sir Robert, returning with apologies—all care must be taken of his dear wife, she had had a difficult pregnancy—seemed to have noticed nothing unusual in Meg's behaviour: as if, thought Christie sourly, he could see nothing beyond the swollen belly that might contain his long-awaited heir. 'I am surprised that you did not leave her at Denby, if you are so concerned for her,' he said.

Sir Robert's eyes glanced sharply at him, as if noting the covert hostility: then, as ever, they shifted to a point somewhere behind Christie's left shoulder. Since he was standing before an arras depicting a most bloodthirsty hunting scene, he hoped that his brother-in-law was enjoying the view.

'Indeed, I did my utmost to persuade her to stay behind,' said Sir Robert. 'But she would not miss the King's visit, and insisted on being brought in a litter. As you well know, my dear wife has a very strong will. But she seems well enough, though somewhat tired, and was greatly cheered by the spectacle—as indeed was I. Now, we have heard nothing but rumours for months—I will have the truth from you about everything that has been happening in London, dear brother.'

Christie was conscious of a stab of annoyance at being called 'dear brother' by a man he disliked and distrusted, and was more brief, obviously, than Sir Robert would have wanted. He knew nothing of how the man's loyalties would lie—whether he, as a Yorkshireman, would follow the King, or whether, as a former member of King Edward's household, would cleave rather to the boy in the Tower. Since he had a shrewd idea that his brother-in-law's heart, at bottom, was given only to his own interests, he was not especially informative, even when pressed by a gently insistent Sir Robert. Then, somewhat to his relief, Sir James Tyrell, now Master of the Horse and Master of the King's Henchmen, joined them, breezily disgusted with the behaviour of one of his young charges, John Berkely, who was only eleven years old and rather inexperienced in matters of Court etiquette. He had none of Christie's misgivings about supplying Sir Robert with all the news he required, and soon the two knights were deep in discussion of the coronation, in which of course Sir James had played a considerable part, and the coming investiture of the Prince of Wales. Christie seized his chance: he slipped gently away, and went to find his sister Meg.

It was against his better judgement, since she had been so cool towards him, and he expected only another rebuff: but there was a germ of hope inside his head, for surely, if she had truly not wished to see him, she would have submitted happily to her husband's desire to leave her safe at Denby, with her precious child so close to birth? She must have known that Christie would almost certainly be in the King's train, and that the likelihood of their meeting at some time in York was quite high. Why come at all, if she did not in her heart wish to see him?

She was not in the chair to which Sir Robert had guided her so carefully. He glanced round the lovely crowded Hall, seeking a rose-coloured gown and a darker, white-veiled cap of carnation velvet. He found her at last, standing without a trace of fatigue by one of the windows in animated conversation with a much plainer young woman of similar age. For a moment she was unaware of him, and he saw the old Meg, her lovely face bright with joy and laughter, her long pale hands dancing expressively as she talked. Then she saw him, and the shutters came down on her merriment. The other girl glanced over, brows raised, and her eyes widened in expectation. There was no doubt she had guessed who he was, and probably, from her expression, she knew of the rift between them.

Meg's face was cold and bitter, her beautiful blue eyes bleak. 'I have nothing to say to you. You may leave us.'

He was made of the same metal as she, and would not be so easily dismissed. 'Meg, I have no intention of leaving you. Madam, will you excuse us? I have matters to discuss with my sister.'

Meg's friend hesitated and glanced at her. Meg's reply was cold and final. 'There is no need for you to leave, Dorothy. There is nothing for me to discuss with my brother. Now will you go, sir? I do not wish to speak with you.'

There was nothing he could do, nothing, no chink in her armour at all: and the presence of the other girl made it impossible to beg, to plead with her for the forgiveness she withheld so sternly, for a return to the happy friendship they had shared for so long. He could not believe that all those years counted for nothing in her view: and yet he knew his Meg so well, and could not expect any mercy. He sought her eyes, desperate to communicate what he could not say in words: but, like her husband, she would not look at him, only at a point beside him. He said at last, his voice low and calm, disguising his distress, 'So be it, Meg. I will submit to your wishes, and take my leave. But, I beg you, remember my vow.'

For an instant, her eyes flashed directly at him. 'Why should I? You had no difficulty in forgetting it. Good day to you, sir.'

Defeated, he bowed to her and to her friend, and abruptly, to conceal the hurt, turned and strode over to where Sir Ralph Bigod, now carver to the Queen, was talking to a worthy citizen of York. At this bitter moment, he could not bear to face Sir Robert Drakelon, and the knowingness in those sly shifting untrustworthy eyes.

CHAPTER TEN

'Overmuch harm, and too great a loss.'
(BOOK 10, CHAPTER 33)

It was fortunate that Christie was kept very busy over the next few days, in the hectic preparations for the Prince's investiture: there was no time to brood on his meeting with his sister, in the rush to organise a suitably impressive ceremony. Robes, banners, horse harness, and even thirteen thousand fustian badges depicting the White Boar device of the King, had been ordered from London: the Wardrobe, excelling themselves, returned the goods within two days of receiving the lists. But there were several nerve-wracking days before the trains of baggage arrived in York, and it was Christie's task to ensure that local tailors and clothmerchants were prepared in case of disaster. It also fell to him to intervene in a trivial but explosive dispute between two of the lesser members of the King's retinue and the worthy citizen in whose house they were billeted, and in addition he was given the task of overseeing the preparation of the ceremonial route between the Archbishop's palace and the Minster, and had to ride about the streets through which the triumphant procession would wind, ensuring that they were raked clear of filth and rubbish, and strewn with fresh-smelling herbs. It was past summer, and there were few flowers, so that statues of saints and crosses and conduits were decked with greenery like Christmas, and here and there a flash of wildflower colour, the yellow of marigolds or the faded blue of meadow scabious.

Despite the haste, the ceremony passed off splendidly: the citizens of York cheered to a man, woman and child, White Boar badges everywhere, as the King and Queen walked hand in hand with their son, almost vanished within the richness of his robes, amidst their joyous subjects. It was a much more informal occasion than the elaborate ancient ceremony of the coronation: and yet, Christie found this the more moving, as his sovereign accepted, with a rare and visible delight on his thin pale face, the tumultuous acclaim of these, his truest subjects.

For exactly eleven days, the idyll continued. The City Guilds

[209]

performed their plays for the King and Queen: there were banquets and feasts at the Guildhall and at the Palace. Hunting trips, jousting, archery contests were all arranged, and it seemed at times to the people of York, sated and dazzled with display and spectacle, that the days following the Prince's investiture were as much a public holiday as the twelve days of Christmas.

On the twelfth day, the blow fell.

A messenger in the red and blue of the Duke of Norfolk's livery galloped into York on an exhausted and foundering horse. He asked to be taken to the King, directly, without wasting time cleaning the mud and lather from his clothes and was ushered into Richard's presence.

It was a charming, intimate domestic scene. The Queen and two of her ladies were sewing in the evening light from one of the windows of this, the absent Archbishop's privy chamber, while the King and his small son were seated together on a pile of cushions in the other windowseat, playing with a very young hound puppy which had been presented to the child by Lord Lovell, whose family badge was a dog not dissimilar. A tall young man with an odd face, all bones and angles and uncomfortable grey eyes, wearing the white boar collar of a Squire of the Body, approached and asked his business.

'I have a message from His Grace the Duke of Norfolk—for the King's ear,' said the messenger, still short of breath after his ride: he had never thought to reach York only on the third day after his departure from London, and bearing in mind the importance and urgency of his errand, he was glad the roads had been good, his horses excellent, and the weather kind. He watched as the Squire approached the King, who greeted him with a smile that faded as the other man spoke, and then turned and assessed the messenger with chill grey eyes. Then the Squire returned to him. 'The King asks me to conduct you to him. All the people in this room are utterly trustworthy—your message may be delivered in full confidence.'

Confident was not the way the messenger felt as he followed the Squire across the herb-strewn flagstones of the Archbishop's chamber. Sweet smells—rosemary, chamomile, thyme—arose to assail him as he walked, searching for words that would convey the essence of the news he brought, without undue alarm or exaggeration. He had no more success now than on the long weary bone-shaking hours of his ride north: the Duke of Norfolk had chosen him for his trustworthiness and riding ability rather than his eloquence. He knelt before the King, kissed the outstretched hand, and rose, twisting his cap between his fingers.

'You have urgent news from His Grace of Norfolk?' said the King, his hands playing with the soft furry ears of the puppy, while the Queen and her ladies watched with interest and the Squire, tall and deferential, stood to one side and waited.

He swallowed, and fumbled within his doublet for the sealed letter. 'I have it written here, Your Grace, though not plain—His Grace of Norfolk did not wish it to fall into hostile hands. But my chief message I must tell you, Your Grace, and it is this.' He took a deep breath, and let the words follow as the Duke had spoken them to him, three days ago in London.

'His Grace of Norfolk bids me say that there has been an attempt on the lives of the children in the Tower.'

The Queen gasped, and put her hands to her mouth: the hound puppy gave a sudden yelp as the King's grip tightened convulsively on its ears. Only the Squire did not move: even little Prince Edward stared in wide-eyed alarm at the messenger. The King said, his voice very quick and sharp, 'An attempt? Was it not successful, then?'

'Not yet, Your Grace, to my knowledge. Both boys were alive when I left London, though the Lord Edward was grievously sick. He took most of the poison, the doctor thinks.'

'Poison?' The King's voice rose, and the Queen, her veils flying, leapt to her feet and ran to him, her hand reaching out to clasp his. 'Does the letter have the details, or do you?'

'The Duke wrote only of what has been done to find the culprits, Your Grace. He thought it best that I tell you the full story—he wished it safe from prying eyes.'

'I don't blame him,' said Richard drily. 'I trust this tale has not travelled? Who knows of it?'

'The Duke, Your Grace, and the Chancellor. The Constable of the Tower, Robert Brackenbury. The children's attendants at the time of the attempt—there were three of them, all trustworthy, as you know, Your Grace. And the physician called to treat the elder boy. No-one else.'

'Save yourself,' the King reminded him. 'Who was the physician?'

'I believe it was your own, Your Grace—Dr Hobbs.'

'Well, he at least can keep a still tongue in his head—a man of

[211]

sense, unlike that excitable gossip-monger Argentine. Now, tell the full tale—from the beginning, as you know or have been told, and leave nothing out.' His keen eyes travelled over the messenger's dishevelled appearance and weary face. 'And wine and wafers for you while you speak, and a hearty meal when you've finished. Christie?'

Christie Heron, who knew exactly what was required of him, went silently to the door to summon the chamberlain, who would relay the request for refreshments to lesser mortals. Behind him, the messenger's dust-thickened voice spoke with the plain words of the ordinary man, of the disaster that had so nearly befallen the two sons of Edward IV.

'It happened five days ago, Your Grace—last Sunday. The children had been in the garden, shooting and playing with two other boys their own age.'

'Who were they?' the King's voice interrupted sharply.

'I do not know, Your Grace. The children of one of your Household in the Tower, I believe. They had all been playing together very well, although the Lord Bastard Edward complained of feeling sick, and seemed unhappy. This is what I was told, Your Grace. Your nephews went back to their apartments to prepare for supper, and it was when they were at the table that the Bastard Edward was taken ill. He was very sick, Your Grace, and seized with a violent griping in his belly. The younger boy seemed fine at first, and then he also became unwell. A message was sent urgently to the Chancellor in Westminster, and he despatched Dr Hobbs to tend the children. The Bastard Richard soon recovered, but at first his brother's life was despaired of, and the Chancellor himself prepared to shrive him, for they could not find a more trustworthy priest, and the boys' illness had been kept very close. I am told,' the messenger added, with a weary smile, 'that it was the Duke of York—I mean, the Bastard Richard—who rallied his brother from death and urged him to live so that he would not be left alone. And by the mercy of God, the boy did not after all die, and lives yet and grows better, though he is still very weak and had not left his bed when the Duke of Norfolk and the Chance'lor bade me come here.'

Christie, back in his place by the windowseat, saw that Queen Anne was silently weeping, and that her son had both his small thin arms around her: his purpose, he further saw without surprise, for young Prince Edward was a kindly, good-natured boy, was to give comfort rather than to receive it.

[212]

'You tell a sorry tale,' the King said, his face sombre and concerned. 'But there is no word of poison in it. Why is the Chancellor so sure that there is poison involved? The children could have eaten tainted meat, or suffered from some contagion.'

'That is what their attendants thought, Your Grace. But when the Chancellor arrived at the Tower, the Bastard Richard told him that he thought his brother was the worse because he had eaten too many of the sweetmeats, whereas he himself had only had two or three. But their attendants knew nothing of any sweetmeats. The Chancellor asked the boys where they had got the sweetmeats from, and they said that they had found a box of them left on a table in their apartments, and assumed that they had been sent as a gift from their mother, Dame Elizabeth Grey.'

'And had they?'

'No, Your Grace. No messenger from Westminster had come to the Tower that day. Dame Grey does not know of this, we are certain.'

'And she would be the last person to try to poison her own sons,' said the King, without a trace of irony. 'All her hopes for the future are pinned to those children. Why did the boys think the sweetmeats came from their mother, then?'

'I think there was a note to that effect on the box, Your Grace.'

The eyes of the King and Queen, grey and blue, met, and held. Then Richard turned back to the messenger. 'Were there any of the sweetmeats left? What were they?'

'They were marchpane, Your Grace—the elder boy apparently has a great fondness for marchpane, his brother less so. All the Tower knows that, according to the Constable. They had eaten perhaps half the box when they were called in to supper. The younger boy says that he can remember putting it down on a window-ledge, but when the children were taken ill, it had disappeared.'

'And you say my nephew Richard is well? What of his brother?'

'The Bastard Richard is indeed well, Your Grace, and as anxious to catch the culprits as the Duke and the Chancellor.'

'I can well imagine it. And Edward?'

'The Duke told that he is weak, but daily getting better, thanks be to God, Your Grace. However, he has been very cast down by the discovery that he was poisoned, and has had much recourse to prayer. He lived in daily fear for his life, the Duke said.'

'Does he blame me for the poison?'

The messenger shot a startled, guilty glance at the King that told its own story. After a long silence, he muttered, 'I—I believe so, Your Grace—forgive me, I believe he does.'

Richard sighed, and turned his head to look out of the window: the yellow stone of the Minster amid the lush grass of the close, speckled with strolling clerics and courtiers ignorant of the crisis within. His son, studying his face earnestly, put a small hand on his sleeve. 'Father, why does my cousin think you want to kill him? He ought to know you better than that—*I* know you wouldn't kill anyone who wasn't your enemy, and he isn't, is he?'

'No, Ned, he is not,' said the King wearily, and his hand rested on the straight light-brown hair capping the boy's head, as if giving a blessing. 'But he thinks I stole the crown from him, and he cannot trust or forgive me. I had hoped to have him and his brother join you at Middleham—you would like that, would you not? I thought so—but now I must think again, for a while at least. Let me read the Chancellor's letter.'

As he scanned it, a deep frown engraved between the dark brows, a servant entered with the wine and wafers. Christie served his royal master with a silver goblet, half-full as Richard preferred, and another for the Queen. The messenger, patently at the end of his resources, received his gratefully, and took a large gulp more in place inside a tavern than the King's privy chamber. The servant, unobtrusive, withdrew as Richard finished reading. 'The Chancellor tells me that the culprits have not been apprehended for this dreadful crime, although he, the Duke and the Constable have made most strenuous efforts to discover their identity. He says, however, that they have not been able to be completely thorough because of the need for secrecy. If it became known that someone had tried to kill my nephews, there would be few men who would not place the blame at my door. There have been rumours of rebellion for some weeks now, though nothing definite, nothing that I can move against—but my informants assure me that the talk is of freeing young Edward from the Tower to place him on the throne again. Men wishing to do that would hardly poison him first, would they, my love?'

'No, they would not,' said the Queen thoughtfully. 'But there must be others who would prefer to see both you and the children eliminated. Adherents of the house of Lancaster, for instance.'

'Lancaster? They have only one poor feeble claimant left, and he's a pensioner of the Duke of Brittany—my brother tried several times to lay his hands on him, but without success. Now there have been the Duke's insolent demands—you remember, he threatened to hand the Tudor over to the French King unless I sent him four thousand soldiers, for which I of course must pay. So I told him he could send Henry Tudor to the King of Cathay for all I cared, and there the matter rests, for the moment. I trust Tudor is too busy worrying whether he's going to spend the rest of his days in Paris or Brittany to concern himself about matters in England, still less the fate of two bastard children.' He glanced at the Queen's sceptical face, and smiled at her in a way that spoke more eloquently than any words of his trust and affection. 'You disagree, my love?'

'The Tudor himself may be of little account,' said Queen Anne, with the political insight she had learned from her father, the great Kingmaker. 'But his value is not intrinsic—he is a bargaining counter, as you yourself have just indicated. Some would crown an ape, if it had blood of Lancaster. And he has powerful friends, both here and in France and Brittany. Might some of them not have acted on his behalf, to clear his way to an attempt on the throne? You are not sure whom you can trust, and these rumours of rebellion are proof of that. If one attempt has failed, another may be made—and it might well succeed, poor Edward and Dickon killed and the blame for their murder placed on you, as yet another incentive for revolt.' She placed a hand on his, looking very earnestly into her husband's thin anxious face. 'I know, you know, your friends and household and government know, that you simply are not capable of such a dreadful, unnatural deed as murdering your own brother's sons. But the people, the people in the country, the people who spread rumour and gossip in taverns, even many of the knights and squires who served your brother, don't know that. They don't know *you*, dearest, as we do. They see only that you have put Edward aside and yourself in his place, and they are hostile and suspicious. You understand that, I am sure—it is natural for the ignorant to distrust that which they do not know. The children are not safe now, whoever tried to kill them will surely try again—and they're obviously subtle and secretive, and very clever. You must *do* something, Richard, you must make sure they don't succeed— I couldn't bear it if those two sweet boys were killed when it could have been prevented, and then their deaths laid at your door.'

'Don't worry, sweetheart—I have a plan in mind already,' the King assured her. He turned to the messenger, who had been somewhat restored by the wine and crisp fresh wafers, aristocratic food he sampled all too seldom. 'Can you enlarge on the attempts made to find the poisoners?'

The messenger could, a little. All the boys' attendants had been questioned most rigorously, but all had strenuously denied any involvement, and their loyalty and trustworthiness seemed beyond question—they had been appointed by the King himself, or by the Duke of Buckingham, and were beyond reproach. Yet no-one else could have had such easy access to the children's apartments, unless taking advantage of a lapse in the watch kept over them. The whole affair was utterly mysterious, and the Chancellor confessed to being baffled: even to suspecting that the sweetmeats had in fact been harmless, and the boys had after all fallen victim to some unpleasant but quite natural sickness. But the possibility of poison remained, and both the Duke and the Chancellor advised that further measures to be taken to protect the children. Only the King could authorise this, however, and meanwhile their attendants and guards had been temporarily changed, as a precaution.

The King, deep in thought, thanked the messenger and dismissed him, with two gold angels from his own purse as a reward for his service, and instructions to seek out the hot meal awaiting him in the chamber allotted him by the chamberlain. Then Queen Anne, at her husband's request, dismissed her two ladies. The room was silent, waiting, only the arras stirring in the draught from the door, and the crackle and hiss of the fire burning briskly in the huge hearth. The King glanced at his son, who was curled drowsily against him, and then beckoned Christie closer. 'Have you heard all of this unhappy tale?'

'I have, Your Grace.'

'And you were in Edward's household, were you not—from Stony Stratford to the Tower. He knows you—does he trust you?'

There was another silence, as Christie remembered with pity the frightened lonely child he had left three months ago. How much more must he be terrified now, knowing that someone had tried to kill him—and certain that the man behind the attempt was his uncle, who had stolen his crown? Honestly, he said quietly, 'I don't know. He might—I flatter myself he had some regard, some liking for me. But I would not stake my life on it.'

'Would you stake his?'

'What do you mean, Your Grace?'

'I mean, that you are one of the few people that I can trust absolutely. You know the messenger's story, one of only a handful who do. It seems clear to me that, despite what the Chancellor thinks, the poisoner must be someone very close to the children; someone with access to their apartments—a guard, an attendant, even a lowly washerwoman or cook or kitchen servant. Short of dismissing half the Tower's staff, and letting the secret out, we cannot be sure of removing the danger. No, what we must do is remove the *children*—and as secretly as possible, so that the assassin does not know that they have gone or, more importantly, where they have gone. It can be given out within the Tower that they are suffering some illness that is not dangerous but infectious, so that no-one will be surprised when most of their attendants are withdrawn. Later, when the danger has gone, they can come north—perhaps join young Edward of Warwick at Sheriff Hutton, or come to you at Middleham, eh, Ned? All these Edwards and Richards are confusing, aren't they?'

'No, they're not,' said his son sleepily. 'I'm Ned, and my cousins are quite different from me, even if we do all have the same name.' He yawned, and the Queen, smiling, said, 'Time you were in bed, my young prince. Your squire will be here soon—give him a surprise and be in your chamber before the time. And you can have the puppy with you tonight, tell him I said so. Now pay your respects to me and your father, and off you go.'

Christie watched as the little boy, small and frail even beside his light-boned parents, made his courtesies and received a less formal kiss from King and Queen before racing, the hound puppy at his heels, from the room. As the door slammed behind him, Anne said, 'I thought it best he go, before your plans are laid. He's so bright and intelligent, he has understood everything, I am sure—and so happy and trusting that we cannot be certain that he will not spill out the truth to someone who might use it maliciously.'

Her husband looked at Christie, a faint sad smile on those inflexible lips. 'Alas, I am growing to realise how many of those there might be. Fortunately, I have my loyal men of the North, on whom I can rely absolutely—and you, Christie, are most emphatically one of those. In the years since you came to Middleham—how many are they? Two? Three?—Since I took you into my household, you have amply repaid my trust and faith in you. Your current position is an indication of that, but I can tell you, if you carry out the mission I have in mind successfully, I will reward you far more lavishly, for it will be a difficult task, and possibly a dangerous one. Is your servant also be be trusted? I have not heard any bad reports of him lately.'

'He is a reformed character,' Christie said, grinning at the thought of Perkin's likely reaction to the news of royal interest in his faults. 'If he is not to be trusted, then I am no judge of a man's nature, nor of anything else.'

'Good. He must of necessity know of this enterprise. Now, would you tell the chamberlain that I wish to speak with Sir James Tyrell? And that we will all take a private and quiet supper in this chamber. You and Sir James may eat with us, and so our secret will remain privy between us four. The fewer who know, the better.'

Sir James Tyrell, honest and square and very evidently somewhat puzzled and surprised by his unexpected summons, soon appeared, as did a splendid supper, fine demain bread and rich crumbly cheese, pigeons roasted brown and crisp, wine and good north-country ale and pottage and crusty pies surrounding tender young pigeons, rabbits and partridges, with baked oranges and quince marmalades, new rosy apples, juicy and sweet, and plums and pears donated by a wealthy citizen of York from his own orchards. By court standards it was a scanty and informal meal, lacking in any ceremony, King and Queen serving themselves and each other, as they might when alone together in their bedchamber. In between mouthfuls, Richard acquainted his Master of Horse with the attempted murder of the boys in the Tower, and Sir James's undistinguished, weathered features grew more appalled as the tale unfolded. At the last he said abruptly, 'So there's still some assassin skulking undiscovered in the Tower? And the boys are still there? You know me, Your Grace, I'm naught but a plain old soldier, but you can't tell me they're safe there until that thrice-cursed murderer is caught.'

'You're right,' said Richard. He had finished his meal, and was absently toying with a dark, purple-skinned plum, tossing it idly from hand to hand. It was noticeable how he had relaxed in the intimate surroundings, and was once more recognisable as the Lord of Middleham. 'And we can't catch him because even to try would be to tell all London that my nephews had been poisoned, and naturally I'd have the blame laid at my feet. So the answer is to smuggle the boys out of the Tower, and spirit them away some-where remote, somewhere that no-one will suspect, a hiding place where they'll be safe until all threat of revolt, from whatever source, is removed. We mustn't forget, either, that murder isn't the only danger they face. My informants have wind of a plot afoot to snatch them out of the Tower and proclaim Edward as King. And that would bring war again, without a doubt.'

It was raining outside, as dusk grew, and drops spattered gently against the small leaded panes of glass in the windows. In the minds of all four there arose dread spectres, death and pestilence, brother fighting brother, families torn apart, slaughter and devastation across the rich pleasant green fields of England. It had happened before: Tewkesbury had been fought only twelve years previously, Sir James had been knighted there, and Anne Neville's first husband, Holy Harry's disputed son, had died: her own father had been killed at the battle of Barnet, fighting against a Yorkist army that included the young Richard, Duke of Gloucester, still in his teens. Their childhood, their youth, had been marred and savaged by war, and the grim possibility of another decade of civil strife seemed all at once to loom very close.

Tyrell, when he spoke, seemed much more cheerful: he was, after all, as he was so fond of telling everyone, a practical man of action. 'So, we smuggle the lads out and take 'em—where, Your Grace? Gipping?'

The King's normally immobile mouth cracked in a sudden smile. 'You have read my mind, Sir James. Yes, Gipping. Your home is small, remote, isolated, I know this from what you yourself have told me. Your wife is a gentle lady, of wit and charm, and you have young children of your own. Further, no-one will think of looking for Edward and Dickon there—they will expect to find them in the Tower, or at Baynards Castle, or Westminster—or they might think I have taken them North, to Sheriff Hutton or Middleham, as indeed I plan to do when all these uncertainties are settled. Then perhaps that wretched woman calling herself Queen Dowager can be persuaded out of sanctuary with her daughters, and they can all live quietly somewhere while we continue with the task of bringing peace, justice and good government to this troubled country. It's a dream, perhaps, but a pleasant one, and please God we will make it come true. Well, Sir James? Are you willing to take my nephews into your household, and keep them secret and safe? It's a considerable responsibility.'

'And one I'll gladly undertake,' said the Master of Horse. 'You needn't fear for the boys, Your Grace—my dear Anne will take good care of them, and there's our four young ruffians to keep them company. The country's quiet thereabouts, and the Duke of

Norfolk looms large in Suffolk. No, Your Grace, I'd be glad to have them at Gipping. How are they to be taken there? Do you want me to do it?'

'You and Christie here. He was in Edward's household for a while, and the boy knows him—and, we hope, will go willingly with you both, and his brother too. They must leave the Tower as secretly as possible, ideally in disguise, but you must decide those details for yourselves, in consultation with Brackenbury. No-one else must know, for the moment. I will inform the Chancellor and the rest of the Council separately, but only the Chancellor will know exactly where the boys have been taken.' He glanced at Sir James, than at Christie, holding their attention with the full force of his personality, suddenly positive and incisive as it always was in action, or under extreme pressure. 'You two are amongst my most trusted servants. This is an enterprise that must not fail. Not only are the lives of those two innocent children at stake—the whole safety of the kingdom lies in question. I cannot give you an armed escort, for speed and secrecy are vital. I must send you out to save my nephews from harm or death at the hands of vicious and unprincipled murderers, with no other help but your own wits. Christie will take his servant—have you a man you can trust utterly, Sir James? What of Wellesborne?'

'You know as well as I do that I would place my life in his keeping, and I doubt young Kit here could say as much of his rogue Hobbes. He can keep a close tongue in his head, too. Have no fear, Your Grace—Kit Heron and I will rescue your nephews for you, and confound those murdering devils—spawn of Lancaster, I wouldn't wonder.'

Sir James could be said himself to be spawn of Lancaster, his father having been executed for conspiring against Edward IV, and his first cousin killed at the battle of Barnet fighting for the Kingmaker, not to mention various other cousins, uncles and more distant relations who had all fought for the unfortunate Harry VI. Sir James's loyalty to York, however, and in particular to Richard, was undoubted, tried and tested.

'They may or may not owe allegiance to the last sorry remnants of the line of Lancaster: it matters little in comparison with their offence against my nephews and myself, not to mention the rest of my family—and the boys' unfortunate mother. And as they must undoubtedly be planning another attempt, your mission is most urgent. You must leave at dawn, ride hard and secretly—three or four days should see you in London, if you change horses at the usual inns. Go straight to the Tower, and give Robert Brackenbury my message and instructions—I will write nothing down, you must carry it all in your heads. Then you must take the boys from the Tower. I leave the details up to you and Brackenbury, and of course Edward and Richard must be persuaded to go with you willingly—carrying them kicking and screaming from the Tower will not help our cause of secrecy,' he added with a dry smile. 'The success of your task depends to a great extent on your own initiatives, and I have complete confidence in your ability to do it. I will give you a token to show to Brackenbury, to prove the truth of your words, and so you must come to me before dawn tomorrow, so that you can set out in good time. Go now, so that you have a good night's sleep, and I will arrange fast horses for you.'

'And go with my hopes and my blessing,' Queen Anne added softly. 'If you save those dear children from danger, then surely you will earn God's thanks as well as ours. May He keep you safe and bring those boys to a secure and happy harbour. Their lives depend on you two alone—take care, Sir James, take care, Christie, for I long to see my nephews again.'

*

'The children are dead.' Sir Thomas Bray shut the door of the parlour at Ashcott behind him, and stared with stricken eyes at his wife and daughter, stitching together, peaceably for once, at an arras. Dame Alice lifted her head and fixed her basilisk gaze on her husband. 'I told you,' was her sharp comment. 'I told you he wouldn't let them live long. He knows they're a threat to him, and your friends are proof of that. Who told you? Is it common knowledge?'

'John Harcourt told me,' said Sir Thomas heavily. He crossed to his chair, a huge oak affair close to the roaring fire, and dropped his bulk wearily into it. 'It's not common knowledge in the sense that it's been given out officially, no. But there's certain word from London, though no details as yet—nothing as to how, or when. On whose orders, I fear, is rather more obvious.'

'The King's, of course,' said Julian fiercely. 'If you can call him King—usurper or murderer would be more appropriate.'

'He was crowned and anointed,' her father reminded her. 'And such a King can only be removed from the throne by death. Of course, the fact that the Princes are dead puts a new complexion on our plans. We cannot now restore poor little King Edward to his rightful throne—we must look elsewhere for the man to dislodge the usurper.' He glanced meaningfully at his wife, and Dame Alice's plain large features were suddenly, extraordinarily, irradiated with joy. 'Aah!' she said, on a long-drawn breath. 'They will ask Henry Tudor?'

'They *have* asked Henry Tudor, or rather, to give him his proper title, the Earl of Richmond. Queen Elizabeth has learned of her sons' sad deaths, and not unnaturally wishes to be revenged on their murderer. She had agreed to marry her eldest daughter to him, should he succeed, and thus unite the houses of Lancaster and York. We also have another illustrious name to add to our supporters. The Duke of Buckingham has agreed to join us, and be leader of the English risings, while the Earl of Richmond invades with his French troops.'

'Buckingham.' Dame Alice's voice was scornful. 'And what's that gilded popinjay seeking that he can't get from his royal master, eh? Or is he after the crown himself?'

'The word is, that he has repented of his former error, in dislodging the rightful King. Moreover, he apparently changed his allegiance because he was repelled by the news of the murder of the Princes.' He crossed himself. 'May God assoil them. We will pray for them: there will be a mass said for their souls in the chapel this evening. But with God's help their murderer will not enjoy the fruits of his sins for long. There is a date set for the rising, and it is the eighteenth of October—exactly four weeks hence.'

'So long,' said Julian. The arras quite forgotten, she stared intently at her father, her face afire with impatience. 'Four weeks! Why not sooner? Surely everything is ready, and all your plans completed?'

'They are not fully worked out yet,' Sir Thomas told her. 'There are men in many counties who will rise with us, but they must be organised. The setting of an agreed date is only the beginning. Arms have to be obtained and made ready, horses organised, meeting-places set. A messenger has gone oversea to the Earl of Richmond, naming the appointed day and a suitable landing place, and the main reason for the delay, poppet, galling as it may seem to you, is to allow the Earl time to gather ships and men for the invasion. The Duke of Brittany has promised to help him, and he has the treasure taken by Sir Edward Woodville when the old King died—it's only just and right, after all, that King Edward's money should be used to help avenge the murder of his sons.'

'And what support have you?' Dame Alice demanded. 'I know there's no love for King Richard hereabouts, but how many have committed themselves to your cause? How many have promised soliders, or arms? Will they keep to their promises? Fine words win no kingdoms, you know, husband.'

Patiently, Sir Thomas gave her the details. 'The men of Kent will rise and seize the City of London. The King, after all, has given us the perfect opportunity by retreating to his wretched north parts and leaving the field clear. London will fall like a rotten apple. Hereabouts it's mainly Sir William Stonor, John Harcourt and myself to lead our tenants, but further south the country's alive with our supporters. Half the country will rise, and the muster places are at Newbury and at Salisbury. Further to the west, the Marquis of Dorset will lead them, and Sir Thomas St Leger.' He beamed at Dame Alice and Julian, delighted with the success of the conspiracy. 'All the South will rise, wife, and tip Richard Plantagenet off his shaky throne. It's true, yes, we're a mixed bunch—some have long cleaved to Lancaster in secret, others are Woodvilles, or owe allegiance to them. But most of us are like me—plain honest knights and squires who have served King Edward faithfully and do not want to see his son ousted, still less murdered. We began our plotting to replace poor little King Edward on the throne—now we must continue, in order to avenge his death. It is God's will, most assuredly, that we do so.'

In the chapel at Ashcott that evening, the priest, Sir John Mitchell, performed Mass in memory of the children in the Tower, piteously and barbarously slain by order of their wicked uncle, and begged God to care for their innocent souls, now surely ascended to Heaven, and to aid those who would avenge their death. It was a very affecting ceremony. The glow of the candles lit the faces of the Bray family and their servants, and filled the tiny stone chapel with the sweet honey scent of beeswax. The soft light glinted also on the tears trickling down Julian's face. She had always indulged her emotions with untrammelled freedom, but they had up until now been entirely on her behalf, or that of people who directly affected her in one way or another. But this was different. Those two little children, done to death in some grim dark room in the Tower, a knife across the throat perhaps, or a pillow over the face, had nothing to do with her. Their deaths could not influence her life in

[223]

any way whatsoever, they were remote, distant, she had not even seen either of those children, could only imagine two angelic, golden-haired little boys, alone and afraid. And yet she wept for them.

And she wept also for those of their family who still lived: for the Queen in sanctuary, also surely lonely and frightened, with the dreadful grief of her sons' deaths to bear. She had lost Richard Grey, executed at Pontefract three months ago with her brother, Lord Rivers, and the elderly Sir Thomas Vaughan, judged by the Earl of Northumberland and convicted by order of the King: now she had lost these more harmless, utterly defenceless children. What anguish must she feel? And her daughters, too. The Princess Elizabeth was near her own age, and already it seemed this Henry Tudor was desperate to marry her. Julian, aware of new, confused and nameless feelings within her, felt unexpected pangs of envy. No-one seemed to want to marry her, heiress or not: it was months since her father had last mentioned marriage, or someone's son who was seeking a bride. Once she would have felt relief: now there was this strange longing to break free of her childhood, to become truly grown up, to have her own home to order and her own affairs to direct, to have the companionship of a male adult who was neither father nor servant nor priest. And all these disparate urgent emotions coalesced inside her as she prayed earnestly for the souls of the Princes in the Tower, and for their mother and sisters, and set the rain of tears falling down her face.

*

A hundred miles away, in a little stone chamber not unlike the one in which Julian and her parents were praying, Elizabeth Woodville knelt before a prie-dieu all set about with glittering, guttering candles, and called with anguish for God's vengeance on the murderer of her children, and his protection for their innocent souls. Had her own feelings not been so grievous, her eldest daughter might have been more dismissive of this very obvious show of emotion: as it was, Bess also was weeping as she prayed. It was not the death of Edward that upset her so greatly: she had last seen him more than a year ago, and at most half-a-dozen times before that, and he was a comparative stranger to her. No, it was Dickon she mourned, the bright, brave, sunny child who had lightened all their days, his life long, and was now so cruelly snatched away from them, his brilliance snuffed out so casually, as a man might crush a crawling insect in his path. She would always remember the jaunty set of his cap on his riotous yellow hair, the enthusiasm in his grey eyes, his joy at leaving the cramped hushed quarters of sanctuary to taste once more fresh air and freedom.

.That freedom had been an illusion, lasting just as long as his journey to the Tower: for months the few visitors allowed to them had spoken of the boys' confinement, the guard placed on them, allegedly for their own safety, the closer withdrawal within the inmost parts of the fortress until at last they had ceased to be visible at all. And then the Countess of Richmond's doctor, a quiet and competent elderly Welshman with a pleasant smile and a refreshing lack of pretension, had come on one of his usual visits to tend Anne and Katherine, who had both been ill. His face had been gaunt and strained with tragedy, and the Queen had known at once. Bess would never forget the stricken look on her mother's face, perhaps the only truly genuine emotion she had shown for a very long time. Doctor Lewis, very gently, had taken her aside, away from the wide-eyed, fearful gaggle of daughters, and had broken the news to her that her sons had been murdered.

Elizabeth Woodville's wail of anguish had filled all their apartments within the sanctuary, had echoed and coruscated amongst the stones and doors and walls: then the sobbing had begun, and Bess and Cecily, themselves in tears, had gone to comfort their stricken mother. Eventually they had persuaded her, now calling down vengeance upon her children's murderer, to her bed, where one of the few women left to them had administered a soothing drink that had at last done its work and left the exhausted, bereft woman sleeping. Lying gaunt in the great bed, her flesh sunk on her bones and her greying hair spread around her, she had lost at last every vestige of her former beauty.

With pity, but no love, Bess stared down at her mother: then she turned to the doctor. She had come to like him, despite the fact that he came from the Countess of Richmond, a formidable woman of whom she had always been rather afraid, and now she gathered all her failing courage to ask the questions that she must. 'Please, I think I can guess, but tell me—are my brothers dead?'

Doctor Lewis, who even at his age was not immune to the tall, sturdy girl's mass of golden hair and large, tear-filled hazel eyes, put his hand on hers with a daring that afterwards astonished him. 'Oh, madam, I do not want to tell you—I wish I had not been the one—your poor lady mother—oh, madam, I wish I could say it were not true, but alas it is!'

The tears gathered at the corners of Bess's eyes and spilled over. She wiped them away with a determined, ringless hand and said in a whisper, 'Tell me everything—please, spare me nothing. Is it certain?'

'The Countess has made sure that it is true, madam. She has many spies and informants, and she has discovered that the boys were indeed done to death—within the last week, she believes, though she has been unable to discover exactly when they died.'

Bess took a deep breath and looked Doctor Lewis straight in the eye. 'Please tell me if you can—how—how did they die? Was it quick? Did they suffer pain? Were they frightened?'

Doctor Lewis looked away, and then down at the scuffed leather shoes emerging from beneath his black furred gown. 'I am told that it was poison, madam. There was no-one found prepared to slay the poor children outright, so poisoned sweetmeats were given to them. The elder boy succumbed quite quickly, but the younger one lingered in some agony before he died.'

I must not faint, thought Bess, and she clutched at the nearest support, which was the arm of her cool, practical sister Cecily. The dreadful image of her brother Dickon, so much beloved, tossing and crying in unbearable pain with none to comfort him, rose to fill her mind. If I had known, her heart cried out in despair, I would have chained him to my side rather than let him go to that evil man—he must have known even then, he must have planned it from the beginning—and Father trusted him, I trusted him, poor Dickon trusted him! She sobbed convulsively and then pushed the tears from her face as Doctor Lewis spoke, with gentle concern. 'I am so grieved to have to tell you this, madam—I could wish, oh how I could wish, that it were not so.' He waited patiently as the girl fought for self-control: her younger sister, though very pale and shocked, was more calm, standing like a rock to support her. At last, when she could breathe properly, he said carefully, as he had been instructed, 'Are you aware of what these cruel and tragic deaths will mean, madam?'

'They mean that my uncle is a vicious, unnatural murderer,' said Bess fiercely, and in the sudden flash and glare of her hazel eyes there was a strong resemblance to her father. Doctor Lewis shook his head sadly. 'That is indeed true, madam, but I meant, rather, what will their deaths mean to you? For you are now the only true heir of York.'

There was a sudden, total silence. He had been told to convey these necessary facts to the Queen, but she was indisposed: the Countess, knowing Elizabeth Woodville too well, had not made allowances for any display of a mother's natural grief and distress. But these matters concerned the Princess Elizabeth even more closely, and over the weeks of his visits to the sanctuary he had come to admire and respect her judgement and common sense. She was seventeen, of full age to be wed, and he had enough sympathy for her situation to feel the urge to give her at least a little warning of what lay in store for her.

'I suppose I am,' said Bess slowly. 'But I can't be Queen—I have no army to fight for me—and I've no desire, no desire at all to subject England to another war over the crown. I think I'd rather go into a nunnery than cause more death and suffering. If my uncle has murdered my brothers, then I hope God punishes his wickedness, and I'm sure he will—but I do not wish to be the instrument of it.'

'But if another was?' Doctor Lewis pressed home his argument. 'You must know, madam, that my lady, the Countess of Richmond, has been conspiring for some time now with certain knights and gentlemen loyal to your father's memory, to overthrow King Richard and replace your brother on the throne which is rightfully his. That of course, alas, cannot now be. But there is another with a claim to the crown, now in Brittany, you must know of him—the Countess's son, Henry Tudor, Earl of Richmond, who is the heir of the Beaufort line, and the last hope of the house of Lancaster. If he were to marry you, madam, the heiress of the royal house of York, all strife and discord would vanish, and the country would be united under your joint sovereignty. It is the perfect solution, is it not?'

It was too much to take in, on top of her anguish for her brothers. Bess could only look at him helplessly, and weep. But later, after he had gone, she turned over his suggestions in her mind, and pondered them, for one must, as Cecily had already pointed out, be practical. Grieving for Edward and Dickon would not bring them back, nor would it dislodge her wicked uncle from his throne. She had prayed, yes, endlessly, for their innocent souls that surely must pass swiftly through the pains of Purgatory and ascend at last, spotless and joyous, to Heaven. But Doctor Lewis had shown her a way in which she could avenge their deaths: and what better way than to unite in marriage with Henry Tudor, and together take the throne?

So she thought, for the first few days after the tragedy was revealed. The long hours of praying and mourning, the duties involved in tending her mother and the little ones, all of whom were now ill with a persistent cough and fever that would not leave them, did not at first give her much time for reflection. But later, as the early rush of grief subsided and she was able, tentatively, to think of Dickon again without instant tears, a little worm of suspicion crept into her mind. *Could* her father have misjudged his own brother so completely? How and why was the Countess of Richmond able to be so certain that Edward and Dickon were dead? And surely, if she wished to see her son wear the crown, their deaths were far more useful to her, and Henry Tudor, than they would be to the King, who was already fairly firmly seated on the throne.

She must not allow herself to hope: false hope, not despair, was the great destroyer. But the doubt remained, and would not be dispelled. Were they truly dead? And if they were, who had killed them? Her uncle, who had already disposed of them legally, and who would incur the greatest odium if he had them murdered? Or the Countess of Richmond and her supporters, who needed to clear them out of her son's path to the throne, and who could place the blame squarely at the King's door?

She did not know. Cooped up here in sanctuary, it was quite likely that she would never know, and almost certain that she would indeed never see Dickon or his crooked grin again, or hear that cheerful voice urging them to dance and sing and be merry. Her prayers took a new turn, urging care for her brothers' souls if they were dead, and their safety from harm if they were not. She prayed to God, to Christ and His blessed mother, to all the saints she could think of until her voice was hoarsened to a whisper and her knees stiff and sore with too much kneeling. And she prayed also that if the Countess of Richmond had planned their deaths, then she, Elizabeth Plantagenet, would never be called upon to marry her son Henry Tudor.

She wondered what the mysterious Tudor was like. No-one had seen him, no-one could tell her: he had been in exile since childhood. All she knew was his age, twenty-six, which seemed old to her at seventeen: she hoped that he did not favour his mother, who was a small, frightening, clever woman with a hint of ruthless ferocity in her piercing eyes and mean mouth, and whose piety was fierce and uncompromising, unlike the gentler, more retiring devotion of God of Bess's grandmother Cecily, Duchess of York. Bess felt, desperately, the need of her grandmother, who had been closer to her in childhood than her own mother. She could not confide in the Queen at the best of times, let alone now, when Elizabeth Woodville was so immersed in her parade of grief and desire for vengeance, nor in Cecily, from whom she had grown further and further apart since they entered sanctuary. Cecily had thought the marriage with Henry Tudor an excellent one: better Queen of England, in her own country amongst her own family, than, say, Queen of France or Scotland, and alone in a strange land. Cecily would not understand her doubts and fears.

Bess turned over the pages of her little book of hours: a plain volume, much worn and loved, with here and there a tiny exquisite picture like a jewel. And as if of their own accord, her fingers faltered and stopped, and she stared at the familiar sonorous words of the Office for the Dead. Her lips shaped the syllables as her eyes lingered on the painting at the head of the page, a little group of priests and mourners standing vigil over a richly draped bier in a church, all set about with candles. If Edward and Dickon were dead, where did they lie? Had there been anyone to lay them with gentleness and dignity in their coffins, or to light candles about them, or keep the long night watch which she herself, and her mother and sisters, should more properly have done? Or had their small broken bodies been stripped to hide their identity, and thrown into the Thames to roll with the ships and the fishes and the tide, to the endless sea?

A tear, then more, fell on the delicate page, and Bess, heedless of the damage, sat and wept for her doomed brothers, and her father, and for the end, absolute and final, of all childhood and all innocence.

*

The landlord of the Bull at Ware ushered in a succession of servants bearing napkins, steaming dishes, brimming jugs of wine and ale, and watched, a satisfied smile on his round scarlet face, as they set his bounty on the snowy white tablecloth. He did not know his guests, and their names—Master Wilkinson and Master Morley —were unfamiliar, but they were plainly gentlemen of some quality, travelling to London from Lincolnshire, they had said. Since no landlord gained custom by being overly curious, he had asked no further, and had assumed them to be connected in some way—perhaps the younger man was married to the other's daughter?—and engaged upon some lawsuit, or buying in winter goods, cloth, spices, furs, from the City. So he contented himself with indicating each dish—a fine fat capon, fattened up for weeks by a neighbouring farmer who supplied all his meat, including this excellent beef and mutton, and the contents of the steaming bowl of pottage. Finally, with a proud flourish, he drew their attention to the pike, a most splendid creature caught that very day in the River Lea, fried in fresh butter and served with a green sauce richly flavoured with all kinds of herbs from the inn's own garden. He waited only to see their appreciative faces and eagerly poised knives, and withdrew.

In the big Hall where lesser mortals dined all together, he distinguished their servants, a tall well-built man of gentlemanly appearance and a small youth with a wide lipless mouth and an insolent twinkle in his blue eyes. They made an ill-assorted couple, and whereas the boy looked perfectly at home, his companion appeared distinctly ill-at-ease in such common surroundings, as if he did not normally frequent such places. Allowing himself another mild stab of curiosity, the inn-keeper ascertained that all was well, no fights, no drunkenness, no complaints, and returned to the private parlour where his more exalted guests were supping. Outside the door, he adjusted his face from the authoritarian to the deferential, knocked, and entered.

They had certainly done justice to the repast. The pike was picked clean to the bones, head and fins, the rich coney pottage, flavoured with herbs, onions and spices and thickened with eggyolks, reduced to a thin coating round the bowl, the roast stuffed capon lying in spectacular ruin, and no trace left at all of the tender beefsteaks that had been browned on a griddle, liberally spiced, and served with a sharp verjuice sauce. Unnecessarily, the landlord enquired whether the meal had been to the gentlemen's liking, and received the expected answer: he then asked if they wanted more.

'No, thank you, landlord, a splendid supper,' said the older man, stretching luxuriously and belching with repletion. 'But some more wine would be pleasant, eh, Kit?'

His companion smiled rather coldly. 'But not that—Gascon, was it?'

'From Burgundy, sir.'

'From Gascony, Burgundy, wherever—not that one. Hippocras, James? Yes, we'll have your best attempt at hippocras, with honey, if you please, landlord, and plenty of cinnamon.'

A servant was despatched, and the older man turned to the inn-keeper. 'What news have you? Any happenings in London?'

Incongruously, the plump professionally jovial face grew long and tragic. 'Why, yes, sir, most sad and terrible news has come to our town—you may not have heard, if you have been travelling, but they are saying that the Princes, old King Edward's poor little innocent sons, have been foully slain in the Tower of London.'

CHAPTER ELEVEN

'A Queen's son shall not fail thee.'
(BOOK 8, CHAPTER 33)

It was raining on London: Heaven's tears, many might think, weeping for those innocent children, murdered, surely, by order of their wicked uncle. The hour was late, near to vespers, and bells were ringing, vying with the raindrops drumming on the roofs and splashing in the waterlogged streets. There were few people about, and those were hurrying to shelter, hats pulled over faces and well-wrapped against the cold and wet. The four weary travellers arriving at the Red Lion in Aldgate attracted little notice: the young groom who took their horses was too damp and miserable to pay much attention to them, and the chamberlain who led them to a pair of rooms off the gallery running round the rear courtyard, made sure their fires were drawing well and took their orders for supper, showed no sign of recognising either Christie or Perkin—who, it had to be admitted, resembled rather a drowned rat than the son of the Red Lion's landlady. But when the chamberlain had gone, promising to have their supper brought as soon as possible, Perkin found himself instructed to find his mother immediately, and ask her to join them. 'And not a word as to what it's about,' Christie finished sternly: and his servant turned wide innocent eyes on him in horrified reproach before fleeing.

Wellesborne was unpacking their baggage, little enough of it bar two changes of clothing apiece. Christie, who felt uneasy in his silent imperturbable presence, glanced at him before turning to the stalwart, rain-sodden figure of Sir James, steaming gently in front of a new fire rapidly gaining heat. 'Do you think the tale is true?'

The news that the boys were dead had not made any difference to the speed of their journey: the twenty-odd miles from Ware would have been accomplished much more quickly had not Christie's horse cast a shoe at a spot distinguished by its total lack of blacksmiths. At least two hours had been wasted while they had searched and then, at last successful, waited further while the shoe was replaced. Then they had continued as rain began, riding too fast for conversation, but all wondering whether their urgent mission would in fact prove to be in vain. The thought had hung over them, darker than the lowering clouds above, and remained with them now: so that Tyrell knew exactly to which tale Christie referred. He look directly at the younger man. 'I don't know, young Kit. It could be—that fat landlord was very certain. But it was only a tale, a rumour—and rumour has given men five wives before now, never mind prematurely killing off two children. Which is why we must have our supper as soon as may be and go see Brackenbury. He'll know for certain.' He coughed. 'I'm only a plain old soldier —and don't you dare mock me, lad—but haven't you thought those boys might be better dead? Solves a mort of problems. I mean, they're harmless enough now in themselves, but what happens when they grow up, eh?'

There was a silence. Sir James, looking harder at his companion, said, 'You disagree?'

'I disagree. To murder two innocent children, for whatever reason, is a heinous sin.' Christie's light eyes rested speculatively on the older man. 'You have children. Would you have someone murder them for the sake of future convenience?'

Sir James, slightly ill-at-ease, shook his head. 'You know I would not. Only goes to show there's more to you than meets the eye, young Kit. For years I've been thinking you an ambitious ruffian who'd slay your own grandmother if it brought you advancement —and now you turn out to have more scruples than I do.'

Christie was saved from a reply by the entrance, all at once, of Perkin, his mother, and a tray of supper dishes borne by the chamberlain. After the servant had gone, Cis folded her arms and fixed Christie with one of her most shrewd stares. 'Well, what's all this about then, that Perkin's closer than a fresh oyster? And who's your fine friend?'

It was fortunate that Sir James, a man of plain speech himself, did not object to it in others, even those who were his social inferiors. Christie, with an evil grin, turned to the older man. 'Sir James Tyrell—Mistress Cicely Hobbes, lady of this splendid establishment. Cis, we must eat quickly—we'll tell you everything in due course, but for now can you just answer me this—how widespread in London is the rumour that the boys in the Tower are dead?'

'Everyone's heard it,' Cis told him, her mouth tightening, and a deep frown appearing. 'But you'd be able to tell me more than that, wouldn't you, given that you've the King's ear?'

'We don't know if it's true,' Christie said, ignoring the

unpleasant cutting edge in her voice. 'Believe me, Cis, we don't. If the boys *are* dead, we know nothing of who killed them, or how—and neither does the King. If they are not, we have come to take them away to a safer place.'

'I didn't think there *was* any place safer than the Tower,' was Cis's caustic comment. Sir James turned to her. 'On the contrary, Mistress Hobbes—we have certain information that there has already been one unsuccessful attempt on their lives. And not ordered by the King, you can be sure of that, but by his enemies.'

Cis looked from one man to the other, still the highly sceptical frown on her face. 'I'll believe it when I see them,' she said finally.

'Well, if they are still alive, you will see them—and tonight,' Christie told her. 'We plan to smuggle them out of the Tower, in disguise, and lodge them here before we leave tomorrow.' He forestalled her next question by adding quickly, 'It's best you do not know where. For the moment, this is all to be most secret: it's vital the boys' enemies don't know they've even left the Tower, let alone where they have been taken.'

'And we need your help to make that certain, Mistress Hobbes,' Sir James added. He had had the gravest doubts when Christie had suggested taking this woman into their confidence, and seeing her in the flesh had not really dispelled his fears. But they needed her help, and he prayed that she could keep a close tongue in her head. If the boys were alive, and could be brought to the Red Lion, it was plain that her attitude would change instantly from hostility to warm unqualified support. It was a rare shame, thought Sir James, that rebellion and unrest could not so easily be cured: but the children could hardly be paraded across the suspicious south of England, especially since the elder boy was probably ailing and there was the real danger of a rescue attempt, or an assassin close amongst their attendants. It would suit the King's enemies very well to have the boys murdered in full public view.

If, of course, they were not already dead.

Under Cis Hobbes' sceptical, sharp eye the two men and their servants swallowed their supper without taste or ceremony. When they had finished, Christie turned to her. 'Thank you for your forbearance, Cis. How long is it to curfew?'

'About two hours. There'll be few people abroad, mind you, on account of the rain, and if you don't act suspicious no-one will notice you. I pray God they *are* alive,' said Cis, suddenly utterly serious, 'and if they are I'll vow a candle to St Nicholas every

Sunday and holy day for the rest of my life—and I'll do all in my power to help you. Good luck to you—and God go with you, Christie.'

*

In the dim light outside, the rain fell heavily, steadily from low grey clouds that hid the last of the day: it lacked at least an hour till sunset, yet was almost dark. As they hurried along Aldgate, trying without success to avoid both the growing puddles and the piles of ordure and rubbish that scavengers had not yet cleared away, doubtless hoping that the rain would perform that task for them, Christie reflected that they could not have chosen a better time for their enterprise. Those few souls hardy or foolish enough to venture out in such inclement weather were hurrying along with bent heads, intent on reaching their destinations as quickly as possible. On such an evening, secrecy would be easy.

In ten minutes' hasty walk through the wet streets, they had arrived at the Tower of London. The grim bulk of walls and ramparts loomed above the rain-speckled moat, the White Tower pale and ghostly behind. The men on the first gate were rather more alert than Sir James or Christie would have liked, however: instead of letting them through with barely a challenge, they were questioned quite closely by the gate-wards, and only the fact that they wished to be conducted directly to the Constable of the Tower was sufficient to allow them through.

Two guards led them swiftly through the maze-like outer defences, under towers and along the bridge across the moat to the main gate-tower, with more soldiers. Tyrell and Christie were handed over to these, and taken on into the chief part of the fortress. And all the while, as they hurried through the rain, Christie's apprehension grew. These precautions, though expected and in some ways reassuring, did not make for optimism. What had happened, to make Brackenbury so cautious? They would find out soon enough, and perhaps the answer would not be to their liking.

Amongst the stern grey stones and towers, the ordinary timber and plaster of the Constable's lodgings struck a friendlier note. Brackenbury had a wife and children, and only a tiny manor in Durham to support him apart from what he had gained in the King's service, and so his family lived with him, in tranquil comfort somehow greatly at odds with the martial atmosphere beyond their windows. When Christie and Sir James were ushered into the

Constable's presence by the latest in a very long succession of guards and servants, it was to find him sitting at a tables board with one of his daughters, while his wife and the other girl laboured over their needles. A fire roared cheerfully in the hearth, and the air was fragrant with fine beeswax candles and sweet herbs strewing the floor. Robert Brackenbury had sprung from origins as humble as Christie's, but the man who rose to greet them as old friends was a tall, rather stooped middle-aged man of scholarly appearance, richly dressed in a furred gown against the cold of late September, while his wife and daughters wore velvet and jewels. It was a reminder of how high Christie himself could reach in the King's household: and of the rewards promised him if this latest, most important mission should prove successful.

Wine and wafers, inevitably, were summoned, and Brackenbury, with keen interest, questioned them as to their journey and the news from the north: but, it was plain, he limited the freedom of his own talk. Given the undisguised curiosity of the wife and daughters, girls perhaps twelve and nine years old, Christie thought it wise: and a sliver of hope crept into his head. If the two boys were indeed dead, would Brackenbury, known for his honesty and kindliness, have seemed so cheerful?

Sir James, obviously well aware of the approaching hour of curfew, intimated before his first sip of wine that they had important and urgent business to discuss privately. Brackenbury glanced meaningfully at his wife, who obediently took the hint and shepherded her daughters away to another parlour. As soon as the door had closed behind her, Tyrell turned swiftly to the Constable. 'Are you certain there is no chance we will be overheard? No-one else at all must know of our talk.'

Robert Brackenbury, glancing at him, said nothing, but rose from his chair by the fire and slipped the door open. The chamber beyond was empty: he closed it and retraced his steps. 'We are alone, Sir James, I can assure you of that. Your servants, I presume, can be trusted?'

Perkin and Wellesborne stood against the carved and painted panelling that lined the Constable's winter parlour. Christie, despite the inner tenison created by the urgency of their task and the fear of its failure, could not help but be struck anew by the difference between them: Wellesborne urbane, tall, respectable, a man as entitled to the appellation 'gentleman' as his employer, and Perkin, short and somehow disreputable despite his fine clothes, his black hair sleek with rain under the cap. 'They can be trusted,' said Sir James. He looked straight at Brackenbury from under thick dark brows, and said bluntly, 'The two boys. Are they still alive?'

An expression of alarm informed the older man's rather thin, pleasant face, as if the question were a harbinger of something he dreaded, and he did not speak at once. The tension in the chamber grew to be a monstrous, almost tangible thing: they are dead, Christie thought, and the intensity of his horror surprised him. And then Brackenbury, warily, nodded. 'Yes, they are—and lodged here, in this house.'

The relief was enormous. Christie felt the tautness leave him, as if a lutestring, drawn too far, had suddenly broken. Sir James, a devout man not normally given to public displays of his piety, dropped on his knees by his chair, his face informed with delight, and mouthed a swift prayer. Robert Brackenbury looked from one man to the other, obviously bewildered. 'Forgive me,' he said at last, softly. 'May sweet Jesu forgive me—I thought you had been sent to kill them.'

The words restored Sir James to his usual self: he rose and glared at the Constable. 'You should know His Grace better than that, Rob—you've served with him long enough, as we have, you've been in Scotland, you've seen how his mind works. Did you honestly think he would have his own nephews slaughtered?'

Robert Brackenbury, honest man adrift in a devious, ruthless and dishonest age, stared at him helplessly and spread his long slender hands. 'It is what all the world believes—you know the story of the marchpane? It is what the boys themselves believe, too. They are certain that their uncle means to have them killed. Edward has not yet fully recovered from the attack—he prays incessantly and makes his confession daily, he is so sure that he faces death. I feared for the health of his mind, as well as his body, and so I brought them here until they should recover. They are lodged in the chamber that lies next to mine, and no-one save my own family and a few trusted close servants know they are there. I consulted with the Duke of Norfolk and the Chancellor after the poison attempt, and we thought it best to dismiss the boys' attendants, letting them think that others would be engaged in their place. The Garden Tower, where they were lodged, is still kept under close watch, and the Tower gates have had their guards doubled, with strict orders to question all visitors closely, as you yourselves have just found. The rumour of unrest is sufficient excuse, and the Duke of Norfolk has been told that there was a plan to rescue the boys. How that marries with a plot to kill them, I do not know.'

'It's possible that the conspiracy has changed direction,' Christie said. 'There are many people who are the King's enemies and ours, who would be delighted to see the boys cleared from their path. The King has his suspicions, but no proof. In the meantime, our orders are to take the children into the country, as secretly as possible, and hide them there until all threat of rebellion is over.'

'And tonight,' Tyrell added. 'If they can be taken out of the Tower disguised, under cover of darkness, no-one will know they have left for some time, if what you say is true. So, Rob, we must hurry you, I am afraid.'

'Have you somewhere safe to lodge them tonight?' Brackenbury's doubts seemed to have vanished: his rather stooped back had straightened, and he looked like a man about to be relieved of a well-nigh intolerable burden.

'An inn not far away. The landlady is my servant's mother: she will be eager to help us, once she knows the children are not dead. Most of London thinks they are,' Christie added, rising pointedly from his chair. 'Once they are safe, perhaps the King's friends can spend a while spreading rumours that are true, instead of these false ones that spring fully-armed from the ground like dragons' teeth.'

Sir James had evidently not had a particularly literary education, and looked blank. Brackenbury, at the door, said softly, 'You said that they were to be disguised. How do you propose to disguise them? They are well-known to the Tower guards.'

The idea, beautifully simple, had already occurred to Christie: he brought it forth with confidence. 'Your own children are of roughly the right age and size. Why not disguise them as your daughters? In the dark and rain, the guards will just see their clothes, their faces can be shrouded in hoods. And if you accompany us, that will convince them.'

Brackenbury stared at him: Sir James, more forthright, laughed and slapped his thigh. 'By all the saints, that's a good one, young Kit! The perfect solution—and the girls themselves need never know. Then once out of the Tower, you can return, Rob—as if you'd taken them to see an old aunt, perhaps. And no-one will know they've gone out—they'll think it was your two little maids!' He gave way to his mirth. Robert Brackenbury gazed dubiously at Christie. 'It's a sound plan in theory, but there's one vast obstacle in your way. How will you persuade the boys to go with you, let alone dressed as girls?'

'There's only one way to find out,' Christie told him: and with a shrug and a smile, Robert Brackenbury turned to lead the way to the chamber in which the sons of Edward IV had found refuge.

It was a wide comfortable room, dominated by a richly carved wooden bed, a representation of the City of Jerusalem on the headboard and handsome hangings with a design of flowers and wild animals. Christie's eyes noted an oak chest, stools, a wainscot bench by the fire, cushions in the window, already well-shuttered against the wet dark, and a table at which sat a small, curly-haired child, whom he had last seen looking out of the Garden Tower at his uncle's coronation procession, writing busily. In a corner stood a little prie-dieu, ablaze with candles, and on his knees before it was the boy who had once been King Edward V, and was now known officially as Edward Bastard. As the door opened, both children glanced round: the younger boy's eyes stared puzzled at Tyrell and Christie, but Edward leapt to his feet, rocking the prie-dieu and the candles, which guttered wildly. Christie, seeing the change in him, drew in his breath sharply. He had thought the child in whose household he had served had been too thin, too tense, but that had been normality compared to this. Edward's face was as sharp and pinched as a starving orphan's, his eyes sunken and ringed with shadow, his skin even in the ruddy candlelight suffused with a bluish tinge. He was painfully gaunt, and the hands that hung helplessly by his sides were knobbled and scaley with disease, and trembled like a wind-blown leaf. As his eyes beheld Christie, they widened: then, as if his legs had given way, he dropped to his knees again, crossed himself, and began feverishly to pray in a ceaseless whisper.

Sir James caught Christie's eye with a significant look that spoke of his own pity and distress. Brackenbury shut the door behind them and said gently, 'Edward? Dickon? Do you know these gentlemen?'

It was plain that Edward was in no condition to give a rational reply. The younger boy got to his feet and gave them a considering stare: no trace here of the fear that transfixed his brother. 'Yes,' he said at last. 'You're Sir James Tyrell, aren't you? You're kin to Dame Haute, who used to be in charge of our nursery at Westminster.' There had been a sudden and perceptible tremor in his voice, fiercely suppressed. 'And you—I remember you, sir. You spoke with my sister Bess in sanctuary once. You were in Edward's household for a while, weren't you? I remember him talking about you.'

Edward IV had never forgotten a face either. Christie found himself smiling at this small, stalwart, and very self-possessed child. 'I hope it was nothing bad.'

'Oh, no—I think he liked you. Master—Heron, isn't it? I thought so. Edward? Edward! Here's Master Heron, who played the lute for you.'

The wild, sunken blue eyes stared at Christie. Gradually, something approaching rationality returned to the boy's face. He got clumsily to his feet, and said hesitantly, 'It *is* you, isn't it? I remember you. You . . . you were kind.'

'I am glad that you recall me,' Christie told him. 'But what's more to the point, do you trust me? Do you trust me, and Sir James here?'

Edward looked bewildered: a frown of suspicion crossed Dickon's face. He said, 'Do you come from our uncle? The man who calls himself King? He's been trying to kill us, *we* know it, whatever the Constable might say. He tried to poison us with marchpane.'

'I never liked marchpane much myself,' said Christie lightly, and was rewarded by an involuntary twitch in the child's stern mouth. He had decided to treat with this boy, since the elder one seemed to have no more spirit than a wet rag: and if young Dickon, with his martial enthusiasms, could be persuaded to see their flight from the Tower as a splendid adventure, so much the better. He went on, 'It's not true about His Grace your uncle. Whatever you might think—and I don't blame you, half of London thinks the same—he wishes you no harm. In fact, we're here now because of that poison attempt—as soon as His Grace heard of it, he sent Sir James and myself here with most urgent and secret orders.'

The boy's interest was caught: he said slowly, 'He doesn't want us killed?'

'No. He thinks you're not safe here in the Tower. Oh, I know the Constable has taken great care of you, but everyone knows that you are here, and despite all his precautions, the assassins may strike again—and succeed this time. So Sir James and I are going to smuggle you both out of the Tower tonight, and take you to safety.'

'Out of the Tower?' said Edward, on a note of alarm. 'But where could possibly be safer than the Tower?'

'Somewhere where your enemies can't find you,' said Tyrell. 'Somewhere they won't think of looking. But you must trust us, both of you, and do what we say. We shall have to disguise you to get you out of the Tower without being suspected.'

Dickon stared at him, his mind obviously working with speed. 'You want to smuggle us out—now? But how do we know we can trust you? How do we know you aren't going to kill us as soon as we're outside the walls?'

'It would be a rather public place,' said Christie drily, noting the way the elder boy had flinched at his brother's words. 'You have no proof that we mean you no harm. You do have to trust us, and I don't blame you for your suspicions. But I will swear by the Blessed Mary, Mother of God, and all the saints you care to name, that we have come to take you to safety, and I know that Sir James will do the same.'

'You're both creatures of my uncle,' said Edward, his voice trembling. 'You're going to kill us, I know it, I know it—please, Brackenbury, don't let them take us!' Tears coursed down his wasted cheeks. It was a pitiable sight, the more so as the sturdy Dickon put a protective arm around his older, taller brother. 'It's all right, Edward—I won't let them take you!'

'Listen to me,' said Brackenbury, stepping forward to confront the two children. 'There is no need for all this—you are nearly a grown man, Edward, it is time you behaved like one, and stopped using your little brother as a prop. Do not give in to your weakness —you must fight it, and grow strong in mind and body. Now listen—*listen!*'

The pathetic sobbing ceased, and the boy stared up at him, his mouth trembling but controlled. Brackenbury put a gentle hand on his shoulder, gripping it, lending him strength. It was obvious that he was fond of the children, and knew them well. 'Do you trust *me*, Edward?'

A pause, and then a nod.

'And you, Dickon, do you trust me?'

'Yes, I do.'

'That's good. Now, you must trust me now, as you have never trusted before, and trust these two men also. They are good men, I know them well, and they have only your welfare at heart. They are speaking the truth, and you must go with them. Do you hear me,

Edward? You *must* go with them, your lives may depend on it!'

'But we're safe here,' said Edward, his voice faint and exhausted. Dickon said slowly, 'No, we're not. They know where we are, they could try again. Do you *want* to stay mewed up in here for ever? Don't you want to see the sky again, and flowers and fields and animals? *I* do!' He shook his brother's arm, none too gently. 'Edward, please, *think!* We *aren't* safe here! If Brackenbury says we can trust them, then we can trust them—*I* trust them! Oh, please, Edward, I do so want to be free again—please be sensible—you can't stay here for ever, you'll die here, I know you will!'

Edward, it was obvious, had long ago abdicated his will to make decisions to his little brother. Drained, defeated, he stared emptily at the floor, and his answer came in an exhausted whisper, barely audible. 'Oh, very well—if you want to go, then I will too.'

Brackenbury's lean face split into a broad smile. 'Thank God. I warn you, though, you may not like our idea for your disguise.'

Dickon, his face wreathed in an answering grin, shook his head. 'I don't mind, whatever it is—is it a soldier? Have you got armour for us?'

'Not very secret, the two of you clanking out of the Tower in full battle harness,' Christie pointed out, marvelling at the sudden light-heartedness that had infused the chamber. Dickon, obviously imagining the scene, burst into rather wild laughter, and even Edward's unhappy face brightened a little. Brackenbury said, 'No, not soldiers. We want you to wear girls' clothes.'

Dickon, his grey eyes wide, looked at the three solemn faces of the men and then laughed again, clapping a hasty hand over his mouth. Edward said disbelievingly, 'You want us to dress up—as *girls*? No, no, I won't!'

'Oh, come on, Edward, it'll be such fun,' his brother urged him. 'Don't spoil it, please don't—it'll mean we'll get away safely, they'll *never* think it was us!' He turned to Brackenbury with enthusiasm. 'Are we going to wear dresses? Anne's and Elizabeth's? I'm about Elizabeth's size, I should think,' he added, glancing judicially down at his short stocky figure. 'Though she's younger than me . . . and Edward, you can be Anne.'

His brother, with the first true spirit he had shown throughout, stared resentfully at him. 'No, I won't. I refuse.'

'Oh, Edward, don't spoil it—please don't spoil it—it's fun, an

[242]

adventure! And you'd make a very good girl, a much better girl than I would.'

'I think that was the wrong thing to say,' Brackenbury pointed out, into the ensuing offended silence. 'Edward, please be reasonable. You must both go in disguise, or neither of you—Mother of God, your lives depend on no-one recognising you! Will you put your brother's life in danger for such a trivial, petty reason?'

'I'd rather be myself,' said Edward, showing the sulky, mutinous behaviour which Christie had seen before. He hunched a shoulder and kicked his slippered foot at a nearby stool. 'I don't *want* to be a girl.'

'Do you want Dickon to go, and leave you behind?' Brackenbury said reasonably: in his place, Christie felt that he would have resorted to shaking some sense into the boy, despite his earlier sympathy. Edward sullenly shook his head, and the Constable pursued his advantage. 'There's your answer, then—for your uncle I am sure would rather have one of you safe than neither, and if it comes to the sticking-point, then Dickon will go on his own. We are quite prepared to do that, if you want.'

There was a fraught silence in the chamber. It seemed suddenly hot, and Christie felt sweat on his body. Then Edward kicked the stool again, so hard that it fell over with a clatter onto the polished floorboards, and said sulkily, 'All right, I'll do it.'

Once decided, all was urgency: the boy might change his mind, and curfew approached, the hour beyond which all citizens were supposed to have a good reason for being abroad. The chance of being stopped and questioned by the Watch was too great to risk unless absolutely necessary: however changed Edward might be from the boy King who had paraded through the streets of London five months ago, there was still the possibility that he or his brother might be recognised, however dark and wet the night, however convincing their disguise. Brackenbury brought their garments, saying that they were a little old, but serviceable: new gowns were needed anyway, so these would not be missed. Dickon eagerly divested himself of doublet, shirt and hose and dived with enthusiasm into the linen kirtle and tawny velvet that had belonged to the nine-year-old Elizabeth. It was a little tight, but otherwise fitted quite well: Sir James briskly laced it up over the kirtle, and finally fitted a plain red velvet girdle, ornamented with curling embroidery. 'There you are, lad—a proper little maid!'

'I don't know how they can walk in these skirts,' said Dickon, trying. His feet kicked the heavy folds and he all but fell, erupting into giggles. 'Let's see if I can curtsey—oh, no!'

He fell over backwards, inducing the first proper smile that evening on his brother's face. 'Go on, Edward—I'll wager you can't do as well.'

With an air of resignation, Edward removed his outer garments and wriggled in his turn into the kirtle belonging to Anne. It hung on him in vast folds: Dickon, aware of the importance of not upsetting his brother further, forbore to laugh as Brackenbury helped him don the murrey velvet gown, laced it up and fastened a blue girdle around his chest. The gown was very obviously much too big, and the coney-fur collar kept sliding off his bony shoulders. Dickon, who had discovered by experimentation how to walk in his voluminous skirts, studied his brother and nodded. 'It looks all right, Ned. Are we going to wear cloaks? They'll hide our hair, it's too short for a girl.'

For answer, Brackenbury produced two enormous, heavy fustian garments dyed a dark greyish colour. 'They're not the children's, theirs will be missed, but my wife's and her waiting-woman's. Hardly articles of high fashion, I'm afraid, but in this weather who cares? And the main thing is to disguise your hair and your faces. Edward, you will find walking much easier if you take little steps—don't stride.'

'Like this,' said Dickon, mincing gracefully around the floor with an elegant swish of velvet, the heavy folds held out in front of him. 'Lift your skirts up a little—see? Then it's easy.'

With faltering steps, Edward copied him: he had not his brother's relish for the task, however, and all but fell when he caught his foot in a trail of cloth. At that moment, the door opened. Brackenbury glanced round in alarm, but it was only his wife, whom he had evidently let into the secret. 'I have some hose here. You mustn't go out without hose, your feet will be so cold! Your ordinary shoes will do, though, they're not so different from the girls' ones.' She stood over the boys as they struggled with the thick woollen stockings, and then turned to the three men. 'Will they need anything else? How far do you have to go?'

'Not far,' Sir James, told her, waving a vague generalising hand. 'And we can obtain further supplies, if necessary, before we leave London. I thank you most kindly, Mistress Brackenbury—you have been a great help to us.'

'I am glad to be of service,' said the Constable's wife softly. She

[244]

was a great deal younger than her husband, by about twenty years or so, and her air of calm efficiency had had a notably soothing effect on the two boys, who stood quite still in their unaccustomed gowns and enveloping cloaks, silent and wide-eyed. With a smile, she went over and bent to kiss each child on the cheek. 'I wish you Godspeed, Edward, Richard. May you have a safe journey free from all harm—I shall pray for you, and think of you always.'

'I thank you for all your kindness, Mistress,' said Edward, formally: and there, in his sudden assumption of dignity, could be seen the child King. Dickon, less inhibited, flung his arms around her and said urgently, 'Thank you, thank you, and *please* don't tell Anne and Elizabeth that we've gone, or anyone else—it's *very* important!'

'Don't worry, I won't,' said Mistress Brackenbury, smiling gently. 'Though I should think Nan and Bess will guess quite quickly. But they're old enough to keep a secret, after all. Now I think you must go—take care, Robert, please. What story will you tell the guards?'

'That a relative is sick, and has asked for their company,' her husband told her. 'It's a poor excuse, I know, but if we make little of it, then the guards will too—and everything must appear as normal as possible. Is all quiet, Agnes my dear?'

His wife went to the door, opened it, and listened. There was no sound from the chamber beyond, nor from the rest of the house, and she nodded, her finger to her lips. Sir James took Edward by the arm and steered him carefully through the door: Christie followed with Dickon, feeling tremors of excitement running through the child's small sturdy frame, and found himself warming greatly to his intelligence and uninhibited enthusiasm. More than ever, it seemed a shame that this boy had not been born the elder: and he wondered how much Edward's less appealing personality and open hostility towards his uncle had contributed to Gloucester's decision to usurp his throne.

In the Hall, otherwise blessedly empty, waited Perkin and Wellesborne. Both children had negotiated the narrow, creaking and uneven stairs, with rather differing degrees of success. Dickon seemed quite at home in his strange garments, and seemed to be practising a walk similar to Elizabeth Brackenbury's: Christie could hear him muttering under his breath, his hand tightening on his arm, and once a small fierce voice upbraiding himself, 'No, stupid, she takes *little* steps!' But Edward several times nearly fell, and was

[245]

only saved by Tyrell's support: he looked thoroughly unhappy, and tears did not seem far away. There was little time left: Agnes Brackenbury arranged a corner of each boy's cloak over their heads, hiding their distinctive shoulder-length hair, and showed them in a hasty whisper how to grip the cloth under their chin with one hand while manipulating their skirts with the other. Then her husband opened the door, and ushered them out into the night.

It was cold but not, thank God, windy: that would have made the boys' skirts even more difficult to manage. The rain was falling heavily, however, and hissed malevolently upon the Constable's horn-covered lantern. By its uncertain light, the six of them made their way haltingly to the gate, and the first encounter with the guards.

They were bored, cold, fidgety: only one torch flared under the archway, the other having gone out, and Brackenbury was able to distract their attention with a reprimand, and a reminder that the portcullis must be lowered. 'But not until I return, I'm only going as far as the Bulwark, to see my girls safe away with their uncles. I'll be no more than a few minutes.' And the four men-at-arms, listening respectfully to their constable, spared not a glance for the 'girls' hovering in the shadows under the gutted torch.

Once that first gateway to the outer ward was passed, it was easier. The duty of escorting his supposed daughters justified the appearance of Brackenbury, who would probably not usually emerge on such an unpleasant night, and their presence, in turn, would not be questioned while he was with them. It began to seem ridiculously easy: Dickon, clinging to Christie's arm, even gave a little hop and skip occasionally as his exuberance got the better of him. The rain pelted in their faces, and they hurried along, heads bent, over the moat and so to the last gate. As they approached it, the rain beat harder, and then suddenly, with arm-wrenching abruptness, Dickon's feet shot from under him on the wet slippery stones and he went down in a great flurry of skirts, squawking astonishment. They were close, too close to the gate: Christie saw as he bent over the boy that his cloak had slipped and the fair, distinctive hair, very different from Elizabeth Brackenbury's dark straight locks, shone in the dim light from the lantern.

'Are you all right, Bess?' Brackenbury called, swinging the lantern so that its light shone away from the boy's betraying head. Christie nudged Dickon with his toe and, prompted, he called, 'Yes, Father,' his wet hands scrabbling frantically for the cloak.

Christie helped him to arrange it once more over his hair, made sure that he had a firm hold of it, and hissed in his ear with no respect for rank, King's son or no, 'If you'd walked *sensibly*, you wouldn't have fallen, would you?'

'Sorry,' Dickon muttered, his crestfallen face hardly visible in the shadows cast by the cloak. Christie helped him to his feet and they made their way with rather more care to the shelter under the arch of the gateway. But the guards beneath it showed no curiosity, no surprise, no interest, only the same cold unhappy boredom. Brackenbury chatted briefly with them, reminded them of their duties, and warned them that he would shortly be returning. Then with a joke and some sudden laughter, he escorted Christie, Tyrell, the two servants and the two children out of the Barbican and towards their last obstacle, the Bulwark Gate. This was the outermost defence: once past this, and they would be safe, yet Christie could not rid himself of the feeling that all might yet go wrong.

The men beneath it saluted Brackenbury respectfully: then one of them, a middle-aged man with a plump, kindly face turned smiling towards the children lurking behind Christie and Tyrell. 'It's a filthy night for little ones to be out, isn't it? Did you like those sugared plums my wife made for you?'

As Christie opened his mouth to say something, anything, in reply, Dickon forestalled him. In a girlish pipe quite unlike his own, he lisped, 'Yes, thank you, Harry.'

'I'm right glad of it, Mistress Elizabeth. And how are you keeping, Mistress Anne?' Plainly he knew the Constable's daughters well: and to answer him might bring disaster, just as to remain silent would also invite suspicion. Again, it was Dickon who spoke. 'She's taken a vow of silence today as a penance. We're going to see our cousin, who's been taken ill, and we must hurry—come *on*, uncle!' And he turned, towing Christie in his wake, and stepped past the indulgently smiling guard into the fresh free darkness beyond the gate. With a muttered comment that provoked the soldiers' laughter, Brackenbury led Tyrell and Edward in pursuit, Perkin and Wellesborne following after, and so to safety.

They hurried through the rain past shuttered houses until they were well out of earshot of the Bulwark: then Dickon halted and turned, his voice shaking with triumphant glee. 'Didn't I sound *just* like Elizabeth, Brackenbury?'

'You did indeed,' said the Constable. Even in the inadequate light of the lantern, his face looked haggard with relief. 'How in the name of all the saints did you know he was called Harry?'

'Oh, Anne mentioned that it was Harry Parker's wife who gave them those sugar-plums—they were lovely!' said Dickon, with a small boy's reminiscent greed. 'So when he mentioned sugar-plums I knew he must be Harry. And it'd be just like Anne to take a vow of silence—she prays almost as much as you do, Edward,' he added to his brother, of whom nothing could be seen but a sodden, enveloping cloak draping his trembling form. 'I'm wet through. Where are we going now?'

'To the Red Lion at Aldgate, God willing,' said Tyrell. He turned to Brackenbury, his plain soldierly face wreathed in smiles. 'I do not know how to thank you, Rob. I think your help has saved these children—and I know we can never repay you. I shall ensure the King knows everything.'

'And he will doubtless reward me, as you cannot,' said Brackenbury drily. 'My true reward is to see Richard and Edward go to freedom and safety—I need no other.' And with a tenderness that was deeply felt, he drew both boys to him for a parting embrace that they were not afraid to return: then, with last hasty words of thanks and farewell, turned and walked back towards the Tower, leaving them alone.

The bells of curfew rang out from St Paul's as they turned into Aldgate, and tavern doors opened to disgorge light and wine and beer-soaked drinkers, returning unsteadily home. Hand on his dagger, Christie guided his small charge through the crowds, but there was no trouble: the revellers were too intent on hurrying home to shelter to worry about four men and two small girls, and they reached the safety of the Red Lion without incident, though both children frequently stumbled on the uneven stones or trailed their skirts in piles of ordure. The gates of the inn were firmly shut, but Perkin's stout fist gained speedy admittance, and it was only a few steps further to their chambers side by side along the galleried courtyard.

It was dry, warm, and a cheerful fire blazed in both rooms. The beds boasted two warming pans, and pallets had been set out, covered with good thick sheets and blankets, for the servants. And in the chair by the hearth of the larger chamber sat Cicely Hobbes, her fingers busy with sewing and her shrewd bright eyes watching the door. Christie saw them narrow as the two children entered, Edward by now drooping and in need of Tyrell's fatherly arm about his shoulders. Wellesborne shut the door and, without orders, gently removed the dripping cloaks, now black with rain, and laid them in a sodden heap by the fire.

Cis drew in her breath sharply, for there was no mistaking the identity of either child, despite their draggle-tailed incongruous gowns and girdles that only emphasised the boyish head of Dickon and the gaunt sick pallor of his brother. With a humility entirely uncharacteristic, Cis Hobbes slid from the chair and knelt before them.

The act of reverence, so long withheld, brought Edward to breaking-point: he bowed his head in his wet scaley hands and sobbed uncontrollably. Cis, her expression one of lively distress, scrambled to her feet. 'Oh, no, Your Grace, I beg you—you're safe here!'

'You mustn't call him "Your Grace",' said Dickon seriously. 'He isn't King anymore. Our uncle Richard is King.' There was no trace of the earlier hostility in his voice: perhaps, thought Christie, who was rapidly coming to admire this undaunted and quick-witted child, he had come to the conclusion that his uncle was no longer to be feared. He added politely, 'Please, mistress, could we have something to eat? I'm sorely hungry.'

'And clothes,' said Cis, reverting rapidly to her normal self. 'For shame, Christie Heron, could you not have thought of a more suitable disguise? As maids, indeed!'

'It worked,' said Dickon. 'It worked, so it was a very good idea—we pretended we were Constable Brackenbury's daughters, it was fun.' He kicked at his soaked, mucky skirts. 'I think I'd like to go back to being a boy, though.'

'And so you shall,' Cis assured him. She looked Tyrell and Christie squarely in the eye. 'Well, you've brought them here, safe and sound and secret as you said, and I'll take back freely all the wicked things I thought about King Richard—though I still think he's a usurper, mind,' she added belligerently. 'But what are you going to do with them now? They can't stay girls for ever—I'll be willing to wager you won't persuade them to ride into the country in skirts and cloaks, you'd never hide them. How are you going to get them out of London?'

'Easily, with your help, dear Cis,' said Christie: and proceeded to tell her how.

*

The dozen men on watch the next morning at the Aldgate, were as usual too beset by the press of people pushing inwards, against those wanting to get out of the City, to pay much attention to the group of gentlemen and servants on horseback who demanded that way be made for them. In the end, the guards had to bar the common herd with their halberds while the three gentlemen, two servants and a page rode under the broad arch and into the street beyond. No-one gave them a second glance as they rode away towards Mile End and the gentle hills of Essex, for the irate landlady of the Red Lion had chosen that moment to ask the gate-wards most urgently if they had seen her rascally kitchen-boy who had run away in fear of a thoroughly deserved beating: and by the time they had leisure to watch the road again, the East Country party had long since ridden out of sight.

It had been easy enough to transform Edward and Dickon back to their true sex, with their fervent co-operation. But this would pose its own problems, as both boys were well-known to the citizens of London, and ran the risk of recognition. In the end, careful use of a stain used for polishing and colouring wood had turned Dickon's golden curls to brown: he looked startlingly ordinary in this new guise, and when clad in plain russet doublet and hose, with a cap on his head bearing the Tyrell knot, he appeared quite unlike his former self. Edward, however, was much less easy to disguise. His delicate looks had prompted Christie to consider keeping him a girl, but the difficulties of having him ride sideways on a lady's saddle, compounded by the comment that would be occasioned by a woman travelling alone amongst men, led him to abandon it. Accordingly Edward, his pallor concealed by a judicious and careful application of face paint, was dressed in plain servant's garb, and instructed in his duties by the indomitable Perkin. Christie and Tyrell had feared that he would baulk at this indignity, but the tensions of the escape from the Tower seemed to have drained all the remaining life and spirit from him, and he seemed happy to do as he was told and surrender all decision to others. Christie could not help wondering how such a spineless creature would ever have coped with the rigours of kingship, and then reminded himself, compassionately, that in the last six months the boy had suffered more adversity than most men faced in a lifetime. Secure on the throne, he would doubtless have been very different.

Cis had provided two extra horses, spare clothing and food to see them on their way: and though she did not say as much, Christie knew that he had won a friend and ally for life. He could only wish that the rest of London and the southern parts might be won over so easily: but to display the boys openly would be to invite their abduction by rebels, or their deaths at the hands of the agents of Henry Tudor. That must wait until all danger was passed, and any rebellion crushed: meanwhile, they would take the children to the safety of Gipping.

They had to travel more slowly than Tyrell or Christie would have liked, because of Edward. He had not recovered from the poisoning, and moreover had not sat a horse for months—since his ceremonial entry into London, in fact. To his credit, he rode without complaint: it was Dickon, his round freckled face anxious, who drew Tyrell's attention to the swaying drooping figure trailing some distance behind them. As a result, they only covered the ten miles or so to Romford that day. The inn they chose asked no awkward questions, and the next day Edward vowed that he was much better, and quite capable of travelling twice the distance. That took them to Chelmsford, where the landlord of the Swan showed rather more interest, but was quite easily satisfied with Christie's casual small-talk. It was a route that Sir James evidently used often, although he took good care to choose inns where he was not known. After Chelmsford, they left the Ipswich road and struck north towards what Sir James declare to be the fairest country in the whole world, his own home, Suffolk.

Christie, as they rode, watched the countryside unfold on either side of him with great interest. Here was not the bleak moors of Northumberland or Yorkshire, nor yet the wide bare common fields of the country around Ashcott or in the middle shires. This was a land of small, intimate valleys lined with woodland and hemmed by hedges: streams ran brightly across or alongside the road, and the wayside trees and bushes bore blackberries and rose hips, elderberries and haws. Strip farming seemed to be almost unknown here: small fields, golden still with stubble, alternated with enclosed pasture where dun-coloured cattle and small curly-horned, dark-faced sheep grazed peacefully on the lush grass. The roads were still very wet, though it was two or three days since the last rainfall, and the earth was heavy, rich clay. And every town and village through which they passed seemed to be trying to outdo the last in the building of its church. He had never seen such wealth so casually displayed, and the sun glittered on glass and flintwork and stone. Sir James, seeing his appreciative gaze resting on the churches of Sudbury, where they lay that night, smiled. 'Ah, young Kit, you just wait—you wait till we reach Gipping.'

If Sudbury was rich, the town of Lavenham was astonishing. Sheep, it seemed, had laid the foundations of this thriving place, and raised the splendid houses lining its streets, as well as the magnificent church, still evidently in the throes of rebuilding. The town had grown fat and wealthy on wool and cloth, and prosperity reigned supreme here as it apparently did all over these parts. But they did not linger, though the sky was threatening, for Lavenham had been the manor of the exiled Earl of Oxford, his house lay here, and most of these fat clothiers had once owed their allegiance to the house of Lancaster. It was not a place to dawdle, and they had already attracted one or two curious glances. Shortly after they left the place, Sir James took them down a track which branched off to the right, and led in a north-westerly direction. 'Better safe than sorry,' he explained to Christie, in answer to the younger man's query. 'No-one will expect us to take this way, and it'll cut miles from our journey—we could be home by nightfall.'

That assessment proved accurate. The sun was setting behind the thick woodland on their left as they rode into the town of Stow-market, with yet another imposing church. After four days of admittedly gentle riding in dry weather, Edward was near to collapse. Dickon rode beside him, talking cheerily to him, keeping his ambling nag on the right path. All through the journey the younger boy's spirits had remained irrepressibly high. He was interested in everything around him, from sheep to windmills to the identity of a hawk seen in the distance or the usual wages of a labourer, and both Tyrell and Christie were subjected to a stream of questions which they did their best to answer. Sir James, who had sons of his own, proved very knowledgeable about all aspects of his own countryside, and Christie, listening, learned much about Suffolk. He had found himself falling under the spell of this green, lush, gentle country, with its laconic, self-possessed inhabitants whose sturdy spirit and independent enterprise was evident, and whose hard, at first outlandish accents and phrases gradually assumed familiarity. He found himself gaining a little understanding of their extraordinary dialect, and the dropping of all unnecessary consonants and the nasal inflections seemed almost normal now, especially since their speech was echoed, more faintly, in the robust tones of Sir James. Typically, Dickon had been fascinated by the strange words. 'What's a hodmedod?'

'It's a snail, lad—a common-or-garden snail,' Tyrell told him. The problem of how to address a King's son who had been stripped of his titles and declared a bastard had not really arisen: to treat his supposed page with the courtesy proper to a royal Duke would have been, to say the least of it, wildly foolhardy, and the directness and cheerful nature of the child his family knew as Dickon had made a similarly informal approach the natural solution.

'And what's "bang"? I heard a man in the last inn calling for bread and bang.'

'Bang is what we Suffolkers call our cheese, it's so hard you must bang it on the board before it's soft enough to eat,' Sir James assured him solemnly. Dickon gave his characteristic giggle, one hand across his mouth. 'I don't believe you, Sir James—it's not true!'

'I swear it is, lad—on my honour. Now look where you're going, there's a great Suffolk pothole in front of you, and it wouldn't do to arrive at Gipping all wet and draggle-tailed—and that's another Suffolk expression for you! How's your brother faring?'

Dickon, at once concerned, glanced back. Edward was riding hunched over his saddlebow, as if too weary or weak to hold his back straight, and Perkin was at his side, guiding the horse. His anxious face was answer enough: he said, 'How much further?'

Christie, who missed the unruly fire of Bayard—not a spark enlivened these mediocre hired horses—was as interested in Tyrell's reply as the child. Sir James, aware of it, glanced at Dickon and smiled cheerfully. 'Oh, not much further, lad—just a mile or two.'

And indeed it was not long before they came to a straggling collection of cottages along a green populous with tethered cows and a few goats. Women coming out with milking pails, in the golden evening light, saw Sir James and greeted him with smiles and curtseys: he was, of course, the lord of their manor. And then, at the end of the green, through trees, Christie saw the gleam of black and white, and knew why Tyrell had smiled when he had admired the churches of Sudbury.

The chapel was tiny, but perfect: the walls made of chequered stone and flint, outlining the huge windows, five along this side, that must make the interior as light and airy as if it were entirely surrounded by glass. Battlements hid the low-pitched roof, and it stood amidst tall oaks and elms. In its own miniature way, it was as beautiful and glorious as the flowering stones of York or Westminster: a creation of love and harmony, writ small.

Sir James, his face glowing with pride, waved a hand. 'I built it to celebrate my marriage to my dear wife Anne. If you look closer, there's her badge and mine all over it, Arundel hearts and Tyrell knots, as well as initials, coats of arms, all manner of what. The master mason wasn't cheap, but he was an uncommonly skilful lad.'

The casual tone of his voice did not reveal the evident satisfaction that Sir James felt in his chapel: Christie was willing to wager that the mason, master of his craft though he undoubtedly was, had had many suggestions from his patron about the design and execution of the building. 'I rebuilt the old house at the same time,' Sir James went on. 'It's not as fine as the chapel, I'm sorry to say—but then it's not right that my own house should be more handsome than God's, is it?'

It was true that the plaster and timber of the house a little beyond the chapel was not nearly so imposing, but its smoking chimneys and air of comfort and welcome were a pleasant sight after the long weary miles of their journey. Wellesborne had been sent ahead from Stowmarket to advise Dame Anne Tyrell of her husband's arrival, and now she stood in the doorway, her children grouped excitedly around her. As Sir James explained patiently to Dickon that the stretch of water between chapel and house was not only a fishpond but dug to drain the water away from the foundations in this thick clayey soil, two small boys and a little girl broke away from their mother and charged up to him, shouting a delighted welcome and showering him with questions. Beaming, their father dismounted in front of the porch, swept the little girl, who was perhaps three or four years old, into his arms for a paternal embrace, and ruffled the heads of the boys, who were jumping around him with joyful exuberance. 'Well, here's a fine noisy welcome home for your old father! Aren't you going to stand still and give me a proper kiss? You've grown, Tom,' he added to the older boy, who was perhaps eight. 'You'll soon be as tall as me. And I've brought you two new playmates—this is Dickon, and the lad over there is Edward. They'll be staying with us for a while.'

Over the bobbing heads of the children, Christie met Anne Tyrell's amused, rather puzzled eye. She was a short, round woman with a square brown face indicating both common sense and a disdain for fashionable fripperies such as plucked eyebrows, face-paint or a pale complexion. 'Husband, do you not think that our guests may need some introduction, not to say explanation?'

Since by now about half-a-dozen servants had appeared, as if by magic, to gape at their master's home-coming, it was evident that to do so here and now would be most unwise. Moreover, Edward had fallen rather than dismounted from his horse, and was being supported by Perkin and Dickon. Sir James called for those standing idly about to take their horses, and ushered his party within the house, while Dame Anne called for wine and wafers, and a servant badged with the Tyrell knot conducted them to a little chamber where they could wash the dirt and dust from their hands and faces. Then they gathered in the winter parlour, which faced south and had a blazing fire in a wide brick hearth, to explain their sudden arrival to Dame Anne.

Her own children had been banished, and she stood by the hearth, a plain but capable figure, her hair hidden by a simple linen hood. A servant had placed a jug, cups and a platter heaped high with wafers upon a table, and poured the wine. Sir James dismissed him, ensured that the door was shut, and turned to his wife. 'My dear, I must apologise for failing to give you sufficient warning of our arrival, but we have come in haste and secrecy from London.'

Dame Anne's brown gaze was resting speculatively on the boys: Dickon bright and alert, one hand tucked into his belt and the other behind his back in characteristic pose, his eyes glancing about the room with interest, and Edward, still drooping with weariness, standing with hanging head beside Christie. Sir James, smiling rather apprehensively, took a deep breath and waved the two children forward. There was no accepted etiquette for this situation: at last he said quietly, 'My dear, I wish to present you to Edward Plantagenet and his brother Richard, sons to our late King Edward.'

There was a startled silence: and then Anne Tyrell, echoing that other practical woman, Cis Hobbes, sank on her knees before them. Edward, his face remarkably composed, extended a thin scabby hand, and Dickon, in his direct way, said quickly, 'That must be a secret, Dame Tyrell. No-one's suppose to know that we're here. You mustn't kneel to us, please, we're just ordinary children now.'

Since he was so very far from ordinary, Christie could not suppress a smile. Dame Tyrell turned towards him, and her husband hastily introduced him. 'Christopher Heron, in the King's service, my dear, and the provider of plots, plans and disguises—he even dressed them up as girls to get them out of the Tower!'

'Merciful heaven,' said Dame Anne, smiling. 'It can't have been an easy task—not many boys would volunteer to smother their legs and freedom in a skirt. Let me give you wine, you all look quite exhausted, and I think that Edward should sit down at once, before he falls down. And *then*, dear husband, you can explain exactly how and why this humble house must entertain two princes in secret.'

*

It was dark before the tale was done, with help from Christie, who found himself liking Anne Tyrell's rather dry, abrupt style, and the irrepressible Dickon. A light supper had been brought and eaten, and the three older children, Tom, James and Nan, had come in briefly with their nurse to say goodnight. Christie was of the opinion that Edward at least would also benefit from an early dismissal to bed, but with that mulishness that he often showed in the face of reasonable persuasion, he refused utterly to leave, and remained hunched in his chair, picking at the sores on his hands and listening in silence to the story of his escape.

'And so the boys must stay here, for the moment?' said Dame Anne at last. 'I am more than willing to have you as our guests, Edward and Richard, but you won't be well-guarded—we have no soldiers here, and if you want their presence here to remain a secret, my husband, you can hardly surround the place with armed men.'

'Secrecy should be their best defence,' said Tyrell. 'You and I, my dear, and young Kit here, and his servant and Wellesborne, will know their true identity. The other servants need know only that they are cousins—of yours, I think, since Cornwall is far away and there are no other Arundels hereabouts. That is all our children must learn, for the moment at any rate. Later, perhaps we can tell them the truth, when all this talk of rebellion has faded and the assassins have been discovered.'

Dame Anne drained her wine-cup with a sigh. She said slowly, 'Will you be staying here for a while, husband? Or must you go back to the King?'

'Someone must take His Grace word that his nephews are safe and well,' Tyrell said. 'Possibly Wellesborne could go, tomorrow. But for now, my dear, you have your husband back with you, and the pleasure of his company for a few days yet. And young Kit here, of course, if you can find room for him as well?'

'Indeed I shall try,' said Dame Anne, laughing. 'He shall be as one of our family.'

Afterwards, Christie was to look back on that time at Gipping as an idyll, a haven of peace and tranquillity between the desperate urgency of their mission to save the children, and the upheaval in his life which came after. As autumn approached with mellow warmth, he could relax and shed the responsibilities and burdens of life in the King's service, becoming for the first time for many years his own man again, no duties to perform, no service, no errands, no formality. He had the freedom to go where and when he pleased, as the guest of Sir James and his wife, and in those last days of September he could almost feel part of their warm, close little family. Edward, his health badly affected by the strains of the journey, did not rise from his bed for many days: and yet, although sick and exhausted, his mind seemed more at peace than ever before, and the sores on his hands and face began to heal up. Moreover, the night attacks which had been so frequent grew less and less, and Dickon, who insisted on sharing his brother's chamber, could report on his progress with optimism. Good plentiful food, ample rest and freedom from fear had been necessary for Edward to begin his recovery, and he was slowly returning to something more resembling the beautiful, accomplished child whom Christie had first seen at Stony Stratford, five months previously.

Dickon, also revelling in his freedom, quickly struck up a friendship with Tom Tyrell, who was two years younger, and the two of them ran wild on their ponies and had to be forcibly persuaded to sit still long enough for lessons with the Tyrells' chaplain. Six-year-old James was under the care of a nurse, with his little sister Nan, who was three: there was also William, a baby. Christie, to his surprise, found himself becoming more and more involved with the children, particularly Dickon and Tom, and discovered that he actually enjoyed their company. Perkin, with approval, watched as his master, unawares, shed in this warm informal household the stiff impassive face of years of service to the great, and began to present a much more human face to all the world. It was a face Meg would have known, and Perkin and his mother too had had glimpses of it: but to relax his guard all the time, instead of just in private, was an indulgence to which Christie had never succumbed since early childhood.

Dame Anne, who had at first thought him rather unapproachable, soon discovered her mistake. At a hint from her husband, she offered him the loan of her lute—for his own, of necessity, had been left behind at York with Bayard, in the dubious care of Sir Ralph Bigod—and from thence their evenings were much enlivened by singing, dancing and music, as their days were spent according to the weather in reading, cards and chess, or riding, hawking and shooting. Sir James, who was after all Master of the Henchmen, was able to teach the boys something of knightly pursuits: butts and a quintain were rigged up, and both Tom and Dickon, in their struggle to become proficient, sported a wide collection of bruises in very varied locations. It was easy to forget that the shouting, freckled child in the old leather jack and mended hose, charging on the plump pony that more properly belonged to Tom, had been born a Prince and had lived all his life amid the exalted luxury of court: and certainly no suspicion of his true identity then entered the heads of Tyrell's household. Edward, too, as he grew stronger, seemed to put away his resentment and unhappiness, and to accept his present, humbler lot in life: but he still tired easily, declined to join in his brother's boisterous games—even shooting at the butts, formerly a favourite exercise, he now claimed to be beyond his strength—and spent much time reading or talking with the chaplain and Dame Anne. She felt sorry for him, but it was impossible to feel thus for Dickon, who entirely lacked self-pity. Instead, she spent many hours with the pale, fragile boy who seemed more inclined by nature for a scholar or a monk than for a King. And she wondered, as did Christie, what would become of these two very different children.

And then the peace was ended, abruptly, with the return of Wellesborne from Pontefract, where the King had gone on his removal from York. He brought written instructions from Richard, phrased in general terms, requesting the presence of his full trusty Master of Henchmen and Horse, Sir James Tyrell, and Christopher Heron, Esquire of the Body. Verbally, the message was rather more detailed and specific. The children were to be left at Gipping, under the care of Dame Anne, trusting in secrecy to make them safe, and the Chancellor and the Duke of Norfolk had been informed of their whereabouts. But as reports were now reaching the King from various spies and informants that rebellion was being planned in the south of England, with the rescue of the Princes as its probable objective, Tyrell was asked to ensure that his house, and its precious guests, did not remain unguarded in his absence: without, of course, giving away the importance of the two children he claimed to be his wife's kin.

So when Sir James Tyrell and Christie Heron and their servants rode away from Gipping on Wednesday, the eighth day of October, they left behind not only a bevy of rather tearful children (even Dickon looked subdued and unhappy, and Edward had had to be reassured over and over again that they would still be safe in Sir James's absence), but a half-dozen stalwart men, armed with swords and axes and halberds, with instructions to defend Dame Anne, the house and the children, with their lives if necessary. The rumour of insurrection was the excuse, although the likelihood of rebellion coming close to such a peaceful little backwater seemed remote, despite the Lancastrian sympathisers around Lavenham. But Sir James explained to his tenants that he would not feel easy in his mind knowing his family to be unguarded, and they must obey Dame Anne in everything. As she was quite accustomed to directing Sir James's business in his absence, he was confident in her ability to keep all the children safe: but nevertheless, as they left that quiet, delightful place, Christie could not help feeling some unease. They seemed so unprotected, so vulnerable.

But nowhere had seemed safer than the Tower, and yet they had almost died there.

He had not wanted to leave Gipping: the wrench as they had turned away from the shady trees, now coloured gold and amber and russet, had been surprisingly sharp. He realised that he envied Sir James very much his happy marriage and his loving, pleasant children. Not long ago he had decided firmly to remain unmarried until he could acquire lands and a home of his own: now, he found himself pondering the advantages of a wife, and not only to breed his heirs. Sir James and Dame Anne had shared a loving, affectionate, congenial relationship that was very attractive, far removed from the dreary mutual dislike of Sir Thomas Bray and his wife, or the storm and passion, now only a faint childhood memory, of his own parents. A woman to love, and who would love him in return, to make music and laughter with, to breed children, sons like Dickon if he were fortunate, daughters like little Nan Tyrell with her dimples and giggles and endearing lisp. He would rise high, it had been promised, and King Richard was a man who kept his promises and was generous in rewarding good and faithful service. But somehow that prospect seemed a hollow sham without the thought of a family who could share and inherit his prosperity and good fortune.

These thoughts occupied much of his mind as they rode north, and Perkin was privately displeased at his master's apparent return to his former remoteness, not guessing at the real reason. If he had known that Christie was pondering the acquisition of a wife, he would have been vastly reassured.

*

There had been no sense of any urgency in the King's letter, and so they did not hurry, spending two days on the ride to Huntingdon before turning north. And on the afternoon of the fourth day, as they drew near to the town of Grantham, they heard the sound of fast-approaching hoofbeats behind them. It was two men, riding hard on lathered horses, both bearing, recognisable even at this distance, the red and blue livery of the Duke of Norfolk. They would have ridden past, but Tyrell barred their way, calling out, 'What's the hurry? Are you riding to the King?'

'Yes, Sir James!' said the first horseman, gasping for breath as he reined in his sweating mount. 'His Grace lies tonight at Lincoln, so I am told—I must not stop—I have most urgent news from the Duke of Norfolk!'

'What news?' Christie demanded, but in his bones he knew already, so that the messenger's information did not come as a surprise.

'The Kentishmen are risen up in the Weald, they plan a march on London—the tale runs that they want the Tudor on the throne.' He gathered his horse's reins and urged it onwards: and his parting words, delivered over his shoulder as the animal galloped away, left Sir James and Christie staring in astonished horror at his disappearing, dusty wake.

'They're saying the Duke of Buckingham will lead them!'

PART
✿ III ✿
1483–85

THE HEIRESS OF ASHCOTT

'Love must arise of the heart,
and not by no constraint.'
(BOOK 18, CHAPTER 21)

CHAPTER TWELVE

**'Full well she knew
the cruelness of her mother.'**
(BOOK 8, CHAPTER 11)

Sir Thomas Bray had been quite open with his wife and daughter: once decided upon joining the rebels he saw no reason to hide any of the details of the plot from them, or for that matter from his neighbours. The Ashcott blacksmith was kept very busy repairing and refurbishing armour and weapons, and many of his tenants had promised their support. All was planned, nothing it seemed could fail: until news came in the second week of October, that the men of Kent had risen fully eight days too early.

Even then, it might not have been disastrous, save for the swift and decisive movement of the Duke of Norfolk, who had been keeping a watchful eye on the country around London for just such an eventuality as this, and was able to spring into action immediately. The City was secured, and the rebels prevented from crossing the Thames into Essex, and thus rendered helpless, cut off from their fellow conspirators in the west.

Undaunted, these remained faithful to their original plan. After all, the men of Kent were but a small part of the overall scheme: the Duke of Buckingham would march in strength from Wales, Henry Tudor's force was to land on the south coast, and they themselves had many promises of support in their rising against the northern usurper and murderer of his innocent nephews. Three days before that appointed for the revolt, Sir Thomas Bray kissed his wife with unusual tenderness, received a passionate hug from his only daughter, and rode away with his dozen or so men-at-arms to his meeting at Newbury with Sir William Stonor and Sir Richard Woodville, John Harcourt and Sir William Berkeley, Sir Roger Tocotes, Sir William Norris, Sir Richard Beauchamp, and many others.

That night, the weather took a hand in the proceedings. There was a storm the like of which few could remember, with lashing winds and torrential rain all across the south-west of England. Nor did it last for one night only: all the next day, and the next, the rain fell and rivers rose and roads became impassable seas of mud. The Duke of Buckingham, assembling a motley and unwilling force from his tenantry, who loathed their harsh and grasping landlord, was not at first concerned: it was when his march eastward was halted by the flooded River Severn that he first faced the possibility of defeat.

His men chose the opportunity to slip away, back to their homes: they were wet, cold, hungry, and saw no chance of any reward for their efforts. The Vaughan family, no friends of the Duke, insolently raided his lands as soon as he had left them, even to the extent of taking and firing his castle at Brecon. Buckingham's world had collapsed in ruins about him, with dreadful speed: within the space of a week, his triumphant march had disintegrated into ignominious failure. He halted at Weobley to rally what remained of his demoralised forces, and woke up to find that the Bishop of Ely was no longer amongst them. The rat had left the sinking ship.

It was the end of his rebellion, but not, please God, the end of Duke Harry. He could find refuge amongst his faithful retainers, and meanwhile Henry Tudor's invasion would surely succeed, even without the glorious name of Buckingham to aid him. Knowing that the Vaughans and Sir Humphrey Stafford were hot on his trail, Buckingham adopted a servant's guise and fled into Shropshire.

The same storm that had put an end to the glorious hopes of the Duke of Buckingham had also removed the threat of Henry Tudor. He had had most generous help from the Duke of Brittany—fifteen ships and five thousand men—and had set sail as arranged with what in his cautious, wary nature passed for optimism. Fierce gales had scattered his fleet on the first night, but, little daunted, he had limped along the English coast with the two ships remaining. Soldiers at Poole had attempted to entice him ashore, shouting that the Duke of Buckingham had triumphed, but Henry Tudor, as wily a fox as his supporter the Bishop of Ely, was unconvinced, and sailed away to safety.

At Newbury, Sir Thomas Bray waited with his fellow-conspirators for news of the victorious Duke of Buckingham. They had committed themselves irrevocably to rebellion, their standards had been raised, the leadership of the Duke of Buckingham and the claim of Henry Tudor to the throne proclaimed: they were exceedingly conscious of the penalties of failure. And the countryside around seemed generally unenthusiastic, not to say apathetic: even the news of King Richard's unspeakable wickedness in murdering his nephews had not brought people flocking to help depose him.

Then devastating news reached them. Buckingham's army had never materialised, and the Duke himself had fled towards Wales: moreover, the King himself was marching towards them in strength, unopposed. Resolution turned to panic, and like Henry Tudor's ships, they scattered.

*

Henry Stafford, second Duke of Buckingham, sat in his homespun disguise at the rough plank table of one of his humbler retainers, and filled his golden head with marvellous plans for the future. This was just a temporary setback. Soon the rest of the conspirators would sweep all before them, the countryside rising to support the mighty name of Stafford and Buckingham. The Tudor would land in force, and together they would cast down the usurper from the throne, just as he had planned and schemed ever since the news had reached him, six long months ago, of King Edward's untimely death. And then, once Richard was out of the way, and with the two boys long dead, he would be able to manipulate Henry Tudor too. It depended on the unknown Welshman's personality, of course, but one who had so successfully duped the great Duke of Gloucester would surely have no trouble in controlling this Lancastrian non-entity.

He was dwelling on this attractive scene when the door opened without even the courtesy of a knock. He had expected the food that Ralph Bannaster had promised him: instead, the room was suddenly full of armed men. Bewildered, protesting, the Duke was unceremoniously hauled from his stool and brought to face a stern-looking man who announced that he was Thomas Mytton, Sheriff of this county. 'And you are Henry Stafford, Duke of Buckingham?' he finished, looking dubiously at his captive's threadbare ordinary garb, so very different from the famous peacock dress of the flamboyant Duke. The disreputable man standing before him reared his golden head proudly. 'I am indeed. What does this mean? Why am I being held?'

'You are declared a traitor by proclamation of His Grace King Richard, and I am commanded to convey you to his officers, who will take you to His Grace. Then, you will be required to answer for your crimes.' The man's eyes were as cold and hard as pebbles. 'Take him away.'

They took him to Shrewsbury, heavily escorted, on a sorry jade of a horse, lean and spavined. Not a soul lifted a finger to help him: several threw mud or filth. He fixed his mind on the meeting with

[265]

the King, knowing that his golden persuasive tongue would win him over, as it had done so many times before. He would beg for mercy—not too self-abasingly, of course—and swear faithful allegiance. He could betray his former associates, claim that he had intended all along to change sides at the last minute and so rid the country of plotters. He would be reconciled with the King—if only he could be granted an hour with Richard, all would be well.

At Shrewsbury they handed him over to two of the King's knights. He recognised them both. One was Sir James Tyrell, whom he knew as an unimaginative, plodding soldier, and whom he had always despised. The other was a much younger man, whom he had left as a plain Esquire, but high in the King's service and favour: and now, it seemed, grown much higher. They were immaculately dressed in velvet and jewels, with the rich ceremonial collars of the royal household, and their faces were stern and implacable. For the first time, a tiny tendril of doubt coiled itself inside Buckingham's devious brain.

They asked him for details of the conspiracy: he refused, saying that he would confess his crimes only to the King. 'So be it,' Tyrell said, without much interest, and Buckingham was taken away, to spend a cold dark night in a bare little room with blankets and a candle thrust in as an afterthought. He was not accustomed to being ignored, and beat on the door for some time, demanding the attention of a servant: but no-one bothered to reply.

It took three days to convey him to Salisbury, where King Richard had halted to ensure the loyalty of the countryside about. Neither Tyrell nor Christie had any more contact with their noble captive than was absolutely necessary. Every time Christie beheld that arrogant beautiful head, undimmed by defeat, or heard again the lovely persuasive voice, his skin crawled. They knew now that it had been on Buckingham's orders that the attempted poisoning of Edward and Dickon had been carried out, and Christie, seeing the smug face unsoftened by any trace of shame, repentance or contrition, felt his fingers itch with the desire to maim or to kill. He thought of the children, so nearly dead, and young Edward's health and spirit so badly damaged, possibly for ever: of the countryside threatened once more with the evils of war and rebellion and foreign invasion: of the grief of Elizabeth Woodville and her daughters in sanctuary, deceived into thinking the boys were dead and thus inveigled into plotting to overthrow the King. It was a long catalogue of sins, to lay at the door of this man's vanity and delusions of kingmaking, and he could fully understand the King's overwhelming grief and rage when the news of his friend's betrayal had reached him. Buckingham was doomed: nothing could save him, and the only person who did not seem to know it was the Duke himself.

When they reached Salisbury, he demanded to see the King. Christie took his request, knowing full well what the answer would be, and found his sovereign lord as hard and immovable as granite, the grey eyes like chips of ice. 'I will not see him,' said King Richard in a voice with the tones of winter: and Christie, understanding, retreated.

Buckingham did not believe it. He cajoled and pleaded and begged, convinced that the malice of his guards alone prevented an audience. Later, embarrassingly, he wept, but in vain. The melodious voice, roughened with distress and urgency, promised enormous rewards if he could only be granted a moment, no more, to plead for his life. The King, however, had already decided, and in the market place the carpenters were hammering the nails into a hastily-built scaffold.

To the impassive Sir Ralph Assheton, newly appointed deputy Constable of England since the previous holder, Buckingham himself, had rebelled, he poured out his confession. The names of Lady Margaret Beaufort, Countess of Richmond, her steward Reginald Bray, her physician Doctor Lewis, the Bishop of Ely, the Marquis of Dorset, Sir Thomas St Leger and other names of interest were noted down along with those of the leaders of the conspiracies in the southern and western counties. Most of them were already known: it was still an unpleasant shock for Christie to hear again the name of Sir Thomas Bray thus branded a rebel and a traitor. This was another crime to lay at Buckingham's door, the callous manipulation of honest knights and gentlemen such as Sir Thomas, pawns in the hands of their cynical leaders, who had been falsely encouraged to rebel, and would now pay the price with their lands, and perhaps even their lives.

Henry Stafford, Duke of Buckingham, paid his dues to God and to the King that afternoon. The wind blew cold, and drops of rain mingled with the whirling leaves and rubbish in the Market Square in Salisbury, as the cathedral bells tolled deeply overhead, and crowds gathered to watch because it was not after all every day that a Duke of the blood royal, however dilute and tainted, was headed in their sleepy city. Some murmured because it was a Sunday, and

All Souls' Day, and not therefore appropriate for an execution, but more held the opinion that, holy day or no, it was a fate richly deserved, and they did not in the least blame the King for despatching his false friend as soon as possible. The whisper went round that it was doubtless the Duke who had compassed the deaths, so widely reported, of Edward IV's sons, and clods of filth were thrown from the back of the crowd, where the soldiers around the scaffold could not reach.

The Duke of Buckingham, still in the mean homespun of his disguise, stood on the scaffold and blinked unbelieving at the grim grey sky. The King had refused to see him—but that must be due to the malevolence of the men around him, and he had bribed one of the guards, with his ruby and gold thumb-ring, to take a message to Richard. Buoyed up with this last hope, he mounted the rough wooden steps unafraid. Richard would forgive him, would accept his protestations of future unswerving loyalty, once he had had a chance to explain his case. He was planning what he would say as they made him kneel: and he was still waiting for the shouts of reprieve when the axe rose, and fell.

*

In Exeter, the failed conspirators packed the town to consider their future which, on the most optimistic level, looked bleak indeed. They had had the news of the death of their leader, Buckingham, and of the dismal failure of Tudor's invasion. Now the King was approaching, swift and relentless, and there were perhaps only two alternatives left: flight into ignominious exile, or into hiding. Many took ship, and sailed to join Henry Tudor, amongst them John Harcourt, the Marquis of Dorset, Lionel Woodville, the Bishop of Salisbury, and sundry others. Sir Thomas Bray chose to go into hiding, professing himself too old and too unwell to go jaunting across the sea into uncertainty and penury. He had plenty of friends who would help to conceal him, and besides, he must get word to his wife and daughter of his situation.

It was unfortunate that he chose, as his companion in escape, Sir Thomas St Leger, who was an old friend of his, and also the widower of the King's eldest sister, Anne of York, who had died some years ago. St Leger, with the Marquis of Dorset, had been the chief stirrer of rebellion in the south-west: he was well-known, but not well-liked. A servant in the house near Exeter where the men were hiding heard of the reward offered for his capture and betrayed him: and Sir Thomas Bray found himself a captive, taken in revolt against his King.

He did not expect mercy, though the friends of St Leger offered huge bribes for their release. He regretted that their plans had failed, and that the usurper remained firmly on the throne, despite their efforts. He could not make a will, since all his goods and lands would be forfeit: and he thought bitterly and sadly of the wife and daughter who had urged him to take this course, and who would now probably be left destitute. And then, in his cell in the castle, he had an unexpected visitor.

He did not at first recognise the tall man in rich crimson and jewels, with the collar of the royal household, who ducked under the stone lintel and stared at him with hard grey eyes. The guard said, 'Sir Christopher Heron,' and shut the door behind the new-made knight.

Sir Thomas got heavily to his feet. The cell was damp and uncomfortable, and smelled foul: Christie could see the water glistening on the walls, and something rustled in a corner. He felt sudden pity and sadness, that the man who had once been his friend should be brought to such a pass, and had to remind himself sharply that Sir Thomas was a self-professed rebel and traitor, well aware of the just penalty for his crimes. It had not stopped him, though, from adding his plea for mercy to the chorus demanding that Richard spare St Leger's life. He himself cared nothing for St Leger, but he could not in conscience allow Sir Thomas to be executed without a word in his favour.

The King, in the matter of St Leger, had been implacable. As for Sir Thomas Bray, he seemed prepared to be merciful, while pointing out the seriousness of his offence. Christie had listened, understanding, and had come away hopeful, with permission to interview Sir Thomas gladly granted.

He saw with disquiet how ill the man looked. His skin was a dirty greyish-yellow colour, and the flesh had become flabby and sunken, the old burn-scars on his face alone preserving an illusion of pink health. He fixed Christie with a tired gaze and said, 'Has he made you a knight, then?'

'Yes,' said the other man, not enlarging upon it: he could hardly give the true reason for his elevation. Sir Thomas looked him over shrewdly. 'It seems to agree with you. Have you come to gloat, then?'

'I've come to give you some comfort and hope,' said Christie. He saw that Sir Thomas had pressed his hand to his chest, as if it pained him, and beads of sweat broke out on his mottled forehead. He added quickly, 'Sir Thomas, are you ill?'

'It's nothing—I've had these pains for some time now. Though it shouldn't matter,' the old knight added wryly. 'Since I'll be headed in a few days anyway.'

'You may not be,' said Christie, dropping his voice. Sir Thomas frowned, staring up at him: it seemed he had not the energy to rise from his stool. 'What's that you say?'

'I said, there is a chance the execution will not take place. I have appealed to the King for clemency on your behalf, and he has listened with some favour.'

'Well, he obviously likes you,' said Sir Thomas, with the ghost of a chuckle. 'I misjudged you, Christie Heron, and I'm sorry for it. And I thank you with all my heart for your efforts, but I warn you, you may be labouring in vain.' He broke off, hand still across his chest, his eyes abstracted as if listening to something, and then resumed with rather less vigour. 'I'm a sick man, you must see it as plain as I feel it. I've seen my father with these pains, and I know how it goes. In a day, or a month, or half a year, I may well be dead, and probably sooner rather than later.' He stopped, doubled over by a spasm to severe to ignore, and it was some time before he could resume. 'Christie—you've risen a great way—we've had our differences and have them still, but there is yet some friendly feeling between us, is there not?'

'The fact that I am here now would seem to prove it.'

'Then do me a favour, lad, if the worst comes and I die here, either of these pains or the headsman's axe make little odds—I've confessed my sins and done penance, and would go to God gladly, but for one thing—my dear Julian. She'll be left alone, friendless, dowerless—will you help her? The King gave a pension to Lady Hastings after he killed her husband—can you put in a word for my wife, and my dear, dear daughter?' Tears stood in his eyes. 'I cannot bear to think of her penniless. I know you don't care for her, and I must admit she detests you, but for my sake, if I should die, do this for me—will you promise it?'

'I promise,' said Christie, and smiled. 'Though I shall try to keep it secret from Mistress Julian—help from me will be as welcome as from the Devil.'

Sir Thomas laughed: it turned into a fit of coughing that was obviously agonisingly painful. 'Thank you,' he whispered, when he could speak again. 'You don't go out of your way to show it, do you, lad—but you've more compassion than most.'

'It's merely for the convenience of my conscience,' said Christie, and Sir Thomas's pain-twisted smile followed him wryly from the unpleasant cell.

He had seen the marks of mortality plain on the older man's face, and said as much to Richard that evening. 'Sir Thomas Bray is a dying man. He may not live long enough for you have him headed.'

'I had not intended to execute him,' Richard said. He was playing chess with Francis Lovell, and the game had reached a point where a bad move from either protagonist would spell disaster. His eyes moving thoughtfully from his remaining knight, wonderfully carved in ivory, to his threatened queen, he added, 'What family has he?'

'A wife, Dame Alice, and one daughter.'

'His heiress, then? How old is she?'

'Sixteen or seventeen, I should think, Your Grace.'

'Of marriageable age,' said the King, pondering. His thin pale hand rose, hovered over the queen, and moved her five squares to the left. 'Check.'

Francis Lovell's face betrayed his dismay. 'The very move I was dreading! What's your concern in all this, Christie? You're not casting your lure for the daughter?'

Christie shot him a startled glance, and laughed. 'The thought hadn't entered my head. The girl's a termagant, a scold in the making like her mother. Sir Thomas may not be happy in his prison cell, but it's undoubtedly quieter than his home.'

'Are you going to move, Francis?' Richard enquired, as Lovell stared despairingly at his suddenly altered fortunes. With a shrug of resignation, the Chamberlain pushed an ebony bishop with a jewelled mitre between the white queen and his endangered king. At once Richard brought up a disregarded castle to take it. 'Check —and mate, I think you will find.'

He was right. With a resigned grin, Lovell conceded defeat and began to set out the pieces on the board again. An esquire brought wine to refill their cups, while another attendant drew the shutters and curtains against the darkness. This moment of intimacy was rare, and more so in the hectic events of the last weeks, when crushing rebellion had been far more important than leisurely pastimes, music or other diversions, and it was only now, in Exeter, that the King and his household had at last taken the opportunity to relax a little. But the betrayal of Buckingham had left its mark: only the most intimate members of Richard's household knew how little he slept. Christie, already high in the King's favour, had found that his part in the rescue of the boys in the Tower had admitted him finally to the charmed inmost circle of the King's friends, and was treated with redoubled trust, courtesy and affection. Richard had found time to dub him knight, in recognition of certain services lately rendered, and to reward him with lands and offices to the value of one hundred pounds a year, proper to his new dignity. Those lands, however, were scattered, most being forfeited properties belonging to Lord Hastings or the Marquis of Dorset: no block of land to call a home, to form an estate. And Christie had realised long ago that the best way of obtaining a manor house he could pass on to his descendants, was to marry a lady in possession of one.

The same thought, evidently, had occurred to the King. His hand toying with the intricate carving of the ebony queen, he said, 'Sir Thomas's daughter is of marriageable age. What lands will she inherit, on his death?'

'There's a fine manor called Ashcott, near Deddington in Oxfordshire, and some quantity of land around it. Where else, I do not know.'

'He has manors near Witney and Broughton,' said Lovell, who lived a few miles away. 'And more in Buckinghamshire, so I've heard—besides which, his wife was born a Clifford, and must have brought him a considerably dowry.'

'A sizeable property,' said Richard, his eyes contemplating the chess piece. 'But the daughter is not yet bestowed?'

Christie knew all at once whence this careful conversation was leading, and despite himself, a smile broke out on his face. It was certainly on the surface an excellent solution for all concerned —save possibly for those two most involved. He would marry Julian Bray and so keep Ashcott in her family, provide himself with a wife and an ancestral home, and quite possibly be asked to make sure that his father-in-law did not stray again into the paths of rebellion. There were only two things wrong with the idea: the first, and most important, was that his prospective bride could not bear the sight of him. And the other was that the groom could not cheerfully contemplate life in company with the indomitable Dame Alice.

'The daughter is not betrothed, so far as I know,' he told the King. Richard lifted his eyes to his newest knight's face, now carefully schooled. 'Then at one stroke you can possess yourself of a wife, and lands to enhance your status,' he said. 'You can also save her family from attainder thereby. You plainly know the young lady well. Is she such a shrew that you cannot marry her?'

Christie thought of Julian, the fierce dark eyes and mass of chestnut hair, the graceless passion and turbulent anger within the overlarge frame, and opened his mouth to answer in the affirmative: lands, house or no, he would not mortgage his hopes for the future to a girl he heartily disliked. And then he remembered something else: that same girl, her hands trembling with emotion, her voice, pure and lovely, soaring in song. And some new, unexpected feeling took him by the heart, and whispered of sympathy and compassion. If he did not marry her, her inheritance might be forfeit, and the King bestow her on someone less merciful, less tolerant of her moods and tantrums. He had sensed the cause of her tangled personality, more than a year ago, and he found himself unable to contemplate her marriage to an insensitive or even brutal man who would treat her with even less consideration than did Dame Alice. She loved music, so did he: it was a beginning.

'No,' he said, smiling suddenly. 'I have some hopes of altering her opinion of me.'

'She's the giantess, isn't she?' said Lovell unexpectedly. 'Very tall, big, red-haired girl with a loud voice? I have met her.' He regarded Christie with some sympathy. 'You'll have your work cut out there. I wish you all joy.'

'You are certain of this?' said the King to Christie. 'It does seem an excellent idea, but I'd be the last to wish upon you a wife you do not want. Have you any doubts? You have plenty of time to think on it, before Sir Thomas is told.'

'No doubts,' said Christie, and as he spoke felt the truth of his words. The aptness of the plan had struck him with some force: he had liked Ashcott, and Sir Thomas, and while he did not have much regard for Julian, he thought that he understood her, and that there was a good chance of winning her over. She was very young yet, and young girls were notoriously easy to mould. Dame Alice was another matter, but surely there was some out-of-the-way manor to which she could be despatched beyond earshot.

'No doubts at all?' Richard gave him the benefit of his rare, attractive smile. 'You surprise me—but I don't doubt you'll deal with Mistress Bray and her mother with your usual efficiency. And that's a small matter beside the lands you will possess. You will have to stand surety for Sir Thomas, of course, but I'll release him

[273]

into your custody tomorrow. I don't doubt he'll be agreeable: he struck me as a man open to reason, and this solution will have as many attractions for him, I fancy, as it has for you. Too late to tell him now, of course, but I'll send for him in the morning, and tell him the good news.'

But the morning was too late: for the official who was sent to bring Sir Thomas Bray into the presence of the King returned somewhat delayed and considerably flustered, with sad news. The prisoner, already ill, had suffered a seizure in the night, and died shortly thereafter, a priest in attendance and his soul shriven. It was too late to inform him of his reprieve, and of the plans for his beloved daughter's future: and too late also to tell him that the main reason for his rebellion was false.

*

The news of Sir Thomas Bray's unhappy death in prison in Exeter came to Ashcott four days afterwards, brought by a royal messenger. The letter expressed formal, stilted regret that Sir Thomas had not lived long enough to be apprised of his forthcoming release, and drew Dame Alice's attention to the accompanying document. This set out in an elaborate secretary's hand the various crimes that her husband had committed against the King, and the penalties incurred thereby: and she, as the widow of a proven and self-confessed traitor, faced a simple choice. She could either see his lands given to another, and retire with her daughter to a charitable relative or a nunnery on a pension which the King would be pleased to grant her: or she could agree to the marriage of her said daughter, Julian Bray, to Sir Christopher Heron, knight of the King's household, and the King's most true and faithful servant.

Julian was out hawking when the letter that brought ruin to her world arrived. It was a windy November day, but the sun had shone that morning, and she had called for her favourite hawk, Gawain, and had her horse saddled, and taken herself and her woman Friday and her alaunt Cavall and an attendant groom to the sheepwalks above Ashcott. They had a good gallop, and Cavall flushed out two pigeons and a pheasant, all of which Gawain killed, clean and swift and beautiful. It had been a good day: feeling happier than she had done for some time, she turned her horse's head around and with her companions walked slowly back to Ashcott and a pleasant supper. Already it was near sunset, and the clouds in the west were angrily red, threatening foul weather. The air was chill, and Julian wrapped her warm fur-lined cloak closer about her, and soothed the hooded goshawk on her wrist with soft words and strokes of her gloved hand, while Cavall, tongue hanging out but still jaunty, trotted at her palfrey's side. Friday Gower followed, her calm blue eyes resting thoughtfully on her mistress's broad back. She did not regret staying in Julian's service: on most days the girl was quite tolerable, and in the absence of her mother it was possible to have a pleasant conversation in which Julian might at times treat her as a human being, with opinions and feelings of her own. That did not mean that the younger girl was not spoilt, arrogant, thoughtless and given to appalling outbursts of temper: but there were signs of maturity now, and Friday had hopes that Julian would one day come to be a friend rather than a superior. It all depended on her father: Julian had been very short-tempered since his departure, obviously very anxious for his safety—far more so than her mother, in fact. If only they could have news of him!

The news was waiting for them: and as soon as they entered the hall at Ashcott, and became aware of the hushed unnatural stillness in the house, Friday knew that something was wrong. Then Dame Alice's woman, a sly girl called Mary whom Friday heartily disliked, came up to them, her narrow face at once serious and eager to impart her tidings. 'Dame Alice says you're to see her in her parlour at once, Mistress Julian. She has bad news.'

Julian's heart gave a great lurch within her, and she stared, transfixed, at Mary's sharp eyes and evident relish. It was as if she had known all that day, as if she had enjoyed herself so much because she would never be so lighthearted again. Her father was dead, she knew it, she could see it in the other girl's avid expression, but she would not give Mary the satisfaction of being the first to confirm the tragedy. Instead, she ripped her cloak from her shoulders, thrust it into Friday's arms, and ran from the hall to see her mother.

Even at this moment, long habit made her stop to compose herself outside the door, to smooth her windblown hair and check that her attire was tidy and comparatively clean. Then she knocked, and entered in response to her mother's command to kneel dutifully before her.

There was no grief in Dame Alice's face, only hard anger, and a look of calculation. She had two pieces of paper in her hands. 'Get up, girl. It's about time you were back—you've been gone much too long. There's news of your father—he was captured in Exeter.'

Her voice clearly showed her contempt. At another time, Julian would have been sorely angered, but now she was desperate to discover what had happened. 'Captured? By the King?'

'Yes. Why he didn't take ship like most of them, I don't know. However, he's dead—he died in prison five days ago.'

It was, to say the least of it, a brutal way of breaking the news to the child who had always been the apple of his eye. The words hit Julian with the force of a blow, driving out utterly the brief moment of hope when she had thought that captivity was the worst. She gasped, and tears filled her eyes, spilling over. Her mother glanced at her. 'Well you may weep, girl. It was your urging led him to this, as I recall. Small use crying now. Your father's dead, God rest his soul, and we must think on this.'

Through her sobs, Julian realised, appalled, that her grief was to be dismissed, disregarded as though of small account. She stared, unbelieving, at Dame Alice. 'I can't—can't think of anything—for God's sake, Father's dead, *dead*—and you don't seem to care at all! I can't think of anything else, I can't—aren't we even going to pray for him?'

'All in good time. This is more important—what we are to discuss, daughter, is your marriage.'

If her earlier words had horrified Julian, this was far, far worse. She felt as if suddenly caught inextricably in some dreadful nightmare, from which she must surely, surely now awake. It could not be true: her beloved father, her only friend in all the world save Cavall, dead, slain in prison, foully murdered by the usurper as he had murdered so many others, and her mother could stand there calmly and tell her she must consider marriage. No chance to pray, to weep, to grieve, to mourn, to adjust her life to this new, bleaker path: she must instead look to her marriage.

It was at that moment that Julian, with a clear intensity that frightened her, began truly and deeply to hate her mother. She took a deep breath, and wiped her tears with her kerchief, and raised her head to look Dame Alice full in the face with eyes that glittered. 'Very well,' she said. 'What of my marriage?'

If Dame Alice noticed the change in her daughter, she did not show it. She tapped the papers. 'As Sir Thomas died a rebel in arms, all his lands and good are forfeit to the King, and we face penury, with Ashcott gone to another and you and I turned out to live on the charity of our relatives. However, the King has offered us an alternative which he doubtless thinks will be more attractive. If you marry where he directs, the lands will not be taken, and your rights

[276]

as your father's sole heiress will be confirmed, so that we may both stay here at Ashcott in comfort.' She bestowed a chilly smile on the girl in front of her. 'I know which I would choose, and I think you will be sensible.'

Julian, bewildered, horror-struck, stared at her, her mind in turmoil. To learn in the space of a few minutes of her beloved father's death, and now of a forced marriage was almost too much for her mind to grasp. She siad in a whisper, 'Who? Who is it? Who does the King want me to marry?'

The answer came like the lash of a whip, seared with contempt. 'Sir Christopher Heron.'

In her state of shock, she did not realise, at first, who was meant. 'I don't know him. Who is he?'

'You do know him, my girl, though he's been elevated well above his proper level, it appears. He's that puffed-up minstrel boy your father sent here last year from Scotland.'

Why cannot I weep any more, or faint, or even run out of the room, thought Julian in despair. Why must I keep standing here with my head high and listen to this? It was only her pride that held her there, taut and upright as a strung bow, her eyes fixed on the heavy, brutal, implacable face of her mother, and the tear-tracks drying on her cheeks. She said with the flatness of despair, 'I can't. I can't marry him.'

'You'll marry him, girl, if I have to beat you black and blue to get you to the church door. Don't you understand?' Dame Alice took three steps forward and thrust her head at Julian's, so that the girl felt her mother's breath and spittle on her face. 'You stupid girl, your precious father can't help you—he's dead, and your only protector is the King, and a poor protector he's turned out to be. It's the King who has the ordering of your life now—and if he tells you to take the veil, to the nunnery you go, and no argument! It's to your benefit he hasn't done that, and taken your lands to give to one of his north-country savages—and it's still in his power to do it, if you displease him. Do you understand, girl? You can't disobey the King.'

Julian remained silent, armoured in pride, wondering remotely why she could not follow her mind's most urgent command and strike those cold, calculating features not a foot away from her. Her mother's fleshy, ringed, powerful hands grasped her shoulders and shook her, viciously. 'I said—you—cannot—disobey—the—King. Do you want to go to some nunnery and leave this place for strangers? You have no choice!'

'I won't—I won't marry him!' Julian said. With a frantic twist of her body, she tried to get away from Dame Alice's painful grip, but the hold on her only grew tighter, and she could not free herself.

'Obstinate—ungrateful—wicked—girl!' the older woman shouted, emphasising each word with a violent shake. 'You've no choice, do you hear me? No choice—none at all—and if you persist in this stupidity we'll both be turned out of Ashcott—do you *understand*, you witless girl? You'll be destitute!' And unable to make her point any other way, her right hand came up to strike Julian's face. The stinging pain of the blow brought tears to the girl's eyes: her hand went to her mouth and came away blood-stained from the place where one of Dame Alice's rings had cut her lip. For good measure her mother slapped her again on the other cheek, and then released her and strode over to the hearthplace and back, her small eyes glaring at the stunned, horrified figure of her recalcitrant child standing numbly in the middle of the floor. 'Well? Are you dumb? Now let's have your answer!'

Aware of her bleeding face, Julian could think of only one thing: how to get her revenge. She said savagely, 'It's the same as it was before! I'd *rather* be destitute than marry that loathsome man! And I know why *you* want me to marry him—you're only concerned for your own comfort, and you wouldn't be able to live so well in a nunnery on a pension, would you? You don't care about me at all—not at *all*, you evil old woman, you only care about yourself!'

With a gasp, Dame Alice lunged at her, but Julian, expecting it, was too quick for her. She retreated to the door, her hands groping for the latch, and said breathlessly, 'You'll have to put me in chains and *drag* me to the church—and you can't force me to say the vows. I won't marry him, never, never, never!'

*

Friday, who had ascertained from the rest of the household the news of Sir Thomas's death and the bargain made with Julian's marriage, found her mistress lying face down on her bed, sobbing despairingly into the softness of the feather bolster. She dipped a kerchief in water and attempted to bathe the swollen, tear-stained face, but the girl would have none of it and struck her hands frantically. 'Go away, go away, I tell you—go *away*!'

Friday, reflecting that Julian was best left alone to indulge her natural grief for her father, retreated. At the door she all but bumped into Dame Alice, grim of face and wielding a birch rod. 'Out, Gower. I wish to speak with my daughter.'

Any anger Friday had felt at Julian's behaviour evaporated abruptly. Overwhelmed with a feeling of sudden appalled sympathy for her mistress, she opened her mouth to remonstrate with Dame Alice, and then thought better of it. Any pleas for mercy on Julian's behalf would undoubtedly lead to instant dismissal, and by the look of it the poor girl would be in desperate need of a friend before the day was out. She dropped a curtsey and went away, finding her own eyes full of tears.

She was summoned an hour or two later by Dame Alice. Still evidently furious, Julian's mother stood in her parlour, two scarlet spots of anger brilliant on her cheeks and her small pale blue eyes glittering with rage. 'You are to attend my daughter. She is being most obdurate, in spite of all persuasion. She is to stay in her chamber until she relents. You are to allow her no comfort, nothing she asks for, and only the food that I permit—no dainties, no sweet-meats, and above all no books nor music. If that accursed lute were not so valuable, I'd have it burnt. Do you understand me, Gower? She is to be confined until she yields to reason. Now go to her.'

Apprehensively, Friday made her way again to Julian's chamber, and listened with compassion to the muffled sounds on the other side of the stout oaken door. Then, gently, she went in.

Julian lay hunched on the bed, her body shaken at intervals by dry, racking sobs, as if all her tears had been spent. She had evidently not submitted tamely to her mother's beating: her face was cut and bruised where the birch had caught it, and her hands were bloodstained. It was her back, however, that had taken the worst punishment. In places the rod had slashed the thin wool of her gown, and blood matted and stained the blue cloth. Friday drew in her breath sharply and then, with great gentleness, set to work. As if tending a very young child, she stripped the ruined gown, kirtle and smock from Julian's abused body, and washed the blood away from her back, head and hands, seeing with shocked sympathy that some of the worst cuts might leave permanent scars. Then she went in search of ointment, and was given a jar, very grudgingly, by Dame Alice from her own cupboard. 'I suppose you must have this. Has she repented yet of her wicked behaviour?'

'She has said nothing, Dame Alice.'

'You must tell me the instant she shows any sign of repentance,' said the older woman, frowning. 'And you may inform her that if

[279]

she persists in this foolish obstinacy, she may expect no mercy from me. You may go.'

Her normally placid soul seething with an entirely alien anger, Friday marched back to Julian's chamber, and slammed the door with uncharacteristic vigour. The girl on the bed sat up unguardedly, and then gasped with pain. 'Friday?'

Her voice at least was fairly normal, though her face was not. Never beautiful, it was now downright ugly, disfigured with cuts and purple bruises, red and swollen with weeping. 'I've brought you some ointment,' said her waiting woman, keeping her voice calm with an effort. 'If you would lie on your belly, I will put it on your back.'

Julian's tear-reddened eyes stared hopelessly at the older girl: then, meekly, she did as she was asked. A muffled gasp of agony was the only sign of pain as Friday, with slow gentle fingers, slipped her smock down, anointed the weals on her back, and pulled the linen garment back up to cover them. 'Is that better?'

'I don't know,' said Julian. She was lying on her stomach, her face pressed against the bolster, and her voice was rather muffled. 'Was it my mother's ointment?'

'Yes,' said Friday , rather warily, but there was no explosion. Instead, Julian went on, carefully, 'Then—then I'd prefer that you didn't put it on again. I'll go without, please.'

There was a silence, while Friday marshalled arguments in her mind and then discarded them. 'Very well,' she said at last, and then added cautiously, 'Do you not wish to marry this man then?'

'I'd hardly be in this condition if I did,' said Julian bitterly. 'Oh, Friday, you fool, of *course* I don't want to marry him. Would you? He's only a common minstrel, for all he's been made a knight, though why I can't think—and he's loathsome, horrible, I hate him, I *can't* marry him, Friday, I can't.'

Friday stared at her in bewilderment. 'Who? I don't know who it is you must marry—only that the King wishes it.'

'You do know him, he's that dreadful minstrel who came here last year. The one who treated me as if—as if I was six years old!'

There were several comments that Friday could have offered, but she wisely held her tongue. She did wonder at the intensity of Julian's feelings, for she herself had thought Christopher Heron a personable and pleasant enough young man, but it was her mistress's way to be perverse—offered the hand of a veritable paragon of beauty, virtue and wit, she would rail against him if she had not chosen him herself. Friday was well aware of the deficiencies in Julian's character: she also knew as well as Dame Alice that there was no choice. The King commanded, and would brook no disobedience, no hesitation, no doubts, certainly not from the sixteen-year-old daughter of an attainted rebel. She wondered how to convey this unpalatable truth without risking verbal or physical abuse: in the end, she said quietly, 'He may not be so bad once you are acquainted with him.'

Julian jerked round: it was obviously painful, for she gasped, but otherwise ignored her damaged back. 'Understand this, Friday—I don't want to be acquainted with him. I am *not* going to marry him.'

'You may find you have no choice,' said her maid. As Julian's face creased with rage, she added quickly, 'Please—I'm not your enemy, nor do I want to be. I don't agree with your mother, nor with what she has done to you—I think it is despicable. But, please, Julian, please remember—it is not your *mother* who commands you. It is the King.'

'I know. But why did he have to choose that Heron man? *Why?*'

'Perhaps Master Heron asked him,' said Friday mildly. Julian stared at her. 'I can't think why. He doesn't like me, he told me so—you remember, you must, you were there.'

'He could feel sorry for you.'

Julian treated this suggestion with short shrift, and a word she had learned in the stables. 'I know why he wants to marry me. He doesn't want *me*, he couldn't care less about *me*—he wants Ashcott, he wants all this.' Her hand waved at the stones, the arras, the carved furnishings, the green lush land without the walls. 'That's all he wants me for—my wealth. I'm nothing, less than a dog or a cow.' She began to laugh, or sob, Friday did not know which. 'Oh, why, oh, why did they kill my father? What had he done? He only rebelled because the little Princes were killed.'

'The word is that he was not executed—that he died naturally, in prison,' Friday said gently, repeating what she had heard from the other members of the household. Julian waved a furious hand. 'You can't believe that! They murdered him, just as they murdered those poor little boys, and Lord Rivers, and Lord Hastings, and everyone else who's stood in their way—in the King's way!' And then, as if the full impossibility of her situation had only now struck home, she added, more quietly, 'Oh, Friday, what am I to do? What *can* I do?'

[281]

Her maid gazed with compassion at the girl on the bed, her hair matted and tangled, her face battered and ugly with cuts and bruises, and a lack of hope plain and piteous in her eyes. 'You must give in,' she said at last.

It was the wrong choice of words. 'No!' Julian cried, and in a savage movement that must have hurt her a great deal, flung herself face down on the bed and abandoned herself to rage and grief. There was nothing further that Friday could do or say: she stood looking down at the other girl for a long moment, and then, feeling suddenly weary and heartsick, turned and left her alone.

*

In the days that followed, Julian Bray, whose life had not up till now been particularly happy, suffered a misery such as she had never known, a dark agony of soul that had no solace, for in her own heart she knew that she was to blame, entirely to blame, for her dreadful predicament. Over and over, in the intervals when she was not praying for her father's soul, and its swift passage through the agonies of Purgatory to the deserved joys of Heaven, she examined her actions, her words, herself, in the bitter merciless light of her guilt. She had confessed to the priest, far more honestly than ever before, her manifold sins—pride, hatred, disobedience, wilfulness, selfishness—and had received his instructions for her penance almost with disappointment: for what number of prayers, of charitable gifts, of candles lit or Aves said, could ever erase the guilt and self-loathing that she herself now felt?

She had urged her father to rebel: she had attacked his self-respect, impugned his honour, and encouraged him to a course of action which had led directly to his death, the end of the person she loved best in all the world. She hoped that he had died shriven, his sins confessed and his penitence noted by priest and God, and that a soul whose faults were more a matter of too much kindness, too much love and compassion, than of any wickedness or evil, would now surely come to safety in Heaven. His punishment had been swift. Hers, she knew, would last her life long: and beside it, even her hatred of her mother and her loathing for that marriage, seemingly inevitable, seemed pale and petty things. Her thoughtlessness and pride had led her beloved father to his death, and she could never, ever, forgive herself.

And in the long lonely hours of torment, when she turned that inward eye savagely upon her character and found that she intensely disliked what she saw, Julian put aside her childhood, unknowing that she did. She had had the knowledge brought home to her, with brutality, that she was responsible for others as well as herself: that she could not live her life thinking only of her own emotions, pleasures, griefs, that there were others whose happiness depended on what she did or said. Through childish selfishness she had eliminated one of those people: but there was still Friday, patient, uncomplaining despite the years of heartlessness, intolerance and downright abuse. Friday had been gentle, had not inflicted her presence, had performed her duties with care and compassion. If I were in her place, thought Julian with disbelief, I would hate me. Friday doesn't—she has said she is my friend—or at least, not my enemy. I will be Friday's friend, for God knows I am going to need one, and my mother most emphatically is not.

None of her self-examination had changed her feelings towards Dame Alice: for she knew that, whatever her own sins, her mother's were the same and greater. Dame Alice had loved neither her husband, for whom she had obviously felt little more than faint contempt, nor her daughter, whose value lay now only in her marriage. Julian knew that she must accept the destiny which had been laid on her by strangers, and go consenting to the marriage she detested: but because the chief beneficiary would be her mother, she could not bring herself to acquiesce in something so repugnant. Her pride, her hatred for the parent left to her, would not permit her to give in, after all her protestations, after that beating which was the worst ever inflicted on her, even after sixteen years of similar treatment at her mother's hands. She wrestled with herself, unable to relent, and as a result found herself subjected to another session under the birchrod, compounded by a withdrawal of all food. That in itself did not much concern Julian, who had sent her meals back untouched for several days now, unable to eat: but Dame Alice was at last struck by inspiration and produced, with malicious relish, the one weapon she knew to be invincible.

'I tell you, you wicked girl, if you don't consent now I'll have that hellhound of yours knocked on the head within the hour. And I mean it, too.'

Her heart suddenly cold within her, Julian stared at her mother's gloating face. 'You wouldn't dare,' she whispered, knowing that Dame Alice was quite capable of ordering such a deed—and of enjoying it, too, for she loathed Cavall, and had only tolerated him because he was her husband's gift to Julian. Now, with Sir Thomas gone, the hound was in mortal danger, and she saw with satisfaction that Julian knew it. She pressed her advantage home. 'Well? I'll have your answer now. Yes, and the dog lives, and you go free. No, and he dies, and you stay here, and at the end of the day you'll be married if we have to drag you to the church door, whatever you may think, hussy. It's your choice—does that cur die, or not?'

Defeated, Julian stared at her, her large brown eyes bleak, abject. 'Don't kill him—please don't.'

'It's in your hands, girl. Will you marry this man?'

Even now, it took a supreme effort to say the words: the silence lengthened, agonisingly, and with an exclamation of impatience Dame Alice turned to go. It wrenched the answer out of Julian, for she knew that her mother went to order the death of her beloved dog. 'Yes—yes, *yes*, I'll marry him—but don't do it, don't kill Cavall—please don't!'

The triumphant leering smile on her mother's face almost destroyed her—if she had had a dagger in her hand, Julian knew that she would have been tempted to murder. 'I won't, though God knows why not,' said Dame Alice with satisfaction. 'I'm glad you've seen sense at last, daughter, after ten days of this ridiculous obstinacy, and especially since Sir Christopher is to favour us with a visit soon, probably after Christmas. That will give us plenty of time to make you at least fairly presentable—your gown is disgusting, and your face shockingly ugly.' She looked the girl up and down, and then added, with an air of imparting a confidence, 'To tell the truth, I'm as unhappy about this marriage as you. To mix our proud Clifford blood with a nobody, a jumped-up northern savage with only the usurper's favour to commend him—it's abhorrent. But we have no other choice—now. Remember, though, this situation may not continue for ever. The rebellion which cost your father his life will not be the last. The country cannot tolerate this usurper, his crimes and his wickedness, his foul northerners. They will turn again to Henry Tudor, and next time we will not fail.' She smiled, a cold, terrible, cruel smile, so that Julian knew how Medea or Medusa must have looked. 'You may not have your upstart husband long, daughter, and then you will be a widow, with a good chance of finding a man much more to your liking. Pray for his untimely death, girl—I know that I shall.'

❧ CHAPTER THIRTEEN ❧

'The man in the world that she most hateth.'
(BOOK 4, CHAPTER II)

Sir Christopher Heron rode up to Ashcott two weeks after Christmas, having obtained leave of absence from the King for a considerable period. Richard and his household were now back in London, the country quiet behind them, all insurgents ignominiously fled. There remained the problem of the exiled rebels: all men of substance, prominent in the local government of their shires, justices, sheriffs and the like, replacements for them must be found. Already, Richard had realised that he must install reliable men in their place, and he had no more trustworthy servants than his own northerners: but the insular, closed communities in the southern counties would undoubtedly resent the intrusion of these strangers. There was no other answer, but he was aware that it would not reduce the simmering resentment still felt amongst influential people in Berkshire, Wiltshire, Kent and all the other seats of revolt. The solution he had found for Ashcott pleased him: a dynastic union was greatly to be preferred, and his most true and loyal servant, Sir Christopher Heron, deserved the lands and status that marriage with the Bray girl would give him. He was a made man now, and had received his dues for safeguarding the King's nephews. Richard valued and rewarded such service most generously: it was a shame that the circles of his trust had now perforce to be drawn so narrow.

Christie halted Bayard, with some difficulty, at the top of the hill leading down to Ashcott. It was a cold and windy afternoon, and the early January sun peered intermittently through the racing clouds and then retreated, as if it disliked what it saw. Christie did not. He stared down at the fertile valley, wet and green even in winter, the marshy half-flooded meadows promising rich grazing the next summer. There were fat sheep, and the cattle he had seen were sturdy and well-fed, despite their winter diet. The people too looked healthy and happy, and were warmly dressed against the chill winds. But it was Ashcott itself which gave him the greatest pleasure. He looked down at it, noting in his mind the glowing golden stone, the tidy wall, the strong tower and general air of well-being and comfort. He still hankered after the intimate inexhaustible wealth of Suffolk, that had so thoroughly laid its spell on him, in those few autumn days at Gipping: but he had been given the opportunity to seize Ashcott, and would not spurn that gift. At last, he had a place he could call home, lands to tend, a dynasty to found, a place to which he would belong, who had never truly belonged anywhere. It was security, the pinnacle of his ambitions, and he wanted to savour this first moment of homecoming.

It was a minute or so before he bethought himself of the girl on whom all this depended, the girl who had reportedly consented to be his wife: her mother had written to the King accepting the terms offered. He realised, with a sudden shock, that consent was not the term to use in this case: Julian Bray had been presented with a choice that was no choice at all, and in his arrogance he was about to inflict on her his presence at her board and in her bed. He wondered, with the first twinges of conscience and disquiet, what would be her attitude towards him. Would she continue to resent him, childishly kicking against inevitability? Or would she have achieved a mature acceptance of a situation she could not alter?

He would not have been reassured had he seen Julian at that moment. She sat in her chamber, while Friday held a mirror to her face, and glared at her reflection. True, it did present a slightly better appearance than previously: the bruises had vanished, and the cuts across her cheek and forehead, and around her mouth, had healed and were scarcely visible. It was not a pleasant sight, though, despite the luxurious frame of chestnut hair, brushed and brushed again by Friday until it gleamed a rich, glossy red-brown. Resisting the temptation to stick her tongue out at her unloved self, Julian turned away from it and got up, plucking dissatisfied at the folds of her grass-green velvet gown, new-made, fur-trimmed, and finer than any she had had before. 'It should be black,' she said irritably. 'And it's much too big, Friday.'

Her woman put the mirror down and studied Julian's tall, large-boned frame. 'You have lost a good deal of flesh,' she pointed out. Ten days of self-starvation had removed a surprising number of bulges from around hips and chest: Julian would never have the slender, willowy figure so fashionable, but her present shape did not seem so large on a girl of her unusual height and sturdy build. The green velvet suited her, brought out the rich rare colour of her mass of hair, and the high waist, cinched with a girdle of intricate goldsmith's work, let the heavy cloth fall straight to the ground, skimming the hips. It was indeed too big, especially around the arms, where the sleeves were supposed to be tight-fitting, but the low neckline, edged with fur and laced over the red kirtle with gold lace, exposed Julian's pale wide shoulders, and revealed that, lost weight or no, her proportions were still generous. All in all, Friday considered that the garment went a long way towards making this relatively plain girl attractive: and certainly she would be more interesting to a husband than the spoilt child he had known before. Julian, however, disagreed. 'Perhaps I am thinner, but it doesn't make any difference to me, does it? I'm ugly and over-sized, and I always will be.'

There was no whining note of self-pity in her voice: she was stating a fact she thought obvious. Friday gave her a look of affection, noting yet another example of her mistress's rapid increase in maturity. 'You do have things that are beautiful. Your hair, for instance.'

'My hair!' Julian pushed her hands through it and smiled wryly. 'I'll grant you, my hair is good. But my wedding day is the last time it will be on show: after that, it'll all be hidden under a headdress, and no-one will see it.'

'Except your husband,' Friday reminded her.

A curious look, compounded of fear, dislike, and resignation, crossed Julian's expressive face, and she turned away to stare out of the window. Finally, her voice came very quietly, faltering. 'Friday —I hate him. How can I live with someone I hate? How can I make conversation with him? How—how can I have him in my bed? That's the worst of it—to have him touch me—I shall try to pretend I don't care, I shall have to make a show of indifference—but I'll shudder every time he touches me, I know I will. How can I hide it, Friday—how can I hide the fact that I loathe the sight of him?' And then suddenly, passionately, the cry burst from her. 'It isn't *fair*, Friday, it isn't *fair*! Why should I be forced to marry someone I hate, someone I despise? And spend my whole life in misery, simply because I'm an heiress?' She jerked round, and Friday saw the old Julian, violently emotional, rebelling vainly against the immovable implacable destinies that shaped her future. 'And all because he's greedy for my land, my money! I wish I'd been poor, oh, Friday, the poorest cottager has more chance of a happy marriage than I do!' And she burst into furious, anguished tears.

Feeling very old and wise, Friday held her, and comforted her, though she knew that Julian's prophecy was almost certainly correct. This marriage, begun in hatred for entirely mercenary reasons, had no more hope of success than a cow had of flying, and Julian knew as well as she, that it was doomed from the start.

Then there was a knock at the door that proved to be Mary, Dame Alice's woman, with the news that Sir Christopher Heron had arrived, and wished to be conducted to his bride. Julian, aware of Mary's maliciously curious eyes on her tear-stained face, said that she would be ready in a few minutes, and asked that wine, cakes and wafers, and fruit be brought to refresh him while they talked. When the door had shut behind the woman's back, she turned to Friday, her eyes hopeless. 'It's no use weeping, is it? I must do this, it's my duty, I can do no other. But I can't be glad, Friday, I can't even *pretend* to be glad—all I can do is try and hide how much I detest him and everything he represents, because if I'm to spend the rest of my life with him, we must at least attempt to be civil with each other—or it would be impossible, intolerable, utterly miserable to quarrel all the time.' She stared sadly at her maid. 'But Friday— please, I know I have been very unpleasant to you in the past. I've treated you shamefully—yes, I have, and you know that as well as I do—but you haven't ever complained, you've never been anything other than patient and tolerant. I know it's a lot to ask, but will you stay with me? Will you be my friend? I—I think I shall need a friend very much, after I am married.'

Friday found that her eyes and nose were prickling at this un-characteristic and suddenly moving humility. She smiled. 'You do not need to ask. Yes, I will gladly be your friend.' She held out her hands, and Julian took them, and with sudden mutual affection they embraced and then stood apart, hands still linked, smiling at each other rather tearfully.

'Thank you,' Julian whispered, her heartfelt gratitude plain on her face.

'You've travelled a long way in a very short time,' Friday told her, shedding her usual deference and speaking straight from the heart. 'And I admire you for it—you have grown up at last, but you have a difficult time in front of you. I'll support you in any way I can, but I will not come between you and your husband in your private affairs—that would be wrong, wouldn't it? He'll be here any minute, I must go.' She smiled, and added softly, 'I know the words are inappropriate, but—good luck, Julian.'

The expected knock at the door came very soon after she had left.

Julian bade him enter: she found her hands were shaking and cold with sweat, and her heart was pounding so much that she felt it could burst from the confines of her body. Then the door opened, and closed, and Sir Christopher Heron stood not ten feet away from her.

He had not changed. The bony, rather mocking face with the cold silver-pale eyes was the same, and the impassive expression that gave no clue at all to the thoughts behind it. The clothes, however, were much more impressive: she saw velvet and fur, a rich jewelled crimson doublet and a black demi-gown over it, giving him an air of distinction entirely spurious. Hypocrite, Julian's inner voice said angrily. But the epithet could, she knew, just as easily be directed at herself, as she smiled falsely and invited him to partake of wine and wafers and little sweet cakes flavoured with saffron and cinnamon.

Christie, for his part, had been astonished at the change in her. Little more than a year ago, she had been a fat, spoilt child: the last time he had seen her, six months previously at Crosby Place, she had still carried more flesh than was pleasing, and her manner had been, to say the least of it, somewhat offensive. The girl before him had the gloriously abundant hair that had always been her chief claim to any looks at all, but she was much thinner, and the lovely gown was obviously too big. The strained, strong-boned face, the freckles standing out like blemishes on the white skin, the bruised circles around the wide brown eyes, were a silent indication of her suffering. Her father had died, she had naturally grieved for him, and to have been told at the same time that she must marry a man she loathed or become a pauper—he began to see the reason for the despair in her eyes. And probably, knowing Dame Alice, her consent to the wedding had been obtained only after violence. He found he pitied her very much: and a strange, unwelcome, astonishing impulse came over him, to take her in his arms and reassure her, that now, however much she hated and distrusted him, she would be safe.

But that insincere false smile kept him away from her. She was painfully unpractised in dissembling: at least before she had never bothered to hide her thoughts and feelings, and he found that he preferred it. She handed him wine with a hand that trembled, and then retreated to the safety of the window before saying, stiltedly formal, 'I trust you had a good journey, sir.'

The Christie he had once been might, with deliberately callous irony, have begun an elaborate exchange of courtesies: but this girl was going to be his wife, and he did not want to embark on a marriage that would probably last for the rest of his days, or hers, in a miasma of distrust, hatred and bitterness barely concealed by false politeness. Most of his own life had been a sham, a pretence of service and servility erected on very different feelings, and only since his employment by Richard, Duke of Gloucester and King of England, had his inward and outward selves begun at last to marry together. He had chosen the opportunity this girl had presented, of acquiring what he most wanted out of life, and it would be hypocritical to pretend otherwise: but he was also concerned for her. He would marry her for her wealth, but the least he could do was to treat her with kindness, courtesy and consideration: and even, if that lay in his power, to make her happy.

He smiled at her: it was intended to disarm her barely-concealed hostility, but in fact only heightened Julian's simmering resentment. 'I had a good journey, thank you. And I would like to tell you that I am very sorry about your father's death—he was a good friend.'

The brown eyes flashed, suddenly, with the strength of her feelings. 'Was he? Are you sorry?'

His gaze holding hers, he said quietly, 'Yes. Yes, I am. He was a good man, and an honest one.'

'And so your master had him murdered!' said Julian, her false civility dropping away from her with all her good intentions, as her grief and anger for her father's death rose overwhelmingly to the surface. 'He was only fighting for what he thought was right—because those two poor children were murdered—and he was murdered too!' Her voice was raw with the strength of her emotions, and her cheeks burned with fury: Christie knew that only the physical distance between them prevented her from striking him. He said, keeping his tones deliberately calm and level, 'Julian. He was not murdered.'

She stared at him with contempt. 'Do you really expect me to believe that?'

'I do, because it is the truth. He was a sick man when he was captured. I went to see him, to tell him that the King might well show mercy towards him. He asked me to ensure that you were provided for, because he knew that he was dying. I went to the King to ask for his release, and His Grace granted it. He sent a man to bring your father to him the next morning, but he had had a seizure in the night, and was dead.'

'How convenient for you,' Julian spat. 'So what did you do? Ask the King for me, so that you could have Ashcott?'

'The King himself suggested it. I'll admit that there were several advantages in such a match.'

'Not to *me*, there weren't!' Julian's furious face came closer. 'If I'd had *any* choice, *any* choice at all, I'd have spurned you—you're detestable, insufferable—as evil as your precious usurper!'

Six months ago he had been angered, and hurt, by her attack on his lord. Now, knowing that in her eyes she had good cause, he stayed calm, marshalling his thoughts and arguments with a logic that might, perhaps, appeal to her reason if not to her emotion. 'But you have not spurned me, have you, Julian? You have freely consented to marry me. Yet I think you hate me as much as you hate the King.'

'You're wrong—I hate you more,' she said viciously.

'And you have some justification for it. We have not dealt together happily in the past, for various reasons, but things are different now. I want you to be my wife—'

'No!' Julian cried. 'You don't want *me*! You want Ashcott—and I'm the means to that end, aren't I?'

'You're wrong,' said Christie. 'I could have had Ashcott without marrying you. The King would merely have attainted your father, seized his lands, turned you and your mother out with a pittance, and given it to me as a reward for my services. He suggested that you become my wife, but unlike you I had a choice. I chose to marry you, Julian.'

'And I wish you hadn't!' The girl took another step nearer, her face contorted. 'Don't tell me you chose me—don't! I'd rather be a pauper living on charity than be married to you—I'd rather lose Ashcott, lose everything! But I wasn't even granted *that* choice. I'll be forced into that church to marry you just as surely as if you and my accursed mother held a dagger to my throat! So don't preach at me, don't play the hypocrite—I'm as much your chattel as that stool or this table, and I've as much choice in the matter.'

For once, Christie did not know what to say in answer. Faced with such passionate hatred, his reasoning and logic seemed inadequate, and his words and platitudes even more so. He saw with clarity his own arrogance, that had assumed that her attitude would be changed because of his supposed act of kindness in marrying her. Rather, the reverse was true. All his plans and hopes of reconciliation seemed ludicrously redundant. He would be marrying a stranger, a girl who had no feelings towards him besides implacable loathing: and all his own well-meant impulses of sympathy and consideration for her plight looked paltry and insulting. He began, most unusually, to regret what he had done: but he would not go back now, for the lure of Ashcott, of everything for which he had ever hungered, the ultimate satisfying of his dearest ambition, was much too strong. And Julian, with her passionate hatred and violent emotions, presented a challenge that, with what he suspected was his usual arrogance, he wanted very much to take up: for her sake as well as for his own.

For now, however, a retreat was not only kind, but politic. He said, as gently as he could, 'Julian, listen to me. I am truly sorry. I never intended to distress you. I hope that your feelings towards me will change, because our life together will be intolerable for both of us if you continue to hate me as you do now—and before God, I can understand your reasons for doing so, even if I do not agree with them. But I don't hate you.'

'Don't you? You've thought of a most excellent revenge on me,' Julian said savagely. She added, her voice suddenly full of a bleak weariness, 'I think it best if you go. The sight of you makes me sick. If I'm to have your face in front of me, day in, day out, I want to see as little as possible of it now. Will you go?'

And, accepting defeat, he went.

*

Those few days before the wedding were possibly the most unpleasant of his entire life. His intended bride quite literally hated the sight of him, and could not, obviously, bring herself to treat him with even the barest civility. Her mother was little better, speaking to him curtly and having absolutely no more contact with him than was polite. Mealtimes were stilted, silent affairs, bound by unnaturally stiff ceremony more suited to a noble household than to a small country manor, and they were the only times he ever saw Julian. Usually, she shut herself in her chamber, or more rarely took herself off hawking with her maid and a groom in attendance. Dame Alice, with her barbed comments and barely-concealed contempt, was poor company. Christie, mindful of his duties towards the estate that would soon be his, asked questions and was directed, coldly, towards Sir Thomas Bray's steward, a man called William Marten.

With Marten, Christie was able at last to converse with a normal human being in a normal friendly manner (as usual, he did not count Perkin's bright and faintly insolent chat). He knew very little about agricultural matters, and was relieved to discover that less than a quarter of the manor's demesne was directly under its lord's control, most of it being let to local men in return for payments in coin and kind. The exceptions were the water-meadows around the house, flooded or marshy during the winter and providing rich grazing for cattle in summer, and the sheepwalks on the hills above Ashcott. He was surprised to learn that Sir Thomas had owned a flock of nearly two hundred sheep, and a score or so of fat kine, in addition to the horses possessed by his family and household. Marten laid the account book out for his inspection, listing all the receipts: rents due every quarter from the fifteen manors owned by Sir Thomas, in Oxfordshire and Buckinghamshire and Berkshire, payments and gifts from his tenants—cattle, pigs, casks of salted meat, sacks of wool and flour and bushels of wheat, hens and geese alive or dead, cloth, vegetables, beer: the list was endless, and capped by the laconic statement, 'Received of Wat Hedger, 1 demi coney.'

'What happened to the other half?' Christie enquired, and found in Marten a similarly dry sense of humour. 'I believe his dog ate it, Sir Christopher.'

Then there were the expenses. Marten's neat clear hand had enumerated everything, from the twenty pounds spent last year on a palfrey for Mistress Julian, to a penny given in alms to a beggar at Adderbury, the village that faced Deddington across the valley of the River Swere in which Ashcott stood. Christie's experienced eye, running down it, saw that the household had lived well, but not too well: Sir Thomas had wisely eschewed such notorious extravagances as legions of idle servants in expensive livery, quantities of vain apparel, or spectacular building schemes. Each year, of the eight annotated in the account book, had shown a handsome surplus, and Marten, with justifiable pride, had led Christie to a huge iron-bound wooden chest in the estate room. It had three locks, and when opened proved to contain perhaps four or five hundred pounds in gold and silver, all neatly docketed and tied in bags, along with all the deeds and documents relating to the manor of Ashcott and the others in Bray's ownership.

With a slightly bemused feeling, Christie stared down at the wealth thus revealed, and realised that his marriage to Julian would make him a rich man—and, coupled with the lands and offices given him by the King, a very rich man indeed. He would never again have to exist on a pittance, unable to afford more than the barest necessities. He could dress as befitted his rank, trick his wife out in jewels and fur—if she would accept them, his cynical self pointed out—have his every wish and need answered by troops of liveried servants, ride the finest horses, eat richly spiced food, buy silver plate, have this cold old-fashioned house wainscotted and the kitchen rebuilt. It was a dazzling prospect to the man who had always been someone's poor relation: and after that first glorious moment, he damped down the fires of delight. He had no need of large numbers of servants when Perkin did all that was necessary, nor of fine horses when he already possessed the swift but ugly Bayard. Nor, he told himself wryly, could he shower Julian with jewels and fine garments when she would most like hurl them back in his face. He realised then, as Marten closed the lid on the fortune inside, that without at least the toleration of the girl whom he had forced to become his wife, all this—all he had ever wanted, all he had dreamed of, all he had worked and schemed to obtain, all his days of service—were empty, hollow, purchased at the cost of the ruination of a young woman's life.

And yet he knew, knew full well that if he could only, somehow, find a chink in that implacable hatred, he could eventually win her over. Music might prove a common bond: he had his lute now, though he was sadly out of practice and his fingers had lost their hardness from lack of use. And he knew she loved hawking, and riding: surely he, who also enjoyed such pursuits, might join her? But there was no chance of her letting him close enough to begin even the most tentative overtures of friendship. It was as if they did not speak the same language.

*

But the language they spoke at the church door was understood by both. It was raining hard, as it had done for most of this wet, cold, unpleasant winter. Fortunately, the wedding party was not large, and most could be crushed into the shelter of Adderbury's church porch where the priest, a short fat man enveloped in his robes and in the throes of a dreadful head-cold, performed the rites with unusual speed. And Christie saw with compassion the white, closed face of the stranger who was vowing to become his wife, for fairer for fouler, for better for worse, for richer for poorer, in sickness and in health, to be meek and obedient at bed and at board, till death them

[294]

did part, and was filled with a sadness that was unfamiliar to him, and disturbing, as he heard the promises she must have no intention of keeping. The finger on which he slipped the ring, a band of twisted gold bearing a small, deep red ruby, lay cold and unresponsive in his: it was thick, with a musician's callous, and the nail had been chewed down to the quick, a child's hand on which the ring looked incongruous. And then it was done, and the wedding mass was performed within the comparative warmth of the church, punctuated by the sneezes of the priest and the drumming of the rain and hail on the windows. Then, bent over their horses, the little party made its way back through the mud and water to the welcome dryness of Ashcott, for the wedding feast.

Feast was, perhaps, not quite the right term to describe the meal that was served in the hall to the happy bride and groom and their household. The Ashcott cook was somewhat limited in his imagination, but had laboured long: so, unfortunately, had the ox before its slaughter. The company at the high table was small: Christie, Julian, Dame Alice, the priest, Sir John Mitchell, the steward, Friday Gower, Mary Norris, two or three neighbours and their wives and, somewhat to his surprise, Perkin Hobbes.

Perkin had regarded his master's impending marriage with mixed feelings. Well aware of Christie's ambitions, he could be glad that he had now achieved a home and estate to call his own, and the wealth that was his deserved reward. But the choice of bride was a different matter, and he viewed Julian with suspicion, knowing full well her feelings towards his master. The girl had had no choice, he must admit, but at least she would not be parted from her home nor from her mother (if that could be described as an advantage), and it might be said by some that his master had done her a favour by marrying her—he was a knight now, had risen high with the King's generosity, and could well go higher. It seemed ungrateful, not to say churlish, for her to sit by her new husband's side, toying with her meat, and an expression on her face fit to curdle new milk. Perkin covertly watched his master cut up her beef for her, serve her with wine, smile at her, talk to her: and all in vain, for he might as well have been speaking to a statue. But when the second course had been cleared away, and the fruit and cheeses brought, Christie beckoned to his servant, who had been enjoying the luxury of having a page serve him with all he desired, and asked for his lute. With pleasure, Perkin brought it to him: most brides were serenaded with minstrels, but few indeed by their husbands.

[295]

Christie had spent some hours in practice for this moment, accustoming his hands and fingers once more to the intricacies of music. He had no hopes that this would succeed in winning even Julian's notice, let alone her kindness, but he found that, once decided upon it, he could not easily discard the idea. Choice of suitable songs had also presented a problem: there was none that would not seem a cynical mockery to her, and make him out the worst kind of hypocrite. But still he must try, to see if she would be bound by her vows of love and obedience.

It was, obviously, a vain hope: but he tuned his lute quickly, and struck a ripple of notes. Julian's large brown eyes were studying the screens at the opposite end of the hall: her mother stared coldly down at him, but the rest of the company seemed eager enough for him to begin. He glanced at Julian's waiting-woman, the plain fair-haired girl with the impossible name, who one day soon might be needed as an ally, and then began.

> Continuance
> Of Remembrance
> Without ending
> Doth me penance
> And great grievance
> For your parting.
>
> So deep you be
> Graven, pardie,
> Within mine heart,
> That afore me
> Ever I you see
> In thought covert.
>
> Though never plain
> My woeful pain
> But bear it still,
> It were in vain
> To say again,
> Fortune's will.

There was a murmur of appreciation as the plaintive little song finished. He glanced at Julian, a smile on his face, that froze at the open, naked contempt on hers. As if unmoved, unnoticing, he launched straightway into part of a song which, sung in full, was more proper for a lady's voice, but appropriate nonetheless.

Grievous is my sorrow
Both evening and morrow
Unto myself alone,
Thus do I make my moan,
That unkindness hath killed me,
And put me to this pain.
Alas, what remedy
That I cannot refrain?

When other men do sleep,
Then do I sigh and weep,
All raging in my bed
As one for pain near dead.
That unkindness hath killed me,
And put me to this pain.
Alas, what remedy
That I cannot refrain?

He did not dare look at Julian's face after that, although the expressions worn by the rest of the high table indicated a certain sympathy. A sudden, savage impulse struck him: 'For my dear lady,' he said formally, and began the last, that he had never intended to sing.

Its irony was obvious from the start to anyone who understood Latin: those not so knowledgeable soon appreciated the joke. Smiles broadened as the song progressed, and Christie, keeping his voice crystal clear and true, made sure that every syllable was heard:

Of all creatures women be best
Cuius contrarium verum est.
In every place you may well see
That women be as true as turtle on tree,
Not liberal in language but speak secretly,
And great joy amongst them is so for to be.

The steadfastness of women will never be done,
So gentle, so courteous, they be every one,
Meek as a lamb and still as a stone,
Crooked or crabbed find ye none.

Men be more troublous a thousandfold,
And I marvel how they dare be so bold
Against women for to hold,
Seeing them so patient, soft, and cold.

[297]

Now say well by women or else be still,
For they never displeased men by their will:
To be angry or wroth they have no skill,
For I dare say they think none ill.

There was no doubt that everyone had seen the point: several of the men were grinning broadly. Dame Alice, of course, was unmoved, and Julian, he saw, had a face like stone: save for the red spots on her cheekbones, and her glittering eyes. Regretting his impulse as suddenly as it had arrived, he laid the lute down and stood up, glancing around the hall—his hall—and all the people within it, his servants, attendants, workers, clad in their brilliant holiday clothes, waiting for his word. Now would normally follow dancing, when the house would be open to any passer-by, if one could be found in this weather, and the bride expected to take the hand of any man who asked her. But he found he could not face the thought of further hours of celebrating an occasion that was so decidedly not joyous for its chief participants. The mourning for Sir Thomas would be sufficient excuse for the lack of merry-making, as if all the neighbourhood did not know of the circumstances surrounding the marriage: but he knew too, that he must not seem mean on this, his first appearance as their lord and master. So, he told them that there would be no dancing, in respect for the memory of the bride's father: however, there was plenty of good wine and beer for the tenants to drink the health of bride and groom. And then, with a cold feeling of apprehension about the forthcoming night, he turned to his wife. 'You are tired, I know. Shall we go to our bed?'

The words came to Julian as from a very great distance. All day she had moved remotely, dazed, as if her real self were imprisoned behind a chill wall of glass and could only watch as the false Julian did as she was ordered, spoke the vows binding her to this hated man for ever, sat at the table that was now his and received food from his hands. She could not eat any of it, the beef tasted dry and all but choked her, and even the sugared subtleties, cunningly wrought like angels or lambs, each girt about with an appropriate text, had no power to delight her eye or her palate. The wine, however, had been a different matter: she had lost count of the times her cup had been filled, but it had seemed to make no difference. Her feelings of remoteness and isolation from the proceedings seemed only to increase, if anything, until he had begun to play.

[298]

And then she had had the strangest sensation that he knew her thoughts, knew that only music was likely to penetrate that armour of despair.

She had listened, trying not to, as he sang the first two songs, and scorn had been her overriding emotion. How dare he presume to speak with a lover's voice, when no words even of affection had ever been between them in this most cold-blooded and mercenary of marriages? She had pretended not to pay any attention, and flattered herself that she had succeeded. And then, appallingly, he had begun the third, and she knew before the first verse was done that it was a deliberate insult, aimed at her, and performed, surely, in the hopes of penetrating her indifference.

It had worked. Her first impulse was to hurl her wine-cup at him: a moment's reflection, as her hand tightened on the silver stem, persuaded her of the folly of such a course. She was a wedded woman, not a child: her pride would not let her now succumb to such infantile passions. She drained the cup instead and glared at him, unable to prevent her rage from showing on her face. How dare he offer her such an open, calculated insult before all her household—her mother, her maid, her servants, people who had known her since childhood. Scarlet with humiliated rage, she stared down at her plate, while it wavered through the tears she could not, in all pride, permit herself to shed.

So she hardly heard, let alone understood, Christie's words to her: he had to repeat them, standing closer, before she realised that the part of the ceremony which she most dreaded, was upon her. She saw his outstretched hand, and for a moment her legs would not obey her: then her mother nudged her, none too gently, and she rose. The room swayed and curtseyed, and she knew that she had taken too much wine: but if she had been able to purchase oblivion by that means, she would have drunk the barrel dry. Her legs moved, seemingly of their own accord, to the end of the table, where her husband took her by the hand, and even now she was unable to suppress the shudder that ran through her at his warm, dry touch. Then amidst the cheering, laughing group of people she was led upstairs to the chamber that had once been hers alone, shared only with Cavall. The dog had long ago howled himself into silence in the stables outside, where he had been tied for the present: for Julian had been desperately frightened by Dame Alice's threats towards her beloved hound. Surely, if her own mother had proved so ruthless, her husband would be similarly intolerant of the place the animal held in her heart, and would seize any excuse to be rid of him. So her reasoning had run, and she had thought it safest to banish him.

Sir John blessed the bridal bed, warmed with hot stones wrapped in towels, and newly covered with a richly worked counterpane that Sir Thomas had bought some months before, intending it for his own bed. Then, with much mirth and laughter, and no modesty at all, his daughter and her husband were bedded, and a huge cup of hippocras, warmly spiced, thrust into Julian's hands. Desperate now to keep at bay the terror threatening to overwhelm her, she gulped it down, though its thick cloying sweetness was never usually much to her taste. And then, abruptly, the curtains around the bed had been drawn, and with final, bawdy exclamations of good luck and tipsy encouragement, the company had retreated downstairs, leaving her alone with the man she had promised, faithlessly, to love and obey.

She drained the cup with hands that shook suddenly, and looked about for somewhere to set it. Christie took it from her gently, and laid it on the floor outside the confines of the bed. She looked very young, her hair, so thick and falling well below her waist, hiding her body as effectively as Lady Godiva's. Her face was flushed with the wine, but her brown eyes, widened in panic, were those of a terrified hind. He had already decided that to apologise for that unforgivable song would only serve to provoke another outburst of temper, so he said instead, quietly, 'Are you tired in truth?'

Frowning, Julian shook her head and regretted it immediately: the dim shapes of the bedcurtains revolved alarmingly. 'No,' she said, with what she hoped was a chilling dignity.

'But you would prefer, perhaps, that sleeping was all that was required of you, tonight?'

Dimly, through the fog of wine-fumes, she realised that he was offering her a way out, a chance to evade the ordeal she dreaded above all others, the last and most appalling of his invasions of her self. A perverse pride prompted her to deny the gift thus generously offered, as if it were a paltry thing of no account. 'I don't care what you do to me,' said Julian, with indifference.

There was a long silence, during which she wondered if this feeling of remoteness, of inhabiting a stranger's body, would continue to increase at such a rate: that hippocras, perhaps, had been a mistake. And then she felt his hand on her shoulder, slipping down through the great mass of her hair to cup her breast and caress

[300]

her body, and she sat quite still, feeling and yet not feeling his touch on her skin, for it evoked no response from her at all, not even a shudder of loathing. Then, with gentleness, he laid her back upon the pillows, wondering that his desire should be aroused at all by a woman who showed no more reaction to his lovemaking than would a wooden effigy, and, meeting no resistance whatsoever, slid down upon her.

It was a dreary, miserable act, and when he had finished, Christie was left with a bitter taste that he wished urgently could have been physically washed away. He supposed, wearily, that this deeply unsatisfying consummation had been necessary, if only to set seal upon the marriage. He would not have put it past Dame Alice to have it annulled, if she thought there was reason, so that Julian could marry someone more to her mother's liking. But he lay for a long time in the dark, listening to the sound of her breathing, long and slow, and hoping that the wine had at least sent her to sleep. He knew exactly the urge that had made her drink so much at the wedding supper, for he had felt much the same impulse himself at moments of crisis in his life, most notably after his quarrel with Meg. He wondered if her wedding night had been like this, and discarded the thought immediately: for his sister had gone to her marriage with gladness, if not with any love, and would not have lain immobile while her husband laboured over her.

With a sharp sadness that surprised him, he wished that it had been otherwise. Using a deliberately hostile eye, he examined his own behaviour over the last week or so, and found it not at all to his taste. He had embarked on this marriage for a reason which, to be true, was common to almost every bridegroom of rank up and down the country, but with scant respect for the feelings of his intended wife. She had been offered a choice so appalling as to be none at all, her mother's beatings and threats had bludgeoned her into consent, and he had compounded his error by treating her quite understandable feelings of resentment, not to say loathing, as a challenge or an obstacle for him to overcome as blithely as a knight in a romance on some quest. The final straw, he knew, had been to insult her publicly at the wedding supper: it would be long remembered by both bride and guests.

And it should have been different. How he could have made it so, given Julian's intransigence, his rational mind failed to see: but the part of him which had wished, with idealism, for a marriage to match Tyrell's, or that of the King and Queen, regretted most bitterly the mistakes and the arrogance which had led him to this disastrous situation. And he realised, too, that his feelings for Julian were strangely mixed. He had gladly agreed to his marriage out of his desire for her wealth and lands: he had thought he disliked her, though he had had some sympathy for her plight. But now, lying awake next to this strange, wild, turbulent girl, so greatly at the mercy of her emotions, he realised that he had not so much control over his own feelings after all. Pity, compassion, yes, he had felt that for her, but now there was something else: admiration, perhaps, for the misplaced strength and stubborn prideful resistance, and an understanding of her feelings that owed nothing to his own rather limited experience of such things. Why he should know so well what lay behind her actions, he could not comprehend: it was a mystery at once baffling and encouraging.

And the body in the dark under his hands had been generous and inviting, defying the wish of its inhabitant. He had not thought her especially well-favoured, despite the glory of her hair, and lust had not until now entered his calculations. He realised that he desired her very much: and more, to have her at last respond to his lovemaking, as a wife should, and as she had that day promised.

But she would not of her own accord change her heart towards him. Somehow, he must woo her and win her, as any knight in a romance must lay siege to a cold-hearted lady who spurned his advances. It was a common enough story in the French books so beloved of court ladies: but in them, the object of desire was usually wed to someone else. The tactics to follow if the wooer were her own husband, were never stated. And besides, nowhere in any romance was there any lady remotely resembling Julian.

He did not sleep at all, or at least did not remember it: and found that, surprisingly soon, it was dawn. He heard the muted noises that indicated the house was astir, and lay still for a moment longer, deciding to ask for their breakfast to be taken in bed—after all, he was now the master here, and could please himself, and defy custom. Then, with a faint feeling of apprehension, he turned his head to look at Julian.

His wife lay sleeping soundly still, curled away from him. The coverlet had slipped down, exposing the pale skin of her back, and it was marked across, again and again, with healed cuts and scars, obviously caused by a rod.

His anger rose in his throat, making him feel ill with it. He had no doubt who had done this, or why, and if Dame Alice had appeared in the chamber then and there, he would have been hard-pressed to resist administering to her a similar beating with whatever had first come to hand. Even at Alnwick, under the strict rule of the Master of Henchmen, he had never received chastisement as severe as this: it seemed possible that she would be marked for life.

Very gently and carefully, he drew the coverlet up about her shoulders: she did not wake. Then, he slid from the bed as silently as he could, pulled on his discarded hose and shirt, and went in search of Perkin Hobbes.

Julian woke with an ache in her head and her mouth uncomfortably dry. For a moment she lay, bewildered, puzzling over these unusual and unpleasant sensations, and then, with horrific suddenness, memory returned. Shame washed over her as she recalled the events of the previous night: the quantity of wine that she had drunk, now settled noxiously in her head, the agonies of the ceremony and the celebration, the indignity, fortunately blurred, of the consummation, and above all, towering over the rest, the song which had told all those in her household exactly what her husband thought of her.

Tears of mortification and misery pricked at her eyes, and overflowed as she realised for the first time the horror of her future. She was married now, to a man she loathed and who, it appeared, hated her in return, and there was no possibility now of altering it, short of death. No chance of annulment, because they were not related to each other in any degree, nor was the marriage unconsummated.

Heedless of whether or not her husband was in the bed with her, Julian rolled onto her stomach and wept despairingly into the soft feathers of her pillow.

A long time later, the door opened, and closed. Footsteps padded over to the bed, and the curtain was drawn back. Like a recalcitrant child, Julian did not move save for the involuntary sobs that shook her from time to time. Then the voice of her husband, as level and unemotional as a lawyer's, said, 'Julian. Would you like to break your fast?'

It was such a normal, unexpected thing to say, that she was taken by surprise. Before she could stop herself, she had rolled over to sit up, quite forgetting her nakedness, and stared at Christie. 'Breakfast?'

'Yes, why not?' he said, sitting down beside her on the bed as if they had done this every day for years, and laying a laden wooden tray between them. 'New bread, and some boiled mutton, salt herring, and beer. Oh, and a mug of buttermilk—I thought that might be more to your taste than the beer.'

Julian stared down at the generous repast. 'I'm not hungry,' she said flatly. It was a lie: despite her headache, her stomach was growling—she had after all had no supper the previous night—and she also had a raging thirst for which the cool bluish refreshing buttermilk was the ideal answer.

'I'm surprised,' said Christie. 'I'm pretty sharp-set myself, and I thought you would be too.' He swung his long limbs up onto the bed to sit cross-legged beside her, surveying the food before choosing a thick slice of bread and a hunk of cold mutton to top it. Julian, suddenly aware of her nakedness, hastily arranged her hair to cover herself, and pulled the sheet up. Her groom did not appear to notice it, nor the fiery blush which accompanied it, at odds entirely with the richer, more subtle red of her hair. Through its veiling masses she studied him, wondering at the calm of the man. How could he sit there as if they had been married twelve years instead of twelve hours, discussing breakfast and eating as if he had not a care in the world?

'What do you know of accounts?'

Julian's head jerked up: she stared at him. 'Nothing.'

'Then why not start today? I shall not always be here to oversee them, and though Marten seems a solid reliable man, it's always a good idea to check his figures.' He took another mouthful of bread, and pushed the pewter mug of buttermilk towards her. 'Have that—don't tell me you don't feel the need of it.'

'I don't.'

Christie's eyes met hers, and he gave a wry shrug. 'It's up to you.'

'My mother can check the accounts,' said Julian, after a silence broken only by noises from the small chamber outside, where someone was evidently raking out the fire. Christie finished the mutton and gave her his full attention. 'I'm not married to Dame Alice, am I?' he pointed out reasonably. 'I'm your husband, and in my absence I shall expect you, not her, to be in charge of Ashcott.' He saw her mouth open in denial, and added, 'I know it'll be a difficult task, to assert yourself. That's why we can use these first few weeks together to show you how a manor is run. A wife should be her husband's partner, don't you agree?'

The tone of his voice held nothing but friendship. Julian stared mutely at this strange, unsettling man who might have been a different person entirely from the savage satirist of the previous night. Cowardly, she evaded the direct question. 'I will be guided by you,' she said, looking down at her big freckled hands lying on the coverlet, for she knew she could no longer meet the intent, pale grey eyes resting upon her, could not pretend a meekness she did not feel.

'If you object, then please say so,' Christie told her. The flat, subdued voice came, a travesty of her usual robust tones. 'I do not object, husband.'

He resisted the impulse to shake her: he preferred Julian angry to this falsely submissive mouse, for at least her rages were honest. 'Good,' he said. 'It should be profitable and pleasant for us both.'

Julian could not think of a reply that was suitably cutting: and besides, the state of her mouth and tongue rather precluded further speech. Of their own accord, her fingers went out to the mug, hovered, and seized the handle. With a covert glance at Christie to see if he had noticed, she took a sip. The cool liquid felt and tasted wonderful: she gulped it down with as much enthusiasm as she had swallowed the wine the previous night, and found the bottom of the mug came much too soon. She lowered it and saw her husband's pale eyes watching her. He smiled briefly as she looked hastily away. 'Bread, Julian?'

She made no objection as he heaped her platter with bread and herring. Suddenly her hunger was overwhelming: she fell on the food with relish, while Christie leaned back on the pillows, one arm behind his head, sipping beer. He said casually, 'Where's that dog of yours? I thought he went everywhere with you.'

She could not answer at once, because her mouth was full. That would not have stopped the old, unmarried Julian: but today she wanted her behaviour, perversely, to be utterly correct. He would not be able to fault her: neither would he receive any warmth, only a cold politeness. She swallowed the bread and herring and said, 'He is in the stables. I did not think it fitting that he share our chamber.'

'On the contrary,' Christie said. 'Why put him out now, when you have most need of a friend and companion? And he ought to have the opportunity to grow accustomed to me, after all—or he might well resent my presence. Does he have alaunt blood?'

'I believe so,' said Julian, with a chill finality that precluded any further questions, however friendly. Christie, aware that his chances of penetrating her hostility were slight indeed, left it at that, finished his beer, and rolled off the bed. 'I'll go get dressed in the outer chamber, and leave you in peace. Will you meet me in the estate room, in an hour or so, to look at the account books?'

'Yes, husband,' came the falsely subservient voice: and he had to be content with that.

Julian, alone at last, had precious little time to ponder her husband's apparently changed attitude, or to feel any satisfaction that she had played her part and kept her temper. Scarcely had the door shut behind Christie, it seemed, than it swung open to admit Dame Alice, Mary, and Friday, all to varying degrees eager for details of the wedding night. It took Julian's desperate, new and hard-won self-control to stand still under the barrage of sly innu-endo, more open bawdry and pointed questions, answered when Dame Alice, not satisfied with her evasions, whipped the coverlet off the bed to examine the sheets. 'You should have kept your legs together,' she told her daughter bluntly. 'Now there's no chance of an annulment—you'll have to make what you can of your lusty peasant Yorkist, won't you, my girl? Until our fortunes change —and pray to the Blessed Virgin that he doesn't get you with child in the meantime.'

Julian, scarlet with embarrassment, stared at her mother, aston-ished at her blunt coarseness. Dame Alice, seeing it, laughed. 'Don't be so squeamish, daughter—it's a hard life most of us live in, and you've been sheltered from it too long. It's time you discovered reality. Nice thoughts and good intentions don't count for much, you know. The world's against honest folk, and we must make what we can of the opportunities that come our way. Now, slug-abed, are you going to rise? Mass was said long since, and it's high time you appeared in the hall.'

'My husband,' said Julian, finding some pleasure in the word for the first time, 'has commanded my presence in the estate room. He wishes me to learn something of casting and checking accounts.'

The contemptuous laugh with which Dame Alice greeted this announcement was, somehow, more insulting than anything Christie had said, or sung. 'You? Accounts? You know nothing of money save how to spend it, thanks to your precious father. It's a waste of time, and I'll tell him so.'

'He wants me to help in the running of the estate in his absence,' Julian said stubbornly: she was beginning to realise, reluctantly, that Christie might have been right in this. Her suspicions were confirmed by Dame Alice's next words. 'That'll be my task, girl, and don't you mistake it. Ashcott may be his property now, but if I have the overseeing of it while he's away with his precious usurper, it's an easy enough matter to add a little expense here, take away a few rents there, and put the difference aside. And don't look so scrupulous, it ill becomes you—there are plenty of uses to which that money could be put, as I daresay you can guess. Henry Tudor could well be glad of any sum, however small.' And she laughed, well pleased with her plan.

Julian, appalled, stared at her mother in disbelief. It would never have occurred to her to resort to such a devious stratagem, however much she hated her husband. Arguments, quarrels, were almost acceptable, understandable in such a marriage. But with cold-blooded calculation, to go behind his back and steal his revenues, to support his sovereign's enemy—it smacked of treason, to Christie as well as to the kingdom. She said, trying unsuccessfully to keep her disgust out of her voice, 'You couldn't—you wouldn't dare!'

'Oh, would I not?' Dame Alice cast a contemptuous eye at the two waiting-women, both loyal to Bray rather than to Heron, and laughed scornfully. 'You've a deal to learn about the world, as I said, and it's high time your eyes were opened. I'll go speak with your husband myself. Accounts, indeed!' And she swept out, followed by Mary Norris.

Frideswide's eyes were sympathetic. 'Was it so very bad?'

Julian choked back the scornful retort that had risen to her lips, and shrugged with what she hoped was convincing carelessness. 'No better nor worse than any wedding night. Friday, quick, help me dress—whatever happens, I must stop my mother taking charge of the accounts!'

With her usual painstaking efficiency, the older girl dropped smock and kirtle over Julian's head in careful succession, lacing the latter up the back. 'The black gown? Or the green? Or the grey with the sable cuffs and collar?'

'Whichever comes first to hand,' said Julian impatiently, and was in a moment or so clad by her waiting-woman in the black. She had worn it nearly every day until Christie's arrival for her wedding, in memory of her dead father. It was laced up, the cuffs and collar of deep purple adjusted, the girdle, her plainest, fastened: then, deftly, Friday plaited the heavy mass of hair and, for the first time, concealed it within an embroidered cap which she pinned to the back of Julian's head. It felt heavy and uncomfortable, but she was a married woman now, and it would not be at all seemly to leave her hair uncovered. Finally, with agonising care, Friday arranged the wires and veil of the elaborate headdress so fashionable at the present. She was not practised in this, and it took a long time, while Julian fidgeted in an agony of impatience. Then at last her maid deemed her fit to face her household, and held the mirror for her approval.

Julian glared at this novel reflection. Bereft of the great mass of hair, her face seemed pale and heavy, the blemishing freckles more prominent and her eyes, nose, mouth, chin, all revealed as too large, while the gauzy wings of the headdress gave her a bovine look. It did not suit her at all, and a glance at Friday's doubtful face revealed that she was not the only one to think thus. However, it could not be helped for the moment. With a mental note to experiment until she had discovered a more becoming form of headgear, Julian picked up her voluminous skirts and fairly ran from the room.

Sir Christopher Heron was not in the estate room. William Marten was, however, wearing a hunted expression, and so was Dame Alice, her head surrounded by the veil and barbe, covering her neck, that were the symbols of her widowhood. Her face, naked like Julian's now was, showed her ill-nature in every line and furrow. 'What are you doing here, girl?'

'I am obeying my husband,' said Julian, pointedly. This next hour would, she knew, be one at best uncomfortable, at worst, exceedingly unpleasant. She would be caught between two warring people, both of whom she hated: and yet the habit of long years of defiance remained with her, and she could not bring herself to take Dame Alice's part, however much she detested her husband. Besides, she knew that anyone acquainted only with the facts, rather than with the transient and reprehensible emotions involved, would doubtless take her own side. She was married now, she must by law and custom and vow obey her husband, and her property was his: and for Dame Alice to plot to appropriate some of that wealth for her own purposes was undoubtedly a crime, if not a sin. The certainty of this gave her the courage to face her mother's glare, and to add, 'He has commanded me here, mother, not you, and so it would be best if you left.'

Dame Alice was not used to such calmly given orders, especially not from the daughter she had spent a lifetime more or less vainly bullying and browbeating. 'You dare speak to me like that, you insolent little jade—you'll go to your chamber, now if you please.'

'You forget,' said Julian, inwardly marvelling at the calm with

[308]

which her mind was marshalling her arguments. The old Julian would long since have spectacularly lost her temper: the new learning that heated words gained her little, was still seething inside, but determined not to lose control. 'I am my husband's now, and it is his place to chastise or upbraid me as he thinks fit. You no longer have any rights of punishment over me—and although I must respect you, since you are my mother, I find it very hard to do so.'

There was a taut silence. Marten, listening perforce to this exchange, applauded the girl silently. It seemed she was learning sense at last: hot words and bluster had never been any answer to Dame Alice, but this reasonable argument could not be refuted, and the older woman knew it. If she thought she could browbeat her daughter's husband in like fashion, however, Marten feared that she was sadly mistaken.

The door opened at that moment, and Christie Heron came in, accompanied by the big tawny hound who had up until now followed Julian everywhere at Ashcott. As soon as Cavall beheld his beloved mistress, the animal slipped his collar with a neat, practised twist of the narrow head and leapt upon her, licking and crying with joy, his tail revolving like a windmill's sails. And Christie saw her face soften, her eyes open wide with delight, and she knelt and hugged him, her own sounds of welcome almost indistinguishable from the dog's. Dame Alice, looking on with a stony eye, folded her arms in disapproval, and then turned to her son-in-law. 'I understand from my daughter that you wish to teach her something of accounts?'

'That is my intention, madam, yes,' Christie said, one eyebrow raised in enquiry. 'She must take my place when I am away at court or on the King's business, and some knowledge of my affairs is essential.'

'With respect, sir, it is not,' said Dame Alice in chilling tones. 'I have always overseen Marten and directed his work, and I see no need for Julian to take my place when she knows nothing of such things. She'd be better employed at her needle or distaff, or learning what goes on in the kitchen or stillroom. Her father allowed her education in such matters to be sadly neglected, and I intend to remedy this state of affairs with all speed.'

'I'm sure that's very true,' Christie said. 'But all in good time. Knowledge of sewing and spinning and other household matters is of little use if there's no money to spend, and in my view a thorough grounding in business is of greater value than these. She's young, and willing, and not at all lacking in wits, and I doubt it will take her long to grasp the basic essentials.'

The impulse to disagree rose to Julian's throat and was ruthlessly suppressed: he did after all, astonishingly, appear to be taking her part. She rose from her knees by Cavall, wondering if she could reveal the full extent of Dame Alice's duplicity: but even now, with her mother's inimical eyes upon her, she did not dare.

'I repeat,' said Dame Alice, chillingly, 'it is not necessary for Julian to be acquainted with business affairs. I am more than capable, I assure you.'

'I don't deny it,' said Christie, in tones that implied that he did. 'But Ashcott, unfortunately for you, madam, is mine now, and I intend to direct my household according to my wishes. I regret, Dame Alice, that you have very little say in the matter. Now, if you would be so kind as to leave us? I'm sure there is plenty to do in the stillroom.'

Julian's mother stared at him as though she could not believe her ears: then, with a muttered imprecation, she turned and swept furiously from the room. To Christie the air at once seemed fresher: he said quietly to the girl standing staring at him, 'I am sorry if I have offended your mother, but such things have to be made clear, or there will never be peace in this household. If you have changed your mind, I will understand.'

At that particular moment, Julian felt she would rather do anything than sit down in front of a musty-smelling old account book, and attempt to make sense of incomprehensible figures and boring lists: but she knew that Christie had won a small victory on her behalf, and she had no wish at all to submit to her mother. 'I am happy to follow your desires,' she said, and lowered her eyes so that he might not see the sparks of anger within.

*

Somewhat to her surprise, she found afterwards that she had enjoyed the morning spent poring over the day-to-day expenses at Ashcott. Her father had always been lavish with his coin where his beloved daughter was concerned, and her clothes, jewellery, dog, hawk and palfrey, books and musical instruments and other expensive presents had all been purchased without a thought to their cost, while she had been given generous amounts of money to spend on whatever took her fancy. She had never lacked for anything that could be bought, nor had she been short of coin when a word to Sir

Thomas had always brought more. As a result, she had no idea at all of how much ordinary things should cost, nor of good value or worthlessness. Her husband, on the other hand, was evidently very well versed in such matters. The book was opened by Marten at Michaelmas the previous year, and Christie ran his finger down the neat lists of purchases, commenting as he went. 'Salt bought in quantity for the Martinmas slaughter—that's a once-year expense. These spices, Marten, from London—were they brought by a carrier?'

'Yes, sir. Sir Thomas had a regular arrangement, and an order with the grocer.'

'Then that can be continued—tallow for candles, rushes, cloth for the making of livery for the servants—who did the making, Julian?'

Surprised at being asked, she answered without animosity. 'Oh, my mother's women, and some of it was put out to a tailor in Banbury.'

'Deddington as well,' said Marten, indicating a lower line. Christie glanced at Julian's intent face. 'You see, each entry is simple enough, there's no mystery to it—Marten here records each expense and its cost. If there's more than one of an item he gives the total—see here, "Bought of the pheasant-taker, twelve pheasants, two shillings." How much then for one pheasant?'

'Two pence,' said Julian.

'And six?'

'One shilling.' Some annoyance at this simple catechism had entered her voice.

'And who's the pheasant-taker, and where does he live?'

She could only look at him blankly, with irritation—how was she expected to know? Marten came to her rescue. 'That's old Will Cooper, sir, lives in Adderbury on the hill. We used to have a man who collected their eggs and reared the chicks under a broody hen in this household, but he died, and no-one else seemed to have the skill.'

'That's a shame. It's also a shame that things like wheat and cheese have to be bought—but if Sir Thomas didn't choose to farm his land himself, that was his option.'

'Much is received by way of rent,' Marten pointed out, and turned to the part of the book headed "Receipts". Here Julian saw, for the first time, something of her father's wealth: the payments in wheat and meat and beer and wool, the considerable amounts of coin received and duly noted. She was glad, too, that they had not

[311]

investigated further the lists of recent expenses, for mourning garb for all the household would have been a considerable item, along with the expense involved in bringing Sir Thomas's body from Exeter, his interment with requiem mass and much singing for his soul, the keeping of his month's mind with all due ceremony and respect, just before Christmas, and the ordering of a brass to commemorate him in Adderbury church. The pain of his loss was still sharp, and she had refused to accept that the man sitting by her side had had no part in it.

Christie had earlier asked Marten to produce two lists: one of his tenants, their methods and dates of payment, and the location of their lands, so that some idea of the estate's income could be drawn up, and the other of all items of regular expenditure, food, candles, wood, cloth, horse fodder, stabling, pewter, linen, clothing and all the other details of country life. Julian, seeing laid out all the sources of the wealth which made her comfortable existence possible, looked at the first paper. 'I never knew there were so many tenants! And not just here and in Adderbury, but in Witney, Broughton, Thame—who collects all the rents?'

'I do,' said Marten, with a wry grin. 'And a thankless task it usually is, Mistress—Dame Julian, especially when the harvest's bad or times are lean.'

Of course, she was not Mistress Julian Bray any more, but Dame Julian Heron. She did not like the unfamiliar sound of it, and moreover she had always tended to associate the title 'Dame' with her mother. She frowned. 'And all these things you've listed here, that we buy—do we *really* drink so much wine?'

The rest of the morning, until the household was summoned to dinner, was spent listening to Marten's detailed and thorough explanations of Ashcott's expenditure. Julian, with growing interest, learned of the difference in price and quality between tallow, beeswax and rushlights, the best time of year to buy good wine, the most efficient remedies for lice and ticks in her father's prized flock of sheep, the dyes necessary to produce the colours of the servants' livery—the cheaper woad for the deep blue, the expensive saffron for the yellow trimmings and laces. She listened, and made comments that did not always appear to strike the two men as trivial or ignorant, and emerged from the estate chamber unaware that she had spent nearly three hours at her husband's side without once exchanging a cross word.

It did not, in the nature of things, last very long. Dame Alice had her own reasons, which were varied, for disliking too close an association between her daughter and the husband she wished to be rid of at the first opportunity, and lost no time in propagating quarrels with the vigour of an enthusiastic gardener, sowing seeds of discord rather than flowers. Christie, who had anticipated something of the sort, proved impervious to suggestions that his wife was frittering away her time in music and hawking when she should have been engaged in more domestic pursuits, and even to the allegation that she had spent money once her father's, now his, on a wildly extravagant set of harness for her dapple-grey palfrey, who was known to the grooms, on account of his less than handsome manners, as Kicker, but to his owner as Cygnus, the swan. Julian, on the other hand, was much easier to goad. Every day her mother brought her examples of Christie's high-handed behaviour to servants and tenants, his cruelty to a faithful Adderbury butcher, spurned after twenty-five years of supply to Ashcott (and almost as long purveying meat that was rotten, poor quality or not as described on his bills), and the ruthless efficiency with which the slack and idle habits encouraged indirectly by Sir Thomas's open-handed rule were suppressed. Four members of the household were dismissed, and Julian, who had known all of them since her childhood, protested and raged and wept in vain—they had formed part of her life at Ashcott, and she did not care if they had been pilfering supplies and selling them to friends for ten weeks or ten years, so long as they were not summarily turned off. But Christie, who knew that he must earn the respect of those he ruled if he were not to be fleeced and cheated at every turn, ignored his wife with calm implacability. And Julian's fury and frustration grew apace alongside her unhappiness.

After the fiasco of the wedding night, Christie had behaved to her with as much consideration in the bedchamber as if there had been a sword laid between them in the manner of the romances. He had not laid a finger on her, and Julian, with anger, found herself harbouring feelings on the subject that were almost of—disappointment, as if he had removed a reason for her to hate him. There were plenty of others, of course, and she catalogued them daily: his callous treatment of the Ashcott servants, his disregard for her feelings in the planning of their marriage, his active support for the evil usurper and shedder of children's blood, and above all the part he had undoubtedly played in the murder of her dear father. But to her now, at bed and at board, he showed her every courtesy, behaved exactly as a husband should, and her complaints, her anger, fell on him like arrows striking steel and dropped, blunted and made harmless by his apparent calm patience. Bewildered, she could not help contrasting this attitude with the mockery and ridicule he had shown to her before their marriage, and her inconvenient conscience told her that perhaps, now they were wed, he wanted to make a friend of his wife rather than an enemy. She remembered, guiltily, her similar, more reluctant resolutions, fragile plants which had all withered away in the searing conflicts between her husband, her mother and herself. She was coming to realise that her married life could not always be like this, until death parted them: one or both of them would run mad, if it was. But they were bound, indissolubly, no possible excuse for annullment—had that been why, as Dame Alice had thought, he had made sure of consummation on the wedding night? But there would be no child of that deflowering, and if he continued to sleep firmly on the other side of their shared bed, the chances of conceiving one looked slender indeed. Why, wondered Julian, enduring yet another of her mother's tirades on the subject, did he not force himself again and again on her, to engender the baby that would inherit Ashcott, and ensure the continuation of Herons there? It was a puzzle, though she had to admit that his neglect of these matters caused her relief as well as that obscure unwelcome disappointment. It did not enter her head that his sympathy with her extended thus far.

Christie, remembering the terrified, unhappy child who had told him that she did not care with wine-induced bravado, could not bring himself to touch her again, and see the shutters close across her face. If he was ever to make a success of this marriage, and to have his wife regard him with more tenderness than her usual hostile glower across their shared plate, then he must be patient, considerate and firm. He would not grovel before her, pretending a passion he did not feel, although he was finding it increasingly difficult to lie calm and still each night, two feet of unsullied sheet between his body and hers. He had never been a great womaniser, his lusts were directed towards less tangible objectives—money, power, status, lands. But he found that he wanted more of the pale, generous body he had dutifully taken that first night: wanted to awaken in her the desires that existed already in him, so that they could share that at least.

It was a foolish dream, he knew: small chance of sharing desire, affection, even friendship with a girl who so plainly detested him and all he represented. And there was the baleful, unpleasant presence of her mother, eager to foment discord with a fervour that would have done credit to Medea. He had a good idea of some of the reasons that Dame Alice might have for making the relationship between him and his wife even worse than it was already, but found her relish for it somewhat disturbing: he did not like to feel that there was something of which he might be ignorant. It was a pity that Dame Alice's dower lands did not boast a house of sufficient standing to contain her inflated pretensions: the only alternative ways of being rid of her were into a nunnery, which was unlikely to say the least, or into the arms of a second husband. Christie, considering the difficulties of persuading a man of suitable age and standing to sacrifice his peace for the sake of Dame Alice's admittedly fairly handsome dower, knew this prospect to be as hopeless as the other. For the moment, his wife's mother was immovably ensconced, and life at Ashcott, in what should have been the bliss of the first few weeks of marriage, was fast becoming intolerable.

A solution to his problems arrived late in February, wearing the familiar livery of the white boar, with a summons from the King. Sir Christopher Heron's services were required, it appeared, sooner than had been anticipated: he had been due to return to Westminster in March, but this request for his earlier attendance was a surprise not at all unwelcome. Julian, seeing the white boar on blue and murrey, knew what the courier's arrival portended: and found, to her annoyance, that she did not relish the idea of being left alone with her mother. The past six weeks had seen Christie establish himself, in no uncertain terms, as master of the household, and the servants had begun under his instruction to defer to her rather than to Dame Alice. In his absence, her mother's overpowering personality would doubtless reassert itself, and although Julian did not lack the will to stand up to her abrasive and abusive tongue, she dreaded the prospect of the endless battles that lay before her.

The ugly bright bay horse that her husband, unaccountably, always rode by choice despite the animal's evil temper, stood, or rather fretted, in the courtyard, stamping his hooves so that sparks flew from the stones, and swishing the long black tail so that one groom, misjudging the distance, was all but blinded as it lashed across his face. On a much smaller, quieter horse sat the scrawny bright-eyed lad that Christie continued to tolerate as his servant, despite the fact that he was all too obviously quite untrustworthy. Julian, in her warmest furred gown, the russet velvet with the deep-bordered hem of fine miniver, stood shivering in the porch, feeling the wind bustle amongst her skirts and frisk playfully around the veils of her headdress, raising the hairs uncomfortably on the back of her neck. It had rained before dawn and, obviously, would rain later: the clouds were low, grey and threatening. Tomorrow, her husband would be in Westminster, at the bright glittering court of which she had seen but a brief glimpse at Crosby Place, last year: and she would still be here, cold, lonely, doing battle endlessly with Dame Alice through the dreary weeks of Lent. She wanted to say to the tall figure at her side, richly and splendidly clad in green and gold, 'Take me with you.' Not for the sake of his presence, of course: never that. But she desired most desperately an expansion of the narrow confines of her life at Ashcott, that had once meant everything to her, and now seemed so limited and frustrating.

And there were the accounts, too. How was she to work with Marten, as her husband had instructed her, when as soon as his back was turned her mother would be meddling, or worse? How could she prevent the woman who had once had such physical power over her, from reasserting that force once Christie was gone to Westminster? Miserably, she stared out at the mud and cobbles of Ashcott's wide courtyard, crowded with servants and horses, and struggled with the unwelcome realisation that the man she detested was also in some sense her protector.

'I am sorry that I cannot take you with me,' he said, and Julian, startled out of her gloom, jerked round to stare up at him. In the dim light of the porch, his face was hard to read, but the concern on it was plain, and had the appearance of sincerity. 'I know it is going to be very difficult for you, when I am gone.'

'Difficult?' Julian opened her brown eyes to their fullest extent. 'Whatever do you mean, difficult? You need have no fears for me, husband.' And with a defiant confidence she did not feel at all, stepped back to indicate that he could go. Christie studied her, frowning slightly. Then he said abruptly, 'I have given various orders which you may find of some help. I hope I will be back soon—or perhaps, if it is possible, I will send for you. In the meantime, God keep you, Julian.'

And he dropped a light kiss on her high, fashionably and painfully plucked brow, that lingered long after his lips had left it, like a burn.

CHAPTER FOURTEEN

'And when she saw her two sons, for joy she wept tenderly.'
(BOOK II, CHAPTER 10)

After the confused hatreds and guilts at Ashcott, the devious atmosphere at the Palace of Westminster seemed as wholesome as mountain air to Christie. He had stood alone at his wife's house, defending himself in almost entirely hostile country, and although he had succeeded in some ways, in others—notably his relations with Julian—his weeks there had been a dismal failure. He was no nearer to her than he had ever been, and on his two-day journey to London had faced the unwelcome realisation that his marriage was probably already doomed. He was trebly damned in Julian's eyes: by his cold-blooded entrapment of her into a marriage that repelled her, by the part he had supposedly played in Sir Thomas Bray's death, and by his loyalty to a King she had dismissed as an evil child-murderer. On the last count, at least, he saw no chance to redeem himself as long as political expediency deemed that the children lay hidden. He presumed that they were still at Gipping, and wondered if this summons had anything to do with the two boys.

At Westminster, he was among friends: people familiar to him, who valued and respected him, with whom he could feel at ease. Even the freckled, undistinguished face of Sir Ralph Bigod, recently a father for the first time, was a welcome sight, and he began to realise how much those taut, difficult weeks at Ashcott had drained his energy and his enthusiasm. Even Sir James Tyrell, robust as ever himself, commented on the weariness evident in his face and bearing, and felt friendly enough to him to chaff him as to the reasons for it. 'I could have told you a thing or two about marrying a sweet young virgin, you know—did it myself a while ago, and she nearly drained the life out of me, the first few weeks we were wed.'

'It's not the lady,' said Christie, smiling faintly: the days when he might have taken offence at the older man's blunt comments were long, long gone. 'It's her mother is the problem.'

'Indeed? I know her for a lady of, er, fearsome reputation,' said

Sir James, whose own wife's mother had long ago left earthly cares behind. 'Poor old Bray used to tell such stories, over a cup of wine or two, as you wouldn't believe—or perhaps you would. Pack her off to a nunnery, young Kit, or find her another poor unsuspecting fool who'll marry her.'

'I could try,' said Christie, with the demure look that often accompanied his dry wit. 'But I doubt I can find another St George.' He wanted to ask Tyrell about the two boys, but their rather public situation precluded it: the Painted Chamber, where they stood, was crowded with other courtiers, attendants, members of Parliament, officials, lesser servants, menials and all the other assorted hangers upon the coat-tails of royalty. Parliament had been in session for a month, and Westminster was correspondingly packed. Christie, out of touch at Ashcott, had been speedily given the news by all his friends: the act of attainder passed against the late rebels, and King Richard's lawful title to the throne ratified and confirmed. There had also been passed various laws which aimed at the reform of diverse notorious and long-condoned abuses of justice, and one, lesser, law which gave a certain Sir James Tyrell, Knight of the King's Body and Master of the Horse and of the Henchmen, title to lands to which he had long laid claim. He had also received other rewards for his loyal service in helping to subdue the rebellion in Wales and Cornwall, and in retrieving the person of the Duke of Buckingham.

An official in the white boar collar stood before them, and told Sir James Tyrell and Sir Christopher Heron that the King's Grace required their presence in his privy chamber: would they follow him? And the two knights were led through the maze of chambers, steps, courtyards and passages to the room overlooking the river which Richard had chosen for his most private refuge.

He was alone in it, standing by the window. Outside, through the greenish glass, the River Thames ran grey and sullen, pocked by boats, with the low dull green line of Lambeth Marshes beyond. Christie, assessing his monarch for a clue to his mind, as he had learned to do at Middleham, saw that the King appeared to have thrown off the hurt of Buckingham's betrayal. The kingdom was safe, Parliament obedient as always, the country quiet and the programme of much-needed reform that he had long urged his brother to carry out had begun. The man who turned to give them his hand to kiss was relaxed, smiling, confident, more like the old Duke of Gloucester when Middleham had been the heartstone of his world. The alteration in his newest knight was apparently less happy: he surveyed Christie thoughtfully and then said, 'Is married life not to your liking, Sir Christopher?'

'I have hopes of it becoming so, Your Grace,' said Christie wryly. 'But I may at some time in the future require your assistance, if my wife's mother proves—uh, difficult.'

'She's a termagant,' said Tyrell, more bluntly. 'The woman's known for it. Only trouble is, no nunnery in its senses would have her.'

'Perhaps, as the widow of a rebel, she could be persuaded,' said Richard. 'I would not want the redoubtable Dame Bray to come between you and your bride, Christie. But that is not why I have summoned you here, and rudely interrupted your first weeks with Dame Julian. It is another lady who concerns us now—Dame Elizabeth Grey, late calling herself Queen of England.'

*

All winter long, the woman who had once been Queen had remained safe in her sanctuary at Westminster Abbey, living on the Abbot's bounty with her five daughters and the few servants left to them. Believing her sons to be dead, she had conspired with the Countess of Richmond, the Bishop of Ely, the Duke of Buckingham and, most heinously, the man known as Henry Tudor, calling himself Earl of Richmond, to marry her eldest daughter to the Tudor and so elevate her and her husband to the throne of England, York and Lancaster united. The failure of her plots and of the rebellion had left her utterly cast down: she had lost everything, and her daughters Bess and Cecily had laboured in vain to comfort her. Then, after the King's return to London, late in November, a certain Sir Christopher Heron had come to the Abbey and asked to speak with Dame Grey, who was now under close watch by John Nesfield, one of the King's most loyal Yorkshire squires, and kept in strict seclusion: the King could be sure that her plotting days were over. The Countess of Richmond was under her third husband's eye on his Derbyshire estates, Buckingham was dead, the Bishop of Ely fled to Flanders, the Tudor, alas, still at large in France. The unfortunate Doctor Lewis, who had carried messages between the Tudor's mother and Dame Grey, was now safe in prison and the other known go-between, Reginald Bray, had been grudgingly pardoned just after Christmas, although he was a cousin of Sir Thomas Bray, whose death in captivity had, in general opinion, only just pre-empted his execution.

Dame Grey had agreed to receive Sir Christopher: her assent was a polite fiction which concealed the fact that she no longer had any choice in such matters. She remembered, vaguely, the tall young man with the interestingly bony face: her husband would have known his name, his family and home, probably his income down to the last halfpenny. King Edward had been famous for never forgetting a face: she had never paid much attention to those who were not immediately within her orbit, or from whom some advantage could be obtained, or who had in some way offended her. Only these last were never forgotten.

He had told her, in a quiet matter-of-fact voice, that report had lied. Her sons were not dead, but alive and well and in a place of safety. There was accordingly no need to plot with the Tudor, nor to linger any longer in sanctuary, to the inconvenience of herself and the indignity of the kingdom.

Coldly, Elizabeth had refused to rise to the bait. One person had told her that her sons were dead: now another informed her that they were alive. Since, as must be evident, a third could tell her that they had each three heads with as much sincerity, who was she to trust? In short, she would believe nothing without proof.

Proof, it had appeared, was forthcoming. Just after Christmas, two letters were brought to her. One, the handwriting straggling across the page as if its perpetrator had forgotten the use of a pen, presented the humble obedience and good wishes of her devoted son Edward. The other, more brisk, also offered filial devotion, but in rather less pious terms, asked pointedly when she would join them, and enquired after the welfare of his sisters. It was signed, defiantly, 'Richard York'.

They had not said where they were held, but the hand of her youngest son was very characteristic, and recognised not only by herself but by Bess, whom she had summoned to confirm its identity. Edward, the messenger added, had been very ill since an attempt on his life in October, a recurrence of his old problem with his breathing and his skin: his mother's presence was obviously needed.

Bess found herself close to tears as she stared at the letter written by the beloved boy whose reported death had shattered all the pillars of her young world. There was no denying it: even her mother, suspicious and ever ready to see malice where none was intended, could not deny it. They were alive. Her wicked uncle was no longer wicked: the dread dreams of Dickon's death and the casual disposal of his body could no longer have the power to terrify her nights and haunt her days. It was as if a great dark mass that during the last months had been blighting everything she thought or did, was lifted: she could breathe easier, and stand taller, and not fear what the dark held any more. 'Oh, thank God,' she whispered, knowing that all those days of desperate prayer had not been in vain: and that her suspicions had been proved correct. The Countess of Richmond, for her own reasons, had most sinfully and heinously lied to her mother.

It was only then that the full impact of the news had struck her. If the rebellion had succeeded, she might even now be wedded to Henry Tudor—a man on whose behalf, if not on whose orders, her brothers had apparently so nearly died. She broke into a cold sweat with the very thought of it. I will marry anyone on earth, vowed Bess with uncharacteristic ferocity, anyone at all, the Sultan of Turkey or the Grand Cham of Cathay if I am asked, but not that man—not Henry Tudor.

Convincing Dame Grey that her sons lived was one matter, persuading her to emerge from sanctuary was quite another. The place that at first had seemed only a temporary refuge from the chill winds of change and opposition had now taken on, for the woman once known as Queen, the quality of a haven. She had at first missed the ceremony, the elaborate rituals of court life, the cohorts of attendants and servants, the power she and her family had wielded at Westminster. In the safety of the Abbey, she had plotted, and failed dismally to bring down the King she hated, a King neverthe-less acclaimed, anointed, and ruling by consent of the people. Whatever the rights of her son Edward and herself, she had been lucky to have been allowed to remain in sanctuary, however closely guarded.

But outside, the court had changed. There were new faces, new alliances, new intrigues, new feuds, new wielders of power, and she was included in none of them. No longer was she the silver-gilt beauty whose glorious face had caused a King to marry for love rather than policy, for the first time in English history: her mirror showed her with hair more silver than gold, a face sagging and discontentedly wrinkled, and flesh flabby and shapeless after bear-ing a dozen children and, more recently, months of stodgy Abbey food without any exercise. She had always relied on her beauty to obtain her desires: now she was just another fat middle-aged widow, utterly lacking her old intoxicating power, that had attracted any man not blind. Her women, loyally, assured her that her loveliness was still as great as ever, but she knew they lied, and wept and stormed at them and threw brushes and pots of rouge.

Even she, who had always manipulated the world to her advantage, could not stave off the penalties of old age. She continued to use the chamomile rinse for her hair, the saffron dye, the face paints and sweet perfumed oils for her drying wrinkled skin, but deep in her heart acknowledged the futility of it. Being a woman of great energies and vigour, however misdirected, and deprived of her previous outlets, namely her power and her appearance, she had turned at last to her neglected daughters for the satisfaction of her needs. The three little ones, Anne, Katherine and Bridget, at first astonished by the sudden overwhelming interest displayed by a mother who had virtually ignored them in the past, soon responded with most gratifying affection. Bess and Cecily, however, were more suspicious, the one too intelligent and the other too selfish to be so easily won over. And when the first of many of the King's advisers—the Chancellor, the Archbishop, the Duke of Norfolk —came to ask her to leave sanctuary, Bess and Cecily added their voices, urgently, to the more sober arguments of the men of church and state. They were bored, resentful, frustrated: they longed, Cecily in particular, to see the outside world again, to dance and converse with young men, to laugh and sing and be carefree and happy after nine months—dear Heaven, nine months!—mewed up in an Abbey with no company but monks and a few attendants.

Between old and young, Dame Elizabeth was trapped. She knew she could not stay in sanctuary for ever, any more than she could stave off the ravages of old age for ever. But she was nothing if not determined to obtain the best possible bargain for herself and her children, and haggled with all the unyielding greed of a Billingsgate fishwife.

*

'She has agreed at the last to leave the Abbey,' said the King. 'John Nesfield, whom you both know well, is to have the charge of her, and ensure she foments no more plots. The younger girls are to be in her care, and I have promised to marry the older ones to suitable gentlemen, with a dowry of lands worth two hundred marks a year, and generally treat them with all courtesy and consideration.' He made a wry face. 'And she will not emerge until I have sworn a solemn oath to this effect in the presence of the Lords Spiritual, the Lords Temporal, the Mayor and aldermen of the City of London, and doubtless any passing carpenter, hermit or beggar. This I have promised to do, for the woman can't stay there for eternity, and more to the point, neither can those poor girls. So, Sir James, I find I must now beg a favour of you—will you have Dame Grey and that gaggle of girls at your house for a while, under Nesfield's care and at my expense?'

'Why, certainly, Your Grace—and your nephews will be right glad to see them, I know. But I,' said Tyrell, with a grin, 'have precious little say in the matter. It's my wife you must ask, she rules my roost—though she's grown passing fond of those boys, especially the younger one, rascal though he is.' He added, more seriously, 'I am sure my Anne will welcome Dame Grey and all her children, for as long as you wish them to stay with us, Your Grace. My only fear is that we—well, I'm only a simple old soldier, as you well know, Your Grace, and we do not keep any great estate at Gipping. It's a quiet life, far from noise or bustle, and not at all like the court. Will not the Queen—I mean Dame Grey—will she not find it too simple for her tastes?'

'She may well,' said the King, with some asperity. 'In view of her past behaviour I think she's fortunate not to find herself in still greater simplicity in a cell in the Tower. If she cannot content herself with country living and the company of all her children, then she is a bigger fool, and a greedier one, than even I ever took her for. She may not like the idea in the least, but it's all she'll be offered— that, or nothing. A spell in decent seclusion is a generous offer in the circumstances, and I think you'll find she is well aware of it.'

*

On the first day of March, 1484, the King swore, as he had agreed, to receive the daughters of Dame Elizabeth Grey, late calling herself Queen of England, out of the sanctuary of Westminster Abbey, to be guided and ruled by himself, and pledged himself to put them in honest places of good name and fame, and to treat them with all courtesy as befitted his kinswomen, albeit tainted by bastardy. The Chancellor and the ancient Archbishop of Canterbury, bearing a copy of the oath, informed Dame Grey that all was now as she wished: she was free to emerge with her daughters, and join her young sons in country peace and quiet. And on the day after

Richard had publicly pledged himself to keep them safe, she led the five girls and the few attendants left to them out of the Abbey precincts and into the Palace of Westminster, to join the horses and escort who were to take them away from London and the devious, plot-ridden court with all its temptations and dangers.

Bess stood in the outer court, breathing the fresh air as if she had been starved of it all her life, gulping it in with all the smells of Westminster, pleasant and unsavoury alike. Her uncle had greeted them as they entered the Palace, with a polite kiss of welcome for her mother, and a much warmer one for the girls, sweeping little Bridget up onto his shoulder and showing no dismay when the child, who had barely seen a man outside a monk's cowl for months, burst into tears and howled for her mother. Katherine was shy and hung behind, gazing wide-eyed at the bustling world she had forgotten, and even Nan, a normally boisterous eight-year-old, was subdued and quiet on this momentous occasion.

'Hallo, Bess,' said her uncle, having handed the wailing Bridget back to her nurse. 'You look well—seclusion agrees with you.'

'I beg to differ, Your Grace,' his eldest niece had said, smiling in her happiness. 'It is *freedom* that agrees with me so well.'

'I am glad of it,' he had said, smiling in return, and she thought how much more pleasant he looked than she had remembered: not tall, of course, unlike her father, and she in fact overtopped him. And he was slender and slightly built, but whatever the deficiencies in his physique, the smile transformed the pale, lined, high-strung face. She wondered how her mother, or herself, could ever have thought this man capable of ordering the deaths of Dickon and Edward. It was not the place, amongst all these curious devious people, to apologise for so drastically misjudging him, but at some more private moment, when she should return to the Palace, she knew she would let him know of her trust and regard.

The Queen, too, was there to bid them farewell in the outer court: a woman with a tired, gentle, intelligent face and mouse-fair hair, undistinguished in person but greatly loved by her husband and her court. She smiled at Bess, and did not comment on the disparity between the girl's height and her husband's. She gave her good wishes, as did everyone else, and Bess began to wish that it could soon be over, so that they could leave this place and go to Dickon and Edward.

At last, the cavalcade set out. They would not go in state, but nonetheless a suitably large escort was both courteous and sensible, when there was always the chance, admittedly remote, that some adherent of the Tudor might snatch Bess, or one of her sisters, and force her into marriage. So there were men-at-arms, attendants, servants, grooms, baggage, and Bess wondered how they were going to keep their destination secret when, obviously, so many would know of it.

She was soon enlightened. They spent the first night at St Albans, as the honoured guests of the Abbot, and woke in the morning to find that all their escort had been dismissed, to be replaced by a smaller group of men who had the look of gentlemen servants, many of them bearing the interlaced knot that she recognised, after searching her memory, as being the badge of Sir James Tyrell. And indeed it was that knight who appeared as they were breaking their fast, to explain the removal of the Westminster escort, and the change in their route. Riding out of London on this road had been a ploy to deceive any spies or traitors. They were instead to ride across country to Suffolk, and Sir James's own house, where her brothers were waiting eagerly for their arrival. Tyrell would lead them, and trusted to his companion Sir Christopher Heron, also a King's knight, to ensure their swift and discreet journey. And beside him, Bess saw the man whom she had first met in the early days of sanctuary, and who had given her those unwelcome tidings about Edward's poor health. It reminded her now that he was still unwell, and she knew, with a little prickle of foreboding, that their sojourn at Tyrell's manor might not be one of unalloyed happiness.

But for Christie Heron, freed of the doubts and complexities of his married life, the four days it took to bring Dame Grey and her daughters to Gipping were blissful in comparison with the unhappy weeks spent at Ashcott. The sun shone mildly for early March, birds sang, snowdrops nodded pale and shy with promise in the bare brown hedgerows, and new lambs cavorted joyously in the fields. A new year was beginning, and beckoned him with hope: Ashcott seemed very far away as he arranged their night stops with practised efficiency, beguiled the younger children with songs and tales as they rode before their nurses, and played at night for the older ones. When he had first met her, Bess had reminded him of Julian Bray, both tall well-built girls with a mass of hair, in Bess's case the true Plantagenet corn-gold of her father: but on closer acquaintance there was little resemblance between the hasty, imperious Julian and this dreamy, thoughtful, intelligent girl who had a sensitivity and sense and warmth that her flower-like younger sister Cecily entirely lacked. He had never met the late King Edward, but from all accounts many of his gifts, and none at all of his vices, appeared to have descended to his eldest daughter who, if matters had turned out differently, might have been the wife of Henry Tudor and Queen of England. Since she was no longer a Princess, and her mother no Queen, there was no need for elaborate formality, however cold and frosty Dame Grey's expression at the sounds of girlish laughter from the cavalcade behind, and Christie found himself in some demand from all the girls, whether for a story, a riddle or a joke, or a snatch of impromptu song. Why, he wondered unhappily, could not Julian be like this delightful young woman, generous with her laughter and her wit?

Then they came to Gipping, riding through Stowmarket without apparently rousing any suspicion that the stout widow with her lively brood was in fact their late Queen, and Tyrell sent his silent servant Wellesborne ahead to warn his wife of their coming. When Bess rode, with proper wonderment and pleasure, past the perfect small chapel in stone and flint, and into the courtyard of Gipping Hall, her first thought was not for the simplicity of this plain timbered and plastered building, nor for the hungry growl of her belly and the ache in her back and seat from too much riding, but for her brother Dickon. The place was crowded, but her eyes flew unerringly to the golden curly head, the freckles and crooked grin of the small boy ten paces away, wearing a blue doublet and demi-gown and surely taller than when she had bid farewell to him last June . . .

Heedless of decorum, careless of accident, she kicked herself free of the cumbersome board on her saddle, and leapt joyfully to the ground. 'Dickon!' she cried, and the boy ran forward to greet her, to be swept up and swung round as her father had done with her when she was still small enough. Breathless, because he was quite heavy, she let go, and found her face wet. 'You're crying, Bess,' said Dickon sternly. 'You shouldn't be doing that, it's supposed to be a *happy* time!'

'But I thought you were dead,' she gasped: laughing and weeping at once had played havoc with her breathing. Dickon, down-to-earth as usual, snorted. 'Well, I'm not a ghost, and neither is Edward, even if he does look like one.'

She was appalled by the appearance of her other brother. Was this thin, stooped, fragile child with eyes blinking in the spring sunlight, and skin painfully raw and red disfiguring hands and face, really the quiet grave pious boy she had known? Admittedly, he had spent most of his childhood in Ludlow, and she had seen him only at brief and irregular intervals, but that Edward had been well and happy. This nervous boy, his lips so pale as to seem almost blue where they were not afflicted by sores, smiling tremulously, bore no relation to his former self. It had shocked even their mother out of her self-absorbtion: Dame Grey, her eyes suddenly overflowing with, surely, genuine emotion, hurried forward to embrace her son.

Christie, too, was disturbed by the change in Edward. Before, he had looked sick, but not beyond recovery—and that had been a scant three months ago. His sojourn at Gipping, far from having a beneficial effect, seemed to have brought him to the brink of collapse. And to add to the boy's troubles, Christie heard with foreboding the fit of coughing that overtook the child as his mother put her ample arms about him.

Though the boy's appearance cast a shadow on the reunion of the family, their joy still overflowed the small courtyard: and it was noticeable how its centre was not Elizabeth, Dame Grey, nor yet her eldest daughter, nor the boy who had once been King, but the small merry figure of Dickon, who had drawn all of them into his circle as the brilliance of a candle will draw moths to its flame. Even Christie felt anew the spell of his vivid personality, and the old longing came over him, for a son like this boy, in whom he could take pride and entrust the future of his line.

*

During the days he spent at Gipping, the richness of the country-side, the small scale of it, the burgeoning hedgerows and the plenty he saw all around, also enchanted him. Gipping, and Suffolk, had stealthily invaded his heart, and here, only here it seemed, would he ever really be at peace. He escorted Cecily and Bess and Dickon, with the eldest Tyrell boy, hunting with hawk and hound, and could not help but contrast their joyful laughter and delight in their freedom with Julian, who had also loved to ride out with her hawk on her fist, but whom, he realised now, he had never heard to break into genuine laughter.

The thought was painful. Here, amongst the children, he had rediscovered the simple pleasures: the keen flight of Bess's hawk, Dickon's face serious and intent over a strange flower pulled from the hedgerow, the high white sunlit clouds soaring over the bare tree tops, the rainbow's brilliant promise against a sky grey and purple with incipient storm. He had always kept people, even those such as Perkin or Ralph Bigod or Tyrell at a distance, had never allowed them too close to his soul: but now, riding by Dickon's side and answering the stream of interested questions, he realised that he was giving away far more of himself than he had ever done before, to anyone save Meg.

That old wound he trusted had healed over at last, but the scar was still there, and a careless probe had the power to hurt even now. Dickon had soon extracted from him the information that he was descended, albeit illicitly, from the great Hotspur, and had been reared amongst Percies, and was highly intrigued. Was the Earl of Northumberland as haughty as he seemed? What state was kept at Alnwick and the other Percy castles? And why had Christie left the Earl's service?

'I saw a better opportunity with your uncle of Gloucester,' Christie said, glancing sideways at the boy's sunlit face. Dickon narrowed his eyes against the light, and soothed the restless little pony. 'And I found that I much preferred life in his service.'

'My uncle isn't proud like Northumberland,' said Dickon. 'I like him, you know, even though he did take my brother's throne away from him—and even though we thought he was trying to have us killed, but we know that isn't true now. Even Edward can see that,' he added dismissively. 'I'm glad the girls have come, though Cecily's grown much too puffed-up and haughty, and Nan's always in the way—I'm glad Bess is here, she's my favourite sister—she thinks about things.' He glanced curiously at his escort. 'Have you got brothers or sisters, Sir Christopher?'

The old pain twisted briefly, but not on his face. 'I have indeed,' said Christie, smiling because it was impossible to be angry or curt with this child. 'Three brothers, though one was killed by the Scots three or four years ago. And two sisters.'

'Are they old or young, your sisters? Younger sisters can be very troublesome,' said Dickon with grave sympathy. Despite himself, Christie laughed, though with some bitterness. 'I have one older sister, Elizabeth, who was unwed when last I saw her, and likely to remain so if she does not mend her tongue. And a younger one, Meg, who is married to Sir Robert Drakelon.'

'Drakelon? Is that a French name?'

'Norman, I think—it's a very old family in Yorkshire.'

'I don't think I know him,' said Dickon after a while spent, evidently, mentally reviewing names. 'What's he like? What's your sister like? Is she pretty, like Bess?'

It was suddenly, astonishingly easy to describe Meg to the boy, who could have no inkling of the hurt she had done him, and he to her. He was no longer the cold-blooded, unemotional young place-seeker who had weighed his sister against his ambition and ruthlessly discarded her. He had risen high, true, but his goals were different now, for he had the tangible, material rewards of service, and lacked only those which carried less obvious, more human advantages. He had learned a great deal since his quarrel with Meg, not least to value other people, their thoughts and feelings, above place and fortune and favour. At that moment he would have happily discarded his glittering future at court, all the benefits and rewards of royal service, if he could only enjoy the friendship and kindness of the two women who figured most in his life, and both of whom, heedlessly, he had turned against him.

'Meg is pretty,' he told Dickon, seeing her as she always appeared in his mind's eye, golden hair flying, the joy brilliant on her face as she danced at Alnwick. 'More than pretty, some would say. You would like her, I think: she loves dancing and music and clothes.'

'Oh—like Cecily,' said Dickon, in tones which indicated his disappointment. Christie shook his head. 'No—not at all like your sister Cecily. Somewhere between her and Bess, perhaps. Meg is warm-hearted, but also—rather ruthless in getting her own way.'

Into the pause, Dickon said slowly, 'Forgive me—I don't want to pry—but have you quarrelled with your sister?'

'Yes,' Christie said, with a sad bitterness he could not quite disguise.

'Oh,' said Dickon. '*Really* quarrelled? Don't you speak to her any more? When did you see her last?'

'At York, when I was there with your uncle last year. The quarrel's an old one—I don't want to say very much about it, save that I broke a promise and did her great hurt, and she has not forgiven me.'

'Have you said you're sorry? Have you done penance and made amends?'

'I have tried,' said Christie, a wry twist to his mouth. 'But I fear my sister has not relented.'

'Well, that's not fair—that's stupid,' said Dickon positively.

'You're supposed to forgive your enemies, turn the other cheek —that's what Our Lord Jesus said.'

'Did you forgive your uncle when you thought he was trying to kill you?'

'That's different,' said Dickon, with a rather shamefaced grin. 'And I've forgiven him now, for taking Edward's place. I can see why he did it. He'd better look to his throne when I grow up, though,' he added without animosity. 'I promised Edward I'd fight him for it. Edward ought to be King, after all it's his right—what do you think?'

Thus challenged, Christie did not find it easy to give a suitable reply, and knew that Dickon, with that unexpected maturity suddenly flashing out from behind the small boy, was well aware of it. He said slowly, 'His Grace King Richard has been proclaimed King by Parliament and people, crowned and anointed. He is the lawful King of this land, and it is a mortal sin to oppose him.'

'I thought that's what you'd say,' was Dickon's comment. 'That's the safe answer. Do you want to tell me what you *really* think? I won't repeat it to anyone else.'

'I know you won't,' Christie said, for Dickon in this respect was to be utterly trusted. 'But in this I think my thoughts must remain private—and make of that what you will.'

'That you don't like what my uncle did, but you're being loyal to him,' said Dickon with approval. 'My uncle is very keen on loyalty, that's the translation of his motto, isn't it—"loyalty binds me".' He added, with endearing directness, 'I can see why my uncle favours you so highly, Sir Christopher. I like you too.'

And Christie was absurdly pleased, as if given this accolade by someone much more important than a ten-year-old boy of tainted parentage and uncertain future. But Dickon had that gift, such was the force of his personality, of transcending such trivial matters as age, birth and circumstance, so that his friendship and liking were bestowed, and received, with honour.

It was a new thing for Christie, to be surrounded by children: with the seven of Dame Grey, and Tyrell's four, Gipping was crowded with them, and the atmosphere was delightful, full of spontaneity and surprise, a lack of ritual and formality that was a most refreshing change after Westminster. Anne Tyrell, with commendable aplomb, played hostess to the woman who had been Queen, and was now plain Dame Grey again: she who had once demanded that her own mother serve her on her knees, must now

[330]

return to ordinary life. She sewed, and worked tapestry, contributed recipes for medicines and cordials to Dame Anne's collection, and helped in the stillroom. She also spent much time with her son Edward, whose joy at the reunion with his mother had not been reflected in any improvement in his health. He was usually to be found by the fire in the solar at the southern end of the house, reading or studying, and the energy drained from him slowly and subtly, so that it was only afterwards that Christie, with hindsight, could realise that the decline was irreversible. A chill caught after Christmas had settled on the lungs, so Anne Tyrell had explained sadly, and she knew, if no-one else could admit it, that Edward, once so briefly King of England, was dying.

By this time, the man who had usurped his throne was moving north, towards Nottingham, and in the middle of March a messenger arrived at Gipping, requesting that Tyrell and Christie join the King. The letter also suggested that Sir Christopher Heron bring his bride to Nottingham, and present her to Richard and his Queen.

Christie received this summons with very mixed feelings. He had come to love Gipping, and he had enjoyed the company of Dickon and his sisters: also, he was increasingly concerned about young Edward. The King would have to be told about his nephew's illness, of course, but it was a task that neither he nor Tyrell would relish.

The suggestion that he collect Julian on his way was not entirely welcome either, though it would give him the chance to spend some time in her company without the interference and malice of her mother driving a wedge between them. Whether she would want to be presented to a King she believed to be a usurper and murderer of his nephews, was another matter: and knowing Julian's old habit of speaking exactly as she thought, Christie felt somewhat apprehensive about her meeting with Richard. But the King had commanded it and, thought Christie ruefully, he would just have to take the consequences.

So, with sorrow and reluctance, he took his leave of Gipping. Tyrell was going direct to Nottingham, so would not be able to accompany him. It was a wet and windy day when he and Perkin left, so the courtyard was empty of waving children: he had already taken his farewells, and wondered, as he turned away from Edward's sick pale face, if he would ever see the eldest son of King Edward IV again.

*

The intimate, small scale closes of the Suffolk countryside gave way to wider, bleaker lands, the huge common fields of each village, some green with autumn-sown wheat, others fallow with pastured beasts, or sprouting freshly with oats or barley. It was the landscape of Ashcott, and though that place was his own, he knew he could never somehow summon up the same affection for it as he felt for the country around Gipping.

But here was Ashcott, and he rode down the hill from Dedding-ton, and saw again the yellow stone and green grass, and felt disloyal: for this, after all, was his home.

The weeks of his absence—there had been four of them—had been difficult ones for Julian. At times, she raged in her mind at her husband—how dare he go off at his King's whim and leave her, neither daughter nor mistress in her own home? He had married her, expected her to give orders, instructed the servants to obey her, and then summarily left her within six weeks of the wedding.

She had tried to assert herself: at first, hesitantly, and later with growing confidence as she saw that, for perhaps the first time in her life, she had the sympathy and support of most of the household. Marten the steward was in particular a great help: he had seen, to his surprise, the makings of an efficient lady of the manor inside the spoilt brat he had always known, and he had besides conceived a liking for her despised husband. Marten greatly admired efficiency, and Sir Thomas Bray's haphazard generosity had always somewhat distressed him.

But of course, it was Dame Alice who was the problem: she who had ruled the roost for so long was not so easily to be dislodged, and Julian's orders were countermanded so frequently that the servants, far more afraid of the mother than the daughter, eventually did nothing that Julian asked them until they had first checked with Dame Alice. And at last, goaded beyond endurance, Julian turned on her mother after her discovery that her suggestions regarding the dinner menu had not been carried out. She had chewed her way through six-month-old spiced salted beef with barely contained fury, and afterwards confronted Dame Alice in the parlour. 'I *told* them in the kitchen to leave the salt beef today—I'm sick and tired of it in broths, in pasties, in meat loaves—why did you order it otherwise, Mother?'

'The beef must be eaten, and before Lent. It'll go rank otherwise —it won't keep till summer.'

'It's rank now,' said Julian. 'And anyway, it doesn't matter what you think—I'm in charge of this household and if I want roast cameleopard for dinner I'm entitled to have it served!'

'Huh!' said Dame Alice, her contempt rich in her voice. 'What do you know of running a household, young madam, eh? Nothing!'

'And whose fault is that?'

'Yours, you insolent hussy, for idling your time away! You'll be ruled by me, do you hear? Married or not, I'm your mother and I've kept this place run smooth for more than a score of years—I'm not handing it over to an untried green girl with none of the wits she was born with!'

'I gave the *order*!' Julian cried, losing her temper altogether. 'My husband gave control of Ashcott to *me*—not to you, you interfering old cow!'

She had gone too far. Her mother, her face flushed and ugly with rage, struck her a tremendous blow on the side of the head that sent Julian, sturdy and strong as she was, staggering back against the big carved chair. Its arm drove into her thigh, but even that sharp pain did not dispel the dizziness and raw agony around her ear. Gasping, she shook her head to clear it, only to have her mother fetch her a second blow, on the other side. 'And that's for your insolence, you wicked, evil, ungrateful child. Now will you go to your chamber, or must I hit you again?'

Julian, dazed and battered, was in no condition to make any protest. She was dragged to her room, her head still ringing from the pain of her mother's fists, and heard the bolts slam with a curiously remote feeling of finality.

She was still there, a week later, when Christie returned, so the bruises had faded and the swelling had gone down. Dame Alice had realised however, somewhat tardily, that for Julian's husband to arrive unexpectedly to find his wife incarcerated in her chamber would not be very wise: so before the lean bay courser had trod wearily under the gatehouse, she had hastened to her daughter's room and swept back the bolt and door with a falsely munificent gesture. 'Your fine and handsome husband's here, madam. Why don't you go greet him?'

Julian, suspicious and wary, walked down to the hall and found that it was indeed true. There was the lean ugly bad-tempered horse, there was the disreputable servant and there, filling the porch, was her handsome husband. He was not, of course: that face had too much strength and individuality to be merely handsome. There was a look on it now that was hard to read, and his face was not expressive at the best of times: but there was something hesitant in his eyes, as if uncertain of his welcome.

For her part, his coming signified the end of her imprisonment, nothing more nor less: that was why, for a brief discarded moment, the sight of him made her glad.

He was going again, he told her, pulling his gloves off in front of the hall fire while Perkin struggled with his boots: this was only a flying visit. But she need not fear, he added, with some irony: when he left, she would go with him.

'Don't I have any choice in the matter?' asked Julian, with more hostility in her voice than she had intended. Christie glanced at her, then at Perkin. 'Are you trying to pull my leg off as well, witless one? *Gently*, for the love of God! No, wife, you don't have any choice, because the King has commanded your presence at his court in Nottingham. Doubtless he wants to see what manner of bride he's saddled me with. You'll need all your gowns and girdles, and as many of those ridiculous headdresses as you can pack—oh, and all your jewels. King Richard's household may not be quite as splendid as his late brother's, but it's still the court, after all. It'll be like Crosby Place, or better. Well? Why the long face? I thought it was every young girl's dream, to rub shoulders with royalty and wear silk and jewels?'

'It probably is—given the choice. But I haven't been—no-one has *ever* given me a choice, except my father. I don't like people telling me what to do,' said Julian, through clenched teeth. To her fury, the old mocking grin of their earliest acquaintance appeared in his face. 'Poor Julian. And you don't even have any choice in that.'

She opened her mouth to tell him about Dame Alice, saw her mother's bulk move into distant view, and thought better of it. With a supreme effort of self-control, she lowered her eyes meekily. 'I will bow to your wishes, husband.'

Christie regarded her with rueful resignation. 'You know, Julian, I think that I prefer you honest, even though your words drip poison and your look rivals Medusa's. At least I know what you're thinking.'

She did not know what to say to that at all: no ready answer sprang hot to her tongue. She spoke at last, still staring earnestly at the floor until the rushes at her feet were printed indelibly behind her eyes: shut them, and the shapes remained. 'When must we go?'

'Tomorrow morning—the horses must be rested, and you'll

have a chance to pack. Take your woman with you, the one with the absurd name.'

'It's a good Oxfordshire one, and Frideswide was a venerable saint!'

'Venerable, yes, easy to pronounce, no—I can see why everyone calls her Friday. I should go now,' said Christie, bracing himself as Perkin pulled off the second boot with a wet sucking noise. 'I know what women are—you take all night to pack two gowns.'

There was no answer to him in this mood, so Julian, longing to kick that infuriating mockery off his face, turned with an angry swish of her fur-hemmed skirts and stamped back to her chamber to summon Friday.

On reflection, however, she could not help allowing just a tiny frisson of excitement to shiver into her mind. She was leaving Ashcott, and above all she was leaving the oppressive, brutal rule of her mother: never before had Dame Alice allowed her out of reach of her hand or eye. And she was going to Nottingham, which was not quite the same as Westminster, but would still contain the King and Queen, lords and ladies in abundance, and all the brilliant life and bustle of the court. It was a shame that she had not had more warning: on the other hand, as Friday was swift to point out, she could doubtless order a couple of new gowns at Nottingham, for when she had observed the latest fashions she could have them copied.

'I'm not interested in fashions,' said Julian, without much conviction. Years of being fat and physically immature for her age had left her with a deep dislike of her appearance: even her now-womanly figure did not satisfy her, her face was too heavy and her features too strong, she was much taller than was comely, she was clumsy and lacked altogether the fair daintiness that was the pattern of every heroine of romance. But she was beginning to realise that judicious choice of clothes and colour could effect some improvement. Green and blue suited her best, contrasting well with her pale freckled skin: black did nothing for her at all, russet and mulberry colours little better, and her saffron gown had been a dreadful mistake that had had to be home-dyed in woad. The high waists and tight girdles of the older styles of gown became her curves much better than the newer, plainer fashion with the low-slung belt, which tended to emphasise her hips, still rather ample despite the flesh she had shed. But she still had not found a style of headdress to

[335]

suit her: she would have to look at what the court ladies were wearing.

The prospect was all at once quite cheering. Julian realised how much she had felt restricted and stifled by Ashcott, which she had not left since before her father's death. Freedom, dancing, music, new experiences, new faces, beckoned enticingly: it was a shame that her husband must perforce be part of this adventure, but it was the price she must pay for her liberty, and at the moment she was so desperate to escape from her mother that even a jaunt in Christie's company was enough to lift her heart.

And she did not, when it came down to it, mind very much about having no choice.

CHAPTER FIFTEEN

'You have saved the fairest flower of your garland.'
(BOOK 8, CHAPTER 40)

It was April by the time they reached Nottingham, and rode over the wide stone bridge spanning the river. The castle lay on its great rock to their left: but there was no banner flying, and the people crowding the streets and markets were somehow subdued. Nor were there the usual signs of royal residence, the packs of gorgeously-clad courtiers and officials shouldering their magnificent way amongst the populace, or riding in state through the common herd. With a sudden feeling of foreboding, Christie led his wife and the two servants through the narrow streets to the castle, rearing gloomily above the town.

All Julian knew of Nottingham had been learned from tales and ballads of Robin Hood, and she had been disappointed to discover that Sherwood Forest, haunt of deer and outlaws, lay to the north and therefore well out of their way. She had, she must admit, enjoyed the journey, the different sights and sounds and smells, the changing landscape and weather, the strange accents of the people, and just the feeling of being alive, and free, her horse moving under her and the sun and wind on her face. It was neither safe nor seemly to gallop Cygnus, for a lady's saddle gave a seat precarious at best, but that did not stop her, on several occasions, from urging the grey palfrey into a canter when a particularly inviting stretch of smooth green opened up on the edge of the road. To this daring behaviour Christie made no comment, a lack of disapproval which she found, obscurely, to be disappointing.

So was his attitude towards her, as chaste as any monk, though the mordant wit was more in evidence, and she saw for the first time how much of it came Perkin's way, and how the servant, cheerful and down-to-earth, gave back as good as he got, without, it seemed, much respect. He was not disobedient, however, and Julian, at first rather shocked, realised later that this relationship between master and servant was not only most unusual, but much more complex than she had at first thought. So was Perkin, whom she had on first sighting written off as a disreputable rogue entirely unsuitable for any gentleman's servant, let alone one employed by a King's knight.

But conversation with the boy had proved enlightening. Christie was supervising the shoeing of Bayard at a wayside smithy: only his voice and hands could control the courser in such circumstances, for fire and noise never improved the big horse's temper. Julian took the opportunity to tie Cygnus to the rail set up outside for such a purpose, and stretch her aching legs: it was afternoon, and they had been riding all day with only a brief break for dinner at a small inn. She strolled over the green, avoiding a flock of geese tended by an urchin gawping at this fine lady in velvet and fur, and turned to find Perkin at her side. He barely came up to her shoulder, and she wondered how old he was: it was so hard to tell, he had a child's body but the face of a shrewd, wise and unscrupulous old man. In response to her haughty stare, he grinned, revealing gapped teeth, and said, 'Beg your pardon, Dame Julian—I feared you was planning to run off.'

'Hardly,' said Julian, knowing he was joking, but unable to take his words as lightly as he did. 'Where would I go?'

'That's a point,' Perkin conceded. 'You ain't likely to go back to Ashcott, are you, lady? Difficult to know where you *could* go.' He glanced at the stony face of his master's wife, and added, 'He ain't such a bad sort, you know.'

Julian turned and looked down at him. 'He doesn't show much judgement in his choice of servant.'

If she had thought this would discourage the irrepressible Perkin, she was unfortunately mistaken. 'I tried to tell him that, when he took me on,' said the boy. 'Proper little thief I was, beggar, vagabond, tumbler—I'd done some wicked things, lady, and here was this fine gentleman saying he'd have me for his servant—I couldn't believe it at first. Here's a soft easy fool to gull, I thought —but I was wrong, there's no gulling *him*. Couldn't get away with nothing,' added Perkin wistfully. 'He's got eyes in the back of his head, that one, if I didn't know better I'd say there was sorcery in it.'

It was not possible, Julian decided, to make her expression any more quelling than it already was. She turned and walked back towards the smithy, where Friday waited, still sitting her placid chestnut ambler. With a leap, Perkin placed himself in front of her, his ridiculous face for once serious. 'Wait, please, lady—I want to say something—even if you think I'm scum of the earth, please, Dame Julian, will you listen?'

Astonished, she stopped and stared at him. Hurriedly, before she could start walking again, he went on. 'I know it ain't none of my business and I didn't oughter speak—it ain't my place. But I can't help saying it, lady. I know my master better than anyone, I reckon. He doesn't let go easy, what he's feeling, he don't like to give himself away, but when you know him like I do, lady, you can tell—you get to know the signs.' He took a deep breath, and added, 'I know you hate him, and you've got cause, you think—but you've misjudged him. He didn't have to marry you.'

'Maybe not—but I had to marry him.' Julian gathered up her skirts and prepared to move on: this strange conversation had disturbed her more than she liked, and she wished it at an end. Perkin, with increasing urgency, grasped her sleeve. 'No, no, listen, lady, please—what I'm trying to say is—you may think he doesn't care for you, but I reckon he does!'

'For *me*?' Julian's face was incredulous. 'You witless little worm, you don't know what you're talking about. Now get out of my way, let me pass, or you'll regret it.'

And Perkin, his face comically rueful, had stepped back, reflecting as he stared at her retreating figure—surely no-one had a more expressive back—that he had messed that one up, and no mistake. He had known exactly what he wanted to say, and somehow it had emerged all wrong. Now he had offended her, and his blundering had had entirely the opposite effect to his original intentions: for he had wanted to present himself as a friendly face in whom she could confide, and had completely forgotten that not all people treated their servants in such an open and informal manner as did Christie. He had misjudged Julian as drastically as he had accused her of doing with her husband, and he had probably done serious damage. 'You witless idiot!' Perkin berated himself furiously. 'Why can't you leave well alone?'

But of course, being Perkin, he could no more do that than take vows of poverty, chastity, and obedience—not to mention honesty.

The seed he had planted in Julian's mind did not have very fertile soil in which to grow. It was nonsense, of course, malicious meddling nonsense, and any fool could see it. Christie had married her for her lands, he had shown every sign of actively disliking her, and any softening of his attitude after the wedding could be put down to his desire to be on slightly better terms with the girl who must be his companion in bed and at board for the rest of their lives.

He does not care for me at all, thought Julian angrily: but she could not help observing Christie more closely, especially in his dealings with her. Since, on the journey, he had arranged it so that she and Friday always shared one chamber in the inns, and he himself and Perkin the other, at least she could not accuse him of lustful feelings towards her, and she had been glad to escape the embarrassment of sharing her nakedness with him in the same bed. Usually, on the road, he treated her with courtesy, but did not talk to her much: it had to be admitted that she was almost always in conversation with Friday, who had made the transition from servant to friend so easily that neither girl had noticed it. By the time Nottingham was reached, Julian had come to the conclusion that Perkin had been wildly inaccurate in his estimate of the relationship between her and her husband.

However, as they approached the castle gates, she had to admit that, on the whole, the journey from Ashcott had been quite a pleasant experience.

It was obvious that something was wrong: and as soon as they entered the great outer bailey, with the twin rocks facing them across its expanse, they learned what had happened. Three days ago, a messenger had come from Middleham. The King's delicate only son had taken a childish fever and, quite unexpectedly, had died from it.

It had been a devastating blow for Richard and Anne. Not only had they lost the heir to the throne, the Prince of Wales, their only child: they had also been bereft of a little boy whom both had loved most dearly.

It had been Tyrell's misfortune to arrive at Nottingham just before the messenger from Middleham, and he was able to tell Christie of the King's reaction. The Queen, as was only natural in a bereaved mother, had been desperately overcome with grief, distraught and inconsolable, her face raw and swollen with weeping: and the King had not even tried to comfort her, but had joined her in her sorrow. The last three days had been filled with prayers, masses said over and over again for the child's innocent soul—he had only been nine years old—and the desperate gloom of a court that had suddenly lost its direction. For who, now, would be Richard's heir? His Queen, though young yet, seemed unlikely to have more children: she had conceived two or three times, but the young Prince had been the only one to survive, and there had been no more pregnancies for years. There was Clarence's son, who lived at

Sheriff Hutton in Yorkshire, a child of nine debarred by his father's attainder and also by a certain rumoured lack of wits. There was in addition the eldest son of Richard's sister Elizabeth, John de la Pole, Earl of Lincoln, who was twenty and a capable, energetic young man of good repute. With the threat of Henry Tudor still well-defined on the horizon, it would be advisable to have a grown and acknowledged heir, and Lincoln was the only possible candidate.

Christie and Tyrell discussed it into the night, after Julian had retired to her bed, and came to that conclusion. But at the back of Christie's mind was the bright, ever-present thought of Dickon, of whom Edward, Prince of Wales, had been but a sickly pale shadow. If the other Edward died as well, then Richard would be left with another option: and who could be a more promising and, probably, more popular heir to the throne than the small, remarkable boy who had once been Duke of York?

Julian lay sleepless in her bed, listening to Friday's snores—it was somehow typical of Friday to snore—and thinking about the justice of God. Surely this was His punishment for the murder of those two innocent children? The King had taken their lives, and now, almost a year after the death of their father King Edward, his own son had been cruelly snatched from him. Julian did not stop to think that the innocent Prince of Wales had been punished more than his wicked father: his soul, after all, was now doubtless safe in Heaven.

She could not help feeling shocked, however, when she beheld the King the next day. The man she had seen nearly a year ago at Crosby Place had been young still, despite his careworn, strained appearance. This one was old, his back hunched under the burden of grief, deep lines grooved around his mouth and between the winged dark brows, and his eyes were full of agony. She had to take a stern hold on herself, so that she was not tempted to feel sorry for him: he was, after all, entirely to blame for this tragedy. But he was able, in a way which she would have described as noble in another man, to give her a tired smile as she knelt before him, and to apologise for the absence of the Queen. 'But she has been laid very low by grief—I am sure you will understand, Dame Julian.'

There was a little pause. Christie glanced at his wife: her face was very pale, so that the freckles and the redness of her lips were very marked, and with apprehension he wondered if she were about to make some appalling remark. But Julian, her head bowed and the gauzy wings of her veil spread about her, said very quietly, 'I am sorry to hear of the Prince's death, Your Grace.'

Julian had no idea why she had said it: she had intended to utter words quite different. But she was rewarded by a smile from the King, albeit a singularly sad one, and a gracious dismissal. Surprised at herself, she wrestled with her conscience all day, through the elaborate ceremonial dinner, the gentle strolls in the privy gardens, the supper and the quiet prayers and pastimes that followed. There would be no great feasts, dancing or merrymaking here: the whole court mourned the boy to whom, not two months ago, the lords and officers of the household had sworn allegiance in the event of his father's premature death.

Julian should have felt cheated, but did not: the atmosphere at Nottingham was so sad, so desperately unhappy, that even to raise her voice seemed a crime, and to laugh or smile impossible. She had Friday to talk to, even if she did not often see her husband, who was frequently at the King's side. After some days the Queen appeared, so pale and so full of sorrow that Julian's heart went out to her: for she was also surely innocent, and had been punished for her husband's crime with the loss of her only child. Julian, with little experience of children, could only dimly imagine the compass of Anne's anguish: she knew only that the despair in the Queen's face made her want to weep. She nearly did weep, when brought to the privy chamber to be presented: close to, the pleasant, undistinguished face bore the indelible marks of her agony, and, like her husband, she looked far, far older than her twenty-seven years. Kneeling, Julian tried to express her sympathy, and found the tears choking her throat.

'Pray for him,' said Anne, softly. 'Pray for him, Dame Heron —and pray for me as well.'

And with her sympathy and sorrow like a hard heavy stone of grief around her heart, Julian did as she was bid: and Friday, older and so much wiser, saw and noted one more mark passed on the long and difficult road to maturity.

Many came to Nottingham to offer their condolences to the King, and amongst them a man whom Julian did not know, and whom her husband knew all too well. She noticed him first at dinner, where she sat with her husband and another lady and gentleman at one of the side tables in the Great Hall: the piercing blue eyes attracted her attention first, and the expression in them as they rested on herself and on Christie's face. He was an older man, perhaps the age of Christie's friend Tyrell, though cast in a much finer mould: this man was good-looking, well and even elegantly dressed, but there was something too evasive, too subtle in his face, and when he saw her staring at him, his eyes slid slyly away.

'Who is that man?' Julian asked of her husband. It was a curious but casual question that received a response out of all proportion to the initial enquiry. He glanced over, and his face seemed to stiffen, and grow cold and remote. Julian, watching, saw the stranger incline his head courteously, and after a long pause, Christie did the same. Then he turned back to his meat, but she noticed that little of it went near his mouth. More quietly, so as not to attract the attention of the people sitting by them, Julian repeated her question. 'Please tell me. Who is that man who keeps staring at you?'

He could not put off answering for ever. Reluctantly, as if the words had been dragged from him, Christie told her. 'He is Sir Robert Drakelon. His wife is my sister.'

Nothing he had ever said to her had had the impact of this one simple statement. Her spoonful of pottage hanging perilously forgotten half-way to her lips, Julian stared at him with incredulous amazement. 'Your *sister*? I didn't know you had one!'

Her voice was loud in disbelief: several heads turned. Christie did not admonish her: he said quietly, 'I have two, in fact. Elizabeth, who is older, and unwed, and my half-sister only. And Meg, who is five years younger than I, and married to Sir Robert over there.'

There was something in the quality of his voice that repelled further catechism, but Julian ignored it, intensely curious: she was beginning to realise how little she really knew this reserved complicated man who had so unaccountably married her. 'Why have you never spoken of her?'

'Because you never asked,' Christie pointed out, with some justice. 'She does not appear to be here: presumably she is at Sir Robert's manor at Denby. She would have had a baby in— probably in September last year. So perhaps she is too busy to come to Nottingham—it's a fair few miles, after all.'

Even Julian could detect the disturbance in his voice. Either her husband had quarrelled with his sister—which she did not find in the least surprising—or he had disapproved of her marriage. Since Sir Robert was obviously wealthy, personable and well-bred, Julian could not for the life of her see why, but put it down all the same upon the ever-lengthening list of her husband's crimes.

Dinner ended, and Sir Robert immediately came over. Close to, Julian could see that he was in fact quite advanced in years: the black sleek hair was flecked lightly with grey, and there were many finely-seamed lines around his eyes and mouth. Julian's fertile mind, nourished on romances, leaped instantly to an alternative conclusion. Perhaps she didn't want to marry this old man, she thought, with sympathy for the unknown Meg, who could not be much older than she herself. And probably my husband forced her into it—that would be entirely like him.

She was presented to the coldly smiling Sir Robert, and found that he made her uneasy, like calm deep water that might conceal a sea-serpent. Her husband was congratulated upon his marriage, and accepted Sir Robert's compliments with a cold incline of the head. He then asked about his sister's welfare.

'My wife is well,' said the older man, with a chilly half-smile that Julian did not trust at all. 'She was brought to bed of a child last September—a girl, alas, a poor sickly puny thing, always ailing and fretful. I do not expect the infant to survive her first year, but my wife will have nothing but the best attention for her. I fear she is wasting her time.'

With a memory of Queen Anne's distraught face fresh in her mind, Julian felt a surge of hot anger against such male callousness. What did he know of a mother's anxieties and grief? She said forcefully, 'Perhaps your wife loves her baby.'

Both men, gave her a startled glance, as if her presumption in speaking at all, as well as her words, had alike been a surprise. 'Little Katherine is hardly worth the trouble,' said Sir Robert dismissively. 'And besides, my wife expects another child, which should be born in October. This time, I trust it will be a boy. That is why she has not travelled to Nottingham with me. It's plain her foolhardy trip to York last year did the baby no good at all—indeed, the physician and the midwife both said it hastened the birth—and I've ordered her most strictly not to stir from the house till this child is born. I will not have her harm this one by such stupid reckless behaviour —I dare not risk losing a son and heir.'

Julian, glancing at Christie, was astonished at the expression of controlled anger on his face. She did not know his sister, had no idea of the girl's character, but could still feel outraged sympathy at her husband's callous treatment of her, his only concern, it was plain, the safety of the unborn child who might be the precious heir. And by the look in Christie's eyes, he felt the same as she did. With the unwelcome feeling that she might in this have misjudged her husband, she heard him say quietly, 'Poor Meg—she must take such confinement hard. She always loved to ride and walk abroad.

You would like her, Julian—she enjoyed hawking too.' He smiled at Sir Robert, and the quality of that smile made Julian shiver suddenly. 'I could only wish, brother, that your concern for your wife and my sister matched your undoubted anxiety about your putative heir. I would remind you of what happened in her first pregnancy, and that I still have a care for her. Come, Julian, we must go see Sir James.' And with a scant courtesy just short of outright insolence, swept his wife away.

Julian puzzled long over this new, strange facet to her husband's personality. It was clear that he was fond of his sister, and loathed her husband—but why did it seem that the sister had quarrelled with Christie? What had happened? She lay several nights in her bed, her thoughts revolving in time to Friday's rhythmic snores, and could arrive at no solution. And during the day there was the ever-present figure of Sir Robert, who seemed to have rapidly insinuated himself into the King's favour, and whose speculative, evasive gaze seemed to be forever watching her husband whenever he did not appear to notice it.

There were other revenants from Christie's past at Nottingham too: the Earl of Northumberland for one, a tall haughty figure in early middle age, a man who demanded the utmost deference from all inferiors, whose pride was legendary and whose rule of the north, once assumed to be his family's right, was now severely limited by the King, who was well-known to be planning a Council of the North, to rule these parts in his absence in London, under the nominal leadership of the young Earl of Lincoln, his only grown heir. It was plain that Sir Robert Drakelon was well regarded by the King: he was also much in the company of the Earl of Northumberland, and Julian heard from Sir James Tyrell, who felt sorry for her and had made a point of befriending her, that Sir Robert was retained by the Earl and was a member of his household. 'And a pair of devious, slippery fish they are too,' said Sir James, who had a surprising relish for gossip. 'Wouldn't trust either of them out of my sight.'

She liked Sir James, and could not imagine why he was so friendly towards her husband. But then several people seemed to hold Christie in high regard, not least the King, on whom he was in regular attendance. Julian, suspicious, and disbelieving, watched her husband as he moved easily about the household, noted the charm and efficiency with which he worked, and the cameraderie he shared with his fellows, and was conscious of envy. She had no

[345]

position, no friends here save Friday: she felt an outsider, a super-numary, an appendage, treated with courtesy but no friendship. She must wear mourning, so that the gowns she had hoped would enhance her appearance had perforce to be made in black, a colour that drained away any good looks she had ever had, and she stared unhappily at the more beautiful ladies, their fair and lovely skins enhanced by the sombre colours, who moved about the Queen. She knew that it was sinful, and had confessed this along with all her other transgressions, but no amount of Aves or Paternosters could prevent the resurgence of the envy she felt of all those more fortunate, more attractive women.

And then, quite unexpectedly, the Queen made a special request for her presence in her privy chamber one evening after supper: and the child who brought the message added that she was asked also to bring her lute.

Anne, still grief-stricken by her son's death, had sought solace in prayer, in reflection and fasting and reading her many religious books: now, as those failed to lessen her pain, she looked for more earthly consolations. The King had suggested music, and had informed her that the wife of his knight Sir Christopher Heron, himself gifted on the lute, was apparently also an accomplished musician and had a lovely voice. So, Julian was summoned to play, and again had no choice.

Not long ago, when still a child, she had demanded to display her prodigious skills to as wide an audience as possible, and had learned that others appreciated her talents, even if she, deep down, did not. But she would rather have gone into the wilds of Ireland or the wastes of Africa than play to the Queen, even if Anne was a gentle soul whom she both liked and pitied.

But she went, trembling with dread, to the Queen's chamber, clutching her lute in sticky hands and wishing that she had spent some of her lonely hours at Ashcott and at Nottingham in practice. Common sense dictated that her choice of music be quiet and sad in tone, no bawdy ditties nor merry carols celebrating the May, and she had run with panic through her repertoire in the desperate search for something suitable. Now, sitting on a stool before Her Grace, a bevy of fine ladies as well as various officers of the Queen's household (including, had she known it, her husband's friend Sir Ralph Bigod) in attendance, she tuned her instrument with shaking hands and launched, a little too loudly, into her first song.

A sad tale of unrequited love, it brought sighs of melancholy pleasure when she ended, and the Queen smiled. 'That was lovely, Dame Julian. Your voice is most expressive. I pray you, sing another—do you know a song of our Blessed Mary, that begins, "Of all women that ever were born"?'

Julian did, and sang it, wondering if the heartbreaking lament of Christ's mother would lessen the pain that Anne felt for the death of her own son. Indeed, the Queen wept a little, but wiped her eyes at the close and asked for something perhaps more light-hearted. Moved herself by the slow sad beauty of the song, Julian felt the request a little incongruous, but obliged. Unlike her husband's, her repertoire was not extensive, but she tuned the strings yet again, and embarked on a song that still had its own sadness, though less intense.

> I have a young sister,
> Far beyond the sea,
> And many be the dowries
> That she sent unto me.

Out of the corner of her eye, she saw the door open, saw by the bows and covert movements that the King had arrived. It was a measure of the confidence that she had gained from her first two songs that her voice barely faltered, then gained strength and soared again, high and sweet and pure.

> She sent to me a cherry
> Without any stone,
> And so she did a dove,
> Without any bone.

Her fingers wrought the familiar pattern: she glanced up and saw Christie in the group of men about the King. He was staring at her, a strange expression on his face: she looked away, and continued the song.

> She sent to me a briar,
> Without any leaf,
> And she bade me love my leman,
> Without any grief.

She could not know the overwhelming memory that had flooded into Christie's mind: the bare bleak tower at Bokenfield, and his own voice and Meg's weaving together the enchantment of that same song, the last time she had spoken to him with love and friendship. And now this girl, so very different, was singing the same verses, and he wished, such was the pain, that he had never suggested to the King that Julian play for Queen Anne.

When the cherry was a flower,
Then had it no stone:
When the dove was in the egg,
Then had it no bone.

When the briar's in the seed,
Then hath it no leaf:
When a maiden hath her love,
Then she is without grief.

The delicate notes died away in the high rafters of the big airy chamber, and Julian's voice echoed louder, in counterpoint. And Christie looked at her pale over-wrought face, at the greatness of the emotions so transparent within her, and something moved and altered in his heart, and would not be denied: the urge to take her in his arms, to give her the comfort and friendship that she so greatly lacked. He could not, here and now, analyse the nature of his feelings: he knew that the old pain of Meg had something to do with it, and his increasing sympathy for Julian. And mixed with it, was the bitter, wry knowledge that, far from welcoming such an approach, his wife would undoubtedly spurn him with all the force and contempt at her command.

*

Easter did not lighten the gloom at Nottingham: for the rest of his life, the King would associate it with the dreadful moment when the white-faced, unhappy messenger from Middleham had told him of the death of his dear and only legitimate son, little Ned. Though the boy had been buried at Sheriff Hutton, and the order gone out for a fine monument to him, with a carved figure in alabaster, though the masses for his soul had been said and his month's mind would be kept with candles and prayers, he still could not believe that he would never see the child again, never rest his hand on that silky cap of brown hair, never see the boy's shy, happy smile, the delight on his face when he realised that it was he whom the crowds were cheering. . .

At the end of April, the King and Queen and their household left Nottingham and made their slow way north, to York. There was a brief pilgrimage to Middleham, where the bereaved parents spoke with those who had attended their son in his last illness: Richard had thought that Anne might want to stay there whilst he went further north to plan a summer campaign by land and sea against the marauding Scots. But though she dearly loved the place, her home in childhood and marriage, the Queen could not bear to stay: better at York, or Pontefract, which held no such memories.

By this time, Julian Heron had been absorbed informally amongst the Queen's ladies. She had small knowledge of court etiquette and ritual, but she learned swiftly, and besides, Anne was no fearsome tyrant but a pleasant and gracious lady whom everyone loved. Julian found her musical talents were highly prized, her neat sewing (a skill only gained after many hours of agonising labour under the lash of her mother's tongue and fist) praised above its deserts, and her love of hawking enthusiastically employed in stitching hoods, jesses and broken feathers for the royal birds. She had left her goshawk Gawain at home, but the Queen, with great kindness, gave her a new bird, a sweet little merlin whom Julian named Elaine, after the lady who loved Lancelot.

They hawked at Middleham, at York and Pontefract, while the King went north with his household and his Council to deal with the Scots: and Julian found that she missed Christie's presence. No, 'missed' was not the right word, she decided firmly, but she was aware of his absence, and sometimes felt very lonely, despite the friendliness and kind words of the other ladies and of the Queen.

So when the messenger from the south eventually found the King and his household at York on Ascension day, his wife was at Pontefract and could not share these new, sad tidings: yet another death, and one which could not be publicly mourned. Edward Bastard, once Prince of Wales and King of England, had died a week before of, ironically, one of the night attacks which had never been thought to be dangerous. He had seemed up until then to be improving a little in health, and had even been walking in the garden the day before: but his struggles for breath had failed, and he had died in the arms of his elder sister, Bess, with his mother, his brother Dickon and sister Cecily by the bedside.

It had been particularly hard for Bess, who had only a few days previously allowed herself to think that Edward, against all hope, might after all recover. He had been so much better of late: and then Dickon, desperate with fear, had plunged into her chamber and

Cecily's in the middle of the night and shaken her awake. 'Oh, Bess, Bess—wake up—oh, please, wake up!'

Cecily, ever practical, had lit a candle: Dickon's face, white, the eyes enormous with fright, stared at her, and she saw young Tom Tyrell, similarly scared, just behind him. 'What is it?' Bess had asked, forgetting the impropriety of such a visit. And her brother said, 'It's Edward—he's having one of his attacks, and it's a bad one—oh, Bess, come quickly!'

So she had flung on a kirtle and gone at once to her elder brother, while Cecily had summoned their mother, Dame Anne, and Tyrell's priest.

Bess had known as soon as she entered the chamber that this attack was the gravest that Edward had yet suffered. The room was filled with the sounds of his desperate, crowing struggles for breath, so that she hardly dared to breathe herself lest it restrict the air he could take in. In the light of the candles his face was blue, his eyes staring, terrified as he gasped and choked, his body rigid and arched with his desperate efforts. While Dickon and Tom watched anxiously, and the priest muttered prayers, Dame Anne rubbed on embrocations, applied burning feathers to his nose in an effort to enhance his breathing, and Bess and her mother held him and attempted to calm him with soft, soothing words. But nothing seemed to work: his struggles grew feebler, the breaths shallower and faster, and the evil blue cast to his skin increased even in the golden glow of the candles that were now in every corner of the room. And then, with a final convulsive effort, he fell back into Bess's arms, and suddenly the room was quite silent.

For a moment, they could not believe it: then, as the priest, knowing the worst, intoned his prayers, Bess bowed her golden head over the lifeless body of her brother and burst into tears.

They could not bury Edward at the church in Stowmarket where all the Tyrells had been laid, not if his brother's safety was to be ensured. The lovely little chapel at Gipping was not a parish church, and had never been used for interments, but to lay the pathetic body of Edward Plantagenet, King of England for two scant months, beneath the soft green grass of Gipping seemed the most appropriate course. So, after the message to the King, wherever he was in the North, had been despatched with Sir James Tyrell's steward, a most trustworthy man, a grave was dug in a corner of the chapel's yard on the evening after the boy's death. The manor's carpenter had spent the day building, with reverent care, a coffin worthy of a King, for with the mysterious process common to most close-knit households, it had not remained a secret at Gipping Hall, after the arrival of their mother and sisters, that the two boys first introduced as Edward and Richard Morley were in fact the sons of Edward IV. Loyal to the Tyrells and proud of the honour in being thus chosen to tend the boys, the servants of Gipping had kept their great secret diligently, and no word nor rumour had ever appeared, in Stow-market or further afield: indeed, rumour still asserted confidently and variously that the Princes were dead, or in Flanders, or spirited away north to their uncle's household.

So in the soft light of evening, the spring sun setting behind the newly sprouting trees, all the birds singing joyously in the country quiet, the people of Gipping Hall, some score in number, joined their own family and the boys' to bid farewell to Edward. The stout oak coffin was lowered into the ground, and by common consent, if not custom, it was Dickon, now to many the rightful King of England, who stepped forward, his freckled face bright with tears and his mouth set firm and straight, to cast the handful of heavy Suffolk clay upon the pale new-hewn wood. Then, the two men who tended the Hall's garden, and who had dug the grave, shovelled the earth back into the pit. Elizabeth Woodville, sup-ported by Dame Alice and Bess, turned away with her face hidden in her hands, weeping.

As the rest of the company followed her, only Dickon was left, staring bleakly at the men working on his brother's grave, until at last only a rectangle of tumbled and beaten earth remained, to be carefully covered over with the turves they had cut that afternoon. By the time of Edward's month's mind, you would never know that he had been buried here.

*

Far away in Yorkshire, in Pontefract Castle whence he had re-moved after hearing of his nephew's death, King Richard was writing to his mother, the Duchess of York, who lived a secluded and pious life at her castle of Berkhamsted. It was a difficult task: the Duchess had disapproved of her youngest son's action in seizing the throne, and had taken no part in public life for nearly a year, declining to appear (ill-health the ostensible reason) at his coron-ation. She had forgiven him, however, and they remained on good terms: now she, who had always striven against great odds, and often in vain, to keep her children united, would want to know of the death of her grandson Edward. He could not tell her in a letter, however: the pious conventional phrases would arouse no suspicions should it fall into the wrong hands, while the messenger could give her more personal details. He had sent spies into Brittany: Henry Tudor, surrounded now by a solid band of English exiles who had fled to join him when Buckingham's rebellion failed, had been by no means discouraged by the abortive rising, and was actively planning to invade again, possibly this summer. No-one knew how many of his adherents remained in England, but it was obvious that one of the chief impediments in the Tudor's path to the throne, was the small personage of his nephew Dickon, one time Duke of York.

His pen poised above the inkwell, Richard was thinking of that child, so much more promising than his elder brother, so abundantly gifted with intelligence and charm, so well-fashioned, it seemed, for kingship by God: a true prince. He had been ousted by his uncle, but Richard, smiling sadly, thought that it might one day be politic to give him back his rightful heritage.

'Madam, I recommend me to you as heartily as is to me possible.' His quill scratched busily: later, one of the clerks would write it up and document it in the archives. 'Beseeching you in my most humble and effectuous wise of your daily blessing to my singular comfort and defence in my need.' Her letter to him, when his own Ned had died, had given him great solace: she knew how he had loved the boy. He continued. 'And madam, I heartily beseech you that I may often hear from you to my comfort.' Two letters since Christmas: he would have appreciated more, but could hardly press her save in these most gentle terms. Now to the most important part of the letter. 'And such news as be here, my servant, Thomas Bryan, this bearer, shall show you, to whom please it you to give credence to.' Bryan was the son of the Chief Justice of the Common Pleas, a loyal servant and utterly reliable: he could be trusted with the news of Edward's death. He went on to more practical business, the temporary replacement of one of her Wiltshire officers, one Colyngbourne, who had been discovered to be an agent of the Tudor, with Francis Lovell, who lived nearby and was at present on his estates. Of course, he must be bound by the Duchess's wishes in the matter. 'And that it please you, that by this bearer I may understand your pleasure in this behalve. And I pray God send you the accomplishment of your noble desires. Written at Pontefract the third day of June with the hand of your most humble son, Ricardus Rex.'

He wrote also, though without provision for a copy, to his brother's widow, expressing his condolences on the death of Edward, and suggesting that, since Gipping must now hold unhappy memories for her, she go elsewhere. There were other places in plenty: or perhaps a nunnery would offer her temporary refuge, if she desired to seclude herself in her grief. He added his wish, that the elder girls, Bess and Cecily, join his household in the north this summer: the younger children would of course stay with their mother if that was what she wanted.

Of Dickon, he deliberately did not speak, partly out of natural caution, partly because he had not yet decided what to do with the boy. There were several possibilities. The most obvious was that his nephew come north with his sisters, and join his cousins of Lincoln and Warwick at Sheriff Hutton. That, however, might not be politic for several reasons. John, Earl of Lincoln, was twenty, very conscious of the fact that he was the only untainted, only grown heir of York. Young Warwick, who was nine and hardly had the wit to write his name, was no rival to John's pretensions: but the bright promise of Dickon surely would be. Without his meaning it, the child might well attract around him people who would want to use him for their own ends, as they had once used his poor brother, and Richard, with a busy summer ahead of him subduing Scots and pirates, would not have the time to keep the situation under his control. And also, everpresent at the back of his mind, was the poison attempt in the Tower. No assassin had ever been caught: the boys had been well watched and guarded, and still had nearly died. If Dickon was publicly brought to Sheriff Hutton, might not that unknown assailant be tempted to strike again, and this time be certain of success?

Secrecy had saved Dickon up until now: instinct told him that it would continue to do so. This Tudor menace would end sooner or later, either in failed rebellion and subsequent execution, or when he could finally persuade the Duke of Brittany to hand the self-styled Earl of Richmond back to English justice—which, despite his royal blood and regal pretensions, would be swift and merciless. Then, Dickon could at last be brought back to court and treated with the respect he deserved, for, bastard or no, he was still a King's son. But where would he be safe, in the meantime?

The answer came to him late that night, so that he sat up abruptly

[353]

in his bed, disturbing Anne. 'What is it, my love? Have you had a bad dream?'

It had been a dream: a face he had not seen for years hovered still in front of his eyes. 'No nightmare,' he told her, 'but my own sister Margaret. I was dreaming of Margaret, in Burgundy.'

'Margaret?' Anne's voice expressed sleepy surprise. Her husband's sister had been Duchess of Burgundy for about fifteen years, and they corresponded seldom, despite her passionate loyalty to her divided family. 'Why dream of Margaret now?'

'Perhaps—perhaps it is a dream of significance,' Richard said quietly into the dark. 'Perhaps God Himself has sent it to me, as a sign—I have been wondering much, what to do with Dickon. Why not send him to Margaret in Burgundy? She will love him and care for him, rear him until the Tudor is defeated and he can live in safety again. Yes—I think that is the best solution. I will send him to Margaret.'

*

It was only appropriate that the two men whose lives had been for so long bound up with his nephews, should be the ones to escort the survivor to safety and seclusion with his aunt in Burgundy. So the following morning, Tyrell and Christie were summoned to the royal presence, and told of the plan. They knew already of Edward's death, as did most of the intimate circle around the King, and both had felt sorrow for the child's tragic end. And yet, thought Christie now, staring at his monarch's pale sharply graven face, it was possible to see the hand of God in this. Two children, both called Edward, both frail, dead within six weeks of each other, to leave Dickon, sturdy in mind and body, a boy surely more fitted by far for the kingdom which many still, if they knew he lived, would consider rightfully his. The Queen was young, but now it seemed barren, and moreover in precarious health: she had lost much flesh since her son's death, and a great deal of her quiet energy. There would be no more children of their marriage, that was obvious. Christie wondered if Richard had at first contemplated making Dickon his heir, although Lincoln, being grown, was a much more sensible choice. Now, of course, there was this alternative plan.

He listened to the details, wondering how he was to explain his absence to Julian—it would probably be of some months' duration, for the King had other business for him overseas as well as the care of Dickon. She might have to return to Ashcott, of course, only being permitted here by virtue of his own presence, and he did not envy her. Perhaps the Queen could be persuaded to keep her in her household, or even allow Julian to join Bess and Cecily at Sheriff Hutton. He would crave that boon of the King, for although Julian's life here was not idyllic, it was surely preferable to a dreary existence at Ashcott under her mother's brutal thumb.

He asked the favour, and Richard, his mind already running elsewhere, gave ready assent: so that when he went to the gardens, where Julian was, he was able to tell her that her place here in the north was assured until his return.

She had been entertaining the Queen and the other ladies with her lute, and he came upon them sitting in the bright sunlight in a bower trained all about with roses, just coming into bud. The air was warm and sweet with the scents of wallflowers and the crushed herbs that had been planted in all the paths: the clear purity of her voice was a sound he would now recognise wherever he went, whether it was Ashcott or Westminster, Burgundy or Spain. And a knife twisted suddenly within him, for she had never freely sung for him.

He stayed in the shade of a blossoming cherry tree, thinking of the songs he had sung with Meg, and watching the little group of sombrely-clad women. Julian sat amongst them in her new summer gown of dark blue silk, caught under her breast with a wide jewelled girdle, the collar and cuffs finely embroidered with long-legged birds, an allusion to her husband's name that she had unwillingly agreed with the tailor, since to refuse his suggestion would have been most shocking. At last she had found a style of headdress that suited her, a lower-crowned bonnet that still hid her hair, but had two lappets turned back to frame the strong structure of her face. She finished the song; it had evidently been a merry one, for the other women were smiling, and Julian's expression changed to a wide and genuinely happy grin, the first he had ever seen.

And it was not for him: he knew, when he stepped into her sight, that it would fade.

It did. He knelt to the Queen, and asked her leave to speak for a while apart with his wife: and then led Julian to a corner of the garden where they would not be overheard. For in this he had given her no choice either.

'What is it?' Julian asked. She was frowning, and looked for a moment disturbingly like her mother. He thrust that unwelcome thought away with speed. 'I have come to tell you, Julian, that I must leave here. The King has urgent business for me, and I must set out for London after dinner.'

There was a small silence. 'Then I am to go to Ashcott,' said Julian flatly, trying to keep the disappointment out of her voice. She was coming to enjoy this courtly life, she liked the Queen and her ladies, and the pleasant existence at Pontefract, although there was rather too much time spent on her knees. To forego all that and return to her mother, the arguments and beatings and endless struggles, would be unbearable.

'On the contrary,' said her husband, and she saw that he was smiling. 'I have asked a special favour of the King, that you be allowed to remain here—and when the Lady Elizabeth and the Lady Cecily come north to Sheriff Hutton, as they shortly will, you have been granted a place in their household.' He studied her face, the frown still deep between her strongly arched chestnut brows, that were still too thick for fashion despite resolute and painful plucking. 'Is this not to your liking, then?'

'You didn't *ask* me,' said Julian, her voice low and savage. 'Once more, you didn't *ask* me, you didn't even bother, you just went to the King and asked, you *assumed* I didn't want to go back to Ashcott, didn't you?'

'I did,' said Christie. 'But you don't, surely—do you?'

'It's my home,' said Julian icily, drawing herself up to her full height: tall as he was, she could almost look him in the eye. 'Of course I want to return there.'

Her certainty rang more than a little hollow: Christie knew, as surely as he knew his wife, that if another had suggested that she stay at Pontefract, she would have welcomed it gladly. Wondering if he would ever gain her trust, he said quietly, 'I am sorry if it displeases you. But the King has granted this as a special favour, and it cannot now be lightly set aside without insulting him. Perhaps when I return, we can go to Ashcott together.'

Nothing in Julian's face indicated that she found that prospect anything other than displeasing. 'Perhaps,' she said, and turned away. 'Pray excuse me, husband: the Queen will be wondering why I am so long.'

'Julian!' His hand came out to detain her: she turned, and the dislike and contempt on her face almost stopped the breath in his throat. 'Take your hand from me!'

He dropped his arm, and from somewhere summoned a smile. 'I

was going to say, God keep you while I am gone, Julian—goodbye.'

With anger, she watched him retreat, her feelings a riot of confused relief and hatred. She woud not have to go to Ashcott after all—but not to be consulted, to be treated as if she were a dog or a horse or a child . . .

'God's bones, I hate him!' Julian Heron cried, and drove her hand against the wall as if it were her husband's face.

*

Edward's death had signalled the end of their idyll at Gipping: Bess had known it in her heart, ever since the day of his burial. Her mother moped, the younger children were fretful, the little house that had once seemed so cosy and intimate now felt cramped and sadly lacking in privacy. The King's letter was brought by a servant in white boar livery, and its arrival signalled a family discussion dominated, as was predictable, by the stout purposeful figure of her mother.

The King had expressed his sorrow at his nephew's sad and premature death, and had offered various practical alternatives to life at Gipping, a place which now, it was obvious, held no attractions at all for Elizabeth Woodville. On the whole, said the former Queen, looking at her son and her daughters, she preferred the idea of a nunnery for a few months. It would give her time to recover from her dear Edward's death (there was a catch in her voice here), and to pray for his poor innocent soul. It would also free Master Nesfield from his task of looking after her, since he had already expressed his eagerness to fight the Scots. And above all, it would give the little girls the chance to catch up with their education, especially in moral and spiritual matters: they had run wild at Gipping, and now must learn civilised and gentle manners befitting their rank and sex.

For a moment, her heart sinking, Bess thought that she and Cecily were also to be confined to a nunnery: but her mother's gaze, chill and grey, was bent in her direction, as she read out the relevant portion of the King's letter. '"And as for your elder daughters, I ask that they be allowed to take up residence at my castle of Sheriff Hutton in Yorkshire, where already live my dear nephews Edward, Earl of Warwick, and John, Earl of Lincoln, and I hereby undertake to provide for them as befits my kinswomen, as I swore before my lords spiritual and temporal, and the Mayor and aldermen of the

[357]

City of London, on the first day of March in the first year of my reign."'

They were to go to Sheriff Hutton—Elizabeth had vaguely heard of it, and Yorkshire by repute was a cold, bleak place, full of wastes and savages. Still, she and Cecily would be away from their mother, they would be free to ride out, free to dance and laugh and mix with their cousins and other young people. She looked at Cecily, and saw that her sister's eyes were shining. That oath, so publicly sworn by her uncle, had also promised to find them husbands. After the events of the last year, Bess had not in the nature of things taken much time to think of young men: now, with a mixture of excitement and curiosity, she allowed her mind to dwell upon the subject, as doubtless Cecily was also doing. And at least if she was wed to some 'gentleman born', as her uncle had promised, she would not have to endure the lurking threat of marriage to Henry Tudor, the man on whose behalf the deaths of her dear brothers had been planned and so nearly accomplished.

'Is there any mention of me?' asked Dickon of his mother. He added, with some firmness, 'I am *not* going to a nunnery with you, Mother. I'd rather go to Sheriff Hutton with Bess and Cecily, if I can't stay here.' He saw Elizabeth's frown and added hastily, 'Of course I didn't mean to upset you, Mother—if you weren't going to a nunnery I'd like nothing better than to be with you. But I don't feel a nunnery would be right for me—I'm nearly eleven now, after all, and I should be in some noble household, learning how to be a knight.'

Bess hid her smile: Dickon was coming to an understanding of diplomacy, even if it did not altogether disguise his essential honesty. Their mother glanced down at the letter and quoted again. '"My wishes regarding another matter will be made to you in due course. In the meantime, I commend it to your care and diligence." I agree, Richard, a nunnery is no place for a growing boy, and I doubt that the one which I have in mind would let you within its walls. Your uncle evidently has plans for you which he must not trust to paper, and we will discover in the fullness of time what they are.'

*

The oarsmen bent their backs, and the little boat leapt forward on the blue, sparkling water. The tide was flowing fast, and less and less mud was left, brown, wet and stinking of seaweed, on either side of the broad shiny river. Above, the sky was azure, clear and cloudless, and even here, out on the water and a hundred yards from land, only a very gentle breeze wafted cool fingers about them. It was hot: Christie had long ago removed his black demi-gown, and his doublet, and Tyrell had laid his own gown on the thwart beside him. At the bow, a small boy crouched, his round black bonnet pushed down firmly over his riotous curly hair, also stripped to shirt and hose, trailing his hand in the water. Without turning, his voice came clearly back to Tyrell and Christie in the stern. 'Father!'

So far, they had had no problems with this mission. Dickon, told he was to be taken to his aunt Margaret in Burgundy, had expressed pleasure and delight at such an adventure, and moreover in the company of two men he regarded now as his trusted friends. His only disappointment had been that he was not to go in disguise: somewhat to Christie's surprise, it seemed that Dickon harboured fond memories of that confused and nerve-wracking escape from the Tower. They had persuaded him that to ride across Suffolk clad in skirts might be tempting God's providence too greatly: instead, he was to pretend he was Tom Tyrell, and treat Sir James as his father.

Dickon had entered into this role enthusiastically, although Sir James seemed to have more trouble in assuming paternity. It took him two or three seconds to respond to his 'son's' call. 'Yes, Tom?'

'When do we board ship, Father?'

'As soon as may be, God willing,' muttered Perkin, who was profoundly mistrustful of water despite his London childhood: a fall into the Thames at the age of nine had not increased his confidence, and he could still remember the choking foul water filling his throat. Tyrell's reply did not add to his happiness. 'In a mile or so yet, lad, and the tide's still against us. We'll be on the *Margaret* inside the hour, if these good fellows bend their backs.'

The four good fellows, stripped to the waist to reveal the said backs, brawny, brown and variously furred, had rowed them already a mile down from the Quay at Ipswich: there was not enough breeze to make use of one of the little ketches and sailboats that normally took goods and passengers to the larger ships moored below the causeway at Downham Bridge, two miles down the river. The tide would soon turn, and the *Margaret* would leave without her passengers if they were late: time and tide, as Tyrell had reminded his companions, waited for no man. Dickon, familiar with the sights of London's river, had stared fascinated at the fat

[359]

shallow-draught wool cogs moored along the quayside, the bales of cloth going aboard, hard yellow Suffolk cheeses and sacks of wool, and unloaded from lighters and barges, tuns of wine, salt, fish, stone. The boy's stream of questions proved difficult to answer: Christie had never seen Ipswich before, with its surprising bustle and general air of prosperity, and Tyrell, more familiar with the place, was too busy ascertaining that the *Margaret* had not yet sailed, and hiring men to row them out to her. In the end Dickon was reduced to wheedling information out of the sailors, the wharfmen, anyone who could spare a moment. Because he was Dickon, they usually did. No-one seemed to think he was anything other than a gentleman's son: in this little provincial town, it would have been remarkable if anyone had connected the small shabbily dressed boy, so obviously the stout knight's son, getting under everyone's feet on the quayside, with the Duke of York, whom rumour still confidently placed in the grave, or already in foreign parts.

Nevertheless, they were both glad when the child, still demanding the name of the ropes used to haul up the nearest cog's sail, was handed down to the hired boat, and they were able to set off on the last but one lap of their journey.

'Is that her? Is that the *Margaret*?' Dickon's voice could probably be heard on both banks. The bend in the river had straightened to reveal perhaps half a dozen ships of varying sizes anchored in the channel, with a cluster of smaller vessels around each. The nearest was also the finest, with much bright paintwork and fluttering pennants.

'The *Margaret*? That in't the *Margaret*,' said the largest, furriest oarsman, with a cheerful snort. 'Thass the *Trinity*—one hundred tons, carrying wine from Bordeaux. No, lad, *that*'s the *Margaret*.'

Dickon looked in the direction indicated by the man's jerk of the head. There was a disbelieving pause as he surveyed the patched sides, the faded paint, the general air of dilapidation: then he said slowly, '*How* far are we going?'

'Flanders, young Tom,' said Christie, unable to hide a grin, although the ship's appearance was somewhat alarming to a landsman like himself. 'I presume that thing is floating, and not sitting on the riverbed.'

'She's not as bad as she looks,' said Tyrell, without much conviction. 'She can't be, if she's so highly recommended.' He glanced at Christie's dubious face. 'Never been on shipboard before?'

[360]

'Never—and I must say I'd have preferred a vessel a little more . . . shall we say, new-looking? Still, I expect she's sound enough. Green already, Perkin my lad?'

'I ain't never been on shipboard neither—and I ain't sure I want to be, sir,' said Perkin, with a gloom quite unlike his normal cheerful self. 'Still, I ain't paid to ask questions, am I.'

'No, you aren't—you're here to look after me and Sir James —hold the basins when we're sick, clean up after us, tempt our wavering appetites with gruel—why, Perkin, you look quite ill,' said Christie, with gentle malice, as his servant stared fixedly and despairingly at the scrubby heathland on the northern bank. 'Come on, cheer up—I'm sure it won't be so bad as you think.'

'And I'm sure it will,' Perkin muttered unhappily. 'I wish Wellesborne was here instead of me.'

'Wellesborne had business to perform, remember? And he's ridden north many a time. You'd undoubtedly get lost—and besides, with a face like yours, you're bound to bring good luck.'

Perkin sent his master a glare that changed to a reluctant grin. By now, the little wherry had passed through the cluster of ships and was fast approaching their destination. One of the oarsmen cupped hands round his mouth as the boat slowed, and hailed her. '*Margaret* ahoy! Passengers!'

There was a bustle of activity along the stern gunwhale, now looming high above them. Close to, the ship was surprisingly sound, though shabby and workmanlike compared with the splendour of that other vessel. A rope ladder tumbled down the side, and the wherry turned neatly to lie beside it, hardly moving in the calm lazy water. Before the men had even slipped their oars, Dickon had his hands on the rope: he had to be reminded to pick up his discarded doublet, and to sling over his shoulder the bag containing the few clothes and possessions it had been thought advisable to bring. Then, thus encumbered, he leapt up the ladder like a particularly energetic jackanapes and vanished over the gunwale, leaving the portly Tyrell, Christie and a distinctly nervous and burdened Perkin to follow in his wake.

The deck was crowded with grinning bronzed sailors, wearing little, for the most part, except for brief drawers, their legs and feet bare. Startling by comparison was the man who approached from the sterncastle, his swarthy face split by a smile of gleaming whiteness. Dickon was staring at him with interest, as well he might, for this big brilliant man would have seemed glorious at

[361]

Westminster: here, amongst the half-naked sailors and plainly-clad passengers, he was as gaudy and exotic as a peacock in blue, green and red, glittering with gold and jewellery. His hair was black, oiled and curled, and a large ring glinted in one ear. On another man, all this splendour might have seemed ridiculous, but such was the force of his personality, not to mention his physical presence, that he carried it off superbly.

The expressive dark eyes rested, smiling, on Dickon's small figure, and the boy said, his eyes bright, 'Sir Edward Brampton!'

'Indeed it is, young sir—and who might you be?'

Aware of the audience of seamen, Dickon said, 'My name is Tom Tyrell, Sir Edward, and that's my father, and Sir Christopher Heron. I didn't know *you* were going to be the captain!'

'But of course,' said Brampton, and exchanged bows with his two adult passengers. Christie, who had heard much of this remarkable man, studied him with quite as much curiosity as the boy. Sir Edward was a Portuguese Jew, who had come to England some fifteen or twenty years ago as a soldier, merchant and sea captain: he had rendered great service to the Yorkist cause, and had been converted to Christianity, King Edward, as was the custom, being his nominal sponsor at the baptism. He had continued to serve King Richard on land and at sea, and had been richly rewarded with lands, money, and trading concessions. His loyalty was unquestioned, his skills of seamanship widely known: if asked, Christie could not have chosen a better captain for such a precious cargo.

He was, of course, well aware of the identity of his smallest passenger, and once below, in a surprisingly spacious cabin in the stern, made it clear that he was honoured and delighted to be entrusted with the responsibility. 'We'll soon have you safe with your lady aunt,' he told Dickon. 'I was right sorry, though, to hear of your brother's death.' He crossed himself, a gesture incongruous on a man of such exotic, not to say pagan, appearance. 'May God assoil him, poor child!'

They murmured their agreement: then Dickon, who with the resilience of childhood had put much of his grief aside in the weeks since Edward's death, said, 'How long to make the crossing to Flanders, Sir Edward?'

'Depends on the wind, Your Grace, could be two days if it's with us, four or five if not. At the moment, there's little at all, but it'll back round to the west afore long, Your Grace, and then you'll see the old *Margaret* fly!'

[362]

'You mustn't call me "Your Grace",' said Dickon seriously. 'I'm the Duke of York no longer. And on this voyage I'm plain Tom Tyrell, Sir James's son—please don't forget, Sir Edward, it's very important!'

The big man reached over and ruffled the boy's abundant hair. 'Don't worry, young Tom—I won't forget!'

The wind picked up, the *Margaret* weighed anchor on the turn of the tide and used its flow to slip quietly down the estuary of the River Orwell, with its banks of red earth, scrub and heath, the crowded shipping, the fishing weirs staked out from either bank, often a danger to vessels, and the bleak low salty marshes close to the sea. Dickon, entranced, followed Sir Edward more closely than his own shadow, asking questions which the Portuguese answered with expansive good humour, in the rich deep voice that held only the slightest trace of his native accent. Perkin crouched unhappily on the stern deck, greenish-hued and in everyone's way: his master, though, had not the heart to order him below. Sir James, an experienced sea traveller, was not averse to lending a hand with the ropes as the anchor was weighed and the sails hauled up, and Christie joined him, feeling the same pull of interest as had fired Dickon, though not to the same level of enthusiasm. Both men were horrified, as they approached Orwell Haven at the river's mouth, to see the small figure of one of the possible heirs to the throne of England capering in the mainmast shrouds like a little jackanapes, hallooing with exuberant delight, and deaf to their shouts. Sir Edward, however, bellowed at him in stentorian tones that had no respect for rank. 'Come down from there, you little rascal, before you fall down—the wind and waves will knock you off once we reach open sea.'

Dickon was quick to obey, and stood, somewhat crestfallen, on the stern deck, watching as Harwich, with its jumble of houses, fishing boats, and bitter centuries-old feud with Ipswich, swept past and the *Margaret* began to roll and buck in response to the waves sweeping into the Haven from the sea outside. Perkin groaned and bent his head over the gunwale, and the small boy at once went to comfort him. 'It's all right, Perkin, you're not going to die!'

'Oh, yes, I surely am!' was the muffled response, and Dickon, who had become very friendly with Christie's servant on their journey from Gipping, gave his back a sympathetic pat and then straightened, watching the flat receding coastline, the banks of the two rivers, Stour and Orwell, merging into one horizon below a glorious sky only lightly flecked with high cloud. Christie, watching, knew what he must be thinking: and indeed, after a while, the boy turned to the two men, his clear grey eyes very bright. 'Will Flanders be like England?'

'Flatter,' said Tyrell succinctly. 'And more water, more rivers and canals—but quite like Suffolk. You'll have to learn Flemish.'

'I can speak French,' said Dickon doubtfully. 'But not very well—not nearly so well as Edward could.' He stared thoughtfully at the gently rocking land, now a deep greenish-blue with distance, and added, 'Will I come back?'

'Of course you'll come back, lad,' said Tyrell confidently. 'Once the Tudor's disposed of and it's safe, of course you'll come back.'

'Will I?' The wide grey eyes caught Tyrell's and held them. 'Will I? Do you suppose I'll ever see Mother and Bess again?'

And that was one question which none of the three men standing by him could answer.

CHAPTER SIXTEEN

'We have foughten for a simple matter, and quarrel overlong.'
(BOOK II, CHAPTER 13)

Like Middleham, Sheriff Hutton had originally been a Neville castle, and also like Middleham, it dominated the village at its foot, its dark walls towering over the little cottages and the church where Edward, Prince of Wales and the King's most beloved and only legitimate son, lay entombed. Bess, arriving with her sister Cecily under a raining July sky, was pleasantly surprised. True, this was not Westminster, but the domestic apartments, ranged round a narrow moated quadrangle, were modern and comfortable, and the surrounding countryside was not the desolate waste she had expected, being green and fertile, filled with sheep and cattle and ripening corn, with the neighbouring hunting forest of Galtres promising good sport. After Gipping, the castle did seem large and formal, and the landscape very open: the towers of York Minster, nine miles away, were visible on a clear day. But Gipping was a lost paradise, with memories both sweet and bitter, and she knew that it was gone for ever. Besides, life at Sheriff Hutton promised to be lively and full of activity, and she could not help but catch Cecily's mood of eager anticipation.

There were all the young people lined up in the courtyard to greet them. She recognised the puzzled, vacant stare of her cousin of Warwick, whose fair hair and freckles were like a dreadful echo of Dickon, without the life and intelligence of her brother: this child was the despair of his tutors and, in her youngest brother's scornful words, unable to tell a goose from a capon. Then there was her cousin of Lincoln, very much on his dignity, and his precocious thirteen-year-old brother Edmund, leering openly at Cecily's dazzling beauty. Her sister, however, was fortunately looking elsewhere, at the ogling stares of one of the other, and more personable, gentlemen. Bess noted the pimpled face of the seventeen-year-old Lord Morley, who was married to Lincoln's sister Elizabeth, and a crowd of assorted ladies and lords, most of them young, the people who would be her friends and associates for the next few months:

then she accepted Lincoln's cousinly kiss, and was drawn within the Great Hall.

Later that evening, after supper, Bess and Cecily withdrew to the Solar above the Great Hall, the better to become acquainted with their companions. Their cousin Elizabeth, Lady Morley, a tall dark girl, very quiet and reserved, they knew already, and Margaret, Countess of Lincoln, and the three others were presented as Mistress Margaret Hoton, Dame Margaret Bigod, and Dame Julian Heron.

Hearing the familiar name, Bess stared with interest at the tall, sturdy young woman standing before her in a sombre but becoming gown in very dark green. 'Are you the wife of Sir Christopher?' she asked, and the girl looked up, startled. 'Why, yes, my lady—Sir Christopher is my husband. Do you know him?'

'Of course I do,' said Bess warmly. 'He escorted us from Westminster when we left sanctuary—he has been a great friend to me and Cecily, and our mother and our other sisters.'

The expression on Dame Heron's face was hard to read, but looked like disbelief. Happy to find someone who would be a link, however tenuous, with the vanished days at Gipping, Bess looked forward with pleasurable anticipation to a cosy chat with Christie's wife when occasion should arise: as it did the following day, when they all rode out with their hawks and hounds to the forest of Galtres, not far distant.

It was obvious that her hawk was Dame Julian's passion, and certainly she showed greater enthusiasm than any of the other ladies. By her pale grey palfrey's side trotted a great tawny dog, a considerable contrast to the fussy little spaniels belonging to the rest of the party, nervous of venturing into clumps of undergrowth in case they snagged their silky hair. The hound, which answered to the name of Cavall and treated all save its mistress with lordly disdain, did most of the work of flushing out the birds, and Dame Julian glowed with pleasure when the forester praised him highly.

On the way home after a most successful afternoon, as the others rode ahead, Bess seized the chance to urge her dappled horse alongside Julian's. 'You are Christie's wife,' she said, smiling. As Julian, surprised at this evidence of familiarity between the old King's daughter and her husband, agreed, she added wistfully, 'You're very lucky, to have such a husband.'

If surprise had been on Julian's face before, it was now increased a hundred-fold. 'Lucky?' Her voice went up into a squawk of indignant astonishment, and then lowered as she remembered, tardily, that this girl, though not much older, was somewhat superior in rank. 'I was forced into the marriage, Lady Elizabeth. Good fortune didn't enter into it.'

Bess said quickly, 'I'm sorry—I didn't realise—' She broke off in some confusion, and then added doubtfully, 'Forgive me—but you must have *some* feelings for your husband, surely?'

'Yes,' said Julian. 'But they're not the sort of feelings you're supposed to have.'

The bleak bitterness in her voice astonished Bess. For a moment she was silent, bewildered: for she had liked Christie, so had Dickon, and she trusted her brother's instinctive, usually accurate judgement of character. Yet this Julian hated her husband, apparently. Not wishing to make an enemy of her, for Bess always wanted to be on good terms with those around her, she weighed her words carefully before speaking. 'I thought myself lucky to count Sir Christopher as my friend. He has done great service to my family, and besides—I liked him, very much.'

'Great service!' Julian, incredulous, jerked on Cygnus's reins, and the palfrey reluctantly halted. Bess brought her own mare to a stop, determined now to sort out whatever misunderstanding had undoubtedly arisen between these two people who should have been close, and appeared instead to be bitter enemies. She did not stop to consider that she was interfering in what was, after all, none of her business: her father had always been concerned to promote good relations at his court, and she had done likewise amongst her friends. With an earnest frown that was not a little like Dickon's, Bess said quietly, 'Yes, great service, for which my uncle has justly rewarded him.'

'And you like him? Don't you care that he's loyal to your uncle?'

'Why should he not be? My uncle is King, after all, and Sir Christopher has been in his service for years.'

'I don't understand,' said Julian at last, her large brown eyes searching Bess's puzzled, serious face. 'You—of all people—you should hate the King. But you don't, do you?'

'No, of course I don't,' said the other girl. 'Oh, I did once, when we were in sanctuary, but I didn't know the truth about him then. Now I don't hate him at all—he's been very kind and good to us.'

'Kind? Good?' Julian felt as if a nightmare had been suddenly unleashed around her. 'But—but he killed your brothers!'

There was silence: then, dreadfully to Julian's ears, Bess began to laugh. For a moment, she wondered if the older girl's mind had been unhinged by her terrible experiences, and then she realised that the laughter was gentle and genuinely amused. 'Oh, dear,' said the Lady Elizabeth Plantagenet ruefully. 'I never thought that you wouldn't know—but as you're Christie's wife it won't do any harm to tell you—though it's supposed to be a most deep secret. Please don't tell anyone else, will you—please, it's most important.'

'Secret? What secret?' Julian, utterly bewildered, all her certainties crumbling about her, forgot all propriety and grasped Bess's arm. 'Oh, please tell me—what is it that you know, and I don't?'

'My brothers are alive—or rather,' Bess amended sadly, 'one of them is. They were not murdered, Julian, and my uncle wished them no harm.'

'Are you *sure*?'

'Of course I am sure,' said Bess patiently. 'I have seen my dear brother Edward die, in my own arms of a natural illness, God rest his sweet soul, and not two weeks ago I bid farewell to my brother Dickon before he went overseas with your husband and Sir James Tyrell. There *was* a murder attempt on them, when they were still in the Tower, but it didn't succeed—the assassins were never caught, and my uncle thinks they were agents of Henry Tudor.'

She did not know then, why Julian stared at her with distraught horrified eyes, and then burst into tears. Distressed herself, Bess urged her horse forward and took the girl's merlin, which was in some danger of baiting, before putting a free arm across the bent, shaking shoulders. 'Oh, Dame Julian—what is it? What's wrong? My brothers weren't murdered, and my beloved Dickon is still alive, and safe—that's cause for gladness, surely.'

But Julian could think only of her father, the person she had loved best in all the world, who had died in vain for reasons that were false, in unwitting support of the man on whose behalf, if not order, the supposed murders that had spurred Sir Thomas to rebellion, had been attempted. His death had been unnecessary, and if it had not been for his death, she would never have been trapped in this marriage. On her father's count and on her own, she wept for all that should have been, and what, alas, now irrevocably was.

'Do you want a muckinder?'

Bess's quiet voice impinged on her distress. Julian raised her head, with somewhere the wild impulse to laugh at the child's common phrase on the lips of royalty. There was genuine concern on Bess's face, and her rather broad, pale hand held the proffered kerchief. 'You must need it,' she said. 'But you'll feel better for a good weep—that's what my nurse always used to say. Can you tell me why you're crying?'

Behind the muckinder, Julian hesitated. Her immediate impulse had been to refuse: but she liked Bess, she liked her directness, her lack of pretension, her sympathy. And the need, after the nightmare of the last year, to unburden her soul to someone other than Friday was overwhelming. She took a deep, quivering breath, and then another, trying to calm herself, while Bess waited, her grey mare cropping the grass, and her own eyes damp with emotion: she had always been able to share too greatly in others' moods and feelings. When Julian finally raised her face, it was not an attractive sight, being red and blotchy with weeping, but her eyes were calm.

'Yes, if you don't mind, Lady,' she said, glancing about them. For the moment they were alone, although it was only a matter of time before the forester or one of his assistants noticed their absence and came back to look for them: a special watch was supposed to be kept over Bess and Cecily.

'You'd best be quick,' the King's daughter said, and added, a little shyly, 'Please, don't call me "Lady"—we are of an age, I think, and friends enough—I am Bess, and you are Julian. Why are you so unhappy? I want to help you.'

'I don't think you can—I don't think anyone can.' Julian took a deep breath, and added starkly, 'My father died in the rebellion last autumn. He only fought in that rebellion—he supported Henry Tudor—because he thought your uncle had had your brothers murdered. So—so you see, if that rumour was false—then he need not have died. And if he hadn't died, I wouldn't have been forced to marry Christie.'

The silence was broken by distant shouts. Cavall turned his sharp tawny head in that direction, and Cygnus pricked up his ears: the other girl's greedy dapple kept on tearing up the grass as if it were her last chance of food. Bess, aware that they would not have long to talk, said quickly, 'What's so bad about Christie? He's loyal, he's efficient and he's good company too—he made us all laugh at Gipping, and he plays that lute so beautifully, *and* he's young, and not ill-looking—I wouldn't mind such a husband at all, when you think of what you could have had—someone old, or a pimply baron like Lord Morley. Why don't you like him?'

Julian stared down at her hands, at the familiar pattern of freckles, the strong knuckles and bitten nails. Her voice came muffled, so low that Bess could barely hear it. 'I think—I think it's because he's never given me a choice.'

There was no chance to elaborate further, although Bess's bewilderment was obvious, for the forester's shouts intruded, and soon his horse came crashing through the bushes. Bess had to offer a lame excuse about looking for Cavall, and they rode back to Sheriff Hutton in silence, surrounded by the chatter and laughter of the other girls.

Julian was still reeling under the impact of news which had altered all her perceptions and crumbled the very foundations of her life. The boys had not been slain—one indeed was still alive, and sent to safety. The King was not an unnatural monster, murderer of his own nephews: on the contrary, he had shown the children every consideration. It certainly solved the mystery of why their mother had emerged from sanctuary and given her daughters into his care. And Christie had given loyal service not to a murderer, but to a just King who, however dubious his accession to the throne, had since then, it was generally acknowledged, ruled well and wisely. And even now, her husband was overseas, with the remaining prince in his care.

So she must revise some of her opinions of Christie. And with reluctance, she faced the true heart of Bess's puzzled questions. Why did she not like him?

She forced herself to recall that first meeting, when she had been a heedless, imperious child. Under the headdress, she grew hot with embarrassment and shame as she remembered the angry words, the thrown stools and cushions, her thoughtless abuse of poor Friday. He had treated her as a child, that was why she had been infuriated, but then she had *been* a child. She had behaved abominably, and he had been provoked into displaying an attitude of malicious contempt. I'd have done the same in his position, thought Julian miserably. And later, when her father had died, and she had been faced with that marriage—it was the lack of choice that had enraged her, and her belief that he had had a part in her father's death. Such had been her agony and distress that she had hit out blindly like a hurt animal, and her behaviour had only served to convince Christie that she was an immature and wilful fool who should be tamed.

But he had had a choice. She had not. That still rankled. And yet, after that disastrous first night, he had treated her with kindness and consideration. He had supported her against her mother, and he

[370]

had seemed to know about her struggles against Dame Alice's overmighty rule. He had not forced himself on her.

She rode into the courtyard at Sheriff Hutton, still not knowing what to think, bewildered by the confusion in her feelings. She had misjudged him on some counts, surely, and perhaps on others. And yet, she had struck her attitude long ago, and her pride would not allow her to climb tamely down, waving the flag of surrender.

If he were beyond seas, she would not see him for some time, probably not until the autumn. She dismounted, feeling her knees wobble, and reflected that, whatever the outcome between her and Christie, she had at least made a friend of Bess. And as for her husband—when he returned, perhaps she would know her feelings better.

*

For what remained of the summer, and well into the autumn, the group of young people stayed at Sheriff Hutton, hunting, riding, watching the men engage in swordplay and even, once, a makeshift tournament: sewing, making music, strolling in the gardens, playing chess or tables, tending their horses and dogs, reading romances or histories or more pious works. And as the days slipped by, in calm and happy pursuit of pleasure and amusement, Julian continued unawares the subtle education she had begun with the Queen at Nottingham and Pontefract. Here there was no Dame Alice to scold and punish and abuse, no arduous tasks, no reluctant servants, but a group of girls of similar age to herself, who accepted and liked her at her own value, genuinely admired her musical talents, and were prepared to have her as a friend without reservation. Unknowing, happier than she had ever been in her life, Julian flowered. Friday, kind and silent and tolerant, counted in her mind as the weeks and months swept past without a tantrum, without even a cross word, for her mistress was so involved in the delights of companionship that all her previous unhappiness had vanished quite away.

Julian was able to say to Bess, one quiet October morning in the castle garden, 'I wish Christie would come back!' And Bess, almost as tall and sturdy as herself, but widely accounted beautiful with her yellow hair and translucent hazel eyes and rosebud mouth, had looked at her with that thoughtful, serious gaze, and commented, 'You would not have wanted that when I first knew you.'

'Things are different now,' said Julian, unaware of how much she herself had changed, how her happiness had spilled over into her face, flushing her cheeks and brightening her eyes and giving her a look of joyous expectancy, as if each new day was a wonderful surprise, and her life now a voyage of delightful discovery. 'I—I'm not sure what will happen when he does return. He might make me angry—and I have a terrible temper.'

'Do you?' said Bess, with interest. 'I can't imagine it.'

Julian, remembering that constantly furious former self, giggled. 'I was insufferable, the slightest thing sent me into a rage. It seems such a long time ago,' she added reflectively. 'But it's not—only a few months, since I came here, and I haven't had anything to be angry about! Though how it will be when I go back to Ashcott, I don't know.'

'Now you feel differently about Christie, perhaps things will be better,' Bess suggested. Julian spread her hands: it was a long time since she had bitten her nails, and they were clean and neatly trimmed on the left hand, longer on the right, for better playing of her lute. 'I don't know. He used to have that knack of saying just the thing that would infuriate me most. But there's one person who will always make me lose my temper, and that's my mother.'

Bess smiled. 'I think everyone's mother does that. I know sometimes mine can be—difficult.'

'She must be an angel compared to mine,' said Julian bitterly. Then, she laughed rather wryly. 'You see—she even has the power to annoy me at a distance. I only have to think of her to be angry.'

'Then don't think of her,' said Bess sensibly. Think of something more pleasant—dancing, or the new gown you're going to have soon.' She put a hand on Julian's arm. And I do hope Christie comes back soon. I'll pray for his return—and then you will be truly and finally happy.'

It was something that Julian doubted, deep in her heart. She did not trust her own reactions, faced with the difficult and complex man who was her husband: if he were in malicious mood, she knew her good temper would not hold, she understood herself too well. And she hardly knew him at all, knew nothing of his own heart or soul, she had been married to him for more than nine months (although that time had been spent mostly apart), and he was still a stranger. She felt she knew the young Earl of Lincoln, self-consciously haughty, much better. She wanted to begin again, to set her marriage on a friendlier footing, but was unsure how to go about it, did not know how to make the first tentative overtures of friendship, and feared that they would be received with mockery.

*

October turned to November, and autumn to winter. Here in Yorkshire it was cold, and the wind howled around the high exposed towers of Sheriff Hutton with an eerie wailing that put some of the more nervous servants in mind of demons or witches. The distant northern moors already had their first powderings of snow, and the season for hawking or riding expeditions had long passed.

The King had spent most of the summer and autumn in Yorkshire or at Nottingham, but had written to say that he expected his nieces would join him in Westminster for the Christmas festivities. It had been a time of mixed fortunes. Peace had been finally concluded with the Scots, and cemented with the betrothal of his niece Anne, sister of the Earl of Lincoln, to the heir to the Scottish throne. This agreement had been accompanied, through tortuous diplomatic alliances, by a better understanding with the Duke of Brittany, harbourer of that menace to the peace of the kingdom, Henry Tudor. Unfortunately, the Tudor had received warning that he would be kept in closer custody, and had escaped to France. He and his exiled supporters were now with the French court, and had very recently been joined by the Earl of Oxford, who had fled from captivity near Calais.

But Henry Tudor, for now, could be dismissed to a dark but distant cloud on the horizon. The King had other problems, mainly in the south of the country, where his replacement of rebels such as Sir Thomas Bray with his own northern supporters in their lands and offices, had caused widespread and considerable ill feeling. But there was nothing that could not be solved by wise and just government, and he looked forward to Christmas at Westminster with some pleasure.

So did Julian, as she and Friday packed their belongings, and prepared to travel south. The glittering prospect beckoned seductively: dancing, feasting, disguisings, festivities, all on a vaster and more glorious scale than any she had ever known at Ashcott or Nottingham, Pontefract or Sheriff Hutton. She would no longer be the outsider, a child gaping awestruck at the exalted unreal people on the dais, or the lonely, shabby girl, too miserable and confused to find companionship. She had the friendship of the King's nieces

(Cecily had proved very helpful in the matter of fashion and enhancement of beauty), the liking of the other young ladies in their household, and in six months her poise and confidence had changed beyond all recognition. Yet she was not aware of it: she knew only that she was happy, and that going to Westminster meant either an increase in that delight or, more unpleasantly, the doubts and uncertainties that would result when—if—she met her husband again.

The journey south took some time, since they travelled in some state and comfort in chariots. At least they were sheltered from the rain and hail that fell frequently, although Julian disliked the cumbersome, jolting contraptions intensely. By the time the vehicles lurched their way under the great gate and into the outer court of the Palace of Westminster, she felt as if every bone in her body had been separated from its neighbour, and the Countess of Lincoln was an unhealthy green colour, as indeed she had been all the way from Yorkshire. Gratefully, Julian emerged blinking into the outer court, and saw the Queen, come to greet her nieces.

For a moment, Julian wondered who was this gaunt stranger in royal garb. Then, with the rest, she sank low onto the warm stones: it was unseasonably sunny. The shock of Anne's drastically altered appearance remained dreadfully acute as she bowed her head, the hollowed, feverishly flushed cheeks and shadowed eyes, the transparent thinness of the white-skinned hands, on which the rings hung loose, indelibly pictured behind her closed eyes. She is dying, thought Julian, with sudden clarity—and the King adores her. The death of their son had been a great enough blow—if she dies too, he will be quite alone.

'I am glad to see you here, Dame Julian.' At least the Queen's voice was the same, low and pleasant. Julian kissed the cold hand and rose, wondering how she could keep the distress out of her face. Apparently she succeeded, for Anne's expression was one of kindness and welcome. 'You must be exhausted after your journey. And I have good news for you, Dame Julian—your husband is here at Westminster. He is in attendance on His Grace at present, but I think you will find his duties end after supper, and then you will be able to meet him. He will be glad to see you, I am sure, and you will have a great deal to tell each other.' And with a ghastly shadow of her old sweetly gracious smile, she led the group of girls within the Privy Palace.

They had been given rooms near the Queen's apartments, and in each one there was a fire burning brightly, warm scented water in which to wash away the stains of travel, comfortable feather beds, sumptuous hangings which had once, though probably some time ago, graced a much grander chamber than this. Julian was seated on a stool by the fire, wrapped in a towel, Friday brushing out her damp thick hair, when there was a knock on the door. Her heart faltered: was it Christie, already?

But it was Cecily's lovely face, framed in her clouds of silvery hair, that came round the door. She said, 'Can I come in, Julian?'

Julian, a little doubtfully, assented. While she and Bess were fast friends, Cecily was a rather different matter, being somewhat sharp-tongued and not afraid to hurt—in fact, Julian thought she might enjoy it. In matters of dress and other concerns which any devout churchman would denounce as sinful vanity, however, Cecily was invaluable, having an instinctive flair for colour and fashion. She fixed Julian with a bright eye and grinned impishly. 'I hear your husband's in the Palace.'

'I hear the same,' said Julian. Cecily came to stand by her, eyeing the glorious length of chestnut hair: if Friday had not piled thick strands of it in her lap, it would have trailed on the floor. After five months of happy proximity at Sheriff Hutton, there was no ceremony between any of them, in private at least, although Friday had bobbed a quick curtsey as she brushed.

'And it's months since you've seen him,' said Cecily. She pulled up a stool and sat on it, surveying Julian's towel-swathed form with a critical frown. 'So you have to look your very best. Pity you're so big.'

Julian glanced at her, but the day had long gone when that sort of remark would induce her to lose her temper, and Cecily knew it. Her eyes flicked up and down Julian's body. 'What are you going to wear? And don't say the blue. It doesn't do anything for you, that low waist. Has he seen the green before?'

'No, I had it made at Pontefract.'

'Well, I should wear that, then. And a little rouge on your cheeks—you look very pale. Your hair is lovely, though,' said Cecily, with the air of one making a comment rather than delivering a compliment. 'It's a shame you must hide it under a headdress. Unless—' She frowned, obviously thinking hard, and then leapt to her feet. 'Put on your green gown. I have an idea, I'll be back.' And with a whirl of skirts, the door shut behind her.

Rather bemused, Julian dressed, with Friday's help, in the green.

It had been hung up as soon as they arrived to rid it of at least some of its creases, and now Julian slid it on over her lighter green kirtle, feeling the soft slither of the thick silk, and the warm tickle of the pale fur at collar, cuff and hem. Friday clasped her best girdle, of goldsmith's work, jewelled and heavy, under her breasts, and stepped back. 'You look—you look lovely, Julian.'

It was not like Friday, self-effacing as ever, to dole out compliments. Julian smiled wryly. 'All this fuss to impress my husband—and I don't even know if I want to.'

'Oh, come,' said Friday quietly. 'I thought—forgive me, I thought that your feelings had changed.'

'I don't know!' Julian said forcefully, realising that, after the happy placid months at Sheriff Hutton, her temper was once more on its old short rein. 'I'm sorry, Friday,' she added more calmly. 'I don't know what I feel—except that I'm nervous. I wonder what the Lady Cecily has in store for me?'

She did not have long to wait: a brisk rap heralded Bess's sister, bearing a peculiar contraption that looked like a rather shapeless bag, in silver-grey silk. 'I borrowed this from Lady Lovell,' she said breathlessly. 'Try it on.'

'What is it?' Julian asked, staring doubtfully at the grey bag. Cecily smiled with a certain amount of superiority. 'Don't you know? It's a heathen turban—you'll be a saracen for the day!'

Friday crossed herself. Cecily, with a pitying glance, crossed to Julian. 'Gather all your hair up—no, your woman can do it.'

Friday did as she was told, reflecting that Bess would have known and used her name. Cecily had no time for menials. She held the mass of heavy hair while Cecily pushed the turban onto Julian's head. It fitted snugly around her hairline, the soft grey silk draped over a light arrangement of wires: the centre was open, and through it the hair hung in rippling waves down her back and shoulders. Julian had never seen anyone wearing a headdress like this before, and had no idea what it would look like on herself.

She learned soon enough: Friday handed her the mirror, and she stared at the stranger with grave brown eyes looking calmly back beneath the high draped oval of the turban, the hair sweeping over her shoulders.

'It looks good,' said Cecily with approval. 'I knew it would suit you. Are you ready for supper?'

She did not see Christie at supper, for he was serving Richard in the King's Great Chamber, while she and all the rest of the party from Sheriff Hutton supped at the Queen's board in her chamber. Bess and Cecily, the Countess of Lincoln and Lady Morley ate with the Queen by virtue of their high rank: Julian sat with other, less-exalted ladies at a lower board, and had not quite the same number of dishes at each course. Nervousness made her reluctant to eat: the food tasted dry and flavourless in her mouth, and she had trouble swallowing it. There would be dancing that evening, music and minstrelsy, and she would undoubtedly see Christie there. What would he think, and do, and say? What would she say? Would she forget all her new-won maturity, and behave again like a spoilt brat? She could not predict her own conduct, for she knew too well how her good intentions always seemed to vanish in the heat of her emotions.

The Painted Chamber, where the court gathered after supper, was a high and noble room, decorated with many beautiful paintings that dated from the reign of the third King Henry, more than two hundred years ago. They depicted scenes of war and battle from the Bible: Julian could recognise, amongst others, the histories of King David, the destruction of the temple in Jerusalem, and the bearded figures of several prophets. The floor was tiled, and the whole effect one of brilliant richness, dazzling to a girl who had only known the humbler decorations at Ashcott or Nottingham, or the primitive pictures that covered the walls of every church in the land. She gazed on the paintings in each window-embrasure, trying to order her mind and body for the coming encounter, and then, deliberately, let her gaze swing over to the group of lords, knights and gentlemen around the King.

Tyrell was there, she recognised him immediately, and other men she knew vaguely: Lord Lovell, the Duke of Norfolk, the Chancellor, other churchmen, some in gorgeous vestments, others gazing with disapproval at the sumptuous display of silver and gold, velvet and fur, the brilliant colours and extravagant clothes. Julian had no thoughts to spare for sinful earthly vanity: her heart knocking like thunder against her ribs, her mouth dry and her courage shrivelling rapidly, she at last located her husband amongst those closest to the King. He was talking to Sir Richard Ratcliffe: then he glanced round, and she saw his eyes wander casually over the group of ladies around the Queen. His gaze swept across her without recognition, which did not surprise her, though she felt a stab of disappointment, as if he should have discerned his over-grown lumpish wife in the person of a court lady. Then his eyes came back to her face, lingeringly, and she blushed and cast her eyes down. When she looked up again, he was still looking at her, and the long thin mouth held the faint elements of a smile. He inclined his head, said something to Ratcliffe, and then approached her.

Christie had at first not known her at all, though he had wondered curiously about the very desirable lady in green and grey, the tightness of her golden girdle emphasising the generous swell of her breasts, surrounded by fine grey fur, and the silken turban, an unusual Burgundian fashion, setting off the high forehead and large eyes. Then, as his eye left her, he noted the lady's height, and the flood of red-brown hair that cascaded from the turban down her back, the only seemly headgear for a married woman that would allow her to display her crowning glory, and he knew her.

She was Julian, and not Julian, this poised, confident, fashionable lady. Then their eyes linked across half the length of the chamber, before she lowered hers in evident confusion. He extracted himself from the men around the King, and went over to her.

The Queen saw his approach, and smiled. 'Sir Christopher! You have come to be reunited with your wife at last—why not take her somewhere more private, so that you can talk in peace?' She glanced at Julian, whose face was set like pink and white alabaster, save for the freckles, and touched her lightly on the arm. 'Go, my dear. You must have prayed many times for this moment.'

With a deep curtsey and her thanks, that sounded unconvincing to her ears, Julian turned to face her husband, aware of the faces of all the ladies, known and unknown, staring at her with some curiosity. The turban concealed her burning ears, but could not hide the flush on her face. Christie smiled at her, and, blushing still more fierily, and ashamed of it, Julian lowered her eyes with a proper wifely meekness, and allowed herself to be drawn quietly from the room, their exit followed by several interested eyes, chief amongst them those of Bess and Cecily.

Outside the Painted Chamber, there was a little ante-chamber before the Queen's apartments: it was empty and only dimly lit. Julian stood still, not knowing what to say: and besides, she doubted her tongue could obey her, for it seemed to have stuck to the roof of her mouth. Her senses heightened in this state of unusual awareness, she heard Christie's soft, regular breathing, felt the touch of his hand warm through two layers of green silk about her arm, found her own intakes of air constricted by the tight girdle high about her body, smelled the sweet aroma of the waxen candles in their stand.

'Are you well?' he said. She could make nothing from the tone of his voice: and his face, when she glanced up at it, was similarly uncommunicative. She said, the words barely above a whisper, 'Yes, I thank you, husband, I am quite well.'

Christie surveyed her, the bent head with its preposterous but strangely becoming burden, the tumbling masses of hair, the low-cut gown, and was disconcerted by the strength of his feelings. For six months he had been absent on the King's business, and he had travelled in Flanders and Burgundy and later, more secretly, in France. In all that time he had had little leisure to think of Julian, of her life at Sheriff Hutton presumably in the company of Dickon's sisters: but he had wondered sometimes how she did, whether she thought of him at all, even, aware of the improbability of this last, if her feelings towards him had changed in any way. He had not been prepared for this metamorphosis in her appearance, the veneer of sophistication quite alien to the graceless child he had once known, and disliked. He did not dislike her now: with a strength that was threatening to master him, he wanted her very much indeed. But he did not want to force his body on her, greatly though he desired her: he wanted her compliance, he wanted, at last, to give her some kind of choice. But there was no warmth emanating from this statuesque, immobile girl, a travesty of meekness with, he knew, a volatile and wilful core. He decided at last on honesty: he said quietly, 'I have looked forward to this moment for a long, long time—and now it is here, I am full of uncertainties.'

So astonishingly uncharacteristic was this confession that Julian, startled out of her state of frozen apprehension, jerked her head to stare at him, her eyes huge and dark beneath the faint, arched brows. '*You?* Uncertain? Of what?'

'You,' said Christie wryly. 'You are not exactly predictable, are you, my lady? You blow hot or cold according to your mood, you are child and maid and woman all in one—how many Julians inhabit your head, beneath all this?' His hand came out, as if of its own accord, and lifted a strand or two of hair. 'I don't know any more what you think of me—I used to be able to tell from the expression on your face, and now that is hidden—and as I said to you once, I would rather have the old honest Julian, however filled with rage and hatred, than a dissembling mask of fashion.'

[379]

'But I don't know what I think!' Julian cried with passionate intensity. 'I used to think I hated you—I used to loathe you—and now I just don't know, everything I believed in is false, I don't know what to think.' She swallowed hard, her eyes brilliant with tears, and said more quietly, suddenly aware of the need to keep her voice low, 'I—I talked with the Lady Elizabeth. She couldn't understand why I hated you—I couldn't understand why she liked you. And I found—she told—she told me the truth. About her brothers. And then I had less reason to hate you—but my father, my poor father—he rebelled and died for it, and all for nothing, he was duped, he need never have died—he need never have *died*, and then I wouldn't have had to marry you!' Tears spilled over: she pushed them away with an impatient hand. 'So—I don't know, I don't know what I feel, I think we ought to change, I think we ought to begin again, and be friends—but I can't—I don't know how!'

Christie, with a supreme effort of will, kept his hands still, so strong was the urge to take her in his arms, to lend her his comfort and affection—and more? He did not know either, it was one further uncertainty in the thoughts and feelings of one who had always been so sure and, it had to be admitted, so arrogant. He said softly, 'I think we both have to begin again. I have thought too little of you for too long—and I know now, I must make amends for the way I have treated you in the past. We are married, after all, and we ought at least to deal more kindly together. Will you forgive me?'

There was a tense silence. Julian stared at his impassive face: she said doubtfully, 'I don't know—I can't tell what you're thinking either, but I never have known you, what you feel—you hide yourself behind a face like a mummer's mask, and I can't ever tell if you're speaking the truth.' She gulped in some much-needed air, and added, 'What do you think of me? What are your true feelings towards me? Do you hate me still?'

'I never have,' he said, with perfect truth. 'I disliked you, yes, but I could see also the reasons for your behaviour. But you've changed, and I have altered too, almost without wishing it, against my will: my sister Meg had something to do with it, and so did you. I want more than money, lands, position, though I have all three, and their possession used to be the lodestar of my life. But now I want my days to hold good companionship, affection, perhaps more, if God grant it. And I want those things with you.'

In the Painted Chamber, the minstrels had struck up—evidently the dancing had begun. A fat, slow tear made its way down the side of Julian's nose, and Christie reached out and wiped it away with one finger. 'Do you not believe me, dear lady? Do I have to spell it out so plain? In the years I have known you, I have moved from dislike, to pity, to fondness and now, I think, to the beginnings of love. Oh, no, no, is that so terrible, that you have to weep?' For Julian, overwhelmed, had buried her face in her hands, and her shoulders trembled with the strength of her feelings. 'There is no need to cry.'

His words evoked no response, save that she sobbed the more. With sudden foreboding, Christie wondered, with a sharp pang of what he recognised to his disgust as jealousy, if she had fallen in love with someone else during the months amongst all those young sprigs of nobility at Sheriff Hutton. He discarded that thoroughly unworthy suspicion as soon as it had been born, but a fear lingered, for he realised suddenly that he could not bear her love to be given to another: and supposed, ruefully, that such a thought meant that he in his turn did truly love her.

'I don't believe it,' said Julian. Her words were muffled by her hands, so that he could barely catch them. 'You can't love me—no-one loves me—it's not possible—you can't—in the name of God, why?'

'Your father loved you,' he said. 'So does Cavall. So, I think, does Friday. And is not the Lady Elizabeth your friend? The Queen has spoken of you highly to me, and in very affectionate terms. Why do you think you're unworthy?'

'I am,' said Julian. She dropped her hands and glared at him. 'I'm too tall and too big and too fat. I've got a scold's temper, I'm proud and thoughtless and I hurt people—I say cruel things. I should be meek and gentle and obedient and I'm none of them. Bess—I mean the Lady Elizabeth—she's shown me favour, but that's because of her own gracious nature, not because of me!'

'It's not true,' said Christie. 'Julian, you don't need to tell the catalogue of your supposed vices—why not list your virtues instead? What I see, and everyone else must see also, is honesty, a great and generous heart, and the courage and wisdom to change yourself. What you say was true of yourself years ago, when you were a child, and unhappy. It's not true of you now, is it?'

'It's not for me to say,' Julian muttered, very low. Christie said impatiently, 'I wish you'd be yourself, instead of what you think you ought to be—and what your mother would like. Why can't you let go your fears? Why can't you believe in yourself? Why can't you believe me when I say I may love you? Do you still hate me?'

'No.' Julian added, after a moment, 'At least, I don't think so. I didn't want you to be here tonight—and yet I did. Why—why do you say you love me?'

'God's bones, girl, because it's the truth!'

'It can't be,' she began, and found that his patience had finally expired. His arms came up to surround her, and his mouth came down on hers, stifling her words and her protests. She had never been kissed like this before, and was utterly astonished and unprepared: then, a traitorous sweetness invaded her senses, there was pleasure in the feeling of his body pressed against hers, and a delicious languid warmth surrounded her skin. With a shiver of delight, she forgot her doubts, her fears, her bewildered anger, and gave herself up to this new and delightful sensation.

When he released her, she found her legs trembling, her body suddenly and disconcertingly cold, her senses bereft and wanting more—much more. To her surprise, his eyes, staring at her, mirrored her own bewilderment at the strength of the feelings he had aroused. He said very quietly, 'There is wine and bread in my chamber. No-one will require us. Will you come with me?'

He had given her the choice, and she assented, moving into his arms again as if she belonged there. This time the pleasure was heightened as she responded with a passion that he had not expected, and aroused him still more. This was not the wooden effigy he had deflowered on their wedding night: this was a young, warm, sensual woman, just beginning to realise the wonders that she had missed.

It took them some time to reach Christie's chamber, partly because it was at the other end of the Palace, near the King's riverside apartments, partly because when they walked, Christie's arm was close about her, and when they did not, which was more frequent, they kissed. To Julian, awash with sensual pleasure, it was like suddenly being given an utterly delightful new sweetmeat, whose delicious flavour demanded she eat more and more of it, as quickly as might be. Christie could not but wonder that the unresponsive hostile girl of that first encounter had been transmuted into this warm, pliant, almost wanton woman, as greedy for his kisses and the increasingly bold explorations of his hands as he was for hers.

At last, after a dim confused journey through dark corridors and covered walkways, lingering at every possible moment, drawing her aside as servants or members of the household passed as if she were some light dalliance instead of his wedded wife, they came to the strong oak door, with its iron-strapped hinges and cumbersome lock. Christie opened it, drew his lady inside, and left her alone for a brief second to fire a candle. Its light showed him the familiar chamber, the hangings of the broad soft bed, the softly glowing fire that Perkin had earlier made up, the simple furnishings, the girl who stood drunk with passion in front of him, her tangled mass of hair hiding her disarranged gown, her lips bruised, her eyes enormous. He locked the door, ruthlessly excluding Perkin, who was doubtless watching his betters disport themselves in the Painted Chamber, and turned to her.

Julian watched him approach her, this tall lean man who was still essentially a stranger, who yet had the power to awaken a desire in her that she had never suspected to exist. And her only goal now was the satisfaction of that desire, with a man she had previously hated, so that everything else faded into oblivion besides the longing that filled all her body, to be touched, kissed, held, invaded.

Words were unnecessary. Their mouths met, their bodies pressed together, his hands running over all her gown, returning again and again to her breasts. She moaned with pleasure: gently, he released her and, linking his hands behind her back, unclasped her girdle. The bright gold lay discarded on the floor: it was joined by the turban, lifted off with great care so as not to snag her hair, and then he slid the upper part of her green gown, the lovers' colour, down to expose her high, full breasts. As he kissed them, she fumbled with his belt, dropping it on the tiles, to be joined by the rest of their clothing, like wreckage on a beach, charting their progress to the bed.

*

Julian woke shivering with cold, and for a moment did not remember; she wondered why her body ached, why her mouth hurt, why her hair seemed to be caught on something so that she could not turn her head without pain. Then, she recalled what she had done that night, and a blush swept hot over her at the memory of it. She had behaved—though admittedly to her own husband—like a wanton, like a common harlot. No lady of virtue should have offered herself so freely: it was her role to be submissive and obedient, to be taken meekly rather than respond so ardently to a man's advances.

[383]

And besides, she loathed him—or she had thought that she did.

Utterly confused by the complexities of emotion jostling within her, where once quite recently there had only been childish simplicity, Julian lay there miserably, wanting to cry, wanting to move, and unable to do either. She had never attempted to analyse her feelings before, they had always been so direct, immediate, overwhelming. Now, she had no idea whether what she had experienced was hate, or love, or, more probably, common lust. And the more she pondered her astonishingly bold and abandoned behaviour the more she disliked it, and herself, disliked the sensation of having laid herself, her soul naked with her body, exposed to ridicule and mockery and gossip. She had wanted, truly she thought, to begin again in their marriage—but not like this, she realised unhappily. Not with an explosion of desire that left her utterly confused, adrift in the dark, but with small gradual steps of friendship, companionship, shared interests, a gentle non-violent progression that would not upset her volatile emotions.

Christie muttered something, and rolled over, away from her, still sleeping. She found she could move her head—he had obviously been lying on her hair. Very cautiously, Julian sat up, and saw the wreckage of the bed, its turmoil of linen and embroidered coverlet an eloquent testimony to the force of their lovemaking. It was still dark outside, and the candle he had lit, so long ago it seemed, was still, just, flickering. The fire had gone out, which explained the cold.

Julian stared at her husband, his long lean body inadequately covered by a corner of blanket, his hair paler than she remembered in the uncertain light. She could not see his face, for which she was glad, but she could hear the slow, regular breathing that told her he was deeply asleep. Suddenly she could not face the prospect of his waking up, the watchful chilly eyes upon her, the rather hard northern voice doubtless commenting on her appearance or, worse, the quality of her performance. With an infinite care that disguised her sudden desperate urge to escape, Julian slid slowly from the bed and in haste set about retrieving her clothing. Her smock was easy enough to put on, but the kirtle laced up the back. She struggled with it in silence for what seemed like hours, aware that at any moment the candle could go out, or Christie wake up, before giving up. In a few moments, after all, she would be back in her own chamber and pulling all these complicated garments off again. The gown came next, hauled over her head with a rustle that sounded terribly loud in the silence. Last of all, her hose: she found one and pulled it on, but both garters and the other were nowhere to be found. Mentally consigning them to oblivion, Julian thrust her feet into her fine green kid shoes, picked up the heavy girdle and the turban, and tiptoed to the door.

Nothing stirred. She glanced back at the quiet figure on the bed, and at that precise moment the candle went out. Refusing to panic, she found the key with her fingers, turned it, and lifted the latch with a click that was eerily loud. She waited, her heart thumping suffocatingly in her throat. Still no sound. Like a wraith, Julian slid round the door, and all but fell over something lying on the floor of the antechamber on the other side. The something squawked and sat up: in the flickering golden light from a wall cresset, she saw that it was Perkin.

'Eh?' His shrewd blue eyes peered sleepily up at her. 'So *that's* why—should've guessed.'

'Ssh!' Julian hissed angrily, and listened. There was no sound on the other side of the door, and very softly she closed it. Turning, she found Perkin standing square in front of her, arms folded and a belligerent expression on his ugly face. 'You ain't going, are you?'

'Yes,' said Julian in the same hissing whisper. 'It's none of your business, is it? Now stand aside.'

'And to think I thought you'd learned some manners,' said Perkin insolently, and his blue eyes glittered. 'Why are you leaving him?'

It was too much, to stand here in this cold and draughty little chamber bandying words with a servant—and a low-born disreputable one at that. 'I said—it's none of your business,' Julian repeated. 'Now let me pass.'

'Going back to your own chamber, are you?' There was a sudden glint in Perkin's eye. 'Do you know the way, lady? You ain't been in the Palace a day yet.'

The shot struck home. Julian stared at him, realising that she had not the faintest idea of the direction in which her chamber lay: her passage here had been in semi-darkness, confusion, with too many other things to think about to memorise the route. 'No,' she said reluctantly. 'No, I don't.'

Perkin gave a triumphant snigger. 'Where are you lodged, lady? By the Queen's apartments? Thought so. Then I'll guide you—you never know who you might meet on a dark cold night like this, eh? Even in the Palace.'

It was insufferable, infuriating. It was also true. Julian fought the urge to hit her husband's servant as hard as was necessary to remove the smug smirk from his mouth. With a superb effort, she succeeded, and said through clenched teeth, 'Very well. You may guide me, and quickly.'

'We are in a hurry, aren't we,' was Perkin's comment as they made their way through the labyrinthine passages of the Palace, scurrying through empty antechambers, down corridors and along pentice-covered walkways where the December cold struck cruelly even through her thick silks. The moon was full and high, laying black and silver shadows on courtyards and tiles and on the clouds torn and ragged above them: Julian glanced up, once, realising that it must be perhaps three or four o'clock in the morning. Possibly, if her mind could let her, she would sleep a little.

And then they were there. She realised, belatedly, that she had done Perkin an injustice: insolent or no, he could easily have left her to find her own way, or not, through the maze. She said, shivering, 'I'm sorry, Perkin. Thank you for showing me the way. Now you must get back to your master. The fire's gone out.'

'And my pallet's warm,' said Perkin. He stared up at the tall girl thoughtfully. 'I know it ain't none of my business, and you've told me that often enough, lady. But it is, in a way, because if he's unhappy he takes it out on me, see? And make no mistake, my fine lady Julian, you've got the power to make him very unhappy indeed.'

'You think so?' said Julian, as witheringly as she could. 'I didn't think he had enough feelings in him to *be* unhappy. Goodnight, Perkin.' And she slipped inside her chamber, leaving him standing disconsolate outside.

She was greeted with joy by Cavall, who had lain all evening bereft by the fire, and for whom Friday was no substitute at all. Her maid was asleep in the big bed—the firelight, dim and glowing, showed her that much. Trembling with cold and exhaustion, Julian pulled off her clothes in the near darkness, not caring if she ripped them, and crawled into the Friday-warmed bed in her smock. Cavall leapt up and curled between mistress and maid, and had to be dissuaded from licking her face in his delight. She had thought she could not possibly sleep: in fact, she succumbed within seconds of laying her head on the pillow.

❧

CHAPTER SEVENTEEN

**'And there was dancing and minstrelsy
and all manner of joy.'**
(BOOK 2, CHAPTER 17)

It was Christmas Eve, and a time of high festival. The court had heard Mass that morning in the Chapel of St Stephen, so cold that the breaths of the singing boys filled the beautiful building with dragon's smoke, and the incense plumed from the censers in great scented swathes, while the lords and ladies, nobles and gentlemen, King and Queen, shivered in their velvet and fur. There was to be a great feast in the White Hall, music, singing, dancing: a day of mirth and joyous thanksgiving for the birth of Our Lord, and to crown it, a midnight Mass after the banquet.

At Ashcott, Julian had always loved Christmas, had laughed uproariously at the antics of the mummers, the cavortings of the village fool, had danced, with the abundant energy of childhood, the round country dances popular in the household. Last year, there had been no merrymaking: last year, they had been in mourning for her father, and she had just been coerced into agreeing to marriage with Christie Heron. So this time, the riotous gaiety of which the churchmen always disapproved should have been welcome.

It was not. She had spent the last week or so trying desperately to avoid her husband: it was not always possible, even in the warren of unplanned buildings which was Westminster Palace. She did not even really know why, save that each sight of that clever, impassive face had the power to bring back, with hideous, humiliating clarity, that one night of passion when she had shamefully succumbed to her baser instincts.

He, of course, had sought her out the day after her precipitate flight from his chamber: but he had, to her astonishment, made no mention of that night. It was as if it had never been. Julian was at first bewildered, then relieved, and then, perversely, affronted. At this point she realised the ludicrous nature of her feelings, and found the grace to laugh at herself.

There was something else, too, a deeper, more powerful urge, that stirred in her body every time she saw him, and must be suppressed. For one night she had given in to her instinctive lust, and she had been appalled by it. She knew that her waiting-woman, though she had never mentioned it, was puzzled by the situation: knowing that Julian had spent a night with her husband, why did she now sleep alone, save for Friday and the dog, and why did she evade his presence?

If it puzzled Friday, it did not bewilder Christie. When he had woken that cold morning to find daylight come and his lady gone, his first emotion had been anger. How dare she run away, after such a night? But he had questioned Perkin, who had confessed his role in guiding her back to her chamber with characteristic aplomb. 'Well, what's a little lad like me to do, sir? She's twice my size, I reckon she could break my arm with one twist, like the Green Knight.'

'Could you not have *called*, Perkin my lad?'

'Doubt if you'd have woken, you was sleeping like the dead. Anyway,' Perkin said, 'she brooked no argument. In a rare old hurry, she was. What *did* you do, sir?'

'Never mind what I did—though I doubt there's been a woman in all history as contrary as this one. How did she seem? Was she frightened, alarmed?'

Perkin shot his employer a very sharp glance, but Christie's face was at its most unrevealing. This in itself told him a good deal. He said cautiously, 'She was angry, mostly, with me for being there—but she's often angry to hide being frightened, ain't she?'

This perceptive remark did not pass unnoticed. Christie gave him a withering glance. 'Is she, indeed? You seem to know her better than I do.'

Perkin, impervious, stared back at his master. 'Perhaps I do, at that. Certainly better than she knows herself. Christ's wounds, sir, couldn't you have found a wife a little more, er, meek?'

'No, you insolent brat, I couldn't—and you can count yourself lucky, for every other master in the land would have had the hide whipped off your scrawny back years ago. Now, is it asking too much of you, dear Perkin, to quit sticking that ridiculous nose into my affairs? Or you may find that the distance between the Palace and the gutter is a great deal shorter than you think.'

From anyone other than Christie, that would have been purely a joke, or purely a threat. Perkin knew that his master was quite capable of treating it as either, and he did not care to put it to the test. He resolved, however, that somehow, soon, this absurd situation must end: and since Christie and that stupid perverse girl were bound indissolubly together for good or ill, it was her mind that must be changed.

There was no chance however for him, a mere servant, to have private speech with her, and besides, the bustle of approaching festival kept everyone busy. He saw her many times, usually wearing the simple veiled headdress she had always worn: the turban, with its unsettling memories, she had returned to Lady Lovell.

The week until Christmas passed uneasily. The whole Palace, it seemed to Julian, must find their strange relationship food for gossip: she was well aware of Bess's silent concern, Cecily's curious looks. But no-one said anything to her, for her manner precluded any approach. And, three days before the festival, she received another grievous shock: for Dame Alice arrived at Westminster.

*

Julian's mother had done much travelling that autumn. In November, in answer to a surprising invitation, she had left Ashcott and journeyed north, to Derbyshire. There, she had spent a very pleasant fortnight in the company of her hostess and childhood friend, Margaret Beaufort, mother of Henry Tudor and now wife of Lord Stanley, living in enforced seclusion on her husband's estates and forbidden to travel to Westminster for fear that she might not be able to resist the temptation to plot again on her son's behalf.

It was speedily apparent that this was not an invitation purely for old friendship's sake, although the two women found themselves companionably united in their grievance against the present King and his rule. They had not seen each other for some years, but had corresponded frequently, and lately Lady Stanley's steward, one Reginald Bray, had been a regular visitor at the home of his dead cousin's wife.

'Your dear late husband rendered my son such valuable help before his death,' Margaret Beaufort had said to Dame Alice one evening by the fire in her solar. 'It was great shame and sorrow that your daughter's marriage was so—unfortunate.' She bent her head to her sewing: it was well known that Lady Stanley's mind and hands were never still, always sewing or reading or praying or, said the malicious, meddling in what should not concern her.

Dame Alice, who was the same age, had known her since they had been children, an ill-assorted pair, one tiny and slight and one big and heavy, but both sharing a relentless determination. The Lady Margaret Beaufort and Mistress Alice Clifford had been reared in Lady Margaret's mother's household at Bleteshoe in Bedfordshire. She had been at the heiress's first wedding, when the tiny, indomitable girl with her ugly sandy-red hair had been married to a tall, young man called Edmund Tudor, Earl of Richmond, whose mother had been Harry V's French Queen, and whose father, scandalously, had been a handsome Welshman who had enticed the lonely widowed Queen into his bed without, it was rumoured, the benefit of a marriage ceremony. The young Earl had died within the year, leaving his fourteen-year-old widow to bear their child two months later, a boy with his mother's sandy hair and his father's greyish eyes. He had been named Henry, and though in the near twenty-eight years since his birth his mother had barely set eyes on him because of his captivity or exile, she promoted his cause with a single-minded devotion that with her piety was the main-spring of her life.

The heavy, coarse woman seated with her had also only the one child, and this a daughter who had turned out most unsatisfactorily. Lady Stanley, whose spies and informers were unsuspected and ubiquitous, knew that the girl and her mother had not had much choice when faced with a marriage to one of the usurper's most intimate and trusted knights, but it meant that they must all be very circumspect to avoid arousing this man Heron's suspicions.

Dame Alice watched the pale beringed hands pulling the needle in and out of the fine cloth. 'We had no option, my lady,' she said at last. 'I dislike the man heartily—a jumped-up northerner with an inflated idea of his own importance—overweeningly arrogant. I was glad to see the back of him.'

'And what are your daughter's feelings about her husband? It could be important, Dame Alice—if she gets wind of what we are about, will she tell him?'

'I doubt it. She's a graceless disobedient jade, but she loathes him as bitterly as do I—and I've made sure of it. Yes,' said Dame Alice, comfortably stretching her hands to the fire, 'you need have no fear, my lady, that her affections are in any way engaged.'

'Good,' said the Lady Margaret approvingly. 'And she is at Westminster, you say? The perfect excuse—what could be more natural than for a mother to visit her only daughter at such a time of happy festivity? I will speak to my husband, ask him to arrange that you be given permission to attend the court. And then, my dear

Dame Alice, you will be able to keep watch on your daughter, and on any others whom you or I deem it politic to observe—I cannot be there, alas,' Lady Stanley finished, with ironic sadness. 'But if you will be my eyes and ears, and my mouthpiece too, then my absence will not matter.'

The winds of rebellion were stirring again, and Dame Alice was already sniffing them eagerly. She arrived at Westminster in a mood of purposeful energy, noted Julian's pale aghast face, saw before the end of her first day that the girl was still, thankfully, estranged from her husband, and made contact with several old friends and cronies also in attendance. She had always affected to despise gossip, but there was no doubt it had its uses, both in the gathering of information and in the spreading of rumour.

From Yorkshire, a black-haired man, impeccably and fashionably dressed despite being in early middle age, brought his lovely young wife to London for the first time. He would rather have left her behind, for she had made it more than clear since the birth of their second child, not three weeks after the death of the first, that she now disliked him intensely. Sir Robert Drakelon, resentfully staring at his wife's upright cloaked figure ahead of him, on the chestnut horse he had bought for her on their marriage, thought that it was the death of the little girl that had done the mischief —though why she should be so distressed over the demise of such a poor puny thing, and a girl into the bargain, utterly escaped him. And of course she was prone to strange fancies in pregnancy: he still sweated at the memory of her madness before and after that first miscarriage, her extraordinary delusion that his own sister had been poisoning her. But she had seemed to get over that quite successfully, although her attitude to him had hardened, he could see now with hindsight, to one of resentfully hostile but dutiful obedience. And when, during her third pregnancy, he had taken her horse away and ordered her to stay in the house, she had given him a look, a brief flashing look from those beautiful blue eyes, that might have chilled him if it had not come from his own wife. He must be imagining it: Meg had her faults in abundance, but they surely did not include wilful harm to her husband.

But she had seemed to accept her captivity calmly enough, after that first moment, and he had been proved joyfully and triumphantly right when three months ago, the baby had arrived. It was a quick easy birth, and the child a large, healthy, lusty boy, screeching fit to be heard in Barnsley. He had fair hair, which immediately fell out, and misty blue eyes. Sir Robert, supplied at long last with an heir, doted on the child. The baby was christened Roger, a rather old-fashioned name, but one that had long been in the family, and born last by Sir Robert's father. He was supplied with a cradle, a rattle, warm coverlets, swaddling bands and a buxom bountiful wet-nurse, who took sole charge of him: Dame Margaret need have nothing to do with him.

To Meg, this was but one more ember to add to the stoked and smouldering fires of her hatred. She could not rid herself of the feeling that her husband, by expecting little Katherine to die, had in fact somehow contributed to her death: for if the force of Meg's will had been enough, the baby would be living still, instead of lying in her cold cold grave under the snow of Denby churchyard.

She had grieved for Katherine, and her sorrow was the sharper because there was no-one to share it with her. Her husband did not understand, and she had no friends who could commiserate: only acquaintances who thought the death of an ailing year-old child inevitable, even kind. Meg, for whom Katherine had laughed, and smiled, and walked her first and only faltering steps, knew differently, and the bitterness grew. Then Roger was born, and it seemed that Sir Robert, having subtly stolen one child from her, was more openly removing the other one as well. And in the little contact she had had with her son, she could see herself in him, could see a baby to love as she had loved Katherine: except that she would not be given the chance. Already his smiles, his reaching hands, were for the nurse Margery, and his mother was a stranger who came every day, stared at him with unsettling hungry eyes, and went away again. Word had got around the manor that it had been Dame Drakelon's lack of care that had led to the little girl's death: she was after all, they said to each other, a bit—well, you know, accompanied by a tap on the head. And definitely not to be trusted with the nurture of the heir to all the lands and name of Drakelon.

She had not gone to her husband to plead with him for the care of her baby: she was too proud, and besides, she knew well that it would avail her nothing, for he would never trust her again, and he had always taken some pleasure in refusing that which she most wanted. And now she was riding to Westminster where once, in her innocence, she had thought the world existed, and had so wanted to dance. She would see the King and Queen, and feast at court, not because her husband wished that she enjoy herself, nor even because he wanted to display her beauty, but because he would not leave her at home alone with her son.

And probably Christie would be there, with the fat sullen girl of Sir Robert's description, whom he had unaccountably married, although the fact that she was apparently an heiress might explain it. She would have to see him and speak with him, and all the time his chilly assessing eyes would see too clearly her unhappiness, and know that he had been right all along, and she had been wrong, wrong, wrong, to tie herself to this cold calculating devious and deliberately cruel man, twice her age, a man who made Christie seem positively open-hearted.

They were welcomed, and given a comfortable chamber in a part of the Palace close to the wall dividing it from the Abbey precincts. It was very cold: Sir Robert's servant stoked their fire while a menial brought hot spiced hippocras. Meg's woman, a quiet girl of Yorkshire yeoman family called Mariot, busied herself hanging clothes and wrapping a heated hearthstone to warm the bed. Meg stared at the plain red-nosed maid, who lacked any pretensions to looks or intelligence: she could not even write her name, and reading the romances that Meg had loved was utterly beyond her. Sir Robert had chosen her, and Meg knew that the girl reported on her behaviour to him. It was another ember on the fire. She looked at the bed, where doubtless her husband would once more claim his rights with pain and indignity to herself, and repressed a shiver. She was trapped, trapped for ever, she could see herself dwindling into dreary middle age, her looks gone, her figure ruined by years of childbearing, embittered by a loveless marriage and her husband's alternating indifference and active cruelty. Only children offered any hope of relief, and it seemed probable that she would not even be allowed to tend them.

I hate him, thought Meg, staring last at her husband's immaculate sky-blue furred gown surrounding his trim shape as he warmed his hands to the fire. I hate him—I wish, oh how I wish he were dead! And it was a sign of the strength of her feelings, that she felt no shock or remorse at this most sinful desire, and did not even cross herself.

*

The feast had been cleared away, the boars' heads, borne in with state and song, and now picked clean to the skull, had been removed with the other courses, and now the servants were packing up the tables and clearing the Hall for dancing and festivity. Minstrels played, the hoarse rebecs complementing the more delicate lutes and the loud cheerful pipes. The King sat in his chair of state amidst crimson velvet, a banner bearing the white boar hung against the wall behind him surrounded by the traditional green boughs of Christmas, and Queen Anne, her face red and white as if painted beneath the heavy headdress, sat beside him, a shrunken figure within her scarlet cloth of gold and ermine, a splendid gown. She sent an encouraging smile at her niece, who was wearing one of her other dresses, as a gift of love this Christmas time: they were both tall, fair-haired women, but Anne had found that most of her garments hung loose on her now, as if made for someone else. Bess, magnificent and stately in the blue cloth of silver, sat with her eyes wide and dreamy as she stared at the bustle in the smoky hall, caught her aunt's glance with a slight, guilty start and smiled in return. Daydreaming again, thought Anne with affection: she greatly preferred Bess to her hard and flighty sister Cecily. That young madam was dallying now with her cousin, Edmund de la Pole, a precocious thirteen-year-old with a bold eye, a ready wit and, already, an incipient beard. Both girls had been presented with gorgeous gowns from the Queen's own collection, and there had been some surprise and murmuring when they had appeared thus arrayed at the feast.

Anne's eye roved further, down the ranks of people who lined the Hall, some sitting, others standing in expectation of the dancing. She caught sight of Bess's friend, the young Dame Julian Heron, who had been reunited with her husband but now, alas, seemed to be avoiding him. Cecily had commented upon this, maliciously, to her aunt, and Anne had upbraided her sharply. But there was no denying that Dame Julian was behaving most strangely: and no denying, either, the nature of the look that Sir Christopher sent her, across the width of the Hall, and which she had not appeared to notice.

Anne stifled a cough, and glanced anxiously at her husband. The King was deep in conversation with the Duke of Norfolk, and had apparently not heard. So far, it seemed successfully, she had managed to hide the severity of her illness from him, pretending that what ailed her was nothing but the after-effects of a brief but severe fever. But, sooner or later, there would come a time when she could conceal her plight no longer: not now, though, she prayed silently. Sweet blessed Virgin Mary, let him enjoy this last Christmas.

Julian had sat with other gentlewomen and ladies, including her mother, while her husband served the King. She had known of Dame Alice's arrival the previous evening, when a page had brought her the summons in her mother's thick, almost illegible hand. The sight of it had brought about an instinctive reaction of sheer panic: her knees had trembled, her heart had pounded, beads of sweat had broken out on her forehead. Friday, concerned, had asked her if it was bad news. Julian, with a bitter smile, shook her head. 'No, not in the way you think. My mother is here, and wishes to see me.'

There was nothing Friday could say: she stared in compassionate silence as her mistress crumpled up the note and hurled it into the fire, then turned on the child who had brought it in a fury. 'I'm not going—I have the headache, and you may tell my lady mother that, if you please. Now go!'

But she could not put off the encounter for ever: and so now there were two people in the Hall that she did not want to meet. Dame Alice she had located some time ago, in the company of several other widows and wives of similar age and wildly dissimilar appearance. At another time, Julian might have found amusement at the sight of half-a-dozen women so utterly different in size and shape: now, however, she felt only cold fear, and the beginnings of a deeper disquiet. Why had her mother come to Westminster?

A movement across the Hall caught her eye, and she saw a black-haired man making his way towards her husband. It was Sir Robert Drakelon: and the lovely girl by his side must be Christie's sister Meg.

Julian stared avidly at her, noting the pale face, the rosebud mouth and blue eyes, the cornflower-coloured gown with the heart-shaped neckline and low girdle emphasising the slender, sinuously fashionable line of her waist. It was a face not dissimilar to her husband's, but cast in a softer mould, with a hint of strength, however, in the firm mouth and pointed chin. Her expression caught and held Julian's attention: it was one of contemptuous dislike.

The courtesies were exchanged, and she saw her husband say something. Sir Robert drew his wife to his side with a proprietorial gesture, and his smile seemed false even at that distance.

A roar went up from those nearest the door. The Lord of Misrule had entered, capering in grotesque costume and mask, with his retinue of similarly-clad attendants, normally at work in the Palace in a less exalted capacity. Their chief, who was just recognisable beneath his gruesome mask as one of the King's fools, stamped his staff of office on the floor and roared for silence. It was Christmas, and they obeyed him: the company, grinning with anticipation, well filled with rich food, flushed with wine, awaited his edicts with pleasurable expectation. At Christmas, the world went topsy-turvey, and inferiors could rule their betters: this licensed foolery was popular from palace to cottage, and even the serious-minded King had a stiff smile on his face, while his Queen, her cheeks hectically coloured, laughed hilariously at the costumes.

The Lord had a rhyming speech prepared, about the holiness of the season and the rightness of celebrating such a happy occasion with mirth and song and dance—'But not yet, good ladies, lords and all, for first some forfeits I must call.'

There was an expectant hush, broken by giggles from a dimly-lit corner where a couple embraced. The Lord of Misrule peered in the direction of the sounds, amid rising laughter, and then pointed with his staff. 'And first I say, that every wife—must kiss her husband, as she loves life!'

Shouts, laughter, ribald comments greeted this. The lady, blushing hotly, was claimed by another gentleman who did not look best pleased at having his dame's affairs thus exposed before all the court. The King, laughing as heartily as the rest, reached over to kiss his Queen: and Julian, who had feared this as soon as the Fool had finished his rhyme, found herself facing her husband. 'Well?' said Christie, and his voice was light, even if his eyes were not. 'Will you not kiss me, my dear wife?'

Because she could do nothing else, she lifted her face, not far, to his, and his mouth slid to find hers while his arms imprisoned her. Deeply shamed, she found her body betraying her once more, and could not disguise it: when the kiss ended, his arms still locked around her, he surveyed her flushed hot face and said, very gently, so that she could hardly hear him above the babble, 'Oh, Julian —why will you not give in?'

'I don't know what you mean,' she said, to gain time: her breathing was rapid and out of order, and she feared that he would kiss her again. Or did she?

'You do. Don't fight it, my love, don't fight it—there's no sin in desiring your husband, no sin in love.'

The voice of the Lord of Misrule broke in, pitched to echo in every corner of the Hall. 'And now I give my second test—each lady must kiss whom she loves best!'

To an observer, the next few minutes might have proved illuminating: not every couple stayed together, and ladies scurried hither and thither, emboldened by wine and the freedom of the occasion, embracing sundry fortunate gentlemen amidst much laughter and ribaldry. Julian could not escape: in panic her body twisted once, and then was still inside Christie's long arms, while he kissed her again. And this time, though she tried to force her mouth shut, to turn her head away, to direct her thoughts elsewhere, still her senses would not allow her. It was as if her body were melting with warm pleasure, clinging to his like ivy on a wall, and his words echoed remote in her mind. 'Don't fight it—don't fight.'

Dame Alice, her lips clamped in a thin disapproving line, had beheld this riotous behaviour with distaste: it seemed that this King, for all his vaunted denunciation of his enemies' debauched conduct, nevertheless allowed such things in his own court, under his very nose. Nor did her companions much care for such freedom and licence. And then her eye fell on the figure of her daughter, arrayed in a splendid gown of tawny damask that showed off her voluptuous shape to too much advantage, almost unrecognisable as the spoilt hoyden of her childhood days, being thoroughly kissed by her despicable husband, and looking, disgustingly, as if she enjoyed it, so tight was her body pressed against his. As she watched, Julian's hands came up to grasp his back, and she seemed to be returning the kiss avidly. With a snort of fury, Dame Alice hastily averted her eyes, but too late: her closest crony had noticed. 'Is that your daughter? That is not her husband?'

'It is,' said Dame Alice with profound disgust and anger. 'I'll swear she loathed him more than the devil—and now look at the fickle jade—no better than a trollop, and in the King's own Hall!'

'He is her husband,' the other woman pointed out. 'And it is not unknown for a young woman of bold character to—succumb to the lusts of the flesh, while still in her mind disliking the object of her desire.'

To which sanctimonious comment, Dame Alice gave only a contemptuous snort.

The minstrels had struck up in response to the Lord's request, and a commoning dance was ordered, a procession led by the minstrels more or less riotously around the Hall. Julian, all her resolve vanished once more in the strength of her desires, found herself pulled into the line by Christie. The minstrels led, directed by the Lord of Misrule, and the line wound up and down the Hall, crossed itself three times, turned back on itself and became inextricably tangled. Amid the laughing crowd, Julian and Christie stood quiet, an island of stillness within the movement and chatter. His eyes held hers and she could not look away: she could see herself reflected very small, the white stiff wings of her headdress, the heavy gold chain she wore about her neck, the swell of her breasts beneath it, and the deep sable fur edging the low bodice. 'I want to talk to you,' he said. 'Will you come with me?'

Outside the Hall the great yard stood white and empty in the surrounding dark, lit by cressets that cast flickering pools of light onto a powdering of snow. It was cold, and a few scattered flakes were falling hesitantly. The Clock Tower stood in front of them, its dial in shadow. Julian shivered as the chill struck her skin, warmed from the hot Hall behind her: a gale of laughter came through the closed doors, and the sounds of dance music. 'You wanted to talk to me,' she said, her voice sounding more hostile than she had intended. In a dark corner of the courtyard, a woman laughed softly, and a man's voice murmured something.

'I do,' said Christie. He sounded suddenly weary, and she glanced at his face: it was shadowed and unrevealing. 'Julian—we cannot continue like this. I think I know what ails you, what you feel, but there must be an end to it, one way or another, and soon. For I do not think I can bear to have you warm in my bed one night, and as cold as stone the next day.'

The thumping of her heart seemed almost to have closed her throat. Her mouth dry, Julian swallowed and said, foolishly, 'Why not?'

'Because I love you, Julian—that's why not.'

A snowflake fell on her face, and she brushed it away with the stupid tears. She did not know him, she did not understand him, she did not even like him—but she knew the truth when she heard it. She said, also speaking the truth, 'I don't love you.'

'I know that. Sweet Christ, I don't expect miracles. I know what you have suffered, and I know that you never wanted us to be wed. But I know also that what was between us just now, and that night last week, cannot be ignored. Julian, dear girl, there is no sin, no crime, no shame in wanting me. I'm not your leman—I'm your husband, and it's only right, even in the eyes of the Church, that we should take pleasure with each other. It isn't wrong, though you behave as if it was. And yet—' He put his hands on her shoulders, where her gown had slid down during the dancing, and the warm touch burned her skin like fire. 'It's a beginning. It might not be the beginning you wanted, but it's there nonetheless. We know very little of each other, we've seen each other rarely, our marriage was started in fear and hatred and arrogance—but we've both changed, haven't we? I want you, your heart and your soul, not your lands—you are my lodestar now. And I don't want to force you, I want to woo you and win you gently, with love and kindness—will you not let me at least do that?'

More tears had joined the snowflakes. She quivered under his hands, and her confusion and uncertainty spoke plain on her face. Mutely, slowly, she nodded.

'And will you share my chamber, dear girl? For when we know what delight we can have of each other, it seems a shame to sleep cold and alone.'

It would be difficult to cast aside the attitudes she had struck for years, and to venture into this new territory, as strange and unknown, and yet as enticing, as the lands of King Arthur. She was not sure, even now, that she could do it. But his gentleness, so surprising and unexpected, had almost convinced her. He loved her, dear Christ knew why, for she was big and fat and ugly, and bad-tempered into the bargain: but he said he did. And somewhere, deep within her, something that had long been starved and withered was nourished a little, and began to grow.

And perhaps there was no shame after all in wanting him, when that very evening half the court had seemingly been lusting after men and women to whom they were not married, when the King had kissed the Queen with a passion undimmed by years of wedlock, when the whole atmosphere within the Great Hall was one of merriment and bawdry, licensed by the season. The minstrels were playing a familiar tune, the tabors picking up a lively beat: suddenly, the urge to dance her doubts away overwhelmed her. 'I am yours, husband,' she said, and gave him a smile suddenly bright with mischief, that almost stopped his heart. 'Will you not come and dance with me?'

'In Ireland?' he said, quoting a fragment of an old ballad, and she laughed. 'No, not if I can help it—but in Westminster, perhaps!'

It was a round dance, a huge circle of gorgeously-clad people stepping and bowing and swaying from side to side in steps that varied from the intricate and neat to the inebriated and unsteady. The King and Queen had joined it, and the Duke and Duchess of Norflok, Edmund de la Pole led out the Lady Cecily, and Lord Lovell partnered the Lady Bess. The musicians stood in the middle, red-faced and perspiring freely, while the tune bounced along and the ring turned and stamped and jumped with it. Julian and Christie, with muttered apologies, slipped into the circle and joined in the steps with enthusiasm.

Meg, at the other side of the ring, saw them, and was filled with a sudden surge of anger. There was her brother, so fine in crimson and green velvet, all furred and embroidered, the golden collar of his office around his neck—an office he had won by ruthless callousness, by such acts as betraying his sister. And in whose service? That of a usurper who, common fame reported, had probably made away with his young nephews. It was true that the slight figure of the King, his face showing signs of strain and anxiety, did not look like a murderer, and his grief at the death of his own son had apparently been heartbreaking. But Meg, in her present bitter mood, was not prepared to give him much benefit of the doubt. Covertly, as she danced with one hand in her husband's and the other in some sweating lord's, she observed Christie's wife. It was apparent that Sir Robert had misled her: this was not the great gawky sullen girl of his description. She noted the pale face, the fluttering headdress, the rather old-fashioned but very becoming gown, the rich girdle emphasising the generosity of her figure: and she saw also the smile, the spring in her step, and the way that Christie looked at her, and her heart grew cold and closed with jealousy. Her brother loved that girl, it was obvious to her who knew him best of all, even now after years of hostility. How dare he find happiness, after what he had done to her?

The dance ended, and those who wished to sit out the next retreated to the walls, while the Fool called another, an energetic Burgundian tune which neatly eliminated the older members of the company: the Duke and Duchess of Norfolk, both perspiring heavily in the hot Hall, already thick with the heat of torches and active human bodies, the odours of perfumes and pitch dogs and wine, sweat and smoke, led the way back to the High Table.

Meg, drawn aside by Sir Robert, saw that her brother had also declined to dance, and that he was approaching them, threading his way through the crowd with his wife, flushed and grinning more than was proper for a lady, held firmly by the hand. Close to, she was not at all pretty, and she was too tall, taller even than Meg: she was nearly Christie's height, and she overtopped Sir Robert by an inch or two. Whatever can he see in her, wondered Meg: but there was no mistaking the smile in his eyes as he looked at her. She's naught but an overgrown hoyden, no grace, no beauty, no character.

The introductions were performed, and Julian stared with scarcely-disguised curiosity at her husband's sister. At close quarters, Dame Margaret was even more lovely than she had thought: her pale skin had the flawless purity of the rose called Maiden's Blush. But the large blue eyes were chill and unfriendly, and the sweet curve of the pink mouth was spoilt by the tight compression of the lips. As befitted sisters by marriage, they kissed, and the touch on Julian's cheek was as light and cold as a snowflake. 'You look very fine in that gown,' said Meg, and her smile was free and false. 'So comfortable—you must have had it a very long time.'

Julian picked up the insult at once, and could see no reason for it—true, her husband had evidently quarrelled with his sister, but was there any need to extend the enmity to her as well?

She refused to rise to the bait: she gave Meg a smile in return. 'I thank you, sister. And yours is delightful—I wish I could wear that newer style, but it does not suit me half so well as it does you.'

There was, in fact, more to this girl than met the eye, Meg decided as the conversation, after its inauspicious beginning, embarked stiltedly on a discussion of other styles and materials bedecking the ladies around the Hall. And from the glances that Christie gave her, looks that were remarkably similar to those that Sir Robert had directed towards herself during the very early days of their marriage, it was not love and affection that moved him so much as lust. Her lips curling in a scornful, contemptuous smile, Meg knew that soon he would learn the same bitter lesson as had she.

The dancing over, the court made its way to St Stephen's chapel for midnight Mass. The snow was falling more heavily now, and, most improperly, some more riotous and drunken spirits started to throw it at each other. This unseemly exuberance was soon quelled, however, and the service, one of the most important of the year, was conducted amid the usual hushed reverence, before the King and his household dispersed to their beds.

It was Christie's chamber to which they went, quiet after the solemn yet joyous service. Perkin, slumbering before the fire, was rudely prodded awake and ordered to serve the bread and wine and ale allowed to all the King's knights for their nightly sustenance. In celebration of the season, the wine was spiced, and warmed by the fire: and Julian, sipping it, her heart thumping with pleasurable anticipation, allowed herself the luxury of studying her husband's tall figure as he sat on the opposite side of the hearth, his feet stretched out to the warmth, his face relaxed, almost smiling, in the firelight. Having seen Meg near to, she could assess the likeness between them: both tall, long and slender, with strong-boned faces that were broader above, narrowing below, to a sharp, prominent chin. In Meg, those features had been softened into beauty. Christie would never be one of those handsome heroes of romance, but his face was interesting, even, some might say, attractive. This is the man I once hated, Julian thought, with something like surprise. And now I am sitting here all aflame by his fireside because I cannot wait for him to kiss me, to hold me and touch me, and lay me down on that bed as we did before. And she gulped the spiced wine and poured more, grateful for the tingling warmth it provided, and that feeling of joyous recklessness.

Perkin had retired to a little closet off the chamber: they were quite alone. It must have been the wine that induced her to say, her voice lazy but curious, 'Why did you quarrel with your sister?'

The quality of the silence changed. With her newly observant eyes, Julian saw his knuckles suddenly pale with tension, and his face become quite still, as if sculpted from stone. Too late, Julian realised that she had blundered, even as he turned those rather disturbing pale eyes upon her, and said gently, 'What makes you think I have quarrelled with Meg?'

Julian faced him, her eyes similarly wide and unblinking: committed, she could not withdraw, though Pandora's box had been opened. She said, choosing her words with uncharacteristic care, 'Because—because she doesn't seem to like you, or you like her.'

'Perhaps we never have,' Christie suggested, his fingers playing with the stem of his winecup: only the silvery eyes, watchful and narrow, gave him away. 'But don't let thoughts of my sister spoil this evening. Come here.'

She swallowed the last of the wine and obeyed those strange compelling eyes, rising and moving across the few feet of floor as if a sleepwalker, or enchanted under some spell. Perhaps it is a spell he's put on me, she thought, with a shiver of superstitious delight, a charm of liking and desire, a love potion, save that I don't love him and never shall, but oh how I want him to touch me—

He pulled her down onto his lap, and poured more wine into his cup: they shared it like lovers, their hands linked around the bowl, and he kissed and drank from the place where her lips had touched, and broke the fine white demain bread for her: she giggled as the crumbs disappeared down between her breasts, and still more as he attempted to retrieve them and then let his hand roam while he set the wine down and kissed her, long and lingering. And once the fires were fully awakened, it became more serious as passion took over and inhibitions were cast to the winds. Some tiny remote part of Julian's mind marvelled at this bold abandoned girl whose hands roved and explored as freely as his, whose body pressed ardently against him as her mouth sought his kiss. And then even that awareness was lost as desire rose feverishly: somehow, still twined together, he guided her to the bed, neither of them able to wait any longer for the consummation.

Perkin, lying drowsily in his closet, knew what they did and smiled his satisfaction into the unseeing dark. All was well now. That witless girl with her rages and perverse ideas and wild moods had finally seen sense: she was wed to his master, and might as well make the best of it. And if she enjoyed his bed-skills, so much the better. With a sigh of relief, he rolled over and slept.

In another part of the Palace, Meg lay wakeful, her mind a seething venomous cauldron of rage and jealousy. Somewhere mixed in with it was a desperate bitter yearning for her children, one dead, one living, who would never be hers. By her side Sir Robert slept, having claimed his peculiar conjugal rights: he had never, in all their years of marriage, made any attempt to give her any pleasure, if the inflicting of pain and discomfort on his wife could be called pleasurable. She lay there still and remote, shutting herself off from the hurt, while he worked off both his cruelty and his urge for another heir on her unresponsive body, and then rolled off her and straight into sleep.

And Christie—he might only lust after his wife, but by the look of it she also lusted after him. Meg could not imagine how this agonising undignified act could bring any joy whatsoever to the unfortunate woman, but it seemed that Dame Julian found it so.

Hot bitter tears of envy and unhappiness squeezed from beneath her tight-shut lids and tracked their way down the side of her face into her hair. It isn't fair, whispered the child within her, who had always gone her own way. It isn't *fair*—why should they be happy when I am so miserable? And it's all Christie's fault—if he had answered my letter, if he had come when I asked, if he had not betrayed me, I would not be in this position—he would have calmed my fears, frightened Mistress Slingsby away, saved my first baby—and then I would still have my husband's trust. He doesn't deserve to be happy, and if *she* knew the truth, I'll wager she wouldn't look at him in quite the same way.

With thoughts of vengeance filling her mind, Meg lay wakeful: nor did Dame Alice Bray, in a chamber not far distant, sleep much that Christmas night. She had been appointed Lady Stanley's eyes and ears, after all, and her mind was busy with plots and allegiances, vengeance and victory. There was, too, a more domestic problem to solve. According to his mother, it was probable that the Tudor would invade the following summer: and if his army succeeded, and the usurper defeated, and, please God, justly slain, then what would happen to her daughter? If she became too fond of her despicable husband, Dame Alice could foresee all sorts of complications: if he were killed, and his lands attainted, what would befall Julian if she espoused his cause too strongly, and grieved for him? Doubtless Lady Stanley would speak for Dame Alice, but this Tudor was an unknown quantity, his mercy a doubtful element: and what if the sorrowing widow refused to marry some worthy supporter of the new King, and thus forfeited the lands on which her own comfort, and of course her mother's, depended?

Better all round, Dame Alice decided, her lips compressed, if the silly jade were to be dissuaded, by fair means or foul, from falling in love with her husband. And her mind was still pleasurably going through the various methods she might employ to that end, as she drifted into sleep.

CHAPTER EIGHTEEN

**'And so he chose her for his sovereign lady, and
never to love other but her.'**
(BOOK 4, CHAPTER 21)

For the traditional twelve days until Epiphany, the Palace of
Westminster was given almost entirely over to dancing, feasting
and other vain pursuits. Tables groaned with food and wine,
minstrels wore out their hands and lips in strumming and beating
and piping dance tunes, roundelays and carols: the kitchens were
full of half-naked, exhausted men and even the fertile imagination
of the Master Cook, so adept at compiling new concoctions, at last
seemed to have run out. Surfeited with rich food and enormous
quantities of wine, dazzling still in glorious colourful clothes that
showed signs of wear to the careful observer, the ladies and
gentlemen of the King's household gathered for the climax, the
Epiphany feast, when King and Queen appeared in state in their
crowns, and the greatest revels of the year ended.

Julian sat, her eyes on her husband at another table: more exalted
people than he served the King on this most royal occasion. By
now, it was a standing joke amongst her friends, Cecily in particular, that her gaze could scarcely be torn away from his. Others had
had too much food or drink this season, but of love's banquet she
would never be surfeit.

Cecily had questioned her until, King's daughter or no, Julian
had asked her rather sharply to desist. It was plain that, if she had
not been of such high rank, the girl would long ago have cast virtue
to the winds. She laughed and flirted with troupes of dazzled young
courtiers, her cold dancing grey eyes sliding from one to the next,
and her gowns, like Bess's, were a gift from the Queen, and
magnificent. It had caused not a little comment: Dame Alice,
coupling the favour shown to the bastardised girls with the increasing pallor and obvious sickness of the Queen, was brisk in spreading rumours.

Bess had not questioned Julian, but her wide gentle hazel eyes had
smiled pleasure and congratulations, and Julian had been much
heartened by her obvious approval. The Queen, also noticing the
new understanding between husband and wife, rejoiced, and

instructed her chamberlain to allot a larger chamber for the happy pair. Their evenings, when the revels were ended and Christie was not in attendance on the King nor Julian on the Queen, took on an almost domestic air. Friday sewed, Perkin tended his master's clothing, poured wine and ran errands. Cavall, happy that his beloved mistress now slept in the same chamber, even if he was no longer allowed on the bed, slept before the fire, his narrow head between his paws, and Julian and Christie sprawled together on a nest of cushions, playing music to each other.

With her happiness, her voice took flight: and the songs he sang her were songs of love, sometimes not without a touch of irony. Julian, however, was apt to take such things rather too seriously, and once had to be restrained from beating her lute over his head as he sang a song uncomplimentary to women, though not the one with which he had so insultingly serenaded her at their wedding feast.

To Julian, that time seemed now impossibly remote. They had been married for almost a year, and yet only now were they making the discoveries about each other that the friends and servants of both had known for much longer. Julian was untidy, leaving possessions and clothes scattered for Friday to pick up: she was a restless sleeper too, sprawling everywhere, muttering and dreaming. Christie, on the other hand, was far more reserved in everything he did: his garments, after a lifetime of great households, were always neatly stowed and immaculate, and he slept tidily and still. She was fascinated by his sleeping face, so relaxed and open it seemed to belong to someone else, but never let him know she studied him, for fear of the mockery he now never showed to her. He could be very amusing, however, about the more curious characters of the court, and merciless about their less attractive foibles: and once, asked to play for the King before all his household, provided an extempore series of verses, sung to an old and familiar tune, that satirised, though gently, several well-known figures.

Now, the hundreds of people gathered on this Epiphany, 6 January 1485, ate and drank to the music of professional minstrels, and each course was borne in to the sound of trumpets, with a marvellous subtlety confected in sugar and marchpane, gilt and colour, between each parade of dishes.

There was a sudden stir at the lower end of the Hall, and a man in the livery of a King's Messenger, grimy with the mire of travel, made his way between the long tables to the dais where the King sat in state, his Queen by his side. The murmur died as it was realised that this courier must bring news of the utmost importance, or he would not have presumed to interrupt the festivities without even the benefit of a change of clothes. Heads turned to follow his progress towards the King, and there was utter silence in the Hall as he knelt before his sovereign, his hand outstretched, holding a paper. 'I bring news, Your Grace—news of invasion!'

There was a hushed intake of breath, mostly by those who had forgotten that no invader of any pretensions, let alone Henry Tudor, whose cunning was already notorious, would consider risking a sea crossing in the depths of an unusually windy and chilly winter. The King took the paper, opened it and read rapidly, his lips moving: then, he raised his eyes to his expectant court. 'We have news here of great importance—of invasion, as the messenger said. Our spies in France write that the Tudor is of a certainty planning to invade our realm in this coming summer. It's welcome news—at last we are to be given the chance to eliminate this thorn in our side, once and for all!'

A cheer, spontaneous and full-throated, rang amongst the glorious hammer beams of the roof: and Christie, who had his own reasons for wishing Henry Tudor dead, as did Tyrell roaring enthusiastically opposite him, joined in with the full force of his lungs.

Dame Alice, not far from her daughter, smiled sourly. They could all cheer now, the fools, but time would send them laughing on the other side of their faces. If God's justice meant anything, then the Tudor, last scion of the house of Lancaster, would prevail, *must* prevail, against the murderous usurper who sat there so arrogantly amid his sycophantic courtiers.

*

'News,' said Christie to his wife. 'Good, or bad, you can take your pick—according to how long you wish me to be gone.'

Julian stared at him, frowning, her eyes narrowed. 'I don't wish you to be gone. What do you mean?'

'I have to leave the country—on the King's business.' He spoke lightly, as if it did not matter. But Julian was coming to know him better, and was aware that he disguised his stronger feelings thus. She pulled a stool to her place by the fire, while Cavall, who never greeted anyone but her, lowered his head with a sigh and went back to sleep.

'Leave the country? Is it anything to do with the Tudor?'

'Not directly, no.' He sat down on the stool beside her and, with the ease of habit, put his arm around her shoulders. 'Do you know anything about the Earl of Oxford?'

'He's a supporter of the house of Lancaster, until lately imprisoned at Calais, and now escaped to the Tudor,' said Julian promptly. She was surprised at the cheerful sound of her voice: the prospect of spending an unknown number of nights alone and, worse, perhaps at Ashcott and once more under the aegis of her mother, was an exceedingly desolate one.

'Imprisoned in Hammes Castle, which is near Calais—since about, oh, I should think ten years ago. One James Blount was in charge of him. The King heard that Blount was becoming a little too friendly with Oxford, and decided to bring him back to England. But before he could arrange it, Oxford and Blount escaped to the Tudor in Paris.'

'It happened last autumn, when I was still at Sheriff Hutton—I remember the news coming. Another viper to add to Tudor's nest, the Earl of Lincoln said.' And Julian added, knowing that she would not like the answer, 'What has the Earl of Oxford's escape to do with your going over sea?'

'Because the King, understandably, wants to appoint a new governor at Guisnes, which is the other castle guarding Calais. And the governor he has chosen, very wisely in my opinion, is Sir James Tyrell, and he has asked me to accompany him on his journey, as we are old friends, and to ascertain that a certain person whom I have not seen for some time continues to flourish.'

There was a little silence. 'You mean the Prince?' Julian asked at length, very softly.

'I mean the Prince. You don't need to know anything about his whereabouts—it's not that I don't trust you, but the fewer people who know this, the better.'

'How many people *do* know that he's alive?'

'Myself, of course, and Tyrell: the King and Queen: Bess and Cecily and Dame Grey and the little girls, of course, and Tyrell's household where we stayed: Perkin, and his mother—and you must meet his mother Cis, she has more wisdom in her little finger than most of this household in their heads. The Lord Chancellor, the Duke of Norfolk, Brackenbury, Lord Lovell and sundry other intimates—Ratcliffe and Catesby, and Kendall the secretary. It seems like a long list, but they're all most trustworthy people. And of all these, who know that Dickon is *alive*, and no more than that, perhaps only three or four know exactly where he is, or even that he is out of England.'

Julian thought of that small boy, threatened, hidden, perhaps frightened or bewildered: he was only eleven. She said curiously, 'What's he like?'

'Dickon? Everyone calls him Dickon. The kind of boy any man would be proud to have for a son. Brave, intelligent, generous, good-natured, he's all those things, but more than that, he's Dickon—he has a maturity, a greatness of spirit you don't usually find even in a grown man. If you can imagine Bess, as a small boy, more lively and less dreamy than Bess, but with that same essential quality—then you have Dickon.'

She was silent, hearing the love in his voice as she had heard it in Bess's at Sheriff Hutton, and for a moment felt jealous of this unknown child, who seemed to have a hold on so many hearts. She suppressed the feeling with the hope that soon, God willing, they might both have a son of their own to cherish: it was early days yet, but it did not seem possible that the intense lovemaking which brought each night to a peak of delightful pleasure would not soon have some result.

'You haven't asked the most important questions of all,' he pointed out. 'When am I going, and for how long?'

'Not long?' Julian enquired, trying not to sound too wistful. Despite the increasing closeness of their relationship, she was still wary of exposing her feelings to him. Once in his arms it was different: then another Julian seemed to emerge, more reckless, less inhibited, interested only in their mutual passion. But she still could not be quite easy in his company at times like this, when love-making was not uppermost in their minds.

'Not long, I hope.' His hand played idly with her hair, that in the privacy of their chamber she always wore loose. 'A month or so, no more—just to be sure that Dickon is safe and well-hid. Tyrell and I will leave in about a week—so we have that time still together.' His hands began to stray, and Julian forgot about hidden Princes, and the future, and knew only the delightful present.

*

For the two weeks since Christmas Eve, both Meg Drakelon and Dame Alice Bray, for their own separate yet oddly similar reasons, had been trying to have a private word or two with Julian. Julian, who disliked and distrusted both of them without knowing their intentions, avoided them with the instinctive ease she had perfected in the drear days before Christmas when it had been her husband she must evade. Evenings she spent with Christie, when he was free: days were fully occupied with Mass, breakfast, attendance on the Queen, whose enjoyment of her music had grown as her health faded, pastimes in the company of Bess, Cecily, the Countess of Lincoln and other young women she had come to know at Nottingham, Sherriff Hutton and Westminster. Eventually, however, a break in the weather disrupted the busy Palace routine. The sun came out, the snow melted, and for a space there was in the air a promise of spring, even though it was not long past Epiphany. In happy celebration, the Lady Bess proposed an expedition along the river bank, perhaps as far as the village of Chelsea, with hawk and hound, for the female members of the court. There would be little sport to be had, but a good taste of fresh air and exercise.

Julian, suddenly aware that she had not set foot outside the Palace environs for weeks, welcomed the proposal, as did many others. When they all congregated in the outer court to find the grooms and their eager horses, there were perhaps fifty ladies altogether, with their attendants, all ready for a little exercise between dinner and supper.

The sun was kind, the wind gentle: it was one of those very still clear winter days, cold and yet invigorating, with haze lying over the marshes opposite the Palace, and the trees very black against the vivid blue sky. There was no snow left, but puddles filled all the ruts and hoofprints in the roadway, and the horses churned it up still more, so that the last to pass, assorted grooms and falconers bringing up the rear, were soon mired from head to toe.

Meg rode with the rest: her husband had business with the Signet Office, something about a manor he wanted. In her innocent girlhood, she would have loved such a ride as this: but now all the complexities of her bitterness weighed her down, and she could not enjoy the stark beauties of the day. The little spaniels put up duck and heron along the water, and the great yellow dog that belonged to Dame Julian Heron did much work too, controlled by his mistress's loud unseemly voice. Guided by that sound, Meg manoeuvred her horse, lean from its winter diet and fidgety from lack of exercise, into the other girl's orbit, and waited her opportunity.

It came when the Lady Cecily's pretty merlin, very similar to Julian's own, refused to return to her fist and sat twenty feet up a willow tree, sulking. One of the falconers, with some annoyance, was attempting to retrieve the bird, while the rest of the party watched, or walked their horses round, or drifted onwards. Julian was one of those who looked on, a little apart: she noticed nothing until a soft footfall and the chink of a bit announced the arrival of another horse, and even then she assumed it was Bess, or Lady Morley, until she turned and saw Meg's chill blue eyes staring at her.

'Hallo,' said Julian, as casually as she could: she knew that her sister-in-law had been trying to seek her out, for what reason she did not care to guess. Her own merlin, Elaine, shuffled on her gloved wrist and shook her head inside the beautiful plumed and embroidered hood: Julian soothed her with soft words and a stroking finger. Meg said quietly, 'I have come to make amends and to offer you my apologies for any distress I may have given you. I would like us to be friends, as well as sisters.'

Julian, surprised by this opening gambit, stared at Meg. The other girl was in rich red velvet today, under the enveloping warmth of her cassock, and it became her well. She still did not trust her: but an overture of friendship was not lightly set aside. 'That is my wish also,' she said, courteously. 'Do you enjoy hawking?'

It was an interest they had in common. In the twenty minutes that it took the falconer to retrieve Cecily's errant merlin, they had exchanged a multitude of stories, information and hints about their favourite sport, and Julian, wondering why she had thought this girl cold, gave way to a sudden impulse. 'You may carry my falcon, if you like. Her name is Elaine.'

With evident delight, Meg took the bird onto her own wrist —her riding-glove was thick enough to shield her from the crooked sharp talons—and caressed her gently. 'I have a hawk of my own in Yorkshire—but I could not bring her south. She stays behind, with my baby.'

'You have a child?' Julian asked, surprised: that willowy waist did not seem to be a mother's, somehow. Meg smiled, a sad smile full of bitterness 'I had two. The elder died . . . five months ago. The new one, the baby, Roger, he is four months old, and a week, and three days.'

'And you left him? You left him behind?' Julian stared at her. 'Couldn't you have brought him with you?'

'No—especial care must be taken of him. He's the heir,' Meg explained, and Julian detected the irony in her voice, reminding her very much of Christie, and realised that there was a great deal more about Meg's marriage than at first appeared. Her suspicions were confirmed as the other girl continued. 'I am not even permitted to sully my hands with his swaddling bands or his feeding—I can only watch from a distance.'

'But why, in sweet Mary's name?'

'Because my husband will not trust me, after what happened to our first child. You don't know? Hasn't Christie told you? But no, I don't suppose he would, would he.'

'Why not? What are you talking about?' Julian asked curiously, seeing the glitter in Meg's eyes and the tightness around her mouth. 'Please explain—that is, if it won't distress you too much to talk of it.'

'Distress? Oh, I've wept all the tears I ever had, they've run dry long since,' said Meg savagely. 'Shall I tell you what happened? Would you like to know what your fine and lusty husband is *really* like, when he has no reason to speak you fair? Shall I tell you?'

An awful premonition had come over Julian, a hideous sense of expectancy. Whatever it was, it had affected Meg very deeply: her whole appearance had changed, her body was as taut and upright as a bowstring, her face hard and grim: no sign of the casual, chattering girl that had sat that horse only a few moments ago. 'Tell me,' she said.

'It's a long story—I'll be brief. When I was betrothed to my husband, Christie didn't like the idea. He didn't trust Sir Robert, and he thought that he would not make me happy.' Meg's mouth twisted in a bitter laugh. 'He gave me a promise—he vowed on his honour, that if ever I were to need him, I would summon him—and he would come to my aid. I treated it lightly, being so sure that I was right—but I respected it too, in my heart, for we were closer than most brothers and sisters, we were reared together in the Earl of Northumberland's household, we knew each other, understood each other, loved each other, as no-one else did.' She glanced at Julian's pale, apprehensive face. 'Have you ever had that feeling?'

Surprised at being asked the question, Julian did not answer at first. 'Yes—yes, I suppose—with my father,' she said eventually.

'So you know that closeness. Perhaps you think to find it with Christie—well, what I'm about to tell you will convince you that you're wasting your time if you do. To continue—at first all was well, my marriage was not blissful, it was not a love match after all, but I had what I wanted, and did not doubt that I had done right.

[412]

Then I became pregnant with my first child. Sir Robert was very careful of me—too careful, perhaps. And he went off to the Scots wars, leaving his sister to look after me. And she—' For the first time in Meg's narrative, her voice faltered and her anguish was suddenly plain. 'She—even now I don't know if it was true or not, pregnant women have strange fancies—but I became very ill, and it seemed to me that Sir Robert's sister was trying to poison me, because she wanted the inheritance for her own son.'

There was silence, broken by shouts of encouragement from those watching the falconer. Julian shivered, despite her thick gown and warm cassock-coat. Meg, her eyes bleak, went on. 'I wrote to Christie. He was in Berwick, with the Duke of Gloucester, as the King then was. I begged him to come to me, I reminded him of his promise, I swore that my life might depend on it. And he received that letter, he admitted it to me. He received it, and he did not answer it, because he did not want to jeopardise his position with Gloucester during the war with the Scots. He saw his chance of rising high—and so he betrayed my trust.'

Belying her earlier words, there were tears flowing down Meg's face now, and Julian, almost weeping herself, put out a comforting hand. Ignoring it, Meg forced herself to finish the story. 'I heard nothing, and heard nothing. I thought he had not received the letter—I couldn't believe that he would break his vow. In the end, I was so desperate that I tried to run away—I think by then that I had gone a little mad. And when I lost the baby as a result, I went mad in earnest. Sir Robert kept me locked up, even after I had recovered my wits—he blamed me for the baby's death, and refused to listen when I accused his sister, even though I had only been ill when she was in the house: when she went to York for a while, I grew better. But it *was* through her that I lost the baby, I *know* it was.

'And then Christie came to see me, full of excuses. I could not believe he had actually had my letter, and had done nothing —deliberately, coldly put it down to womanish fancy, and pursued his ambition. And if he had come to me, my first baby would not be dead, and my husband would not have taken my son away from me because he feared I'd go mad again and harm him!'

And Meg put her head in her hand and sobbed as if her heart would break: as, thought Julian miserably, hastily taking charge of the fluttering merlin again, it probably already had. The whole dreadful tale had induced in her a complex tangle of emotions: anger at Sir Robert and his unknown sister, a remote bitter satisfaction that her suspicions of him had been proved correct, sharp grief and pity for Meg, so beautiful, so apparently blessed, and yet so desperately unhappy. But her chief rage was directed against Christie. So clearly could she see him weighing his ambition and his sister in the balance, and discarding Meg as casually and callously as he had once picked up her, Julian, for his wife. Like cards, we are to him, she thought savagely, like cards in a hand he's playing, collected when he has need of us, thrown away when we've served our purpose. And the thought came creeping after, chill: when he no longer wants my body, when—if—I give him his heir, will he discard me too, as both he and Sir Robert have done to Meg?

A cheer announced the retrieval of the falcon: the party was preparing to move on. Bess came up to them, her face concerned. 'Dame Drakelon! Are you all right? What's wrong, Julian?'

'She's grieving for her babe that died,' Julian told her sadly, with partial truth. 'May we return to the Palace?'

'Of course—you don't need to ask! Take one of the grooms,' said Bess, and urged her horse up to touch Meg gently on one trembling shoulder. 'I am so sorry, Dame Drakelon. I have lost a dear sister, and my father too—I know something of what you must feel. May God lend you the strength to overcome your grief, and give you solace.'

But Meg was too desolate even to hear her words of comfort.

With bitterness and anger in her heart, Julian led Meg back to Westminster. Listening wet-eyed as the other girl struggled to control her sobs, the old rage at her husband grew to a grim cold fire within her. What amends, what justification could he possibly make for having ruined her life? And it had not been an ordinary relationship he had had with her, either: closer than are most brothers and sisters, Meg had said. Julian could not imagine Christie being close to anybody: even she and Perkin, who knew him better than anyone, were kept still at a distance. She had learned to guess something of what he thought and felt from the few clues offered by his face and voice, but apart from those two occasions before Christmas, he had never once told her anything of his real emotions. And not even in the wild heat of their lovemaking, had he spoken again of loving her: and she, since she would only speak the truth in such matters, had said nothing of loving him.

I was gulled, thought Julian with fury. I was seduced into his bed and all he wants now from me is an heir, just as all he wanted before

[414]

was my lands. He has no more honest feeling in him than—than a pike or a carp!'

She led Meg to her own chamber, because it was nearest, and installed her by the fire. Friday was sent to cajole ale from any sympathetic chamberlain, and in the absence of Perkin, doubtless with his master or elsewhere in the Palace, Julian prodded the fire into redoubled vigour with a poker and piled fresh wood on top: it would use up most of their allowance for the night, but she did not really care. The ale arrived, still warm, and spiced: 'I told him you were sick,' Friday said to her mistress, while staring with curiosity at the girl by the fire, her tear-streaked face and reddened swollen eyes. 'I had to give him a kiss for it, though.'

Despite that leaden lump of rage in her belly, Julian smiled. 'Be careful, Friday—you don't want the reputation of a wanton.'

'Small chance of it,' said her waiting-woman, though the smile on her face and the flush in her round cheeks indicated that the payment had not been forcibly taken. 'Shall I retire to the closet, Madam?' she added formally. 'I have some sewing to do.'

'Yes, if you would,' said Julian, aware of Meg's pleading eyes upon her. She watched Friday gather up needle, thread and a neat pile of hose, and other mending, and disappear into the tiny chamber next door. Then, drawing up her stool, she sat down by her sister-in-law's side and poured the ale for her. 'Drink this—it will warm you, and cheer you.'

'I don't think the fires of Hell could warm me,' said Meg bleakly: but she took the pewter mug and sipped it, her teeth chattering against the rim. Julian studied her with an agony of pity, knowing that there was no help that she could give, nothing that she could do, now or ever, to ease the terrible pain in Meg's soul. And silently, as she looked at the girl's despairing face, she vowed that somehow, her husband would pay for the dreadful damage he had done to his sister.

Meg put the mug down at last in the smoky warm embers of the hearth, and turned to Julian. 'Thank you—oh, thank you. I feel—a little better now.' She managed a wan smile. 'And now I think I ought to go—Christie might be back, and I don't—I don't think I could face him.'

Neither could I, thought Julian bitterly. Aloud, she said, 'You don't need to worry. He is in attendance upon the King, I think, so we have an hour or so yet. Please—don't go—I can't let you go back to your chamber like that.'

'Oh,' said Meg, with a desperate attempt at humour. 'Do I look so bad, then?'

'It might arouse—curiosity,' said Julian carefully.

Meg touched a hand to her eyes, and brought it down again to clasp the other in her lap. Julian saw that they were shaking. She stared for a long while into the fire: then she said in a low voice, 'I am sorry—so sorry. I had thought myself far stronger than that—I did not mean to give way to my grief. But—there has been no-one at all that I can talk to—no-one else at all.'

Julian stared at her in surprise. 'No friends—no family?'

'I have no friends—I have lost touch with those I had when I was in attendance upon the Countess of Northumberland, and Denby, my husband's manor where I live, is very isolated. Besides, since news of my madness became known, few have cared to visit. Family? My own, the Herons, live their own lives at Bokenfield in Northumberland, and they are like strangers to me, for I spent nearly all my childhood at Alnwick. As for my husband's family, they ignore me at best, for when I gave him his son, I disinherited them. I have had no-one to talk to, all these years.'

Julian found tears creeping down her face. She brushed them away impatiently, and put a hand out to hold Meg's. 'You have a friend now. *I* am your friend.'

Meg stared at her. 'You—you don't hold it against me? That I told you the truth about your husband? I only wanted to warn you—so that you didn't suffer too.'

'I know,' said Julian fiercely. 'And I thank you for it, I don't blame you. It's the truth, and will out, as they say—I would have discovered it one day, I am sure.' She glanced at Meg's white, blotched face and added softly, 'Was it only to warn me, that you told me?'

'No—I wanted revenge as well,' said Meg.

The silence was broken only by the crackle of the fire, the snuffling dreams of Cavall, and distant sounds from the rest of the Palace.

'You may have it,' said Julian at last. In the heat of her anger, her mind was made up: for what was her desire, no, lust, that now seemed to be tainted and repellent, compared with the callousness of the man to whom she was wed? She added, 'I don't think I could bear—could bear to have him touch me again—not after what he has done to you. And he hasn't changed at all: he only married me because I could bring him the lands he wanted, and when I made my hatred plain, he tempted me with soft words, until I climbed into his bed willingly, thinking that he loved me—' She broke off, remembering with shame how she had been gulled, and drew a long quivering breath, fighting to stay calm. 'But now, thank God, you have truly opened my eyes.'

'What will you do?' Meg asked. The ugly colour on her face was fading, her beauty gradually returning: she leaned forward avidly. Julian said slowly, 'I shall go back to Ashcott, I think—he will not follow me, he leaves for Guisnes with Sir James Tyrell in a few days' time, by the King's command.' She laughed, bitterly. 'After what you've said, I doubt he'll cast aside a royal order, even to bring me back. And then—I don't know. Perhaps I'll take a vow of chastity —it can be done without entering a nunnery, I believe. And I shall pray to Our Lady of Walsingham that I am not with child, for if I am not, then he will never have his heir of me!' And she laughed again, with a fierceness worthy of her mother.

At that moment, the door opened, without a knock. Both girls jerked round in surprise, and beheld the brother of one, the husband of the other, standing in the doorway.

His eyes, glinting silver, took in the little scene, so outwardly cosy, and all its hidden, sinister implications. And he saw the malicious triumph of Meg's face, and the blazing, dreadfully familiar rage on Julian's, and his heart beat like a passing bell with the intimation of disaster. As if it might, somehow, stave off the reckoning, he said casually, 'I thought all the ladies had gone hawking—you are back early?'

'Your sister became very distressed,' Julian said. 'I escorted her here to comfort her.' Her eyes held his, the wide brown eyes that had looked at him with passion and desire only last night, and now stared stark with hatred. 'And she has been telling me a tale.'

'A tale?' he said, his voice level, and she smiled, but not with pleasure. 'Yes, a true tale, and a sorry one—it speaks of the betrayal of a sister, and a brother who put his ambition above everything else.' She rose from her stool and walked towards him, her eyes on him still. 'You have no more need to speak fair words of love to me, sir. I know now how thoroughly I have been duped, how I have been enticed and seduced by you, because you could not get your heir on me any other way!' She laughed, a harsh loud sound that echoed nightmarishly in his head as he stared at her advancing figure. She stopped, just a few feet from him, and he realised suddenly that he had not shut the door. He closed it, hoping that

Perkin would not appear, and said, making his voice reasonable, 'Julian, listen. You have heard only Meg's side of the story. Will you not consider mine?'

Behind her, Meg's face was white, greedy, triumphant. He had never seen her look so lovely, nor so cold: and in his heart he faced the terrible fact that he had lost them both. Julian's next words confirmed it. 'Your side of the story? Is there one? Do you deny you ignored Meg's letter in favour of your own ends?'

He was silent, knowing defeat, and it was answer enough. Julian laughed again, scornfully. In her rage she was magnificent, tall, strong, her face brilliant with the force of her hatred, her red-brown hair, unconfined, pouring down her back and breast. 'You cannot deny it. And I can't deny that I loathe you, Christopher Heron, loathe and despise you for ever!'

His own anger was rising now to match hers. 'Julian, will you *listen* to me?'

'No, I will not—I have heard all I want, and I've had enough of your sweet lies to last me for the rest of my life. Understand me,' said Julian savagely, 'I never want to see you again, to touch you again—ugh!' She shivered involuntarily, and saw with triumph the sudden, unmistakeable hurt in his face. 'Never, never, *never*—do you understand me?'

She would have turned away, but his hands shot out to grasp her arm. It was as if he had burned her: Julian cried out, and twisted violently. 'How *dare* you—let go, let *go* of me, let *go*!' With her free hand, she struck out wildly, as hard as she could. The ring he had given her on their wedding day carried a cut ruby: the sharp edge of the gem raked his face, narrowly missing his eye, and left a sudden welling track of bright blood in its wake. Julian felt the grip on her arm loosen, and with a last, urgent effort tore herself free and retreated, gasping, to Meg's side.

Christie stood quite still, feeling the blood running down his face. Even now, with his world, his future utterly in ruins about him, the irony of it was plain: slashed with the ring he had given her, to symbolise their marriage. By the fire, the two girls watched him, their faces white, implacable, vengeful, like the Furies confronting Orestes. He made one, last, desperate appeal, knowing it would be in vain. 'Julian—will you not talk to me, alone?'

'And have you wheedle me into your bed again? God's blood, I will not!' She glanced at Meg. 'I am going. You will give me shelter? I don't want to stay here any longer with—with *that*.'

He stood and watched her gather her things, because his pride would not let him do anything else. She called Friday, who crept white-faced from the closet and began to throw garments into bags, and then turned to him, with those great brown eyes full of the contemptuous loathing he thought his love had banished for ever. 'Farewell, husband. You are finally rid of me.' And cloaked with dramatic fury, she swept from the room, with Meg, Cavall and Friday in her wake.

It might have been laughable. It was not. Standing there, he was conscious only of the desire to weep, that he had not experienced since he was a lonely homesick child first at Alnwick. Then a helpless, desperate fury took control instead: he turned and smashed his fist against the iron-clad wood of the door.

*

Perkin found him, a few moments later, washing his hand in the little basin of water kept on the clothes-chest. His master's face was masked on one side in blood, and the basin was tinged with pink. Perkin stared in horrified astonishment. 'Sweet Jesus! What's happened here?'

'I lost my temper,' said Christie, looking down at his hand. The knuckles were a mass of torn, bleeding skin, leaking into the water. Perkin came to his side and peered at the damage. 'What in God's name did you do?'

'I hit the door. As you might guess, the door won the battle with some ease.'

'I can see that,' said Perkin 'I'll bind it up for you, sir—wait a moment.' He vanished into the closet and re-appeared a few seconds later with some strips of old linen, and an expression of bewilderment on his ugly face. 'All Dame Julian's clothes have gone.'

'I know they have, witless one—and so has she.'

There was a moment of appalled silence. Perkin said at the end of it, 'Gone? Dame Julian, gone? Where?'

'Ashcott, Wales, Araby the blest—I don't know. All I know is, she's gone—and for good, knowing Julian. Can't you do that without hurting?'

'No,' said Perkin. He strapped up the hand with brisk, uncaring efficiency and then stared at his master's haunted, damaged face. 'Did she do that?'

'What do you think? I'd hardly do it myself. If I wanted to cut my own throat, I'd be slightly more efficient.'

'Why?' Perkin demanded doggedly. 'Why did she do it? Why did she go? I thought—I thought it was all set to rights between you.'

'It was—until my sister took it upon herself to interfere. She told Julian about the letter that I didn't answer—and how she lost her first child, and her husband's trust in consequence.' He smiled, bitterly. 'And I suppose you could say it was justice done, in a way. I put my ambition first, and in so doing ruined her life. Now she has told Julian the truth, and turned her utterly against me: and if by that she has destroyed all my hopes, then perhaps it is a fair revenge.'

'It seems to have addled your wits as well as your face,' said Perkin roundly. 'Fair revenge? Justice? Don't give me that!'

Christie laughed, a bitter weary sound. 'I should flay your skin from your flesh for your insolence—Perkin, lad, your concern for me does you great credit, but there's nothing you can do about it, nothing at all—you didn't see her face.'

'I may not have done, but you're wrong—I'll alter this, I'll set it right, if I take a year doing it, nor my name ain't Perkin Hobbes!'

*

Dame Alice, reading a pious work lent to her some time ago by Margaret Beaufort, looked up in affronted surprise as the door to her chamber burst open unannounced. It slammed shut behind the wild, dishevelled figure of her daughter Julian, her meek bovine maid behind her. 'Daughter! What are you doing here, girl? What does this mean?'

'Help me,' said Julian. 'Please, Mother, I can't bear it here any longer—never want to see him again—please, Mother, take me home to Ashcott!'

And Dame Alice smiled blithely at the unexpected fulfilment of all her hopes. 'Of course, my dear child—as soon as you wish.'

*

'She's gone,' said Perkin flatly.

It had been an unhappy evening, and a worse night. Christie had retreated into silence, but not, to Perkin's heartfelt relief, to the wine-jug. He had not gone to supper, and his livery of wine, ale and bread remained untouched. Tyrell had appeared at one point with a curious, slightly anxious face, and Perkin, firmly barring the door, had explained mendaciously that his master was suffering a slight sickness and would undoubtedly be well again tomorrow. Tyrell expressed his concern, was told that there was nothing he could do, and went away reassured. Perkin had bathed Christie's slashed face, and privately hoped that there would be no permanent scar, while running various possible explanations through his mind that could be offered to his master's friends and colleagues. Then, mentally cursing the stupid hot-headed impetuous girl who was the cause of all this, he had retired to the closet, but not to sleep.

And very, very late that night, when even the ceaseless hum of the Palace had died away into silence, Perkin heard the first soft notes of Christie's lute, falling into the stillness. He did not know that it was in a minor key: he heard only the sadness, yearning and desperation, in the intricate sound of the notes. Christie played for some time: some of it, Perkin recognised, and one, over and over again, as the tune that began, 'I have a young sister'.

Curse her, thought Perkin viciously: curse them both, for what they've done. And tomorrow, bright and early, I'll do all I can to put it right. God damn all women to Hell!

He went in search of Julian the next day, but discreetly: he did not want it noised through all of Westminster that Sir Christopher Heron's wife had left him. No-one had seen her, there was no sign of her: and in the end, in desperation, he tried the chamber he knew had been allotted to Dame Alice Bray.

A Palace servant opened the door, broom in hand: behind him, the chamber was bare, neat, empty. 'Dame Bray is not here,' said the man courteously. 'She has returned to her home, I believe: she left at dawn this morning.'

Then Perkin knew the worst: but he still must ask, and make certain. 'Was she alone?'

'No, she wasn't—her daughter was with her, so I've heard,' said the servant, without interest. Perkin thanked him, and returned with leaden feet to convey the news to his master.

Christie was writing something when he entered: disaster might have struck, but there were still estates to be run, offices to be performed, duties to be done. He did not look as if he had slept at all, and the gash along his face was red and angry. 'Well, Perkin the diligent? What have you discovered, since you've undoubtedly been about my business again?'

And Perkin gave his news.

There was silence, in which Christie stared at the paper before him. Perkin, craning surreptitiously to look, did not think it was a letter, nor yet an official document. He could not write his own name, but he knew a song or a poem when he saw it.

'To Ashcott?' Christie said. His voice, to his surprise, sounded almost normal. 'She has gone to Ashcott with Dame Alice? Things must be bad indeed.'

Perkin, his eyes on the bandaged hand, the scarred face, said nothing. After a while, Christie said, still in the same conversational tone, 'I'm sure you can find something to occupy you elsewhere. For the present, my own company is enough for me. Go visit Cis—she hasn't seen you since Christmas. You're free for the day, Perkin my lad—go do what you will.'

And he did: and not what Christie would like, for with righteous anger in his heart, he went to find Meg Drakelon.

He had already seen Sir Robert in his earlier travels through the Palace, on his way to some official. There was a good chance that he would find Meg alone in their chamber, and so it proved: a maid let him in when he said that he had a message for her mistress, and he came face to face with the tall willowy girl he had only previously seen at a distance.

She was like Christie, but beautiful: and like him, thought Perkin, cold and calculating. But did she have a heart and soul as he did, however deeply buried? Or was she chill stone all through?

'I crave a word with you alone, Dame Drakelon,' he said formally, and in the superior accents he had learned to assume on important occasions. The girl's fair, almost invisible eyebrows rose: they were finely and artfully plucked, much more effectively than Julian's, and Perkin, who had assimilated many stray scraps of knowledge and wisdom in his scant nineteen or so years of life, noticed the delicate rouge cunningly concealing her pallor. 'Alone? You're my brother's servant, aren't you? Very well. Mariot, you may leave us.'

The waiting woman, a diminutive figure in a gown of dull blue, crept from the room. Meg sat down on the windowseat cushions and leaned her back against the stone. She wore one of the new hoods in the French style, the edges turned back to frame her lovely face, and the clinging lines of her blue damask gown and the gold-threaded girdle emphasised her sinuous waist. Perkin could understand why Sir Robert had wanted to marry her: half the men of England might have felt the same. But was she like the old Queen? Did her beauty hide a nature that was chill, rapacious and uncaring?

[422]

There was only one way to find out, and he was not afraid of her for himself. He came straight to the point. 'I've come on behalf of your brother, lady—but he doesn't know I'm here, if you follow me.'

One fair brow was raised, in a way extraordinarily reminiscent of Christie. 'Perhaps I do. What do you want?'

'Peace,' said Perkin simply.

There was a small silence: then Meg laughed. 'Peace? What has that to go with me?'

'Everything, since you destroyed it,' said Perkin. He knew he was being rude, but he could not help it: he had to risk alienating this woman, to drive his message home. He saw her mouth open, and hurried on. 'Listen to me, lady, and I'll tell you plain. My master may have done you wrong years ago, he doesn't deny it, and I don't. You've paid for it, true enough—but *so has he.*'

'Really?'

The cool tone infuriated Perkin. 'Yes, lady, *really.* Sweet Virgin, if you'd seen him—oh, yes, he has paid, he loved you, that's plain, and still does—even before yesterday, your quarrel hurt him. I know him better than most,' Perkin said, and added angrily, 'Better than you, it seems. Ever since then he's been wanting to make amends—he's changed. God's bones, he *loves* that girl—you should have seen him last night, and this morning—and I suppose you're satisfied now, ain't you, three lives spoilt, not just one —well, you've had your revenge, lady, are you enjoying it?'

Meg rose to her feet, her face pinched with anger: no need of rouge now, with the fury blazing on her cheeks. 'I think you've said enough, you impertinent little rat—now go, before I forget myself. Go on—get out!'

Ladies in a rage held no terrors for Perkin, who had survived both his mother's and Julian's. He stood his ground, a small slight figure with the hard-won assurance of any street-reared child, and delivered his final hit, to strike home or not, as she pleased. 'There's a tune, Dame Drakelon. Do you know it? It goes something like this.' And in his dry throat, hummed the first notes of 'I have a young sister'.

Meg's face changed for an instant, and he saw something there —regret? reminiscence? grief?—before the mask of fury returned. 'I know it. Get out.'

'He was playing it on his lute last night,' Perkin said. 'Over and over, till I got sick of hearing it. I thought you might know it. Good

[423]

day to you, Dame Drakelon.' And with haste, he made his bow and retreated, shutting the door just a little too loudly behind him.

Meg stood in the middle of her chamber, wishing that she had thrown something, anything, done whatever was necessary to reduce that dreadful upstart impertinent little knave to his proper level. Her hands clenched, her teeth gritted together, she turned and paced restlessly about the room like something caged, unable to keep still, and then flung herself down onto the cushions on the windowseat. Her elbow knocked the stones, sending a tingling, agonising pain through her arm: but it was not that which caused her, suddenly, to bury her head in her hands and burst into heartbroken tears.

She did not know then why she wept. Only gradually did some semblance of normality return, although the nameless grief still remained as sharp and agonising as a knife, stabbing anew at an old wound. Why am I crying, she wondered, with surprise. Why am I weeping, when I have won? I have what I have wanted all these years, I have had my revenge—and oh, how sweet it was!

It was not sweet now. She forced herself to face reality. She had carried three children: the first two were dead, the third denied to her. There was a chance that further children might be allowed to stay in her care, but she doubted it: and besides, she loathed Sir Robert, his deliberate cruelty, his evasiveness and coldness and the perverted lechery which had led him to marry her, and which ever since had repelled her, even as she had encouraged it, desperate to hold his interest in any way possible, with her close-fitting gowns and skilful use of cosmetics. Their marriage was a mockery, a sham, as hollow and worthless as a shrivelled hazel husk: she could seek no comfort there, nor from her own family, who had washed their hands of her with relief on her wedding, and were now pursuing their own concerns. The only true friend she had ever had was her brother: and she had destroyed his happiness too.

I must have been mad, thought Meg, staring out of the window at the privy garden below, deserted and bleak on this cold January day. Sweet Mary, mother of God, help me—forgive me. What have I done?

She remembered the agony she had felt during the early days of her marriage, when she had believed that Mistress Slingsby had been poisoning her. That had not been Christie's fault. He had betrayed his promise, true—but he has paid, had said that disgracefully impudent servant. And she remembered the pain on his face as Julian berated him, and the look in his eyes as they left.

And he had played that tune, over and over again, late at night, the song that had once been their own.

> When a maiden hath her love,
> Then she is without grief.

'I will have what I want, and be happy.' The words of the young Meg echoed chillingly down the years, tragically, criminally confident in her ability to mould events, and people, to her wishes. She had failed: she had learned that in some things she was utterly powerless. And her overweening arrogance had brought her here, to this chamber in the Palace of Westminster, with no love in her life: husband, brother, children, all denied her for one reason or another. And the vengeance for which she had hungered and planned and longed for nearly three years was as ashes in her mouth.

For a long while she sat there, the tears drying on her face, irresolute, her heart pulling one way, her pride another, while she looked into the lonely tunnel of her future, and found no comfort. Her maid appeared, obsequious but sly: Meg knew that she reported everything to Sir Robert, and had undoubtedly heard every word of her conversation with Perkin. She found that she did not care: all her thoughts were concentrated, increasingly, on her brother, and that image, desperate and haunting, of the song played over and over again in the silence of the night.

She came to a decision, and stood up. 'Mariot, go into the closet, and look over my best gown—I think the hem needs cleaning and brushing, and I wish to wear it tonight.' And when the woman had vanished to do her task, Meg slipped silently to the door, lifted the latch and slid through it.

She found her brother's chamber easily enough. She did not know if he would be there: his duties were irregular. Most likely, she would be faced with the knowing insolent servant. She took a deep breath, and knocked.

Silence. She knocked again, and before she could take her hand away, the door opened. Disconcerted, Meg stared at her brother. He was clad only in shirt and hose, and he did not appear to have slept, nor shaved. He looked older, and tired, and desperately heartsick: and suddenly, Meg knew that she had done right. 'May I come in?' she asked quietly.

He would have slammed the door in her face: but he saw the

tear-tracks upon it, and the reddened eyes, and something stopped him. His eyes took on a wary, suspicious look, but he said evenly, 'Yes—if you must.'

She walked past him into the chamber where, not twenty-four hours previously, she had persuaded his wife to leave him. To her relief, it was empty. There was no servant: no dog slumbering by the fire, though of course that was Julian's. Meg glanced around, and then said, 'Can we talk?'

'Talk away—I'll listen or not, as I please.'

The level voice told her nothing. Meg, with unhappiness, knew that this would not be easy: to understand her change of mind would be hard enough, to accept it still more difficult. He had every justification for throwing her out of the room as soon as she tried to offer her inadequate apologies and overtures of friendship: and somehow that prospect was hardest of all to bear.

With a gulp of air, she said abruptly, 'I came to say—that I am sorry. Sorry for what I did. I wish to make amends.'

There was a moment's disbelieving silence, and then he laughed, a cold bitter sound. 'Amends? You? That's rich indeed! Why should you? You've had your vengeance, you've turned Julian against me—now get out.'

'No,' said Meg. 'No, I won't. Christie, listen. Please listen. I have wronged you. I have bitterly wronged you, and you have every reason to hate me now. But I—this morning I realised what I had done. Whatever you did to me was in the past. We have both altered since then, and I think you've changed for the better, while I have not. I—I've been alone for a long time, with my dreams of revenge. All my life has been chained up with it, and now that I have freed myself, I can see how empty it is, how cruel and stupid I have been—and you are my only friend in the world, or you were once.'

The words sounded glib, but he could tell, he had always known, the quality of her sincerity by the tone of her voice. And now, she was speaking the truth. He wanted to believe her, and yet he did not, for if she was not lying, then Julian was gone for nothing, and tomorrow he must leave for Calais with Tyrell. He searched his sister's face, the reddened eyes, the trembling mouth, and found there only remorse, and guilt, and desperate sorrow.

'Do you love her?' Meg whispered: and Christie, his control suddenly slipping away from him, turned savagely and buried his face in his hands. It was answer enough. Her tears suddenly flooding her face, Meg ran and flung her arms about him: he turned and seized her in an embrace that almost cracked her bones, while she wept into his shoulder, sobbing her regrets, and his hand stroked her hair: her hood had fallen on the floor.

She drew back at last, dabbing at her eyes with a tiny kerchief that was quite inadequate. With a wry smile, he offered her a larger one. She saw clearly for the first time his bandaged hand. 'What happened?'

'I hit the door in a fit of temper,' said Christie ruefully. He surveyed his sister, her wrecked and drowned beauty, as she scrubbed at her swollen face with the rough linen. 'I think I have some wine, though it might be rather stale—it was my nightly livery, and I didn't drink it. Remarkable self-control, don't you think?'

'You never drank much anyway,' Meg pointed out.

'True. I dislike being out of control of myself—it can be dangerous, on occasion.' He did not tell her of the last time he had set out deliberately to get drunk, in the aftermath of their estrangement. He had thought then that she was lost to him for ever: even now, with her wan face echoing her remorse, he could not quite believe it. He poured wine for her, with a hand that was not quite steady despite all his efforts, and some for himself. It tasted flat and metallic after twelve hours spent in a pewter jug, but its fortifying effects were undiminished. He led Meg to the bed, which had been made up for the day, and she sat down, her golden hair in glorious disarray around her. He hitched himself onto the windowseat and surveyed her as she sipped the wine, seeing the changes in her, the hard lines about her mouth and the narrowed eyes shadowed by strain. She had not been happy, nor had she achieved her desires: and her vengeance was hollow, desperately regretted as soon as accomplished.

'Do you mean it?' he asked. Her eyes, vividly blue, lifted abruptly to meet his, with nothing in them but the bitter truth. 'Oh, yes,' said Meg, very low. 'Oh, yes, I mean it—you have paid the price of our quarrel, and so now have I.'

'You have left one person out of the reckoning,' he reminded her. 'Julian. And she's the innocent one in all this. You only used her as a weapon to strike at me—a weapon all too willing, as it turned out, but still innocent.'

'I know!' Meg cried, her hands twisting on the stem of the wine-cup. 'Do you think I don't know that? Though she surprised me,' she added after a while. 'I didn't expect her to be so ready to hate you.'

'It's because she hated me before: and she's an impetuous person, at the mercy of every mood and feeling. We have been married nearly a year: it was only here, this Christmas, that I could persuade her to look at me with something other than loathing. She has a nature passionate and generous in every emotion: love, hatred, desire, she can overflow with them all. I aroused her hatred first, then her passion—I had hoped that love would follow.'

'Perhaps it still may,' Meg suggested, after the sad silence had lingered too long. 'Can we not go to her, and explain?'

'I can't, for two reasons. Firstly, Julian left for Ashcott this morning, in company with her mother, who's no friend to me either. And secondly, I go to Calais tomorrow, with Sir James Tyrell, and I may not be back for some time.'

Meg stared at him despairingly. 'But there *must*—there must be something we can do—I can't just leave the situation like this!'

'Why not? You caused it.' He caught himself up with a muttered curse, and came over to take her into a warm and brotherly embrace. 'Meg, I'm sorry. Sometimes my bitterness gets the better of me. I will write to her, before I go, and try to explain—though, knowing Julian, I doubt very much she'll even bother to read it, let alone believe me.'

'I can write to her,' Meg told him. 'She might read my letter, and place more trust in me than in you—and if I write to tell her of my sorrow, of how we have mended our quarrel, how it was all a misunderstanding—'

'But it was not. I broke my promise to you, and you suffered for it. That is the simple, basic truth, however much you or I might try to disguise it.'

'Yes, I suppose it is,' said Meg slowly. 'But—but I know now that it doesn't *matter*, not so much as I thought it did, and nothing besides our friendship, and your own marriage. And my other babies—Katherine, may God keep her sweet soul, and Roger—they came to no harm because of you. Katherine's death had nothing to do with you, or Sir Robert, or me—she was sickly and ailing from birth.' And she sat staring at her hands lying in her lap, while the tears dripped onto the fine damask of her gown.

'Meg.' Christie's voice was very gentle: she looked up and saw his face, concerned, loving, as she had never seen it before, save when he looked at his wife. 'Meg. Has it been very bad? Tell me about Sir Robert—tell me about your children.'

It took a long time. She had never confided any of this before, and guilt, as well as emotion, tied her tongue and caused her mind to falter. But in the end the pitiable tale was told, of a loveless marriage based on perverted cruelty, children dead or taken, grief and fear and mistrust. Words of comfort, regret, sympathy, seemed inadequate in the face of Meg's tormented life at Denby: so Christie held her trembling hands, and listened, and said nothing: for in the end, if their love was strong again, there was no need of words.

CHAPTER NINETEEN

'I trust she will have pity upon me at the last.'
(BOOK 4, CHAPTER 21)

Julian stared at her face in the little mirror that Friday held, surveying the pinched mouth, shadowed eyes and lack of colour with weary unhappiness: then she turned away. 'That will do, Friday.'

The waiting-woman put the mirror down and retreated, brush in hand. 'It will soon be supper-time, it's getting dark. Will you come down, Julian?'

'I might,' said her mistress, listlessly. 'Will you bring me my book? The *Romance of the Rose?* It's in the winter parlour.'

When Friday had gone, she picked up the mirror again, moving it up and down to reflect her body as well as her face. No sign, yet: the new-styled, clinging gown disguised little, and did not flatter her, but the curves it revealed had always been there, though sometimes to a greater degree than now. But sooner or later, her mother would discover the truth.

Later, rather than sooner, she hoped fervently. The unfortunate fact of her pregnancy was bad enough news for Julian: she trembled to think of the effect it would have on her mother.

They had been back at Ashcott for three weeks now, and Dame Alice had not let an hour, let alone a day, go by without expressing her satisfaction at the rift between her daughter and her husband. At first it had been balm to Julian's sore, betrayed feelings: but over the last ten days or so, her reaction had changed first to annoyance and then to intense dislike. In that first agony of rage, she had turned to Dame Alice for help and support, but her mother's jubilant attitude, and her frequently-spouted pleasure in being proved right, had rapidly galled Julian.

She had begun to wonder, instead, whether she had not made a grievous error in so high-handedly dismissing Christie from her life, at Meg's greedy behest. With the other girl's despair still fresh and appalling in her memory, it had been easy to allow herself to be swept along by her sister-in-law's very natural grief and anger. But at Ashcott, with only Dame Alice's hostile, contemptuous comments on her husband for company, the habit of years had reasserted itself: Julian found, to her confusion, she was beginning to hold the opposite opinion. Doubt crept into her heart, and would not be ignored, despite all her efforts. Meg's hatred, whilst harboured for apparently justifiable reasons, really had nothing at all to do with the fragile, growing flower of Julian's relationship with Christie. Meg had wanted her revenge on her brother: and due to Julian's eagerness to believe any tale that could be told of her husband, however damning, and the ease with which the older girl's emotions had swept her into a return of her own hostility, she had succeeded.

It was with difficulty, and shame, that she acknowledged to herself she might, possibly, have been wrong. But she would have died rather than admit it to Dame Alice, secure in the certainty that her daughter would never be reconciled to her husband: and there was no chance to acquaint Christie with her doubts, her tentative change of heart, for he had gone overseas, and she had no idea of his whereabouts, nor for how long he would be gone. She was alone, save for her garrulous, malevolent mother: as she listened to tirade after tirade on the subject of her absent husband, Julian longed to tell her roundly to hold her tongue, but still, somehow, could not quite dare. The habit of years died hard, and she had no-one to support her.

Save Marten. The steward had come to her in the first week when Dame Alice was busy in the kitchen, and craved a few minutes of her time. Julian had followed him, slightly mystified, to the estate room, stacked with account books and papers, the chequer board to reckon the sums, dominated by the great chest with its three locks, that contained the surplus wealth of the estate. Marten had pulled up a stool for her, and had showed her the accounts for the ten months or so since she and Christie had left Ashcott to go to Nottingham. For a moment she stared blankly at the neat columns of figures and details: 'Paid Thomas the Grocer of Oxford, 2 loaves of sugar, 7lbs at 6d a pound, ½lb of cloves, 16d, cinnamon, ¾d, 1lb of ginger, 2 shillings.' Then Marten's calm practical voice began explaining, detailing, turning pages to show her the totals for the months and, at Michaelmas, for the year: wages, expenses, receipts.

'There is a discrepancy,' said Marten. Julian was staring at the signature on the bottom of the page: 'This checked by me Alice Bray Michaelmas 2 Ric. iii'. The heavy spluttering hand contrasted strangely with Marten's neat writing: but the signature of her husband, a few pages earlier, had produced in her a surprisingly sharp pain, compounded of doubt, and desire, and regret. She returned to the present with an effort. 'Discrepancy? Where, Marten? I can't see one.'

'Not here,' said the steward patiently. 'As is usual, the receipts from your husband's estates far outweigh the expenses incurred. The discrepancy is *there*—in the chest.' He jerked a thumb towards it. 'I checked it last week. According to my reckoning, over three hundred pounds is missing.'

For a moment, she was too stunned to speak. It was a vast sum: almost enough to keep a family in lord's estate for a year. Finally, her voice came out in a strangled squeak. 'Three *hundred*? As much as that? Are you sure, Marten?'

'I'm sure,' said the steward soberly. 'Like you, Dame Julian, I couldn't believe it. But I've checked, and checked again. Since Michaelmas, someone has taken three hundred pounds in coin from that chest, and replaced it with stones in the same bags.'

There was a taut silence. Then Julian raised her eyes to his and said deliberately, 'Who keeps the keys?'

'I have one set of them here.' He patted the ring hanging from his belt. 'And your lady mother has the other. No-one else.'

This time, the silence threatened to go on for ever. Julian broke it at last, with a deep breath to gather her courage. 'So—the probability is that my mother has taken the money.'

'It grieves me deeply to say so, Dame Julian, but yes, that is my thinking.'

'But she has her dower—the marriage agreement settled her dower on her! She has no *need* to take money—and certainly not so *much* money.'

'Dame Julian—' Marten coughed and carried on, diffidently. 'Lady, you have been absent for almost a year, during which time there have been many comings and goings here at Ashcott. I am not sure, lady, I repeat, I am not *sure*—but I think that the money may have gone overseas, to Henry Tudor.'

'Oh sweet Jesus Christ,' said Julian, and stared at him, horrified, her hands to her mouth. Marten shook his head sadly. 'I wish it were not so, lady, I wish with all my heart it were not so. But I have eyes, and ears, and a good mind, and I can put two and two together as well as anyone else. Did you know that your mother had visited the Lady Stanley?'

Mute, Julian shook her head.

'Or that your cousin, Reginald Bray, who is a pardoned traitor, has come to Ashcott quite frequently?'

'No.' It came in a whisper. Marten stared at her compassionately, and with hope: this girl, if made of the stuff he suspected, might be able to withstand her mother. And certainly her sojourn at the King's court had made a great difference to her appearance and her manner. Her response now, obviously, was to think over the implications rather than to rage or wring her hands, undoubtedly not the old Julian. He waited, watching the deepening frown between the strong chestnut brows. Her head came up abruptly. 'Is my mother plotting with the Tudor, do you think? Tell me—honestly.'

'Yes, I do think so.' Marten hesitated, and then added, 'When is Sir Christopher expected?'

There was a startled silence, with another, deeper quality woven into it, which he could not interpret: then she said slowly, 'I don't know. He has gone to Calais on the King's business. I don't—he didn't tell me when he would be back.' And a blush, bright and telling, suffused her face, as she met Marten's serious gaze.

'That is indeed a shame,' said the steward, with deep regret. 'A very great pity indeed—surely he will not be long gone?'

'I don't know!' Julian cried suddenly. 'Oh, dear Christ, I don't *know*—I wish to God I did!' And she jumped up and ran from the room.

That had been in the first week, and the first time that she had admitted to herself that she wanted him back. Now, what she had suspected had come to pass. She was pregnant. She had kept her secret from Friday, though the maid would surely guess sooner or later. But Ashcott, that had once seemed a refuge, was now rapidly coming to be something more akin to nightmare. She could have stayed at court: instead, she was here, expecting a child whose existence she dared not confess, under the eyes of a mother who was stealing huge sums of money from her estate, and plotting treason behind her back, and her only hope of salvation was the husband she had impetuously rejected, and whose departure she was coming to regret with increasing bitterness.

If it had not been happening to her, she might have laughed.

It had taken an enormous amount of willpower to endure the loneliness of her nights. She had banished Friday to the truckle bed, and slept alone, restlessly, with Cavall creeping on every night illicitly to warm her. But all her pride, her confused memories of hatred, could not obliterate the empty ache that her body felt, the awakened hunger unassuaged, her cold skin touched only by the night air, the prickly sheet, Cavall's rough warm fur. With bewildered misery, she realised that she missed her husband—no, not him, his lovemaking—with humiliating, insufferable force.

And the result of that lovemaking lay curled and minute in her belly, to grow and swell into that which he most wanted, and her mother most dreaded: a Heron heir to Ashcott. She could see now, as clearly as if writ before her in letters of stone, what Dame Alice planned. Henry Tudor would invade that summer. It was inconceivable, of course, that he would succeed against the King, who was also the best soldier in England, but doubtless her mother hoped for miracles. And if he did—she forced herself to ponder the hypothesis with logic and reason. If he did succeed, and the King was killed or sent into exile, there was a good chance that Christie, one of his most intimate lieutenants, would share his fate. She, Julian, would be left the widow of, probably, an attainted traitor whose lands would be forfeit if Dame Alice did not use her friendship with the Tudor's mother, and her help for his cause, to good effect. In that case, she would be a rich widow, a magnificent prize for anyone in search of an heiress: and doubtless she would have as little say in her second marriage as she had in her first.

But if she had a child, a son who was the lawful heir of his father, then she would be no prize at all, her child would be put in the new King's wardship, perhaps brought up in another household, a stranger, while the new King controlled his lands and kept his mother in a nunnery—

She shivered, and bethought herself of Meg, who had believed that her husband's sister was trying to bring about a miscarriage by poison, and whose own son had been put in the care of another, leaving her bereft. The memory of the distress and grief on Meg's face lingered still, sharp and clear, a potent reminder of what, at the worst, might lie in wait for her.

And more than anything else, she dreaded confessing it to her mother.

But the day of reckoning was unexpectedly delayed. Late in February, on a day of cold steady rain, a man arrived at Ashcott in the King's livery. At first Julian, peering through the distorting glass of the hall at the hunched sodden figure dismounting in the courtyard, thought that it was Christie, and her heart gave a great leap. She had not heard from him at all, had not expected to: and the absence of any communication had at once caused her sorrow and, more disconcertingly, annoyance: as if she wanted him to lay proofs of his love before her, like a knight in a romance, wooing his scornful lady. It was one more tangle in the already hopelessly confused skein of her unruly emotions.

But this messenger might bring news of her husband. She hovered by the door, and behind her, Dame Alice, who had seen the man's arrival from an upstairs window, entered the hall in some haste. She had made the same deduction as her daughter, and was anxious to intercept any message. There had been one a few weeks ago, not long after their return to Ashcott: the writing had not been Christie's, but it had been addressed to Julian, and Dame Alice was taking no chances. She had guessed right: the letter had been from Christie's sister, asking to mediate in a reconciliation between him and his wife, and Dame Alice had had no compunction in throwing it on to the fire.

But Julian was already in the hall: and the man entered, escorted by Marten, dripping water everywhere. 'I bring a letter from the King's Grace to Dame Julian Heron.'

'I am she,' said Julian, her heart thumping suddenly: what news was this?

Behind her, Dame Alice relaxed slightly. The man drew a letter from the oiled leather saddlebag he carried, and handed it to her. She broke it open and scanned the few, neat lines, in the hand of the King's secretary, Kendall, before raising her eyes to her mother's avid face. 'The King commands me to Westminster, as soon as may be. The Queen is sick, and desires my attendance.'

Dame Alice let go a long heavy sigh of relief. She would welcome her daughter's absence for a season, the better to further her plots. 'Then if you are commanded, of course you must go.' She smiled. 'I shall order Friday to pack at once.'

*

And so Julian rode again to Westminster, hunched in a soaked travelling cloak on her subdued palfrey Cygnus, with Cavall trotting gloomily beside her through the mud, the King's Messenger their escort and Friday similarly enveloped and moreover in the throes of a head-cold, plodding miserably behind. It took four days because of the parlous and mired state of the roads, but on the first day of March, she saw again the white stones of Westminster Palace, and entered the familiar courtyard.

[435]

She was allotted a small chamber within the Queen's apartments, and had barely time to wash the stains of travel away with warm water, and to change into her best dark green gown, before she was summoned to Anne's chamber. She had prepared herself, remembering that the Queen had already been ailing at Christmas, but she did not at first recognise the skeletal woman who lay listlessly on a daybed strewn with cushions, while her niece Bess read to her.

'Dame Julian! My dear, I did not look for you so soon.' Anne gave her hand: it was pale, the skin translucent, the veins standing out stark and blue like those of a very old woman. Appalled, Julian's face mirrored her distress too plainly. Anne shook her head. 'Do not look so sad, Julian. It's naught but a winter sickness: the doctors tell me I shall be well as soon as the days lengthen and the sun dares to show his face again. And there's one thing shall make me better, and that is your sweet singing and playing. I hope you have your lute? I have longed to hear your voice again.'

'I have tried,' said Bess, with a rueful grin. 'But my singing is like a corncrake's compared to yours, Julian.' Her hazel eyes met those of the younger girl, significantly. 'So I suggested that you be sent for. Cecily and I have missed you, too.'

The lute was brought, and Julian, with sadness, began to play and sing. And as her fingers moved effortlessly over the strings, and her voice soared in plaintive lament, she saw Bess's gentle dreamy face turn away, to hide her tears.

It was plain to all at Westminster that Queen Anne was dying. The doctors had done everything in their power, urged on by a desperate King who had lost his only son and now could not bear to lose his beloved wife, the companion of his childhood and adult years, as well. They had banished him from her bed, for fear of contagion, but he came to see her every day for hours at a time, reading, talking, listening to the music of Julian or other, more skilful but perhaps less moving players. And Julian, seeing his tenderness, his love, his grief, wondered how she could ever have thought this man a monster.

Only the Queen seemed to be cheerful, and at first Julian could not believe that she knew nothing, felt nothing of her approaching death: especially when the flesh had fallen from her bones, leaving only the gaunt travesty of the Queen whose grace and gentleness had won her many friends. But, seeing her with the King, Julian realised that her confident belief in her imminent recovery was a false show, put on for Richard's benefit and that of her nieces, so that they might be heartened. Anne knew as well as everyone else, that the slow, agonising consumption of the lungs from which she was suffering, would soon kill her.

Not a week after Julian's arrival, the day came when the Queen could not muster the strength to rise from her bed. Her ladies tended her: Bess was never far from her side, and Julian played music, soothing, merry or sad according to the Queen's request, until her fingers were sore and aching and her head numb with songs and sorrow.

And on the sixteenth day of March, when the sun was darkened by an eclipse that frightened the credulous, who saw it as a certain portent of disaster, the Queen died, her husband at her side, his tears falling as openly as those of her ladies, and of his nieces Bess and Cecily, who were also in attendance. And Julian grieved as much as any, both for the dead Anne, who had suffered greatly at the end but was now assuredly safe in Heaven and reunited with her son Ned, and for the King, bereft now of all his family, and bewildered by his loss. At the suggestion of Lord Lovell, he threw himself into hawking and hunting, and birds were brought from all over the country to the royal mews at Charing: while the Palace mourned with sincere grief.

Julian spent much time in the company of the King's nieces. They had been much favoured at court, and gifts had been showered upon them. Bess had become very close to her aunt Anne, and even Cecily, hard and bright and sharp as a diamond, had shed tears at her deathbed and at her funeral, splendid in its black and purple display of sorrow, in Westminster Abbey, where, not two years before, she had been crowned with such high hope. But they, and the old Queen Elizabeth Woodville and her younger daughters in seclusion at Bermondsey Abbey, depended utterly on the King's benevolence.

In the aftermath of the Queen's death, those who had been closest to her became closer still to each other, as if the bond that joined them in loving her had been drawn still more tightly when she died. The King was often in the Queen's apartments, inhabited now by his nieces and their ladies, to bring comfort to them and to himself: and the whispers began.

Friday brought the rumour to Julian with a shocked face. 'They're saying the King plans to marry the Lady Bess as soon as he can!'

Horrified, Julian stared at her. 'That's impossible! He couldn't —dear God, he's her *uncle*! The Pope himself couldn't grant a dispensation for that marriage.'

'That's what I thought,' said Friday, unhappily. 'But everyone's whispering it—all over the Palace.'

'Poor Queen Anne,' Julian said, and crossed herself. 'And the King! What will he say to these rumours?'

The King had at first tried to ignore them: they were too ridiculous to take seriously. It was true that he had shown Bess great favour and friendship, but his wife had shown her greater: and besides, she was his niece, and he had publicly sworn to treat her and her sisters honestly and courteously, as his kinswomen. He was fond of the girl, too: her face, her stature, reminded him daily of his brother Edward, whom he had loved and served so well, and also, to a lesser degree, of the small valiant boy he had sent to safety in Burgundy. But marriage—it was disgusting, unthinkable. Neither England, nor Europe, were so short of young princesses and noblewomen that he must marry his own niece: nor was his seat on the throne so shaky.

But when rumour, the lying jade, began to assert that to further his incestuous passion, he had poisoned his wife, he knew he must act. That the south of England, never better than suspicious, should credit such calumnies was bad enough: but if it should ever be believed in the North that he had poisoned the daughter of the Kingmaker, whom all Yorkshire had loved, then he would be lost indeed.

So he called his Council to deny any such intention: and swore too, before the Mayor and aldermen, the citizens of London, his lords and household, in the Great Hall of the Knights of St John in Clerkenwell, that rumour and gossip lied: it had never come into his thought or mind to marry in such a manner, nor was he glad of the death of his Queen, but as sorry, and in heart as heavy, as any man might be.

He was not the only one distressed by the tales. The other subject of them had wept most bitterly when first she heard the gossip: it seemed to Bess an insult first to the poor Queen, who had loved her like a sister, and she was glad that her aunt was now dead, and beyond the reach of such lies. But her uncle was not. She had seen his terrible despair at Anne's death, and her heart, itself sorrowful, had gone out to him in pity. Bu she could not believe, never, not though she lived for a hundred years, that the desolate, haunted figure of her uncle, withdrawn and isolated in his grief, had ever seriously entertained thought of marrying her. He must marry somebody, the need of an heir was now desperate as the menace of Henry Tudor, with firm French support, loomed across the channel: and Henry Tudor had sworn to marry her.

Bess thought of going to her uncle and begging him to marry her to someone, anyone, so long as it was not Henry Tudor. But he had enough problems without hers. She confided instead in her sister, whose keen mind was unclouded by sentiment, and in Julian Heron, who had given the Queen such pleasure in her last days in this world. And Julian, encouraged by this sharing of intimate thoughts and feelings, confided her own secrets in return.

Not all, of them, of course: her suspicions of her mother she could not, even now, bring herself to voice, and besides, she had no proof. But she told Bess of her pregnancy, though it did not show yet, and, making sure that Cecily was not within earshot, of her quarrel with Christie.

'And you have not heard from him since?' Bess asked. She sat on a stool by the fire, serene and lovely in black velvet, her yellow hair falling down her back like a cloak. Julian, whose mourning gown robbed her of any pretensions to beauty, shook her head so that the veils surrounding trembled gently. 'Not a word—and to tell you the truth, I'm sorry for it.'

Bess looked at her intently. 'Are you, Julian? Are you really?'

Faced with her gentle pressure, Julian felt the bright colour flooding her face: but she did not falter. 'Yes, really. I do want to see him again.'

'And you're going to have his child? Does he *know*?'

'He doesn't. He left for Calais before I knew myself.'

'Perhaps you ought to tell him,' Bess suggested softly.

'How can I? I don't know where he is. Calais was only his first destination. After that—I think—' She glanced around and lowered her voice to a whisper hardly audible even to Bess. 'I think he has gone to see how your brother does.'

'I guessed it.' The older girl was whispering too, and her eyes shone. 'Oh, how I *wish* I could see Dickon again—you ought to meet him, Julian, he is—he's not like most people's little brothers,' she finished rather inadequately, but hastened by the approach of Lady Lovell.

That night Julian dreamed of Christie, a hot, shameful dream that woke her sweating, and shivering with desire. She rolled over, despairing and unhappy, and buried her face in the pillow to stifle her sobs. Her feelings now were very far from that one regrettable lapse into her old hostility.

She had wondered if Meg were still at Westminster, and had asked on her return to the Palace: but Sir Robert Drakelon had taken his lady back to Yorkshire at Candlemas. The news left Julian feeling acutely disappointed. She wanted urgently to talk to her to discuss more fully their different feelings towards Christie, and to express her own confused doubts and grief at their separation.

The Queen was dead, but she made no move to return to Ashcott. Sooner or later, she would have to face her mother's wrath: her body was beginning to thicken, as April passed and the warm spring days that the poor Queen had so longed to see, lightened the gloom of the court a little. But the centre of it was hollow: no matter how the officials bustled, or the Council discussed grave matters of state, in the middle of all the busy routine and glitter and feasting of the Palace, the King had lost all heart for kingship.

It was not at first apparent, save to those who knew him best: but since Anne's death, the fire had gone. In one bold stroke, two years ago, he had captured the throne, and defeated all opposition. And yet, since then, his luck had steadily drained away from him. His dear son, hope of his future, had died: and hardly had he recovered from that terrible blow than his sweet wife had been taken from him too. It might seem to some like God's punishment for his transgressions: and certainly the miasma of poisonous rumour that proclamations and threats had entirely failed to disperse, insinuated that the King's bereavements were the direct consequence of his usurpation of the throne, and his murder of his nephews.

This despondent time would not last: his friends rallied round, encouraging him, putting forward new plans, new futures. He was young yet, only thirty-two. There was plenty of time to marry again, and beget a string of heirs. He might well have twenty, thirty years even, of kingship ahead of him, of balancing feud and faction, fighting off the Scots, bringing England to wealth, prosperity, peace. He could strangle rumour easily, for he had only to marry some other princess—a Spanish one had been suggested—and to produce the person of his nephew Richard, once Duke of York. But to all, the King made the same answer. 'I will defeat the Tudor, and end that menace for ever. *Then* I can look to my dynasty, and silence wagging tongues.'

The Tudor gathered his forces in Rouen, his little band of exiles exhilarated by the promise of French troops and money, while at her home in Derbyshire his mother, the Lady Stanley, spun her sticky webs of intrigue. The King had sent out Commissions of Array to every county in the winter, warning his supporters to be ready and vigilant in case of invasion: now, with rumour rife, he prepared to strengthen the southern ports and the fleet with the help of Lord Lovell, while he himself decided to move north, to be nearer those parts which could be trusted to offer him support. The Ladies Bess and Cecily were to return to Sheriff Hutton for safekeeping, where lived their cousins of Warwick and Lincoln, well away from the Tudor's reach, while Dame Grey and the younger girls could stay at Bermondsey, secluded from the turbulence of court life.

Julian, unhappily, knew that she must go back to Ashcott, if only to try and undo the damage that her mother had done. The last time she had made that journey she had been eaten up with hatred and bitterness: she still sometimes felt anger, for it was hard even now to acknowledge that she was in the wrong. But the Queen's death and the King's suffering had taken her mind from her own petty problems. And she vowed as she gathered her courage for the coming battle, that she would do everything in her power to thwart her mother's designs.

So, she bade a sad farewell to Bess and Cecily, and with her waiting-woman, her horse, her dog, and a royal groom for escort, rode back to Ashcott. It was the last day of April when she came down the familiar lane from Deddington, with a cuckoo shouting welcome from the trees along the river, to face her mother: and on the same day, many miles distant, her husband landed at Dover.

*

He had seen Dickon, lodged with a prosperous family in the Flanders town of Lille. They had taken him to their hearts, as did everyone: he jabbered away in Flemish to the children of the house, in French to its Burgundian mistress, and in English, breathlessly, to Christie and Perkin, both of whom he greeted with enthusiastic delight. 'Hullo! How are you? How's Bess? Is my mother well? Did you have a good journey?'

He was able to answer the boy's questions, smiling, while the woman who had temporarily taken the place of Dickon's mother looked on with her crowd of boys and girls. It had been easy enough, last summer, to slide the English prince into this respectable household, whose master and mistress both had strong connections with the Burgundian court. He had been introduced as a cousin, son of a Burgundian merchant reared in England, and for the first few months had applied himself to learning Flemish, with spectacular success. He was now, obviously, completely accepted within the family and amongst their circle of acquaintances, without rousing any suspicion. With regret, Christie left him and travelled, very quietly, to Paris and thence to Rouen, in the guise of an English merchant. At Rouen was Henry Tudor's headquarters, and King Richard's urgent instructions to Christie, as to all his other agents, was to discover when, and where the Tudor planned to land his invasion force in the summer.

He failed: it was only to be expected, for the group of exiles had all the closeness of oysters and the cunning of foxes, and strange Englishmen were automatically suspected. Only a warning by another agent saved him from attack, or worse: and he and Perkin left Rouen, frustrated at their lack of success, able only to report that the invasion plans were well advanced, and ships to transport the expedition were fitting out at Harfleur.

Tyrell welcomed them at Calais: there too was the King's bastard son, John of Gloucester, fourteen years old and appointed Captain of the town, a small serious dark-haired boy who reminded Christie very much of his father. Then, at last, they were able to take ship, and return to England where, as Perkin put it, the coin was good and the people spoke honest English, not all the tongues of Babel, and the food not apt, unless you chose your inn very unwisely, to give you belly-ache and the runs. Bayard, foul-tempered and flat-eared, was collected from the farm where he had been stabled for the past three months at exhorbitant rates, and Christie rode back to Westminster to report to the King.

He had heard, of course, of the Queen's death, but Richard's face still came as a shock, deadly pale, new grim lines around his mouth and brow, the cheekbones standing out sharp above the sunken flesh. Christie told him of Dickon's progress, gave him letters and despatches from Calais, and reported, finally, on the state of Henry Tudor's invasion plans. The King sat with an impassive expression on his face, and Christie had the disconcerting impression that he was not really listening. Lovell was, though, and asked several pertinent questions. Then Richard raised the shadowed grey eyes to his knight's face. 'You have done well, Christie, though we're still lacking that most vital information—but they're impossible to penetrate, close as limpets. Still, I have hopes—there are other agents burrowing into their secrets. Now, you have spent three months on my business: I expect you would like some time to spend with your wife at Ashcott.'

He had been expecting this: the King had always taken a friendly interest in the marriage that had after all been his suggestion, and had watched its sudden flowering at Christmas with evident approval and satisfaction. It was only natural that Richard should assume that Christie's most urgent desire at this moment was to return to Julian's side.

As indeed it was: but he had no idea of the reception he would have. Had Meg managed to explain that her desire for revenge was now infinitely regretted, and that brother and sister were reconciled? What had Julian thought of the letter Meg had promised to send her? Would she believe it? Would she change her mind? Or, if he returned to Ashcott, would he be met with that same implacable hostility?

He did not think he could bear it, if that was so. The thought of embarking on another long, weary, desperate effort to capture her affections appalled him. He wanted the Julian who had been his at Christmas, her generous, inviting body, her eyes smoky with passion: not the Julian of their earlier acquaintance, touchy, hostile, short-tempered. He smiled tiredly at the King. 'Doubtless I soon shall, Your Grace, but in the meantime, I would very much like to take up my duties here. I would like nothing better than to assist in the trouncing of Henry Tudor.'

The King gave him a long considering look, as if aware of the reasons for his decision. But all he said was, 'I shall be most grateful for your aid, Christie. We have missed your stalwart service most sorely.'

*

The Lady Elizabeth came upon him in the Privy Garden, the next afternoon. She was in black still, damask silk patterned with a duller weave of roses, and against the mourning gown her bright sunlit hair shone brilliantly. For the moment they were alone. She gave him a meaningful look. 'May I speak with you, Sir Christopher? On a private matter.'

'Of course,' he said. She reminded him so strongly of Dickon, with that quality of serious and thoughtful enquiry that was

[443]

characteristic of them both, but which the other children of King Edward seemed to lack.

Bess glanced round: the garden was not empty, and her sister Cecily's bright laugh could be heard from, inevitably, a group of young gentlemen and fewer ladies. But there was no-one near them. She said softly, unawares echoing Dickon, 'Forgive me—I don't mean to pry—but in the last few weeks I have had much speech with your wife.'

Christie stared at her in surprise. 'With Julian? Is she here at the Palace, then?' And hope suddenly sprang free in his heart.

Bess shook her head, displacing the neat streams of yellow hair about her shoulders. 'No, no—I'm afraid she's gone—she left for—Ashcott, is it? A week ago, it must be. She was here to tend my poor aunt in her last illness, may God rest her soul.' She sighed sadly. 'The Queen did so love to hear her singing: she recalled her from Ashcott so that Julian could give her comfort, and when Her Grace died, she stayed here . . . we are great friends,' said Bess, and her hazel eyes gazed earnestly into his. 'She told me you had quarrelled.'

'Did she?'

'Yes.' Bess continued to study him, wondering how much to tell him, for Julian's revelations had been in confidence, and she did not want to betray her friend's trust: moreover, there were certain things—Julian's pregnancy chief amongst them—that she did not think it right to reveal. Best to learn them from his wife. So, healing the rift between them was her first consideration, and she tackled the task with her usual honesty. 'She said little of it, but I had the impression that she was—confused, I think, in her own mind. About her feelings for you. I think—I think she had felt almost *compelled* to hate you at first, but she did imply that her real thoughts were quite different.' She hesitated, and then added carefully, 'Are you—are you going to see her, soon?'

As with Dickon, it was impossible to feel offended by her genuine concern. He smiled rather ruefully. 'I don't know. I have written to her, begging her forgiveness. What I do, depends on her reply.'

It had taken a large part of the night, three pens, a bottle of ink and most of a stack of paper to compose that letter. In the end, he had restricted himself to a brief explanation of the facts, and a simple appeal: to receive him, and listen to his side of the story. He had acknowledged, honestly, his undoubted error: he had also told her that he had learned from this mistake, and paid for it too. Whether this would have any effect on Julian's enmity remained to be seen: but he would wait for an answer before riding to Ashcott.

It was easy enough to do: not so easy to wait, here in the busy unhappy court, for her reply. Whatever it was, he prayed it would come quickly: the long, lonely, empty nights, sleepless until the scant drear hours before dawn, were an agony he knew he could not tolerate for long.

*

A servant brought the letter down to Ashcott: it had been left at Deddington by a gentleman travelling from Oxford, who had been given it at his inn there. Such haphazard arrangements were not very satisfactory, but Christie had hardly been able to command a King's Messenger to take his private letters: it had been nearly a week on its journey. And as luck would have it, the first person the servant saw as he entered the hall was Dame Alice.

'A letter, Tom? For me, or for Dame Julian?'

'It's addressed to Dame Julian, lady. Shall I take it to her?'

'She's out with her hawk and dog,' said Dame Alice, with unconcealed disapproval. 'I'll give it to her when she returns.' She held out her hand: he put the letter into it without anxiety, and thought no more of it.

Dame Alice recognised the writing, neat, clear, and as straight as if following an invisibly ruled line. She carried it upstairs to her parlour, slit open the seal-string with her knife, and cast her eyes swiftly down the single page. Another offer of reconciliation, couched in plain and simple terms, and yet suffused with his affection. Fool to fix his heart on that obstinate perverse jade: greater fool, to trust to paper. And with a satisfied smile, she tore the thick paper across three times, and watched it curl and blacken and smoke into ashes in the hearth.

It had been obvious on the girl's return, to her suspicious eye, that Julian was expecting a child: she had berated her roundly, and Julian, to Dame Alice's astonishment, had answered back in no uncertain fashion, that this babe was her and her husband's business, and would be kept thus. And she had added, with a blaze of furious dislike that had taken her mother quite aback, 'Why are you so displeased? It's your first grandchild, after all, perhaps an heir for Ashcott. Or do you have some scheme for my future which you haven't told me?'

[445]

Dame Alice had for once been silent, and since then, had been much more circumspect. She had written to Reginald Bray in most general terms, but warning him not to visit Ashcott again until she gave the word. There was still some money to be given him: she would rather have contributed the family's pieces of silver, plates, cups, chalices, the magnificent silver-gilt salt that graced every dinner table, but their absence would immediately be noticed. Something had made Julian suspicious: those suspicions must be allayed.

So, she set herself to be pleasant to the ungainly, unlikeable, unamenable girl who, most unfortunately, was her only surviving child. She gave every appearance of concern for Julian's health, ordered titbits for her from the kitchen, encouraged her to eat and to be lazy, and even countenanced the expenditure of an iniquitous amount of money on oranges, for which the stupid girl had developed a craving.

Julian, for so long the subject of her mother's unrelenting hostility, could not at first believe this abrupt change in attitude: then, her suspicions rose up anew. It certainly made life much more pleasant, to be free at last of Dame Alice's constant nagging and harping criticism, but she would not relax her own vigilance. There were no mysterious comings and goings, no sign of the sinister Master Bray, but on her suggestion Marten, on his next visit to Oxford, returned with a new lock for the coin-chest, which he fitted himself, and to which he alone kept the key. No mention of this was made by Dame Alice: but there was no chance now, short of her stealing the key or breaking open the chest herself, of any more of Ashcott's hoarded wealth going to the coffers of Henry Tudor.

Knowing that she had done her best, Julian immersed herself in the comfortable routine of Ashcott in summer: and as the baby grew within her, so did the desperate longing for her absent husband diminish, and her nights at last were peaceful, feeling the child's movements inside her, her turbulent emotions growing serene and placid as they drifted together towards birth. And she thought often of Christie, wondering when he would return, waiting with uncharacteristic patience for the letters that would surely soon arrive to herald their reconciliation.

*

Christie thought constantly of her: but as the days went by with no word, his hopes drained steadily away. During the day he could

[446]

submerge himself in the hectic preparations for war and the removal of the court to Nottingham: it was the silence of night that drew his spirit down, and awakened his longing for Julian. Over and over again his mind relived the days around Christmas, that now seemed to have the quality of enchantment. He knew that he had never had her love, perhaps not even her affection, only her desire: but that had been beginning enough. And then Meg had destroyed it all with her jealous urge for vengeance, and the fragile relationship had shrivelled instantly to ashes. Perhaps he had been a fool, to hope that someone as volatile as Julian could be brought to accept, even to love him: and it was hard, so hard to realise that his own love and need for her had not created in her an answering emotion.

She had not answered: he knew in his heart that it had been hopeless, that Bess must have been mistaken. His only chance lay in confronting her, in trying to persuade her yet again to give her quarrel over.

But he could not go now. He had once more made himself indispensible: the King depended on his efficiency as he did on the work of Lovell, Catesby, Ratcliffe, Brackenbury and all the other hard-working, trusted men around him. The Tudor must be defeated: then, he would go to Julian. Separation had done no harm before, and might even smooth the path of reconciliation.

He wrote to her again, the night before they left Westminster, telling her where he would be, and expressing his hopes for her safety and happiness: and he signed it, simply, Your true and loving husband. He paid a man a shilling to take it to Ashcott as soon as might be, and mounted Bayard with the hope that somehow, that letter might succeed where the other, and Meg's, had apparently failed.

Dame Alice did not even bother to read it before she cast it in the fire.

CHAPTER TWENTY

**'I love now him that I have
most hated of any man alive.'**
(BOOK 4, CHAPTER 22)

The Castle at Nottingham, a vast and gloomy pile hanging like a threat over the unfortunate town below, was part palace, part fortress, and unquestionably the most suitable place for the King to prepare for the invasion and defeat of Henry Tudor. It had plenty of room for his household, and it was centrally placed in the heart of England, so that wherever the Tudor landed, Richard's army could move swiftly against him.

It was also known to him as the Castle of Care: here, he and Anne, a little more than a year ago, had heard the news of their son's death. The Queen had never really recovered from that dreadful blow, tormented by the certainty that she was now barren and that, while she lived, he would have no heir of his body. When at last she had realised that she was dying, she had bid him, gently, to be of better cheer: for when she was at peace with little Ned in Heaven, he would be free to marry and have more sons, for his sake and for England's.

Of such a measure had been her love: and now he was bereft of it. He had his friends, his household, his loyal and trusted servants, but none shared his heart nor his soul, as Anne and Edward had. He dealt with the business of government, of military preparation, all the machinery of war put in motion to vanquish Henry Tudor, with a curious and strange feeling of remoteness, as if all this activity was detached from him and meant nothing: empty actions performed, like a Corpus Christi play, because there were people looking at him. He smiled and spoke and gave orders and signed the papers that Kendall or his clerks put in front of him, but his soul was echoing hollow, because he had lost Anne, and knew in his heart that this must be God's judgement on him, for his seizure of the throne and his betrayal of his brother's children.

Edward had died, true, but Dickon was safe, and Bess and Cecily secure in Sheriff Hutton, so that if the Tudor struck at London he would find only their little sisters, too young for marriage. He had done his best to assuage the wrong he had done them, but nothing

[448]

on this earth could displace the single inalienable fact: that he had usurped the throne that had rightfully been Edward's, and thereby almost certainly hastened his death.

And after him, that throne was Dickon's. He had treated the Earl of Lincoln as his heir, given him the North to govern: but when the Tudor was beaten, he would bring Dickon back from Flanders, rear him at court, and see whether that brave and brilliant promise flowered with maturity. And if so, and if he did not by then have a son to succeed him, then Dickon, who had reminded him of his own Ned, would be made his heir. It would cause problems with Lincoln, and with the young Earl's mother, but that was a bridge to be crossed many years hence.

Defeat the Tudor: it was the litany that ran through the castle from the Mass at dawn to the ceremony of All Night in the evening. And sometimes it seemed to Christie that the world had stopped, and held its breath waiting, until Henry Tudor invaded, and was beaten.

To Nottingham came many lords and gentlemen, to offer support and assistance, or to bring news of others, and amongst them was Sir Robert Drakelon, retainer to the Earl of Northumberland, and Meg, his wife.

The reunion between Christie and his sister was at once joyous and sad. They had not seen each other for six months, and in the interval, despite an exchange of letters, the reconciliation, brief and heartfelt, had taken on for both of them the quality of a dream. Had it really happened? Had the years of estrangement been erased? Or was it only a creation of the imagination, destined to vanish instantly in the flames of long-held enmity?

It was true. She stood at the door of Christie's chamber, and her smile was bright with happiness. 'Hullo. I thought I would come and see you before dark. We have just arrived.'

They hugged, and he offered her wine, which she declined. She looked happy, but preoccupied: there was a faint frown between her arched, plucked brows, and his request for her news at first went unanswered. Then she smiled, and gave him her full attention. 'Oh, I am very well, thank you, and Roger is cutting teeth, and God willing there will be another child—though not until Candlemas, I think.'

He was not pleased: too many women died in childbirth, or exhausted their strength and their looks producing babies in rapid succession. There was no thickening yet of Meg's trim slender body, and her beauty was undimmed: doubtless Sir Robert's lust had got the better of him again. Christie crushed his distaste—did he not lust after his own wife?—and asked the question that was uppermost in his mind. 'Meg—did you write to Julian?'

Startled, she stared at him. 'Yes, of course I did. I wrote a few days after you left with Tyrell, just as I said I would. What has happened, then?'

'And you had no reply?'

'No—but I didn't really expect one, to be honest. I suggested she write to you, if what I said had changed her mind. Why? Have you had no word?'

'None. I wrote to her when I returned from Calais, at the beginning of May. I heard nothing. I spoke with the Lady Elizabeth who gave me some hope. Then on the eleventh, we left Westminster, and I sent another letter direct to her, in the hands of a servant, so that she would be certain to receive it. I told her that I would be with the King, at Nottingham. We arrived here the second week in June, and it's now the third in July. More than two months, Meg.'

'There are other possibilities besides the worst,' Meg pointed out. 'Your letters might have gone astray, or hers. It happens frequently, though not I admit when you pay a man to take it direct instead of trusting it to some carrier or passing traveller. She may have made you a reply which went to Westminster—or she may never have received your letters.'

'That she never received one, I can well believe. But all *three*, Meg?'

There was a silence. His sister stared at him thoughtfully. 'Unlikely. But there's the chance that she did not answer the first, but decided to write to you when the second letter arrived—and if you'd already left London, there would be ample opportunity for it to go astray.' She put her hand on his, broader and browner than her slender pale fingers. 'There may be no reason to think she's ignoring you—that's what I'm saying. There is still *hope*. And even if she has the letters, and chosen not to answer them—well, I hardly know your Julian, but she seems to be one who changes her moods very frequently. Am I right?'

'You are, to a certain extent. But she was sure enough in her loathing of me, for years. It's the usual situation between us,' said Christie ruefully. 'Last Christmas was a brief illusory interval, in which I thought, poor addled fool that I was, that she had truly changed. I am beginning to see that I was wrong, and she had not.'

'Don't speak of that! You don't *know*! And when all this is over, and the Tudor is beaten,' said Meg, suddenly quiet, 'you can go back to Ashcott and woo her.'

'Under the eyes of the she-dragon, her mother? I think not —Dame Alice loathes me quite as much as her daughter did, if not more.'

'Does she?' Meg looked up with sudden interest. 'Does she, indeed? Why?'

'Because, as a man of undistinguished birth—bastard Percy blood notwithstanding—and a trusted intimate of the murdering usurper, I am a less suitable husband for her than a crawling viper.' Christie smiled. 'Besides, she is a woman of singularly unpleasant character, and doubtless she'd object to me were I a lord of royal blood and saintly personal habits. And of course, I'm not.'

'No,' Meg agreed, straight-faced. He caught the irony in her voice and laughed suddenly. 'Oh, Meg, Meg, little sister, how I have missed you!'

'And I have missed you,' she said softly, and kissed his cheek, lightly but lovingly. 'We were so close once—to quarrel was like stabbing each other to the heart. And now we have found each other again, it's as if I'd discovered that you were alive after all, when I'd been thinking you were dead.' She smiled at him, and then added, 'To return to our earlier talk. This Dame Alice—could her hatred of you extend to—to destroying your letters?'

There was silence. She had given him reason for hope after all, and it blazed suddenly in his face. 'Yes—I would not put it past her malice, not at all. She is a Clifford, and her husband died supporting the Tudor, so she is a Lancastrian born and bred—and she would doubtless like one of the same breed for her daughter, if I were killed. Do you think it likely, then?'

'You know the woman—you be the judge.' Meg looked at him, and added, 'It seems to be a possibility—and certainly more likely than all of the letters being lost. But it doesn't alter Julian's feelings—they could be still exactly the same, despite what the Lady Elizabeth told you.'

'I know. I know only too well, as I know her only too well. But at least there is a good chance that she might be brought to change her mind—again!' He drove his fist into the soft coverlet. 'If only I could go to her, *now*, and see her for myself—but I can't.

[451]

Richard needs us here, in readiness for when the invasion comes.'

'Do you think it will?'

'Of course it will. Tudor has French help now—the French fear that the King will invade France and try to regain the lands England has lost. Doubtless they feel this Tudor is of a less martial disposition, and will be grateful to those who helped him to the throne. I went to Rouen and Harfleur to try and discover their plans—I saw the ships fitting out with my own eyes. It's now or never for the Tudor, he must gamble all on one throw of the dice—invade this summer, to win or lose, or dwindle into a harmless and pathetic pensioner of the French. And with Richard's son dead, and his brother's children discredited, he probably feels he had a good chance to establish his own dynasty—at least as good a chance as Richard, whose heart for the moment is not in it.'

There was a silence: then Meg said quietly, 'Christie—what has happened to those boys, the Princes? Do you know?'

He trusted her, but he did not trust her husband. She saw his hesitation, and said swiftly, 'You need not tell me, if you do not wish it. But it has been puzzling me. Everyone has assumed they are dead—yet their sisters dance at court and are on friendly terms with the man who's supposed to have had them murdered, their mother placed her other children in his keeping and has a pension from him. *Are* they dead?'

Christie glanced at her: he said slowly, 'Richard has not harmed them, nor has he ordered them to be harmed. He has taken every thought for their comfort and safety.'

'Then they *are* alive!'

'I didn't necessarily say that. I know where they are, yes—but I will divulge it to no man or woman living, save on the orders of the King, or until times change. And with that, dear sister, you will have to be content.'

She looked down at her hands, frowning, as if making up her mind whether or not to speak. At last, as he waited, she said, her voice low, 'I think—I should not be telling you this, but I think that my husband . . . that his loyalty isn't as firm as the King believes it.'

This time the silence threatened to stretch out for ever. He saw a tear drop onto her hand: he wiped it away, gently, with a finger, and tilted her chin up so that she faced him. 'What makes you think so, little sister? Can you tell me?'

Meg had mastered herself, and her gaze did not falter. 'A man has

[452]

visited Denby, twice now, to speak with my husband. I would have thought nothing of it, except—except that his name is Bray. I noticed it, because that is Julian's family name, is it not? But then I heard something from a neighbour. . . Is he in the pay of the Tudor?'

'He is his mother's steward. God knows why the King did not clap him into prison with the rest of the conspirators in Buckingham's rising—but he pardoned him instead, and since then, Master Bray has lived in Lady Stanley's household. Are you *sure* that was his name? Because if it *was* Bray, then Lady Stanley is probably plotting rebellion again—and the King must be warned.'

'I'm certain of it,' said Meg. 'I didn't have speech with him—I assumed he had come on business, and he didn't stay for any meal, on either occasion. I only caught brief glimpses of him, but I can tell you exactly what he looked like: a short man in early middle age, with a funny squashed-looking nose. In fact, he reminded me a little of your servant, what's his name, Perkin, grown old.'

'Poor Perkin! I've never seen Bray, but there are many people here who have.' He looked at Meg's pale face, and added, 'Thank you. I can guess how much that cost your conscience—a wife's loyalty must always be firstly to her husband after all.'

'No longer,' said his sister. 'Your King has done wrong in usurping the throne, but he will be a wise and just ruler, given the chance—and now that I know he has not harmed his nephews, my conscience is clear. What do we know of Henry Tudor? A Welshman of dubious birth who's been in exile for half his life, supported by the Regent of France, who'd doubtless give ships to a jackanapes if she thought he could take the crown of England—all else I know of him is that he has the colouring and cunning of a fox. And besides, the King is our crowned and anointed ruler—it's treason to oppose him, and against the laws of God as well as man.' She shivered suddenly. 'And I will not be party to treason, even if it is my husband's.'

*

He sat for a long time alone, when she had returned to her own apartments, turning over her information in his mind. He had no doubt at all that Sir Robert's mysterious visitor was the Lady Margaret's steward. But that in itself, though highly suspicious, proved nothing. The purpose of his visits might be quite innocent, connected with land or other lawful business. The secrecy, the care with which he had been kept away from Meg, whose brother was a knight of the King's household, suggested otherwise, but still there was no proof.

In his bones though, with intuitive strength, he felt that treason was planned. He had never trusted Sir Robert, his cold evasive nature, the eyes that were always sliding elsewhere. But why Sir Robert, whose wealth was not especially great, who did not command many armed retainers, whose principal manor was an old-fashioned fortified house in an isolated part of Yorkshire? Why had he been singled out for the Lady Margaret Beaufort's subtle approaches and suggestions of treason?

Money, perhaps—rebels were always in need of coin, to pay their soldiers and equip them. Or perhaps Sir Robert, wishing to support the Tudor, had made the initial overtures himself. Why, was hard to imagine—he had no court appointment, true, but he was a man of substance in Yorkshire, retained by the Earl of Northumberland and highly regarded by him . . .

Retained by the Earl of Northumberland. That was the key, he was suddenly sure of it: and the implications made his flesh creep.

The woman born Lady Margaret Beaufort had married, firstly, Edmund Tudor, Earl of Richmond, when hardly more than a child, and had borne Henry Tudor two months after her husband's premature death. She had then wed the uncle of the late Duke of Buckingham, which on reflection could explain several things about that vivid, brilliant, treacherous man, and finally, Thomas, Lord Stanley, whose wife she had been now for twelve years.

Lord Stanley, who two years ago, when Richard was Protector and Duke of Gloucester still, had plotted with Hastings and the Woodvilles against Richard's life. He had been briefly imprisoned, speedily pardoned, and made steward of the King's household. It was a post that had not been affected by the plottings of his wife, whose punishment after her conspiracy with Buckingham had been moderated, so it was said, by reason of her husband's service and loyalty. But it was a post that required Stanley to be ever at the King's side, and the court was aware, as Stanley himself must also be aware, that the noble lord's slippery loyalty could not be called into question while he was under Richard's eye.

And Stanley was one of the most powerful magnates in England: he controlled large parts of Cheshire, Lancashire and the borders of Wales, and was capable of putting two thousand men into the field. His lands were close to those where Henry Tudor, the Welshman, might most certainly command allegiance. At one time or another during the past twenty-five years, Stanley had supported nearly every faction that had fought over England: King Henry, the old Duke of York, the Earl of Warwick, King Edward, had all received his aid, usually while his brother Sir William was assisting the opposing side. True, he had given King Edward years of good service after the collapse of the house of Lancaster, but now this exceptionally wily and devious man had every reason to support Henry Tudor: for if the pretender won, Stanley would be stepfather to a King.

But Stanley was not now at Nottingham: he had sought permission from the King to retire to his estates for a space, as he had been so long absent, and attend to much-needed business. It was a perfectly reasonable request, on the surface: but Christie remembered, with cold clarity, the look in the King's eyes as he granted it—on condition that Stanley's capable service was performed in his absence by his eldest son, Lord Strange. With a thin smile on his bland face, Lord Stanley had agreed, knowing that he thereby gave the King a hostage for his good behaviour, and departed to his estates and, of course, the company of his ruthless, pious, and treacherous wife.

And now her steward was in contact with a trusted retainer of the Earl of Northumberland, and if it's on a matter of innocent business, thought Christie, then I'm the Duke of Burgundy. The prospect of a link between the untrustworthy Stanley, the power of the northwest, and the haughty Northumberland, whose dreams of power in the northeast had been largely thwarted by Richard—it was enough to turn the blood to ice.

The more he thought about it, the more he disliked it and the more certain he was that mischief was being planned. The King must undoubtedly be told: but since the Queen's death, Richard had retreated into a private world of grief, his heart no longer in the business of government. It was as if, thought Christie with disquiet, he had become seized with a sense of fate, God's will, call it whatever you might: as if he felt that he could do nothing against the slow-gathering mass of treason and conspiracy and vicious rumour that was opposing him, as if the outcome of his struggle against the Tudor would be decided not by the King's own efforts, but by the judgement of Heaven.

Which was all very well for Richard, thought Christie grimly, as he waited to speak with the King: but what of his supporters, and his friends?

[455]

Richard received him with some surprise: he was not on duty until the next day. Those others in the Privy Chamber were utterly trustworthy, like Christie owing everything to the King's favour: Will Catesby, Richard Ratcliffe, John Kendall.

'I have news for Your Grace,' he said. 'It may be significant—indeed, I believe it is.'

'Tell me, then.'

'I have reason to think that Sir Robert Drakelon might not be so loyal as you suppose, Your Grace. He has been visited privately by Master Reginald Bray.'

Out of the corner of his eye, Christie saw Catesby stiffen and nudge Ratcliffe in the ribs. The King looked up at him: his face was pale, weary, with none of the resolve, the fire of plan and action that had once burned there. 'Your sister is married to Drakelon, is she not? Is she your informant?'

'Yes, Your Grace. He was not presented to her, but she heard his name mentioned, and realised who he might be.'

'And did she see him?'

'She did. She described him as a short man, with a squashed-looking nose. Is that a fair portrait?'

'It is.' Richard stared into space, his hand twisting the finger-ring round, and round, and round, the old gesture of stress. 'Bray, visiting the Earl of Northumberland's retainer. It may mean nothing, of course—Sir Robert may have sent him packing.'

'According to my sister, Bray has made at least two visits.'

Richard gave him a sharp glance. 'What is your opinion of all this, Christie? Is there something in it?'

'Yes, I think so—mischief at the least, and probably some danger. Can you not seize the Lady Stanley, or at least her steward? While she and her son live, she will never cease plotting on his behalf.'

'It has never been my practice to make war on women,' said the King, 'however much they might seem to deserve it . . . and besides, her stepson Lord Strange is here in Nottingham, and should prove ample surety for her good behaviour—and her husband's. And also, there is no proof of his disloyalty. If I should move against his wife, I risk pitching him wholeheartedly into the Tudor's camp. And that I cannot afford to do. I have given him the opportunity to justify the trust I have place in his loyalty. If he betrays it, he knows what punishment he can expect. As for Northumberland, you know him as well as I do—he is after all your uncle. He and I have worked well together, governing the North, for close on fifteen years. I doubt very much whether he has ever entertained thoughts of treason—he knows his position with me, whereas the Tudor is unknown, untried. You did right to warn me, Christie, and I shall be the more vigilant for it: but I can take no action until Tudor lands.'

And he had to be content with that.

*

The hot days of July succeeded one another with blazing skies and distant thunder, and still there was no news of invasion. The castle of Nottingham seemed sunk in a strange limbo of waiting, as if time had ceased until the Tudor came. All the preparations had been completed: Lovell held the south coast in readiness, Norfolk watched the East and London, the King himself guarded the North and the Midlands. Commissions of Array had long ago been sent to the principle men in each county, proclamations against Henry Tudor, 'which of his ambitiousness and insociable covetousness encroacheth and usurped upon him the name and title of royal estate of this realm of England', had been read in every town up and down the country. They had only to wait: and when news of invasion finally came, the web of loyalties in which the King had placed his trust, would at last be tested.

Late in July, an agent more successful than Christie had managed to send word that Henry Tudor's fleet was about to sail. The King sat still in Nottingham: but, as he had done when warned of Buckingham's rebellion, he sent for the Great Seal, kept by the Chancellor, the Bishop of Lincoln, in London. Thomas Barrow, Master of the Rolls, brought it north, and presented it to Richard in the chapel of Nottingham Castle, in the presence of the Earl of Lincoln, Lord Morely, the Archbishop of York, and sundry other lords and gentlemen.

It was seven o'clock of a warm, humid summer's evening, on the first day of August. Thunder grumbled far away, and flies buzzed against the windows. The sun still lit the chapel, and laid the brilliant colours of the stained glass across the stately figures: the King, royally robed in crimson and ermine, the Earl of Lincoln straight and tall and young in a sky-blue gown and darker doublet, the Archbishop in his gorgeous robes and Master Barrow, washed and fed after his arduous journey, kneeling, bareheaded, the blue of

[457]

the Virgin's robe colouring his bald pate, handing to Richard the Great Seal in its bag of soft white leather.

A few hours earlier, a young russet-haired man with pretensions to the crown of England, had set sail with the tide from Harfleur, with fifteen ships and two thousand Frenchmen.

*

The King went hunting from Beskwood Lodge, in Sherwood Forest. It was a way of releasing tension that was welcome to most of his knights and esquires: some, more nervous, worried that the invasion would catch them by surprise. What the King thought as he pursued the swift, lovely deer through the trees and open scrubland once haunted by Robin Hood no-one knew, save that he too seemed to find some release in sport, and freedom from the gloomy, memory-laden buildings at Nottingham. And on 11 August, when they returned from a successful foray—the King himself had killed two stags and a hind—there was a messenger from the castle waiting for them. The news had arrived that morning: Henry Tudor had landed at Milford Haven, in the south-west of Wales, on 7 August.

Christie, watching the King as he listened to the messenger's hasty words, saw Richard change and grow as the man spoke, stand straighter, gather fire, as if he had sloughed off old skin. 'At last!' he said, when the man had finished. 'The Tudor is landed, and now we will defeat him, and wipe this menace from England for ever!'

That afternoon in Beskwood, clerks hunched over desks and tables, writing over and over again the King's commands to his followers:

> Trusty and wellbeloved, we greet you well. And for as much as our rebels and traitors accompanied with our ancient enemies of France and other strange nations departed out of the water of Seine the first day of this present month, making their course westwards, being landed at Nangle besides Milford Haven in Wales on Sunday last past, as we be credibly informed, intending our utter destruction, the extreme subversion of this our realm and disinheriting of our true subjects of the same, towards whose recountering, God being our guide, we be utterly determined in our own person to remove in all haste goodly that we can or may. Wherefore, we will and straightly charge you that you in your person with such number as you have promised unto us sufficiently horsed and

harnessed be with us in all haste to you possible, to give unto us your attendance without failing, all manner of excuses set apart, upon pain of forfeiture unto us of all that you may forfeit and lose. Given under our signet at our lodge of Beskwood, the eleventh day of August.

Ricardus Rex.

Knights, esquires, household officers, all not present at Nottingham were summoned. The Duke of Norfolk: Thomas, Lord Stanley: William Herbert, Earl of Huntingdon, husband of the King's bastard daughter, Katherine: Richard Williams, Constable of the castle of Pembroke, where had been seen the beacon fires telling of invasion, and who had sent the news on to Nottingham: Sir Robert Brackenbury, Constable of the Tower: and Harry Percy, Earl of Northumberland.

Carrying that letter had been Sir Robert Drakelon. Christie could have suggested a different envoy: but his brother-in-law was the obvious choice, and moreover had volunteered for the job with the loudly-voiced opinion that he would do anything that he could to hasten Henry Tudor's downfall. He took leave of his wife, Meg, adjuring her to return to Denby as soon as might be, to organise the safety of his household: and then rode off northwards with his servants, towards Yorkshire.

With misgivings, Christie watched him go: and then, the next day, must say his own goodbyes to Meg.

There would almost certainly be a battle. He would be in danger of capture, injury, death. She remembered the child he had been, at Alnwick, a thin serious boy, conspicuous for his overwhelming urge to succeed despite the taunts of the other children, for his comparatively humble birth and his bastard blood. He had learned with the other boys the essentials of a knightly education: swordplay on foot and on horseback, the use of a lance, the care of armour, the training of a horse. But apart from his brief experiences in the Scottish wars, he had never had the chance to put his training into practice. Meg looked at him as he stood before her, tall and lean still, his sharp face unsmiling, like his royal master cast in a more severe mould than his years would warrant. He is only twenty-five, thought Meg. Twenty-five years old—too young to die, too soon—oh, God, sweet Mary and all the saints keep him safe! But all she said to him, trying to smile bravely, was, 'Take care, Christie —please take care. Now that we have found each other again, I couldn't bear it—'

[459]

She broke off, and Christie said drily, 'I have no intention of being killed—and though others may have every idea of killing me, I shall do my best to avoid them.' He smiled, and put his hands on her shoulders to kiss her, lightly, on the smooth brow below the plain red velvet of her hood. 'And when the Tudor is beaten at last, you can come to visit me at Ashcott—it's a little like Denby, but richer and more beautiful. And perhaps by then, Julian will be my friend.'

'I have a request to make,' said Meg. 'Will you send this letter to Julian for me? And you write to her, Christie, please, write to her again—and tell whoever takes them to give them only into Julian's hands.'

'I have written a letter already,' he told her. 'And I will send Perkin with them—if he cannot outwit Dame Alice, then no-one can. If indeed it is Dame Alice who is to blame.' He grinned suddenly. 'Besides, Perkin is probably the only knight's body-servant in all the land who doesn't know a sallet from a barsanet. If I relied on him to clean and scour my arms and harness, I'd be known as the Rusty Knight—and if I let him buckle it on me, I'd have fingers on my feet. Sir Ralph Bigod has found me a good lad to do the job, and Perkin's nose has been well and truly out-jointed.'

Despite herself, Meg giggled: a girlish sound he had not heard from her since the bright days before her marriage. Suddenly, impulsively, she flung her arms around him and hugged him. 'I must be gone. Oh, take care, Christie—and I'll see you soon, God willing.'

'When we beat the Tudor,' said her brother, and kissed her again, and watched her go as he had watched her husband, but with love.

*

Perkin Hobbes rode down the long hill towards Ashcott with deep apprehension, the two letters safe inside his doublet. It had taken him three days of riding: he had spent the first night in Leicester, the second in Daventry, the third (he had got lost) only fifteen miles or so further on, in Banbury. Now, on a bright fresh Monday morning, the day of the Assumption of the Blessed Virgin Mary, he had reached his destination.

He could guess what the letters must contain: pleas for reconcili-ation and forgiveness. Small chance of that with Dame Alice looming, thought Perkin drily: he could deduce as well as any man the reason why Christie had adjured him to give both messages only to Julian, and especially not to let Dame Alice have them, or indeed even allow her to see or know of them. All the miles from Nottingham, Perkin had been rehearsing in his mind all the various stratagems he could dream up for speaking with Julian alone: they turned out to be unnecessary.

As he came down the hill, his lean chestnut hackney's hooves slipping a little on the stones in the red earth of the track, he glanced to his left and saw, in the distance, two people riding along the hill towards him. Seeing that they were women, and that one of the horses was a grey palfrey, he pulled up his own and sat waiting for them.

It was indeed Julian: her height was quite recognisable. He saw as she drew nearer that she had grown much stouter since he had seen her last, and then realised, with greater astonishment, the reason. It was yet one more complication in his master's life, one that Perkin suspected had not been welcome to his wife, however much Christie might rejoice at the possibility of an heir.

Cygnus walked up to him, ears laid flat, and was pulled up with difficulty by his mistress: he snaked his grey head out wickedly and attempted to bite Perkin's hackney, who sidestepped. Julian, without fuss, dealt her errant horse a brisk thwack with a switch she carried, and then turned to Perkin. There was no hostility, yet, in her unsmiling face, only a wary curiosity. Pregnancy agreed with her, her skin glowed and she had an air of unbounded good health: the heavy hair was confined in a simple unfashionable net, and shone like fire in the sun. 'Well, Perkin? What news do you bring?'

Friday sat behind her on her own undistinguished ambler. Perkin glanced up and down at the empty lane, the distant house, and then fished inside his doublet. 'Greetings, Dame Julian. I bring you letters, from your husband and Dame Drakelon.' He held them out to her: Julian sat still, her hands tight on the reins, and stared at him. Fearing rejection, he added hastily 'I beg you, lady, *please*. Listen to me. Have you had any other letters since you came back here?'

'None,' she said, obviously puzzled. 'Why do you ask?'

'Because my master has already sent you two letters. Have you received them?'

'No, I haven't.'

'Nor the letter that Dame Drakelon sent to you, oh, six months ago?'

This time, there was more than a flicker of interest in Julian's still

[461]

face. 'Meg? Meg wrote to me? But I have never had any letter from her.'

'Nor have you had the two letters from Sir Christopher,' Perkin reminded her. He added significantly, 'Now do you see, lady, why I was commanded to give these into your own hand, and yours alone?'

'You mean my mother . . .' Julian's voice tailed off as she considered the implications. 'Does my husband suspect that my mother has intercepted his letters?' And then, as a sudden thought struck her, she added, 'You said that Meg—that Dame Drakelon had written to me too. But how do you know that? She is my husband's bitterest enemy.'

'No longer,' said Perkin with some small satisfaction. 'That honour, lady, may well belong to yourself.'

There was silence. 'You sound just like him when you say that,' Julian said, and there was a trace of wistfulness, of regret, in her voice. 'But the quarrel—the quarrel between my husband and Dame Drakelon—what has happened? They loathed each other— he betrayed her, ruined her happiness—what's happened to alter it?'

'I don't know, lady,' said Perkin. 'I only know it's all changed between them—as doubtless his letter will tell you. And if that don't convince you, here's the other, writ in Dame Margaret's own hand, and given to me to bring to you and you only. Read it, lady, please, even if you don't read the other—and perhaps it will change your mind.'

For a moment, Julian sat still, while behind her Friday's face mirrored Perkin's, full of urgent, hopeful appeal. The situation had not changed—Christie had betrayed Meg's trust, he had not denied it. So why had they apparently become friends? She would never know if she did not read their words. She took a deep breath, her heart hammering suddenly inside her ribs, and said, 'Give me Dame Margaret's letter.'

They were easy to tell apart, even for one who could not read: Meg's hand was as neat as her brother's, but smaller, and written with a pen cut very fine. He put it into her hand, anxiously watching her face.

Julian studied the crest imprinted on the red wax of the seal. It was a dragon's head, very appropriate for Drakelons. She pulled the string away from the stiff shiny red blob, and opened the letter.

It was not long. It was dated 12 August, three days ago, and told her, with simplicity, that although Meg's brother had done her great wrong, she had forgiven him at last, and made amends for the wrong she had done him in return. She begged Julian's forgiveness for destroying her happiness, and urged her to reconsider her attitude to her husband. 'For if you could see as I have done his grief at your leaving, you would surely consider a different course—he loves you as well as any man loves his wife, and more, and this I can swear who knows him best. Vengeance was not mine to wreak, and now most bitterly do I regret what I have done. In the name of all the saints, I beg you, turn back to my dear brother, for he loves you right well, and has no comfort without you.'

She found her eyes watering. Mentally upbraiding herself for such foolishness, she brushed her hand across her face, to no avail. A fat tear blotted the ink. She thought of the long empty nights, the loneliness, the endless battles with her mother. She thought of the child, vigorous within her, due to be born in two months' time, and whose existence he did not even suspect. And she thought of Meg, whose life had been an expression of her bitterness and hatred, and now, it seemed, had found love and a measure of happiness instead.

Abruptly, she folded Meg's letter and pushed it up inside the long tight sleeve of her gown, where it would not be seen. 'Perkin—may I have the other one also?'

Scenting victory, he nodded, and gave it to her. The seal bore a prancing unicorn, shallowly impressed, as if in desperate haste. It was Christie's badge. With a beating heart, she broke it, and scanned the contents swiftly.

She had expected an appeal, excuses, justifications. This was nothing of the kind. It told her in plain words that the Tudor had landed, that he rode to battle, that there was a chance that he would not see her again. He advised her to equip those of the household who could bear arms, and to take any other measures she thought necessary for the defence of Ashcott until, God willing, the danger was past. And finally, he urged her to put her trust only in those she was sure of: Perkin could enlarge on this, if she did not understand. He signed it, 'Your true and loving husband', and for a moment she sat bewildered, disappointed, and curiously angry—could he not commit that much-vaunted love to paper?

Then she saw that there were lines below his signature. The words, plain and clear and unequivocal, burned into her soul.

Go, heart, hurt with adversity,
And let my lady thy wounds see!

And say her this, as I say thee,
'Farewell my joy, and welcome pain
Till I see my lady again.'

'Oh sweet Christ,' said Julian, softly, and put her hands to her face. The reins, the switch and the paper dropped to the ground, and her tears followed. Perkin, seeing Cygnus about to take advantage of his sudden freedom, leaned over and grabbed the grey's bridle. 'Oh, no, you don't—stand still!'

Friday, unbidden, kicked her way from her own horse's back and ran to steady her mistress as Cygnus sidled restlessly. 'Julian —please, don't distress yourself—what is it, why are you weeping?'

Julian, obviously, was incapable of answering. Perkin dismounted, letting his own docile hackney at liberty, and stood by Cygnus's lean, deceptively beautiful head, ready to punch him between the eyes in case of trouble. Friday, her hands about her mistress's waist, helped her down from her suddenly precarious perch on the restless palfrey: Julian sank down in the dusty red road, all the while sobbing as if her heart had broken.

For in the end, as he had hoped, his love had worn down her resistance, and forced her to realise that, astonishing as it might seem, another cared for her deeply and unfalteringly, and would not be discouraged. She wept for him, the man she still hardly knew, because he had always kept his soul closed to her, save when he sang to her, or made love. And above all, she wept because after all, at the end of these wasted lonely months, it might still be too late, her change of heart: for he went to battle with Henry Tudor, and only God's care could keep him safe. And he might never know that she had realised her mistake.

'Julian!' Friday's voice intruded on her despair. 'Julian—you'll make yourself ill, oh, Julian, please stop—think of the *baby*!'

As if in echo, her unborn child delivered a healthy, irritated kick as a reminder. She pressed her hands to her belly, feeling the tears trickle down her face, feeling the new life moving under her fingers.

'It's all right,' said Perkin, his London voice unwontedly serious. 'Please, lady, there's no need for this—did the letter—did it upset you so much?'

'I'm sorry,' Julian wept, gasping for breath. 'I'm sorry, so sorry—tell him I'm sorry, Perkin—if it isn't too late—when will the battle be?'

[464]

'Battle?' He stared at her in honest bewilderment. 'There ain't no battle, not yet, anyway, and what's more, you know him as well as I do—if anyone's born to be old, it's Sir Christopher. Anyway, he's got me to look after him, ain't he, and you and his sister to pray for him, so he's as well guarded as any man could be.'

Julian, suddenly aware that she must cut a ridiculous figure, sitting in the road, tried to get to her feet. Friday, solicitous, helped her to rise. Gently, her mistress set her aside and stood, a little unsteady but unbowed, in front of Perkin. Her battle for self-control had succeeded, despite the tears on her face, and her voice trembled only slightly when she spoke. 'Thank you, Perkin. Thank you for bringing it to me, and not taking no for an answer. Thank you, for giving me hope. Will you take a letter back for me?'

'Of course I will, lady,' he said, his wide mouth smiling so much that it seemed his face would split in half. 'But first, lady, may I crave a favour? Please don't turn me round and set me on my way back to Nottingham without a meal and a good night's sleep!'

*

Over England, that week, the strands of destiny wove and joined and ravelled together towards their end, as the messengers scurried here and there, bearing news, instructions, orders, reports. From York, where the defence of the city was put in hand, and a messenger sent to the King to ask what help he required. From Thomas, Lord Stanley, who explained that he had recently fallen sick, and would thus be unable to join the King; and, more privily, to his son Lord Strange, telling him to make his escape in all haste. The young man was unfortunately discovered as he tried to leave, and revealed a tale of treachery: his uncle Sir William had conspired with him to aid the Tudor, but Lord Stanley himself—or so swore Lord Strange, frantically, thinking his own life at stake—meant to remain loyal to the King. Given pen and paper, he wrote desperately of his plight, and begged his father to ignore his illness—in which none believed, knowing Stanley's reputation—and to lend Richard his unqualified support. That messenger went westwards, towards Lancashire: just as he left Nottingham, another galloped in with the tidings that the Tudor's army had three days ago entered Shrewsbury, having marched entirely unopposed through half the length of Wales.

It meant betrayal, by those Welsh chiefs who had earlier sworn not to let the Tudor, one of their own, pass through their lands. But at the last, it did not disturb the King: he longed for the chance to defeat his opponent himself, rather than leave it to some obscure ambush in the wild Welsh hills. It did not matter, either, that Tudor's little army had been swelled by several hundred of those same Welshmen, nor that others, Englishmen, were rumoured to be joining him. The King could still command the loyalty of many men, far more than the Tudor could scrape together in his march across the Midlands.

The arrival at Beskwood of the men of York, John Nicholson and John Sponer, was more disturbing. They had had news of the invasion, but nothing more, no requests for men or arms: what did the King want them to provide?

The Earl of Northumberland, who was Commissioner of Array for the East Riding, should long since have summoned the city. Evidently he had not. It was unlikely to be incompetence: it was more likely to be the unpleasant fact that the haughty Earl, knowing the devotion of the men of York to their King, had deliberately ignored them.

But elsewhere, the news was good. Norfolk had sent word that he would fulfil the rendezvous at Leicester with a strong force, and Brackenbury's message was in similar vein. Nor had Lord Stanley actually joined with the Tudor, but was hovering in front of him with his troops, committed neither to one side nor to the other. The King's only comment was, that he wished that the noble lord would make the secret of his miraculously swift recovery available for the benefit of all.

On Saturday, 20 August, Perkin rode into Nottingham, cursing himself for the biggest fool in Christendom. Sped on his way by Julian's urgent desire that her letter reach Christie before he should march to battle, he had urged his lean, long-legged hackney to enormous efforts, and disaster had struck. The animal had stumbled on a rough, isolated piece of road, fallen, and lamed itself. Perkin, unwilling to leave the injured horse, which had cost a fair amount of money, had had perforce to lead the chestnut several painful miles to the nearest town, only to find almost all horses of any quality gone to war, for, so his informants told him with bulging eyes, the Tudor's army was at Lichfield, only twenty or so miles away, recruiting men to his banner, and the local lord had taken his tenants, and their horses, to join him.

Perkin thanked him through clenched teeth, made sure that the hackney was comfortable in the inn stables, and went in search of a substitute mount. The only one on which he could lay his hands was a large solid farm horse with furry feet, a benign eye and a back like a trestle. Its owner, seeing Perkin's desperation, haggled greedily, and he ended by paying far more for the animal than it was actually worth. Then, surveying his much diminished quantity of coin, given to him by Christie for his expenses on the journey, he took his purchase back to the inn and stayed the night, it being then dusk and the moon too old and dwindled to help night riding.

His purchase of the plough horse, although it was willing and sound enough, soon appeared to be a grievous mistake. He was unable to persuade it out of a lumbering canter, and most of the time it was content to trot, despite his frantic urgings. Nor must he risk an encounter with the rebel army. He made a big sweep to the west to avoid them by passing behind them, succeeded but lost himself twice, found himself, to his dismay, in Derby, and finally arrived exhausted and sweating in Nottingham late on the Saturday evening.

The town and the castle were empty. The King, and all his household, and his soldiers, were gone.

Perkin could have wept. There was no chance of following them tonight: still, he knew where they went. He put up at a small cheap inn for the night, tried without success the next morning to exchange his stout nag for a swifter animal—Nottingham was almost denuded of horses—and, after a hearty breakfast, set out doggedly to try to cover the twenty or thirty miles to Leicester before darkness fell.

*

Leicester was also the destination of Henry Tudor, who had early abandoned his original intention of marching on London: his advisors, his uncle Jasper, Earl of Pembroke and the Earl of Oxford, both experienced military commanders, had urged him against it. Better to stake all on the bold throw, and meet the King in pitched battle before he had had the chance to gather all his forces.

Near Atherstone, on Sunday, 21 August, Tudor rode to a pre-arranged meeting with Lord Stanley and his brother. He was too cautious to feel any more than the faintest pricklings of hope: he knew their reputation, and even without the advice of Oxford or his uncle Jasper, was aware that it would be foolhardy in the extreme to place any trust in them. Meeting the man whom his mother had so unaccountably, married, and whom he had never previously encountered, he took an instant dislike to the blandly smiling face, the ready promise of loyalty, the glib proposals for a master strategy. Nor did Sir William, fat, pale and shiny-looking like a very well-fed slug, inspire any more confidence. Slug-like, both men slid from his grasp with promises to join his army as soon as the time came. Lord Stanley at least had the genuine excuse, which he reiterated at every turn, that he feared for the life of his son, hostage in the King's army. His brother's pale bluish eyes watched Henry Tudor, and slithered away from contact. They rode back to their forces, leaving him with the feeling that the air had been cleared of some noxious smell, and knowing that, whatever the outcome of his battle with the King, stepson or no, they wished only to be on the winning side.

The previous night, as Henry Tudor lay restless and anxious near Tamworth, and Perkin unhappily at Nottingham, Henry Percy, Earl of Northumberland, at last arrived in Leicester to join the King, at the head of some two or three thousand men, exhausted after their hasty journey south. Richard welcomed the tall, hawk-faced, blue-jowled man who, surprisingly, was uncle to Sir Christopher Heron, and listened impatiently to his reasons for this tardy arrival. He dare not call Percy's loyalty directly into question, for his troops would comprise perhaps a third of the royal army. But he knew that the man's allegiance, as it had always been with his family, was in the end only given to himself.

And Sir Christopher Heron, making discreet search and enquiry, could not find Sir Robert Drakelon amongst Northumberland's men.

The next morning was Sunday, and once more hot and sunny. The people of Leicester gathered to marvel and cheer as the King's forces marched westward out of the town, towards the enemy. The troops of the Duke of Norfolk, solid East Anglians and Londoners for the most part, came first, many bearing his badge of a golden lion. They were followed by the King, riding the great white courser, given to him by Norfolk's son, and called White Surrey after its donor: the Duke himself, and the Earl of Northumberland, came just behind, at the head of the knights, esquires and other officers of the royal household. Amongst them, in the armour he had scarcely ever worn, and which he had not trusted Perkin to put on him, using instead the services of Bigod's lad, and riding his fretful Bayard, came Sir Christopher Heron.

He was glad that the day of reckoning approached at last. Scouts, sent out from Leicester in some numbers, had reported that Tudor's army, comprising less than five thousand men even after their desperate recruiting efforts on their march through Wales and the shires, was probably about twenty miles from the town, and were even now most likely moving along the line of Watling Street towards them. It seemed that Henry Tudor, though he had never seen any fighting, was as eager to have his cause subjected to the judgement of God and the outcome of battle as was the King.

The scouts had also reported that the Stanley brothers, both Lord Thomas and his brother Sir William, were hovering in the vicinity, unwilling it seemed to commit their forces—in combination they appeared to have more men at their command than did the Tudor —to the side of either King or rebel. The King had said little to this last piece of information, but everyone present had thought of Lord Stanley's son, the young Lord Strange, a hostage for his family's loyalty. Knowing his father's reputation for treachery, it was not surprising that Lord Strange exhibited signs of anxiety and stress.

Christie, his sallet tipped to the back of his head, glanced round at his companions, all men he had known for years. Sir Ralph Bigod, his freckled face rather abstracted: presumably he was thinking of his young wife Margaret, and their small child. Sir Robert Brackenbury, Constable of the Tower, who had shown such kindness to Dickon and his brother, was easily recognisable by his height, though his characteristic stoop was reduced by the elaborate plates of his fluted Flemish armour. There was Lord Lovell, hastily returned from the south, Will Catesby, Sir Robert Percy, Sir Richard Ratcliffe, clanking in harness which none of them had worn in serious anger since the Scots wars three years ago. In every face there shone the same grim, purposeful hope that illuminated the King. This was the test, the ordeal by battle, the judgement by God as to which man had greater right to the crown of England. They followed their anointed King, whom they had served, and loved, for years: not even the murmurings of disaffection, even of treason, amongst the fringes of the great host could disturb their determination to wipe the Tudor menace, once and for all, from the face of the land. Some, who had more exact knowledge of their enemy's previous tactics, thought of the attempt on the lives of King Edward's sons, and silently vowed vengeance. They had eight or ten thousand archers and men-at-arms behind them: in comparison, the Tudor's paltry French mercenaries, rabble of attainted English exiles, and motley collection of wild Welshmen, seemed no great obstacle.

The thought of defeat was at once too absurd, and too dreadful, even to contemplate.

*

Sweating, exhausted, Perkin Hobbes came in sight of the town of Leicester late on Sunday afternoon, having taken all day to ride from Nottingham on his stolid horse. He muttered a prayer of desperation, and enquired of the men on the gates, whether the King was yet within the town.

Derision greeted him: this undersized jackanapes, on his humble giant of a horse, both lathered and dripping with sweat, and with a definitely alien accent, commanded no respect. 'The King! He wants the King!' And in tones of cheerful contempt, 'You're too late, lad—the King and all his host rode out this morning.'

'Oh, Christ,' said Perkin despairingly. To his weary mind it seemed that he would be fated to follow his master up and down the country until the end of time, always just one day behind. 'Where have they gone? I have a message for my master, he's in the King's household—please tell me where they've gone.'

The solid faces stared belligerently back at him. With rising desperation, he fumbled in the flapping purse at his belt. 'There's a penny for you if you'll tell me.'

The coin disappeared with alacrity. 'Rode west, they did,' said their leader, with a toothy sneer that might have been intended for a smile. 'Heading for Atherstone, that's where the rebels are supposed to be. But you won't find them afore dark.'

And dark was rapidly approaching. Perkin thought of the dwindling store of pence in his purse: of the fact that he had once spent many nights under hedgerows or trees, and doubtless could do so again. But he had been three years in a gentleman's service, and the prospect, even on a warm summer's night, did not appeal. He asked for directions to a cheap inn, and made his way there, reflecting that one night could make little difference to his errand, nor could a penny for his horse, two for his own food and lodging, much deplete his already scanty coin. He had a hearty supper of bread, ale and mutton, and slept the sleep of the just, or the exhausted, until dawn.

It was Monday, 22 August 1485.

❧

CHAPTER TWENTY-ONE

'And never was there seen a more dolefuller battle.'
(BOOK 21, CHAPTER 4)

The hill stood above the wide rolling countryside of Leicestershire, red earth showing through the golden ranks of wheat and barley, almost ready for the harvest. In itself it was not especially high, but it commanded a splendid view of the lands about, and its steeper sides made it a most suitable position for the King to draw up his army and plan his strategy.

The royal host had spent the night encamped in and around the little village of Sutton, perhaps a mile from the hill. Since the only building with any pretensions to size was the church, tents had been pitched for the nobles and men of the household, and the King. The night was warm and dry, and men-at-arms and archers had spent it under hedgerows or in barns and outhouses, watched by the startled, apprehensive villagers, who had been suddenly and rudely pitchforked into momentous events of which they had only the vaguest knowledge.

Christie had served the King with wine, bread and meat for his supper, and had waited, quiet and watchful, as Richard conferred with his chief captains, Norfolk, Northumberland, and Lovell.

Norfolk, a big, plain, grey-haired man in his sixties, was, with the King himself, the most experienced commander. His words were brief and to the point as he moved bits of bread around the board at which they sat. 'Here's our camp, at this village, what's it called? Sutton? And over here, roughly speaking, is the Tudor at Atherstone, which must be five or six miles or so distant. In between is that hill, with the marsh at its foot.'

'The hill is the key,' said Richard, leaning forward. 'It's steep on its westward side, and on the southern slopes too. The ideal place to draw up our host, and wait for Tudor's approach. Once in position, we can adjust strategy according to the Pretender's position—and Lord Stanley's.'

There was a pause. Lovell coughed, and raised his eyes to the King's face. 'Your Grace—what will you do with Lord Strange?'

The unfortunate scion of the house of Stanley was under guard in another tent. The King smiled thinly. 'That depends on the out-come of the battle—and upon his father. I will decide on the morrow. Meanwhile, there is much to do. At first light the army will move onto the hill—therefore, you must rouse the men early, an hour before dawn, and make all ready to march as soon as there is sufficient light.' He looked at Norfolk, grim, powerful, solidly reliable, his capable son behind him. 'You will have the honour of commanding the van, Jack.'

Norfolk's face broke into a broad smile of satisfaction. 'I'll be right glad to have the first chance at that Welsh bastard, Your Grace.'

'And the blue Percy lion will fly over our rearguard,' the King continued. 'Here, to the east of the hill, would be the best place, I think—but all will be decided in the morning, when we have had a chance to survey the ground. Are you all in agreement? We shall confer further in the morning. Meanwhile, I think a good night's rest is essential for everyone.'

But it was doubtful whether any, in either army, slept sound that night. From the archers and more humble levies, huddled together in whatever shelter they could find, to the King and the man who would snatch the crown, none lay easy. Sentries patrolled the royal army, watching for enemy activity, watching also for those whose courage had failed them, and who might try, usually successfully, to slip away under the friendly cloak of darkness. Scouts had reported on the rebels' position near Atherstone to their commanders, but only the day would bring the fullest information about the Tudor, his captains and the strength of his force: and that of Sir William Stanley and his brother, of whom the best that could be said was that if they were not committed to the King, neither were they apparently intending to join with the rebels.

The King, contrary to his own instructions, passed a disturbed night. Christie, lying with Sir Ralph Bigod in his sovereign's tent, heard Richard move restlessly on his bed, turning again and again. At least once, he rose to pray at the little prie-dieu erected in a corner of the tent. Christie listened to the soft, indecipherable rush of words, and thought of his own future. There was still no word from Julian, no sign of Perkin, and he knew that he must face reality, unpleasant as it was. Why should she alter her opinion of him? His reconciliation with Meg did not alter one jot the truth that had so appalled his wife: that he had betrayed his sister's trust, putting ambition before his vow, and in so doing had ruined her

[472]

marriage. No amount of penance, of excuses, of forgiveness, could wipe away his crime: he knew it, and so, he did not doubt, did Julian.

He had a wife, living, who might hate him. The King had a wife, dead, who had loved him. They were both utterly alone. Richard had his crown, his kingdom, his cause against the Tudor to sustain him. What did Christie have? A wife he loved, to no avail, and a home where he was a stranger. When the Tudor was defeated, he could look forward to more rewards in the King's service, the pinnacle of achievement: for one so young, so high in favour, ennoblement after further years of loyalty seemed quite possible.

But what were lands, a title, honour, if he could not pass them on to his descendants? Christie stared bleakly into the dark at his brilliant future, and found it empty.

*

Long after her sister had retired to bed, Bess sat by the shuttered window of their chamber at Sheriff Hutton, her mind nearly empty of thought. She had been there so long and so still that the fancy came upon her, she had turned into stone herself, and become one with the castle in which she had spent the last two months, waiting, always waiting, for news of the invasion which everyone seemed to welcome: for only then would all the doubts and uncertainties of the future be cast away.

Not for her, of course: her own future was dim, cloudy, full of faces she hardly knew, amongst which there would one day, soon, appear the man who would be her husband. She hardly cared about that: so long as she could be with the people she knew, and loved, she did not really mind, for hers was a generous, affectionate nature, and she trusted her uncle's judgement in this, that he would not shackle her to a man she loathed.

But Henry Tudor was a different proposition entirely. How could she wed the man who had attempted to kill her brothers, who would have slain or defeated the King? She did not want to be Queen on those terms: she would rather live out her life as plain Mistress Plantagenet. Her father, however, had given her some knowledge of the harsh realities of her position, and the events after his death had shown her how little choice she would ever have to follow her own inclinations.

Cecily slept, snoring slightly: it was the only blemish on her delicate, fastidious beauty, and one which, waking, she hotly denied. Bess smiled wryly, and wondered what future lay in store for her sister; for all her sisters, and her mother; for Dickon, alone and valiant in a foreign land, amongst strangers; for her cousin John, Earl of Lincoln, and his brothers and sisters; for her other cousins, Edward, Earl of Warwick, a vague child in a world of his own who had hardly the wit to write his name, and his older sister Margaret, a pert vivid girl with her father Clarence's fatal charm.

They were a family: despite death, treason, dissent, they were still a family. What would happen to them all, if the Tudor proved the victor?

They had had no firm news for days, beyond the fact that the rebels had landed, and were marching to meet the King. The battle might take place tomorrow, next day, next week, next month: it might already have happened.

'Oh, God, sweet Virgin Mary, Holy St Michael and all the angels, give him the victory,' she prayed desperately: and did not mean Henry Tudor.

*

The day dawned fine, blue sky above, a mist hazing the low ground around the foot of the hill, emanating doubtless from the marshes. The King's camp had begun to stir well before dawn. Commanders who had had little sleep moved around the quarters, waking men who had rested little more. Soon the village and the ground about it were thick with soldiers yawning, stretching, snatching bread from their baggage, checking their equipment, wiping metal clean of the night's dew. In the slow-gathering light, they began to form up sluggishly with the gentlemen and knights who led them, and whose tenants, friends or kinsmen they generally were.

In the King's tent, Richard was being arrayed in his battle harness, while giving orders, swift and terse, to his captains for the deployment of their troops. In a corner hovered various men of the cloth, quavering to no-one in particular that Mass must be said, and the wine and bread were with the baggage and could not be found.

'Your Grace.' A man in the household livery, murrey and blue, shouldered his way into the tent and knelt, catching his breath. 'Your Grace, the rebel army is on the move from Atherstone. The scouts have just reported it.'

'Then we must move also.' Richard, his armour complete save for various straps and buckles, turned, the hapless squires following him with urgent hands. 'Is Surrey saddled? Good. We go to survey the ground. Norfolk, have your men formed up in readiness. You also, Northumberland. Brackenbury, marshal my 'household. Heron, Bigod, Percy, ride with me.'

The sun had not yet risen, as the King, the knights and a small bodyguard rode out from the camp towards the low bulk of the hill which would form a barrier to Tudor's progress. Overhead the heavens were blue, and innocent of clouds, but around the base of the hill the mists wreathed tortuously, masking the land beyond. There were scouts already on the hill, their eyes trained keenly on the ground where the battle would take place, and they turned as the horses galloped up the slope towards them. Their leader, a man in half harness and armet helmet, trotted his horse over to the King. 'There's no sign of them yet, Your Grace.'

'And where is Lord Stanley?'

'There, Your Grace—over to the north.'

The Stanley forces were about two miles distant. Evidently the noble lord had not yet committed himself to either side: he would doubtless play the same waiting game as he had done so often before, and delay until the outcome of the battle was decided, or in doubt, before throwing his forces in to aid the winner. His younger brother, Sir William, bolder despite his sluggish size, was a more dubious quantity: and, being a proclaimed traitor, had nothing whatever to lose by supporting the Tudor from the outset.

Yet there he was, his men somewhat in advance of his brother's.

It was some grounds for optimism. The King turned from contemplation of his possible enemies, to consideration of the ground. The hill was a fine defensive position, with steep slopes running down to the marshy land below. The rebels would have to negotiate that mire, that hill, to come at him: he could attack at his leisure, and aim his archers, his harquebusiers and his field guns at the puny forces ranged against him.

Christie felt the breeze on his face, turned and saw the sun's first bright rays climb above the distant church of Sutton Cheyney, to drive away the last of the mist. It would be a glorious day: and it might also be his last on this earth.

He had never faced open battle before: the fighting in Scotland had been risky, the wounding of Sir Thomas Bray had proved that, but for the most part brief, frantic hand-to-hand encounters. He had no experience of the desperate confusion of a mêlée, vicious and exhausting. Last night, as he had lain awake, listening to the King's

[475]

uneasy dreams, the thought had crept into his head that perhaps, it might not be so dreadful to die: his life was bleak and bitter, there was no joy in it. And then he had thought of Meg, and her children, how her need of him had not ended: and of Julian. He wanted to see her again, to see the heavy curling hair, the wide dark eyes, her sturdy strength and blistering honesty: and he wanted, above all, to hear her singing voice once more, that high breathtaking purity that had no match anywhere.

As if in echo of his thought, high above the bare hilltop, scattered with scrub, rough grass and sheep, a lark began its song, joyous in the morning.

Life was sweet after all, so long as he had ears to hear, and eyes to see, and love to give, even if the recipient were unwilling. He turned Bayard, who stamped and snorted, and rode back with the King to the camp.

An hour after sunrise, the royal army left Sutton and made its ponderous way towards the hilltop. Norfolk commanded the forward section, with archers and men-at-arms and harquebusiers accompanying his field-cannon, which would be chained together to avoid being overrun. His lieutenant was Brackenbury, the gentle scholarly man of a family as obscure as Christie's, determined like him to fight for the King who had favoured him so highly. These men of the south and the green close countries of Suffolk and Essex viewed the wide tree-scattered spaces around them dubiously, but marched on doggedly, and deployed around the ridge of the hill in a great straggling line along the southern and western slopes. The white lion standard of the Duke of Norfolk floated above them, surrounded by the banners of lesser men: the three sable chevrons on silver of Brackenbury, the Earl of Surrey, the knights and gentlemen of London and East Anglia. Behind, crowding the comparatively long and narrow hilltop, the King set up his great standard, the white boar bright against a background of murrey and blue, the livery colours of the house of York. Around him on their restless horses, nervously taking their mood from their riders, sat the lords, knights and gentlemen of his household, united in their devotion to his cause. There had not been space on the hill for Northumberland's men, who were grouped on the lower ground, to be held in readiness should the day unaccountably go against the King.

Even without the men of Northumberland and Yorkshire, it was an awe-inspiring display of strength, calculated to strike terror into their opponents. Christie, glancing round at the seething, murmuring, clanking mass of men, took a deep breath and smiled faintly under the shade of his sallet. It was a good company to fight in. He thought of the men he himself had been able to raise: not from Ashcott, but from manors once belonging to the Duke of Buckingham, that had been given to him on his knighthood. He had sent his command to his bailiffs and stewards without much hope of response, and had been pleasantly surprised when a score or so of archers and soldiers, variously equipped, had trickled into Leicester. From the talk he had had with them, they had hated the Duke, who was a harsh and exacting landlord: they had not fought for him in his rebellion, but were prepared to risk their lives with their unknown new lord. He had placed them with Norfolk's vanguard, for he himself must ride with the King: but he had promised them a fine reward for turning out to fight Henry Tudor.

From his position in the centre of the field, it was not easy to view the enemy's approach: his sight was blocked by standards, banners, bills, lances and the solid and astonishing variety of helmets of all ages, some of which might well have seen service at the Battle of Agincourt, or even of Crecy. His belly growled sullenly, although he had at least been able to snatch something to break his fast. In the haste and confusion of making ready for battle, the King had not even had that benefit: but since he had not heard Mass, had vowed not to let meat or drink pass his lips until the Tudor should be defeated.

The sun rose hotter. Bayard ceased his fidgeting and slept, his eyes half closed and his tied and braided tail swishing futilely at flies. Christie thought of Perkin, doubtless lurking in some tavern, and his mind strayed, almost unwillingly, to Julian, to wonder what she did at this moment—riding out on the sheepwalks, perhaps, or in the little garden at Ashcott?

At last, as the sun approached its zenith, there was movement in front of them: shouting of orders, a standard dipping and swaying, men surging forward. A great sullen roar cracked the air: one of the King's field-pieces had been fired. It was swiftly followed by its fellow: as their ears rang and a great double plume of smoke rolled back over the army, the answer came, fainter. The Tudor evidently had guns also.

The vanguard, Norfolk's men, were moving steadily down the hill, pausing to loose their arrows at the rebel army below, before smashing into the Earl of Oxford's men. From their position

[477]

behind the King, Christie and the other members of the King's household could see little, but the sounds of battle came up to them clearly, mixed with a faint stalwart thread of larksong: the screams of the dying and wounded, shouts and battle-cries, the tremendous explosions of the huge guns and the smaller popping noise of the harquebusiers. Then, slowly, the main bulk of the army moved forward to occupy the place left by Norfolk's force, and the struggle below them came into plain view. The marsh at the hill's foot had drastically limited the rebels' line of attack: away to the northwest could be seen the men of Sir William Stanley, distinguished by their red jerkins and his standard of a white hart's head, while to the south, much further off, hovered his more cautious and devious brother, whose badge, unsuitably, was an eagle's leg. The banner of the commander of the rebel van—which seemed to comprise most of their army—showed the famous silver star of the Earl of Oxford, the Tudor's most experienced captain.

It was apparent that the Pretender himself was not yet engaged in the fighting: more distant from the main battle, Christie saw a group that must hide him. From here, no detail could be picked out, merely a surprisingly small body of armed men on horseback, thicketed with standards, predominately green, white and red in colour. It was unquestionably the Tudor. Christie glanced automatically over to the north, where Sir William Stanley's forces waited under their cynical commander, and saw signs of movement.

Below, a great wailing shout arose: Norfolk's banner wavered and fell into the confused press of men, the lion vanquished. The King, from his position on the crown of the hill, could see everything: Norfolk probably dead, the battle between the vanguards undecided and hotly contested, the forces of Sir William Stanley apparently preparing to enter the field, and above all, offering overwhelming temptation, the distant presence of Henry Tudor with a dangerously puny escort.

Richard looked round at the men nearest to him: his household, the knights and lords and esquires who had served him so devotedly, who would follow him anywhere, to the jaws of Hell if necessary. The time was ripe for boldness: one quick stroke now would bring the battle to a decisive end, and the key to it was the person of Henry Tudor. He gave swift orders to Lovell and Lincoln, instructing them to hold the hill and to throw the remainder of the main army into battle as they deemed necessary, and then turned to his friends and servants. 'There is the Tudor! He is ours for the taking—will you follow me, and bring an end to this canker, once and for all?'

The question was rhetorical, the shouts of assent eclipsing even the tumult of the fighting, furgher down the hill. With a great worldless cry of challenge, the King's company lowered their visors gripped sword and battle-axe, and urged their horses charging down the slope towards their quarry, swinging right to avoid the doggedly struggling vanguards. The great destriers thundered through the thick rough grass, ears flat, nostrils wide, their riders jolting between the high steel-clad pommels of their saddles, wedged tight in readiness for the impact, lances, axes, swords, flails or hammers at the ready according to preference.

Christie preferred in the last resort to trust to his sword, though he held the great war hammer, its heavy steel head designed to crush the strongest armour, in the hand that was not attempting to control Bayard, who was completely unprotected by any metal: he had always fought off any efforts to put armour on his head or chest. The ugly bay was in his element now, a weapon of war in his own right, trained to use his iron-shod hooves and impressive teeth, if necessary, against opposing men and horses. Flecks of foam flew from his mouth. Christie, filled with the wild sudden exhilaration of the charge, found himself shouting with the rest: Bigod, Catesby, Ratcliffe, Robert Percy, the King's standard-bearer Sir Percival Thirlwall, a hundred armoured fighting men all around him, and in the van, the slight, fierce figure of their King, his crowned helm glittering gold and steel in the sun.

It was a sight to inspire awe and terror: certainly, the Tudor made no attempt to flee or fight, but sat his horse in the middle of his soldiers as if transfixed with horror, as the White Boar smashed into the little force of rebels. And suddenly the euphoria of the attack was gone, as Christie found himself fighting in close, desperate, hand-to-hand combat. The hammer crushed the helm of a man who loomed in front of him: as that opponent fell away, he turned his sweating, furious horse with all the strength of his arm to face another who came at him with an axe. The sharp weapon chopped at the wooden shaft of his hammer, shattering it: he wrenched his sword from the scabbard and thrust its long narrow point through the gap between breast-plate and shoulder. As the man fell, blood spurting, he dragged his blade free and glanced swiftly around. Several men were down already, Ratcliffe amongst them, and as he urged Bayard forward the great standard of the Tudor, white and green with a red Welsh dragon spurting flame, crashed to the ground. A shout went up: with sudden wild hope he plunged into the fray. Richard was there, his battle fury lending his slight figure an almost super-human strength: he had slain the standard-bearer, and the tumbled blood-stained heap of armour on the ground was massively big. It was not, however, Henry Tudor: and Richard gathered up his axe and the reins of his white horse and shouted for his men to follow him to victory.

And it was at that precise and critical moment that Sir William Stanley's men attacked.

The force of their assault pushed the royal knights off balance, towards the softer ground of the marsh. Christie, suddenly and desperately fighting for his life against a swarm of foot-soldiers armed with bills and swords and axes, saw someone, Percy perhaps, frantically urging Richard to flee: but the King threw him off, and turned again towards the Tudor. The ground under Bayard's plunging hooves was treacherous: the horse stumbled, and then abruptly was down: Christie found himself on the ground, fortunately clear of the horse, who was thrashing in his death-throes, gutted by a foot-soldier who had crept under his belly. In this prone position he was most vulnerable, he struggled to rise, saw a man-at-arms come at him with mace swinging, and flung himself out of the way. There was no time to remove the lower part of his sallet so that he might see better: peering through the narrow slit of the visor he thrust at his opponent, saw the man fall backwards, and beyond him the figure of the King, standing over the body of White Surrey, similarly brought low, wielding his sword against a great press of foot-soldiers attacking with pike and bill. His shouts came quite clearly to Christie, almost in reach of him, as Sir William Stanley's men closed in for the kill.

'Treason! *Treason!*'

It was the last thing that Christie heard, before a pole-axe smashed into helmet and shoulder, and ·laid him down on the marshy red earth of Redemore Plain.

*

Late in the afternoon, a small young man in servant's livery pushed his sturdy horse into the humble village of Sutton Cheney, hoping that at last his journey might be at an end. He resolutely ignored the dreadful possibility that his master might have met his death in the battle that everyone had assured him would take place that very day. He thought instead, with pleasure, of Christie's face when he opened Julian's letter, and saw how her heart had changed. 'All's well,' Perkin hummed happily, with the high-soaring larks. 'A fine day, and all's well.'

The village was virtually empty. A few ancient, toothless faces peered at him from the doorways of their hovels. He hailed one. 'Where can I find the King's army?'

There was a completely unintelligible cackle, but the pointing finger was guide enough. With a light heart Perkin urged his somnolent horse along the track that led to the pavilions and tents beyond the village, noting the plentiful signs that a large host had lodged there, and was almost at once confronted by a small body of soldiers who emerged from amidst the camp.

They looked very efficient, and unsullied by battle: and they wore a livery that was a fresh, clean scarlet, with the badge of a white hart. With a dawning and awful apprehension, Perkin halted his nag, and watched them approach.

Apart from his dagger, he was innocent of weapons: only his glib tongue might save him now. He watched the leading soldier unsheath his sword and survey him. 'What's your business here?'

So far, honesty seemed to be the best policy. 'I'm seeking my master,' said Perkin. 'He was with the King's force.'

A collective snigger arose from the watchful men. 'You mean, the *late* King,' said their leader. He was a big man, with unfriendly eyes below the open sallet. 'Your master is most likely dead, or captured, or run away. King Henry has won the day, God bless him.'

'God save King Henry!' his minions echoed dutifully. Behind them, Perkin could see many other men, looting tents, piling arms and supplies into carts. Appallingly, they must be speaking the truth. His mouth dry, he said, 'I want to find out whether my master is alive or not. I bear a letter for him, from his wife.'

The soldier's contemptuous gaze flicked up and down Perkin's insubstantial form. 'What's your master's name, then?'

'Sir Christopher Heron, of the King's household,' Perkin told him, his heart crashing against his ribs, while he prayed with a desperate urgency to a deity he had never troubled before, that Christie was safe.

'With the household, eh? There's precious little hope for him, then. The King's knights died fighting most valiantly around him,' said the leader, in a sarcastic parody of chivalrous romance. 'Cut 'em down almost to a man, we did—the men of Cheshire and Lancashire and Wales, to slay the Hog himself—that's a great feat of arms to boast of, eh, lads?'

The men brayed with laughter, while Perkin, in the grip of nightmare, sat his broad-backed horse and sweated coldly, despite the heat. He said, his voice even more reedy than usual, 'Where's the battlefield? I want to look for him.'

'No, you don't, lad,' said the soldier, with something approaching kindness. 'Nasty, it is, down there behind the hill—wouldn't go there if I were you. Besides which, you might meet more of Sir William Stanley's men, and we're known as the soft ones of his lot—so they wouldn't treat you so well. Kill first, ask questions after, that's their cry, and we wouldn't want a nice lad like you splat like a pike, would we?'

Another snigger from his comrades. Perkin stared at him, despairingly. 'But how can I find out if he's alive?'

'Go to Leicester, lad. That's where the King's going, with all his soldiers, and if your man's been taken prisoner, he'll be in the King's train with my lords Northumberland and Surrey. And if he's not a prisoner, then he's dead, and someone will tell you—or he's fled, in which case you'd best seek him elsewhere, eh, lad? Now be on your way.'

Heartsick, defeated, he had no alternative. He tugged the horse's head around, and plodded back through Sutton Cheyney, and the route he had already travelled in such hope.

*

The news was brought to Bess at Sheriff Hutton, the day after the battle, by the men of York. It was much, much worse than she had ever imagined. The Tudor had won, her uncle was dead, and she, like the prize in a tournament, was to be bestowed upon the victor.

Perhaps, she could have escaped, taken horse for the coast and got ship for Flanders. But she was only Bess, dreamy, gentle Bess, not some fierce and valiant knight—and besides, she could not leave Cecily, nor her mother and sisters in the south, nor the slow, pathetic little Earl of Warwick, nor his twelve-year-old sister Margaret, whose pert chatter delighted her as Dickon's had once done. She would stay, and accept her fate, and be Queen of England, for she could do no other.

And perhaps, she could use her influence to soften the harshness of her unknown betrothed's retribution against her friends and her family.

The men of York, distraught, told her that they were all dead: the King, her cousin of Lincoln, the Duke of Norfolk, his son Surrey, Lovell, Brackenbury, Ratcliffe, Lord Ferrers, even the King's secretary Kendall: all slain at Richard's side. Cecily's hand crept out to grasp hers, but she did not need her sister's comfort at this, the worst moment of her nineteen years of life. She was a King's daughter: gentle and thoughtful she might be, but beneath her softness there was steel.

Later, however, she wept, thinking of the treason of which the York men had spoken, the strange inaction of the Earl of Northumberland, the treachery of the Stanleys, the tragedy that had befallen them. The world had changed, and the future was dark.

A group of men appeared at the gates the next morning, below the banner of the red dragon. She received them with her sister, and Lady Morley, and the children of her late uncle Clarence, Edward staring vacantly into space, Margaret straight and severe, their women and servants clustered behind them.

The leader, a man called Willoughby, told her to make ready, for she would soon be conducted with all due ceremony to the capital, there to await the long-delayed, so deeply welcomed marriage with His Grace, Henry Tudor, King of England.

'Very well,' said the tall, stately girl before him; she had never looked more like her father. 'But I must ask, what provision has been made for my dear sister? And for these, my cousins, who are also most dear to me?'

'They are also to travel south with you, my lady,' said Willoughby, glancing with contemptuous pity at the young Earl of Warwick. His newly royal master had been most concerned to seize the person of the child, the last male Plantagenet if it could be assumed that this lady's brothers were indeed dead, but by the look of the poor wittol he would scarcely be worth the bother. He had also orders to discover the whereabouts, or fate, of those two lost princes, and later had the opportunity to question the Lady Elizabeth more closely. Was there any other of royal blood within the castle?

'None,' said the Princess, staring at him in surprise. She was a fine-looking girl, with her commanding height and flowing harvest-yellow tresses and gentle face, and his royal master, not a tall man and rather sparse and sandy of hair, would inevitably be at a disadvantage beside her. Willoughby coughed. 'Forgive me, my lady, but I have been instructed to make enquiries—discreet, of course—as to the whereabouts of your brothers.'

There was complete silence. Bess sat quite still, her mind racing, fighting the surge of grief and anger that would lead her to say something foolish. Best, safest for Dickon, for anyone who had survived that dreadful carnage, to disclaim all knowledge.

Tears, today, were easy. She looked at him sadly, and spoke the approximate truth, thereby committing herself to a lifetime of lying, for her brother's sake. 'I—I am sorry, sir. I do not know where they might be, or whether on earth or in Heaven. I have not seen either of my brothers for a very long time.'

He saw her evident distress, and believed her, and with that answer, must be satisfied.

*

The townsfolk of Leicester, never ones to risk royal displeasure, gave to King Henry a welcome quite as lavish as that they had offered to King Richard a few days before. The landlord of the White Boar, hearing of the Tudor's unexpected, astonishing victory, sent a lad up a ladder with a pot of blue paint, to convert his unfortunate sign to the more appropriate badge of the Earl of Oxford. The new King marched into the town at the head of his victorious troops, banners flying in the late summer sunshine, trumpets blasting his triumph. The curious people, lining the streets with sycophantic cheers, saw a slight, pale-skinned man with a thin clever face and sparse reddish hair. It was the face of a young man who had always been old, the lean mouth unable to smile, even at this glorious moment.

Behind his soldiers, with their captain's banners—Oxford's boar and star, the golden horse of the King's uncle the Earl of Pembroke, the three sable ravens belonging to the Welsh chief Rhys ap Thomas, and the Stanley eagle's foot—came the standards and banners of the defeated, trailed ignominiously in the dust, then the wagonloads of spoils from the abandoned royal camp, plate, armour, and other valuables, and those captives who were hurt, piled in open carts.

Last of all, naked and slung over a broken-down nag, a halter round its neck, reviled and spat upon, came the battered, grotesque corpse of the dead King. It was flung into a horse trough so that all might see in what contempt the victor held the vanquished: and it was two days before the brothers of Greyfriars were allowed to give King Richard, third of his name, a decent burial.

*

Perkin had spent the night after the battle under a hedgerow, but despite his weariness had hardly slept. Over and over again he thought of Julian's letter, of the battle, of how he might have come sooner had circumstances been different: and above all, how it seemed quite likely that Christie had died with his King, without ever knowing that his wife had relented, or that she expected their child.

He slept at last, dreamed badly, woke weeping: scrubbed his face with his by now filthy sleeve, clambered aboard his patient horse, and plodded the last few miles to Leicester that he had still to travel when darkness had overtaken him the previous night.

To his relief, there were different men on the gate this morning, and they let him through cheerfully, especially when he enquired as to the whereabouts of the King. Whereas the White Boar had been sufficient for King Richard, it seemed that Henry Tudor had a more inflated idea of his royal dignity—or felt less secure—and had taken up residence at the castle. Here, presumably, were his captives lodged.

The castle proved to be a neglected, crumbling building, obviously long untenanted. Perkin hoped, sourly, that their night had been less comfortable in their derelict estate, than if they had used the humbler but more sumptuous inns of the town.

He had not expected to be allowed within the gates, and so it proved. The guards were foreign mercenaries, French by their jabber, and capable of speaking only the most basic English. Since Perkin knew not a word of their language, conversation was limited to shouts of single syllables. Their halberds barred his way, and their expressions became more irritated: and then Perkin saw, making his way across the bailey behind the gatewards, a figure he knew. Desperately, he hailed him. 'Sir Robert! Sir Robert Drakelon!'

The immaculate, dark-haired man turned and stared at the gatehouse. Perkin shed all dignity and leaped up and down in the air like a Fool at Christmas, flapping his arms in the air while the Frenchmen gaped at him in astonishment, and screamed. 'Sir Robert! Please hear me!'

There was a long agonising moment when Christie's brother-in-

[485]

law did not move. Then, with a studied lack of haste, eyebrows raised in well-bred enquiry, he strolled across to investigate this bizarre supplicant.

Perkin was not interested in polite etiquette: as soon as Sir Robert was within the gatehouse arch, he said urgently, 'Sir Robert—I beg you, have you any news?'

'News? News of whom, pray? Do I know you?'

'Yes, you do, surely, sir—I'm Sir Christopher Heron's servant —have you any news of him, sir? Please?'

'I have news,' said Sir Robert, suavely bored. 'He is the King's prisoner, to be held at the King's pleasure. Doubtless he will be taken south to London in due course, when he has recovered, to answer for his crimes.'

'What crimes?' Perkin demanded in fury. 'He only fought for his King!'

'Who, as you know, committed many crimes. Catesby is also to face the penalty for his misdeeds, but since he is unhurt, and was captured while fleeing the field, the sentence will be carried out forthwith.'

'Sentence? Unhurt? What do you mean, for Christ's sake?' Perkin could have shaken Sir Robert's well-groomed shoulders in his frustration, but for the menacing presence of the mercenaries, separating them. 'For the love of God, sir, for his wife's sake—tell me—is my master hurt?'

'He is sorely hurt, yes, but the physicians seem to think he will recover to face the hangman, as Catesby will soon face death also. You can tell Dame—Julian, is it? You may tell Dame Julian that there is every chance that she will shortly become a widow, as I believe is her ambition.' He smiled coldly, and said something in French. Roaring with laughter, two of the mercenaries picked Perkin up, one hand under each arm, hauled him across the stones in front of the gate, and tossed him contemptuously into a pile of ordure swept up from the street for the greater convenience of the King's procession.

Swearing, sobbing, Perkin cursed their retreating backs: then he struggled free of the filth and dung, brushed off as much of the mess as he could, collected his horse, which had gone to sleep, and left Leicester with hate and despair in his heart.

It did not occur to him until much later, to wonder what Sir Robert Drakelon, retainer of the captive Earl of Northumberland, was doing at liberty in the company of Henry Tudor.

'Hey, Will, this one's not dead!'

The uncouth voice, shatteringly loud, was the first thing that forced its way into Christie's aching, reluctant consciousness. Someone was pulling his armour off with brisk, uncaring hands: the air struck his hot body and he struggled, trying to push them away. Someone cursed him, and a blow on the side of his head smashed him back into acquiescence. He lay there, jerked this way and that as the looters dragged the fine, expensive armour, German-made, from his arms and legs, wrenching his shoulder and sending him dizzy with sudden agony. Confused, he tried to marshal his thoughts with the cold logic that had so often served him in the past. He was alive, but hurt—his head spun and ached, and his shoulder throbbed with a great burning stabbing pain that chimed unerringly with the beat of his heart. The rough handling had reopened the wound—he could feel blood, warm and wet, all around his right upper arm.

Apart from that, he thought wryly, no harm done—fit as a flea! And then abruptly he remembered the battle, the long waiting, the tension, and even, dimly, the great charge down the hill towards the Tudor. But after that—nothing.

They had finished. With difficulty, he opened his eyes: blood had run over the lids and dried them stickily together, and he tried to wipe it away clumsily with his good left hand. The deep blue sky met his straining gaze: then, into his field of vision loomed a huge grubby face, its features blurred so that it could have been man or monster peering at him. 'What's your name, sir?'

The polite address startled him: he had no experience of the aftermath of battle, but common sense told him that looters did not usually behave thus. The face drew back: he tried to speak, but the words stuck dry on his tongue. Abruptly, his head was raised and a water-bottle thrust at his mouth. Despite the sudden pain in his skull, the cool liquid poured gratefully down his throat, and he drank thirstily. At least, he could take comfort from the fact that they would hardly waste good water on a man they intended to kill.

The bottle empty, he stared up at the face, trying in vain to bring it into focus. 'Your name?' it repeated, and Christie, suddenly exhausted, told him.

The next moments were confused: he was lifted by several hands, and tried to tell them of the wound in his shoulder, but it was no good; an iron fist gripped the place, agonisingly, and he slid gasping into unconsciousness.

The cheering was the next sound, so unlikely that his mind reeled in astonishment. He was in a cart, jolting, every movement sending flames of agony through his body. The cheering rose in waves: he could not make out what they said, until suddenly a stentorian bawl seemed to erupt almost in his ear. 'King Henry! God bless King Henry!'

He tried to say that she was wrong—King Henry had died years ago, it was King Richard now. But the words would not come through, and he gave up and lay there, too tired and weak to make any attempt to understand. He was alive, and for the moment that was the most important thing.

His next clear period of consciousness came as he was unloaded from the cart, bringing on such pain that it forced him awake, and he cried out. Soft voices washed over him, and he was carried on some kind of litter within a cool building, where sounds and footsteps echoed. He was laid upon a bed, and someone set about stripping off his mail shirt, bathing his wounds in warm herb-scented water, and ministering to him with welcome gentleness. Then he was lapped in soft warm blankets, and instantly fell asleep.

*

'Sir Christopher!' A voice, low and urgent, interrupted his slumbers. He opened his eyes, his mind quite clear, and beheld a monk or canon of some kind, he could not distinguish the exact colour of the dark habit behind the brilliance of the candle he held. The brother continued, unhappily, 'Sir Christopher. Please forgive me, there is a man here who would speak with you urgently—I told him you were hurt, but he insisted, in the King's name.'

'The King?' Christie stared at him. 'But the King—' His voice trailed away as the memory came suddenly back to him, that slight figure wielding the battleaxe, and shouting—

'Treason,' he whispered softly, and a familiar voice spoke above him. 'Treason? Whose treason, Sir Christopher? Yours? Against His Grace, King Henry, King by right of God and conquest?'

It was true then. The satisfaction in Sir Robert's voice could not be denied. Christie, narrowing his eyes against the candlelight, could not see his brother-in-law's face, but the pale glimmer of his smile told him all he needed to know.

'I fought for my anointed King,' he whispered. 'What else would you have me do—betray him, as you have done?'

The glimmer disappeared abruptly. 'Enough,' said Sir Robert

sharply. 'You may show defiance now, but the time will come soon when you will be more—amenable. Your royal tyrant is dead, and so are most of his associates, and his household, and the rest have fled. There are few survivors in our hands, and you are one. So tell me, the King must know—*where are the children?*'

For a moment, Christie did not understand—whose children? Sir Robert's? Then, he knew what information was required, and smiled. 'Hasn't he looked at Sheriff Hutton yet?'

A blow from the other man's fist smashed across his face. The brother cried out in protest, and Sir Robert turned and snatched the candle from his trembling hand. 'Get out, and stay out. This is the King's business.'

The monk backed out of the chamber, and the door shut. Sir Robert put the candle down on a stool that stood by Christie's pallet, and knelt over his wife's brother. The one, slanting source of light gave his sleek face a terrifying, demonic look. 'Now that your confessor has gone, you may speak freely. The boys. Where are they?'

Christie's rare anger was aroused, threatening to choke him. If he had been well and hale, he would have risen from his bed to throttle the life from his brother-in-law's smooth pale throat—but he was weak, and hurt, and his arm was bound tightly to his body. He said softly, 'And if I do not know?'

He thought Sir Robert would strike him again: the man's hand moved slightly, and then was still. There was a long silence: then the older man sat back on his heels. 'It would be better for you, believe me, if you do know. You are known to be a close and intimate friend to the usurper. You have undoubtedly shared in his crimes, and have treasonably fought against His Grace, King Henry.'

'Treason?' Christie stared at him in disbelief. 'Since what misbegotten hour has it been treason to fight for a crowned and anointed King?'

'His Grace plans to date the beginning of his blessed reign from Sunday 21 August,' said Sir Robert, smiling. 'So, all who fought against him, as you did, are guilty of treason.'

The audacity, the cunning of it, took Christie's breath away. Finally, he said quietly, 'A King may make laws, and carry out punishment under them as he pleases. But in the end, God will be the judge. And I do not think that Heaven will find me, or any other of our company, guilty of treason. We kept faith.'

[489]

Sir Robert made a sound of contempt. 'And much good did it do you! You are doomed, Christie Heron, and only your wounds have preserved you thus far. Your associate, William Catesby, is to be hanged tomorrow, or the day after. The King is not disposed to show mercy to any who had a part in the usurper's crimes, or who did away with those poor innocent children.'

Christie saw the trap in time. He said, refusing to rise to the bait, 'I do not know where they are—nor, if I did, would I tell you or your master. And who are you to talk of treason, or death? You plotted with Northumberland to betray Richard.'

'Perhaps,' said Sir Robert. 'It brought no result, however, as you might be interested to know. The Earl of Northumberland, your uncle, is at present in the King's custody.' He smiled thinly, with that glimmer of pale, perfect teeth. 'He promised to fight for His Grace, and unaccountably did not. He therefore quite naturally comes under suspicion of disloyalty.' He leaned forward again, and gripped the younger man's injured shoulder. Seeing, dimly, the avid expression of Sir Robert's face, Christie braced himself for the pain that would surely follow, while he vowed wordlessly to keep silence, whatever the cost, for only then would Dickon, and Tyrell, and the rest be safe.

The door opened abruptly: the tiny room seemed suddenly full of monks, their robes swirling, and at their head a tall, commanding man who must surely be the abbot, or prior. 'What means this, Sir Robert? The man is sick! Kindly leave at once.'

The elegant black-haired man rose, his expression smoothed away to one of bland apology. 'I fear Sir Christopher is faint: he needs succour. Yes, I will depart, of course—a thousand pardons, Prior.'

Christie lay still, sweating, as the brothers settled him once more for the night: but he knew that this respite was only temporary. Henry Tudor was King, by right of conquest, and must marry Bess to add her claim to his, as King Edward's heiress. But if Henry knew that Dickon lived—he would do all in his power to seize the child, or murder him as his agents had so nearly done before.

'Keep faith,' Christie whispered, into the comfort of the dark, when at last the brothers had gone. 'Keep faith, all those who still live, and know—I at least will not betray you, Dickon.'

CHAPTER TWENTY-TWO

**'When sickness toucheth a prisoner's body . . .
then hath he cause to wail and to weep.'**
(BOOK 9, CHAPTER 36)

The thunderstorm that heralded the end of the fine weather broke over Ashcott on 5 September. The harvest was safely in, by God's mercy, and had been a good one: no-one in the cottages need go hungry that winter, whatever else the wheel of fortune might bring.

There was a new king in the land: they had learned the news some days ago, with disbelief, horror or delight, according to their various sympathies. Dame Alice, of course, had been exultant, her expressions of triumphant glee aired for everyone to hear. She had not at first noticed Julian's frozen silence, but later, after supper in the parlour, she had taken her daughter to task. 'You're looking peaky, girl. You'll need to tend your looks if you're to catch that fine new husband I promised you.'

'I don't want a new husband.'

'Hoity-toity, girl, don't argue. I'm sure there's one King Henry will want to favour with your hand—I must write to the Countess of Richmond at once, and ask her to use her influence with her son. She dotes on him, and he on her, though she's not seen him for nigh on fifteen years.' Dame Alice placed her elbows on the carved arms of her huge box chair, and stared at her daughter's white, mutinous face. 'Shame about the brat. Let's hope it ails.'

Suddenly, something inside Julian broke free from the years of injustice, the beatings and brutality and subjection. With calm dignity, she rose to her feet, her bulky gown almost concealing the swell of her child, her arms crossed protectively over it. 'I wish to make certain things clear, mother. Firstly, you merely *assume* that my husband is dead. There is no news yet—and *I* prefer to assume that he is still alive. Secondly, even if he is dead—and I will mourn his death, have no doubt of that—I will wed no-one whom I do not choose, even if the King himself commands me otherwise. I would rather take the veil than go again unwillingly into a loveless marriage. And third, madam, understand this. The child is *mine*, mine, do you hear me? And it will be the heir to Ashcott, and I will

[491]

guard its life with mine, with my body if necessary.' Her eyes, dark and hot, held her mother's unwaveringly. 'Your reign is ended. You have what you wanted, what you've worked and plotted for, a new king in England. Be content with that—you can cow me no longer.' And she had turned on her heel and walked out, her head high, leaving her mother, impotent, thunderstruck, alone by the hearth . . .

Reaction came later, with shivering and sweats, but she did not regret her defiance. The servants, the rest of the household, were on her side, Marten and Friday were her friends. Dame Alice had only her own maid Mary to support her, and her power, though enforced in the past with sticks and abuse, was waning. Julian had faced her down, and as she supped the rich thick posset that Friday had coaxed from the kitchen to warm her mistress, she found to her wonder and surprise that she feared her mother no longer.

But despite her brave words, she must face facts. King Richard was dead, and many of his attendants and friends with him: Norfolk, Lincoln, Lovell, all had been proclaimed slain in battle, according to their informant, and it seemed probable that Christie too had been killed. She prayed, desperately, that he had died knowing of her change of mind, that he had not gone to his death in despair of unrequited love. It all depended on Perkin: she calculated, with feverish intensity, that the servant would have had ample time to reach his master before battle was joined, and tried to find some comfort in it. It was impossible: the sharpness and desperation of her grief overwhelmed her. She had been so convinced that this time it would work, that a second—or third—chance had been given to her, to redeem herself. And now the unthinkable had happened, and the King was dead—and Christie, if still alive, probably at the mercy of Henry Tudor.

But he might have fled. That hope buoyed her up for a day or two, until it occurred to her that he would most likely have come here to Ashcott, and that if he had not appeared by now, he would never do so.

Marten tried to comfort her, in his gruff diffident way, by pointing out that Sir Christopher had other manors to which he could flee, and that Ashcott, home of Dame Alice as well as his wife, might not necessarily be his first choice of refuge. She took a little heart from that: but knew also that in such a situation he would have sent Perkin instead. Perkin was not a squire, only a lowly servant, he would not, surely, have become caught up in the fighting. He should have returned to her with news—it was only two or three days' journey to Leicester, where the battle had been fought. Why, then, did he not return?

There was, in fact, a very good reason. Perkin, only a day's hard ride from Ashcott, had gone to sleep in the little inn at Daventry, tired but healthy, and had woken in the night with a raging headache and thirst, sweating profusely: already his thick coarse sheets were soaked. Confused and feverish, he called for help to the others who shared the chamber, only to have them flee precipitately as soon as they realised that he was ill, for fear that it might be plague.

It was not, although at first the monks to whose infirmary he was taken were reluctant to admit him. This was a new kind of sickness, which they had never seen before: the sweat washed from him like water, his head seemed to burst with the pain, the fever raged unchecked. Tossing and turning, desperately but dimly aware that he had a most urgent task to fulfil, Perkin in his delirium tried several times to leave his bed: in the end the brother who tended him had to enlist other monks to share the watch, so that he could be guarded night and day.

They thought he would die: it was a surprise to them, that he did not, but on the fourth day was cooler, lucid, and hungry. He wolfed down all that they could give him, but when he tried to rise from his sickbed, found that he was weaker than the proverbial babe.

'You must rest,' had said Brother John, gently. 'There is no matter so urgent that it cannot wait. Leave it in God's hands, and regain your strength.'

'How long?' Perkin demanded, and the monk spread his hands. 'I do not know. You are young, and strong—a week, perhaps longer. Be patient, and trust to holy Saint Luke the healer to aid you.'

He knew that it made sense, and he tried to swallow his frustration. It was seven days before he was again capable of bestriding a horse, and he bid farewell to his benefactors, leaving almost all his remaining coins—to the sum of six pennies and a groat—in gratitude for their care. Then, he urged his placid horse south, for Banbury: was overtaken by exhaustion and forced to break his journey after only ten miles: and finally, in the middle of a thunderstorm, arrived shivering, soaked and utterly weary, at the gates of Ashcott, two weeks after leaving Leicester, and asked to be taken straight away to Dame Julian.

She was in the estate room, sorting through a pile of documents

with Marten, kneeling dustily on the floor like a servant girl with
her head covered only by a plain linen hood. She saw him, and with
a cry of delight, struggled to her feet. In the three weeks since he had
last seen her, she had grown bigger still, but with her height and
build she carried the child well. 'Perkin—oh, thank God, Perkin!'
And such was her joy that she flung her arms around him, and then
retreated. 'Ugh, you're all wet.'

'It is raining outside, lady,' he reminded her. She stared with
sudden concern at his sodden state, his livery, washed by the kind
monks, run so that the colours were almost unrecognisable, his face
white and hollowed by the marks of recent illness. 'Oh, Perkin, are
you all right? You look dreadful—where's Briggs?'

The chamberlain appeared after her shouted summons. 'Briggs,
something *warm* and reviving for Perkin—mulled ale, perhaps, and
plenty of food—get what you can from the kitchen and bring it
here—no, the fire's not lit, to the winter parlour.'

'I've been sorely sick,' Perkin said, as the man retreated with his
head whirling from Julian's hasty instructions. 'Like to die, I
was—but the good brothers at Daventry saved me. I'm all right
now, lady, honest I am.' He glanced at Marten's unsmiling face and
said, in a hoarse whisper, 'Is he to be trusted?'

'Marten? Of course he is—he's my dear friend and ally. My
mother's visiting a crony near Adderbury, and will not trouble
us for some time, and perhaps not until tomorrow, if this rain
continues.'

A loud rumble of thunder gave point to her words. Julian glanced
about at the piles of papers and parchment. 'I've taken the chance to
go through some of these—there's a grant of land here from the
third Edward to my father's grandfather!' She turned to him, and
her expression grew suddenly taut with apprehension. 'Perkin, you
have news of him, don't you—please, tell me now, whatever it is it
can't be as bad as the things I've imagined.'

'He's alive,' Perkin said bluntly. Marten crossed himself, and
muttered his thanks to God. Julian, more perceptive, stood still,
looking earnestly at the boy's face. 'What else, Perkin? Is he hurt?'

'He is, or so I was told—I haven't seen him, I couldn't, he's a
prisoner—but I saw Sir Robert Drakelon,' said Perkin, and added
viciously, 'Curse his black treacherous soul!'

'Sir Robert?' Julian queried, puzzled. Perkin nodded grimly.
'Yes, Sir Robert Drakelon—he boasted to me how he'd plotted to
betray King Richard with the Earl of Northumberland, only the

Percy didn't strike—not that it made any difference to the battle, by all accounts, the King was still killed, fighting bravely so I've heard, with all his knights around him.'

'And Christie?' Julian whispered. 'He survived it—is he badly hurt?'

'I don't know,' Perkin said honestly. 'Sir Robert said he was —but I wouldn't trust his word if he swore my name was Perkin Hobbes. And—he said—I don't know how true it was, but he said it was only his hurts that were keeping him from a hanging —Catesby was hanged—and he said the King was going to take him to London, and—"Make him answer for his crimes", Sir Robert said.'

'Oh, sweet Christ,' Julian whispered softly. She found that she was trembling, but otherwise outwardly calm, surprisingly considering the frantic, overwhelming rage and terror within, not, now, for herself, but for her husband. She forced herself, with that new calm, to ascertain the facts. 'Perkin—when did you see Sir Robert?'

'Day after the battle, it was—St Bartholomew's Eve.' He looked at Julian's bewildered face, and added with a gulp, 'Lady—I ought to tell you—I didn't get to the battle in time—my horse went lame—by the time I got there it'd been over for hours.' His gaze dropped guiltily to the ground. 'I'm sorry, lady, I know how much it meant—and now I've failed you.'

'No, you haven't,' Julian said instantly. 'No, Perkin, please don't think that. I know you've done your best—and no-one could have done more. Will you help me now?'

Perkin, with gratitude, lifted his head to see her face, firm and purposeful with hope. 'Anything, lady—anything at all!'

'Then come with me tomorrow,' Julian said. 'I must go to find the King, and beg for his life.'

'You can't,' Marten put in anxiously. 'You can't, Dame Julian —for pity's sake, think of the babe!'

'I am thinking of him, or her—would you want my child left fatherless, when I might have saved my husband? The babe is safer in my belly than out in this cold hard world,' said Julian bitterly. 'Have the carpenter or a joiner check the horse-litter—it hasn't been used for years, I think it's kept in the stable. And, Marten, I shall need an escort—if the countryside is full of unrest, there may be danger. Can you find a half dozen or so men who would be prepared to come with me to the King? And some harness they can wear, even if it's only a helmet and a leather jack. And livery coats for them.' She glanced at the great chest, open now so that its store of documents could be removed, the stacked bundles of coin plainly visible. 'And we must take some of that—in case a ransom is demanded.'

Briggs appeared to inform them that the winter parlour was now ready, and as silently faded away. Julian looked at the man and the boy, standing one on either side of her, the solid reliable middle-aged steward, the small ugly sodden rogue of a servant, and smiled at them suddenly, dazzlingly, such as neither of them had seen before. 'Well? Will you help me, and save my husband from the Tudor? Or are you just going to stand there and tell me to stay here for the sake of my babe?'

'No, lady,' Perkin said quickly, and Marten added, 'You are right, Dame Julian. The King should have reached London by now—it is an easy journey, even for a lady in a litter. I will make all the preparations. Do you wish to leave tomorrow? There may not be enough time.'

'Tomorrow, if possible,' said Julian. She added grimly, 'My mother will doubtless object. If you must, humour her—but neither she or any other power from hell will stop me now.'

*

Dame Alice Bray rode under the gatehouse at Ashcott the next morning, in bright and breezy sunshine, her maid and two grooms at her back, and stopped her fat white ambler abruptly in astonishment at the sight that met her gaze. A horse-litter stood in the courtyard, and her incredulous eyes recognised the blue and yellow hangings, rather faded now, of her husband's livery. Beside it, seven men sat horses of varying colours and quality, all clad in the blue and white livery introduced by Sir Christopher Heron. And as she stared, her daughter, wearing her warmest gown, a blue velvet, emerged from the porch.

Dame Alice recovered from her shock and urged her horse forward: she gestured to the grooms to stay where they were, blocking the gateway. 'And what do you think you're doing, girl?'

Julian's head jerked up at the all-too-familiar bellow. She had been about to step into the litter: now she took a pace back and stood, her hands at her sides, and watched her mother approach. Behind her, Friday and the puny rascal of a servant that Sir Christopher had affected, watched warily.

'I am going to London, Mother,' said Julian. For the first time in her life, she felt exhilaration, joy, at the prospect of defying Dame Alice. 'Doubtless you will be fully occupied while I am gone, poking and prying. However, I intend to be back as soon as may be.'

'To London? Why in God's name are you going to London, you stupid girl? And in your condition!'

'That's the first time you've ever shown any consideration at all for my baby,' Julian said. 'Why do I go to London? I go to procure the release of my husband, who *is* alive, Mother, as Perkin here has told me.'

There was a startled silence. Dame Alice's heavy face became suffused and mottled with red. She dismounted and advanced on her daughter. 'You'll do no such thing, girl, do you hear me? Now get back inside and give over this nonsense.'

Julian stood her ground. Behind her, a step in the porch announced the arrival of Marten, whom she had asked to watch in case of her mother's arrival. 'No, mother, I will not. I am a woman grown now, and a wife, and my duty is to my husband, not to you. I would rather leave with your blessing, but I am quite prepared to go without it.'

'You heard me!' Dame Alice raised her hand threateningly. 'You know what to expect if you disobey me—now go inside!'

Julian glanced behind her, and nodded. Marten came out of the shadow of the porch to stand beside her, his long serious face and grey hair lending her support and substance. 'Perhaps it would be best if you let Dame Julian pass, lady. She is determined to go, and you surely cannot wish for unpleasantness.'

Dame Alice carried a hazel switch in her hand, for the control of her stubborn horse. She raised it menacingly. 'You dare defy me—you'll be turned off, Marten, if you persist in this! And as for you, you insolent jade—do as I say this instant, or you'll feel this!'

There was a low rumbling sound that, for a moment, no-one could identify. And then the yellow hound, Cavall, all his teeth exposed in a terrifying snarl of fury, advanced to take up his position protectively in front of Julian. Her mother hesitated: the dog growled again, all his hackles stiff and stark on his back, and took a step forward.

'Call it off,' said Dame Alice harshly. 'For sweet Mary's sake, call it off!' She lowered her arm: Cavall took another step forward. Julian, suppressing the sudden desire to laugh at the sight of her formidable mother forced to retreat by a dog, said loudly, 'Will you let us go in peace, as is our right?'

The woman's mouth opened and closed: she was now pressed up against her horse, who appeared to have gone to sleep and stood as steady as a rock, and still Cavall advanced, slow, threatening, one step at a time, his eyes blazing, the embodiment of all the hatred that Julian had stored up inside her over the years of subjection. He was quite as capable of tearing out a human throat as a deer's, and Dame Alice knew it: her high furious colour had fled, leaving her face greyish with fear. 'Call that dog off—I beg you, daughter, call it off!'

Julian, somewhat to her consternation, found that she was enjoying this. From the expressions on the faces of the servants and others clustered around the courtyard to watch their detested mistress receive her just deserts, so did the rest of the household.

Cavall's nose was almost touching Dame Alice's ample skirts when the priest, Sir John Mitchell, arrived protesting at Julian's side. 'Child! You cannot continue this—what are you doing? Call off your hound, your mother is in grave peril!'

'I know it well,' said Julian. 'I have only to give the word, and Cavall will attack. Or another word, and he will retreat. My mother has had that power over me for years, as you are surely aware, and it is time that she learned that I am no longer to be brow-beaten. Mother! Will you tell those grooms to stand aside now, and let us go?'

Dame Alice, supported by the unyielding bulk of her horse, was obviously incapable of speech, but she nodded her head at last, despairingly, and jerked her head at the two men blocking the gateway. They moved aside. Julian glanced round, seeing the quantity of witnesses, and knew that her mother's power was broken, over her household as well as her daughter. She snapped her fingers, and Cavall, with one longing look at the woman he had always hated, turned and trotted back to Julian's side, hackles retreating, tongue lolling, the image of the faithful hound.

The tension drained suddenly away. Dame Alice's maid got down from her own horse and hurried to her mistress's side. Julian left her dog held rather reluctantly by Perkin, and walked over to her mother. Dame Alice, mute, stared at her as if the child to whom she had given birth had unaccountably turned into a monster. Julian gave her back look for look: then she said softly, 'Marten will look after my affairs until I return, with my husband. Then I suggest that we discuss your future, since it's evident we cannot live together in harmony, and I will no longer tolerate your meddling. You may go where you will, do what you will, your dower is more than sufficient for your needs, Mother—but I do not want you at Ashcott, and I know that my husband will feel the same.' She paused, and then added, more gently, 'Goodbye, Mother. I will not long be gone, I hope.'

Dame Alice watched in stupefied, humiliated silence as her tall, awkward daughter climbed into the litter, which was then lifted up and strapped between the broad backs of the two horses. Then the escort, Perkin and Friday mounted their own animals, and under the fascinated eyes of the rest of the inhabitants of Ashcott, the procession moved slowly out of the courtyard.

Only then did Dame Alice recover some of her usual self-assurance. Her cry came harshly like a crow's to Julian as she was carried in the swaying litter underneath the gatehouse arch.

'You'll rue this, my girl, you mark my words—you'll rue it!'

*

'You crave an audience with the King,' said Margaret Beaufort, Countess of Richmond, Lady Stanley and mother of Henry Tudor. 'Half of England, it seems, requires the same. Why come to me, child?'

'You have been good to my lady mother, madam, and it is said that you are not without influence with His Grace.' Julian knelt, uncharacteristically humble, her best deep green gown spread about her, her head bent and the white gauze of her headdress spread over her shoulders like a butterfly's wings. 'It is not for myself, but for my husband, who I am told lies within the Tower, sorely hurt. For his sake, madam, and for our unborn child, I wish to see His Grace.'

There was a silence. The Countess sat still in her splendid chair by the Bishop of London's roaring fire, and surveyed the girl before her. 'Get up, child, and pull up that stool—you cannot be comfortable thus. When is the babe due to be born?'

Julian did as she suggested, glad of the respite. 'Early in October, madam.'

'It was perhaps foolhardy to risk the journey here, with the child so near?'

Julian looked up at the Countess. The feared, revered, devious mother of the King was an astonishingly small woman, with bright shrewd eyes and a clever face. She had the reputation of being utterly ruthless, at least where her son's welfare was concerned: and, incongruously, was also famous for her piety. But there was a certain kindliness now in her bony, lined face beneath the elaborate jewelled headdress, and, seeing it, Julian took courage. 'Some might think it so, madam. But I found that I could not endure the thought of my husband, hurt, alone, in prison, perhaps under sentence of death.' Her voice wobbled, treacherously, and she took a deep breath and struggled on. 'I have heard that he may be executed, as was William Catesby. At the least, I fear our lands —the lands I brought to him as my father's heiress—may be forfeit. And as my dear father lost his life in your son's cause, madam, it would seem harsh indeed if His Grace were to leave us destitute.'

The silence was filled by the cheerful crackle of the fire, and the distant murmur and soft laughter of the Countess's women. The older woman stirred in her chair, eyeing the girl sitting before her, the pale, strained face, the pleading expression in the wide intense brown eyes. She smiled gently. 'I know your plight, and your husband's, but only His Grace can help you. I can ensure, however, that he will see you as soon as may be. Will that content you, child?'

And Julian's radiant, delighted smile was assurance enough.

*

On arriving in London, on the afternoon following Holy Rood day, the third week in September, she had gone straight to the Bishop of London's palace, hard by St Paul's, where the King was lodged. His Grace was not available to petitioners today, she was told by an officious man in the green and white Tudor livery: but Perkin, wise to court ways, slipped the man a coin or two and asked if his lady could see the Countess of Richmond instead.

And it had proved successful. She had been told to return early tomorrow, and the King would certainly grant her an audience, if not her request. She left the palace light-hearted, the Countess's blessings ringing in her ears, and greeted Perkin with a broad smile. 'Tomorrow, he'll see me tomorrow—I have the Countess's word on it! Where shall we spend the night? Do you know a good inn?'

Perkin stared at her, slightly bemused. 'Don't you know, lady? Me mam has an inn, the Red Lion in Aldgate, none better in London! We'll go there, and she'll give us a right good welcome for sure.'

*

The news that England had a new King had startled Cis Hobbes, as it had done most of London. Her thoughts had gone instantly to her son and his master. She had not laid eyes on either of them since the previous winter, and in the day-to-day bustle and bother of running the inn, they had not occupied much space in her mind. But now, as the news raced through the city, as people gathered on street corners, by conduits and in taverns to discuss the astonishing fact that they had a different sovereign—and one who two or three years ago had been an unknown, poverty-stricken exile—she wondered how Perkin and Christie had fared. She trusted her son to survive almost any situation unscathed: he had given ample proof of his ability to slide out of certain retribution from earliest childhood. And besides, battles were fought by knights and men-at-arms, and humble servant-lads, unless very unlucky or foolhardy, did not become involved.

It was another matter for Christie. She knew, because Perkin had told her, something of the current circumstances of his marriage, and had cursed them both for fools: the girl for being at once so volatile and intransigent, the man for being such a fool as to fall in love with her. She had liked Perkin's master very much, for the combination of the calm, unemotional exterior and quick logical mind, with something much less cold within, had greatly appealed to her practical, shrewd nature. She found that the very real possibility he had ended his life in the slaughter of the battlefield at Redemore, caused her genuine grief.

Accordingly, when the new King arrived in London on 3 September, nearly two weeks after his victory, she had taken care to be foremost among the cheering crowds around St Paul's to see the Tudor, after his reception by the Mayor and aldermen, proceed through the packed streets to the cathedral, where he dedicated his three standards. In common with most other Londoners, Cis found him physically insignificant. True, he was taller than the late King Richard, but his face was cautious and wary, prematurely lined: she might have thought him ten or fifteen years older than his actual age, which was twenty-eight. And even the joyously bawling citizens could not induce a smile.

'Not like King Edward,' said her friend Joan, wistfully. 'Now *there* was a man who looked every inch a king!'

Cis made a coarse comment, and Joan sniggered. 'D'you think he'll marry the Lady Bess? She looks fit to wear the purple and ermine, even if he doesn't.'

[501]

'Of course he'll wed her,' said Cis. 'She's the heiress of England, ain't she? And he's got precious little more right to the throne than the King of Castile—or me, come to that. And that's another thing. If he's to be King through the blood of the Beauforts, why don't he give the crown to his sainted mother, eh?'

Joan, alarmed by her outspoken comment, glanced around in some agitation. 'Sh, please, Cis—you don't know who mightn't be listening, these days.'

'Stuff,' said Cis, and followed it up with a more downright epithet. 'I'll say what I like, and King Richard was a good king, for all he got precious little chance to prove himself. But I'll save my judgement until this one's proved himself good—or bad.'

But she had wondered afterwards: for Elizabeth of York was not the heir to the throne of her father. That honour belonged to the child whom she had last seen, small, fair-haired, irrepressible, pulling off his rain-soaked skirts, telling her that his uncle Richard was King, and so she must not address his brother as 'Your Grace'. The other boy, an attenuated, fair, delicate lad, had since died, she had heard from Perkin: but young Dickon, apparently, was safe. She hoped that he was out of Henry Tudor's reach: perhaps one day, he would come into his own.

She had made enquiries, after the King had entered London. There had been many prisoners in his train, amongst them Norfolk's son, and the young Earl of Lincoln, who like Lord Lovell, now in hiding, had been falsely proclaimed dead by the Tudor in order to discourage rebellion. They had all been lodged with honour in the Tower: plainly this new king sought for reconciliation, and a new beginning, and had already issued a proclamation to that effect. Certainly, here in London, people were willing to give him the benefit of the doubt. They had mistrusted King Richard, for he was a northerner and favoured men from those parts, and London had been the chief source of the evil rumours that had haunted his last few months.

Cis had eventually, with the expenditure of a coin here and there, and the exploitation of her youngest daughter's friend's betrothal to a minor Tower official, ascertained that a Sir Christopher Heron was indeed amongst those held there. The strength of her delight and relief surprised her: she was not after all so very friendly with him. But there was no word of her errant son, and that disturbed her.

So, she was greatly cheered when her head chamberlain knocked on the door of her private parlour, just before supper, and announced, in tones of some disapproval (he had a long memory), that her son Perkin wished to see her.

And there he was, a little higher perhaps, even thinner if that were possible, and ushering within the parlour a tall stately girl in a fine gown that did not disguise her advanced state of pregnancy. 'Dame Julian Heron,' he said formally. 'My mother, Mistress Cicely Hobbes.'

'You can forget that,' said Cis roundly. 'You call me Cis, Dame Julian—everyone else does.' She glanced at her son. 'I can guess why you're here. Do you know he's in the Tower?'

'We thought he must be,' said Perkin, as his mother brought a stool to the fireside and led Julian to it. 'May Dame Heron stay the night, Mother? Your best chamber, if it's free—we've good coin to pay for it, and a fine supper too.'

'Nonsense,' said Cis. 'You won't need to pay me, for as long as you stay here. And there are some fat capons in the kitchen, ready for roasting, and a couple of geese as well. And when you've eaten—and you look as if you want feeding up, young Perkin—then we can talk.'

*

The chamber that Julian had been given was, as Cis had promised, the most luxurious in the Red Lion. Called the Half Moon chamber because of the designs painted on the walls and embroidered on the hangings and counterpane of the large and superbly comfortable bed, it also boasted a huge and roaring fire, and a window looking over the galleried courtyard behind the main part of the inn. There was a closet within, and Friday, as loyal a servant as Perkin, had hung out their gowns on the peg and brushed them free of dust, mud and creases.

They had eaten a good hot supper at the table placed between the fire and the window, the three of them sharing the courses, and when they had finished, and the chamberlain had cleared the dishes away, Cis joined them. Julian could not help but be struck by the resemblance between her and Perkin: both small, spare, blue-eyed, with that wide lipless mouth. She had possessed no beauty even in her youth, evidently, but Julian could readily see the strength of personality that had kept the Red Lion running smoothly and efficiently after the early death of her husband. She sat on one of the stools by the fire and said abruptly, 'I'd heard you quarrelled with Christie.'

If Julian was startled by this direct opening, she did not show it. 'I had,' she said. 'But . . . various things have happened to persuade me to change my mind.' She stroked the cloth covering her belly. 'The child had something to do with it. So did Perkin, indirectly. I don't deny I used to hate him—'

'But now you don't?'

'No, I don't. I want him free, and whole, and with me at Ashcott. And the terrible thing is—he doesn't know I've changed, he doesn't know about the child. And I'm so afraid that they will kill him—or that he will die in there—without ever knowing!'

It was obvious that she was, suddenly, near breaking point. It had been a long day, of travel, disappointment, hope. Cis put a gentle hand on her shoulder. 'You have a good weep, if you want to. It won't do you any harm, and you'll sleep better for it. And if you're to see the King in the morning—well, what man could resist the pathetic pleas of a woman heavy with child, for the life of her husband?'

'I can't plead pathetically at will,' said Julian, behind her kerchief. 'If I can't have what I want, I get angry, and throw things.'

'Best not do that to His Grace,' said Cis drily. 'Or you'll find yourself clapped in the Tower alongside of your husband. Come on, girl, all women know how to wheedle a man.'

'Not this one,' said Perkin. 'She's right, Mam.' He turned to Julian. 'Please don't lose your temper tomorrow, lady—his life may depend on it.'

'I won't,' said Julian. 'Of course I won't—I'm not the child I used to be, Perkin. I've changed, and not just in my attitude to my husband. I'm—I'm older, somehow.' She grinned suddenly through the drying tears. 'I think my mother has had some influence.'

'And her mother makes you look like an angel in Heaven, Mam,' Perkin added, with a quick glance at Cis. 'She tried to stop us coming here—and Dame Julian set her dog on her!'

'Is she alive still?' enquired Cis, looking dubiously at Cavall, slumbering by the fire: his size was a threat in itself, even if his present pose was not. Perkin laughed. 'Just, I think, if she hasn't died of shock by now.'

'I shouldn't have done it,' said Julian suddenly, her face serious. 'I really should not—she is my mother, and I should respect her, honour her—though she has had neither respect nor honour nor even love for me, ever. But I don't really regret it—it frightens me, Perkin, but I enjoyed doing that, I enjoyed humiliating her in front of all the household. And she's ruled them so long, I don't know if she'll ever recover her authority.'

'Pray God she doesn't,' Perkin muttered, uncharitably.

*

'Dame Julian Heron, Your Grace,' said the usher, deferentially, and stepped aside to allow her to approach the King.

He was seated at a table by the window, through which the morning sun slanted. Clerks surrounded him, handing him papers, murmuring: by his side sat a much older man with dark, greying hair and the same lean, clever cast of countenance, who must be the King's uncle, Jasper Tudor, Earl of Pembroke, and who raised his gaze, cool, experienced, assessing, to the girl who stood before him, outwardly calm, inwardly shaking with apprehension.

It was the most important interview of her whole life. On its outcome depended not only Christie's fate, but her own, and that of their unborn child. Succeed, and she would be given one last chance to mend her life and her marriage, one last opportunity to snatch at the happiness that had always eluded her.

Fail, and he would die, and the rest of her days would stretch out in front of her, bleak, loveless, shattered, hedged darkly with the malevolent presences of her mother and the second husband that would be chosen for her.

She did not want anyone else: she wanted Christie. All her doubts, fears, confusions had disappeared, burnt to ashes in the sudden agony when she had realised that his love was not a pretext, not a game, but as real and warm and living as he was himself: and that she, incredibly, was the object of his passion.

She still could not see how she was worthy of it: memories of her past behaviour still made her blush and cringe in shame when she recalled them. But at last, she could accept what he offered, with the same, new maturity that had given her the strength to defy her mother, and act on her own desires. She did not love him, not yet, she thought; but love would surely come quickly, once they were together, and her mother banished. She had broken free, and whatever happened now, she would never again be in thrall to Dame Alice.

So she stood, straight and calm, with Cis's down-to-earth advice ringing in her ears. 'Don't make excuses, don't beg or whine: remind him of the fact that he's promised to be merciful. He wants to reconcile everyone, this King—that's one reason why he wants to marry the Lady Bess. Your Christie could be of use to him—I'd stress that, if I were you.'

Remembering her husband's loyalty to King Richard, Julian had wondered unhappily if he could ever be persuaded to pay homage instead of Henry Tudor, especially since that Tudor's agents had attempted the murder of the boys in the Tower. But she must obtain his liberty, and in furtherance of that aim was prepared if necessary to swear that the sun rose in the west if it would sway the new King.

Henry Tudor signed the last paper with a square, angular mono-gram, laid down the quill and looked up, lacing his hands in front of him. They were fine-boned, long and pale, with freckles that also marred his face. It was his eyes that chiefly struck her: they were not large, and a pale blue-grey that gave his countenance a strangely chilling effect, contrasting oddly with the thin rust-red hair and sharp nose. She thought, involuntarily, poor Bess: for there was little human warmth in that pale, unemotional face.

Yet Christie, with a similarly unpromising appearance, had turned out to be very different from the cold, ruthless man of ambition she had once thought him to be.

'How may I be of service to you, Dame Heron?'

She had, stupidly, thought that his voice would show traces of his Welsh ancestry, but his accent, though slight, was probably that of France, where he had spent the latter half of his life. Disconcerted, Julian found herself gaping, and pulled her mind back to its path. 'I am here,' she said with simple dignity, 'to plead for the life and liberty of my husband, Your Grace.'

Silence. The King continued to look at her: she wondered whether he were assessing character, sincerity, or something more basic. There was none of the leer of the lecher, however, in that cool unrevealing gaze. He said quietly, 'Your husband? That is Sir Christopher Heron?'

'Yes, Your Grace.'

'Late servant to the Duke of Gloucester, calling himself King Richard the Third, and taken in treasonous rebellion against ourself: I remember him,' said the man before her, as if recalling a property transaction. Julian set her jaw and wisely said nothing; the King continued. 'He is a rebel and a traitor, taken in arms, as I think you well know, Dame Heron. Why should I set him at liberty, when others less highly placed than he have already suffered the just penalty for their crimes under the usurper's rule?'

Julian, temporarily at a loss, found panic rising in her brain. With a supreme effort, she took a deep breath, forced it down, and made herself be still. She said steadily, 'On three counts, Your Grace. Firstly, as you may plainly see, our first child will be born in a few weeks, and we have been wed less than two years. Would you leave my babe orphaned, never having known his father or his father him, and myself widowed, when my husband has committed no crime save that of fighting for his anointed King?'

She thought that her passionate defence had gone too far: the King made a sudden movement, as swiftly stilled. She went on doggedly. 'Secondly, Your Grace, you may one day find that my husband is of use to you. His old master is dead: he owed allegiance to none other. He is a realistic man, Your Grace: he will know that you are the true King, and worthy of service. And I know that King Richard thought very highly of him, and whatever else may be said about your predecessor, Your Grace, he knew how to judge a man.'

Again, she thought she had gone too far: and there was much more that she could have said. I have ruined my chance, she thought desolately, and felt her eyes fill with tears. But she continued, striving for the calm dignity which she had assumed before she first spoke. 'And thirdly, it—it seems to me that you greatly desire to reconcile all the factions in your new kingdom, Your Grace, and to begin your reign in a spirit of forgiveness. Is it your desire to be considered a merciful king by your subjects? Or will you execute my husband, as you executed Catesby and the others, and forfeit that title?'

The King's reddish, thin brows drew together in a frown: his compelling, cold eyes held hers. 'You plead most eloquently, madam. Unfortunately, others are also most insistent that I do execute him, as I had originally intended to do, had not Sir Christopher been so sorely hurt after the late battle. It is not my practice, I can assure you, Dame Heron, to inflict that penalty on a sick man. He is not yet well enough to face execution, and besides, there is information that we require of him, as we do of all King Richard's intimates—alas, very few—who have fallen into our hands.' His eyes bored into hers, and she stared at him helplessly, feeling the tears slide shamefully over her cheeks. Furiously, she brushed them away, and said fiercely, forgetting circumspection,

[507]

'What are you trying to tell me? Does someone want his death? Who is it?'

'There is someone, yes, who has old scores to settle,' said the King imperturbably. 'It would, I think, be best for you not to know his identity. However, I can tell you that at present my heart is inclined to mercy, whatever others may try to urge on me. Your evident concern for your husband's welfare does you, and him, great credit, Dame Julian, and I will bear it in mind when I decide his fate.'

'When—' She found her mouth had dried up, swallowed, and tried again. 'Please, Your Grace, when will that be? I don't think I can bear very much—very much more uncertainty.'

'It will not be long. He must recover, in any case, before he can be questioned properly. In the meantime, he is being well cared for, you can be sure of that.'

She was being dismissed, with none of her questions properly answered. Suddenly furious, Julian clenched her fists, and cried angrily, 'At least let me *see* him! Mother of God, surely you are not so cruel as to stop me even *seeing* him?'

The clerks looked up, shocked and startled. Jasper Tudor, an expression of dismay on his face, rose as if he feared she would attack his nephew. The King's face did not change: the fine fingers rubbed, delicately, at a wart above his chin. 'I did not say that you could not visit your husband,' he pointed out, with perfect truth. 'And you may, although his state of health and his close confinement is such that you may not be allowed to stay for very long. Master Fox?'

A tall, thin man in clerical robes, with a narrow, severe, rather cadaverous face, approached. 'Your Grace?'

'Dame Heron will require a paper, authorising her to visit her husband, who is held in the Tower at our pleasure. Pray arrange for the necessary warrant to be made out at once.' He turned his attention back to Julian, who stood, still fighting her tears, before him, and spoke more gently. 'My lady mother has talked of you, Dame Julian. She has also told me of the great service rendered to her by your mother, Dame Alice Bray. Do not despair, although it may seem to you at present that all is lost. I have no intention of turning such a loyal servant of my cause against me, by executing her daughter's husband. You are among friends, Dame Julian—do not despair.' He added, 'Have you a house here in London?'

'No, Your Grace. I am at present lodged at an inn in Aldgate.'

'Then I suggest that when you have seen your husband, you return to your home. It would be only fitting and seemly for the child to be born there, would it not? And you will have your mother by you, and those you know. Ah, Master Fox, the warrant? Excellent.' He put his monogram on it, blocked and uncompromising, sanded it and handed it to Julian with a twitch of the tight mouth that must, she realised, be his interpretation of a smile. 'Goodbye, Dame Julian. I trust we will meet again under happier circumstances.'

Perkin's small face, pinched with fear, awaited her below. She felt as if she were borne on wings of hope: she could have taken his hands and whirled him around the Bishop's Hall in a glorious celebration of dance and delight. 'I've got the King's warrant, Perkin—we're going to the Tower!'

His face dropped comically. She laughed, still relishing the irony that Dame Alice had indirectly inclined the King to mercy towards her detested son-in-law, and clapped the servant on the shoulder. 'No, you wittol, to visit—not as prisoners!'

'Ain't he going to be let free, then?' Perkin demanded. 'And if he ain't, why are you looking so cheerful, eh, lady? He's still going to execute him, ain't he?'

'No,' said Julian, remembering what Henry had said, and, much more important, what he had not said. 'No, I don't think he is. He said he'd been advised to, but—I think he'll let him go, Perkin, eventually—I hope, and pray.'

'Well,' said Perkin, unwontedly gloomy, 'That's always reckoning he don't die before he's freed.'

*

They would let only Julian see Christie: Perkin must cool his heels on the Tower Green. She had never before been in this fabled fortress, residence of kings and queens on coronation eves, also palace, ordnance store, royal wardrobe, and prison. The great White Tower dominated all, its pallor startling against the dull September sky. Bemused by the succession of gates, guards and entrances, Julian hardly knew where she was going: her whole being was concentrated on the coming interview with Christie, the words of reconciliation she would speak, the hope she would hold out to him.

A man soon appeared who was apparently her husband's gaoler, a lean silent individual with a thin, pinched expression, and very greasy dark hair straggling under his bonnet. It was not a face to inspire confidence. She accompanied him to a dilapidated double tower hard by the White Tower and guarding the approach to the royal palace. The staircase was narrow, spiral and dark: she ignored the burden of her baby, shifting uncomfortably within her, picked up the heavy skirts of the blue gown she had worn for her interview with the King, and followed the gaoler and his lantern, her heart juddering frantically in her breast.

It was a small room, circular, with one narrow window giving on to the Green below: as it faced north, no sun could penetrate. She stood in the doorway, appalled at the foetid atmosphere within, the primitive bed heaped with rough blankets, the evil-smelling bucket against the wall, the utter lack of comforts. In horror, she took three steps forward and then stopped, retching, her eyes watering, to stare at the man on the bed.

For one ghastly moment she thought that there had been a mistake, and that the grey-skinned, unshaven, desperately sick man under the blankets was not Christie at all. Then, as she blinked the tears away, she began to discern the familiar features beneath the damp shadowed skin, and the blurring stubble over the lower half of his face. His eyes were closed: very gently, uncaring of the filthy straw, she knelt beside him and touched his forehead. It burned with fever: he muttered something, and tried to turn away from her fingers. Heartsick and furious, Julian saw that he was in the grip of delirium: she shook him gently, feeling the heat of him beneath the dirty shirt which was apparently all he wore, and although he appeared to wake, his eyes, half-closed and bloodshot, wandered past her without seeing her, and he muttered something completely unintelligible.

She brushed away the tears and looked around for water: there was a scummed, slimy and crusted wooden bowl on a stool by the bed. She took a kerchief from her sleeve, dipped it into the noisome inch left in the bottom, and bathed his face. The cloth left dirty green slime marks on his forehead, and a stench pervaded the room. Julian, suddenly consumed with fury, leapt to her feet and turned on the gaoler, her eyes brilliant with grief and rage. 'You animal! He's sick—how dare you leave him to die like this! The King said that he was cared for—if this is care, then the King lies!'

The man stared at her coldly. 'Your husband has no money, madam. And I understood that it was by the King's orders that he be kept thus. Sir Robert Drakelon assured me that he was to be kept close and in discomfort—he has valuable information to give.'

'Sir Robert?' Julian said in astonishment. 'Sir Robert Drakelon? *He* gave those orders? But—but he is wed to my husband's sister!'

'He could be wed to the King of Tartary's sister for all I know, or care,' said the gaoler with contempt, and spat. 'He said it was by the King's orders, and he's appointed Constable here, and who am I to judge, eh? Orders are orders.'

'The King does not know of this, I am sure,' said Julian. 'Sir Robert has not agreed with my husband in the past—he may be settling old scores.' She fixed the gaoler with a stern eye. 'I shall return at once to His Grace and inform him of this lamentable state of affairs. What was your name?'

To her satisfaction, the man blenched. 'No, madam—please do not mention my name, I beg of you—I'll lose my position— my wife and I have four children, they'll be left to beg if I'm dismissed—please, madam, say no word of me!'

'I will not, then,' said Julian magnanimously, to disguise her own contempt for his sudden descent into abject supplication. 'But I must insist that from now on, my husband is properly cared for. Someone must tend him night and day, keep him clean and warm, give him medicines, see that a doctor is brought. He must have proper food and water—not this muck, it's fit only for rats. And he must be moved to a chamber with a hearth—the nights are drawing in colder now.'

The gaoler said, cringing, 'Yes, madam, yes—but for all of this I shall require to be paid for my services. That is the general rule, madam—prisoners are at their own finding, or their friends.'

Silently, Julian thanked God for Perkin's foresight in insisting she take a good store of coin with her, for, as he had put it, 'You never know who'll you'll need to bribe.' She took her purse from her girdle, and tipped two golden nobles into her palm. In the dim little chamber, their promise glittered bright: she saw the gaoler's eyes widen with astonished greed, and knew that she had offered far too much. But she was not without wealth: and for Christie, and their future together, she would have given all she had.

'That's for you,' she said, dropping the coins into his grimy hand. 'For you to ensure that my husband has every comfort—*every* comfort, do you understand? For the King himself assured me that he would, and since His Grace has allowed me to visit my husband, I cannot imagine that he lied to me deliberately. There has been a grievous mistake, whether through malice or ignorance need not concern you, but if I find the error has continued, I shall petition the King for your immediate punishment and dismissal. Understand me?'

The man nodded his head earnestly, his hand clutching the coins with whitened knuckles. Julian glanced back at Christie: he lay still and silent, save for great shivers that ran through his body. She turned and knelt again beside him, feeling her tears wet on her face, and drew his hand out from the blankets. It was hot and dry: she could feel the swift pulse battering at her fingers as she laid it against her damp cheek. He stirred and muttered, as if it pained him and then she saw the scars, and the swollen misshapen fingers, and knew what had been done to him, and why.

And within her, something changed and altered, irrevocably. She had been concerned for him, yes, but her thoughts had also been for herself, and the baby. But now her imagination leapt, to encompass his ordeal over the past few weeks: the battle, the wound that had laid him low, concealed now with a great lump of filthy bandage around his right shoulder. And then, doubtless by order of Sir Robert Drakelon, this sick, hurt man had been tortured, to extract the information which Henry Tudor wanted above all else, the information which would confirm Sir Robert in his favour: the whereabouts of the sons of Edward IV.

And he had not given it: the gaoler had said so. He had kept silence, kept faith, for the sake of the little boy called Dickon, whom all who knew him loved. And not just for Dickon, but for all those who had helped in his escape, and held him safe still, though England's King had changed, and the world was altered.

I must have been blind, Julian thought, her mind on the years when she had thought this man despicable, contemptible, when she had hated him so much. Blind to his quality, behind the cold mocking mask: blind to the truth. And the truth now is that I don't hate him, not at all. I think I love him.

I love him. She said it to herself again, in the silence of her mind, and it had the triumphant ring of utter truth. She looked up, her eyes glowing with the joy and the power of her discovery, and beheld Sir Robert Drakelon, standing watching her in the doorway.

'It's time you left, madam,' he said, cold and hard. He did not look evil, standing there, his beautiful blue velvet uncreased, rich with colour in the gloom, his eyes chill and hostile. The gaoler, with the expression of a rabbit transfixed by a stoat, or a weasel, had flattened himself against the wall, the whites of his eyes shining. Julian got clumsily to her feet, feeling the rage building up inside her, suffocating her. 'Why have you done this?' she cried, her voice high, sounding quite unlike herself. 'What in God's name are you trying to do? Kill him?'

Sir Robert's face did not alter. He said to the gaoler, 'You should not have let her see him.'

'You gave no orders,' the man whined. 'You never mentioned he had a wife—how was I to know?'

'I did not think she would take sufficient interest,' said Sir Robert grimly. 'It seems I have misjudged your feelings for your husband, Dame Julian.'

'A great many people have done that,' she said. 'Including myself. *Why?* Why have you done this? You can't bear him such a grudge—and the King said he was well-treated, and gave me leave to see him—so this is *your* doing. Why?'

'The King?' Sir Robert said, his voice sharp. 'You have seen the King?'

'I have—and I intend to go straight back to him and make my complaint about your actions,' Julian said. She saw his face alter, and knew that she had found a weak point. She pressed home her advantage. 'I know that you have his ear, but I have also the ear of the Countess of Richmond, yes, *and* the Lady Elizabeth, and them he will not ignore. Will he be pleased, do you think, to find that you have wilfully deceived and disobeyed him in this matter?'

'He might, when he discovers the reason,' said Meg's husband. He had recovered some of his self-assurance, but his eyes still looked at a place past her shoulder. 'I have reason to believe that your husband is in possession of information that would be of inestimable value to His Grace. His present condition is merely the result of attempts to extract that information.'

Julian stared at him, horrified. 'So that's why you tortured him! *What* information? What could he possibly tell you that you and all the King's men don't know already?'

'The exact location of the sons of the late King Edward,' said Sir Robert.

She had known that it must be the reason: this was confirmation that, despite his suffering, Christie had not revealed what he knew. And she must not give away her own knowledge, either. One of them lived—and if King Henry guessed it, he would not rest until he had the child in custody, or worse: for the boy would, above all others, be the one behind whom all England would rise to drive out this Welsh interloper. And so, he was the greatest of all threats to Henry Tudor.

But if the King thought him dead, there would be no danger. She said, putting all the bewilderment and sincerity possible into her voice, 'But didn't he tell you? He told me. The boys are dead. The Duke of Buckingham had them murdered, two years ago.'

Another silence. She wondered if he believed her: even if he thought she was telling the truth, there was the probability that Christie had lied to her. Sir Robert surveyed her: she saw his eyes on her directly for the first time. 'A likely tale,' he said coolly. 'Your husband says the same. Unfortunately, so did Catesby, but he was executed before he could be put fully to the test. Lord Lovell doubtless knows, but he has fled. Perhaps others knew also, but either they are dead, or it is not possible to question them as fully as I would wish. Your husband is in custody, perhaps facing death himself.'

'Then he would have nothing to lose by telling the truth,' said Julian quickly. 'And the same argument also applies to poor Catesby. But that—that doesn't excuse your despicable torture!'

'I did not harm him . . . personally,' said Sir Robert. His eyes had left her.

'No—but you gave the order to torture him, didn't you, and I expect you watched while it was happening, and gloated over him—you disgust me!'

'I dislike the word torture,' said Sir Robert fastidiously. 'It has unfortunate connotations. I prefer . . . persuasion, or pressure.'

'That doesn't excuse it, you reptile! And the King doesn't know of it, does he?' Julian said challengingly. 'Nor, I'd guess, would you want him to know of it, despite your reasons—but he will, if you do not treat my husband as he should be. And I should warn you that the King spoke most kindly to me, and gave me to understand that my husband would soon be set at liberty.'

Sir Robert, she was pleased to see, had gone quite white: he looked, suddenly, almost as sick as his prisoner. She added harshly, 'Well? Do I go now to the King and tell him of your actions and your neglect? Or do you give my husband the proper care that the King himself promised me that he had received from the moment of his capture?'

There was silence. Then Sir Robert drew himself up. There were bright drops of sweat on his forehead, and his eyes blazed hatred. 'I will order now that proper care be given,' he said, spitting the words like venom. 'Now will you leave, madam?'

'No,' said Julian. She did not trust him, any more than she would have trusted a serpent. 'I will stay, and see right done. If you eject me now, I will go directly to the King.'

There was nothing he could do, and he knew it as well as she. With a muttered, furious oath, he capitulated. 'Yes. Yes, I will do it. Do you wish to wait here, madam? Or shall I have you conducted to a more suitable chamber until Sir Christopher is lodged in his luxurious apartments?'

She ignored his bitter sarcasm. 'Yes, Sir Robert, I will stay with my husband.'

The gaoler, thoroughly cowed, stayed to watch her. Christie seemed to sleep: she thought that he was a little easier. She forced herself to sit calmly by his side, though inwardly she shook with the force of her emotions: rage and disgust at Sir Robert, the strain of her battle with him, when for the first time in her life her powerful anger had been used entirely for someone else's good, and the love and fear for her husband, that she had never before had the strength to acknowledge, and accept. Desperately, she prayed that he would recover, that she had not come too late to save him: for, if so, then her own life would also be at an end.

Soon, four men appeared, carrying a litter piled high with soft warm blankets. Under Sir Robert's jaundiced eye, and Julian's stern and exacting gaze, Christie was gently transferred from the squalid filthy bed to the litter. Then, ignoring the discomforted knight's livid expression, she swept from the chamber to escort her husband to his new quarters.

Sir Robert had reluctantly ordered that his prisoner be taken to a more comfortable tower on the western wall of the fortress. A fire had already been lit, and though small as yet was crackling busily. There was a wide, glassed window with shutters to keep out the draughts, a proper garderobe closet, a comfortable-looking bed with hangings, and various lesser items of furniture. A woman, middle-aged and kindly, stood there, evidently the wife of one of the Tower officials, accompanied by two serving girls with water and linen.

'Mistress Sawyer—she has some skill with healing,' said Sir Robert curtly to Julian. As the woman drew back the sheets and blankets, the men lifted Christie from the litter and laid him gently on the bed. She exclaimed in shocked pity, and one of the girls crossed herself. The men rolled up the litter, which consisted of two poles with stout canvas sewn between, and retreated silently from the chamber. When Julian looked round, she saw that Sir Robert and the gaoler had gone too.

In the bustle of tending to Christie's needs, she had little leisure to think on the perfidy of Meg's husband. She had never seen injuries inflicted in war: the worst that Dame Alice had ever had to deal with had involved a young man at Ashcott, who had fallen onto a scythe at the haymaking. The great half-healed gash that lay under the filthy crusted bandage which Mistress Sawyer unwrapped, clucking in distress, from Christie's shoulder, was entirely outside Julian's experience, and she recoiled in horror.

'I've seen worse,' was the older woman's comment as one of the serving maids, shuddering, cast the foul linen into the furthest corner of the chamber. 'Praise to St Luke and St Anthony, it's not gone bad.' She glanced round at Julian's white aghast face, and added kindly, 'Are you his lady? Don't distress yourself, my dear—in your condition, you have to be careful, you know. Sit on that stool by the fire if you don't feel well—I can do all that's needful, I've seen many such in my time.'

'Will—will he die?' Julian asked hesitantly. It did not seem possible that anyone could survive a wound like that: and yet Christie did, and had for the three weeks since the battle.

'No, it's none so bad,' Mistress Sawyer said. 'See, it's well on the way to healing, the edges are knit together sound enough. If he does die, it won't be that wound, it'll be the lack of decent care afterwards.'

Julian swallowed her fear and nausea, and approached. A sharp-edged weapon had obviously struck a savage blow from above, breaking the collar-bone and rending skin and muscle: she wondered what had saved him from further injury, and then remembered that he had, of course, been wearing the expensive, originally German armour that he had ordered early in their marriage. Apart from that, a variety of yellowed bruises and the dreadful damage to his hands, he seemed apparently whole.

She watched, ashamed of her weakness, as Mistress Sawyer washed and bathed and poulticed and bandaged, and eventually replaced the blankets with gentleness. 'He'll do for now. The fever's still high, but I've known higher.' She beckoned Julian over. 'There you are, lady—he's more a sight now for your eyes.'

Julian wanted to say that she was not usually so squeamish—that

[516]

it must be a product of her pregnancy. But she knew the real reason, deep within her, why she could not bear to see him hurt, helpless, who had ruled her life and her emotions with such easy arrogance. She swallowed this new, peculiar feeling—it was so strange, to care for another person so deeply. She supposed she had loved her father, once: it seemed so long ago, shadowy, so insubstantial, compared to the force which had swept over her when she had first seen his distorted hands.

She came closer. He was sleeping: during Mistress Sawyer's gentle ministrations, he had muttered and struggled, had said words that seemed to imply that he thought he was in the King's household still: and then, suddenly, shaking her to the heart, the cry that had echoed round the marshy ground of Redemore Plain.

'Treason! *Treason!*'

That cry still haunted her soul, although she knew nothing of its significance. She wanted to hold him, to whisper her feelings, to make him understand how she had changed. The need was desperate in her: and yet she knew she could not wake him, could not disturb his much-needed sleep. She must leave him to Mistress Sawyer's care: but now at least, if Sir Robert attempted to go behind her back and return Christie to that stinking cell, Mistress Sawyer, a formidable lady, would not be in ignorance. And she had the King's letter in her purse: she could visit every day.

She knelt by him, and kissed his cheek briefly: the bone felt sharp and hard under the rough hot skin. Then, with every muscle in her body aching to stay, she turned, and left the chamber.

*

The letter was waiting, when she and Perkin returned to the Red Lion. How it had managed to find her, she could not at first guess, for it was from Ashcott, and bore Marten's neat well-trained handwriting, addressed to Dame Julian Heron, in the care of the Red Lion in Aldgate.

'Oh, he knows where my mam lives,' said Perkin. 'Told him we might be coming here. What news is it, lady?'

But Julian had broken the seal and was staring at the level lines within, that yet showed signs of being written in extreme haste. She looked up at last, her face pale with shock, and the realisation of the terrible choice she must now make. 'It's my mother. She has fallen grievously sick, Marten says—the day before he wrote this, so four days ago, and apparently she's like to die. She—' Julian swallowed suddenly, and went on, her voice wobbling. 'She wants to see me before she dies. And Marten says that I must make haste if I am to see her while she still lives.'

'You can't,' said Perkin roundly. 'She don't deserve it—and what about my master, eh? You can't just go back to Ashcott and leave him mouldering in the Tower, can you? That Sir Robert, he'll be up to all his old tricks again as soon as your back's turned.'

'I don't think so,' Julian told him. 'For one thing, he knows that I can tell the King everything that he has done, and not done, to my husband. And I think his present favoured position with King Henry is more important to him than the vague chance that he might wrest information out of Christie that could be valuable, but also risks the Tudor's displeasure. It's ironic, isn't it, that my husband has the King's protection? But he does, and it's much more effective than anything I could do. And there's a very capable woman, a Mistress Sawyer, who has the tending of him. I have told her the situation, and she knows what to do if Sir Robert tries to move Christie back to that terrible place.' She shuddered. Perkin, appalled, stared at her. 'You can't—you can't leave him—and go back to that woman—dying or not, she ain't worth your care, lady, and you know it!'

'I do know it,' said Julian sadly. 'But she is my mother, she gave me birth, she reared me—and like it or not, there is much of her in me. I was brought up to honour her, even if I found it impossible —even if, in the end, I came to hate her. And I can't desert her now, Perkin. She is dying, she needs me, she wants me at her side, for whatever reason—she may want to make amends for the way she has treated me, I don't know—but it's possible, dying people do want reconciliation, don't they? Christie is as safe as I can make him, but my mother is dying, Perkin, dying, and I don't think I could live with myself if I deliberately hardened my heart now, and ignored her.'

There was silence. Perkin and Friday, uncomprehending, stared at her in disbelief. Cis, more practical, handed her a kerchief. 'You dry your eyes on that, girl. You're right, of course, you must go. We know where Christie is, I can keep an eye on things, I have contacts in the Tower. You and he, you have your whole life ahead of you together, God—and the King—willing. Your mother, whatever's been between you in the past, has no time left. You go to her, and pay no attention to my son—and I hope he don't treat his own mother the way he's urging you to treat yours.'

[518]

Perkin had the grace to look guilty. Julian, her mind made up, smiled tearfully at Cis. 'If—if he's released while I am gone, will you give him this letter?'

She brought it from her purse. It was the one that Perkin had carried in vain across half of England, and looked like it: the paper was creased and dirty, and marked with sweat. Perkin's mother stared at it dubiously. 'Don't you want to write a better?'

'It says all that I want to say,' Julian told her softly. 'I am sure he will come here first, if he's released—and the King gave me to understand that he might be. The conditions he was kept in, that was Sir Robert Drakelon's doing. He wanted to find out about the Princes, Edward and Richard.' Her eyes locked with the older woman's in mute appeal, and Cis smiled. 'You know about that, do you?'

'Perkin told me.'

'Rogue, you were supposed to keep your mouth shut! Well, you knowing can't do any harm, can it? And you don't need to fear for me, Dame Julian. I know when to keep my silence, unlike some people, and why should I be expected to know any more than any other hard-working citizen, eh? As for my rascal here, he's only a gentleman's servant, like your girl, and they can't be expected to know of affairs of high estate, can they?'

'And I'm just his wife,' said Julian. 'And I told Sir Robert they were dead.'

'Well, it's half true,' Cis said drily. 'And did he believe you?'

'I don't know. I doubt it—why should he? I'd say it to save them, and Christie, and he knew it. But Catesby said the same thing, apparently. And it's best if they all believe it, for Dickon's sake.' She smiled. 'I've never met the boy, but to hear the Lady Elizabeth talk of him, not to mention Christie, you'd think he was the hope of England.'

'And so he is,' said Cis. 'If this King Henry proves himself a good and well-loved ruler, then perhaps there will be no need to bring the boy back, when he's grown. But if Tudor earns the enmity of his people—well, then, we have a true flower of the White Rose, ready to challenge his right!'

༄

CHAPTER TWENTY-THREE

'And yet shall I love her to the uttermost days of my life.'
(BOOK 10, CHAPTER 86)

For many years afterwards, men remembered the autumn of the year 1485, not as the aftermath of the battle that had slain one King and given them another, not for the coronation of their new sovereign, splendid though it was, nor for his first Parliament, which petitioned him to marry the heiress of England, the Lady Elizabeth, and so unite all factions behind the throne. Those months between the battle at Redemore Plain and Christmastide were spoken of as the time of the Sweating Sickness.

No-one knew for certain whence it came. Many pointed the finger at Henry Tudor's French mercenaries, who were partly comprised of the dregs from the gaols of northern France. But they themselves showed no sign of the illness, which was characterised by a raging fever, thirst, agonising head-pains, redness of skin, and the copious sweats which gave the disease its name. Many who took the sickness died quite quickly, their bodies exhausted: and it was remarked upon with fear and awe, that the young, the country folk, the poor (who died in great numbers anyway) were spared, or quickly recovered, while the disease cut great swathes through the wealthy, the rich merchants and leaders of London: two Lord Mayors, half-a-dozen aldermen, and many other noteworthy citizens succumbed.

The Tower, with its many hundred close-packed inhabitants, officials, families, gaolers, warders, lion-keepers and all the rest, suffered as much as the City. The poorer prisoners, ironically, were almost unharmed in their chilly cells, and even the more exalted captives, such as the Earls of Surrey and Northumberland, escaped lightly. Again, it was the middle-aged and elderly who died, often very quickly. And amongst them, one Mistress Sawyer and her husband, certain gaolers, and the man put in charge of the fortress, Sir Robert Drakelon.

His demise came with shocking swiftness—alive and well one morning, complaining of feeling unwell before dinner-time, delirious at dusk, and dead before dawn. Word was sent to his wife, residing still in Yorkshire, and his body, undignified in death, was shrouded and hastily put below the ground in the chapel of St Peter, in order to avoid further infection.

Christie did not know of his enemy's death for some time. Recovery came slowly: gradually his mind cleared, and the events of the past weeks, coloured by fever, assumed the shape of a confused and nightmarish dream. Had he once been held in a chamber smaller and darker and more chill than this? Had Sir Robert really stood over him with those endless questions? Who was the woman who had ministered to him so carefully, of whom all he could be certain was, that she was not Julian?

He could not be sure. He knew now that he was warm, and comfortable, fed by a cheerful young man who gave him all the news, great and small. And it was he who let fall the information that the Constable had died of the sweats.

It mean nothing to Christie, unaware of Sir Robert's post: for a moment, he could not dissociate the title with Sir Robert Brackenbury, forgetting that he had probably died in the vanguard of King Richard's army, along with the Duke of Norfolk and many others. 'Poor Brackenbury. And now his wife and daughters will be left alone and friendless.'

The young warder looked at him in surprise. 'Brackenbury? You mean Drakelon, Sir Robert Drakelon. He was put in the Constable's place when King Henry entered London.'

'Sir Robert *Drakelon* was Constable here?' Christie stared at the young man, and the warder, puzzled, nodded. 'Yes. And now he is dead of the sweat: this morning, it was, and they're saying he died raving of demons, unshriven.' He crossed himself, and glanced around as if an eavesdropper was concealed in the garderobe, before continuing in a whisper. 'And the word is, he betrayed King Richard before the battle—so it's only right and just that he's dead.' He looked at Christie with indignation. 'And they say he treated you shamefully when you were ill, Sir Christopher, and you nearly died from lack of care.'

'Did I?' Christie looked down at himself, or rather the humps and lengths of his body as it lay under the piled blankets and embroidered coverlet. He knew he was weak, that his muscles had wasted in his sickness, that the great gash in his shoulder had knitted together, although crookedly, leaving an ugly scar, that his head still ached and spun at some moments. But worst of all, his hands were badly damaged, and would not properly obey him. He had tried to force that terrible truth to the back of his mind, but, lying awake in the long dark silences of the night, he had faced the bitter facts. He had lost everything: he had no wife, no home, no friends, no land, no King. He was a prisoner, at the mercy of Henry Tudor, and he no longer had the power to make music.

The tunes he had once sung danced mockingly in his head, and it was in his head that he played them, every swift movement of the fingers on gut and neck, every touch of the shivering strings. And in desperation he had forced his distorted, aching hands to imitate those patterns, on the coverlet, on his arm, on a piece of wood, anything to train them back to the skills he had lost. It was slow, painfully slow, but by this time the desire to regain his previous perfection had been an obsession. He had nothing else but this: he must at least succeed, or lose all hope.

He knew why they had been hurt: he could even remember, with a dreadful clarity that had fortunately been very short-lived, the moments when the pain was worst, when he had tried not to cry out and failed, when Sir Robert Drakelon had hung above him like some dark avenging angel, and demanded the answer that he could not give, for it would surely condemn Dickon to death.

'*Where are they?* Where are the Princes?'

He had repeated, over and over like a litany, that the boys were dead: and in the end they had stopped, frightened that he would die, or, he supposed now, that the new King would discover what they did. He had never thought that Sir Robert had believed him, even though it was true enough that Edward was dead. Ever since his awakening in this warm, comfortable tower chamber, he had waited for Sir Robert to return, for the agony to begin again, and he had not been sure that he would have the strength of mind and body to resist the man whose delight in cruelty seemed truly evil, and who was also, appallingly, married to his sister Meg.

And now, thank God, he was dead, and Christie was safe, and Dickon's secret kept: and Meg was free. He asked for pen and paper, and wrote to her, in a travesty of his former neat hand, telling her that she was a widow. And below he had added, unable to help himself, his anxieties for Julian, that he was in prison and could not go to her, that he did not know if she had ever received their letters, that he did not know what had happened to Perkin. And he finished, uncharacteristically, with a plea for her help.

'Will you go to her, and put my case, as I cannot?'

It would be to no avail if he were executed, or attained, his lands forfeited, perhaps he himself sent into exile. He did not allow himself, then, to think of it: he put his mind, now that he knew there was no longer any danger from Sir Robert, to regaining his former careless strength.

It took weeks of patient, intensive exercise in his chamber: later, somewhat to his surprise, he was allowed to walk the Tower Green, and gradually, day by day, the unused muscles, aching and feeble at first, grew more and more powerful.

And then, in the second week in October, he was told that he could go home.

He did not believe it at first: the new Constable, a friendly little man quite unlike his sinister brother-in-law, showed him the warrant, with the King's sign manual and seal upon it. He was free to return to Ashcott, on condition that he fought no more against Henry Tudor: and he was required to present himself before the King at the end of the month, for the Coronation, and to swear allegiance to him on pain of forfeit of his lands.

And that was all. He was at liberty to leave. The Constable had provided him with clothing, adequate for the colder season and his position, though not what he himself would have chosen: and with nothing in his hands, he walked out of the Tower of London, to taste the free and empty air.

It was so unexpected that he stood outside the last gate, where he had once hurried on a rainy night with two King's sons dressed as girls, and felt for the moment completely at a loss. The future, vast and empty, yawned before him. He should return to Ashcott, but he knew what it held: a hostile wife, whom despite himself he still loved, after nearly a year of separation, and a mother-in-law who detested him even more. He could not face the thought; and so, for want of anywhere else to go, he turned and set his feet stubbornly on the brief familiar route to the Red Lion at Aldgate.

Cis Hobbes did not recognise him at first. Told there was a man who wished to speak with her, she swept briskly into her parlour, her mind elsewhere, busy with food supplies and the ostler who had been selling off the horse fodder to other, less scrupulous innkeepers, and the perennial problem of her youngest daughter Agnes, who wanted to marry someone wildly unsuitable who would ruin the Red Lion in a week if left in charge. She stared at the long, painfully thin man sitting in her only chair, noting the plain clothes and the air of recent, severe illness, and said, 'What can I do for you, sir?'

[523]

'Don't you recognise me, Cis?' he said, rising with some difficulty: and then she realised who he was, and was so horrified that
she stood still, staring, her mouth open.

'Caught any flies?' he teased her, and she closed her lips and
responded with the brisk forthrightness with which she concealed
surges of undesirable emotion. 'Look at you! What do you think
you're doing on your feet, eh? Sit down at once!'

Obediently, with a rueful glint in his eye, he sat. She saw there
was sweat on his forehead, and his face was grey. 'Wine? Ale?
Supper?'

'It's too early for supper. Wine will do very nicely, thank you.'

She gave the necessary orders, and returned. He was apparently
asleep, but as she shut the door he opened his eyes. 'Do I really look
so frightening, Cis?'

'You look as if you'd been starved for a year. What in God's name
has happened to you?'

'I've been prisoner, in the Tower. I suffered the tender mercies of
my dear brother-in-law, but now they've set me free.' He twisted
his mouth wryly. 'On condition that I swear allegiance to Henry
Tudor.'

'And will you?'

Christie was silent, staring into the bright hot fire. He thought of
King Richard, whom he had followed and served loyally for four
years, until that last fatal charge when the King had staked his life
and his kingdom on the chance of slaying Henry Tudor, and lost.
He thought of Dickon, suddenly endangered by his uncle's death,
living his secret life at Lille. He thought of Tyrell, who had escaped
the slaughter by reason of his post at Calais, and of the other men,
less fortunate, who had died with their King.

They had all kept faith; their loyalty had bound them. Did he not
owe it to their memory, and to those who still lived, to carry on the
fight, to champion Dickon's cause, or that of the Earl of Lincoln,
rather than to bow the knee to Henry Tudor? He had nothing to
lose, after all: there was no future for him in England now.

'I can guess what you're thinking,' said Cis, breaking in on his
unhappy reverie. 'And this may influence your decision, one way or
the other.'

She handed him a letter, one that had suffered many vicissitudes
by the look of it, though the seal was unbroken. He looked at it, and
saw with bewilderment that the rampant unicorn was his own. And
the thick smudged writing, almost illegible, seemed to be Julian's.

He had thought, in his bleak emptiness, that all feeling was numbed, departed. Now, the sudden, shattering beats of his heart gave him the lie. 'Go on,' said Cis. 'Open it. You won't find it ill news.'

He broke the seal, and stared down at it. For a moment, his eyes could not focus on the words: with an effort, he forced them to make sense of the blurred, hasty lines written in her swift, large, untutored hand.

'My dear husband, I know now how gravely I have erred, and most meekly and humbly do I beg your forgiveness, and pray that you will return safely to your most humble servant and bedes-woman, J. Heron.'

And below, eschewing empty formality, she had added, 'Please come quickly, for the sake of our child.'

The last words stunned him: he read them over and over again, unable to believe it, and then lifted his eyes to Cis, completely bewildered. 'She says—a *child*? How did you come by this? Have you seen her?'

Perkin's mother chuckled. 'Yes, I've seen her. She and that rapscallion servant of yours and son of mine were here, oh, three weeks ago. She came to beg your life and freedom from the King,' Cis said. 'And it would seem she succeeded, despite your cursed brother-in-law. Did you have much trouble with him?'

'He's dead,' said Christie, and told her how. As she crossed herself, and muttered a prayer, he added grimly, 'Don't trouble to pray for his soul—it's undoubtedly in hell. He was cruel beyond even my imaginings—and I never did like or trust him.'

'And your sister? Will she mourn him?'

'I would be astonished if she did. She did not suffer quite as I did, but her experiences as his wife nearly drove her to madness. May he answer for his crimes before God, for he never atoned for them on earth.'

'But why? I know he wanted to discover where the Princes were—Julian told me that. But there were others he could ask—and to use torture—' Cis crossed herself again. 'Why you?'

'I was the only survivor they had, apart from Catesby, and the King made a swift example of him. And the Earl of Surrey, of course, though he's hardly a candidate for torture. And Sir Robert hated me—for my championship of Meg, I think, and because I knew that he had tried to betray the King. It's a long story,' said Christie wearily. 'But it's over now, and I'd sooner forget it, and look to the future—and I didn't even know I *had* a future, until you gave me this.' He looked her in the face, honestly. 'I left the Tower devoid of all hope—I thought I had lost everything, and without Julian there seemed no point in returning to Ashcott. I was planning to go beyond seas. And now—' He picked up the letter again. 'Is she really with child? Has she truly changed?'

'She's certainly going to have a babe, yes,' said Cis. 'In fact, it may already have been born—she told me it was due early in October. Yours, is it?'

'Of course it is,' said Christie, thinking back to those dim glowing nights that had given them both such pleasure, and in which the baby must have been conceived.

And in which, also, some affection for him must have been implanted in Julian's heart, without either of them being aware of it, to flower now, months later, for reasons which he could not guess. Then, he saw for the first time, the date on the letter, and said in surprise, 'This was written months ago—in August, before the battle.'

'Yes, and my Perkin wore himself to a shadow carrying it round half of England in your wake,' said Cis. 'He came to the battlefield too late, found you were hurt and captured, and went back to Ashcott to tell Julian. She, poor girl, was well-nigh distracted by the thought that you would die without knowing of the babe, or that she'd changed her mind about you. She came here to plead with the King for your life, so it's her you must thank for it: she was given leave to visit you, and found you were being held by Sir Robert Drakelon's orders in some stinking cell. She threatened him with the King, and, thank God, persuaded him to take better care of you. There was a woman to look after you, she said, and a new and much better chamber for your comfort.' She looked at him. 'Didn't that woman tell you any of this?'

'I remember her, vaguely, from when I was still very sick. But apparently she died of the sweat too, at about the same time as Sir Robert.'

'Then thank God you didn't have it—or perhaps you did, with that fever,' Cis said thoughtfully. 'Perkin had it, you know—that's the reason why he took so long to reach Julian with the news of the battle. For about two weeks, she assumed you were dead.'

He thought of her, whose courage and perseverance had certainly saved his life and given him his freedom, alone and bereft in great agony of mind, and bowed his head. 'Where is she now? Why didn't she stay here?'

[526]

Cis looked at him, with pity. 'She went back to Ashcott. There had been a letter sent, you see, from your steward. Her mother had fallen sick, and was asking for her.

'And I have to tell you this, lad. I've been thinking about it. It could have been the sweating sickness, though she didn't know it. And if I'd realised, I'd never have let her go.'

*

He would not stay more than one night, though she begged him, saying he was not strong enough yet to ride the miles to Oxford, that whatever had happened must already be long over. That was probably true, but it was fear that drove him on—fear for her, and his child, and love for them both. Their life together had been full of mistakes, misfortunes, confusion, misunderstandings: he knew that he could not bear it if now, just when the chance of real and lasting happiness seemed miraculously to be offered him, it was snatched cruelly away at the last minute.

Cis lent him a horse, a good steady hackney, reliable and strong, and the money for his journey. He had nothing else. He had set out years ago from Bokenfield alone, with just his horse and his lute, to seek his fortune with Richard of Gloucester: and since then he had acquired lands, wealth, a faithful servant, a wife and, apparently, God willing, a child. Yet he went with empty hands to Ashcott, to begin his life again, owing all to Julian's resourcefulness and intelligence and bravery, and to the mercy of Henry Tudor.

He said goodbye to Cis with love and gratitude, and she, with a great effort, restrained herself from fussing over him. He was a man grown, with his own life to make. But she did say, quietly, as he sat the bay hackney, a more handsome and amenable horse than poor Bayard, in the inn yard, 'If you should find that—matters do not turn out as you would want—then you'll be welcome here, always.'

She had reminded him of the tragedy that might await him at Ashcott: the pain of it showed briefly on his face, and then he smiled, looking at last a little more like the strong, self-assured, arrogant man she had once known. 'I thank you, Cis—and I will always remember what you have done for me,' he said, and gripped her hand as if she were a man. 'And for Dickon,' he added, very softly. 'God go with you, and may we meet again soon, in happiness.'

'And God go with you,' she answered, smiling, and watched him ride, a lonely figure, into Aldgate.

[527]

It was surely the sun that made her eyes water: she blinked, and when they had cleared, he was gone.

*

He rode down the hill to Ashcott as darkness was falling. Away to his left, the sunset still glowed fiery red, promising fine weather on the morrow. It had been a long day, and he was exhausted, keeping in the saddle by sheer force of willpower: all the muscles in his body screamed at their unaccustomed jolting exercise. He had been three days on the journey, and with every mile he drew nearer to Ashcott, so had grown the certainty that Julian, if not the child, was dead. The combination of disease, especially one as virulent as the sweating sickness, with childbirth, was almost too dreadful to contemplate: and yet he could not find it in himself to hope that she and the baby had been spared.

The hackney felt its way down the rutted stony hill: he must have that track repaired before winter, he thought, and then added the qualification, if he was still here. If Julian had died . . . he did not think he could stay at Ashcott. He would seek employment overseas, in one of the mercenary armies that were always in demand in France or Germany or Italy . . .

There were lights, faint and hesitant, in the dark humped jagged bulk of Ashcott. But as he drew near to the gate, he saw that it was shut. A prickle of fear sprung the hairs on the back of his neck: he leaned from the saddle and with his remaining strength hammered on the wooden panels with the hilt of his dagger. The sound echoed around the walls within, and died into silence. Then a voice, quavering and fearful, spoke on the other side of the gate. 'Who's there, in God's name? Who calls so late? We've sickness here.'

The fear increased, chiming with his heartbeat, but he managed to make his voice calm. 'Let me in, Harry, for Christ's sake. It's Sir Christopher Heron you keep out of his own house!'

There was an astonished pause, and then bolts were slammed back, keys turned, and the great gate swung open. Harry Tyler, the gateward, stood there gaping foolishly in the light from his lantern. 'Sir Christopher! It is you, praise God! Forgive me, sir, forgive me.'

He stood aside as Christie rode under the arch and dismounted. 'Find someone to look to the horse—he's had a long journey.' He did not ask Tyler about the nature of the sickness: whatever had happened here, he did not wish to hear of it in Harry's blundering words. He walked across the dim earth of the courtyard, the stones

[528]

strategically placed to provide a causeway over winter mud: in the failed light he all but fell over one, and swore. Then he was at the porch, made his way inside it more by memory than anything else, and hammered on the great iron door-knocker that he found by touch. 'Open up! Open up in there!'

There were faint sounds of haste on the other side, and the bolts were drawn back. A face, Perkin's, like a benevolent goblin, peered round the latch and gaped. 'God's bones, it's you, sir—you're free!'

'Yes, I do appear to have been set at liberty,' Christie agreed with tired asperity. 'May I enter?'

'Yes, oh, yes—come in, sir!' Perkin cried, stepping back and flinging the door wide with a joyous flourish. Christie walked through into the hall passage, behind the screens. As Perkin shut the door, he saw ahead of him, half way up the stairs, a woman peering down, candlestick in hand. She gave a sudden glad cry and ran down, the wild flame illuminating her rounded, black-clad figure.

It was Meg.

He had just time to realise it before she had thrust the candle at a startled Perkin and hurled herself into his arms, her head against his shoulder, fortunately the uninjured one. 'Oh, Christie, is it you, is it really you?'

'It is,' he said, laughing weakly, and hugging her. She pulled back from him and studied his face earnestly. 'You look very tired. Are you free? Are you truly free?'

'On condition that I swear to follow the Tudor, yes,' he told her, and added softly, 'The gateward said there was sickness here. I have been fearing the worst all the way from London—what has happened?'

Above, faintly, threading through his words, came the wail of a baby.

He stiffened, listening, and Meg said quickly, 'That is your son. He was born a week ago. And Julian is well, it was a very easy birth—she has the right shape for it, unlike me.' She glanced down at her figure, swollen already with the child, the posthumous child of Sir Robert Drakelon, that would be born after Christmas.

'Then what sickness have we here?' Christie demanded, finding his hands shaking with his unutterable relief. Julian was safe, and the baby—and his world was whole, against all the odds. 'What was that old fool Harry Tyler talking about?'

'Oh, one or two of the kitchen boys have taken the sweats, though not very badly—it doesn't seem to affect the young,' said

Meg. 'But I should tell you—the priest is dead, and so is Dame Alice.'

And the last load lifted from his heart. He crossed himself automatically, and said, 'When? Was it indeed the sweating sickness?'

'It was, I believe—though she died before I came, about two weeks ago. I had your letter,' said Meg, and she touched his face gently. 'I know about what my husband did. He is better dead, Christie—he was a cruel, evil man.' She shivered, staring into the darkness at things he could not see, and then she turned and caught sight of his scarred, twisted fingers. 'Oh, sweet Jesus, was that what he did to you?'

He nodded, and she wept. He remembered Perkin, hovering anxiously in the background with the candle, and sent him for wine and other refreshments. Meg said, in between sobs, 'Why? Why did he do it? What could he hope to gain?'

'The greater favour of Henry Tudor, I would guess, if he could extract from me the whereabouts of King Edward's sons. Perhaps my lands, also—that thought did cross my mind. But mainly, I think, purely for the pleasure of it. He enjoyed watching me in agony—and I do not think it was simply because we were enemies. I think he would have had that satisfaction from watching any man—or woman—being tortured.'

Meg shivered again. 'As he did to me. Oh, I would not have told you of it if he had not died—but he used to do things to me, in our bed, especially after Katherine was born—they were not natural, normal things between a husband and wife.'

He saw her tears flow, and kissed her. 'You have suffered more than I have, and for much, much longer—but now we are free, and we can take joy in a new beginning.' He smiled at her. 'Send for your son, if you like—make your home here for a while. We have several wasted years to catch up on, all of us.'

She caught up his hands, and kissed them; her tears still fell hotly. 'But your playing—will you ever make music again?'

'Of course I will. I intend to try my hardest. Already I can handle my dagger, and my horse. I have been practising on bars of wood for weeks. It won't come back all at once, but I am determined that it will, eventually—you know how stubborn I can be. And even if I can't play again as I used to, I can still sing, and I have Julian to make my music, and her voice, I'd swear, can rival the angels.' He smiled joyously. 'And in the end, what does it matter, when I have her, and my son, and you, and my freedom? I have everything that I have ever really wanted, and I cannot complain.'

'Are you going to see her?' said Meg, wiping away her tears. 'She has been in agony all these weeks, not knowing if you would be freed or not—though now Sir Robert is dead, her mind has been eased a little. But it is all she longs for, to see you at her door, and show you the child.'

'Then she will, and as soon as may be,' he said. 'Will you be our servant, and carry up the wine when Perkin eventually appears? But give us a few moments alone.'

'Of course,' she said, and watched him as he wearily climbed the stairs: then, her heart filled with love and happiness, she went in search of Perkin and the wine.

*

Julian sat in her bed, the baby in her arms, rocking it to sleep. He had opened the door very softly, and she had not noticed him, so intent was she on her son. Her hair was loose in this private place, and it poured over the bed in a great chestnut fall, like brown gleaming water. He saw the soft look of love on her face, and knew that it was echoed on his own.

And then, she glanced up, and saw him. The joy that illuminated her features made them beautiful, and told him all that he wanted to know of her feelings. She made as if to leap out of bed, but remembered the baby, and sank back on the pillows. 'Oh, thank God—thank God you're free!'

'I think *I* should rather thank *you*,' he said, crossing over to the bedside. 'Cis told me that it was you who spoke to the King, and you who threatened Sir Robert Drakelon so menacingly that he had to treat me as a guest in his own house.' He smiled down at her, and added softly, 'I owe you my life. Let's hope you do not have cause to regret it, ever.'

'I don't think I will,' said Julian. Her heart was hammering loudly beneath the veiling mass of her hair, and her palms were sticky with sweat. She wanted to reach out and hold him, so thin and tired and ill did he look, though better than the skeletal stranger she had seen lying in the filthy bed in that squalid Tower chamber. But the baby already occupied her arms, and besides, she felt suddenly shy of him, as if she could not believe that at last, after all the years of hatred and misunderstanding, there was now no obstacle to their happiness together.

[531]

He was staring at the child, and his face was very gentle, with a love and wonder in it that she had never thought to see in him. 'He is a week old, Meg said? What have you called him?'

Julian took a deep breath, for in this she had trusted her own instincts, certain that it was the only name the child could be given. 'I hope I did right—he was christened Richard.'

'You did right,' he told her. The smile was becoming broader, and she saw the delight shining through the old impassive mask, now almost gone. 'Though how Henry Tudor will take the news that I have called my eldest son after his enemy, I do not know.'

'You could say he was named after his great-grandsire, my father's father, Sir Richard Bray,' Julian suggested. She added, 'Have you made peace with the Tudor, then?'

'I am free on condition that I fight no more against him, and swear allegiance to him.' He was still looking down, enchanted, at the child, seeing the tiny clenched fists, the button nose and creased mouth and eyes, the faint snuffling breaths as he slept. 'I suppose that could be called making peace, yes. But if I had come here to find you and the baby dead, as I thought I might—then I had decided to go overseas, and fight as a mercenary—or perhaps help Dickon win back his throne.'

She glanced up, her shyness forgotten as she voiced the question that would, he suspected, one day return to haunt him.

'If you serve the Tudor—what will you do, if Dickon comes back to claim his crown?'

There was silence. Christie said at last, slowly, 'I cannot say. There are so many things that could make a difference to my decision—my opinion of King Henry, for instance. And Dickon himself—I would not want to throw away everything which I had gained for a man who might not have fulfilled all that promise. But if he had . . .'

She said, understanding, 'Then your heart would be torn in two.'

'Yes,' he told her, reluctantly. 'Yes, you are right. My heart would be torn in two—because now that I have you at last, and Richard here, and Ashcott, I have everything that I have ever desired. Could I bear to risk it all, to help Dickon regain his right?' He paused, and then added in a different tone, 'Let me take the child, and lay him down. Then I can greet you properly.'

For a babe so tiny, he was surprisingly solid, even heavy. He did not stir as his father put him gently down in the wooden cradle, carved with the child's arms, the three fleurs-de-lis of Bray and

Christie's single heron. He covered him with the soft lambskin, and stood for a little while smiling at his son, the same look of delight on his face. At last, with a gesture she found deeply moving, he touched his finger to the boy's round brow, and said softly, 'Sleep well, Richard Heron.'

'His eyes are blue,' Julian told him, to disguise her sudden rush of emotion. 'But then all babies' eyes are blue to begin with, or so the midwife said. And his hair was pale, until it all fell out, and now he's as bald as an egg.' She smiled tentatively at him, exploring this new feeling of union, of kinship between them, and added, quickly, before her resolve could fail, 'I am sorry—so sorry—I have been a very bad wife to you, and I want more than anything to make amends, and start afresh.' She swallowed, and he saw the tears in her eyes. 'I've treated you so abominably, I've been so very stupid—can you forgive me?'

'Sweet Christ, dear girl, you know that I love you—and so of course I forgive you.' He sat down beside her on the bed, and took her hands in his. 'And you saved my life, without a doubt—and so we owe each other nothing, and everything. You said you had changed your mind, in your letter. Have you?'

'Of course I have,' said Julian, with something of her old indignation. 'Or I'd be throwing cushions at you and telling you to get out.' As he grinned, she went on, more seriously. 'I have been thinking a very great deal—about how wrong I was—all the things I used to think about you that weren't true at all. All I know now is, I've changed so much—and so have you, I think—and we have the baby—and my mother is dead, God rest her soul.' She smiled with wry resignation. 'Do you know what was the last thing she said to me? I'd come back here hot foot, thinking that she wanted to be reconciled—and she lay there and told me that she would never allow you in the house if the Tudor was fool enough to set you free—and then she said, "Take that stupid hood off, girl, why aren't you wearing a proper headdress?" And an hour later, she was dead. And the terrible thing is, she was my mother, my own mother, she gave birth to me as I have given birth to Richard—and I felt nothing more than relief when she died.'

'Don't feel guilty—she made your life a misery. How could she expect any love or honour or respect from you? It's something that must be earned, as you have earned mine.'

'I can't see how,' said Julian, when he had finished kissing her. She found that her breathing was wildly irregular, and that bearing a child had made no difference whatsoever to the intensity of her response to him.

'You are yourself—isn't that enough reason? And the fact that you defeated the King and Sir Robert single-handed is proof positive of your marvellous uniqueness. I love you, Julian—for yourself and yourself alone.'

'And I love you.' Her voice was so low that he could scarcely hear it: his arms tightened about her. '*What* did you say?'

'I said, I love you.' Her voice held a prickle of irritation, and he laughed from pure delight. 'You love me? You do? And I thought that miracles happened in far-off lands and distant times, not here and now. Do you, dear girl? Do you really?'

'I love you,' said Julian, for the third time, slightly louder and with more firmness. 'I didn't know it till I saw you in the Tower —till I saw your hands, and knew that you'd kept silence, and why—are they better yet?'

'They're not mended, but they'll serve well enough, given time and effort.' He spread them out and she took his fingers in hers and stroked them, gently. 'Will you play music, ever?' she asked, very low.

'I most certainly intend to. And meanwhile, I have you to delight me instead. Will you be my minstrel, my lady fair, and play for me? Shall I bring you your lute?'

She tuned it, with a deftness he had lost, but would soon regain with practice and dedication, and thought for a moment before striking the strings in a pattern that he knew.

Meg, coming up the stairs with a laden tray, stopped on the last step and listened as the notes spilled out from Julian's room. She knew the tune that was played: and as she smiled in recognition, their voices leapt together at last in joy and harmony, singing the words that had brought Julian in the end to acknowledge the power of Christie's passion for her, and the beginnings of her own love for him.

> Go, heart, hurt with adversity
> And let my lady thy wounds see!
> And say her this, as I say thee,
> Farewell my joy, and welcome pain,
> Till I see my lady again.

❦